To Face It

A Novel by

Lupe Family

Lupe Family Media

ISBN-13: 978-069 2026977

CREDITS

Cover photo of author by Lance Watson from Jamaica
http://jamaica-gleaner.com/gleaner/20111107/ent/ent3.html

Cover art by Jennifer Forest
http://www.facebook.com/jennifer.forest1 (There are many Jennifer Forests, so add Belchertown to a search for her.)

To Pat Murphy Robinson (born 1926, died April 11, 2013, 11 p.m.)

Editor of *Lessons from the Damned*

&

To all workers unpaid or paid on this earth

CONTENTS

PREFACE

After many years working in street theater in Europe and New York City, and giving many workshops and talks for activist causes, my life brought me Pat, the woman I dedicate this book to. She taught me how to bring history into everything I did, so that I began to comprehend the inescapable connections among the many issues people and communities confront. Inspired by Pat, and by the questions I was continually asked, I decided to write *To Face It* in order to bring this reality to a wider audience by, as Malcolm X instructed us, saying it "plain," with regard to Women's issues, particularly in relation to Black women dealing with white supremacy; Recovery from Racism, domination and forced submission, including rape, of individuals and the earth; the pivotal importance of the Inequality of power relationships under Capitalism; the struggles of the Working Class; and how victory is achieved by standing up to domination in the nuclear family, the workplace, and relationships. Why a novel? To try to make the reality *real* by showing it *lived* through characters who jump and twist and come to understand and face their past and present so they can face the future with courage and integrity. Even in fictional form, however, there's a lot to take in—too much to understand at one time, so I invite you to read the story aloud, put it down, pause when you want, and return to it.

While working on the novel, I have also pursued these themes by creating with other people in Playback Theater; the W.O.W Café Theatre (excerpts from several chapters of the novel have been performed as one-act plays); the Black Women's Blueprint (BWPP); and of course, in the everyday world, including the teaching and practice of Reiki and yoga.

To meet me, go to www.pmrbio.wordpress.com and sign up for the next Free Webinar, four of which are held each year, in the fall, winter, spring and summer. If the date of the next one is not listed, keep checking the website until it is.

I am available for workshops, talks, and performance webinars for people (including families with children) who want to make a difference. As Malcolm said, "transform yourself, transform the world." To contact me about arrangements and fees, email me at patisback232@gmail.com. Include IN THE SUBJECT LINE your name, the name of your organization (if you have one), a 1-3-word description of your event and an estimate of the fee you expect to pay.

To order copies of the printed book, go to Amazon.com. You may also order the book through Sister's Uptown Bookstore, Harlem, New York City. Website: wwwSistersUptownBookstore.com. Email: sistersuptownbookstore@yahoo.com. Phone: 212-862-3680

Lupe Family
New York City,
March 2022

ACKNOWLEDGMENTS

Thanks to all the workers who went to mines and carved out the minerals to make this computer so I could write, and *gracias* to you, dear audience—listeners and readers who are part of this book and whom I hope to hear from/do workshops with in the future.

In addition, I'm thinking of the uplift and corrections from the New Mexico writers' group and, in New York, the writers' groups of the late Louis Reyes Rivera and the late George Edward Taite. And of Little Star and all the other creators who shared their ears; of Cecelia McCall, an editor who helped shape this; of Virginia Hampton, who brushed it up; of Nadia Wynter and all those from that part of my life who kept me going over the years; of the late Joyce C. Duncan, Ph.D., who read the whole first version & kept the encouragement going; of Pat Robinson (always), who advised me to "Just get it out"; and of editor Corona Machemer, who insisted this meant getting it out "right," and who worked tirelessly, with great insight and empathy, to see that the development of the novel's characters and interlocking narratives work together to achieve its aim: helping victims of violence and injustice—racial, sexual, economic—to face the facts, expose truth, and begin the process of transformation.

Thanks also to Lucas Rivera for insightful touch-ups & to the crew of women and men over the years who supported & laughed & donated (too many to mention). And to the National Writers Union folk like Tim Sheard, who make sure writers can keep on creating.

Dearest Randy for your spirit, and the late D.S.K. for your inspiration; all the visitors to the W.O.W Café Theatre who have seen this in production over the years; Phil, who takes notes, and Tantra Zawadi, poignant enactor; Jennifer Forest, delightful illustrator; and all who gave comments and took part in the process—thanks.

This novel was co-created with the idea that the character "Pam" could become her historical self, Pat Murphy Robinson, in video form: "Pat! A Revolutionary Black Molecule!" (TRAILER Pat! A Rev Black Molecule to contact : patthevideo86@gmail.com. YouTube LUPE TOFACEIT). Thanks to all who helped make this a reality.

Finally, Ashe to the Universe and all spirit guides, including Millie: may we all do this again.

PART ONE

(Note to the reader: As a child, Tania was called Buttercup.)

1 NO LONGER SPRING

In the bathroom there is a sliver of blue sky that can be seen through the window unblocked by the next building. Tania, surprised, says "Damn, this is getting worse." Pink bubble-like things grow on her slender wrist.

"Run the cold water over it for a while," Agua suggests, staring at the mirror, checking her parts on the side and down the center of her hair.

"I don't know, maybe I ate something that's filled with crap like I used to when I was a teenager."

Agua fools with her hair as she watches, averting her eyes now and then.

"*Tan feo*," Tania blurts out, something she's picked up from one of the students who talks with Agua in Spanish sometimes.

"It's not real ugly." Agua reassures her. "What kinda crap did you used to eat back then?"

"Oh, I'd eat Drakes coffee cakes, orange sodas, barbecue chips, all together. Then I'd act like a crazy girl."

"Crazy? Whaddya mean?"Agua asks.

Tania, distracted by the itching, screams, "Oh, what's that?" More bubbles form on the outside of her hand and start immediately to widen and become larger on her fingers. It's an attack of an ant colony, but it's in her skin. She stops staring at her skin and rushes to the sink, looking up and down because she can't remember what to do. There's no medicine cabinet in the bathroom.

"How are you going to fix this?" Agua asks, her voice cracking with anxiety.

"I'll just run cold water over it!" Tania is crying, barely able to turn the faucet. It's too much for her this time. "This happened when I was a kid in the bathtub sometimes. I'd have to put Phisohex on it or it would itch something terrible."

"No, this time it'll be okay right away." Agua tries to stay positive.

"Maybe there's a drugstore down the block." Tania's tears are now streaming down her cheeks. "Why does this happen to me?" she wails.

The running water from the faucet keeps up a cooling hum, soothing Tania after a while. Breathing deeply, she remembers. "When I was small, I sucked my thumb for years . . . until I was maybe a teenager."

"A *teen*?"

Agua's shocked face reminds Tania of how Older Sister and Younger Sister used to taunt her for being "too old to be sucking her thumb." She calls them that as a game she plays instead of using their names. "I was at least twelve." Her voice drops to a whisper, and she moves urgently towards Agua. “Can I tell you about it?” She wants to laugh or wildly cry. The itch feels like it’s deep inside her body. It makes her want to jump around. She prays silently to the spirit guides to clear the rash. “Thank God this stupid rash isn’t on my neck, like when I was a kid.” She talks over the sound of the running water, putting her hand back under the faucet. Then, holding the sink, she allows the laughing to start. “Agua, I couldn’t stop sucking my thumb. I was almost obsessed. Any time I saw my parents, but especially my dad, coming toward me, I put my thumb in my mouth. And you know what? My father HATED it. He was real mean.”

Agua looks at the tiny pustules, spreading fast, but flattening out, too, on her friend’s wrist, then says, “You know, I didn’t like my stepfather. He stayed drunk and high all the damn time. My Puerto Rican mother stayed with him, though.” She adds as an afterthought, “’Cause she was so effing weak.”

Tania is surprised to hear herself say, “You know, I think there was something wrong with my father. He would really go off on me about sucking my thumb.” She speaks faster, her voice higher. “He’d almost beat me for having it in my mouth. I mean he spanked us at other times, but when I started developing breasts and still insisted on putting my thumb in his mouth. . .” She stops and corrects herself. “I mean my mouth, he would go off.”

“What did he say?” Agua feels queasy. Touching her stomach, she remembers her girlhood in the projects.

“He’d say, ‘Take that hand out of your mouth, girl, or I’m gonna yank it out.’ ”

“Yank it out?”

“Yeah, like I was embarrassing him or something. I felt so stupid and dumb, and little, but I needed my thumb.” Tania laughs to cover her shame.

Agua turns and looks out the small bathroom window at the tree leaves in the park down the block. “Probably you were exposing him or something.” She fixes her eyes on one cool cloud. “And I know this. People who are crazed don’t like to be exposed.”

Tania’s gaze meets Agua’s when Agua looks back over her shoulder.

“Huh?” Tania blinks.

“Why your thumb? The shape is something like a man’s . . . well, I don’t want to say, Tania. I hope you find out yourself why. But maybe you were trying to stuff something back in!” In the silence that follows, Agua wonders when the glazed expression is going to drop from Tania’s light “colored girl” face.

Finally Tania says, “Let’s go to the park for a breeze. It’s too damn hot in here.” She shakes her wrist, which is feeling cooler, and thinks about buying a cold bottle of water to put on her arm when they go out.

* * *

By taking the F train, anyone can find their way to the University of the Streets, where Agua helps out at a workshop studio. A year earlier, Tania had walked into Agua's life there. Now, every time Tania enters, she hears the creaks of the building welcoming her as she walks up to the studio's floor.

The University of the Streets is a place where young people and older folks, too, do art and talk for hours about a society where actors and dancers feel supported. The founders organized theater classes, ballet—all kinds of arts workshops at very low rates. Creative people who walk in off the streets don't need long applications and interviews, and the workshops are held in the evening and on weekends, so working people can attend.

That first time, Tania, tall and slender, with long legs, had climbed the stairs too fast, so when she finally reached the top, she was hunching her shoulders from exhaustion. When she entered the little room off the hall, Agua, the volunteer office worker, stared at her, chewing gum.

"Hi," Tania says. "Can you repeat that thing you told me over the phone?"

Agua, taken aback, barks, "I said, 'University of the Streets is not some-high-cost-capitalist-style competitive college.'" She pushes her glasses up. The wire frames slide right back down her café-au-lait colored nose.

"Oh, so a lot of people who wouldn't usually cross paths can get to know about each other here?" Tania waves a hand back and forth in the air, thinking about what this really means.

"Yeah, you don't have to be rich and white to get *this* degree!"

Tania crumbles up the flyer she's found in a local restaurant telling about the place and its creative classes. At that moment, she feels a lot freer than the summer she graduated high school, and started her first theater classes.

Agua is a radical-looking woman with big, bushy black hair, an "afro" that sets her apart from some in her community. On top of that, she doesn't use lipstick, nail polish, eyeliner. In other words, she keeps herself away from what, during this era, the Latin culture views as "all woman." She searches the desk, with its piles of unpaid bills, for the registration forms.

"I had a boyfriend once who went to Cuba, 'cause he hoped the Cubans really had universities and film schools that were free," Tania announces, waving her pen in the air in the middle of filling out the form.

"Were they free?"

"Yes! For people from the Caribbean, anyway."

"Oh, yeah? Well, I'm Puerto Rican and that's in the Caribbean." Agua looks over the form. "In fact it was another Latina who told me to check out the mime classes here." She asks how Tania heard about the University of the Streets, but Tania, excited, doesn't hear her and jumps back in.

"Um, yeah, Puerto Ricans go free in Cuba, too," she says. "My ex told me if I lived in socialist Cuba, then from babyhood through graduate school, I could get my education completely for FREE! But at least I can get training here at a very low cost, not like at some prestigious snooty-ass place."

Agua nods, a smile forming that grows even bigger as she looks at this woman who resembles her, with skin the color of cashews, wide-apart eyes and bushy hair similar to her own, but who she doesn't feel is Puerto Rican.

Tania and Agua talk about the people who founded University of the Streets. "Guess they were kinda profound, even revolutionary, thinking that every young person and older person who wants to educate themselves and evolve has the right to NOT have to pay up the wazoo," Agua says, summing it up. She smiles. "It's almost like Cuba's free system."

Tania's eyebrows go up. She feels Agua! "You mean this street college isn't a tall-tales place where they go on and on about how good education is for you, but then you graduate with nothing inside to help you go further. Do we really need to pay for classes about what we already know about?" Tania pounds the desk.

"Um, I don't . . . um, what do you mean?" Agua looks back at the form, not sure how to take this young Black woman. "What did you say your name is?"

"Tania."

"Yeah, well, I don't like to get all up into that heady kind of talk. I prefer to stay clear and simple." Agua laughs, circling the date on the form.

Tania doesn't know whether to take this as a back-handed jab or just a straight-up difference of opinion and style of talking. She steps into the hallway to use the bathroom, tossing a comment back to Agua, "Oh, I'll be here to sign up for the Politics of Arts and Finances: An Education Workshop. It sounds great!"

In the bathroom she worries whether this Latina will like her. She usually feels off-balance in new situations and, as the night darkness enters the room, her thoughts turn to other nights when she was little and called Buttercup.

* * *

Nighttime is coming. Buttercup has to go inside, her freedom over. She has to bring herself into the family house and listen for the footsteps coming up the stairs. Daddy said she'd better not be up "reading by the desk lamp." Quickly she turns off the light. She shivers. He enters. She knows because she smells him.

Daddy tempted her the first time when she was little. "I'll give you my favorite key ring if you let me get in bed with you." He was breathing hard when he touched her leg and then her thigh as he slipped into her bed. She loved him. She thought, He must love me very much, but it doesn't feel good.

Saturdays, he practices his life insurance speech on her.

She sits, his captive audience, her hands under her thighs, back arched. Her head feels like swiveling around, but she sits still at the Formica counter-table. The housekeeper, Miss Duffy, used to stay in the kitchen, but when Tania was little Daddy said she had to go back to Jamaica to take care of her mother.

He moves like an important person, filling out forms, and she doesn't move. "Mr. and Mrs. Brown, you will see the Mainstream Mature Life Insurance benefits help you to be at ease and in comfort even though your loved one is deceased."

Her father used to sell houses, but then one day he said, "There's no money in real estate," and he switched to selling life insurance. At least he didn't have to work in an office all the time and be stared at by the white office staff. He worked out of the house and sometimes his clients came by, but most of the time they called and Buttercup had to take perfect messages on the pink message paper and check the correct box, if they were returning his call. Mommy didn't think it was fair to ask this of a kid, but Buttercup still had to do it.

He sits on one stool, Tania perches on the other. A round fluorescent bulb, the overhead light, glares. It is quiet outside, an eerie stillness. Her father reads to her from his manual: "Our company prepares you for the unexpected, keeping money available at the time of the great loss of the family breadwinner." This word breadwinner leads her to look over at the empty bread-basket. Her feet swing and bang together. She freezes. Maybe he'll finish soon.

He drones on and on about insurance and money. She can't concentrate. He hated selling insurance. Maybe that was why the life insurance chatter didn't sound like he was talking for real. It sounded stale. It sounded like he was just trying to grab people away from their money.

* * *

Closing the door of the stall in the bathroom near Agua's office, Tania thinks, What a child I was, remembering the man with huge brown glasses on his long broad nose under sad deep-coffee-brown eyes . . . the brown-haired man with the neat nails . . . the 5-foot-10-inch-tall Black man, the color of tree bark, whom neighborhood Black women said was good looking, when her mother, the white Jew, wasn't in sight. Of course she knew from her parents' talk that a man named Joe McCarthy, sitting there in Washington, had had a lot to do with her life, but she'd had no idea then that his followers and the U.S. military industrial complex had come to rule the unions, too—the unions where her organizer father had helped rouse the regular guys who listened to the radio and went out on a Saturday night to fight for their rights. Workers who once were strong and militant and had successful sit-down strikes like one in Flint, Michigan, when they took over factories, were now at the disposal of a new breed of union bureaucrat who complied with the government's prying into their leaders' private lives and views on how to run an economy. The militant union leaders like her father, like thousands others deemed influencers, were fired and then blacklisted so they couldn't do the work they'd been doing because they were suspected of being communist sympathizers (and that was just about all Black people who weren't Uncle Toms, because for a long time the Communist Party was the only one that backed civil rights and stood up for the oppressed). Even in those unions that still made a show of standing up to corporations, the new leaders, big, white guys, eventually let their inner racism and their willingness to go along with the way the U.S. economy was run for the rich decide who should be on their staff.

As a child she didn't understand any of this. Only many years later did she realize how the anti-worker and racist purges had forced her dad, one of only two Black leaders in the union he worked for, to find other work; how he forced himself to be good at the selling job he hated because it provided his family with the food, clothes, house, car, ballet classes, music lessons and summer camp—the life her mother demanded. And it was years after that before she would begin to understand how, after he was fired, he became a leader of nothing.

Again, her thoughts turn to the child she had been, who had decided towards the end of the summer after fourth grade that, when "art education" camp was over, she wouldn't go home because she couldn't stand any more of daddy sitting on her bed, mommy never saying anything about it, and her sisters not wanting her in the family. She would go live with her art teacher, Mrs. Stash, who was a caring woman with black curly hair and a thirteen-year-old daughter who was one of the few big kids at camp who listened to the little ones.

* * *

Buttercup just *has* to run away today. She rounds up her artwork, which the teacher has given back. She's sure Mrs. Stash will ask her to go home on the bus with her and her daughter. Glancing at her sandals, she takes a deep breath, hesitant about asking Mrs. Stash to let her visit. She smiles tentatively.

Mrs. Stash and her daughter stop loading paint brushes and cups into the sink and smile back. They're almost ready to leave.

"See you next summer, Buttercup," Mrs. Stash says.

"Okay." Buttercup giggles happily. She believes she'll see Mrs. Stash outside at the bus stop in just a few minutes. Then she'll reveal her secret wish to live with her and her daughter. And they'll say yes!

Buttercup waits. Now it's after 3:30. People are coming home from work. Where can Mrs. Stash be? Buttercup has to run off and live with her *today*.

Her mother's car, a gray station wagon, turns the corner, coming toward her. She could run, but the car will overtake her. She could go back inside. Instead she bends down as if she has to fix her shoe strap.

The car stops in front of her.

"Buttercup! What happened? Where have you been? Why didn't you walk home?" Mother's voice is very tense, but controlled. She never raises her voice, though each word comes out with a push. Her face is taut and her curly hair spreads all over the place because of the heat. Her eyes, which usually seem interested in life, are now two slits, glaring at her daughter. She jumps out of the driver's side. "Get into the car," she says, slapping her thigh hard. It is a habit she has when she's angry.

Buttercup doesn't move.

Her mother steps toward her. She's wearing a dress made of madras fabric. Sweat sticks on her face. "Did you hear me?" she snarls.

Buttercup is sure that if she says it aloud, then Mrs. Stash will come and make everything all right. So finally she says, "I'm leaving with Mrs. Stash."

"What? What did you say? That's foolish." Again the sound of her mother's hand slapping her thigh reveals her fury.

"I'm going to live with my teacher and her daughter," Buttercup says.

"Hah! So that's what you think!" Her eyes flashing with anger, Mother grabs Buttercup's hand really tight and pushes her into the car.

"What did you think . . . that no one was going to come for you? You are not going to watch any television tonight, my dear. The nerve . . ." She slams Buttercup's door so hard the backseat rattles. She starts the engine.

"You wait 'til I tell your father about this."

Buttercup looks out the window, which she has rolled down all the way. The sweet summer air blows her tears away. She stares back at the school building, which is smaller than before. Okay, so Mrs. Stash must have already gone. But at least she'd tried. Maybe next year she'd try again.

Mother parks the car in their driveway. As she opens the door to the house, she calls back in an icy tone, "Remember, don't turn on the TV."

Buttercup's feet drag her into the house straight to her room. She stands on a chair to haul down the school compositions from the shelf above her bed and rips every single one to shreds. She throws the pieces around the room, covers herself in them. Then she beats up her pillow with her doll baby, grabbing it by the head and throwing it at the pillow. She twists one leg around and then the other, then smashes its face over and over into the pillowcase. She fixes her own face into as many ugly, monstrous styles as she can. She scoops up all the bits of paper, twists them together, and sticks the wad between the doll's legs.

She climbs back up to her shelf and pulls down a baby picture of herself and her grandma. She notices she's sucking her right thumb. Her gaze lingers on Grandma, standing next to her holding her other hand.

* * *

Agua grins when Tania strolls back into the office. "What took you so long?"

Tania, ready to leave the memory behind, laughs. "I'm here to sign up," she says. Her bright mind, always searching, had been drawn to a flyer she'd seen on the bulletin board about an Art and Social History workshop for "those who want to understand the world they have lived in."

"Can I start with this now and pay for it with other things later?" she asks.

Agua agrees to this and registers her for the course, and later that week, in the back room, Tania works on her first project for the class, an essay about money and family history assigned by a "womanist" guest instructor.

ESSAY by Tania (For Art and Social History)

My father had some great ideas—like socialism as an alternative to the cut-throat system in which you always have to worry about basic needs like a place you can live, a job or even medical treatment. Also my father stayed stable financially in the face of the racism that told him you are a nigger and you best not act too damn smart in front of these white life insurance salesmen. Those men were not as smart as my dad. He acted like them so they didn't get jealous and gang up on him.

Did they do things to their little girls, too?"

Squeezed in at the bottom of the page in tiny letters, this last sentence had written itself. Tania crosses it out and lingers for another hour or so at the University of the Streets to rewrite, chewing her pencil the way she used to do in high school, when she first became Tania to her writing teacher, Mrs. Green, and to her true friends. Everybody else called her "Butter," the nickname her father gave her when she got too old for Buttercup, because she loved to eat gobs of butter, with a teeny bit of bagel.

* * *

"Um, Mrs. Green, um could you use my middle name, Tania, from now on?"

"Sure," the teacher replies. Her pale face is lined from fatigue. She hadn't gotten much rest during the summer because she had taken a bunch of students abroad on a school learning trip.

"And I'll use it for my pen name when I hand in stuff, okay?"

"Okay." The teacher, rushing to get to her next class before the bell, stuffs her papers into her briefcase and scurries off.

Later that month, when the teacher hands back the outlines for the first assignment, she asks to sit with Tania during her free period.

"Do you have to? Can't you just write the stuff on my paper?" Tania whines.

"No, come to the room at the end of the hall. We can go over it together."

They sit facing each other, Tania's teacher at a desk piled with books for another class and Tania at a kid's desk, her legs crossed.

"Would you read the paper to me?" Mrs. Green asks.

"Okay, but remember, please, it's just the *outline*."

In a small voice, Tania begins to read. "*Story of Butter* by Tania. Background and Intro handed in already. Concluding part of paper:

> *"One Sunday after spending the weekend with the relatives in Brooklyn, my menstruation shows up. No one helps put the fears that I'm dying out of my mind as I look at my panties, red, and blood on the toilet paper. I realize that, like my girlfriend L., I got 'my time.' I call up L. who tells me, dip your hands under the faucet, rub the cotton underwear with soap and only cold water. Rinse that bloodstain out. Can't I ask mother about this? No. That's a stupid idea I have to get out of my head. She'd just blame me for Daddy's visits to my bed. I blame myself."*

Tania finishes reading, but keeps her head down, staring at the paper. Finally she looks up and says, "I'm hoping the details helped keep your attention. Did they?"

Instead of replying, Mrs. Green returns Tania's gaze and says, "Is there anything you want to explain to me, Tania? I mean, the paper we can deal with, but is there something you need to talk about?"

"No." Tania folds her hands in her lap, thinking, this white woman doesn't like my writing. I never get along well with teachers like Older Sister does and that's why Ma loves her and not me.

Mrs. Green wipes the sweat off her neck. "Well, if you ever want to talk to me, find me before I leave class and I'll make a time for you, okay? I'll keep the outline over the weekend and then give you some ideas about connecting things."

"But how *is* it?" Tania asks, looking down at the desk, studying every mark where some kid wrote on the wood. She wonders if the teacher will just laugh.

"It's a beginning that you definitely can work with."

They get up and Tania walks quickly to the door, tossing back in her teacher's direction, "Okay, see you, Mrs. Green. I gotta meet my friend."

Lorna, her weary best friend, who's been waiting outside for her forever, demands to know why she's so late. Her Blackness shines along with her usually pleasant personality of smiles. Her tiger eyes set her apart from other girls.

"Oh, Mrs. Green wanted to go over that stupid paper I put all that truth in. Next time I'll just write about the summer heat and . . ."

"But she wanted it to be about *us*, remember?"

Tania cocks her head to the side and rolls her eyes.

Lorna shrugs. "Okay, forget that. I want you to sleep over after the dance this weekend."

"I have to ask."

When she gets home Tania puts James Brown on the record player to lift her into the mood as she thinks about the outfit she'll wear. From downstairs she hears her mother yelling, "B!"

"Yes?" she calls down from the hallway outside her room.

"Turn off that vulgar music. Who is that, anyway?"

"James Brown, 'Hot Pants!'" She goes back into her room and turns the music off, then chooses a white dress with no sleeves, straight line and a simple neckline. It shows her knees, but no thigh. Now hearing the music only in her mind, she preens in front of her mirror, lacing up her sneakers to the rhythm of Marvin Gaye's "What's Going On." Suddenly she remembers Lorna will be waiting outside for her answer. She runs to her mother and asks, then hurries through the side door to the front of her house, where her friend is waiting with her dog. As usual, her mother said she can only walk the dog with Lorna and then must come straight home.

Hugging Lorna, Tania says, "My mom says yes, I can sleep over, 'cause my parents know your father will pick us up from the dance."

The two young women dare to practice dance moves every afternoon, at the corner of their street. In addition to going over dance steps, at school they practice for track. Sports are Tania's savior. Every week, she stretches, placing her legs in front and pumping her belly to her thighs. Yes, she feels flexible. Then she does fifteen minutes of free running around the small track, 'cause the fellas have the main track on the big side of the schoolyard. But she knows she won't be able to join the track girls at Randall's Island for the 440-yard relays at the next meet, because if she asked to go to a dance and a track meet around the same time her parents always replied, "Choose! A girl has to decide what is important."

In the bus on their way to the Community Center for the dance, Tania starts complaining. "I wish I could run with you all and stay out late, whatever that means. I'm sick of my parents' rules."

"Your parents are real strict," Lorna agrees. She pats her afro into place, runs her tongue over her light pink lip gloss.

"It's my mother! My father isn't even into what we do," Tania says.

"My father helps me," Lorna insists.

Tania can't imagine how anyone could ever think "Stonedad," which is what she and her sisters call their father, whose name is Sadstone, might come to her assistance. "Well, mine doesn't help me," she says. He just bothers me. He even comes upstairs at night and stares at me and . . . Her voice trails off.

"While you're sleeping?" Lorna thinks Tania's father is weird.

"Yes. Or at least he thinks I'm sleeping."

"My father doesn't do that. What does your moms say?" Lorna asks, looking in her bag for her lipstick.

"Oh, forget her . . . she doesn't pay attention to anything but work," Tania says, fidgeting with her fingers.

"Oh God." Lorna stays cool, remembering now that talking about her father and even her mom upsets Tania.

The bus hits a bump, propelling both girls into the air.

"Oh, man," Tania yells. "Now I don't feel good about my dance steps. Let's get off and walk the last few blocks, so we can practice our moves."

"Ohhh," Lorna moans, wondering why her friend suddenly seems so tense about her dance steps.

"Please."

"Why, Butt?" Lorna uses an old put-down nickname for her friend.

"No, don't. Don't call me Butt or Bcup or any of that tired stuff. I'm Tania," Tania says. She's smiling, but inside she feels a little let down.

"Hey, T-a-a-nia." Lorna drags out the sound. "You know I'm your best friend and am okay. But all right, let's get off and practice since this raggedy bus keeps jolting." She rings the bell. "But just for a few minutes," she adds.

"Yay."

The two girls jump down the back steps of the bus.

Later, at the dance, Walker, a young man the color of molasses, lets Tania in on his feelings. "I like your moves, baby." Tania grins. Lorna has a chocolate-skinned boyfriend, too, who wears a leather jacket and doesn't say much.

Red dance-party lights blur the harshness of life as a teen. All the kids can see are bodies moving as a turntable spins a backup of "ooh baby" and violins and little touches of bass guitar. The black velvet musical smoothness eases over slavery and indentured sharecropping and migration and then living in these big cities far from the coconut trees of Jamaica, where Tania's father came from, and the magnolias of Mississippi, which Lorna's parents had left years before. Queens couldn't compare to either, in humidity and sweltering, sexy heat, but the beat and the stylish butts and curves of the girls and the great moves and finesse of the guys ease Tania's heart. She melts into the party. She lets go of her mother's ice cold words, "a girl has to choose," which she only says to keep Tania from hearing the allure of that male singer's high-pitched croon. Mother warns her with her eyes while still letting Daddy hurt her.

She melts inside her thighs and in the place between them where the legs meet. She doesn't dare let her fella touch her there, but he drops his finger to just on top of her butt, and strokes her with what Marvin Gaye would call sexual healing, caressing the sides of her hips where they curve out. She definitely ain't no skinny girl. Her wide-set eyes soften.

In that small four-walls-with-no-decorations community center filled with teen bodies, beautiful, just-at-the-brim-of-life bodies, the steady trap drum and guitar riffing keep them safe for a while, because here, at least, they can rest with their own generation. None of the older women and men who are destroying their innocence is in that room. The highlight of the evening for the young, blossoming women comes when, as a junior track team member, Tania jumps up with the other girls and they dance a line number all together. But when slow drag songs come on, by the Moments or the O'Jays, or "Didn't I Blow Your Mind This Time?" Tania backs up. That's not her specialty, grinding in some corner with a guy, sweating and getting a hard-on, breathing heavy in her ear, while she holds him at his shoulders and prays his hand doesn't slip below her waist.

Suddenly, Tania gasps. Her father is standing in the doorway waving a flashlight as if the dim light prevents him from seeing her. "Lorna," she cries. "Don't turn around but my father's here."

"I thought your mother said my parents could take us home and you could spend the night." Lorna, too, regards Tania's father. As usual, he looks like a snarling dog, though he has beautiful eyes.

* * *

Soon after signing up for "Art and Social History," Tania puts her name down for three workshops Agua is also taking: "Movement," which is ballet and mime; "Scene Study," which involves not only conventional theater, but, thanks to the heritage of one of the instructors, role-playing around the spiritual relationship between Indigenous Americans and the land, and how the degradation of their land is not only an environmental injustice but a spiritual catastrophe; and a creative writing workshop for Black and Brown sisters focused on revolutionary themes.

As the weeks go by the two women begin to know each other better, working together on scenes from Tennessee Williams after the teacher pairs them, and usually practicing their moves in ballet and mime side by side, along with the yoga exercises and meditation each Movement class begins and ends with.

Agua, a single mom, brings her six-year-old son, whom she had named Heru Jade Verde, to the center. Verde means green in Spanish, which feels fruitful to her. He plays quietly in the ballet classroom, his thin body bent over a coloring book, mostly using his favorite color, red. It's a real ballet room with a barre just about the height of Heru, and with special wood floors for the shoes/slippers of the students. Windows face a busy Lower East Side aka "Loisada" street where lots of working-class folks and folks who live in the housing projects a few blocks away, walk fast, shopping and in general taking care of business. The glass panes rise up like huge drinking glasses. Rents in this part of Manhattan are low, so supporters of the arts and artists can afford to run a not-for-profit like University of the Streets.

Today, Clay, an older Black man with a heavy moustache, who is Agua and Tania's artistic mentor, is teaching the battement . . . kick the leg high, then plié, bend the knees out like an accordion, fold. Pointing to one distracted student, he calls out forcefully, "You need to plié twice, then after that, do the battement."

The student, who happens to be male, obeys the teacher. It's good to have another Black male in ballet class doing position two on the hardwood floor.

Clay cuts a concerned stare at them all. "We are artists," he says. "This practice keeps us in shape. Even for writers, our body is our instrument. We need it to be toned so we can do theater or anything else!"

Agua and Tania gracefully complete the routine. Tania lingers as everyone else leaves, including Agua, still in her ballet slippers. She has suddenly remembered, as her classmates shout, "Bye!" that she has to pay for her ballet class today. After changing, she finds Agua waiting for her in the office.

"Oh, so you're only paying for last month." Agua counts the wrinkly dollar bills Tania places in her palm.

"Yeah. It's not the end of this month yet . . ." Tania, who never had to live hand to mouth when she was growing up, doesn't identify with Agua's irritation at the way she continually pays late. She's more concerned that her low-paying part-time jobs can't really cover the luxury of classes.

Agua sighs, remembering how she used to help her mother juggle the bills, especially after they moved out of the projects. Rent always came first. Then, one month, they would pay Con Ed electric so they could cook, then the next tell the monopoly phone company their money was late and beg for an extension on the bill and no late fees so they could buy school clothes or, sometimes, even food She peers into Tania's face and rolls her eyes as she watches her check her appointment calendar. "You know, Tania," she says, "we're running a 'community' thing here, and because of that, the fees almost always carry the expenses. There are no big funders or grants, or anything. We used to operate out of a bar that one of the students ran, with classes during the day when the bar was closed. We don't want this creative place to shut down." Agua presses her afro down for emphasis.

"Okay. I hear you," Tania replies, but some time later, a stream of morning sun-rays glides into the office as she checks in with Agua about her bill, although she's really on her way to the restroom. "I'm finally getting my act together, right?" She smiles.

"Do you realize that if no one pays their fees, this little University of the Streets will have to close? You can't pay Con Ed bills with smiles."

"Oh, God, Agua, you're right. I'm learning that in my class background they just cover up money issues and are tense 'cause the kids don't understand."

"Yeah, I dig that." Agua smiles, too, as she cleans up in the office, straightening out papers and organizing the large desk. To point the subject elsewhere she says, "Is this Saturday mime class your favorite?"

Tania responds with a movement, pretending to be in a box and pushing to get out. "It's amazing to watch Clay when he shows us a new mime step like this one, isn't it? See you in a bit." She strolls to the bathroom, changes and arrives in the studio, where she takes a seat on the floor in the sunny spot by the window.

Agua, already there, joins her. Smiling, she says, "I feel like I've known you before this lifetime." She stretches her body down from the waist. Tania stands up again, and walks her first and second finger up Agua's back as Agua unrolls her spine, vertebra by vertebra.

Agua then sits and starts pounding her strong, supple calves into the floor with her fists to release the buildup of tension from her week as a mother alone with Heru Verde. "Sometimes I wish I'd had more choices," she says.

"Oh? Like how?"

"Well, I was so unhappy with my mother and stepfather, he wasn't helping out with the finances . . ."

"You told me about the viciousness of growing up on welfare."

"Yeah, and the U.S. of assholes lets these corporations be on wealth-fare!"

"Tell me about it!"

"I'm so glad me and you can work out our differences," Agua says, smiling.

Tania smiles back.

Agua rubs her face. "Yeah, the Marxist School talks about doing self-criticism when working with other companions in any movement," she says, revealing more of her hopeful attitude toward clear thinking.

"Agua, it means a lot to me," Tania says, "and it does to you, too, right? . . . The way we can talk with each other about almost anything?"

Agua nods. "Yeah, even though you're not a single mom, or even a poor mother at all, you really listen and follow what it means for me to watch my son, and have to be available to him all the time, or as much as I can."

"I hope I get it. It seems like a big weight."

"Yeah, and that's what I mean. I wanted to be studious, I guess you could say, but back in high school, those shitty schools don't give a damn about anything more than controlling you. The dean told the boys, even though you ain't white and rich you can be like John Wayne and make it. What bullshit."

"So did you hang out a lot?"

"Yeah . . . But Tania, you said you had a track team for the girls, right? And an open running field?"

"Uh huh." Tania nods.

"Well, girl, we didn't. We were lucky we even had a boy's basketball team with an inside gym. Hardly anybody had any space in the classes, they just crammed us in. We didn't have books half the time, always sharing these raggedy ass books that didn't tell you the truth about slavery or even mention it happened in Puerto Rico. That's why my *abuelita* was dark. But she didn't hate herself because of it. She loved her dark skin, and I'm proud of my grandma for that."

Tania interjects, "The other day I heard a program on W.B.A.I. . . ."

"W.B.A.I.? What's that?"

"You know, the progressive radio station, 99.5, the one where you can hear the real news without any ads. Anyway, the program was about Pedro Albizo Campos and the struggle for the end to Puerto Rico as a colony of Spain."

Agua grabs the moment. "Yeah, he was one of the *independistas*!"

"Huh?"

"Independence movement leaders! Puerto Rico was a fucking colony of Spain and now it's a so-called Commonwealth, dependent on the USA of shitty assholes, thieves and all. We want to be a free nation, not even a state. You know, Tania, we Puerto Ricans can't even swim on our own beaches, 'cause the corporations like Hilton or whatever have bought them up and made them P-R-I-V-A-T-E!" Agua raises her voice as she spells out the word.

More students show up in leotards and stretch out on the wooden floor in various poses to warm up. It's time for their mime class to begin. Rolling up and slapping five, Tania and Agua find their space in the middle of the room. Agua, not a dreamer and very practical, concentrates hard in the class. She has to be practical and has little time for dreaming, even though she and Tania were born just a few years apart. Tania, on the other hand, is remembering a poem she has been writing in her mind about a girl she saw in the park one day.

I want to please
daddy please let me be good
A good girl
Don't make me a bad girl
I'll do what you say
Just please
Don't say I'm bad
Daddy you told me to do it and I did it
And I'm a good girl
Right?
Right daddy?
Come home and eat at home and look at me,
In my chair (sitting properly) and tell me

I'm a good good girl
I'm growing up now and you still want me to do it,
And I'm your good little girl and daddy's good big girl.
I'm a good, very good girl, Daddy . . .
Right?

Turning around, Tania notices in the classroom mirror that her face has tears. The classroom is empty.

She searches for Agua, and finds her back in the cluttered office, sweeping the floor. Is this a good time and place for them to talk? They have no more classes that day.

But while Agua cleans, in comes Heru Verde. "Mom, I'm hungry. Can we go now?" There's no space for Tania's thoughts. She waits in the corner.

Using her gentle voice, Agua reminds her son that it isn't time yet, adding, "In the other room in your backpack, I think you'll find the sandwich we made together, remember? Go look." His short legs full of energy, he skips to the other room, in which he has a special corner that is his space, where his coloring books and very own notebook are kept. Agua knows he will occupy himself for a time while she tackles the University of the Streets account ledgers.

After she takes up the broom again, Tania bends down, holding the dustpan. "Your son has hair that's curly like mine," she remarks.

"We are Puerto Rican. Well, he is Puerto Rican and African-American. Or Black is what folks say in my neighborhood."

"Oh, like me, a mixed-race person."

Agua murmurs, "Uh huh."

Tania goes on. "Usually in groups of people who are Black, I don't feel comfortable saying I'm also Jewish and had a Jewish grandma who loved me. It's not like I have white friends, 'cause this city is racist as hell and not many white folks hang out on the Lower East Side or at the University of the Streets or work with me at my low-paying reading-tutor gig at the Brooklyn Child Care Center."

Agua replies, "Yeah, the white folks are either landlords of the building, or a 'stupervisor/boss' at the job."

Trying for a little bit of "get close" talk before Agua starts on her office work, Tania says, "It's not necessary to tell white folks that I'm of color. They can smell it—the telltale stream of brownness flowing through my skin tone."

"Lightly, yes," Agua jokes. "But the all-knowing scrutinizing racist will know that you got African or something different than them at the roots, once they check out that hair." She gestures at Tania's gorgeous puffy hair, pulled to the side and springing out with joy.

* * *

Buttercup is eleven years old. Her father is teaching the Negro history class, which is held in the basement of the church. He is a good teacher. She listens gratefully as he reveals to her for the very first time how an enslaved woman had escaped and led others away from slavers, and returned thirty times to help more enslaved folks escape. All would be hanged or whipped if caught. They looked like her and Daddy and her classmates in the colors from chocolate to ginger.

At home she complains, "Why didn't you tell me about any of this before, Daddy?" She wants to scream it, but he will hit her if she raises her voice to him. He had never even told her she was a Negro, much less that she had a history!

"You were only a child!" he says, dismissing her younger self.

Buttercup realizes this conversation has been a long time coming. Her mouth says nothing, but the face of the underground railroad conductor Harriet Tubman comes into her mind. Oh, yeah, Harriet ran like a rabbit from home, 'cause she was owned on a plantation by a master who beat her.

After five silent deafening minutes, she says, "You told us Harriet carried a gun, right?" Her hands are folded in her lap.

In the stark quiet that follows, Buttercup wonders, "Will I have to become a runaway, too?"

After many minutes more, since he was obviously finished, another question pops out. "Can I go outside?"

"Yes."

"Daddy . . ." She starts to ask him why he never comes to her shows or ballet recitals or dance performances at school. She wants to have a little conversation to cover up the other one, but instead she almost trips over her feet trying to run out of there. Jumping down the step to the sidewalk, she checks out the block for anyone playing double-dutch. She hears voices and races to the corner by the attached houses where the kids play tag. She cries, "Can I play? Can I play too?"

"Yeah," they yell back. "You're 'it.' "

She jumps into action, racing like a wild horse after first one kid, then another. They all elude her, but that stops her only for a minute. She feels on fire. With a vengeance, she reaches out to hit them hard with her tagging. They fall out, cracking up as they jump to the side. Finally she is about to snare a boy. He volunteers to be "it," and she runs from him, shouting, "You ain't got no sense, but okay you're it, you're it now." Her hands reach for her two braids and she pulls them. It hurts her head, but she has such a headache, it also feels good.

"You're crazy. Why are you pulling your hair?" One kid taunts her.

"I don't know" she replies, skipping off.

* * *

"Tania, come back. Stop daydreaming, please."

Without missing a beat, Tania says, "You know what, Agua, this hair is the curliest, but yet not nappy, hair in my family."

"I know what you mean, Tania. We Latinas got that same bullshit hair texture obsession."

Tania's laughter fills the room. "Yeah, Older Sister has let her hair get into a pulled-back ponytail, then braids it up, or at least presses it down into a barrette. She no longer wears an afro. She's in law school, you know! Younger Sister always had straight hair, so it's still that way."

"Wow. Why do you call them those names, anyway?"

"Well, my older sister always said, 'I'm your older sister, you have to obey me,' and the younger one used to say, 'I'm younger than you, you can't expect me to help.'"

Agua breaks up. When she stops laughing, she says, "So, tell me, how do you really feel about all this hair stuff?"

"I hate the crap that folks attach to whether you are more elite or better than poor folks of color by how white your hair looks. My sisters used to call me frizzball. You know, class snootiness."

"Do you see those sisters? You hardly ever mention them."

"Rarely. They live out of town."

Having finished sweeping the floor, Agua sits down at her desk and takes up one of the record-keeping ledgers.

"I guess I'd better go," Tania says, but Agua motions for the younger woman, who is her first real friend outside her family since high school, to sit down.

"Hey, you might as well cop a squat, Tan," she says. She sounds sixteen in her use of street talk all of a sudden.

"Man, why did you use that short form of my name?" Tania says. "That's so . . . freaky. I was sometimes called Toni by my parents, and hated it."

"How come? Did it show they really wanted a boy and had you instead?"

Pulling on a few strands of her hair, Tania says, "You know, I never thought about it like that, but yeah maybe that's why." She wrinkles her nose, wondering.

"You know, I think about changing my slave name legally," Agua says.

"Well, at a lotta jobs, whatever one I have at the moment, I usually let the boss just call me T. That way I know I'm in the world of work bullshit."

In an instant Agua catches her friend's thinking, "And then with us in the real world you are your real self, Tania?"

"You got it. You know how phony and most paying gigs are."

Tania sits down in the chair in the corner of the room that has become "hers" and watches as Agua buries herself in her work. Still, she can't resist saying, "Hey, one more thing, okay? . . . Our mother is white."

But Agua, who is trying to match the numbers up, can't involve herself in the whiteness thing at the moment and doesn't catch it.

Tania persists. "Agua, let me just tell you one thing about my mom."

"About your mom?"

"She used to tell her white and Black friends that she knew what racism really is 'cause she had Black kids."

"Oh God."

"But you know, Agua, her mama, my white grandma, did understand."

"Wow." Resigned, Agua closes the ledger.

"I loved her so much. She kept me safe, you know?"

Agua nods.

Tania goes on, "My grandma liked old Jewish singing, having been a peasant in the 'old country.' Nobody told me grandma was sick, so I stayed in the dark, just like with all the other family secrets. The night she died I dreamed of Hanukah songs and grandma saying, 'Let's go swimming in an outdoor lake.' When I woke up I felt like going right to the lamp she made to turn it on even though it was morning. She'd given it to my parents when she finished making it. On the way to brush my teeth I overheard my mother on the phone saying, 'Mom died last night, Pop She asked for you, but you weren't there.' I ran to the living room and climbed into the armchair by Grandma's lamp. I kept staring at the shade, trying to bring her back in my mind."

"What did she look like?" Agua asks.

"Grandma? She was a short woman with white skin and peasant style-hair—two long braids piled on top of her head—and light brown eyes. And her fingers were short and stubby, without rings. I loved her spirit. She gave money for the little Red Cross fund that I was collecting donations for, back when I was in the second grade . . ."

Agua shakes her head as Tania's face collapses into sadness. Wondering if she will go deeper, she asks, "How did you feel?"

But Tania shakes her head. "Feel? My family didn't deal with feelings."

She says nothing more, and after a while Agua goes to check on Heru, who's creating happily in his notebook, then returns to the accounts. She really does have to get some of this stuff done. As her work engulfs her, a line forms on her face, which has a tight look, with lips pursed.

Tania settles back into her chair and reads over one of her free-write poems:

Life of My Grandma

Even as a young teen B learns
A dying person goes in female and comes back in a big, new aeroplano,
Comes back from death

Comes back from a side of life
those who only stay on earth for now don't know.
Comes back in pretty molecules of air.
Smell her hair
Smell her coat, long and black, like sacred night
Smell her smile.
Smiling with her human earth teeth,
This woman from Death World
does her work.
No longer in a human body
Grandma has no need to carry arms and hips,
or long shoes with cushiony soles for those old hurting feet.
Grandma, a beauty maker, erases B's sounds of alarm.
For a visitor to earthside
from deathside
this is Not Easy
no es facil
there is a Queasy Feel to this Deal.
"Grandma, come back," B wants to squiggle
in her black and white marbled book.
Or, bike riding on sidewalks filled with cracks,
she wants to round a corner and see her.
Grandma, come on, be here, be B's guardian on earth,
Angel in front of this budding girl's sad eyes.
But instead, a wise Grandma speaks to B in a dream:
"I never laughed so much
as when you flew your paper airplane
and it twisted up and away, out of reach
and you just climbed on top of
your sweet flat bike seat,
untangled it from that fence.
I laughed 'cause no one knows, except you,
little teen—yarns of years old—
how to still be a kid
while you develop bosoms and hips."
Grandma speaks in B's dream:
"I'll cut a piece of cake for you,
celebrate with you every birthday you know is coming,
(without my short grandma presence
in front of your black black hair),

I laugh, dear little one.
You, with eyes of Lilith.
I laugh, smile and stand still as a big oak.
Help you stop those boys in school
from trying to choke
all female love of self outta you!
Not with that same pudgy, friendly belly
will I come back,
but in all sound, in all music, and when you sing, calling out for me . . . to come back as I visit your Self later,
with my hand, spirit and powerful soul."

Tania roots around in her bag for the orange she'd bought at the deli around the corner from the University of the Streets instead of the sugary doughnut she really wanted. Sighing as she sucks on a section, she recalls how she used food to avoid facing how hard it was to have a white mother who never acknowledged, much less confronted, her own racism. Her random thoughts are laced with messages: don't use sugar to avoid thinking about mama's racism; don't stuff yourself with strawberry shortcake 'cause you can't stuff the loneliness inside and there's no one to talk to about it; don't stuff yourself with chocolate like Younger Sister, who, it occurs to her, must have been stuffing her feelings inside, too.

She leans her head back on the office wall, and remembers her mother, grandma's daughter.

* * *

While listening to mother directing things, Buttercup thinks about strawberry shortcake. She asks, "Can we have shortcake with red berries and white icing?"

"It could make your tummy hurt," says Mama.

Buttercup doesn't care and touches her lips. At least, after eating a piece, I'll have a smile made of white icing on my brown lips. She doesn't know she can tell someone that sometimes Daddy asks her to kiss him, even on the lips when he comes upstairs. Best to surround her mouth with sweets.

It is her birthday. She is four. Younger Sister and Older Sister have both had their birthday celebrations, within the past month, and now it's time for hers. Buttercup still has a few inches over Younger Sister, but both sisters taunt Buttercup with bursts of laughter. "You're adopted," they shout when she comes home from school. Younger Sister wears nice clothes, always matching, and pulls her long, almost straight, hair back with pins. It flows down to her shoulders. Younger Sister prefers Sarah Lee pound cake to strawberry shortcake. Neither sister wants to come to Buttercup's birthday. They have their own friends. But all birthday parties have to be carefully planned, with party favors for their guests.

It is another birthday, several years later. Older Sister takes over for Mommy, standing over Butter, who leans on the kitchen counter. She and Younger Sister ridicule her idea for a bowling party.

Butter asks, "So what was your agenda for the party you just had, Older Sister?" She notices how Older Sister wears her hair in a single braid. Her sophisticated sister, who has the lightest skin of all the sisters, pulls the braid to the side and tries to force it to hang over her shoulder, sexy like.

"I planned on the straw and tissue paper game." Older Sister spells out the instructions for the game on pink index cards.

Butter tiptoes into the dining room, with its long table covered by a fancy tablecloth and no plastic on top of it, and six antique style chairs, two with arms, set around it, to write out her party cards. She sits in one of the armless, straight-backed chairs to work, giving each card a fancy border with shearing scissors, then writing the invitations. Her feet still don't quite touch the floor; the chairs have no foot rests to accommodate a kid's legs. It's hushed in the room today. When her absent father doesn't have time for the family, which seems like every day to her, only four people sit in these chairs. She misses him, even as she feels mixed up about their "special" relationship. Upstairs, later on, she writes in her diary "Daddy ate out every night. After all he's Daddy."

She wishes she had had the courage to invite Ygerken, the boy from school, to the party. His first name and his last name all become one word so she has created a special fantasy name for him when writing in the diary to hide the fact that she has a crush on him. Ygerken has blond hair.

The day of her birthday, Ygerkin raises his hand when the teacher asks, "Who is against the Vietnam War?"

She worries about the way some of the other kids jump on him with their comments. "You should go back to Russia," they say. "You aren't American."

The other white kids in her Special Progress class, who are bused to her junior high, don't say it aloud, but think, "You're a nigger lover."

"He's an anti-war extremist!" Aaron shouts, his glasses shaking. His face is red, especially his nose.

"Who are we there to kill?" Ygerken raises his voice. "We kill civilians. We kill babies. We kill people that aren't soldiers."

The girls in front of Butter shift in their seats. Are they also thinking Ygerken is a traitor to the U.S.? Sharon, a good-looking classmate, tosses her hair and taps her nails on the showy red, white and blue flag pasted in the center of the cover of her loose-leaf. Butter notices the way Louise Perak pushes her glasses up on her nose, warily looking around. Louise had mentioned to Butter that her older brother was drafted. She's scared the Marines will send him right to Vietnam to die fighting "the good ole fight for America." Butter hopes Louise's hand will do what her own hand does not. Both do nothing.

School ends for the day. Ygerken lightly taps Butter's bookbag with his as he rushes past her out the school door. She runs to tap him back, but can't keep up with his longer legs running down the tree-lined block. She worries that she is boring. She likes him so much because, just like in her house, the school has lots of go-along-to-get-along type rules, but Ygerken doesn't follow them. Yet, he also never notices that she follows him on the bus. Maybe he thinks she just likes to ride past her stop? For the first time she walks in front of him off the bus, trying to force him to give her some attention. Stopping suddenly, he tells her, "Quit following me around. You don't belong here."

"I thought we were friends," she pleads.

"Only in school. Go away." The wind lifts his blond hair as he walks off.

When she turns around the white bus driver is staring at her.

* * *

For a while the silence in the office is broken only by the sound of pages turning as Agua works on the ledgers. It is little Heru who ends it as he comes strolling in, holding his notebook by the middle five pages. The book hangs down like the cover on a bed when you're folding it.

"Hey, Heru." Agua motions for him to come get a hug.

"Mom," he says. "Guess what, mom. I wrote a poem."

"Let's hear it."

Heru looks at his five special pages. Each one has a different topic. Children. He turns the page. Big people. Food. Sleeping. School. On the last three he has gone over the letters with dark crayon and underlined them. Then at the end, after a picture of a lot of homeless people looking like their hands are hoping someone will share some food, he has written: *Everybody shopping / Shopping for this / Shopping for that / But / In my neighborhood / It's only hungriness.*

Both women clap. "Yeah, Heru, you are thinking!" Tania shouts.

Heru's mom hugs him tight as Tania says, "Agua, you know my parents claimed to be for putting a stop to North American values of buy, buy, buy, but don't think about the workers in the sweatshops making the stuff. But they didn't want to face that they were going for this system's consumerism too. We used to go shopping when the fear of standing up to all the shit got too depressing."

"I hear you," Agua says.

Tania goes on: "This system has people so scared all the time, we can't be real, 'cause nothing is sacred or secure. We definitely didn't get that Full Employment bill passed, did we?"

They laugh and shake their heads. Tania interrupts the laughter hiding their pain. "It ain't socialist here, that's for sure. I've been reading how the Cubans rid their homeland of the U.S. domino sugar plantation corrupt wealthy thieves and I'm searching for a different system here, too, but . . ."

Agua grins, appreciating Tania. The younger woman even kind of looks like her. Their eyes smile differently, but their similar attitude shows in their body language as bold and ready to do something with life, "You know," she says, "I wish more folks would wake up. My sisters and brothers hardly do anything and neither does half the U.S. population. I try not to feel hopeless, but I think it's gonna be a life-long struggle, and—"

"Mom, can I play in the park before we go home?" Heru knows he can feel free on the swings.

"Yes," Agua says. "Put your notebook away and we'll be outta here."

All three of them chase that free feeling once they go through the gates of the city park. Then Agua and Tania sit on a bench watching the child swing.

"I know something about the whiteness thing," Agua says, picking up on what they'd been talking about in the office. "And about being color-struck by the grade of hair you have or the lightness of your skin. That happens a lot in the non-socialist Caribbean. Even in Cuba they are still dealing with what colonialism by Spain and the U.S. of assholes did to the native folks and Africans to prevent healthy mixing. I told you my grandmother was dark . . ."

"So what was she like?" Tania asks. But Agua doesn't say any more. Suddenly she's remembering how shamed she felt as a girl when people in her Puerto Rican neighborhood silently walked by as her mom made her stand naked in front of the window. She begins to gather her things.

Wanting to keep her friend with her a little longer, Tania says, "Hey, why are you into acting?"

"Why are you?" Agua says.

"Because I'm hungry for a chance to get out of me some of the stuff that's stuck inside. You know I've been reading Tennessee Williams . . . even though so many of his characters are Southern whites. I relate to these repressed women. I feel like screaming sometimes, Agua, and this way I can do it without people, my neighbors, wondering if I'm crazy!"

"I hear you," Agua says. But before she can say more Heru comes running over and starts pestering mom by peeking in her shoulder bag, because sometimes she keeps an apple or raisins there for their subway trip home so he doesn't feel too hungry and start wanting McDonalds. She utters a quick, "Gotta go, Tania, 'cause Heru is damn near starving." Getting her things together now like one, two, three, she and her son prepare to take off.

"Okay, catch you later. Call me, okay?" Her voice floats behind Agua as her friend heads toward the park gate.

With New York's polluted breeze blowing, Tania looks up to the city's sky and thinks how she could be with more sky in Queens, that outlying borough where she grew up, far from her now by subway, but right in the back of her mind all the time. She sits on the hard green park bench for hours, almost in a trance, lost in remembering.

* * *

"At least the parents have given her a pad and colors. She can make very straight lines. But nothing is connected." These words had been written in the notes of the observant nurse who came to give Buttercup shots for a bout of pneumonia when she was a 2-year-old baby. Buttercup was Black, the nurse noted, but not really. Buttercup was white, but not really.

G- R-A-N-D-M-A ! Buttercup has written capital letters on the lined paper she uses to write a letter. Sitting on the sparkly linoleum floor in the kitchen, she wrinkles her forehead, worrying.

Her little girl writing looks wobbly. GRANDMA GRANDMA GRANDMA in the big letters that are what she knows how to print. That's all she wants to put on two more sheets of paper. She wants her grandma to come back. She wants grandma to come over. She wants to go be near her grandma. Smell her grandma. Play with her grandma or let grandma do her hair. She wants her grandma to come and get her. She thinks about how grandma would come over again, if only she and Mama wouldn't argue so much.

While thinking, she scratches an itch on her nose. Her fragile little tan fingers suddenly feel like they're holding her bedcovers. Her thumb is red from sucking it soooo long every day. She is thinking and thinking and thinking about her bedroom. She just can't get it out of her mind. She worries about when she goes to bed at night and something itches her legs. What is it?"

Buttercup is sitting on her sweet little girl's behind, legs sprawled out, peaceful in the fresh smelling kitchen with Miss Duffy. Suddenly Miss Duffy drops a pot top. Bang! Its clanging brings Buttercup back to reality. She laughs delightedly when Miss Duffy jumps.

"I had a dream last night," Buttercup announces in a small voice.

Miss Duffy turns from watching the pots on both front burners of the fancy new stove; she is listening with her whole round body. Her bosom spans two continents, North America and the Caribbean. Miss Duffy has her feet in this New York kitchen but her heart is in the islands with the family she left behind so she could make American dollars and send them back home to Jamaica, the same island Buttercup's father comes from. Miss Duffy feels scared. The last two dreams Buttercup told her were nightmares.

Buttercup's mother walks in, home from work.

"What *are* you doing!" she explodes, slapping her thigh.

"Oh, Buttercup and I are just talking about her dreams."

"Buttercup is always making up stories," her mother sneers.

As this white boss, a woman of average height with curly Jewish hair and freckles, walks by the hired woman, her soft-soled shoes squeak. Miss Duffy can feel her tension from the stiff way she holds her back, from her stony face and cold eyes, and knows this is the wrong time to mention anything.

Her red-faced boss washes her delicate, ladylike manicured fingers while she orders Miss Duffy to make a green salad. "And you should have put my meatloaf in a lot earlier!" she snaps, wiping her hands hurriedly on a paper towel.

"But I didn't know you were coming home. You usually don't get here until 4 p.m." Miss Duffy's voice, as she tries to defend herself, is quiet, submissive.

"And . . . I want you to get that vegetable dish ready immediately as well," Miss Duffy's boss barks, and turns on her heel. Her dress swishes, slapping Buttercup in the face. Buttercup winces; only Miss Duffy notices.

"Mommy . . ." Buttercup looks up.

"Later, I'm busy right now." She walks off. Buttercup's mama rarely looks down at the floor where her brown and white child, Buttercup, sits most days. Buttercup's mama mostly pays attention to this skinny, eyes-of-sorrow little one only when she sits at the dinner table in a proper chair.

Now, as Buttercup starts to tell her worry to Miss Duffy, her face wrinkles up.

"Ok, honey pie, tell me your story." Miss Duffy smiles.

"Miss Duffy, it's my dream remember?" Her tan fingers came out of her mouth, reaching up for Miss Duffy's skirt. Miss Duffy scoops her up into her fleshy Hershey's chocolate arms.

"Yes, yes, I'm sorry, it's your dream, not a made-up story," Miss Duffy apologizes. Her rugged eyes look deep into Buttercup's. She and Buttercup know it is okay to be going there with this dream. Miss Duffy will hold me, Buttercup thinks. She won't drop me like Daddy did the other day on the side of the table. She touches the big line on her leg where the blood had come out.

"I dreamed I was driving Daddy's big car, and I was driving all around," Buttercup says slowly. Then her round mouth with the lips and tongue of a little person goes to suck her thumb. Buttercup just loves her little thumb. It sticks to the roof of her mouth and stays there.

Usually, no one really knows what she is doing. She covers her thumb with the other fingers. Sometimes it hurts, from being sucked for such a long time.

The last time she'd sucked it in front of Daddy, he'd shouted at her, "Don't suck your thumb!" as he stormed past her into his office room.

Leaning against the wallpaper in the kitchen, seeing the faraway look in the child's eyes, Miss Duffy nudged gently, "Is that the dream?" Miss Duffy's "Come Mr. Tally man," song-voice brings Buttercup's mind back to the kitchen, takes it away from her worry thought about her very tall Daddy.

Miss Duffy puts Buttercup down on the floor, since she really is too big to be held for very long. Suddenly the yellow plantains start to fry too loud. Miss Duffy turns down the blue flame on the stove. When Miss Duffy was little, she got burned by a wood stove. She shows the burn on her hand to Buttercup. Buttercup gently smoothes Miss Duffy's scar. This is their ritual. They have talked many times about staying away from the stove, so Buttercup's hand will never have an ugly scar on it from the fire.

"An' then I remember I can't drive." Buttercup barely gets the words out of her mouth. She cringes even now. Miss Duffy has to strain to hear her.

"I look at the car and the seat next to me. No one is there, Miss Duffy. Nobody is with me. I'm by myself. I'm all by myself. Miss Duffy, nobody is there to help me. I can't drive. I . . . I can't."

Miss Duffy's eyes try to reassure Buttercup as she leans down to pat her head and says over and over again, "It's all right, it's all right."

"Oh, Miss Duffy, don't go to church this week, please. Stay here with me. Miss Duffy let me stay here with you. Take me to church. I don't wanna stay in this house when you go to church, Miss Duffy."

Miss Duffy stands bewildered, staring at this American child.

Then more words stumble and tumble from the youngster's lips: "It's cold in here now. It's very cold."

In a soft voice filled with the smell of plantains, Miss Duffy says, "Maybe you better put on your sweater."

Up near her thin thighs, a pretty, embroidered, child-size red sweater lies across Buttercup's legs.

"Oh, my leg hurts, Miss Duffy." Buttercup's voice is very high pitched now as she smoothes her leg with her sweater. The room seems suddenly very big and the ceiling too far away from Buttercup. The scary sound of rain pounds on the window. It is a big storm.

"I don't want to sit at the dining table tonight, Miss Duffy. I wanna stay here with you in the kitchen at your chair," Buttercup begs.

Miss Duffy wipes Buttercup's face gently. She uses her big thick, work-roughened little finger. The child's skin feels nice and soft, like puppy fur.

Buttercup starts to cry. The tears fall down her cheek like the raindrops on the windowpane. But this is Buttercup's very own chocolate-vanilla skin, not just a sturdy sheet of glass. Buttercup cannot stop the tears.

"I don't never want to be at that table trying to eat those beets with my Daddy looking," she thinks. Finally, she blurts out, "Why is Daddy always watching me?"

But Miss Duffy cannot explain what she is unsure about and says nothing.

"Mommy, where's Mommy?" Buttercup wonders.

"She hasn't come to tell me it's time to serve dinner yet," Miss Duffy replies.

"She hardly ever says hi to me when she comes home. She just talks to you," Buttercup complains. She never asks Miss Duffy to explain her mama's behavior.

No matter how much Miss Duffy takes her apron and wipes the slow-moving rain on Buttercup's thin face, this child being has no other words, just tears. Miss Duffy doesn't know how to stop those tears. Finally she just rocks back and forth in the creaky kitchen chair, holding Buttercup against her good leg.

Miss Duffy only works for the family. She can't say a word. It could get her in trouble with immigration. But Miss Duffy can have carrot-chewing races with Buttercup. She can smile big broad toothless smiles at this small girl. "Come on, let's have our carrot-chewing race with these carrots," she will say, pointing to the bag of orange vegetables lying on the Formica counter, close to the sink.

But now Buttercup is holding on even tighter to Miss Duffy and Miss Duffy doesn't put Buttercup down. She doesn't throw a carrot up in the air, catch it, then start munching on it with her toothless gums. Miss Duffy can't even manage a smile now.

Cradling Buttercup, she stares way past the kitchen's windowpane and the gray, gloomy day to her own childhood in Jamaica. She remembers her own rigid childrearing. She knows the father is harsh with Buttercup, but that's because he, too, is Caribbean. Miss Duffy stays in this house as only the "housekeeper," and she knows that. But she wants to stop Buttercup's weeping.

"Miss Duffy, can you stop Daddy's car from coming into my dreams?" Buttercup whispers.

* * *

Copies of *The Daily Worker* lie on the sturdy green glass coffee table in her parents' home. But the headline in one issue, "The Fight Against White Baseball," blazes up. Buttercup's dad cuts out the article. He wants to show his wife later how clearly racism is being denied by much of the mainstream press, where the "follow Joe McCarthy folks" omit any mention of Negroes fighting against exclusion from white sports. Instead, they attack progressives as "sickening" and scare ordinary people by producing articles about a "Red Tinge." Everyone is supposed to get distracted and think the "Commies" are the problem instead of realizing that the U.S., long after Jackie Robinson first played for Brooklyn, still doesn't really want Negro players in the major leagues. Or the Women's League, for that matter, but that's no longer around.

Father sees Miss Duffy sitting in the kitchen and thinks about the bad news he has to give her. She turns toward her boss and he motions to her to pass the guava jelly jar. Her eyes rest for a moment, as do his, on the trees from Jamaica on the label, then return to his, which seem forlorn. He murmurs, "Guess it'll be better when we're fully independent of those ruthless British."

Miss Duffy says nothing, but in their look they feel both their island and their cold lives here. She drags the garbage bag outside.

As he walks past the table to the phone after another fruitless job interview, Father has no thoughts about baseball. He needs a new job.

He calls out to his wife, who's in their home office alphabetizing their bills. She swivels the desk-chair around to face him. He says, "A white man named Johnson told me there were no positions available once he saw my black face!"

"Oh no!" Buttercup's mother replies, her tone shocked, but not really. She sighs and drops her head. She knows the strains on their relationship when she, the white woman, barks at him, the Black man. These were the kind of face-reality talks they'd been having lately. What had happened to the love that brought them together during the war? What had happened to the ideas they'd shared, she the Red Cross worker, and he, the Army man, who together could overcome Jim Crow and the quiet, vicious Northern color bar.

These disappointments are routine now. She keeps confronting bigotry in her own life, no longer just reading or talking about it with her brother, the former City College activist. She hadn't really known what her parents thought about race. None of them had been able to relax when she was growing up, with the store they owned being the major preoccupation. Both she and her brother worked every day after school at the cash register. She often fed her brother dinner because they came too late after closing the deli to make a meal and put their kids to bed. But her parents had refused to come to her wedding, because she married a Negro. Her brother hadn't come either. This had created pain in her relationship with her husband even before they married. Her parents had only shown up in her life again when Tania's grandmother insisted on knowing her grandchildren. Her brother and his family had remained disconnected.

Buttercup's dad complains bitterly, "Yeah, even though the newspaper with the ad was for this week and came out yesterday, which was Sunday, that white guy told me it had been filled already, and I arrived at 8:30 a.m.! Then, when I walked out to the reception area, I noticed a white man going into the office. He asked me whether this was the place where the insurance salesman interview was. Before I could tell him the job was filled, the receptionist ran out and waved him in. Damn!" He covers his mouth with his fist and turns towards the door.

Buttercup, at the end of the hall, fears the rage in her dad's forehead, his eyebrows stuck up in the air. She doesn't really understand his last words, just watches as he grips the doorknob. Is Daddy scared? She wonders.

Shutting the door, he leans against the frame. "Damn! These racist bastards don't give a Black man a chance! Now we have to let Miss Duffy go." His coffee skin shines in the sun as he stands at the dining room window. He squeezes the back of his wife's chair, staring through the blinds. Their Desoto car, his in-laws' gift to make up for their absence before the kids were born, suddenly looks too big in their driveway. Frustration lines deepen around his nose. He mutters, "How much longer?"

* * *

Tania comes back to the park. She takes her thumb out of her mouth, unaware that she's been sucking it. She wipes her wrist underneath her watch where her skin has started to break out. She shifts on the bench. Her foot has fallen asleep. She shakes it, thinking it was her fault Daddy had ugly moods. But what meanness in the world was responsible for his rage?

On this warm, sunny afternoon both women are wearing sandals and they look at each other's toes as they sit side by side. Agua wiggles hers to lighten the mood. Agua has lovely feet. They hold this sturdy woman. Tania has got on running pants that someone put a fringe on the outer seams of, to dress them up. That's why she picked them out. Yellow, the color of sunflowers . . . For once her pants match her Mexican style top. Aside from the rash on her wrists, health streams out of her arms. She takes Clay, their mentor, seriously when he says women need to do pushups, too, if they're going to be toned for acting on stage.

They rest a while in silence. Then Tania says, "It's been so great getting to know you, Agua."

Agua smiles. "Ain't it something that you used to dislike me 'cause I reminded you about fees and shit? And now we're close enough to share just about everything."

Tania nods and opens her journal. Out drops a fading black and white picture of her parents.

Agua catches it and wordlessly hands it back.

"Listen, Agua, I wrote something," Tania says as she accepts the photo of her white mother with curly hair and her dark, handsome dad. "Can you hear it?" She is hoping Agua will be willing to help her comprehend what she has written, believing that somehow her friend will understand what she herself does not.

"Sure. Better yet, can I read it?"

Tania nods and starts to hand the journal, where the photo holds a place, to her friend. Then she stops herself and explains. "I wrote this because on the subway the other day I watched this little girl and her father and mother."

"What was happening, exactly?" Agua asks. She and Tania make a practice of closely observing other people as part of their creative training.

"Well, he kept on touching the child's hips, and all of a sudden she would just swivel her butt, kinda sexy or something."

"Really?" Agua encourages Tania to get the meaning of this.

"Yeah, and the mother, or whoever she was, but she knew them, 'cause they were all talking, well, she seemed to be ignoring the whole thing and looking out the window. You know how the train is above the ground for part of the time."

"Yeah."

"Okay, so ready to read it?" Tania passes the book to her friend.

"Yup." Agua chews her gum a little quieter as she reads: "*A Little Girl Speaks.*

'I did it
I did it.'
Do I know I can say no
When Daddy touches my butt and winks at me?
Do I even know I can tell my Mommy to look at Daddy and me?
And why won't she see?
Do I know I can say 'help me big big sky'?
Why?
'Cause Daddy likes me when I do it
And I wanna make Daddy happy
But I don't feel good. My tummy is sick.
'Can I have a glass of water?
I did it.'

Agua looks up from the journal. She feels tears welling up as she takes in the meaning of the piece, her eyes blinking fast.

"Wow," is all that comes out of her mouth, however. Tania's friend chooses to wait before saying a whole lot. She knows it took a breakthrough for Tania to trust her and let her read the poem, much less talk about it now. But her eyes behind the glasses on her butterscotch cream face silently say, "I believe you."

"Well?" Tania, herself, is not sure why she had had to write the poem, or even what she is expressing, and she hopes Agua will give some insight.

"Abuse," says Agua. "Yeah that's what this is about. And for me it's about a mother taking part in abuse by nonchalantly turning away."

This truth pains Tania like a burn. She wipes her wrist under her watch, where her rash is itching fiercely again. Her eyes scan the people all around. She feels bodies everywhere, the odors of cigarettes, coffee and too little deodorant mixed in the heat. People don't talk about sexual abuse out loud.

Squeezing her shoulders toward her ears, Agua groans.

Tania asks, "Tense?"

"Yeah."

They decide to go farther away from the noise of busses and trucks on the avenue, deeper into the park, to share an exchange of healing energy.

Agua says, "Let me rub your palms and massage the reflexology points."

This really lifts their energy and Tania returns the favor. "Is it okay to do my own version of a shoulder rub?" she asks. "I can do a back massage like I give my boyfriend if you want. We both took a meditation class once and the teacher showed us some good pressure points."

"Okay," Agua agrees.

As Tania does percussion taps on her friend's shoulders she realizes Agua holds her back very tight, and her hurting hangs in there. Tania's efforts can't seem to release it, whatever that stinging, biting agony is. Finally, as Tania keeps tapping, sometimes on Agua's back, sometimes on the top of her shoulders as she faces her, the pain connects and begins to flow out, as Agua digs further in emotionally to discover her own connection to what Tania has written. Finally she says, "Tania, my Puerto Rican-thinks-she's-almost-white mama used to hold my head between, yes, between her own fat thighs!"

Tania stares at Agua and then down at the pavement.

"Yeah, she put my face up by her vagina and that is wrong, Tania!" Agua looks into Tania's eyes.

It feels ugly to Tania when Agua tells her this. It feels like they've known each other for longer than they have. "God." Tania looks around now and breathes. Her shoulders feel just a little tight, so instinctively she moves them forward, then rolls them. The people in the park look like they're enjoying the sun and the sweet temperature, but Tania has forgotten about the weather. Dumb mother. How horrible. Tania feels her friend just thinking quietly. "I'm learning about the way you do things, Agua," she says. "I can wait. . . Do you want to say more?"

She hears Agua's light voice, not in reply, say, "I am so glad I could tell you, Tania. You're the first person besides the therapy/social worker guy from that program I ever told outside my family. I am so proud I got the guts to tell you. I didn't know you last year. Just meeting you has helped me so much."

"It's helped me a lot too. I've been lonely even though I have sisters. They just . . . you know . . ." Tania fools with her hair, not sure whether to keep talking about herself or to let Agua get more out. They both look at their watches.

"What time do you have?" Agua asks.

Tania laughs. "You have a watch, too."

"I know, but I just wanted to hear that it isn't time yet for me to go pick up Heru from the neighbor." She shifts on the bench.

Tania says, "Okay, just a few more minutes. I know you're under pressure."

"Yeah." Agua checks Tania's wrist where the bumps seem to be fading. "Anyway, Tania, I was lonely most of my life. I wanted to tell teachers and people at those religious summer camps. But I never could." She stops to take a breath.

"Why?" Tania's earrings jingle as she shakes her head in bewilderment.

"They didn't act like that was something they wanted to listen to." Agua adjusts her tight jean shorts around her thighs.

"Why?"

Agua places one finger on top of a seam in the shorts, then runs it over the seam's edge. She replies, "I don't know. Maybe because they never really asked me how did I feel about anything."

Tania pulls at the ring on her right pinky. "I remember last winter or whenever, I said something and you asked, 'How do you feel, Tania?' and I had no idea what you were even talking about."

Agua laughs. "I know that's the damn almost-rich bullshit way. Even the working class just shuts it all down and stuffs it in, pretending we don't have any feelings. Don't talk about any kind of feelings. Stay numb or just act them out. Act them out on each other. I mean even my mother was probably acting out shit that was done to her back in P.R."

Tania looks at her wrist. The bumps are almost nonexistent now. "Thank you so much for trusting me, Agua," she says. "I wish my sisters would trust me, too, but they just seem to get into talking about where they've been and what they've been doing to keep busy. We can't seem to talk honest like this. I wish we could."

"Oh?" Agua's tone invites her to go on.

Relaxed enough to share her soul, Tania complies. "I deserved to be trusted, you know, not told that I was always making up stories. Of course I told about events in exaggerated ways, I was trying to get them to pay even a little bit of attention to me, instead of ignoring me. But they'd only get into one of their haughty moods. One day Older Sister just put on a color-coordinated tennis outfit, picked up her racket, and jumped in the car and left me."

"Tennis racket?" Agua chuckles. "We were lucky if we had a glove when we played handball at the local rinkydink high school court."

After a silence during which both are tinkering with the idea of what to do or say next, they seem to think then say at the same time: "I love that we got to go to good old University of the Streets."

Tania worries that "Well I gotta go" is going to be coming out of Agua's mouth in a minute. When Agua's neighbor watches Heru Verde, it's usually only for a few hours. Well, I can spend time with myself, she thinks, facing her underlying lonesomeness. She holds on to what Agua has just shared.

2 CONNECTING TO AGUA'S CLASS

Coming back from hours of intense daydreaming prompted by Agua's revelation, and the way they had opened up to each other, Tania rubs her eyes and stretches her hands overhead, patting her behind, sore after sitting so long. She's amazed she even wrote that poem down, and sifts through her scribbled notes, but finds no clue. Finally, as evening sets in, pushing her to move, she stands up, picks up her journal from the bench, packs her backpack, and heads for the subway.

Underground, at the station where the F train from Queens and the D train from the Bronx, both bound for Brooklyn, come together, she feels her train, the D, coming out of the tunnel towards her. Graffiti, huge images of cartoon characters and letters, cover every car. They look like the pictures some of her University of the Streets classmates paint. She steps with a new confidence into the train, but then, finding no seat, she grabs a bar and disconnects from her feeling self. The subway map facing her makes her think how different parts of the city along the D line, like Harlem, in Manhattan, where most New York City Black families live real close with one another, are from Queens, with its trees and garden apartments and single family houses like the one she grew up in. In that place called the outer borough, where the F train reaches the end of the line, folks in Tania's old community don't have to share a room with sisters. Holding tight to the bar while the train shakes its passengers on the way to Brook's land, Brooklyn, she thinks the tree spirits in the blocks around her old neighborhood, where the F train ends up, must wonder where that little Buttercup moved to.

Since she left, Tania has grown and grown—come to know things, like how to find and keep a few part-time jobs without her father's suggestions. Sometimes she makes enough money for her jobs to amount to almost one full-time gig. Recently she got lucky and through someone at University of the Streets, landed work with theater ensemble workshops in rehabs that touches her heart.

She has found out how to sign a lease, conscious that this was a contract with a Brooklyn landlord—her Very First Apartment. She has learned to be able to stay home alone, just her. She has found out how to shop for vegetables, with Agua sometimes, picking out the ripe avocadoes to make salads with tofu, once she became a semi-vegetarian.

Even in her relationships with men she believes she is making progress. Until now her boyfriends have in a strange way seemed not really to be part of her life, not really to matter, the way Agua has come to matter. But a while ago she had met her current boyfriend, Buster, in mime class at University of the Streets. He, she was sure, would be different.

A seat opens up right in front of her and she quickly wedges herself into it. Clutching her backpack, she lays her head on her shoulder and closes her eyes. She thinks about her dad and mom. She likes that her family now lives far away. Her mother phones fairly regularly, but the calls consist mostly of criticisms of her choices and efforts to keep track of what furniture she has scrounged for her apartment and to make sure she is scouring her pots and pans "until they shine," as she had been required to do when she was a girl. Her father does not call and only now and then even comes to the phone. She rarely visits them. When she does, it's at their second home on the island off Cape Cod, and she sits on the beach wondering what she's doing there. They don't talk about feelings of any sort. Time with them is an endless parade of tennis court dates for her mom and re-reading clippings from the *New York Times* for her dad, who often isn't even there. She seldom says anything about herself and they don't ask.

* * *

B's dad realizes the guys at the insurance company where he works do not want the government to make Martin Luther King's birthday a national holiday. "Hey, everybody can't get a holiday made for them," the white guys say. Then they stop even talking about it.

Martin Luther King gone! That's hard for the adults around B to digest. Yeah King and Malcolm (who the government paid Black men to kill) didn't agree. But Martin spoke for peace. It must have been the speech he'd had the guts to give at the Riverside Church near Harlem about how America is a violent society and needs to stop its wars, that made the establishment gun him down. B's dad has gone on year after year trying to be a so-called loyal employee selling insurance for this mediocre company and not really getting anywhere.

"You've found them a lot of new clients," B's mother says.

"But you don't understand," her father replies. "A Black man has to slip into his boss's office almost hat in hand, look down at the carpet until his white boss, who is on the phone with someone from Central Office," motions to him.

"I know you detest keeping your eyes lowered and you shouldn't have to."

"Yeah, but every other Black man who got to my job level was demoted almost immediately. So in my pretend-humble, hunched-over back that I wear at the job sits the knowledge that a boss won't tolerate a man. A boss wants a 'yessir' guy. Wants a Black man to stoop low with his tones, and not ask for any new, more lucrative assignments."

"And not one raise have they ever given you in your commission rate. The white guys get increases regularly at evaluation time, but not you."

"You're so right. Every month I plot a new strategy and get nowhere. So I've decided to make a change."

"What do you mean?"

"My cousin, you know, the one who left the city, called me yesterday. He says there's a company up near him that pays better than mine and he can get me an interview. I'm gonna take that interview."

"You have to, of course," Mother says, but without much enthusiasm. She is worried about leaving New York, where she has lived all her life.

When her father interviews for the job, as a real over-the-road insurance salesman, not some assistant, which he's always been before, he gets it, and the family plans to leave Queens. B overhears him say to her mom, who is crying, "Hell of a country where you gotta move outta state to be treated like a man!"

As her family actually begins the process of moving, Tania decides she is not going with them. She's finishing high school in a few weeks and has already filed local job applications, using only her grownup name of Tania now, though her family stays stuck on calling her B. She particularly wants to stay in Queens because this summer she will be taking a class at the National Black Theater in Manhattan. Starting in July she'll live with Lorna's family around the corner, so both Mom and Dad will live away from her, in a smaller house for a family of three. Older Sister is away at college.

Mother packs up Younger Sister and herself, while Daddy works his last week at the old job. The plan is for B's mother to take her car and, with Younger Sister, follow the moving van north. Daddy will stay behind to keep a business appointment the following Monday. Then he, too, will be on his way.

"Can't I go over to Lorna's tonight?" B begs her mother, after everything is stowed in the car. But Lorna's parents are away this weekend, so she has to wait until Monday, and her mother doesn't even respond, except to remind her that they've already discussed this.

B can't let up. She looks down at the top of Mom's head—she's taller than her mother now. She's clear her mother should do something. "I don't understand why I can't go sleep at Lorna's *now*," B complains.

"Your father will be back any minute. You won't be alone for long." Mother's reply is broken up with grunts as she struggles with one last bag that won't get into the right place in the backseat.

"I know. That's just what I don't like."

"Which do you want? To be alone or not?" Mother's irritation shows as she surveys the car, filled almost to the brim.

"I don't want to be alone . . ."

Before B can finish, her mother's voice overrides. "Well, there you go, you'll be with Daddy."

"No, please, Mom, no." B's wide-set eyes get big, her forehead wrinkles, and her mouth sags.

"I know you girls think he's boring, but he's not that bad."

"No . . . it's not that . . ."

Her mother trips over a dropped salt shaker, which she thought she'd packed securely in the front seat with the roast chicken snack.

"Ouch." She bends down to rub her toe, not quite held in by the strap of her sandal. She hisses, "See what your whining made me do, B?" She limps with short stiff steps toward the car, pops in and slams the door behind her.

"Get in here, right now," she shrieks at Younger Sister, who drags herself over to the car, too scared to wave bye to B.

Mother revs up the motor and waves stiffly back at B, as if she's brushing her off. The car pulls out, waits for the moving van to pull out in front, then follows the truck away from the home the family has lived in most of B's life.

Watching her mother and sister drive off, B numbs out. She looks down and counts the cracks in the pavement in front of the house, as the gentle breeze blows her T-shirt and the sun begins to set. It's her track team practice shirt. She didn't tuck it into the loose culottes she wears. Daddy hasn't come back from the store, where he went some time ago. He probably got sidetracked as usual. While she waits for her father to return, she worries about where she will rest and where he will sleep. She checks the phone, and it still works, but there's nobody to call since Lorna is out of town. Now she sits on the lower step of the stoop, inspecting her stubby fingernails. Her suitcase for the summer stands just inside. She leaves the screen door closed and the front door open, to keep the inside of the house cool, for whenever she goes in.

She hears him pull into the driveway and watches as he opens his driver-side door. She stares down at her PF flyer sneakers. Maybe he'll just offer to take her out somewhere for something, like Chinese barbecue spareribs

He turns off the car radio, which is set on the news station, locks the car, and comes up the walkway, taking long strides. He's carrying takeout. "Come inside and eat," he says.

"I'd like to have my dinner right here outside," she says, hoping to get a few more moments to herself.

"No. Come indoors and eat."

"Why?" She scratches hard at a mosquito bite on her back.

"There are too many bugs out here, with the porch light on."

Her movements, left foot then right foot up the steps, are slow, weary. She holds the door a moment, looking at a June bug, then lets her body in. The slam of the screen door—they never fixed the pneumatic door closer—reminds her she's alone with him.

They have to sit on the floor and he settles on the step to the sunken living room. She's on the floor by his feet. They eat with napkins spread out as if it's a picnic. He blows his nose with a handkerchief he always seems to have handy.

The phone rings, and he says, "Get it."

She complies quickly. "Hello?"

"Hi, it's Ben Graves. Is your father there?" Lucky for B her father's one friend, a Black man, also Caribbean, has called to say goodbye.

Standing by the window with the receiver in his right hand, her father seems moved to tell Graves some things now that the house is bare, his wife is gone, and their life is changed, responding to each of his friend's questions, which B can almost hear, with a release of energy and, for him, a torrent of words.

"Yes, we're going," he says and manages to chitchat for a few sentences.

Then Mr. Graves asks about church.

"Listen, I don't need spiritual guidance, Graves. I live in America, where my co-workers joke about the 'commies' and read the *Daily News*, as if that paper ever tells the truth."

Mr. Graves persists: "But what about your children? What about direction for the future?"

"You know what, Graves, it's not clear, the future. But I know what I'd like to do. I'd like to do the same thing to what Eisenhower called the Military Industrial Complex that Fidel and those Cubans did to Batista."

Mr. Graves says something about how hard it is to be patriotic these days.

"Yeah, it's hard to be patriotic when they really just use that as an excuse to get Black guys to register for their wars, and then they get drafted 'cause they don't have the right connections to get out of it, and some of us still think of it as a good 'job' when what it is really is going to kill other brown poor people."

Mr. Graves agrees.

B's father is shouting now, the loudness of his voice a release for pent-up frustration. "It's just like at the job I'm leaving. They never want to include me in the decisions. I should have been a lead salesman, but they keep reminding me they elevated me from the elevator job."

"Yeah," Mr. Graves says.

"You know why they promoted me in the first place?"

Mr. Graves does know, but Daddy tells him anyway. "'Cause I could quote the insurance rates faster than the top sales guy. But even now they tell me shut up and sometimes call me nigga almost to my face. Mostly they say things like, 'Boy, you better be careful or you'll be back manning that elevator!' " He shakes his fist.

Mr. Graves knows all too well how Black men are treated every day.

"It's why I had to take this new job, so I could get away from them."

Mr. Graves recalls the time long ago when, bad as things were, it looked like workers might force them to get better.

"You're right again, Graves. It was the sit-down strikes and solidarity with other workers that made the difference. That's how we can stand up to the owners' violence and the killings, like the so-called industrial accidents that only the *Daily Worker* covers."

Mr. Graves says he really doesn't read the *Daily Worker* much anymore.

"Why don't you read it? The *Daily Worker* speaks the truth more than a lot of other publications. You should read *The Crisis of the Negro Intellectual,* too."

Mr. Graves says, "I will, man. Listen, I gotta go."

Daddy says, "I gotta go, too.

They both say "goodbye" and "be well" and hang up. As he replaces the receiver in its cradle, B's dad looks around at the four walls of the living room, feeling the emptiness of the house as he sits down again and eats silently, worrying, wondering if it's worth it to try again to deal with these white guys in another state. He looks at his daughter. She has such young skin and looks so innocent. She has no idea of the world's misery. She has had a good life. He wants to tell her about his mama and him . . . But no, he was just a child, and men don't talk about those things. The loneliness of his life overtakes him.

B chews in the quiet, too, thinking that what Daddy said to his friend about racism and how he can't get treated right by white bosses is all true. She finishes her two spareribs and reaches for another.

* * *

Tania races up the four flights to her cheap walk-up. She realizes as she checks for dust on her plants that she hasn't eaten anything, but feels exhausted and stretches out on her mattress without even brushing her teeth.

Not being around her father still feels unfamiliar to Tania even though she's long gone from that house, with its front steps and bedrooms. Back then she couldn't bear to sleep. He might come and she wouldn't know what to do. Eyes-half-open sleep was what she had developed as a teen, leaving her eyelids slightly open to try and give him the idea she was still awake. No longer sleeping in a house where her parents sleep, she feels a precious beginning of freedom, but now, having buried those girlhood memories, stuffed them deep into her belly, she often feels cramps and stomachaches that knock her socks off. "Shit, I hate my body," she wails, hauling herself out of bed to take any pill she can, herbal or not. Lying back down, she waits until some relief comes from this festering soreness in a frozen form of ache and shooting knives in her womb. She remembers watching Older Sister suffer through migraine headaches. That had to be painful, too! At last, in the quiet dark, she falls asleep in her clothes, wrinkling them as she tosses and turns in a chaotic dream, which as usual she will block out.

* * *

"Let's pretend you're getting married, B," Daddy says, showing a small smile, unusual for him.

Startled, she almost swallows down the wrong pipe. "What? How do you mean?" She knows he likes to have discussions at dinner. Mostly she used to just listen. It was Mother and Older Sister, when she still lived at home, who would engage in long conversations after his first opening statements.

"I will show you after you've eaten."

"Oh."

She chews as slowly as possible. What does "I will show you" mean? Her stomach cramps. Now her mouth finishes chewing and she goes to wash her hands because they are sticky from the barbecue sauce. There are no towels, but Mother has left a roll of paper ones.

It's after 10 p.m. and she knows they will have to sleep soon. "Where will I sleep?" her voice asks, but her mind doesn't connect with his answer. Furniture-wise there is only one sleeping bag left.

"Right over here." He points to the green bag. Shifting her weight, she sighs. Then she returns to the bathroom for her washing routine. She washes her face and brushes her teeth. Then, peering at herself in the mirror, she checks for blackheads. She uses her fingers to curl her eyelashes and fiddles with her hair. She gargles with mouthwash.

"Come, B," he calls to her.

She hears her nice new sneakers squeak on the wood floor of the hall, as she approaches the living room.

His hand reaches out to her. He wants to show her how a newlywed bride would be carried over the threshold on her wedding day. She brightens as she thinks of her boyfriend Walker, and wonders if he would know how to lift her up. At least she can still see him, since she won't be moving. Her father only talks about it, for a moment. Then he demonstrates it for her by sweeping her into his arms, placing one hand under her knees and his other strong arm under her armpits. Walking and smiling, so that his gold fillings show, he carries her to the sleeping bag. She has to put her feet on the floor herself as he lowers her, because she is taller and heavier now at age seventeen. "Get down," he says. With one hand on her chest, he presses her down, so she is lying flat, and he looks her over, feeling his power.

He tells her she'll make a great bride one day. She wonders why he keeps talking about marriage. She remembers when she would put his thing into her little girl mouth and suck. She needs to think about something else now. She decides she doesn't ever want to get married and be placed on a disgusting sleeping bag after being carried over the threshold, so she imagines herself as one of those women in the soaps on TV. She sees the clothes and handbag, even the coat the woman wears. It has a big collar. She is leaving her husband.

"You know you are my special daughter and special little girl." He props her up. "This is our special thing, not for your mother or your sisters to know about. You know that, don't you?"

"I wish Mommy was here," she says.

"Look, I want to tell you about marriage, sweetheart." He touches her knee. She moves it away.

"Don't be afraid, sweetheart. I just want to show you a few things so you will be ready."

"Ready?"

"Yes, ready for your big day." He places his hand on her kneecap and this time she doesn't move.

"This is a very special daughter I have here in front of me." He kisses her cheek. Then he kisses the other.

"And I want to be very special with her." He kisses her forehead and unzips his fly. He pushes her completely down onto the sleeping bag.

"Daddy, I'm not getting married."

"But you will one day." He pushes aside her culottes and reaches under her panties.

"But Daddy. . ."

"Be a good girl. You are helping yourself learn to be a good wife one day."

Hearing her own heart thumping she feels like screaming, but also feels good with Daddy's fingers now inside her. Her mind continues to race, even as she, having learned to be a zombie, stays motionless. What should I do? I can't get up. I want to go somewhere. But Lorna isn't home. The pain inside her feels too bad now, as he puts something else in there. She pushes on his chest and he pushes his body into her one more time, then sighs his hot breath into the air.

"Good girl." He strokes her head. "Good girl." He lies back.

She feels like throwing up. She will never sleep in this four-bedroom house again. "But," she says in her mind, "I will remember this green sleeping bag with two silver zippers forever. He took me. He is my Daddy. He is my only Daddy."

She covers her body with a sheet and rolls over. Her eyes want to close, but they stay open, waiting till she hears Daddy snoring at last. It's over for now. He won't be back again. She has to rest, but her eyes won't close. She stares at the ceiling and the empty walls. Her mind is a blank. Where is Mommy? Where is everybody? She gets up to pee, and remembers, oh yeah, they left already in the car, after I begged her not to leave me here. But I am Daddy's good girl. I am good and he is pleased.

Entering the bathroom, she sees the toilet seat up, since Daddy, even after all these years with girls, still never puts it down. Standing up, she decides to pee like a man, without sitting. It hurts. It hurts a lot, even after all those ballet classes and splits and wide open stretches. After flushing, she takes a paper towel to wipe her fingers dry.

A dog barks next door. "Stop barking, you dumb dog," she shouts silently to the mirror, where a sliver of moonlight and the glow from the streetlamp outside give her just enough light to see her face. Rivers of tears roll down her cheeks. Her own eyes answer back, "You can't make me."

A steel door shuts in her brain, blocking out the dream.

* * *

Tania smiles most of the time when she's with Agua. She knows her friend isn't going to criticize her constantly the way her sisters and her parents did. Today she's come to Agua's apartment for rice and beans, as she often does now, before going home to Brooklyn. The apartment has one bedroom where Agua's son, Heru, sleeps. There is a pull-out couch in the living room. Sometimes the place feels cramped because of the window bars by the fire escape. Luckily, however, the kitchen, where Agua cooks, is separate and big enough for a table. A cat curls up by the four-burner stove next to the fridge and the metal sink. Once anyone opens their nose they smell *sofrito*, onions, garlic and all kinds of spiced teas—mint in spring, clove in fall, cardamom or star anise in winter, when Agua creates her warm drinks. On this occasion she has cooked up a delightful tofu mashed with cilantro, *ajo* and soy sauce to go with the rice and beans. Tania brought avocado for a salad.

At the moment, Agua is clearing dishes for Tania to wash. The music of La Lupe, which Agua likes to keep her company when she's cooking, still plays on the tiny cassette player plugged in where she sometimes hooks up her blender to concoct wonderful cantaloupe juice, skin and all. When she is alone, she pumps up the cassette player's volume until the singer's cries, sometimes along with a conga player's insistent fingers, beckon her well-groomed feet to tap, making Africa's beat a part of her home.

"My family lives far away and you know what, I really like that," Tania says. "How about your family? Any of them close by?"

"It's complicated," Agua says, focusing on stacking the plates. "It's too much to go into right now. Let's just say I wouldn't want my mother to help my son with his reading. That's why I moved here."

She sits down next to Heru to go over his homework.

After the dishes are done, Tania walks over to the light, rubs her eyes and asks, "Anyone want to go for a *paseo* by the bridge?" While she loves spending time at Agua's place, she still wants to run from being confined indoors.

"Sure." Agua smiles.

Tania often goes along on the walks, or *paseos*, that Agua takes with her son. Sometimes the six-year-old an' mom walk arm around a shoulder—Agua's arm draped over her son's shoulder, and Heru Verde's wrapped around her waist. Agua's calves are graceful as they slide into casual pants and then down into her shoes' brown straps. Anyone can tell she was a gymnast or something as a teenager. She and her son look gorgeous. Sometimes they walk along the Hudson or the East River in Manhattan. Today they end up down on the waterfront by the Third Avenue Bridge. Walking behind them, Tania overhears Agua confide to her son, "Look, Heru, I'm sorry I get so caught up with other people on the phone sometimes I'm too tired to spend time with you."

Tania appreciates the way Agua admits some of her mistakes as a mother. She walks fast to catch up with them.

Heru Verde picks up sticks and drags them behind him, as his pets. As he looks back at one particularly long one, he says, "That's Fanta."

"Does she need to be walked every day?" Tania walks side by side with them now that they've finished their quick private "talk."

She questions Heru more about how to be a good dog-lover for his imaginary stick dog. Then she turns to Agua and compliments her.

"Agua, you're the kind of parent I would like to be: an adult who has the courage to see in her child's eyes a light of pain, and say, 'Oops, I'm sorry for my mistake.' You know, almost no one admits their mistakes to their kids. And certainly not in our parents' generation."

Agua, tapping the railing overlooking the river, smiles. "Thanks. Yeah, mature women are ones who tell our kids, 'I'm sorry I got so distracted by my boyfriend I forgot to read you your bedtime story.' It's a lot to change the way we raise our kids, admitting we're not perfect. So different from the way our parents raised us, you know?" Tania nods and Agua says, "Thanks for hearing me."

Later, as they reach the well-used bridge over the river, the two women discuss going to visit Heru Verde's *abuela* Enid sometime in the future. "I want you to join me and Heru," Agua says.

"Is Enid your mom, Agua, you know, the one who . . . ?"

"Yeah." Agua cuts her off, glancing at her son to remind Tania that he has big listening ears. Tania shifts gears and gazes up at the bridge's steel girders. To change the subject, Agua shouts, "Tania, let's go dancing!"

"Where? When?"

"At the Casa de las Americas. Tonight."

"Why there? 'Cause there'll be those cigar-smoking guys wearing some kind of *gorra*?" Tania uses one of the Spanish words she's been picking up from Agua.

"Yeah! You mean those tipped-to-the-side hats?" Agua laughs. "There's a benefit dance for El Salvador's liberation movement."

"Yay!" Tania does a salsa step, then sings, sounding off-key to Agua's ear.

It's late when they get back to Agua's place, but at least mass transit works in this town, so women can fly around when they want to, even without wheels. They beg Agua's neighbor Maria to watch Heru. Agua lends Tania some clothes.

On the subway platform, they race to the middle car so they'll be riding with the conductor. Breathing hard, Agua smiles and turns to view Tania's full face. "I'm glad we made it," she says.

"Me, too. Better safe than sorry."

At Casa de las Americas, they wait in the extremely cramped half-hallway. The dingy, gated elevator, clanging as if it might fall apart, arrives to carry them up to Casa, where they can hear music, flirt and show some skirt.

As the elevator cranks upward and they check their skirt hems, pulling a little to fix them, Tania says suddenly, "You remember in our writing workshop, we once heard a poem about being victims no longer by some writer named Sary, from a book called *Fight Back!* with an exclamation point. It was about feminist resistance to male violence." She pauses after every other word to make sure her skirt isn't riding up. "Do you ever think about . . . are you willing to reminisce?"

"Not nostalgia, Tania . . . you know that fake, capitalist shit trying to make us think that 'back in the day' things were better."

Tania's eyebrows rise and she shakes her head. Her hair with its non-African locks looks very bushy because she had to leave Agua's in a rush, with the neighbor shouting, "Don't stay out more than a few hours."

"No, I mean, just think of the sisters in that class, you know, and how everybody liked that piece . . . yeah, it was called "No More Willing Victims."

They have stepped off the elevator and the horns are screaming Latin music so loud Agua can't really hear. She motions to Tania to get to a space between two guys standing next to a counter. Maybe it's a bar?

When they feel situated, watching the dancers, Tania starts again, screaming over the music. "You know that feminist piece . . ."

"Oh, yeah, I 'member now, Agua shouts back. The rest of the title was 'How Fascism Is Fought,' right?"

"Yeah, or something like that, but it was about women of Blackness and cars and getting messed around by white guys in a white, racist Queens neighborhood, out where Black folks are not supposed to go." Against the music, Tania sounds like she's whispering. Just then, the trumpet hits a high note.

Agua is chewing gum, but not smacking it. She agrees that if the women had a chauffeur and some money, then and only then maybe they'd be just colored girls and not a threat. "Okay, yeah, I guess if there's a chauffeur driving you in a white limo, then you ain't gonna be attacked."

Tania summons up her mental images of some of those wanna-be type Black folks who now work filling Coca-Cola and Pepsi boardrooms as token managers. Seeing a photo of Lolita Lebron, who is still in the man's jails, on Casa's walls dredges every racist thing back up for Tania. Those Puerto Rican, Jamaican, African women from South Africa, African-American and Jewish sisters of womanism had to cry when the part about not riding with a conductor came up in the poem. Her thoughts are turning back to tonight, when suddenly Agua busts out: "We sure better have rode with that conductor, the way you got all that leg showing." She laughs and her red lipstick smiles up.

"Shit!!!!!!! There's that other poem in *Fight Back!*" Tania says, batting her eyelashes the way some women are trained to be coy.

"Which one?"

"You know, the one titled 'Man, you ain't got no business under my short skirt' or something."

"Oh, yeah, that's right, 'cause these *muchachos* think they get to say something about how we dress. You're right. Tania, I take it back. You wear those yellow fringes, girl. Ain't none of no man's business!"

"Yeah, but I don't like those skimpy ass shoes those male designers put out all the fucking time."

"My style is sneakers ALL WAYS," says August-born Agua, who is wearing some bronze-tinge rouge as well as eyeliner. She heads to the ladies room to freshen her makeup. When she gets back, the Latino singer Ruben Blades is singing about a plastic woman, "Era Una Chica Plastica."

"I like this music, the horns especially, don't you?" shouts Tania, saucily welcoming her best buddy back.

"Let's dance. Nobody's asking us, let's do it ourselves," Agua says.

They break into fancy footsteps and lots of breaks. Suddenly the guys' eyes are on them.

Later, alone in her apartment after that high, mighty salsa music and the dance, and the risky late-night ride home on the subway, Tania sits crying, staring at the window with its bamboo shade. She thinks of all those people in her adult and child past who didn't like her going to parties. It's impossible not to be angry. Tonight she tried to dance all that raging, caged shit out of her. But it still holds up in there. She tries wiping the tears from her eyes with her soft and fluffy pillow, covered with a brightly colored sham. Its blue and light yellow flowers stare at her puffy face.

3 PARENTS VISITED AND REVISITED

It's been a while since Tania and Agua discussed visiting Enid, and Heru has been pestering his mother to take him to see his *abuela*, so today they've made plans to meet at the bridge near Enid's place in upper Manhattan. Tania is coming from her boyfriend Buster's place. They had had a fight over her body and clothes. Again. She feels like not talking to him. As she walks her anger rises in her heart. She has no intention of returning to his apartment or even calling him. But when she meets Agua, she will pretend to be relaxed and won't mention any of this, since Agua doesn't like Buster and will think, even if she doesn't say out loud, things Tania doesn't want to hear right now.

When she reaches the bridge, Agua and Heru are waiting. Heru is eager to take off to see his grandma, despite having trudged the forty or so blocks from home. Not using the subway or the bus gives Agua time to think—visiting Enid requires a lot of emotional stamina. Besides, she has no extra money for tokens, so she and Heru walk just about everywhere.

It's only a few blocks from the bridge to Enid's building. Agua presses the buzzer outside the apartment door. Her mother yells, "It's open, I unlocked it when you buzzed from downstairs."

Pushing the door open, Agua says, "Ma, my friend Tania is here with me like I told you."

"Okay. You know where to go," Enid yells from the kitchen.

Tania, Agua and Heru sit on metal-backed chairs with cushions in the dining area of the overcrowded, tiny-roomed uptown apartment, looking out on a brick wall through windows with bars, waiting for the meal to cook, listening as Enid asks herself at the top of her lungs where she put the *sofrito* she made. She doesn't want anyone else in the kitchen while she fixes everything.

Leaning over to tell Tania what she's thinking, Agua whispers, "My son should at least try to know his grandparent. I think he will never meet his dad's parents. His connection with his Puerto Rican, Spanish-speaking side is through this woman, *mami*. Heru's dad stays uninvolved these days. I told you already about that." She feels guilty talking about her mother in her mother's house.

Tania tries to hear Agua. But Enid shouts at them often from the kitchen, speaking now to Agua, now to Heru, who is called "HeruGreen" by his USA-identified *Puertoriqueña abuela.* Though Tania already knows that his grandmother doesn't respect his mother's choice of an African name for her son, and won't use it by itself, actually hearing her call him "HeruGreen," making one ugly word, is shocking. If she won't call him "Heru," can't she use the Spanish word "Verde" instead of "Green"? Once she'd heard Agua say to Enid over the telephone, "Can you at least call him "Heru Verde!" but obviously Enid will not.

Agua starts talking about cooking plantains. But then Enid joins them at the table and interrupts, saying without preliminaries, "Pass the *plátanos*." Tania passes the white oval plate piled with yellow plantains, then retreats to her thoughts again, wondering when Agua will finish her sentence about how she cooks this great dish that Tania's nana, her father's mother, used to make also. Wondering when Agua is going to say something, *anything*, like she usually does.

A loud attacking voice, Enid's again, jars Tania out of her thoughts. "Give HeruGreen some *pollo* too," she says. She is talking to Agua as if Agua were a girl, or too stupid to know how to divide up the few pieces of chicken left on the plate.

Tania remembers that Agua is trying to encourage Heru to be a vegetarian, but she doesn't dare say anything.

Enid goes on and on without letting anyone else squeeze a word in. "I have some yo yo on my job who . . ." She's complaining about a woman, and then a man, on her gig, but her outburst is just about talking, without looking for any real solution.

After the chicken has been passed, Enid says, "I may sign up . . . Agua, listen to me—" She insists that Agua look up from cutting the chicken wing off the breast for Heru. "I may sign up and take one of those classes you told me about at the Marxist School downtown. I have the schedule here somewhere."

Tania thinks she is probably just trying to impress her visitor, since Agua had told her Enid liked people to think of her as kind of progressive. She shifts her position by leaning on the table and, having finished her food, asks, "Do you want help with the dishes?"

Enid says, "No, no Agua will do them," and goes on with her rant about her job and how she's going to sign up for a class at the Marxist School.

Tania leans back, thinking, I'm sick of Agua's mother acting like she cares about the things that matter to me and Agua. As for signing up at the Marxist School, she ain't gonna do it. She wears all these new clothes that look hang-out and cool, but she ain't gonna take no action. And I'm sick of the way she treats Agua. I can't even help with cleaning up or say anything. She's not my mother, but I have to sit here while she rages. I know I had privilege and plenty of things growing up, and was isolated from the way life is for a lot of people. But at least I'm learning. Is this woman from the working class ready to band together with other folks to change things? I don't think so.

She changes position again, resting one elbow on the back of her chair, her head in her hand. The cheap chairs have threads busting out of the cushions.

"Do I have to listen to her?" Heru whispers to Agua. He can't understand the big words his *abuela* uses in her tirades.

His mom whispers back, "Okay, go look at your coloring book as soon as you finish that last bit on your plate. I know it's good to see your *abuela*, but you feel like playing now, right?"

"Yeah," he agrees.

Tania covers her face, scared that Enid might have heard and will cuss him or someone else out. But nothing happens, and as Enid talks on. Tania stops listening, and hears only the complaining sounds. Noticing a few gray strands at Enid's hairline, she remembers her own Grandma, picturing her sitting in this room, going back into the kitchen and coming out with a plate of fruit. It's the only thing Tania really liked that her Grandma served. She remembers her poem about her grandma, the one Agua enjoyed . . .

Her grandma comes to her in all music, and Enid has turned on the cassette player. Tito Puente wails as Tania daydreams. Grandma enjoyed singing to her granddaughters to put them to sleep. Even at the table she'd hum a tune and Tania remembers humming with her to be close.

Heru, who had wanted so much to make this visit, now looks like he wishes he could stay as far away from Enid as possible. No music between them. His face, with eyebrows raised, seems worried. Usually he grins and the gap in his front teeth makes everyone smile.

Unlike Enid, Grandma could not put real flavor and spice into a meal, but she put it into her life. Her love was spice. Tania can't believe she's been dead almost twenty years, how much she still misses her! If she were here, she and Agua could go visit her, and eat, instead of dragging Heru to his own *abuela*'s. At least he'd have a sense of grand-parenting, from a gentler, less phony woman. She fixes her gaze on Agua, hoping her friend will signalthat dinner is over, and they can leave and still be considered polite in Enid's book.

But Agua, clearing the plates and putting water in the pots at the sink, has all she can deal with just to focus her attention on the mother who's messed up her life and to smile at her jokes, while mentally beating herself up for doing it.

Enid is back on the subject of the guy at work. "He's driving me crazy," she screams. "*Ay que pendejo*!"

Agua laughs along at the put-down in Spanish, even as she's recoiling inside, her tummy aching, remembering the days and nights of slaps across the face and taunts of "*Que estupido*" and being made to kneel on raw rice when she was late coming home from school or talked out of turn. She keeps smiling as she washes and dries the dishes, until at last they say goodbye and she slips out the door, Tania and Heru hurrying after her. As she pushes her glasses back up on her nose, Tania detects the rage boiling within.

When they hit the street, there right in the gutter, they see a man stagger and almost fall. "Oh my god," Agua says. "I gotta get Heru out of here."

"Okay, we'll talk later." Tania urges her on her way.

The man gathers himself up and moves slowly off. He has only one leg. Tania wonders whether he's a war vet like so many men her age who went to Vietnam. She'd heard on W.B.A.I. about how lots of Black men weren't receiving any health benefits after doing the man's dirty work in the Vietnam War, and therefore had become homeless, like this guy seems to be.

She hears the train beneath the grating and rushes to catch it. It's a long ride to Brooklyn, but thank god she has her own place to go to.

The next day on her way to the local Laundromat Tania has the good fortune to run into her new neighbor, Lynn.

A short African American woman with a huge butt, originally from the mid-west, Lynn had moved into a place a couple of blocks from Tania's a few weeks before. Tania, seeing her on her own surrounded by boxes, mostly of books, had helped carry them in. It was just after one of her break-ups with Buster, and she had complained about him for an hour as she helped. She realized Lynn would become a friend when she noticed among her books *Revolution and Evolution* by James and Grace Lee Boggs, along with some Last Poets tapes. Now they sit in the Laundromat watching their washing machines. Tania has a lot to do—she's left her clean things at Buster's, with whom she has made up. Again.

Street noise, especially cars honking and the always-present police sirens, and the persistent drone of the TV, disturb any real peace inside the Laundromat, so the two Black-conscious young women automatically use a New York style of conversing, meaning they try to block out the sounds by talking over them, all the while loading and unloading washing machines and dryers.

"What's your column on this week? . . . What's it called?" Tania shouts, referring to Lynn's job at a local, radical newsweekly that turns out stories like "Woman and Man Beat Up by White Police."

"It's 'Anti Racism through the Eyes of the Left,'" Lynn replies. "You know, some poor folks are starting to side with us about the despicable US refusal to pay reparations to the Vietnamese after our massacres of children and women in the war." She pauses for a moment to wait for a police car to pass, then goes on. "Damn it! What North America needs is a weekly paper with wide distribution that publishes real analysis. I was just home working, and I discovered that when you go to the dictionary you won't find a good definition of the word 'leftist'!"

Tania, who hates to iron, carefully folds some of her tops, as Lynn, her bright, round, brown eyes piercing the air, talks energetically about how the definition of "leftist" doesn't say anything about how a leftist is a person who concentrates on the root of an issue instead of being diverted. One who looks for effective ways to rid the U.S. of its crapitalist system and replace it with a collective one, so all people can have housing, jobs, healthcare and, damn it, food! "The economic part of the amerrycaca shit system is based on nothing but greed for money and power," she says finally.

"Yeah, I hear that and I wish I'd learned it in high school," Tania shouts, although, in fact, still obsessing about Buster, she is only half-listening. She rolls a braid in her fingers, then sucks on the end. She thinks Lynn doesn't notice.

"Why don't you have anything but tops, socks and overalls to wash?" Lynn asks, looking into Tania's basket. Her tone is concerned, not nosey.

Tania is taken aback that Lynn has asked her this. "Because I don't wear tight pants," she says. "And I hate having bellbottoms just to be in style."

"But you have such a nice figure. It's almost like you're hiding your body."

"My body is not for all the idiots on the street who are constantly seeing us as pieces of meat," Tania asserts roughly.

"I hear you, but even when we're up in your apartment you keep it all covered up. Aren't you comfortable in your female self?" Lynn tries to be gentle, but it just strikes her as odd that Tania is all baggy tops and bottoms. Only occasionally does she wear a belt to show off her slender waist.

But now, seeing how Tania's face has a scrunched up look—clearly she's too uncomfortable to answer—Lynn returns to her previous topic. "You know what the essential values in this country are, Tania?"

Tania is now staring out the window at the overflowing garbage cans on the corner. "Well one thing I know—it ain't equality," she says. "The city only picks up trash regularly in the rich neighborhoods. I bet Wall Street's sidewalks have a lot more trash bins, too." She feeds her second dryer more coins, then turns back to Lynn. "What do *you* think this system really values?"

Lynn throws her scarf around her neck and laughs as if to say, you know, but I'll tell you anyway. "Well of course, making money at the expense of everyone and anyone else." She points out that it all started with the buying and selling of land. The native peoples, who white America beheaded and cut off the hands and feet of, tried to tell the first invaders you can*not* own and sell land. Land belongs to Mother Earth. Mother Earth can*not* be traded. "I bet before long, they'll be buying and selling everything a human being needs, like water and maybe even air," she concludes.

Tania beckons to Lynn to help her put her now dry and folded clothes into her shopping cart. Lynn is a little annoyed that Tania would interrupt her with a small job like this, but she comes over and holds open the plastic bag inside the cart so Tania can lay her clothes inside without wrinkling them. Then the two women sit side by side to wait while Lynn's last load finishes drying.

A rerun of an episode of "Julia" has just come on the TV. Most of the other customers have been glued to the idiot box since they arrived, hardly talking at all. Tania glances at the screen, then immediately turns away from the phony Julia and back to Lynn. "Hey," she says, "do you ever notice how Julia, although she *is* a person of color, never seems to have any problems with being Black in this system and trying to find an apartment or a job?

"That's because TV is all about conning us into believing this system works for Black folks." Lynn shows a warm smile, and after pointing out that Tania has left a pair of socks on the table, resumes talking about the connection between economic motives in history and now. She explains again how the first invaders were all about buying and selling, including African people and their children, after the suckers used guns to steal them from their homeland the same way they used guns to steal the land of indigenous peoples so they could sell that.

"That's it, that's it, Lynn," Tania exclaims, caught up in the energy of Lynn's clarity. But before long the hum of the dryers sends her back into her worry about whether Buster will come over tonight and demand sex right away. In spite of how she had gone on and on about Buster to Lynn the day they met, she is not now prepared to get into a discussion of her relationship with him—with Lynn or anyone else. It's another item on the long list of secrets Tania doesn't feel she can share with the world. Only Agua sometimes knows the real Tania behind her intellectualizing wall, but not many other folks do.

Lynn notices Tania's suddenly downcast profile, and intuits she's thinking about Buster. She wonders if something she said about men imitating the bosses in this system after Tania's tirade about Buster and his messed up behavior when they first met had scared Tania into silence, and tries to engage her again on the subject of Amerrycacan values. "Do you know Howard Zinn's *People's History of the United States*?" she asks.

"Yes I do," Tania replies. "We read it in a course I took at the University of the Streets."

"Great place! I didn't know you went there." Lynn smiles. "Okay, let me see what else, umm, what other values. You know, I feel so worked up about this system 'cause it's in every area of our lives." She strains to talk a bit louder as the siren of another out-of-control, speeding cop-car breaks into their conversation. "You know, I'm glad I met you, Tania. Sometimes I feel so lonely trying to get folks to turn off their TV minds and recognize what's really up." Her face glows.

As the sound of the siren recedes, Tania says, "Thanks to those cops blasting their siren, I almost didn't hear you, but damn it, Lynn, you put in ten hours every day, except weekends, to provide this type of information for us, week after week. This week it's police brutality against poor folks, and last week how they protect property not people, and kill poor folks who haven't done anything, except possibly be 'emotionally disturbed.'"

"You got it, Tania." Again Lynn's voice rises with enthusiasm, although her whole body aches from exhaustion. "Besides, how can you *not* be emotionally disturbed under a System that disturbs life itself."

Tania, checking out Lynn's purposely unpolished nails, says, "Your thinking helps me see more clearly the danger of the po-lice"—like Lynn she divides the word in two. "But you have hope. Your paper talks about Cuba's green medicine and healing domestic violence by building community. 'Best neighbor,' that's my nickname for you!" She grins.

"Speaking of Cuba," Lynn says, "some folks see the contradictions there and act like theCubans aren't working on them. But the Cubans do a lot better than other places with a colonial history and herstory, like the Dominican Republic, where the US is still the overlord and Dominicans with dark skin are kept out of political office and off the TV, just like here. Most of them haven't yet begun to revolt and wear African-style hair and be proud of their African roots. Cuba may not be fully socialist yet, but at least they're facing a lot of things . . . at least more than us here in this colonizing, racist, homophobic nation that not only blockades Cuba but stops us from going there to see for ourselves what it's like. How in fact no one is homeless in Cuba. Poor yes, but housing is a *right* there."

Tania grins again and they slap five. Then Lynn puts the last of her laundry in her cart and the two women walk out the door into Brooklyn's streets, talking even louder over the noisy street traffic.

"You cover the world, Lynn!" Tania shouts. "Your piece about the Bantustans in South Africa was great. I mean, homelessness is bad, but being forced to live in 'homes' like that . . . You're so clear about issues, like Africa being re-colonized and how it's time South Africans get support for ridding their homeland of white South Africans who enforce apartheid." A car that almost runs the red light honks at them as they cross. Lynn puts her arm out to shield Tania. "Hey," she says when they make it safely to the other side of the street, "Hey, you know when I was a kid we used to all go to the Laundromat together, me and my sisters and even my brother. It feels homey with you, too. How was it for you?"

"Huh?" Tania pulls away from the sudden intimacy.

"You know, tell me about your sisters and you and laundry day."

"Oh, I really hardly remember."

"Well, what *do* you remember about when you were a little girl?" Lynn knows sometimes her political conversations overwhelm folks.

"I don't remember. Really, Lynn, I truly don't remember hardly anything, except that we lived in Queens and I had some racist teachers who put even smart Black southern-background quote-unquote street kids in the JD track."

"JD?"

"Juvenile delinquent. And some white kids didn't want me to like this white boy," Tania adds.

"Did your father say it was okay?"

"My father?" Tania is shocked Lynn thinks her father had anything to do with her day-to-day life.

"Yeah, 'cause you told me when I first met you, your father had picked your mother, who was white, so was that okay with him for you?"

"My father is so far from my memory I don't think I could tell you anything he did with me or talked about with me."

"Nothing he did?" Lynn had had no father in her home because he had been in jail. Now she thinks maybe Tania is a lot more like her than she knew. "Damn!" she says. "My dad was locked up for years for some petty crime, unlike President Tricky Dick Nixon, who got pardoned. Don't you see what this damn system did to our Black fathers?"

But Tania has shut down. She copes by leaving things in her life unattended. Like her relationship with her father. Like her body. It seems sexy to women who see her when she is in her place and the outside temperature is over 90 degrees. She can't wear those tee shirts and heavy overall tops covering her breasts then. But the same way she left her socks on the table in the Laundromat today, she forgets to look at her body in her mirror. Her body feels ugly and useless, only good for having sex with Buster when he wants her to.

A few weeks later, Tania and Lynn decide to attend an African Liberation Support Committee benefit focused not on the relatively well-funded end-apartheid-free-Nelson-Mandela campaign embodied in the posters lining the venue's walls, but on the struggle of the Eritreans for independence from Ethiopia in East Africa. They choose seats in the second to last row, in front of a young man with black curly hair and a small goatee, who wears a tee shirt proclaiming, "I Am Taino. Before the Spaniards Invaded, Puerto Rico Was Our Peaceful Land." He's there by himself, no doubt hoping to break out of his lonesomeness in this crowded town, and they can feel him eyeing the backs of their heads, Tania's with cornrows, Lynn's cropped afro. With nearby seats empty, they're at ease feeling him out as a "friend" type of guy, turning around now and then to ask questions like, "Do you know how to pronounce the name of the next Eritrean dance?" When he answers, they note his deep voice. It gives him presence.

As the performances are coming to an end, Tania, who isn't interested for herself because of Buster, thinks she can help Lynn attract some more attention from this guy. Besides, she doesn't want to be alone with Lynn because she might ask her about her time with Buster last night. The jumpy feeling in her belly about their fight has her wanting to have someone else around to keep the focus off her. "Hey," she says, "wanna go with us to find something to eat?"

"Sure. I'm Hugo, by the way." He grins as the women rise up in all their young-body glory and introduce themselves. Lynn's breasts curve up and her sensuous back curves down. Her behind sticks out and gives that petulant umph at the end, where her jeans ride down over her sweet butt. Tania's expressive hands are perched on her waist, so you can actually see she has a sweet figure. Her trusting smile and Lynn's fabulous grin have obviously captured this brother. Bangles jingle and ankle bracelets sparkle as they walk out of the hall.

From the outset, Hugo talks so openly about family issues it's as if he's known them forever. Tania takes to him in right away and laughs, slapping five, after he says, "My moms just couldn't imitate those bourgie mf's enough." Definitely a new friend and a "potential guy" for Lynn, she thinks to herself.

A *comidas criollas* restaurant on Broadway reaches out to them when someone opens a swinging front door and delicious aromas from *mole* and *bacalao* stew grab them. "Cuban-Chinese," Hugo says. "Love that *mezcla*."

Tania tucks a napkin into her top to cover her chest. Her father used to wear a bib when eating lobster, and she figures it's important to keep at least some of her loose-fitting tops from having to be washed every single day.

They've been talking about one of the white American speakers at the event. Lynn says, "That guy was one of those talkie types who go on and on about racism. I hope he means to take action on it. But—"

Tania cuts in, the way folks eager to make their point do. "My mother is white, you know. She thought about racism, but then when her friends the Steinbergs said they wouldn't sell their house to us, 'cause what would their *neighbors* think, she didn't stand up and say anything really."

"Damn, I think sometimes these white folks gots to go to hell and be born again, to be rid of that racist shit," Hugo exclaims, laughing lightly and shaking his head in a way that said we all know how deep this shit goes. Lynn looks over in Tania's direction to see how she's taking this last statement.

"Well, yeah, my mother really hurt me, too." Tania speaks slowly. She's never said this to anyone before. It's as if Hugo's free expression of the problems in his family let her know that everybody has issues and it's okay to talk about them.

"How?" Lynn asks.

"Well, she looked like she cared about Black folks 'cause she lived with us in the neighborhood after all the wanna-be-rich Jews and Italians had moved out."

"White flight," Hugo chimes in.

"But she still seemed apart from us. She didn't want me to listen to rhythm and blues on W.W.R.L."

"Huh?" Hugo raises an eyebrow.

"You know, on the radio. We didn't have parties where we danced. And the folks who came over were only . . . What did you call them?"

"Talkies?" Hugo grins. They all laugh, remembering the white speaker.

"Yeah. Talkies. In general she just seemed to give me the attitude she was better than me. I mean everybody in my family kinda jumped on my case when they were uptight about something. Like when we played United Nations . . ."

Lynn interrupts. "What do you mean, 'played United Nations' ?"

"It's a board game. When we played, I got to be South Africa. I don't think I wanted to be South Africa, with apartheid and all, but they gave me that role, and I was too scared to speak up. I distrusted my family, I guess. No one really wanted me to play . . . They just let me 'cause I was supposed to be part of the family."

Hugo looks up from his plate at Tania. His gaze is very tender. This brother understands, she thinks. She hopes he and Lynn do hook up.

While Lynn excuses herself to go to the bathroom, Hugo responds to what Tania has just said. "Yeah, my moms was always telling me and my brother we were *chicos malos*, bad boys, and saying the white folks at school were right. She never came to school to defend us. She thought her English was too bad, and besides, we kids from the projects were always wrong."

"Oh wow." Tania slaps her forehead, surprised a guy is so open about criticizing his moms. "What about your dad?" she asks.

There is silence as Hugo finishes chewing his plantains. Then, as if realizing something for the first time, he says, "He just let that emotional abuse keep happening, I guess." He sits back and puts down his silverware.

As he rests his head against the booth, Tania keeps on eating in the uncomfortable quiet that unexpectedly comes down as they wait for Lynn, the great talker, to return. Stray thoughts wander through her mind until she hovers over her home life. Usually when people ask her things about her girlhood she can't think of anything. She remembers photos of the family, all smiling, but she has no happy memories to go with them. In fact, except for snatches, she seldom sees anything but a haze for the years before she left home. And this remains true despite rare times like tonight, despite the sense she now has that she *can* share family struggles with new friends like Agua and Lynn and Hugo, and the way this sharing leaves her feeling more relaxed and less oppressed by her demons than she ever felt with the girls she practiced dance steps with in Queens.

A couple of weeks later, Lynn phones Tania from her office and tells her that Hugo has given her the phone number of a radical therapist named Pam. "He's funny, he just wrote her name on a dinner napkin the other night," she says, referring to a meal she and Hugo had shared a week after the Eritrean benefit.

"Why?" asks Tania, confused about why a man would even know the name of, much less how to get in touch with, a counselor.

"Why what? Why did he write it on a napkin?"

"No. Why did he give it to you?" Tania says, with an edge to her voice.

"'Cause he thinks young folks, but women especially, who have been so put down by this sexist capitalist system, need a place to be able to express themselves and speak their truth. Anyway, I'm passing it along. Maybe you can share it with your other friend, the Latina sister."

"Are you serious? He really said that?" Tania feels doubtful. Though she takes down the phone number, she continues to question her friend. "Why did he call her a radical therapist?"

"I guess 'cause she's kinda political. He said, 'She's into Marx and has him reading things like this book called *Lessons from the Damned*. It has a chapter on the Black family by four teenage Black girls."

"Wow this is deep . . . all these connections. Lynn, this guy is for you! I'm so happy. To think that I had something to do with you two hooking up." Tania smiles loudly over the phone.

"We are not hooked up, Tania. We are talking." Lynn corrects her.

"Naw, you gonna hang together soon, just like me and Buster."

"We'll see."

"No, Lynn, I know it, I know it."

"Look, Tania, I just called to give you the number in case you ever need it." Lynn, who has covered domestic violence from the angle of how men beat women more often when the economy is bad and folks are more isolated, has long been troubled by what she knows of Tania's relationship with Buster.

"Why would I need it? I don't have half as many problems as some of the folks out here, like these young girls being constantly harassed on the street. The other day I saw a guy actually smack a girl in broad daylight."

"Well at least it was in the daylight," Lynn says pointedly. "A lot of stuff we push under rugs and it stays hidden in our communities of color because . . ."

Cutting her off, Tania jumps in, but avoids the real subject. "I know! You write about it all the time . . . so many brothers in prison, no damn jobs, but white folks say things are 'better.' That's why Hugo is great for you."

"Look, will you please stop pushing me to be involved with a man as deeply as you are." Lynn has to get Tania to back up.

"What's wrong?" Tania, now hurt, doesn't see how trying to get people to do what she thinks is best for them doesn't work.

"Nothing. It's just that I have a different level of need for a man in my life. My work fulfills me and I want to know someone as a friend for a good while before I involve my dear body sexually."

"Oh." Tania shuts down, suddenly feeling ashamed at how much she needs to be around Buster. She's a lot more comfortable talking with Agua about men than Lynn. Maybe Lynn is just more into books.

"So anyway, Tania, call her if you ever want to, and . . ."

"Lynn!" Tania, losing it now, raises her eyebrows. "Why should I? Just 'cause I told you my private and very personal issues with my boyfriend does *not* mean you can tell the world. Besides, I am *not* sick." She begins to chew hard on her braid, the way she once sucked on her thumb.

"Hold on, Tania, I didn't mean . . ." Lynn, sensing finally that this is a conversation that has to be had in person, so Tania can see her eyes and trust her a little bit, suggests gently that maybe they can talk later.

As abruptly as she flared up, Tania calms down, remembering Lynn is at work. "Oh, are folks coming back from lunch so we can't talk private?" she asks.

"Yeah, that's it"

"Okay, tonight then, Lynn. Bye."

"Awright woman . . . See you."

Tania slumps to her knees and hangs up the receiver.

Two days later, hanging out with Buster in his latest rented room, Tania watches Kool smoke rise up past his nostrils. His unemployment benefit is about to run out and still, everywhere he searches for a job they say, "nothing available." He owes back rent on this hole of a place, where there's no privacy unless one of them goes into the bathroom, and shuts the door. And even when you close that thin piece of plywood to take a crap, it's easy to hear what's going on right through it, even with the TV running, which it usually is.

Picking a fight, Buster explodes. "I'm too disgusted with you." His thin body is stiff in his hard chair, his hazelnut hand stroking his sharp pointed goatee and fiddling with his mustache.

"Why are you disgusted with *me*? Maybe you're really disgusted with this shitty system that hates Black men and won't hire you even though you don't have a record and are really good with your mind." She's sitting in the corner on one of his few chairs, her hands on her thighs. "Is that it?"

But a jeans commercial comes on and, not wanting to talk about anything real, he seizes the moment to change the subject. "Look." He points at a white lady cavorting on the TV in skin-tight jeans. "Tania, why won't you buy some tight-ass jeans to show off your butt?"

"Well, it's my ass." Tania speaks up for herself, but when Buster balls up his fist she falls silent.

"What do you mean it's *your* ass?" he snarls. "Who else have you been giving your ass to?"

She looks over at him with one eyebrow raised. Tania has never said anything about any other guys. "I'm only standing up. *Ms.* Magazine is telling us women we have the right to define our own body style and what we will put on it."

Buster glares at her cute body, hiding in her overalls, and pulls his cigarettes out from where he stuffed them in a pocket. His smell begins to have that rank odor, like a bull about to charge. He can no longer really *see* Tania, even as he watches her sitting in the corner by the curtains. He thinks: Well she does have a nice ass. I hate that she won't let me show her off. Her legs are crossed. He remembers she never smokes. He remembers how they met at the University of the Streets, where they clicked and he told her he could be into her. She told him she liked listening to him review the scenes she and Agua rehearsed. He'd told her his mother started hangin' out at dances after his father died.

He never told her more than that—how his mother was a big breasted, wide hipped Black woman who wore sexy black clothes. How once, when he was army age, he went to a small-town dance that served liquor and saw her dancing with some guy none of her ten children even knew. How she denied her son, waving to him across the room like he was just some Black youth she "happened" to know.

As he looks at Tania now, his momma's betrayal rises inside him. Momma denied him, didn't take time to understand him, didn't even introduce him to men she was interested in.

He says, "Tania, you are *my* girlfriend! You got to dress the way I tell you to."

Tania pouts. "I don't have the money to go buy some ole jeans."

"Well then, I'm gonna buy some and you're gonna wear 'em!" Buster shouts. His deep baritone voice, so sexy when they make love, feels frightening.

"No I'm not."

"Yes you are. Shut up!"

The voice of the weatherman on the TV is mere background noise to their yelling. Buster's body looms in front of Tania's small, thin face. She can smell the hot air coming out of his mouth when he leans in to make his point.

Tania lowers her voice, but keeps on talking. Buster realizes that, just like his momma, she won't listen and try to comprehend what he says. He reaches out and slaps her mouth quiet.

Her face begins to ache. She slaps his face. Then she cries, holding her cheek.

Buster walks away, real cool, no expression. Heading to the bathroom, he lights another cigarette and blows smoke rings into the tense air.

Tania opens her mouth. She pushes her breath and it sounds like a scream but nothing comes out. Buster keeps moving until he has the bathroom door closed, putting it between them. Then Tania screams, pounding small fists on the cracked door. "Come out here and apologize. You, you damn asshole . . . You ain't man enough to hit on some man!"

The landlady bangs on the apartment door. "Stop that carryin' on," she yells.

"Out!" Buster rages at Tania through the flimsy bathroom door. "Out! Now!"

"You can't throw me out." Tania sneers, though her hands are shaking.

"I'm in trouble with the landlady 'cause of you!"

Tania gropes for her bag, puts her journal in it, ties on her sandals. She wants Buster to hug her goodbye.

From inside the bathroom he hears her packing up and opens the door. She's standing by the window, facing away from him. He taps her on the shoulder.

Turning and looking up, she begs, "At least apologize!"

No deal. His hands fall back down to his sides.

She cries all the way to the subway, wondering for the umpteenth time why this had to happen, grateful as always that she has an apartment to go to and doesn't have to live with him like so many other women she's heard about.

When she reaches her stop, she finishes crying. She walks up the dirty subway steps to the street. She looks for a pay phone to call Lynn, but block after block, past all the stores in her neighborhood including the Laundromat, she doesn't find one working. She decides to call from home instead.

Click, click she dials her neighbor's number. Thank God, Lynn picks up. As she had when they first met, Lynn listens to the story. When Tania, sobbing, ends it, Lynn opens her blocked mind by asserting past her tears, "You don't have to take that, you know!"

Lights of memory flash as something bursts in Tania's heart.

"Why don't you call that therapist I told you about?" Lynn asks gently.

Tania's mind fills up, her thoughts churning. She tells herself she is *not* crazy. But she does have at least one problem—Buster! Going back to him over and over and letting him hit her in the face *is insane.* But a therapist? Some time ago, not too long after she had first gotten together with Buster, she had almost decided to let him move in with her. But the prospect of the continual forced intimacy had scared her, and before she said yes, she had looked in Brooklyn for a counselor, someone just to *talk* to about it, since she couldn't talk to Agua, who had disliked Buster from the start. But the therapist she went to kept checking his desk clock during her session. He told her she had to have identity issues since her parents were from different races in America. Tania never went back. But maybe this lady would be different. Maybe this woman, what was her name? . . . Pam . . . could be a good person to talk to. Maybe *this* therapist . . . oh my god, what does therapy really mean for Black people? But Pam is Black, Lynn says. So maybe she can understand what makes these things happen.

"Okay, give me the number again," she says. "I lost it." This time she writes it down in her phone book, in the basket on the shelf by the window. "I'll call her, I really will," she says, and the very next day she does.

Different from most traditional counselors, Pam believes that relationships, including social relationships, in this society, are affected by racism and the economic system. To all her colleagues, she shows her very radical aspects. Some say approvingly, "Pam goes for the core of an issue and also connects the family with what society has not allowed. The nuclear family has often been unable to make a living under this economic system, and Pam exposes that." Others disagree. Still, even though Pam associates with many kinds of therapists, she doesn't change, but stays for sure on her own path towards leftist clarity. And she doesn't cover up her convictions, ever.

She lives outside the city limits, in Westchester County. Clients who are city folks agree to make the subway ride to the end of the line, where she picks them up and drops them off. She usually starts at 9:30 am, though some days she starts earlier, like 8 am on a Saturday. She is always available late into the evening, sometimes until 9:30 pm, though most often she ends her work day at 9, having taken breaks only for lunch and dinner and for a workout at the Y. She then spends time with her husband, who teaches at the nearby high school; shortening his commute was one reason she had finally agreed to leave her inner city social work and move out here. Besides, she knew it was just a matter of time before her politics got her fired again. And the move had made it possible to open up the private practice at very low rates, not only because her children could go to the public schools, which had a lot fewer kids than the city schools with their overcrowded classrooms and deteriorating conditions brought on by drastic budget cuts, but also because she could see people for a longer time without the heavy rent she would have to pay if the office were still in the city. So she makes sure to keep her fees affordable to people who are ordinarily denied access to any kind of real counseling.

As her schedule shows, when she sees clients depends on their work schedules. She sees them whenever they're off work, which may be during regular business hours Monday through Friday—or not. But especially on Saturdays, on what some people call the "weekend," she sees cab drivers, truckers and bus workers who go off to work their shifts after the session. Other workers come evenings, from a variety of spots and jobs ranging from loading and unloading at boxing companies and warehouses, to driving medical emergency trucks, to office work, to cultural work at centers for the arts.

Also unusually, Pam does not string her clients along for years. Instead of putting people down for regular weekly appointments to keep her mortgage money churning in, she allows spontaneous appointments so people can move through their pain at their own pace. At the start of counseling she permits some regularity, but she expects that once Tania moves deeper she will join the others, contacting her when she feels she needs to. Like leaves on a windswept day flying in, folks from Caribbean, Jewish, southern Black, Puerto Rican, and many other backgrounds arrive when they feel the pain and call again. She even gives them just five minutes on the phone, rather than forcing a formal appointment, when they call from a trucker's break to get off their chest some anxiety or frustration.

Her home office feels like a huge pushcart supporting workers, who arrive with personalities as different and colorful as the various fabrics moving through New York's garment district. She listens, learns and asks those questions that engage each of her clients—working class, poor, or almost elite. Like Tania, they all struggle for consciousness. If they just want to adjust to this monstrosity of a system, Pam tells them, "Call somebody else, I am *not* a bourgie therapist." Her clients want to demystify their delusions, or some say illusions. In both their hearts and minds they learn to stop making historical mistakes at their workplaces, where they face oppression.

Time with this wise, caring sister relieves them all—time and the fact that she welcomes them into her home, which has turned out to be an integral part of the therapy she offers. It is a reflection of herself, especially the kitchen, with its food pantry filled with the smell of fresh marjoram and rosemary, the small sleek black radio on which she listens to the news, and the wall phone with its long cord that lets her walk around while talking on it and even wash and put away dishes. On the table her *Mother Jones* coffee mug sits on top of her paperback copy of *The Communist Manifesto*. Mother Jones's gleaming eyes in the photo on the cup fight fiercely to speak to Pam's consciousness. "Fight like hell for the living!" inscribed at the cup's bottom, calls out to her. Mother Jones often screamed and shouted those very words to encourage miners coming out of the pits. Another book, *Lessons from the Damned*, lies next to the cup. When she picks it up, it falls open to the chapter by four young Black women called "The Capitalist System's Family," which Pam has marked up heavily, with a red line under the words "I am the most powerful part of capitalism—the family." Further down, red circles surround three consecutive passages describing what the authors call the "Dick-Happy Momma":

> She is closest to the children early in their lives when they must be taught to be slaves. . . . She'll do anything to keep her man, including having children just for his satisfaction, not hers. She is the one who can destroy her child from the day she gives birth. When her man is mean to her she makes her children pay for this oppression. She is just a weak woman who provides the father with strength to oppress. I let her know that she is to feed the man first and the children later. . . . That is why I make the momma Dick-Happy and dependent on daddy and the ruling class Master." The last word in the last circle is "Master."

Tania, who knows almost nothing of any of this, has decided to drive her car all the way from Brooklyn through Queens and the Bronx to Pam's office instead of taking the subway, so she won't have to depend on Pam to pick her up at the subway station or drop her off there after their session has ended. The truth is, she feels reluctant be alone with this new counselor in her car, especially if the counseling session in her office doesn't go well. Besides, she enjoys having the car, which she had gotten a few weeks before she met Lynn, when she and Buster had traveled to Michigan to pick it up from Older Sister, who had gotten it from their parents. It gives her a feeling of independence, even though she rarely drives it except to move it from one parking place on the street to another, according to the city's "alternate-side-of-the-street-parking" rules.

Now, feeling ever more anxious as she leaves the city behind, but driven by the pain of her relationship with Buster, and remembering the commitment she made to her supporter Lynn to honor herself, she forces herself to keep going until finally she arrives at the address she's been given. A Black woman in her middle fifties, short and thin, thin, thin, wearing lots of silver bangles, with sharp reddish Indian-like hands, sparkling eyes, and an especially warm smile, is waiting on the porch, a green-eyed calico cat at her feet. As the cat watches, she extends her hand.

"Tania, you made it," she says.

"Yes." Tania feels naked emotionally, standing here with this stranger. What will this woman tell her? What will she ask her?

"Come in." Pam gestures toward the door and Tania goes up the steps to the porch and follows the counselor into a small but airy room off a hall next to the dining room, which, she will learn, also serves as a waiting room. Sometimes another client will be there when her session is finished, and, during the first few weeks, before she has learned to trust Pam fully, she will bury her head in her scarf and rush out, hoping the person won't recognize her back in the city.

The first thing she notices in the office, which is decorated in warm colors, is a large poster, a photo of a woman looking over a fence, with the legend: "Class Consciousness is knowing which side of the of the fence you are on. Class analysis is figuring out who is there with you." In front of the poster is a chair with its seat covered in blue fabric and facing both chair and poster is a blue couch, soft and comfy, set against the wall. Tania assumes this is where she will sit. A desk behind a small screen with papers on it gives the room a sense of being used, but it's not at all stiff and stuffy the way Tania had expected it to be. The window, without blinds, looks out on a very large tree. She likes the feel. Even the phone rests gently on a tiny table. Its ring does not disturb them as the session begins because Pam walks right by it, letting her answering machine, set to "silent record," take the call.

"So what about a cup of tea?"Pam asks, offering a selection.

Tania chooses chamomile, and Pam pours the hot water over the tea bag. Try and relax, Tania tells her hands as she taps her fingers on the sofa.

Pam asks about the drive from Brooklyn and listens while Tania replies. Tania's tone and manner are very formal, as if she's at a job interview.

". . . so then I took the Hutch— . . . What parkway is that?"

"Hutchinson River."

"Yeah." Tania stops. The travelogue must end soon, and then what? What can she say to this woman? In desperation she turns to what little she remembers about her childhood, which is what she assumes Pam, like any other therapist, is probably waiting for. "So driving on that pokey parkway, I was twirling my hair around my finger, kinda like when I was called Buttercup and used to sit in the kitchen by Miss Duffy watching her cook dinner. Miss Duffy was this woman I loved who used to listen to my dreams."

"Ummm." Pam has a clock, but it is behind her, where she can't see it, though Tania can. She keeps her gaze on Tania as Tania describes Miss Duffy and the house she grew up in. This feels good, so unlike her one and only session with the therapist she had gone to just after she started being with Buster.

"I want to check my car. Is that okay?" Tania obsesses about parking.

"What makes you want to run out right now?"

"Well, in Brooklyn you get huge parking tickets designed to feed our corrupt city government if you park on the wrong side of the street on the wrong day."

"So you know how this system lies." Pam nods approvingly. "We don't have alternate side parking out here, though we definitely have a lying power elite. But go ahead and check if you feel like it." She nods toward the door, but Tania decides not to go out after all. She can't think of anything more to say, however, especially anything that won't lead Pam to the subject of Buster, whom she suddenly doesn't want to talk about.

"What kind of therapy do you use, Pam?" she asks finally, filling time. Thank God the session is almost over.

"I just try to open up your head a bit," Pam replies, smiling. She has many intellectual but defensive clients and knows it's best to wait until they feel comfortable enough to volunteer, on their own, the reason they came to her office for counseling.

Despite this unpromising beginning, Tania continues to see the counselor regularly, gradually opening up to her about when she was called Buttercup. Perhaps it is because Pam is short, like her grandma, and despite otherwise looking nothing like her, glows with the same caring inner spirit. She continues to avoid mentioning Buster, Instead, at the outset of each session, Pam puts out a general question and somehow Tania finds herself going on about things that hadn't crossed her mind in years. "My grandma who first called me Buttercup came from Poland," she says today.

Pam stands, walks over to the wall, and pulls down a huge wall map. "Look at this map of Europe," she says. "My last client needed for me to pull it down so she could see the place her mother migrated from."

"Okay." Tania gets up and goes to look.

"Where was your mother from?" Pam asks.

"The Bronx, but Grandma was born in Poland." She speaks so softly Pam strains to hear her.

"Oh yes. Here's Poland." Pam touches it with her finger.

Looking at the old wall map, Tania realizes Pam has given her a space to put her yearning in. "I loved Grandma's Jewish Polish self," she says when they sit back down.

"Did you tell other kids about her?"

Tania doesn't answer right away. She focuses on Pam's gorgeous dark blue pants. Finally she whispers, "No. The Black kids would never have understood."

"Why?"

"'Cause we were supposed to be Black and that's it. The old teachers in elementary school were angry at us for being Black and we couldn't all of a sudden say, 'Oh, my mother is white like you, Mr. Washington, but not Christian. She was a Christ killer, a Jew.'" Tania spits this out, fury rising.

"Did you say a Christ killer?"

"Yeah, but that's only 'cause that's what Mom told me her growing up was filled with. Irish kids in the Bronx taunting her with 'You killed Christ, you killed Christ.' That's why she didn't make us wear the Jewish gold star necklace Grandma bought for us. She didn't want us to have another thing to deal with."

"So you are Black and Jewish, right?"

"Yeah. But Pam, Black people don't like to hear that."

"I'm sorry, sweetheart, it's not what they like, it's what is."

Tania bursts out crying. "I don't want to be damn Jewish."

"*Why*, Tania . . . ?" The question hangs in the office. Pam waits patiently. This session has reached a critical breakthrough point.

Regaining her voice as her sobbing subsides, Tania chokes out: "Because I hate that I have to stand up to folks and be white too. White poor folks don't seem to like Black folks and yet I trust Black folks more than Jews."

"There are poor Jews too."

Man! Just now Tania wants like anything to be in her cozy little car going . . . going away from this woman who's making her face these things. But she stumbles on. "Well I am, yeah, I mean, Grandma . . ." She shifts from sitting straight up on the couch to resting her head back on the back. "Grandma was my best friend, Pam."

"There it is, it's out."

Letting her life's images pass before her while tears drip, Tania reflects on her revelations. "Yes, I can't deny you, Grandma . . ." she whispers.

The cold wind that blows long and steady outside makes a whirling wintry sound through a small window off to Tania's right.

"I hear my Grandma, Pam."

"I hear her too, Tania. You found her today. People feel better here, and it's important to take what you found with you, through the week."

Hearing Pam's verbal cue to end the session and face her week, Tania nods. "Okay. I know it's time . . ."

"Have an interesting week." Pam's words make Tania laugh, bursting out of the repression that had lurked around corners during most of her teen years. "I love when you say that, Pam . . . Not 'good' or 'nice,' but 'interesting'. 'Have an interesting week.' It's check it out and bring it back . . . for us to work on."

Later, Tania tries to write down in her journal what Pam had said, the words that had helped her see clearly for the first time the conflict between her Black and white selves that had tormented her as a child, and how she had tried to resolve it by becoming Black, and putting away from her heart, along with other "childish things," the Polish Jewish grandma whom she had loved and who had loved her and named her Buttercup. She writes what she remembers, but is not sure she's got it right, and regrets that she hasn't taken Pam up on a suggestion she made that Tania tape their sessions if she wished. It hadn't seemed important then, but now, suddenly, Tania feels strongly that Pam will be the mentor, teacher, counselor she has never had, and she decides to take a cassette recorder to their next session.

Perhaps it is because of this, because on some level the recording confirms the significance of the conversation, that, after spending a fair stretch of time crossing and uncrossing her legs, staring now out the window, now at the rug on the floor, Tania finally gets to the subject that brought her to Pam in the first place and so begins the climb out of the cage she's been crammed into her entire life. "This stinking boyfriend I have treats me wrong," she announces. "And I'm sick and tired of taking it from the bastard . . . He treats me like a piece of shit. I don't do anything to deserve it. In fact that's what really got me in here in the first place, Pam. I told my friend Lynn, who knows your other client Hugo, and she said I don't have to take it and gave me your number. I don't like it when Buster slaps my face."

As in previous sessions, Tania really doesn't know what she's talking about exactly, or even where she is going with what she's saying, only that her stomach, neck and back have ached on and off for weeks. She may have begun her escape from the cage, but she doesn't yet know the lock's combination.

From the time she started seeing Pam, she's been more and more avoiding Buster when he starts to rage, leaving his place and returning to her own safe apartment to sleep. Still, his rants leave her waking up in a panic a lot of mornings, like today. Her headache puts her heart into a low pound, her body trying to show her what an ass-kicking she takes staying with him, even when he doesn't actually assault her. But she does stay.

Now, however, after struggling to stand up to him without talking about it with her counselor, she can't hold back any longer, and blurts out: "I'm scared, Pam. I'm scared of continuing to be a doormat for him. Since I started seeing you I've tried to change things, but I can't seem to stop seeing him."

Quickly taking her own seat to set the session, Pam validates what Tania has just said, intuiting what she has not articulated. "Okay, Tania, so you're clearer now. You're becoming aware how you have allowed this man to put his need to dominate, in a physical or emotional way, totally on you."

"Yeah, I see that now," Tania says. "Thanks, Pam."

Pam's clients usually don't realize it, but whenever one of them is prepared to break through, this counselor intuitively knows it and takes a chance. Sometimes with very few words she shows them how they are victims who are in fact *choosing* whether to stay in intimate relationships that are replays of nuclear family oppression or to revolt. This night feels sharp. Tonight, out of Tania's mouth, will come a revelation allowing her to grab the moment.

Tania, seeing from the clock that her scheduled time with the counselor is almost up, opens her pocketbook and takes from her wallet the ten dollars she pays for each session.

Pam shakes her head. "I can see you have only begun, Tania. Tonight we'll take all the time you need."

Suddenly tears are filling Tania's eyes, spilling over. "Thank you, Pam," she says again.

As if there had been no interruption, Pam continues to affirm Tania's self-esteem. "You have worked very hard to stop taking in his sarcasm, his disdain, his utter disregard for you as a person, his verbal put downs."

"Yes, so what the hell, Pam, that shithead gots the nerve to hit me. Again! Again!" Even now, she feels too ashamed to mention what set them off this time: that he almost got sex from somebody else and she caught him.

While Tania stays stuck in shame thinking, Pam offers another option. "Or you could leave him," she says, then goes deeper. "I'm telling you flat out, Tania, all of us submit to oppression, even I have." She smiles. "Or we revolt."

Tania moves way over in the couch to the other armrest and announces, "Recently I dreamed something I wanna tell you." She thinks she'll have a chance to figure out how to respond to these comments if she deflects Pam's attention.

But for Pam, the universe perks up. She has been waiting for Tania to become ready. All along she knew that, as with other clients, the relationship with the boyfriend, girlfriend, job, boss or outside issue is a replay of old family dynamics. She suspects this dream will reveal a lot to work with. "Okay, tell me," she says.

Tania squirms, struggling to recall all the details of her dream. "My father sits at the head of the dining room table. He throws chicken bones out the window after he finishes eating. The bones land in the driveway and he yells at me to go outside and get them."

"Hmmm . . ." Pam listens, her head tilted in that thoughtful, gentle way she has. She senses that there will be a connection in this dream to both past and present, and that therefore she has no need to force Tania to face her fears of being on her own and let go of Buster. Tania will make the discovery for herself.

"And I don't like that. I don't wanna go. I guess I do, though. I don't remember that part of the dream. I think I woke up. . ." She stops. Pam listens to the silence. "I don't know. . ." Again, silence. "I do know I don't like the way Buster yells at me and orders me around." Subconsciously aware that in her dream she has headed into territory even more dangerous than Buster, she avoids going deeper by turning back to her relationship with him.

Now, kindly, gently, Pam probes, staying focused on the dream instead of veering off to talk about Buster. "Is that how your father used to treat you? Telling you to go and get his throwaways?"

Truth begins to surface for Tania. She blinks, hears her own voice, just above a whisper: "Oh my God. Buster represents my father. My father is why I picked this guy. My father used to hit me!" She finally remembers just this much, and she folds her arms to protect herself. "When I was a kid, my father used to scream at me, 'Don't cry or I'll give you something to cry about.' That was after he'd beaten me with the belt and I couldn't stop the tears. He wanted me to just take it and shut up." Suddenly she has a desire for pizza. Maybe on the way home, she thinks, I'll buy a big fat slice to fix all this and then I'll feel better. Yes, a cheesy slice with nothing but extra cheese. "Please help me Pam." Her nose is stopped up, making her voice nasal. "Help me stop this. I can't leave, just like my stupid mother couldn't leave my dad. I thought Buster was different, 'cause he talked about his feelings sometimes and was at the University of the Streets. But damn it, he isn't different! He *is* my damn father."

"What a breakthrough!" Pam makes the OK sign.

But Tania is too shocked by her own insight to respond. Instead, she tries desperately to avoid this new reality by going back to the nightmare. "Remember in my dream . . .?"

"Yes?" Pam encourages her.

She begins to cry, trying to explain through her tears why her father might have thrown the bones out the window. "Probably it was a game," she says. Then she switches gears again and returns to Buster, speaking more calmly as she finds false safety in intellectualizing. "I can understand why Buster does the things he does sometimes," she says. "He has too much pressure on him, trying to pay child support for his daughter, not having more than a high school education, always on unemployment, 'cause he can't find any jobs that pay enough." Then she adds, "But my father is educated, not like Buster. So he must have just been playing a game with me. In my dream." She justifies the behavior of both of them.

"Well, maybe," Pam says. Once again, however, she probes gently: "But what about you, Tania? How did you *feel* in the dream?"

"I didn't like it. The game, I mean . . ." She crosses her leg. "Oh God, do I have to go through this?" she wails.

"You and I will work it out together," Pam says soothingly, then inserts a clarifying question: "So if you didn't like the game, why did you go along with it? Why did you pick up those bones?"

Again, truth surfaces. "I did it because he told me to. I always did what he told me to. I guess he really didn't like me very much. He was always having intellectual conversations with me, but he was just impressing me. Underneath he thought of me as a slave, to go fetch things for him."

Pam leans towards Tania and suggests a deeper interpretation. "Could those bones have been you?" Tania sobs uncontrollably. Did her father really think of her as garbage, to be thrown away? Of less value even than a slave?

But Pam doesn't pursue it, and instead calms her, explaining how relationships can be a manifestation of the outer system's domination. "So both Buster and Daddy act in that dog eat dog way, 'cause these are capitalist-style social relationships, Tania."

It's hard for Tania to follow everything Pam clears the path for. She just lets it flow into her and, though the words are too far from where she is at the moment, she is comforted by the knowledge that they are on tape and she can go back to them. What she does understand now is that she had not been remembering that her father treated her bad, but it was what she was familiar with, and so she had gone with Buster. Has stayed with Buster. Has complied with Buster's wishes. Has followed Buster's orders more often than not. Now, through her relationship with Buster, and thanks to Pam, she has glimpsed a piece of the truth about her relationship with her father. It's as if Buster has served his purpose and so she can leave him the way she left her father's house. Yet still she hesitates, overwhelmed by her sense that, however right it is that she leave him, she is on the brink of losing the one male friend who, unlike her father, can reveal some of his sadness.

"So now I can choose, right, Pam?" she says tentatively. "But if I leave him, then who would be with me? Who would I be with?"

She is staring at her hands, clenched in her lap, and barely hears when Pam replies, "Tania, you're not alone. There are many other father-fixated sisters out there stuck in abusive relationships, trying to face their obsessive need for daddy's approval. You can find solace in that. And you have at least one sister in your life you can call up and share this with."

As her denial crumbles, Tania manages to lift her eyes to meet Pam's. "Yes, I do. Agua will be right there for me around this when I tell her, I know." After a long silence, she commits: "I'm gonna leave Buster."

Pam affirms her decision. "Yes. Now he's done his job. He gave you the connection to Daddy."

4 BURST THROUGH NUMBNESS

All during the day after she made the connection between Buster and her daddy, whenever Tania thinks of Buster, she picks up her phone and holds it for minutes, obsessing. Then she doesn't dial, but simply adjusts her white peasant blouse with the empire waist, worrying that she still looks ugly, the way she always felt she did as a child. But after a week of this, just before her next appointment with Pam, she goes through with the call. "I have to let you know something," she says, keeping her voice calm, controlled.

After an endless minute of harsh silence, he retorts, "I'm here."

"I'm effing sick of you being quiet and not responding to me," she screams.

"What's there to listen to?"

"You know, Buster, you never gonna face your pain. You just like my father and it's time for me to go." She imagines him looking out the window, lighting up a cigarette. "I care about myself and I don't want to be in this messed up relationship anymore."

"Okay. Then I'll bring your clothes back from here and be done with this."

Her fear of his rage returns. She coughs nervously. But he says nothing more, and listening to the silence, she takes a risk. "Well, come to my place and leave them in a bag on the doorknob. I may not be home."

"You better be there. You owe me money for that time you broke my table."

"When was that?"

"You better be ready to find twenty-five dollars when I come over."

Tania paces, wondering where to hide her money. Finally she opens her closet and buries her wallet under the tee shirts. She worries that Buster will try to hit her again now that she's announced she's leaving. Or will he be silent and cold? No matter. Whatever happens, the most important thing is to take back her own self. Glad he's not a big man, no taller than she is, in fact, she figures she can run out of the apartment if he tries anything. But she rubs her rumbling belly.

An hour later he arrives, pounding on her door. She checks through the peephole to be sure it's him. "Just leave the stuff on the doorknob," she shouts through the door.

"No, Tania. You open the damn door."

"No."

"Awright, then. I'll use the key and come right in."

That he had a key was one reason Tania had stayed home. If she'd gone out, he might have come in and destroyed her clothes and books and everything in sight. She has to get it back.

She hears the click of the lock opening and sits down at the table.

He walks in and tosses a bag with her clothes in it and her red knapsack on the floor in front of her. "Listen," he growls. "You busted up my table and you never paid me back for it. Give me my twenty-five dollars, you lousy slut."

"You know, Buster, you're just mad 'cause I'm finally daring to leave."

"I'm glad you're leaving. You ain't nothing to me. Never was." His eyes rage, now glaring at her, now darting around the room, searching. Where does she stash her cash?

She looks up as he looms over her, placing one hand on the table and reaching out with the other to press her down into the chair. She jumps up before he can touch her. "Okay, you asshole. I'm gonna pay you to get you outta my life. Give me back my key first."

He throws the key onto the table. It spins, crashing into a glass.

She goes to the closet and takes five five-dollar bills out of her wallet. "Here," she says, handing him the money. Then she opens the door. "Goodbye," she says.

"Good stinking bye!" He laughs and kicks a book that dropped out of her knapsack when he first came in, then stomps out, not wanting to have some nosey neighbor call the police.

Tania looks down. The book on the floor is *Lessons from the Damned*. She kicks the door, making sure it's slammed shut tight. Tears well up in her eyes as she bends down to pick up the small paperback book that Lynn had given her as a parting gift when she left town on some long-term assignment and that she had tried to get Buster to look at. She rubs her finger over the inscription inside the front cover: "To Lynn from Hugo/To Tania from Lynn." Pam often gives copies of the book to her clients to help burst them awake, but Tania is glad somehow that her copy has come to her indirectly, through connections to friends. She cries hard now, and collapses on one knee to the floor. Pounding her fist on the wood, she cries out, "Damn it. I jump into the most stupid relationships. I can't do it right. I hate men. I hate Black mfs. Those bastards think they can run me over." Minutes later, wiping her eyes with a tissue, she mumbles, "Oh God, Pam, but I'm glad you cared enough to help me see he *is* my damn father."

Thumbing through the pages of *Lessons*, she stops at the passage about the family she'd tried to share with Buster and reads aloud, skipping a little, as she had with him: "I am called 'family' from the Latin *familia*, meaning a household, the slaves or servants of a house. . . . Now let me show you how I structure myself. In the family I have the father, He's at the top. He's the master under the big ruling class Master. I call him the money-maker and provider. Therefore I let him know that he's supposed to put his woman second and his children last. . . . I make the father the oppressor of the family. He oppresses the momma and in turn the momma oppresses the children. I call the children the slaves."

She wonders now how she ever imagined this would help Buster change. Buster wasn't going to change, unless he admitted he had problems and wanted to grow.

Heaving a huge sigh, expelling all her pent up hope, she stands up to bolt the door and presses her body against it for a second, her forehead on the wood panel in the center. Then, pushing away and trudging back to the table, she hears her heart: I'll find someone to love me, I'll try again, but not with him. Never again with him. Feeling a desire for peppermint gum, she chews her last stick, having fished it out from the bottom of her knapsack.

***

Tania can no longer remember exactly when she first realized that Pam is much more than a radical therapist; she is a core part of an ever expanding network of leftist women, clients and colleagues and seekers, who are engaged in transformation. Once one of her clients makes the breakthrough that will begin to validate her as an agent in her own life, Pam will say, "I want you and all my clients to share your new ability to deeply listen and be listened to with someone else in order to help others," sending them out into the world of "crapitalism" as consciousness-raisers.

When she got to know Agua and others at the University of the Streets, and, of course, Lynn, Tania had entered a world of leftists and pan-Africanists—Pam's world, though neither she nor Agua had known that at first. They had learned it when Agua, on Tania's recommendation, had also started seeing Pam, to help her deal with being a single mom. Not long afterwards, Agua had suggested they form a women's writing and reading group that would also be a support group, with everything they did focused on the family. And with Pam's encouragement, they had done it, becoming the center of a network of women writers who concentrated on raising consciousness about the realities of the family under capitalism. They met every so often in groups of five to eight, connecting by phone tree to tell each other when and where.

Now, today, a group is meeting in Agua's home: women twenty to thirty years old sitting around on the long couch and on pillows on the floor, their winter jackets rolled up behind them. Almost everyone expected to come today is already there when Tania arrives. Agua motions for her to sit next to a slightly older sister nicknamed Smoke, a sepia-toned, broad-hipped woman with an afro hair style. A colleague of Pam's, she has come from a presentation and panel discussion on women in the movement, where the two of them had shared the platform with other radicals. Tania and Agua had gotten to know her when she was an instructor for a while at the University of the Streets, and early on had invited her to be part of the new group.

There is one new member, coming today for only the second time, a ginger-toned woman whose straightened hair lies flat on her head. She sits on the sofa, curling her long legs under her. Agua has nicknamed her Newbie. All the women except Agua and Tania have nicknames in order to keep their membership in the group confidential. What they're talking about is too private to let outsiders, even some in the movement, know what they're saying.

Now that enough folks have gathered to share a pleasant yet activist vibe, Agua lights evergreen incense, placing it in a pot near the fire escape window. Her cats find a small spot near the couch to curl up on as the meeting begins.

The group has scheduled Tania as reader today, and she is grateful that she has another way to move verbally through to her rebirth. She prints her name in large block letters on a piece of poster paper taped to the wall over the seat of honor: T A N I A, as in "Tania la Guerrillera," Che Guevara's compatriot. As she prepares to take her place beneath this "poster," she coughs a huge, choking cough, clearing her throat of her paralyzing fear of displeasing daddy and her unconscious rage at the fact that it lingers despite all the years of being on her own. As if channeling Che's *compañera* gives her courage, she takes her seat on the pillow on the floor under her name, studies the page she has marked in her journal for a moment, and begins reading aloud.

"The way the powers over us in jobs, school, and the world of government keep us thinking we're stupid is absurd. Few folks peek through the lies of silence and shout No!!!! I am going to say something! The system uses blame and shame to keep people quiet." She looks nervously at the women's faces. Newbie's eyebrows arch up, but Smoke nods encouragingly. She continues: "It was my mother's denial and the female relatives' silence that shamed me."

She hopes these other sisters understand. She rubs her soft inner elbow skin the way she did when she was a girl enduring her father's disapproval, though she's now in her mid-twenties. Since most of the group has a political, womanist consciousness, she doesn't have to explain all that much. They're familiar with Shulamith Firestone's *The Dialectics of Sex*. This and several books by Zillah Eisenstein, including *Capitalist Patriarchy and the Case for Socialist Feminism* are on the floor. Articles about Lolita Lebron, who took herself right to the US Congress and stood up with more than words for her motherland, Puerto Rico, and Los Borinqueños, her people, rest on a table near Tania. She has papers marking the pages she wants to read from later. She knows how important Latina leadership is to the group.

Right now, however, she says focused on the family. "Older Sister and Younger Sister are less important to me this decade. I don't even want to tell my two blood sisters about this women's group. Those two females identify strongly with our daddy and think he is always right. Their views are very far from mine on how men oppress even as they are oppressed themselves." Lowering her head, she mumbles, "It's as if my family's thinking is crazy."

The group listens intently. Several are now lying on the pillows with their heads resting on the wall behind the couch.

Tania reads the piece through to the end: "It's almost as if my nuke-liar family enjoyed living in a 'Lie-Now Machine.' The way women keep the fear held close to our bosoms is now so unreal to me!" Putting her journal down, she notices Newbie whispering something to Agua. Suddenly she feels like Buttercup again, remembering the way her sisters were constantly edging her out of their closeness, even ganging up on her and complaining about her. 'Work it out girls,' her mother would say, as if those two would ever listen to Buttercup.

As she cuts her eyes briefly to the women whispering, she feels her shame button pushed again. Maybe she shouldn't be talking bad about her relatives. Maybe the women here will think bad about her. She was criticizing women who go along with daddy as king. Maybe she will be in trouble with some in the group. The phone tree messages inviting the women to the meeting had stated, as always, that the readings might lead to emotional distress as well as cathartic release. But even so, some might be put off.

She moves her eyes to Agua, who has just returned from the bathroom. As she sits down, Tania tries to connect to her, but Agua is zipping her pants up tighter and focused on that. Somewhere deep down inside, Tania feels like her little baby Buttercup self has to come out, whatever the others may think. She can feel herself shrinking like Alice in Wonderland, smaller and smaller until she is Buttercup having nightmares about Daddy's car. She wants to scream but Daddy will hit her if she does. But Daddy isn't here. She screams.

Her yell starts out low and then it roars louder and louder and many of the sisters cover their ears. Curdling inside Tania are all those years of shut it down, shut it in, be careful or your family will think you're crazy.

She looks up at Newbie, her back rigid on the futon sofa. Both cats are startled up and leave, though not hurriedly. The scream ends.

Agua walks over to Tania to wrap her in a long soothing hug. "Wow! Women's consciousness raising at its best," she says, then bows her head in what seems to be prayer, chanting the Yogic Om. Others also hum "Oms," following her lead, so that the feel is of an African call and response. Braids and Afros and straight down locks create a circle of hair as the women bend their heads. Since most of them love Tania, they understand her need to yell. They believe a power greater than anyone they know had helped her and would continue to help her and all of those who came to these "rooms" or "encounter groups," so that they will no longer be blind victims of the vicious tight lips of many of the women from their girlhoods, including their own moms.

Later, while most folks stay chatting in the kitchen after they've eaten, Tania and Agua return to the living room and create their first joint poem on the floor by the window. "Let's See What's Revealed" aka "Saying Stuff —Through Words Out Loud" becomes the title.

As they sit easily on the floor, both their young bodies very flexible, Agua suggests the first line of the poem:

"Most, if not the entire gang, of the female gender has also suffered. . ."

Tania responds dramatically, finger in the air: *". . . But we spoke not a word . . ."*

Agua suggests more lines: *"Stick your soul in my hole. / When my body self was alive to you, you felt good. / No more dead dicks in my bed. / Cold as rock candy, hard and dead."*

Inventing together, they further expose "no-feeling" men, scribbling furiously as the poem carries over to the back of the page.

"We be busting through this father fixation," shouts Tania.

"Hey hey," Agua agrees, slapping five.

As the group leaves, Agua offers to walk Tania to the subway. On the way, they step on each other's sore spots.

Despite her wanting to be her new self-assured self, Tania's grievance pops out first. "Why didn't you call me back like you said you would last week?"

"I had so much to do with Heru I got overwhelmed."

"Yeah, but I'm your friend. Sometimes I feel left out."

"Well, my boyfriend came over, and we got into an argument."

"Oh," Tania says. "But you *said* you'd call me. Am I important to you or not?"

"Of course you are." They pause at the red light before crossing the street.

"As important as your married boyfriend?"

"Well, Tania, it's different, how I feel for you and how I feel for him."

"So are you agreeing with me or what?"

"Stop it, Tania! You sound like my mother. I need a friend, not a nag."

"Well, I came to meet you at that Cuban documentary last week and you didn't show up. And a couple of weeks before that you left me sitting by myself at the WOW meeting."

"What?"

"That's what I mean! You don't even remember. The Women's One World Theatre meeting we were going to go to together."

By now they have reached the subway station, and the sense of sisterhood they felt writing poetry together back at the apartment has disintegrated for the moment. They part without the usual "take care, sister."

As Tania starts down the stairs, Agua stalks off, her face flushed, but before reaching home, she's ready to make amends. She recalls one of the first things Pam had said to her: "Agua, look. Your friend Tania is not your nagging mother, though she has similar traits. You can learn to see where you're mixing them up." And a few days later she calls Tania in a panic. "Hey, Tania, I'm sorry about the other day, but I'm scared," she says. "I've got this thing from the landlord and I'm scared to open it. I just can't. You've got to come help me."

Tania arrives to find Agua sitting at the kitchen table with a letter, still unopened, in front of her.

Without ceremony, Tania pushes. "Well, are you going to open it?"

Agua hates the way Tania goes right at a thing, and out of habit she rolls her eyes. But in fact, this time she's grateful for Tania's insistence. Slowly, she picks up the white business-shit-sized envelope. "It's so scary to face the corporate owners and real estate liars, Tania. They kept me and my moms in roach-infested places when I was growing up."

"I know. I hear you."

"I really don't want to open it." Agua gets up and walks into the hall.

Tania follows her. "But Agua, you could be evicted," she says urgently.

"God! Then where will me and Heru go . . .?"

"Yeah, but if you open the damn envelope, we'll at least know what the next step is from the enemy's side. Come on, we'll read it together."

The gurgle of the continuously running toilet, which the landlord hasn't deigned to fix, inspires Agua to decide to face her fear. She tosses the envelope on her bed and the two women sit with the thing between them, stark white on the India cotton spread.

After trying in vain to tease the envelope open with her forefinger, Agua rips it apart and extracts the letter gingerly, as if she's afraid it will bite. Before unfolding it, she says, "Thank you Tania, for helping me to face stuff. Sometimes I want to hide in a closet, like my damn mother taught me, and not face any of my fears. But I'm glad you're paying attention instead of changing the subject like you do when I ask you to do the same thing."

Tania shakes her head, smiling. "Same thing like what?"

"Face your momma." Agua smiles, too, but because she has such a wide mouth, as always it seems like a grin. Suddenly they're laughing together and hugging each other in relief. Agua unfolds the letter and reads it silently.

"Well, what does it say?"

"That I have to get out."

"Well, you can go to housing court tomorrow morning and set up a date to fight this in front of a judge. I've been listening to *Housing Notebook* on WBAI and they say the no-heat and the roaches and the broken toilet you're always complaining about are legitimate reasons for making your thieving landlord have to wait for the rent. I'll go with you."

"You will?"

"Yeah. I don't have to work until afternoon. But you gotta stand up and deal."

"Oh God, Tania, I'm gonna go. With you there I can do it."

They slap five and Tania says, "I'll meet you in front of the court house at . . . What time does the court open?"

"Eight-thirty!" Agua is so relieved she shouts, waking the cats.

About a week later, after long hours of waiting and then a surprisingly short proceeding, Agua wins more time to find the money to pay the rent for her shitty apartment, though there's still no guarantee there'll be heat. But the judge says she deserves an inspection before the landlord sends any more eviction notices.

Racing away from the constraints of the courthouse, the two women shout "o-o-o-o-o" with relief.

"I'm real glad you came and helped me open that dumb envelope, Tania," Agua says. "And thank you for coming with me to court."

"I'm glad I could. But you did great in there yourself, saying you were withholding the rent 'cause of all the violations."

Back at Agua's they sit reflecting on the day and looking out the window at the unkempt park filled with garbage that is Agua's "view."

"I wanna talk about Pam," Agua says after they've gotten really settled. "I think she's radical, 'cause a lot of people in therapy have told me their counselors say they have to adjust to their family." She looks over her nails, then reaches for the polish bottle, to touch them up while they talk.

Tania nods. "Pam tells us to stand up not only to the family but to these bastards like landlords, who make the family so uptight."

"And we did it. Yay, Tania! Sometimes I hate when you push, but this was really good. I even got the right to an inspection."

"Yeah. But even if things are fixed by the time the inspector comes, you still got to go back and at least *ask* for a set-off on your past-due rent," Tania says.

"Okay, we'll see. I'm still afraid of the landlord. But I faced my fear of the courts and shit. That's good."

Arching her back and letting this night's moon glow on her through the window bars behind her, Tania almost hums, "It's like Pam says. We'll always have each other as part of our foundation."

"Damn, I love that Pam," Agua says. "She helps me to break this shit open. You know what, Tania? I loved my mother, but I adored my step-father, even when he was two-timing my moms. Do I hold men up high? Oh God, I still have contradictions. The yada yada yada of my family!"

Tania joins in the self-revelation. "Yeah, Agua, mine, too. I loved my mean dad and my mother, his enabler, and even my sisters, when I wasn't hating them. I grew up with them. They were all I knew. I trusted them." She strokes her eyebrow. "That's the sick shit they train us into being so familiar with torture that eventually we end up subjecting ourselves to it again and again in our relationships with people we think we really like."

Agua nods her head in agreement. Then, swallowing, and remembering something about her family and her older brother, she laughs. "You know Tania," she says, "both you and me either played ping pong, like you did with your sisters of blood, or stood on the sidelines and watched, like I did with my brother. 'The Boy in the Family plays baseball,' everybody said. She laughs again. "One day he just put the bat down and spoke out, talking in a great big voice, you know, Tan, like when a boy's talking the sound is deeper?"

"Yeah . . ." Tania nods.

Agua pushes on. "And with a big, almost man's, voice, although it kept cracking, he said to my dumb mother and stupid-ass step-father: 'I don't like baseball.' " She is about to slap five with Tania, when an interruption comes. "Mom, I wanna glass of water." Heru has woken up. Agua walks to the bedroom to give him a drink.

Looking around the apartment, which seems cramped partly because there are so few closets, Tania sees one of Agua's poems pasted on the wall. As she waits for Agua to return from the bedroom, she fishes in her bag, the green one with fringes on the bottom, for a creation she's been working on.

"Hey, Agua," Tania stage whispers. "When you come back I wanna ask you to read something I wrote, okay?"

Heru shows how really tired he feels after having played hard that day, because when Agua asks, "Do you want any more water?" he shakes his head. He's not ready for anything but sleep and falls back on his pillow.

Seeing him settled again into bed, Agua smiles to herself. Thank God the child only wanted water, and doesn't need to be held or coaxed back to sleep. Passing the bathroom she thinks, thank goodness water in this Bronx building can be trusted, unlike in her last apartment, where the pipes were corroded. When she rejoins her friend, she holds out her arm and Tania places her latest poem into her sweet hand— the hand of her best friend. A peace bracelet, Heru's gift, adorns Agua's wrist. She wears it proudly.

"Okay, here goes, Tania," she says, and adjusts her glasses to read.

Thanking her friend with a nod of her head and light touch on her knee, Tania lies back. She closes her eyes and listens closely to the way the words she wrote sound in someone else's voice.

5 VISIT WITH LOVE AND FEAR

Some weeks before their appearance in Housing Court, Agua had found Tania a job as a helper in the back room of the day care center where she worked. It was Tania's first union job, and while the weekly paycheck wasn't going to put her on easy street, it was a regular income and not dependent on tips. From the first, she appreciated the informality; with no waitress uniform required, she can wear comfy pants and a sweatshirt to work. And she has come to enjoy the way the kids work out their problems with one another on the swings or in the sandbox. She listens to them the way Pam listens to her.

Lately, however, she has begun to feel insecure. When she was hired, the center had been over-registered with four year olds, but the numbers have been dropping. Now, pressing her hands hard on the wood rim of the sandbox and munching furiously on a Tootsie Roll a kid has left, she sees Agua signaling to her that they can leave. Since all the kids are gone, today they won't have to stay late the way they do on the many days when some parents don't come on time to pick up their kids—overtime work they're not compensated for, since it's not "assigned" as per the union contract; they're just expected to do it.

Noticing her worried look, Agua lays a consoling hand on her shoulder.

"I overheard the cook saying there's gonna be layoffs soon," Tania whispers, looking around to make sure no one else is nearby.

"Are you shitting me?"

"No, Agua, I'm not kidding. This junk never ends. I'm scared."

Agua glances in the direction of the boss's office, then signals with her head that they should leave so they can talk freely. Once they are outside, she says, "So, why not start looking now for more work, so you don't end up unemployed?"

"Yeah . . ." Tania mumbles doubtfully.

With a push in her voice Agua encourages her to try to find something where there's not only a union but where once you're qualified, you're in solid.

"But there's a union here . . ."

"Yeah, but you're the last hired and since the job doesn't require any very special skills, you're going to be first fired in any case. Still, with our union contract, you're legally entitled to sick leave and vacation pay, and even a couple of personal days, and you get them *and* severance pay if you're laid off. You can't be laid off at the boss's whim, either."

"Oh yeah? I heard the other teacher's assistant has connections with a friend of the boss, so I'd be out even if I wasn't last hired."

Agua smiles. "That's why you always gotta watch your back and always have a back-up plan."

They walk the rest of the block to the subway. At the newsstand on the corner, Agua picks up a copy of *The Chief* and as soon as they're inside the station, opens it to the page where the notices for city job exams are posted. She laughs. "Hey Tania, you could take this exam and be bus driver."

"What!? Drive a big ole city bus?" Tania's eyes open wide and almost sparkle.

Agua is reading the fine print. "Wow," she exclaims. "You don't need a bus-driver's license to take the exam. They'll train you and they have some agreement so you get your C D L as soon as they say you're ready to go."

"C D L?"

"Commercial Driver's License. But I also hear places like the transit authority will send people to spy on you when you're on the road driving. They don't tell you they're evaluating you when they come on the bus."

"Who told you that?"

"A bus driver in my building." Agua tosses this over her shoulder, speeding up because she hears a train coming. "But don't let that put you off. Here."

Tania grabs the paper from her and reads about the job. The very next day, she sends in her application.

A few weeks later she is standing with hundreds of men in a line stretching around the corner from the entrance to the Metropolitan Transit Authority's testing center for Manhattan and Bronx surface operators. There's not a velvet hair clip or band in the bunch, and she wonders what happened to all the females. Didn't any apply? Male heads bob in conversation as they wait, but once inside the bass and baritone voices hush as they madly fill in bubbles on the answer sheets. Staring at the paper in front of her, she realizes she doesn't know the answers to any of the questions about headways and schedules or air pressure breaks and what to do if the windshield of your bus falls out. Had there been materials to study? She almost gets up and walks out, but realizes that this would draw unwelcome attention and certainly derisive snickers, not to mention it would be letting her sisters down. Besides, she soon realizes that many, if not most of the questions are framed so they don't require much more than common sense to answer. She is among the first to finish the test. There is nothing more to do but wait to hear whether she has been accepted into the training program.

Their Housing Court triumph draws Agua and Tania even closer together, and they get into something new for them, becoming more serious about their art. They do lots of writing. They are "bad." They go to the "Y" in "boogie down" Brooklyn to read their writings aloud, including the first poem they wrote together, performing it as a public duet. They go with other members of their Working Women Poets group to anti-imperialist teach-ins about wars, covert and overt, where they support each other through impromptu performances of their work. They keep reading, sharing with each other. Phone conversations during this time often go like this:

"Hey, guess what?"

"What?"

"I wrote something. Wanna hear it?"

"Sure."

"Oh great." They share their pride in their creations with each other.

Then maybe Agua will say, "I can make time to go with you to that fundraiser you told me about, the one to raise money for the defense of that guy, you know, the activist who got arrested demonstrating against police brutality."

Both write about the color thing—how difficult it is, as Black women, and for Agua as a Latina sister as well, to realize that after all the so-called progress of the movements of the sixties and the seventies, they are still considered skanks by what is now Ronald Reagan's Amerika. In some ways it's as if nothing has changed. Even the Afro hair style, which both Agua and Tania still wear at times, and which was such a badge of honor and defiance only a few years ago, is now rarely seen. When employers started retaliating against those who wore them, most of the self-proclaimed "proud Black men and women" surrendered. Tania writes an essay that begins: "We are still considered ugly by some Black male comics. Maybe Moms Mabley isn't making as many of her self-hatred jokes as she used to . . . but the kids I tutor sure still call each other 'Blackie.' 'Ugly!' 'You Black so and so.' The system has done too good a job of instilling self-hatred of the people's African roots."

She also further develops her feminist consciousness, coming to realize that not all men are the enemy, that Hugo, for example, whom she is glad to bump into at a Mumia rally, isn't the only man who realizes sexism is embedded in every aspect of society, even among radicals. One day, after a performance she and Agua have given that included the poem they wrote together about sex and Black men (which was really about wanting a little bit of love and forgiving yourself for settling just for sex) she bumps into one of these "guy-friends," whom she and Agua had come across several times at demonstrations, where he often manages the sound equipment, tapes proceedings and takes photographs for a number of radical publications, for which he also sometimes writes. The boys 'round the old way had given him the name Purple, he'd told them. It seems that reciting the poem has freed up something in Tania, and she responds to Purple's overtures, giving him her number.

It turns out that this overweight brother-man with the smooth, youthful skin and hair that reveals he can't be that old 'cause he still has it—later she will learn that he's just turned thirty—shows when he calls that he's available to *listen*, instead of being full of himself like so many men. In fact, he actually talks very little, and gives Tania space to release some emotional junk with him.

"You know these bastard capitalists at the MTA make me so effing mad, raising the fare. They don't give a damn about the working people."

"I hear you, Tania." She can see his smile in her mind's eye. He may be a young man, but the tone of his voice reveals an ancient soul deep inside him.

Her antagonism to unfairness seems to inspire him. He is a man who appreciates a woman who is about more than painting her fingernails, going to the hair salon every week, and waiting for a man to take her to a dance club, then ride them both home in a taxi, even if he really only makes enough money to pay his share of the bills and maybe go to a movie every now and then. Purple is real. He's down-to-earth, receptive. And yet . . . Purple is a man who wears *glasses*. And he doesn't have a body. Can a fat man, no matter how simpatico, be sexy? She doesn't know.

What she does know is that she enjoys spending time with him, time not doing anything in particular, except talking. They meet in a park in Brooklyn, on a bench by a small meadow that they have pretty much to themselves. And while they often talk politics, they also talk about personal things—childhood memories, things that Tania hasn't shared before with any man. Purple tells her about the summers he spent with his grandma in Gullah-Geechee country on the southern coast of North Carolina, taking in the culture of his people, who for 400 years had held on to West African ways, creating a language and a cuisine all their own based on what had been theirs before their enslavement. His grandma had taught him to cook some of the dishes. But mostly he had grown up with his moms and pops in an apartment in the city, where they still live. His pops worked in a factory, and still does.

She talks about growing up in Queens as the child of a white mother and a Black father. When the buttercups bloom, she confides that when she was a small child her Polish grandmother had started calling her Buttercup, and the name stuck until she got too old for pet names. Purple listens in a caring way, speaking only occasionally, and always in a gentle voice, comforting her when the story is a sad one, about her grandmother dying or Miss Duffy going back to Jamaica. Occasionally, also, he touches her shoulder or her hand, again in a gentle, accepting way, completely unlike any other man she has been close to. But then, one day as he and Tania prepare to leave the park, he reaches out his arms and gives her a hug. Fearing that the gesture of friendship is going to turn into a long squeeze indicating something else, she quickly pulls away and jumps up, saying "Oh, I gotta go. Bye now."

She runs to her apartment. Once the door closes, she leans back on it, asking herself why she didn't want him to hug her, why she didn't feel the urge to kiss him. It's only a fleeting question, and though it has come up over and over since she started seeing Purple, she doesn't *really* ask it and then sit down to think about it and figure out the answer. Instead, she simply writes in her journal: "I guess he ain't my type. He's not cute like the men in *Essence* and *Ebony*"

Her wall phone rings. The sound easily snatches her away from her journal. She reaches over to the corner, where her second phone, still with a rotary dial face, sits on the floor.

"Hello?"

"Tania?"

"Oh hi, Agua. You know when you call, I always know it's you, but if Purple calls, I hate that he expects me to know his voice. . . Does he think he's the only man in my life?"

"But Tania, isn't he?"

"I know, but . . . He doesn't like to go for long walks the way me and you do. When we go to the park, he only wants to sit and talk."

"Tania, did you ever think of telling all this to Pam?"

"Why? I mean I'm not really into him like that. I want to talk with him about stuff like the African Liberation group. Being able to do that helps me. He really does know the facts. Like sometimes I think about the effing racism all around New York, in the way Black people generally don't have apartments in the wealthy parts of the Upper East Side. But he helps me see that our struggle is so much wider than New York, like the way apartheid has stolen the South Africans' country and they're being murdered for protesting it by a government backed by the U.S. I'm clear now that colonialism kills."

"Yeah, I totally hear you. He sounds like he's clear that these rich white corporations take over everywhere they go."

"And today he showed me this radical paper that printed an exposé about how the fat cats, with the help of the CIA, get countries to take loans they can't pay back, supposedly to develop their economies. In order to get the money the countries have to give U.S. corporations access to their land and resources."

"Oh, man! It sounds like what they do in Puerto Rico."

"Yeah. The CIA hires guys to keep those loans going. It all works so the corporations don't have to deal with international union organizing." Tania rubs her shoulder where Purple had hugged her earlier.

"Damn! Purple sounds like someone you could really be with."

"I know. But Agua, he has no finesse. I mean, I like a guy to approach me and when he wants to kiss me he does it . . . and then we laugh and we can keep going or stop."

"You mean he talks to you about touching you, instead of going ahead and taking care of business?"

"I mean like even with Buster—that asshole—well, at least he put a strong voice into the mix."

"How?"

"Well, with Buster, you know, even though I was thinking of him as a quote-unquote friend for a whole summer, walking all up and down the streets of Manhattan at eleven p.m., but not going home with him, or letting him go home with me, 'cause I was still living with my previous boyfriend at the time . . . Well, he finally confronted me and said he wanted me to sleep with him. And I couldn't do that and still live with my old boyfriend."

"Well, you had some integrity," Agua says.

"So-o-o, I actually told what's-his-face that I had been seeing someone else. That was the weekend before I finally did sleep with Buster. But at least Buster forced the issue."

"Damn. How did your old lover deal with you telling him?"

"He threw a glass across the kitchen." Tania laughs.

"Oh shit, Tania." Agua can't help laughing too, though she is reminded of her own old choices and realizes she has to face them. She sighs and says, "You know, I went through the same thing . . ."

"Yeah . . . but can I finish telling you about me and Purple and then I'll hear about what happened to you?"

Agua is flexible. "Sure sure. We don't even have to get into me today, 'cause I talked so much the last conversation we had . . ."

"Thanks, Agua. I was just getting to the fact that I wish I *could* be turned on by Purple, 'cause I *say* that looks ain't important, but here I am trying my damnedest to avoid him, somewhat anyway, only 'cause his body ain't quote-unquote built like Buster's was." She peers into the bathroom mirror as if she half expects to see a reflection of Buster standing in the doorway. She has dragged the phone in there to wash her hands as she talks, with the cord trailing behind her.

"Do you trust him?"Agua knows this is a hard question and almost doesn't ask it, because unlike Tania, who blurts stuff out, Agua usually thinks things through a lot more.

"Trust him? What has that got to do with anything, Agua? I guess I over-trust men or under-trust them. My mother and Older Sister never schooled me as to what signals to look out for or what I need to do. I mean, I watch TV and do what they do, as crazy as that sounds."

"I don't know about that and I don't mean to push, Tania, but sometimes I know, for me, I put it into my head that 'cause a man can actually think, he ain't Puerto Rican or something. I mean my so-called stepfather was so messed up and yet he was 'Rican. That's all I saw as a girl growing up: him, a Puerto Rican drug addict, dumb and high. But he did dress fancy. And he'd be coming on to me, even though my moms was supposed to be his woman! And sometimes I had to pull the sheets really tight around me to stop him. So now I can't believe an intellectual Puerto Rican guy is gonna be good for me. That's what seeing Pam has helped me understand, anyway. 'Cause he wanted me and was the only one paying attention to me, I have a hard time imagining anyone who's not like him wanting to be with me. What I'm saying is, even though Pam has helped me realize how mixed up it is to feel the way I do, I still like to put my hair up sometimes and walk in the neighborhood, just to hear the comments I get from the men lounging around on the stoops the way he used to do."

Agua's openness—both what she has said and her willingness to say it—surprises Tania and for a moment she doesn't respond. Then she laughs. "You mean you believe those guys in the neighborhood are really thinking about *you*, Agua, when they shout "Hey, *mami*?"

"Well, I am working on not thinking that, but I wanted you to know my contradictions for real. The fact is, if a guy isn't a dresser, it's hard for me to imagine us in bed one day." She giggles, then coughs, and then, even though it's hard for her to get it out, she says, "It's the same for you, isn't it, Tania?"

Tania, caught up in giggles of her own, readily agrees. "I still want the bad boys. Can you believe it, after Buster?"

"Yeah. You seem to go for guys with leather jackets. And not the flashy red, white and black striped Michael Jackson leather jackets, either; only Michael wears those."Agua stops talking for a moment. Then she says then says abruptly, "Can I ask you something? All the women of your girlhood used to comment on your dad's looks the way me and you are talking about Michael, didn't they?"

"Yeah . . . I guess so . . ."

"Don't you make the connection that your father was the 'pretty man' in the neighborhood, and that's why you're still looking for a pretty man with brains. But how about brains with caring but not so pretty?"

A little taken aback, Tania giggles. "No-o-o. It has to be brains with looks."

Agua persists. "But don't you remember you told me Pam said real emotional intimacy could still be scary for you and that's why you keep going with men who it turns out don't really care? You're afraid of having them care 'cause it makes you vulnerable."

Again Tania doesn't respond, but merely giggles, and as often happens, the two friends join in covering the revealing moments with their laughter.

On a windy day not long after this conversation with Agua, Tania is once again hanging out with Purple in the park. She asks if he'd like to hear something she wrote. He is enthusiastic, and she pulls several pieces out of her bag to read. The wind, however, has other ideas, snatching the pages away. Laughing, he runs and catches them—he's surprisingly light on his feet for a heavy man—and then suggests she come over to his place, which is nearby, to get out of the wind. Somewhat to her own surprise, she agrees.

As she rearranges her windblown hair, she envies his neat Afro, which the wind has left undisturbed. His apartment, a one-bedroom floor-through with bare hardwood floors on the third floor of a brownstone, is as neat as he is, though the handsome furniture is mismatched. One corner is filled with recording equipment and cameras. As he gets them each a glass of ginger beer, she compliments him on the place.

"Thanks," he says. "It's not bad. It's taken me a while to furnish it, but you find better quality stuff on the streets of Brooklyn than I could ever afford to buy. I'd rather spend my money on that." He nods towards the recording equipment. "Anyway, better enjoy it while you can. I may not be able to afford it much longer if the thieving landlords who are beginning to make this part of Brooklyn as unaffordable as the Heights get their way."

She sips her drink and nods her head.

"I've been organizing tenants on and off for various housing organizations, trying to do something about it. The rent stabilization laws are still keeping New York City affordable, but the realtors and so-called developers keep stealing smaller places so they end up on the open market."

"Smaller places? I don't get it."

"If a building doesn't have more than a certain number of apartments it usually isn't rent stabilized."

"So?"

"So the landlord can just raise the rent as high as he wants with no law to stop him. New York landlords are like the feudal lords and the plantation owners of yesterday."

Watching her as she settles into one of his treasures of found furniture and begins sorting through her pieces, he says, "What is that you've got on, that top? Is it African?"

"No, it's a huipil." She corrects him.

"Huh? Huipool?"

"No! Huipil. H-u-i-p-i-l."

"Oh, South American," he says, nodding.

"So you know where these fabrics are from?" She's surprised.

"Tania, I'm a New York City activist. I know about CISPES."

"Cispes?"

"The Committee in Solidarity with the People of El Salvador."

"Oh yeah, they buy goods from collectives in Latin America. I bought a few of these tops, the huipils, through them."

"Yeah. They do a lot more than that, though. They started up a little while ago to support Central American fighters against U.S. imperialism. I go to some of their events and help them by volunteering to do the sound and anything technical they need. There are other groups, too, standing up for the rights of people down there and protesting against what the U.S. is doing, like the School of the Americas."

"What's that?"

It's a horrible place the U.S. Army runs in Georgia that trains the officers in the armies of the dictators down there in so-called "counter-insurgency" techniques, including how to torture people."

Tania is shocked.

Purple goes on. "Yes, this so called free-speech U.S. government does that." He leans back. "All kinds of activists outside and inside New York protest that shit, it's so horrible. What about you, Tania?"

"Well, like I said, I support CISPES."

Purple nods. "It helps for people to wear the beautiful pieces they sell, spending money for them instead of for the stuff you get in make-money-off-sweatshop-labor department stores. He sits down in a chair across from hers, "Anyway," he says. "I want to hear you read your poetry."

"Okay," she says. "This one's called 'Sisters or Fakers,' aka 'Changing Class Identity.'" Then, moving around the room, almost singing, she recites:

"My class of workers—unemployed,
My class of students taking up classes,
While corporate colleges

Shove student loans up their asses.

"My new class of people,
in line at housing tenant court.
Instead of sitting at a table/bench,
pretending to "hold forth,"
My new class . . .

"My new class
done stuffed up the old one's silk-covered jacket
A racket!
A din!
We're coming back to win!"

She sits reads several more pieces. Then she says, "Listen, how about hearing what someone else I admire wrote." She then reads Agua's line: "'Stick your soul in my hole . . .'"

He laughs. "That's good."

Usually responsive to his moods, this time she doesn't join in. She looks him in the eye. "Purple, me and Agua hope there are some men who really are soulful. Are there?"

He doesn't engage or even ask her what she means. Instead he says simply, "I could help produce your poetry for the public. I do that, you know."

"You do?" You really want to come through for me?" She looks into his eyes, shining behind his glasses.

"Sure. Come by again one day next week and we'll tape some pieces to put out there."

"Okay."

She laughs and he smiles as they agree.

A week later, she calls up to Purple's window from the street.

"Be right down," he shouts, sticking his head out. He hurries down the stairs and leads her up.

She takes her shoes off as usual and parks them by the door. "I try to keep the street vibrations outside, the way they teach us in yoga." She smiles.

He smiles back. "You got some kinda outfit on today, girl!" he says.

"Huh?"

"W-e-l-l . . ." He stretches out the word to make it sound funny. Suddenly he asks,"Do you want to see my collage of Malcolm X?"

"Yeah. Where is it?" Tania's eyes search the walls of his front room for it.

Standing up and leading the way toward his bedroom, he says, "Its hanging on my wall in here." With her following, he adds, "Hey, it comes to me that

Malcolm once said something like, We Black people say we didn't leave anything in Africa, but we left our minds in Africa. He talked about reclaiming our minds."

She agrees. As she steps into the room, listening to him talk, she feels the strong sunshine on her arms, coming through the big bedroom window. He never approaches her body, but she feels his soul approaches hers. He notices she doesn't stand near, much less sit on, his bed and decides not to touch her, even as they connect mentally.

They start fooling around with words, challenging each other about Malcolm, because they don't dare challenge each other about what may be going on between them.

"Even though those *Negro* cowards shot Malcolm X, I'm still against the death penalty," he says, looking at Brother Malcolm in the collage, murdered by U.S.-government-paid lackeys."

"But Purple, you mean you don't want the death penalty even for the bastards from the U.S.C.I.A. who infiltrate Cuba and destabilize the Dominican Republic?" Tania retorts, at once laughing and serious.

"Yes. I'm against it here and everywhere." He crosses his arms as he leans against the wall beside the collage. To her he suddenly seems almost rigid.

She tries to think of a way to change the subject to the taping, which, after all, is why she came today. "Hey Purple," she says, leaning against the opposite wall, not far from his bed, and crossing her fine legs over each other.

"Yeah?" His eyes are on her outfit, orange drawstring shorts and a red huipil.

"What?" she asks.

"Tania, yeah ah damn." He is tongue-tied.

"What?" she asks again, looking up at him from the drawstring she's retying.

A car alarm goes off, banging their ears for the minutes.

"God! Why the idiots don't fix those damn things. . ." He goes to the window and almost sticks his head out to see. "Which mutha' is it?" he wonders, then leans back in.

"Okay, so what were you about to say?" she asks, smiling up at him. "Tell me about the way I look, from your point of view." She likes to joke around with him, but joking aside, even if what Purple says sometimes sounds like it could be a put down, it also shows he's really paying attention, closely observing her—not like so many of the fools out here she has even gone to bed with "almost," but who didn't know what color socks she had on.

"Your hair is so cute. And bushy." He makes a big circle with his hands in the air, demonstrating bushiness.

"Yeah. And?"

"And the orange color of those shorts . . ."

"Um hum . . ." She presses her finger down along the top of a seam. Maybe he wants into these shorts.

"Yeah, they're great, and um, but . . ." He stops. "Do they go with that red top? He is smiling, a big grin, and his glasses shine. Then, suddenly, they are laughing. Both their bellies jump up like jellybeans. His fat one, bigger than hers, jumps higher.

"Okay. Go on." Relaxing again, she slouches back against the wall.

"Tania, you have on a red top, orange shorts, then those yellow socks and your sneakers are pink. WOW! Mama, WOW!"

"I do?"

"Don't you know what you put on today . . . or was it yesterday?" He is grinning broadly now.

"Okay, Purple, watch it." She kind of jokes back, figuring he meant to imply she'd just grabbed up the same clothes she'd worn the day before, not that she was out sleeping at some guy's house.

"Yes, I know what I put on," she says. "I'm trying, to dress with the season and the day of the week. In this naturopath's book about alternative healing I read, they talk about aligning with the astrological planetary colors of the week."

He nods. Her spiritual side attracts him.

With a smug air of confidence, she adds, "Monday is, let me see, oh yeah, white, Tuesday . . . something else, Wednesday another color, and so on . . . Saturday is gray. I always put on flashy colors with the gray to round things out."

"Oh wow! I've gotten myself with a wild one." Purple exclaims, doubling over with a good feeling. "I love that you're free!"

"Do you mean free thinking?" She asks, throwing her hands up.

"You can say that again! And again!" He smacks his thighs.

"Okay, Purple, be ready for my comeback. . ." She is laughing too.

"What? When is it coming?" Purple teases to get close. She's not put off by it because his tone is gentle.

"Oh, whenever." She reaches out as if to touch his arm and he dodges to the left. She heads toward the bedroom door.

Walking past the collage she checks out Malcolm X's eyes one more time, then returns to the front room and goes to her bag to choose which poem to read first. She and Purple smile into each other's eyes from a distance. He still stands in the doorway to the bedroom.

After she has rifled through her papers and he has turned on his machine, they sit in chairs near each other. He fiddles with the dials to find the right pitch for her, then, handing her the mike, he asks her to recite the first line.

"*They say the personal ain't political, but to keep it real. . .*" she begins.

"Okay, that's good, hold up." He adjusts the mike again.

For the next hour they go through her pieces about the world of Black women in America as she sees it, one piece about South Africans demanding their land back, and end with a piece about hair and how crazy it still is that some professionals can't wear cornrows on the job if they are in the public eye.

After lots of stops and starts and silence from him as he concentrates on making a clean copy, he announces, his eyes bright, "Tania, I think we got it!"

"Thanks so much Purple. I know we'll be able to use this at our next event."

"Who?"

"Me and my friend, you know that Latina sister I told you about, Agua."

He nods and lowers himself again into the soft chair he sits in when he taping. Working the machine, he puts on low jazz with a steady bass pumping a sexual beat.

"I really like how you connect the way we activists act as activists with the way we act with each other and how that's as political as the cause we support."

"Thanks." Tania smiles and begins to collect her poems and her shoes.

"Hey, why don't you stay over?" Purple suddenly reveals a desire besides listening to her poetry.

"Oh. Wow." His proposition unsettles Tania, and she says nothing else as she finishes putting her loose papers together, then ties up her drawstring bag. When she stands she looks at him, still sitting in his chair. The music's beat is insistent.

He smiles.

"I'm shocked, Purple," she says finally. "I thought we were going to be able to be real *friends*. I still hope we can be. You're the first man who . . . anyway, I thank you so much for this taping; I didn't believe you really were willing to do it. Um, I'm going so can you, um walk me to the train?"

Purple looks down. "But in the bedroom you seemed . . ."

"I'm sorry, I didn't mean..."

Shifting his heavy body forward in the chair he rises, not smiling anymore. He bends over to take the tape of her pieces out of his machine and hands it to her. "Okay," he says. He looks up into her face. She still wants to go, hasn't changed her mind. He gets up, opens the door for her, follows her out, and locks it behind them. As they walk to the subway he reaches for her hand.

6 EYES THAT DON'T FLINCH

"I want to tell you about a dream I had." Tania stares at the floorboards in Pam's office. "It was about a Black man flirting with me as if he'd like to have sex with me. I'm lying in a hospital bed in the dream. I call out 'Purple,' but he doesn't answer me. And when I see his face, it's not Purple, the man I thought it was. Is this a dream of rejection?"

"It has many facets to it. Do you ever think you were trained to flirt with men like they flirt with you?"

"Trained?"

"Pam doesn't answer directly, but guides Tania to tell her about Purple, whom she hasn't mentioned before, and then the specifics of the taping session the previous week. "So how did it go? Did you like his apartment?"

"Oh, yeah. He even has a Malcolm X collage in his bedroom."

"Did you flirt with him?

"Oh God, maybe I did. . . . Let's see. I remember I was leaning against the bedroom wall and fiddling with the drawstring on my shorts. . . But I kept my legs crossed and didn't sit on his bed.

"Did you feel uncomfortable?"

"Yes. I felt like he got me into his bedroom 'cause that's where he said the Malcolm X collage was, after I had already committed to wanting to see it. I *should* have said, well if the collage is in your bedroom I don't want to see it. I feel ashamed . . ."

"Don't 'should' on yourself, dear Tania. 'Should' is when you manipulate yourself into feeling bad. It's okay to look into the past and see where you were conditioned to follow men's suggestions whether you wanted to or not."

"Oh." Tania looks down at her lap and feels a heat rise in her back, straight up her neck. To stop herself from saying any more she covers her mouth. From behind her hand she mumbles, "Well that's it Pam, I just wanted to share the dream before I forgot it."

"It shows how your unconscious is ahead of your conscious self." Pam wonders how far to go and chooses to suggest something, nodding encouragingly as she speaks. "Maybe something from girlhood could arise? I think you can continue uncovering."

"Okay." Tania's tone is dubious, but she makes another face-to-face appointment some weeks into the future and jots it down in her new datebook, with Marx's bearded face on the cover. She is no longer a weekly client, but calls for appointments when she's in pain. Still, she likes to have one appointment, way in the future, to look forward to. Keeping the tie with Pam grounds Tania. While growing up she'd longed for that kind of rooting. As Pam clears away the teacups, Tania puts the fee of fifteen dollars on the table.

When she gets home she finds a Transit Authority letter in her mailbox announcing her high number in the list. She'll actually be called for the job. The notice has come just in time, given the increasing chaos at the day care center.

Thanks to the union, from her first day of bus operator training, and for the first time in her life, Tania really pulls in some bucks. But unlike most of her female friends, she has to face an unfriendly, all-male workforce. She had thought the Black guys would welcome her, but they do not. Bus-driving and other good Transit Authority jobs didn't opened up for Blacks and Latinos until the 1940s, after Adam Clayton Powell, Jr. led a bus boycott in Harlem, and even in the mid sixties, there were fewer than 1000 in a work force of 35,000. As the men see it, for every woman hired, one less Black man will have one of the best jobs for people without a college degree in the city. They don't unite with the women the same way the white guys didn't unite with them. So every day during the week she spends on the training bus with her fellow trainees, standing in the back, she overhears the men putting her down.

On the last day, a comment from one of them does reveal that they all probably have fears and maybe some like hers. "Yeah yeah, it's been good here the last five days." He laughs. "Five days of learning to drive this huge thing without passengers. But check it out, new drivers get assigned according to the crazy schedules set by the fill-in board. By next Thursday, when you start for real, you got to be ready to answer all the passengers' questions while you try to stay awake 'cause you been called to drive at 5:00 A.M. The next day the boss may tell you come to start at 5 in the damn afternoon. How are you supposed to get your eight hours with a work week like that?"

And so it goes. The very next Thursday morning at 5:00 o'clock, she sits in the driver's seat and looks in the mirror at her uniformed self. Her hands are trembling. Her eyes stare back at her. Who is going to drive this thing? The mentor driver shouts "Let's get down the road." She releases the air pressure brake. The bus moves. The mentor driver rests, watching her work as she drives his route. The first male passengers of the day shoot her hostile glares as they board. Fortunately at this hour they're mostly on the way to work and don't ask questions. But they're a grim bunch, bearing no resemblance to the little boys at the day care center—little boys just like the ones they must have been. Back at the bus depot, when she's on her swing break, she passes a fat-faced Black bus driver with a goatee who snarls, "I hope you fall outta your shoes, bitch."

Bastard, she thinks to herself. She walks away from the man and heads outside to stand with the mentor, who doesn't talk to her, much less pal around with her the way he would with a man. They wait to make a relief and drive back down the street. The lack of any camaraderie between her, a working woman, and her mentor, a working man keeps the soul-destroying vibe going. She's scared but determined to face it.

The next day the routine is the same, though the mentor and the schedule are different. After five days of this she's on her own, wheeling the bus up and down the avenues of Manhattan on her own according to the fill-in schedule, which means her hours of work can change day-to-day and she's driving exhausted a lot of the time. But on the day when she picks up her weekly pay check, her mood lifts. The amount, even with deductions, is more than she has ever earned before in a whole month. With this job, if she sticks it out, one day she'll actually be able to take care of herself completely, maybe even buy a car that isn't a hand-me-down from Older Sister. She'll be able to take vacations on her own and not simply go visit her parents at their summer place. Never again, she hopes, will she have to ask for back-up funds from Daddy. Loneliness hugs her shoulders, though. The only other woman in the depot's crew of almost 500 men works a different shift, so Tania never catches even a glimpse unless the woman works overtime so their schedules overlap.

North and south on the avenues of Manhattan, with (except in Harlem) their lines of shops and double-parked delivery trucks. East and west on the streets. The wind carries the car horns, and the smells of the city's overflowing garbage cans and gutters. The lies of the dispatchers in their white cars, who always blame the drivers for being late, however gridlocked the traffic, rattle nerves. Every bolt in every damned bus in the system seems to fall on the passengers' heads and the seats all face the center aisle so people stumble over the bags and legs of those who are seated as they try to push their way through the standees to the back. Whenever she takes over from the previous driver, she has to adjust the mirrors and the one on the right isn't opening out because the guys don't ever seem to open them out and use them, having been conditioned to doing without them by years of not having right-side mirrors that worked due to management's neglect. "You don't need the right-side mirror, just DRIVE," the boss yells, forcing her to pull out unprepared.

"Where in the hell do they get the idea that people's lives and well-being aren't important?" Tania mumbles to herself. She mumbles this a lot, though sometimes the passengers make her as mad as the bosses, especially the stinking crowds on Wall Street, where the clerks and admin staff identify more with the bosses than the other people on the bus, especially the driver. Almost once a week there is one who demands her badge number so he or she can register a complaint about the bus being late or some other damn thing that's not her fault.

North and south, north and south, east and west and back again. The routine often makes her want to scream. The twilight feels best. The soft sunlight gazes over the twenty-story buildings, and the moon is only felt, not seen. She calls Agua from home on Tuesdays and Wednesdays, her regular days off.

"Did you see the moon Tania?" Agua often asks. But they hardly ever dance together in the light of the moon anymore, since Agua is asleep while Tania drives weekend nights, and is preparing school lunches for Heru and going over his homework when Tania's nights are free.

Summer is the worst. Where in this country except New York, can the bosses and management get away with keeping old un-air conditioned busses on the road, torturing both passengers and drivers—especially drivers, who don't have the option of hopping off? The sweat on the driver's seat makes a stink like onions. Between trips, at the depot at the end of the line in Harlem, Tania runs up the stairs to the restroom and splashes her entire body with water, soaking her polyester uniform, then, slides dripping back into her seat. "Why," she moans to herself, "can't we wear shorts? The post office does!"

At the bus depot on her swing break all the men, Black and white, stand by the 50/50 club's spread of bagels, muffins, coffee cups and sugar containers talking like guys do, with every other word a curse word. The club, supported through the drivers' purchase of raffle tickets, has a supply of coffee and tea and soft drinks and sometimes eggs. The cooks make fast food for workers to buy in the few minutes they have before they have to run off to make a relief of another bus operator.

The cook asks, "Do you want a coffee?"

Tania takes his question as a peace offering and smiles. "You know what, um I don't drink coffee." He turns away.

The cook scrambles eggs on toast even though it's afternoon. Because his Latino buddies are nearby, he's brewed up a pot of Bustelo coffee, which they like, not the Maxwell House she remembers from the song in the TV ad when she was growing up: "Maxwell House is a heavenly coffee. . ." As happens at least once a week on her way to the bathroom, she again passes the Black driver with the goatee and chubby face. As usual he snarls at her. This time it's, "I hope your heels fall off your shoes."

After several weeks of all this, she uses the last few minutes of the short break to make the first of what will be several emergency calls to Pam from one of the pay phones tucked away along an outside wall far from the loud, rough voices and heavily built bodies of many of the male operators. To avoid the evening dispatcher, who constantly ogles her, she takes the stairs at the rear of the depot and walks all the way around the block and back inside. Her tense fingers make retrieving the dime from the coin pocket sewed into the front of her uniform pants a chore.

"Pam, I just can't keep driving this damn bus. The scene's too heavy with all these sexist coworkers around, yelling comments about my shoes, my uniform. I want just one good, caring co-worker. But even on my dinner break, I get treated like an object by them, and a pretty messed up one at that. These men aren't my father, but I give them power over me."

"What happened?" Pam has taken the call while preparing soup.

"The men just keep calling me names and they put up a sign."

"A sign? What kind of sign? Where was it?"

"At the depot. When you finish for the night you drive the bus into the garage and a couple of nights ago they tore down a poster board ad, scribbled 'Lesbo' on it, and hung it on a pole at the back of the depot. I wanted to scream 'Who did that!' but of course I didn't 'cause they might jump me."

"Tania, when you started you were so scared you didn't think you could learn to drive the bus. But you faced your fear and you do drive, just like you're going to face this fear and learn to stand up to these guys. You know, this job is giving you clarity about most of the men in this system, not just these guys in the depot. Why don't you write it all out, how they attack others because they're too afraid to face the bosses who attack them? Remember, you're a poet, sweetheart. Write it down and share it and wake others up."

Tania doesn't respond. She stares at the ledge outside the depot window, perturbed as much by Pam's challenge to go deeper as by the high-pressure, exploitive nature of the transportation industry. The streaks of dirt on the window make it hard to see anything. A stray cat jumps onto the ledge. She laughs. "I wish I could jump like the cat that just landed on the window sill, Pam." She looks down at her unpolished nails, twirls the silver bangle on her left wrist. "I want to come see you," she says, "but I gotta go make my relief bus now."

"Any time. Call when you're ready."

On Tania's evenings off mid-week she tries to arrange time with her women friends, hoping they will listen, but they're mostly too busy with chores, since they have to work next morning. And she rarely goes to group meetings anymore because they don't usually meet when she's off. She misses them. Driving the bus every day she sees the women going to work in back-office jobs on Wall Street wearing gold earrings with matching bracelets. She's forced to dress differently, but they're all wearing a kind of uniform, really. She sees that these women workers are, like her, essential to keeping the structure going, but she has nobody to talk with about it all for hours at a stretch the way she used to.

Often after work some tie-up that no bosses ever explains keeps the busses from reaching the depot as they line up, finished for the night. The company doesn't ever let the guys who shift the busses around the depot come out to the street and relieve the drained and exhausted operators waiting there, so they often don't clear out until 1 a.m. Whenever this happens, to save on travel time Tania accepts Agua's standing invite to sleep over at her apartment, which is just over the bridge from the north-Manhattan depot.

Inevitably she wakes up the next morning rubbing her sore eyes. She yawns and, from her make-shift bed of pillows on the living room floor, yells to Agua, who is in the kitchen: "Hey, Agua. I gotta leave now for work."

"Damn! I know. I'm fixing food. We both gotta eat before we head out." Agua cracks eggs into a bowl, then asks, "How do you feel?" She and Tania have both learned from Pam that a woman, when first breaking into a male-ruled industry, will grow stronger if she reveals her feelings. No more good-girl repression. She has learned it from experience, too. Not long after Tania started driving a bus, she had left the day care center and taken a higher-paying job with a company that maintains cooling and heating systems in large buildings, another field where most of the workers are men. Though adjusting hasn't been as tough for her as for Tania—her hours and her work-week are regular, for one thing, and she always works as part of a team—she has also faced resentment from some of her co-workers.

Although it's the beginning of their work day, Tania snarls "Messed up! Women have a right to a job that makes more than 59 cents to every man's dollar. I have a right to this good-paying job. But the bosses and everybody else wished I'd quit from the moment I started training on those 5000 series busses without power steering. I'm okay with the driving now—wrestling around busses without power steering is great for the back muscles. But there's no training for how to deal with male supremacy junk."

"Okay, girl. You know we be with you on your shift. I'm sure those men who hate it that we non-traditional women have taken to being electricians and bus drivers will move outta the way some day. They'll stop calling you a bitch just because the force of the ancestors is in the air around you!" Agua often laughs to urge Tania on, and she comes to her friend now, giggling and twirling around. "You know how to work *magic* with that brutal job, girl." Her hair, all wild, stands out like bristles on a new brush coming off the factory line. Heading back to the kitchen, she calls toward the living room, "Tell me what you're going to tape for the Non-Traditional Employment for Women fundraiser."

"Whaddya talking about?"

Agua stops at the kitchen door and turns around. "You know, the group that helps us women deal with breaking into these male-controlled industries, the one where we did the role playing. They want responses to the questionnaire they sent out. I know you gotta work on Saturday night, but you said you'd write something for me to read, right?"

"Yeah, I remember. I brought it with me to give you. You wanna hear it?"

"Yes! It'll help me do it to hear you read it."

"Okay, it's . . ." Tania is rummaging around in her backpack. She is still half asleep. "Sorry, it's right here under my points."

"Your what?"

"My time points, the list of where my bus is supposed to be and when it's supposed to be there, to keep me on schedule."

While Tania digs out the piece and finishes getting her things together, Agua puts the eggs in the pan and turns the heat on low. Then she returns to stand near the kitchen door. "Okay," she says. "I'm listening."

Tania puts her backpack on the sofa with her badge and other work stuff and says in a tired, throaty voice, "Okay, here goes.

"On New Year's Eve I go to the races with rage. The old timers have pulled off the road early, if they had to work at all. I'm a newcomer, green and not too long in the seat, so I gots to pull these loads for all the busses that are now off the road. Maybe I gotta get out of this job.

"It's almost midnight and some yoyo decides his white ass is better than all the passengers stuffed in my old 5000 bus. The well dressed phony (probably cocaine addicted) moves in front of my bus. Better move slow, but get the hell outta here, before he dies in front of my wheels, or jumps under the back tires, like some nut on Ward's Island tried to do when I was picking folks up by the mental hospital there.

"Anyway, this guy steps off the sidewalk in front of my bus's fender and shouts, "Run me over! Hey, bus driver, run me over!"

"Sweat positions itself between my thighs as I wanna actually kill him, but my mental chatter tells me NO, NO.

"The public is stacked around my ears, and they keep talking and chatting, 'cause to them it's a holiday, party night. To me it's One More God Damn Night of Misery with These Crazy Assholes Who Louse Things Up! I sit still, pull up the hand brake and gaze into the rear view mirror.

"Some jerk yells from the back of the bus, "Hey, what's up, start this bus moving, bus driver!"

"Shit, he don't know what this other dummy is doing in the front. So I honk once or twice and then give up.

"Damn it, I won't make it uptown to my 3-minute rest at the end of the line before 12 a.m. I'll be right here with these suckers bringing the New Year in.

"P.S. I grew up in a family that wanted me to go to a private college and tell lies, like they do at their white-collar jobs. Many white collar workers struggle with inferiority complexes as they push papers that sometimes don't mean anything, or try to look busy. I wonder as I drive back and forth, do my mother and father actually FEEL less than their working-class-identified child? Is that why they ignore me when I talk about a real job that's essential? Do they want me to pretend I don't work in a different-class job than they wanted? They talk

about change and caring for workers, but they don't really mean to align themselves with that class."

"That's great!" Agua grins. "But you didn't get outta the job, you went back to work! So you're clear you can keep doing it, especially now you're done with probation!" She smells the eggs burning and races back to the stove, calling out, "Remember I'm with you!" She licks the spoon she used to stir the breakfast. "My god, I love how you put that writing together. It'll live way past you and that friggin' work you gotta slave at, girl."

In the middle of the week on payday at the bus garage, a white man with a walrus moustache hanging over his lip sits in the payroll office, which is on the top floor.

"Hey, lady, move your butt. You're in back of those guys," he barks. To emphasize the point, he repeats, "I *said* they're before you." He sits behind an opening in the wall of the locked office. No driver can ever think about entering that office, even when the Transit Authority messes up their paychecks. The door looks like it never opens. Certainly it doesn't when there are drivers around.

Tania moves to the end of the line and mumbles to a guy who comes in behind her, "Is this big check worth it? I smelled the ratson the way up here."

He grins and his Adam's apple bobs in the white skin covering his skinny throat. He has cancer but has to keep driving, fumes and all. He wants his daughter to finish college and have a better life. "Yeah, and what about and the stupid line dispatchers yelling at you to go on down to the end of the line "*They* don't have to turn your bus around. They force overtime on you 'cause you're already an hour late and won't make it off the depot pull-in line before it wraps around the corner, with all the busses pulling in for the night."

"Yeah, yeah. And what about the no heat in the busses in winter and the crowds of people who never go home," Tania exclaims. "At all hours they bang on your door when you already out of the stop or fighting crazy traffic."

"Yeah, it's not just the lousy MTA. It's the lousy city. Too many people." A man at the back of the ever-lengthening line who overheard her and the white guy talking chimes in. "You think New York's bad. I remember the last run I had when I was stuck in traffic at rush hour, this passenger told me that the only time New York didn't feel crowded to him was after he got back from China. In the big cities over there millions of Chinese are pushing, pressing and surrounding you every minute of every day."

"Wow!" Tania laughs, at ease for a moment. "That's unreal. Worse than here."

During the middle of the next short session with her busy counselor, who has squeezed her in, Tania listens with eyes wide open. It is her first appointment since she got off probation, and now that her job is secure, Pam is encouraging her to confront honestly her relationship with her family, not to change them, but to strengthen herself. She hasn't seen them since she started driving. While she was sweating out her probation year she couldn't take an extra day to visit them. Her mother calls periodically, her father never. The fact that they made no effort to visit her, making it quite clear that they disapprove of their working-class-identified daughter, has deepened her inner conflicts. Somewhere inside she still wants to be their "good" daughter, and make them proud.

Well aware of all this, and of the stress that was the inevitable result of her constantly shifting work schedule while she was on probation, Pam is just glad there have been no accidents with the bus. But though the situation at work has improved, Tania's continuing anxiety is all too evident in her inability to sleep, and in the fact that when she does, she is awakened repeatedly by the recurrence of the dream she had about the Black man coming on to her as she lies helpless in a hospital bed. Now Pam puts it to her that, as a bus-woman who has people's lives in her hands as she carries them around the city; as a woman who earns her own keep; as a woman who works side by side with men without just hoping they'll be her boyfriend and who has learned how really fragile they are inside, how vulnerable, how their inferiority shit shows through their sexism—as this grown-up woman, she has the inner strength to confront her parents about the hypocrisy of them being people on the political left who look down on the workers whose cause they say they support. "And maybe," she says at last, "you have the inner strength to face the past." She pauses, then adds, "I wonder, Tania, if you're ready now to confront Daddy, the man who covers up his vulnerability so well he doesn't seem to be vulnerable at all."

Pam is at once giving her confirmation and challenging her, and partly because Tania isn't used to hearing long speeches from her, she's unsure how to respond. She's sitting on the couch next to the end-table, where her cassette recorder sits beside a neat stack of books—*Das Kapital* by Karl Marx and the collection of speeches titled *Malcolm X Speaks*. She runs her finger over the photo of Malcolm on the cover. Such a good-looking man . . .

Noticing Tania's hands, Pam says, "You know, Malcolm, toward the end, advanced to suggesting that women in the movement be in leadership roles, unlike other Black men of your younger years."

Finally Tania finds her voice. "I love you, Pam. You're the best therapist . . . right on target. Brothers, I mean the guys, feel less than . . . not more than. I get it. Okay, I can go back on the line today and deal with all of them and their whole lying top-down boss mentality, even when they're trying to pinch my cheeks."

Pam nods. She knows that, though Tania hasn't followed up on her last question, she has taken it in. And though she may not yet be ready to confront her parents, simply by going back on the line she's confronting the ideas and values they represent.

Still, Tania continues to have the same dream. On a wrinkled page of her journal, she writes.

> *6 am . . . the traffic hasn't really started up yet, so it still seems like nite. But my stomach is nauseous. My neck aches. I try to rub the soreness away.*

Her handwriting looks craggy. Putting down the journal she crawls to the medicine chest for some Chinese healing oil. The aroma of the Tiger balm helps silence her screaming muscles. She reaches for her journal again.

> *Where does this much fear come from?*

Life beats hard on Tania as week by week, month by month, she becomes a bus driver, defined, as most people are in this system, by what she "does." On the entrance test she'd passed with high marks, but now she faces the test of living a working-class manual labor reality. Though with the end of the probationary period her schedule is regular, her low seniority puts her at first on the least desirable shift, working nights and on weekends. And if, thanks to the union contract, she has some job security, she experiences daily the contempt of passengers whose white-collar, office jobs give them higher status in the view of the system and in their own. To an extent she is armored against their written complaints and their insults by the fact that many of them—the "executive assistants" who ride the bus, anyway—actually earn less than she does. She is not, however, a spendthrift, largely because of Pam, who studies the man's economic system, as well as counseling folks, and keeps urging her to force herself to save by putting a down-payment on a place that can be her base. "If you don't arrange your affairs so as to create some back-up, the man's way of refusing to plan for people's needs will catch up with you when you're older," she says. Tania takes this advice to heart, and some weeks after the end of her probationary period, on her days off, she begins to search for a place that will be truly hers. Pam also tells her she should buy a better car instead of taking high-cost cabs whenever Older Sister's clunker, which she's still driving, breaks down, but for some reason, she doesn't want to do this.

Slowly, as she shows up day after day to drive safely during the snows of winter, the downpours of spring, and the blistering, toxic heat of summer, Tania is allowed breathing space by at least some of the men. As her schedule now allows, she becomes involved once again in the women's consciousness-raising and writing group that had meant so much to her, though she never gets to stay for the whole time, since they meet on weekends. But her relationship with her family remains loaded, and she is never free from the nightmares. Eventually, however, thanks to Pam's insights, she will make a move to break through the walls and deal with the hard edges of the truth of her childhood.

A phone message from her mother leaves a sour smell. She twirls her hair on her forefinger as her machine plays back the strident voice.

"Hello, Tania, I have to talk with you. Todd is such a slacker. These Black men don't like to work."

Tania thinks, "Just because Older Sister's boyfriend doesn't work in his professional field and, for the time being, is painting houses for a living doesn't mean he's lazy."

She calls back, but almost gags when her mother picks up.

"Hello?" Her mother holds the phone too close, breathing into it.

"This is gonna be a short call 'cause I wanna keep my phone bill down."

"I can just call you back, darling, and pay for the call," her mother says.

"No!" Tania is annoyed. Her mother is acting like she's still a girl who doesn't know how to prioritize and decide for herself. "The truth is, I really don't want to talk with you now except about what you said in your message, 'cause . . ."

Her mother interrupts. "Well, I know your father and I have to have a . . ."

Throwing her free hand up in the air in frustration, Tania continues as if her mother hadn't spoken, determined to finish her thought. ". . . it shows how you don't value those of us who grow the food, get it from the farms to the cities, drive the shoppers to the supermarket to buy it—yes, *and* paint the houses you live in—you don't value us one bit. But we're the ones who do the kinds of jobs you can't live without. So I really don't want to talk to you now except about the message you left." She's scared to add, "you don't really care about me, never even ask how I'm feeling, with my backaches and eyes burning from exhaustion."

Her mother's voice drips condescension. "Okay, darling. What about it?"

"Well, Todd, you know, Older Sister's, I mean your oldest daughter's, boyfriend *is* working. Just because he's painting houses doesn't mean he's a slacker. And a Black man I know, a tech guy named Purple . . . He works three part-time jobs. That's discipline! You can't work like that and be a damn slacker."

Avoiding this undeniable truth, her mom says, "I hate how you use that nickname for your sister. And Purple, what a name!"

"He got it from the poor kids in his neighborhood growing up 'cause he wore purple suede shoes and that meant he had cash to buy more than sneakers. Why don't you ever like the people I like? It's not the name. What's wrong is, he's not from the almost rich Black folks you like, right?"

Again, her mother changes the subject. "Your father and I want you to come visit . . ." She pauses, then adds, "We think you should stop doing the bus job."

"You're not *listening* to me! We weren't even *talking* about me . . . I want . . ." Suddenly she falters, then sneezes.

"Gesundheit."

"Anyway. . ." Tania's tongue still feels tied when she tries to disagree with her mother about anything, especially about men or work. "You know what, oh forget it . . ." She cuts herself off, but when her mother says nothing more, she regains her courage. "Well, another thing, and this is hard for me. But you know what . . . I feel like it's not just my job you don't like. I feel like you've looked down on me ever since I was a little girl. It's like the racism of this country got inside you and you stayed white and I stayed Black, even though I am your daughter . . ."

"I did better than a lot of those Black mothers out there!" Her mother interrupts.

Tania's throat tightens, but she keeps going. "You don't like it that I see myself as Black without also being bourgie like Older Sister is."

"Ah, you're incorrigible!" Mother yells.

"Incorrigible? Well, I'm staying that way," Tania retorts. When her mother says nothing, for the moment Tania feels grown up. "Well," she says, "my phone bill is high, so I'm hanging up."

Her mother attempts to control with a long silence. When Tania doesn't rush to fill the emptiness, however, she backs off. "Okay, darling . . . Bye."

Tania slams down the phone. She reaches for her journal to scribble down whatever, after dealing with her mom.

Hi Journal . . .

A couple of days later, the warmth of Pam's office again welcomes Tania, who starts crying almost from the start.

"Pam, I realize my mother is still a mountain for me. I can't stop her voice from invading my brain. My inner judging mother 'tape recorder' is always on."

"What do you mean?" Pam sits still in her chair, watching her client fidget.

"Well, in my consciousness-raising women's group . . . we explore our mothers' generation and how most feared life without a man. My mother and my friends' mothers all worked outside their homes, but also had to clean, cook, help with homework and were not respected as the family leader. 'Wait for Daddy' was what my mom told us girls. We had to wait for him to sit down just to start eating in my house. One sister who comes to the group, you know, Smoke, says it was like a little kingdom, with a special chair in the living room only the father could sit in. My dad had a chair like that."

Pam validates Tania: "Damn, you sure get the connection between dad and king. And the idea only the big man has the privilege of sitting in that head chair didn't disappear with the fifties." Mentally, she notes Tania is stepping closer to confronting her dad. She crosses her legs, sitting forward now.

Tania wrings her hands. "It wouldn't be so bad if there was genuine respect instead of just the fear the man was gonna fool around with another woman and make another family that kept those women bowing to 'their' men."

Near the end of the session, Pam suggests that Tania, when she "feels strong and solid," send some of her writings about this to her family.

When they next meet, however, Tania is on a different track. It's early morning, and she will go to her midday shift when she leaves.

Crossing her legs in a yoga position, though still sitting on the couch, she plunges in. "My parents never explained various essentials like, bosses are usually liars who keep you hopping . . . you have to have one face at the job, and keep it stony. They didn't warn me some coworkers might try to wriggle into my spot. They used white folks' English. They really liked the hoity-toity crowd." As an afterthought she adds, "They did say unions are necessary, yes that was good."

"Where is this going, Tania?"

Tania stares blankly.

"I was hoping you were beginning to think of how the job and all this connects to Daddy. Did you send any of your writings to them? "

"I will, but . . . I still feel so much pressure to be what my parents want—work in an office or for some shyster politician."

Pam returns indirectly to the writing. "You have the writing group to support you, and we're working on how you can keep defining who you are, okay?"

"Okay," Tania says.Then her eyes water. "It's damn hard how these men treat me, like I don't belong. They say, 'This is a man's job. You don't need to be here.'"

Pam nods encouragingly. She wants Tania to reveal more of her hurt and anger. Maybe she will see the roots of the abuse and from there move to uncover her first abuser.

A bird chirps outside. After another long silence, Tania says, "Pam, the vibe here is comforting . . . kinda reminds me of a big afghan with green crocheted squares that grandma made me once, all tied together."

"I'm glad, Tania." The electric tea kettle Pam keeps on a side table is boiling. "Choose your teabag," she says.

Reaching for the chamomile, Tania starts to make the connection about not talking with her dad. "You know, the fact is I'm scared. I've talked about how hard the job is with all these men. And I see the connection to my father. I hate him, but I need his approval at the same time, just like I need the men's approval at the job. Why can't he just love me? Why can't both my parents just love me?"

"Now we're moving to it. Tania . . ."

"Yeah, Pam, I loved my daddy and he doesn't even call me. It's like I just dropped out of the life in that family and the only one who tries to keep in contact is her."

"Your mother?"

"Yeah. But I hate when she calls. And I feel she does, too. Hate it, I mean."

She stops for a minute, but Pam sits still, waiting, and she goes on. "Pam, you know it's so shocking to me . . . "I feel . . ." Her heart starts to ache and she cradles herself by wrapping herself in her arms. "You know what? My parents didn't ever know who I was. I was dearest little Buttercup to my grandma, but to those parents I was only one of the daughters for them to brag about to their friends when I passed a swimming test or . . . I could never just sit down and say I wanna tell you something, and have them listen."

Again Pam suggests she send them something she has written.

"What for, Pam?" They're not going to change and start to like me. Not ever. It's all effing phony words . . . She always says, 'I love you, darling' . . . Bullshit."

"It's not to change them, Tania. You're becoming the self you want to be, not a willing victim, a sucker, like they taught you to be. You're letting yourself think for yourself and face the fear of letting go of your idealistic notion that they were truthful. You are seeing through the myth that under this American capitalist system you can have a perfect family. The nuclear family's too small to help with all the needs of children. We need a more collective support net." Smiling with both her lips and eyes, she adds, "Whenever you're ready, Tania . . ."

Pam—-so gentle, thank God. Tania resists the urge to jump up and hug her counselor. Her safe nest was never with her parents, it is here on this blue couch in front of the wooden coffee table. Still, she says, "But, Pam, they must have loved me somewhere inside there. How could they just have me, and then 'cause I don't go to the schools they wanted, or live in the type of condos they wanted, or marry the light bright guy or at least a guy with a college degree, they start to look at me strange."

"I don't know how far back and deep the patterns go in your family, but you're breaking the mold. You're not willing to repeat your parent's model. You're saying it's up to you how to live your adult life, that you have a right to be your own person and not to have to defend yourself against their need to control. That's shaking them up."

"The nuke-LIAR family is the little American dream isn't it?" Tania is almost standing. Her hips sit on the very edge of the couch.

Pam's face brightens. "Now you understand, Tania. Unless the people in the family tell the truth, yes it is a dream, just like most myths about our 'democratic' country." Her fingers make the sign of quotation marks in the air. "And, Tania, you can face that dream like you did when you quit Buster. You can grow up and create a better reality." Pam's eyes twinkle with hope.

Days later, after listening to the tapes of this session, Tania follows through on Pam's suggestion that she send her parents some of her writings—or at least makes a start. She writes a long letter to her father, then sets it aside, and instead puts into an envelope addressed to him a poem she has written expressing her feelings about his domination. She doesn't send it, however. Instead, it is still lying on the table by the door "to go out" when the ringing of the phone awakens her, the sound signaling what will turn out to be the prelude to an historic moment. Rubbing her eyes, she fumbles the handset out of the cradle, then lies back down. It feels like the crack of dawn to her, the night worker.

Her mother jumps right into a subject dear to her heart: her daughter's relationships with men, and in particular with Buster, whom Tania had left long ago, but whom her mother thinks she could have married. She doesn't say out loud that "sex outside marriage is bad," but that's the implication as she never stops trying to steer her daughter's behavior as if she were still a teenager. "Don't you want to marry someone and have a family?"

"I suppose so," Tania says. "But Mom, what I'm trying to say is, I couldn't even get, you know, 'cuddle-time' with my 'ex-honey,' 'cause he was always working, hustling to get money . . . so how could I even think of marrying . . ."

"So you do think about it . . ."

"No I don't, actually. I can have sex any time with a man, if I am married or not, so why should I?" Tania shocks even herself with this outburst and stops, hoping her mother will be upset enough to jump off the phone. But her mother is not one for backing down.

"How can you say that, Tania?" she says.

"I'm not talking to you about this anymore, Mom." Tania can hardly believe she has just said this out loud.

"But darling, I was only saying that you could have cooked for Buster instead of always bickering with him. You could have kept the relationship going."

"That's ridiculous. You hear me? That man hit me in the face. Do I have to remind you of that?" She sits up.

"That's what I do with your father . . . If you'd just listen to me."

"What for?"

"Because when he falls into one of his moods, then I just go into the kitchen and beat up the pots and pans."

"I don't think that's good enough. I'm not going to talk to you again, ever."

"What?"

"I want space. I'm becoming clear about things right now."

"No, Tania, you can't just cut us off completely."

"I'm telling you I've gotta grow. It's time for me to face my own problems without your advice, which I don't feel is doing me any good. I'm hanging up."

Before she can do so she hears her mother yelling, "I'm going to tell your father to call you."

Pressing the phone hard into its cradle, she looks at the walls, which feel like they are closing in on her, and then through the window to the trees. I gotta walk she thinks. Her heart races. Despite all her conversations with Pam about boundaries, the mother who used to scare her to death with her words when she was a girl still turns her brain upside down. Abruptly she jumps into drawstring pants and a sweatshirt. Putting on an old corduroy jacket, she figures she'll just walk to the park and rushes out of the apartment, keys dangling from her hand. How can her mother think that the solution to being slapped around by a man is to go into the kitchen and cook and bang on the pots?

A week later, on her Tuesday off, she turns on W.B.A.I. for companionship, since everyone she knows is working. A man is accused by the New Jersey police of beating his activist wife. His wife had called the police, saying she had been slapped and punched in a domestic dispute. As the report comes to an end, Tania mutters to herself, "Damn! Just like my father the activist, except my bourgie mom would never call the cops in a million years, so nobody ever knew he was violent except us." Realizing she is talking to herself, she stops, reflecting that no matter how well she understands intellectually that men like him beat up on their women and kids—and in this system, they are "theirs"—because the system beats up on them doesn't make it stop. The fact is, she's still scared of him, even though she moved out of his house years ago. The fact is that she both yearns for him to call and is terrified that he will. What will she say to him?

As if the news report and her thoughts have some magic power, the phone on the wall in the eat-in kitchen rings.

"Hello, sweetheart," her father croons when she answers.

Her body curls up on the little painted-wood chair almost into a pretzel, one leg crossed under her. "Hi," she says, staring at her beat-up sneakers. Despite her mother's threat to have him call, she is as unprepared for it as she would be for snow in July.

"I am planning to come to New York, and thought I would stay with you."

"When?" She responds as if he had asked and not, with his tone, simply advised her that he was coming.

"This weekend."

"Oh" is all she can manage. She can't believe he would deign to visit her.

"Okay, so I'll call you before I leave."

"Umm." She twirls a curl of her hair around her forefinger and thinks of the poem addressed to him on the table by the door. She thinks of the way he used to ask her to come to the bathroom and talk to him as he stripped off his shirt and cleaned up his stubble. She didn't want ever again to be that near his naked brown chest leaning over the bathroom sink.

"Um, you know what? I won't be around this weekend so I don't think we can do it."

"What?"

She can see him in her mind's eye, agitated, switching the phone from one ear to the other.

"Sorry. This weekend isn't going to work out. Um . . . I'm sorry, but I gotta go now, I really do. So bye for now." She hangs up before he can respond.

Leaving her seat, she double checks the towels in her bathroom to make sure they're clean. "Now what made me do that?" She surprises herself by asking this aloud. On her way out the door she picks up the envelope addressed to him and drops it in the corner mailbox.

"My father used to come up in the middle of the night, just to catch me reading," Tania remarks offhandedly during her next session with Pam, who is totally affirming of her decision not to let her father come to visit her.

"Catch you reading in the middle of the night?"

Pam feels something new is coming up. Tania knows this because she lights another cigarette, looking intently at her client.

"Pam, I think he . . . No, what I am trying to say, is . . ." Her belly sighs.

"That was a deep sigh," Pam says. Her glasses catch the light for a second.

"He might have, you know, 'wanted' me. He was supposed to bring me sanitary pads from the store when I was eleven and he came into my bedroom, even though the door was closed tight."

"Did he knock?"

"No, he didn't."

Tania is now huddled in a corner of the couch. "Pam, I saw his eyes and there was a look in them," she says in a baby voice. "I was laying um naked from the waist down, 'cause I had cramps and had got blood on my panties."

"So you were just turning into a woman."

"Yes, he gave me the sanitary pads, but I think I remember a horrible look in his eyes, like he wanted to do something to me. But all he said was 'Here.' Then he tossed them at me. He kept staring, didn't say cover up. His eyes ran over me, up and down. I remember they stayed a long time on the soft hair between my legs . . . Then he left the room." She rubs her thighs.

Pam allows the stillness to absorb her client's revelation.

"My mother never. . ." Tania starts again, stops. Pam keeps still, waiting.

"I hate my mother," Tania says finally. "She never wanted to leave him, just complained to me about him. I couldn't get a word in, half the time. Every phone call after they first moved away from New York she'd complain that he was at the office, or, on the weekends, off with an assistant."

"Assistant?"

"Yeah, I think he probably had sexual interludes with them, too."

"Too?"

"Well, affairs with them."

Pam ignores Tania's avoidances, which continue despite what she has revealed today. "So . . ." she says. "Is the family hierarchy or the lies the biggest thing for you?"

"The lies . . ." Tania stares at Pam. Suddenly tears are streaming down her cheeks. "I wanted . . . I wanted just . . . I just wanted . . . to have them care."

A week after sending the poem, she phones them. Her mother answers.

"Did Daddy read my poem? What did he think of it?" She plunges in, attempting to lead the conversation, the way he would.

But her mother puts her off. "Let's discuss it whenever she comes up,' is what Dad told me, Tania."

"Mom, I remember I started: *'Dear Daddy, I'm disowning you now / I won't love you no more. / I've loved you for / 26 years, and now . . .'*" Her throat tightens. Discouraged, but determined to stay on the phone and confront the mountain of her mom's dismissal, she allows a curse to well up. "Damn it, did he read any of it? I wrote that I am sick of loving him."

No answer.

"Oh never mind. I gotta go." Her breathing is labored after she hangs up, her lungs constricted, and she drops to the floor into the yoga fish pose, her chest raised up, her heart exposed to the sky. She tries more deep breaths, then reaches for the small, red pillow and throws it. "I'm through with them," she screams.

And she *is* through with them, or so, for a while, she believes. During the next weeks she stops returning her mother's phone calls, and eventually her mother stops calling. After a long search, she finds, bids on, and, with the help of a union-backed loan program, purchases the cooperative apartment Pam had suggested she buy as "back-up." It's in Brooklyn, a cozy one-bedroom on the top floor of a small, turn-of-the-century building not far from her old place. The windows have shutters and window-seats, and are high enough so that sometimes she can see the moon. Moving is easy. She has decided to buy all new furniture, so there are only personal things to transfer, a process she manages with Agua's help on one of the rare days they both have off. But it is exhausting work, and though it is still early when she says goodbye to Agua, who has to pick up Heru, and locks the door behind her, she yearns for sleep.

As she looks at her new futon with its scarlet sheets and bedspread, the teddy bear on the pillow, a feeling of peace comes over her. It is a real store-bought futon, not something donated by somebody who was moving on. And stretched out in the very center, already in full possession, is a beautiful black cat, a gift from Agua. Tania has already named her Black Power.

Thinking of Agua, she realizes there is something else she has to do before curling up with Power. She goes to her new writing table, where the bulky computer she recently bought waits beside the pile of notebooks she still uses to "journal," and locates and unfurls a scroll. It is a poem Agua had written out by hand and decorated with cartoon-like drawings for Tania's birthday last year. She decides she must hang it now, and, crossing her fingers that the hammering won't disturb her new neighbors, fixes it to the wall.

Since her new apartment is in the same neighborhood as her old one, her phone number remains the same, so her parents do not realize she has moved. But contacting them in any way, even just writing to them and facing their coldness feels like slipping into quicksand. She ends up stashing draft after draft of a note. Why does writing to the king feel like the act of a serf saying I left your colony and am now coming back to ask for the blanket I had to forget because I was gone in such a hurry?

But the old dreams keep recurring. Over and over she is lying helpless in that hospital bed. Again and again other dreams reveal the lies of her childhood, yet she hardly remembers them when the nightmares awaken her.

And in session after session with Pam, the counselor urges—almost commands her—to face her family. Her directness on this subject—Pam is rarely direct—is a reflection of her concern. "You've faced up to all those men at work, so the authoritarians who lied and trained you to be afraid will be less terrifying. Go face your daddy, the first male who dominated you, and your mama, too."

Back home after one of these sessions, she sits on the futon in the corner of her bedroom and reads the rough draft of the letter she wrote but did not send, when she sent the poem instead. The edges have started to turn up and it is stained with roach droppings it collected in her old place, lying in the bottom of her open jewelry box. She remembers the beginning of the poem she sent: *I'm disowning you now / I won't love you no more. / I've loved you for / 26 years, and now. . .* The letter reads straight. No rhymes, no images:

Hello Dad!

I have been too scared to really deal with men anywhere in my life today in an honest way, because I find myself reacting to them on or off the job as if they were you. What I mean is that you scared me as a little girl. I got beatings and I think you did other things too.

When I involve myself with a man and he ignores me with hostile silence, raises his voice or says mean things, like he is leaving and doesn't want to talk to me anymore, I immediately try to make up with him, because you were so rejecting of me. I can't stand the temporary tension, 'cause it reminds me of your abandonment for my whole girlhood.

You came home and changed clothes, ate dinner and tuned into that damn European classical music. You ignored me while I was growing up. You didn't go to different places with me as a kid. I remember you came up to school, once. Yeah, just once in all those years, and it was to find out what the school wanted because the teacher was mad at me for something. I wanted you to tell them to stop treating us like animals.

But I still loved you. I wanted so-o-o bad to feel your attention, but the news or the things in the outside world were so much more important for you.

And mom and dad, I thank you for the kind of upbringing that taught me unions are good and we should stop these wars to steal from the third world, but I AM also ANGRY that I did not have your time. Your respectful attention seemed to be on anything that was not a kid or female, like the way the guys at my job act today. I was both a child and a girl.

SO I am gonna ask you some direct questions when I see you, even though I'm trembling inside. I hate to disappoint you.

You still seem like a God to me dad. I know now, that's my problem. You are not that big. But why didn't you love me and give me a moment in your schedule?

I am glad we had a place, of course, to live and you did buy me things, but Daddy, I really wanted your love.

Tania

Having reread the letter for the umpteenth time, she moves over to put it on the end table made with crates she'd scrounged for the move from one of the local liquor stores. Carefully, as if it were dangerous, she sets it beside the phone, which is bright red. Later that night, crying, she writes:

Hi Journal.

She pauses for a long time, then finally scribbles,

"It" is decided. Or I'll say I have decided, made this choice to stand up to my patriarch. I got to . . . Still, despite what Pam says, am I strong enough?

I <u>am</u> stronger than I was. It's not only sticking with the bus driving. It's owning my own place (though that should please him, it won't because of the way I earned the money to get it). It's actually saying no to him coming to stay.

It's understanding the system and fighting back. It's the writing, and Voices of the Working Women using some of my anti-patriarchal poetry in performances. So maybe I can actually go up there and have a face-to-face with my daddy!

She underlines this last sentence twice, then adds:

But could there be a problem I never faced . . .?

She stops writing and clicks the ballpoint pen in and out until the spring breaks.

The decision is made, but still she puts off calling to tell them she's coming. To the plant on the small dining table, as she cleans its red and green leaves, she murmurs, "I could mail the letter, but I won't. I have to find the courage buried under my fear and go up there myself and speak these truths out loud."

The afternoon sunlight streams through the window in the kitchen onto her hanging spider plant's green and white striped leaves. Power watches intently as she runs water into a big bottle, walks over to pour a tiny stream into the plant's clump of earth. Ms. Spider is her favorite. As she dowses her she says to them both, "In our home here we're safe. We don't have to be bothered by their crap."

The plant starts to ooze liquid over the edge of the saucer. Tania takes a tissue to wipe up the spill, then the dust on the table.

"It's been weeks since Mom left me a message, ever since I stopped returning her calls. And the notes she used to send she can't send 'cause she doesn't have this address, though I suppose the post office would forward them if she wrote any. Since I haven't received one, I guess she hasn't written, and I won't have to worry about holidays or birthdays or anything anymore."

Finished with the plant grooming, she uses a spray bottle to mist, then reaches into the pot to adjust a sandalwood incense stick she'd stuck in there, adding, "No smell of their stupid trappings ever comes into my bathroom or my bedroom closets or ever will. I'm my own person here."

But she isn't, not really, as Pam continues to point out, and as all along she has known in her heart. "And I won't be, not really, until they—until I—stop sweeping the elephant of the truth under the mother effing rug." She reaches for the telephone to dial the number at the vacation house. Her thoughts stampede: He's not just Father, he is GOD, who can decide my fate in life. She can hear him saying, "You'll live to regret this." Her arm shakes and she drops the receiver. She picks it up again and uses her left hand to steady her wrist as she holds it to her ear. Letting go for a minute, she misdials the first time, then slowly, with her eyes glued to the keys, presses them one by one a second time. The machine answers, and she leaves a message: "I'm coming up in a few days. Bye."

7 FORTRESS / MOTHER

She's scared, but Tania's feet succeed in marching her onto the subway and into the Port Authority Bus Terminal to take the early-morning bus. She has planned carefully, making arrangements for Agua, who has a key to the apartment, to look after Power The long, slow bus trip will delay her arrival until after lunch.

She has time before the bus leaves, spies a pay phone, drops her coin in.

Agua answers. "Hello?"

"Hey, I'm really going. I don't have much time. I just called to let you know I'm on my way. Look after Power."

"As if I wouldn't! Are you going to stand up to your father?"

As usual, Tania avoids answering.

Agua persists. "I mean, are you really going to confront him about everything, the whole truth about the way he abused you?"

"I guess so, but . . . What do you mean, the whole truth?"

"Do you remember that poem you wrote and shared with me way back when, not too long after we became friends? You know, the one about the little girl on the subway talking about being sexually abused. The one that when we read it to folks we got tears from girls and women in the audience."

"Are you saying . . . ?" Suddenly it's as if Tania is one with the women in the audience hearing the poem for the first time, choking back tears. "Are you saying maybe that little girl was really me?"

Agua sighs in the silence that follows, then says, "So, do you feel strong enough to question your father about that?"

Again there is silence. A mechanical voice intrudes: "Deposit five cents more for the next five minutes."

"Oh, I gotta go, Agua. Bye."

"Bye, Tania. My spirit is with you!"

When Tania flashes her city bus driver's badge, the interstate driver, a middle aged Black man, laughs and waves her aboard. As a professional courtesy, she doesn't have to pay.

"Oh thank you." She smiles and walks to an empty seat in the back near the bathroom. Traffic, once the bus has lurched through the crowded city onto the interstate, isn't heavy. For hours she sleeps, her head tossing on the headrest, waking briefly whenever the bus pulls into a stop along the way. When she finally climbs down off the bus she doesn't remember her dreams. But standing on the deck of the ferry as it approaches the island, she can't get the poem out of her mind. At the dock she rents a car and heads for the place where, until she stopped visiting, she would spend vacations away from hot, humid New York

City. Island vacationers like Tania's parents—like her previous self—know that "riffraff" from the big city can't easily find their way here.

She's a careful driver and keeps her eyes on the road, fighting her anxiety with reflections that don't entirely fortify her: They won't hold me or do anything to me. I'm an adult and can leave when I have to. I have Pam in my heart and Agua, too. Her nose sniffs the ocean air. A breeze whistles by as she pulls up to the house and parks. Turning the engine off, she mutters to herself, "I don't think they'll even listen, but I have to go through with it." The clouds in the east sky signal there may be rain. It often rains in summer here.

Stepping over the wild grass and past the bushes in the back by the large oak trees, she has to force herself to open the door. Her hand goes up, hangs on the doorknob. Instinctively her body tightens. Then, with the inner force of a jackhammer, she pushes in the screen door, ready to start dredging up the past.

A surprised face stares at her as her mother turns from the sink when the door opens. "Look who's here!" she shouts over her shoulder to her husband, who enters the kitchen and stops.

Noting his now totally gray hair, her mother's wrinkled face, Tania thinks, "Aging looks hard—but so was what I went through in their house." Her heart fills with rocks. Both parents had known she was coming, because she'd phoned them. But they act surprised. And they do not say the most important thing: "Oh my god, it's so good to see you after all these years. How we've missed you!" Instead, as they all walk into the living room, they ask questions.

"How are you?" This from her father, lightly. He's standing by one of the African masks.

"Fine," she replies automatically. "I came to find out how *you* are."

Her mother disappears into the kitchen almost immediately, saying, "I'll fix us something to drink. By the way . . ." she calls through the door, "by the way, I'm okay. How was your trip?"

How could she have expected the sharing of feelings, which she knew they would not deliver? She focuses on the living room fireplace, bordered with round fieldstones. Her father's Special Chair faces it, the chair for the king, on which the children were never allowed to sit. He moves slowly toward it, seats himself on his throne, and looks around as if surveying his possessions, which seem to crowd the room: the dining room set with more places than they ever used, the mahogany desk, the alcove filled with books, the Charles White paintings and the African death masks and sculptures with their hollow eyes.

Her throat feels very dry. All her life her parents used Africa's treasures to avoid thinking about how un-African their lives and the way they raised their children were. Mother never wanted WWRL radio, with its African American beats and booming drums, playing her daughter's bones into sexual dancing.

Tania's clear they are up-tight people, and wonders whether they even know what love is. The Charles White paintings also fail to move her right now, though she remembers half-listening to her father as he held forth about White's artistry and the work of other famous Black artists, when she was little Buttercup running in the back yard in Queens.

Her father shouts, "I was recently published in the Island News." He shouts even though she is standing within three feet of him in his living room. She rubs her forehead.

Entering with cool drinks on a tray, Mother asks, "Did you hear about the publicity Daddy got in the Island newspaper when he retired?"

Tania tells herself not to smile and nod, and stays still. But she doesn't say, "I don't want to talk about that." Instead she takes a sip from her glass, then sets it down. She won't touch it again. They do not ask: "Why have you let our family go for so long?" And she doesn't put a stop to the phony chit-chat about the article in the paper, the pretense that there is love between them.

"Well, darling," her mother says eventually, "I've got to go bring in the clothes before it rains. I'm sure you and Daddy have lots to talk about."

Tania nods, but realizes she can't, not yet. Besides, her father has picked up the Sunday *New York Times*, which is lying, as always, on the table beside his chair, and has pulled out the real-estate section. She turns away and follows her mother out through the glass door into the garden. The afternoon sun is almost blinding. The lilacs and the other flowers need water, she thinks. She watches her mother, who is inspecting the buds and petals for bugs. There's no sparkle in her face and her shoulders are hunched. She used to stand so straight. Tania still exercises because of her mother, who played tennis religiously. Her interest in movement and dance stems from her mother's enjoyment of moving, at least her body, though her style of dress didn't reveal her sexuality much. When she'd go out she'd do her hair, put on makeup and a girdle, but today, around the house, she looks frumpy, with her slacks covered by a big top that hides a paunch. Suddenly Tania realizes that, while her own figure is slim, and her style is not exactly frumpy, she, too, dresses to hide her body, her sexuality. She blinks out of her daydream, pats her hair. At least she tries to style her hair in a cute way.

She hears her mother sigh, and says softly, though loud enough for her to hear, "That's the sigh of a woman who's been married too long . . . the sigh of the female who kept this family going. While her husband gets his name in the papers, she makes dinners. It's the sigh of a woman whose big, adult body covers up a little Jewish girl who didn't know how to make her Polish and Russian parents listen." Her mom says nothing.

Frustrated, Tania speaks louder. "You confronted your parents by marrying outside your race, a Caribbean man, my father."

When her mother still says nothing, Tania's voice becomes tender. "Those are the lilacs you planted for your father, when you got that outrageous attack of poison ivy, right?" She wants her mother to hug her, to see that her daughter understands. But she replies only with a frozen stare. She bends down to pick up the clothes basket and turns away. Tania throws up her hands, then thrusts them behind her back and walks toward the house.

Inside, her father is standing by the desk, scissors in hand, reading a clipping of the most recent article he's written for the Island paper. She thinks, "He stands there like one of the political elite, those so-called leaders who are really death dealers. A curled braid sticks in her right eyelash. Shaking her head to release it, she sets her lips firmly together, pressing them over her teeth. "Sit down fast," she tells herself. "Finish it."

He looks at her over his glasses. "Well, well, well," he begins, keeping a few feet between them, looking toward the open window. "Good cross ventilation," he says. His gray hair shoots up into an Afro. He looks good, she thinks. She also thinks, this good-looking man is a bastard."

She refuses to chit-chat about cross ventilation. Preparing herself for the deeper subject, she asks him whether he read the poem she sent him.

"Well . . ." he says, growling like a tiger talking to a cat who won't scratch back. "Well. . ." But he doesn't answer her question. Instead he tells her she'll find the article interesting and tries to hand it to her as he heads for his chair. He doesn't ask whether she wants it or not. She moves too, and sits cross-legged in one of the armchairs with wicker backs, soft cushion under her butt. Keep your hands to the side, she reminds herself. Don't take his stuff.

Her voice quivers. "I need to ask you something." But when he blows his nose with great force, she shrinks back, and instead of pushing forward her question, says, "I feel mixed up when I'm dating men, because you weren't emotionally there. Because of you I think men who are emotionally unavailable are okay."

He finally actually takes a look at this young woman who used to suck her thumb. He fingers one edge of the Sunday paper ruffling in the breeze, scratches an itch above his eyebrow with a gesture like flicking off a bug, dismissing what he sees as a young adult tantrum.

A couple of minutes pass. Not a word is exchanged.

"Do you want to see this article from the Island paper or not?" he asks finally.

Tania tries to snatch back the conversation. "What do I care about the Island paper?" Every fiber in her body shakes.

"There's a whole series of them. I'll go get the file. "

Tania sees this discussion, like a hummingbird fluttering its wings to hover in the same place, is going nowhere.

He walks back toward his Chair, but stays standing, eyes on another clipping he's just pulled from a thick accordion file he brought with him.

She knows she has to speak up. She raises her head to look at him, maintaining her seat to force him to stay near. "We *are* going to talk about this," she hisses. "I hate you." She puts her hands up, as if to ward off a blow.

"Why?" He stands very still.

"You are a . . . monster. You were a monster when I was a kid. You said all kinds of good words about how the bosses were mean to working folks, how white racists had to be confronted as exploiters, but you wouldn't listen to my feelings. And you never even showed up. It's monstrous to pretend you were a dad. You just dominated us. Every day we had to do just what you said or we'd be punished. We didn't have rights. We were like your property."

"You *were* my property, just like I was the boss's property," he shouts back. At this moment, his skin, bronze like the teddy-bears Tania used to play with, changes to gray. Still, he doesn't appear flustered. "You are my daughter."

Tania, despite her fears, is having none of it. "No person is rightfully another person's property, and I'm sick of men in this effing system who think that way. They ain't got a caring feeling in their body. I keep picking men like you. What did you do to us?" She looks out the window, checking her mother's whereabouts, then sighs. Her mind whirls with images. Which one to pinpoint and confront him with? Lying in the bed so scared, keeping the light on, then quickly shutting it off when she heard footsteps approaching her bedroom? Tania remembers how her stomach sank back then. He'd punish her for still being awake. It never dawned on her as a girl that his behavior was strange. Now she thinks, "He came to bother me, never to comfort me when I felt like leaving a night light on to keep away monsters."

Raising her head again, she blurts out, "Listen, I came here to raise this with you and face my fear. You fall off the hook because I let you. One day you, um, walked into my bedroom . . . when I was um about twelve."

"Buttercup . . ."

She hates hearing him use her old baby name. Her raised hand stops him.

"You walked in and woke me up."

He rocks, toe to heel, on his feet.

"Why don't you sit down?" she asks, realizing he towers over her. Slowly he bends his old knees and sinks into the Chair, then puts the articles back in the file folder and picks up the real estate section of the Times, which he sets in his lap in front of his fly.

"I need to ask you something," she says. "Why did you lust after your daughters?" Terror has her heart pumping. She wants a look of, I'm sorry. Nothing.

"I loved all my daughters," he replies. His eyes shift.

Tania can only sit on the rattan chair. She looks up at him. "But you used to spank us too hard. . ." She has lost the thread. Her voice trails off as the old submissiveness reappears. He's going to beat me again, she worries. As a hot surge spreads over her face, she notices that her hands have become like ice.

His eyes dart sideways. He takes his left hand, strokes his face starting at his forehead, scratches his nose, ends with it perched on his chin, as if he had a wise man's beard on his clean-shaven face. "Well, the way I was raised, spanking disciplines children," he says.

"But it was too hard. You used your belt like a whip."

He remains silent, begins leafing through the newspaper. Tania throws her feet to the floor. "I can't believe it. Your thinking must be something like, let's see what's for sale today." He lowers the paper. "Do you want me to just shut up? Is that why you're so damn silent? *I can't!* I can't be quiet anymore. Please just . . ." A shot of her saliva winds up on his sleeve, just pops out of her mouth. She stops herself from making an automatic apology, but apparently he hasn't noticed.

"Do you need some help paying for your creative arts classes, Tania?" he asks. He apparently also hasn't noticed that she's been earning good money for years.

"No, keep your dirty money."

"It's not a bribe."

"Well, what is it then, a threat?"

"Of course not." His tone is contemptuous. "Why don't you go help your mother bring in the laundry?" He picks up the newspaper again.

"I won't be dismissed. I am grown up. Let me be a real person."

Crossing his leg, he folds the paper and fixes his eyes on her. "Okay," he says with the exaggerated patience of someone talking to a small child. "But either we talk about something really important or stop." His look penetrates her.

Swallow, catch a little air. It's only a few seconds, but history is stopping. Tania cannot let him just shut her up as if she's still the little kid she once was, not the property-owning young woman she is. Still, she's whimpering inside like an injured dog, hoping against hope he will stop being this phony guy, who she knows doesn't care, and be her real daddy again. Was it the crass "dirty money" crack that upset him? "Please, Daddy, please smile like you did years ago if I pleased you," she wants to say. "I want you to hug me, Daddy. But you'll have to tell me, how did I please you?" Aloud she only manages to squeak out, "I want you to tell me *something* happened."

He sits in total disconnect, turning the page of the newspaper. He's like a stone, only his body sucks in air. In the stiff silence she realizes again how much Buster resembled him, Buster who hit her and disrespected her and didn't talk to her for hours. Her father is oblivious of her very existence. She wants to snatch the paper from his two well-manicured hands, even makes a move to bat it away, then remembers if she gets too close he could grab her, and stops herself.

Finally she says again, "I need to ask you something." It's as if they're playing a scene on looped videotape. "Why did you lust after your daughters?"

"I loved all my daughters," he replies as before.

"You did not love us." She pauses, then chooses to speak of the one clear memory she has, of the day when he brought her the sanitary pads. "Do you remember? I was curled up in bed with cramps. I wasn't wearing anything but my panties. You threw the pads at me and looked at me with those eyes . . . you know . . . like you wanted me . . . Those eyes also told me not to say anything to anybody. They told me to shut up. And they're saying the same thing now."

"We don't say shut up in this house, we say please lower your voice."

His response causes her calves to cramp. "Reach for it." She urges herself to force the pain out.

"Don't you remember, Da—" The last word tangles up in her throat and she clamps her mouth shut, then purses her lips, blows air out.

"I don't remember," he says.

Now she is crying, yet continues to force words out through the gurgles. "You sound like Nixon with his 'I don't recall. My memory doesn't serve me now.' Those are a phony fat cat's lines." Her hands won't stop shaking.

He doesn't respond violently to the insult as he would have once. Instead he returns to the newspaper, as if to say, "Too bad for you, my daughter . . . Your time with this royalty is up."

But his lack of response spurs her on. As Pam says, he's just a man, not a bogeyman who can kill. She *can* tell him her truth. "Aren't you going to hear me out?" He doesn't move.

Rubbing her eyes, she murmurs, trying to make herself talk louder, but still swallowing the words. "Listen, my life, like me, is black and white, like those Charles White drawings. Fear and love." She sputters, strains for air. "I *know* you hurt me as a child."

He struggles to stand, steadying himself by pressing hard on the Chair's arms. Turning his back on her he walks out. She watches his grey and tan shirt recede, hears the creaking of his rubber soles as he strides away. She's done it. Agua had said "tell, tell him your truth. Tell it, girl." And she's done that and feels it has ended her hell. Her fear of facing his disconnect is over. She knows now he won't talk. He won't hug. She grabs the seat of her chair and forces herself up. She needs oxygen, like a June bug flying around in a small covered jar with just a few teeny holes in the lid. She has just enough air in her lungs to call after him, saying his given name, "Sadstone," out loud, one adult to another, for the first and last time. She runs to open the door, but brakes when her mother comes in, carrying the full laundry basket. They almost collide.

Time stops. Long ago she had learned to read her mother's erratic moods in her coloring. Now her face is cherry red, even raw looking, and sweat beads on her upper lip. She blows at a strand of her gray-flecked hair that has fallen over her eye. Did she hear me? Tania wonders. Her belly sinks. They avoid looking at each other. Yes, she decides, her mother had heard what she said to Daddy.

Of course Mother always used to do a little spying on her daughter. She also used to control the amount of time her children were allowed to have with the feudal lord, so Daddy wouldn't be disturbed by their outbursts. "Let's go shopping," she would say—anything to distract Tania from engaging with her father, anything to protect him. Never to protect her *from* him. She fishes a tissue out of her pants pocket to blot the tears. Each tear has a number—1950s, 1960s, 1970s—the years of her childhood popping out of her eyes. Her hope that Mama would finally leave him turns to dust, like the white sifted flour for the Christmas cookies they won't bake anymore. "You're going to have to face this," she says.

"What are you talking about, Tania?" Her mother heads for the kitchen.

Tania follows, still hoping she can talk to her mother, woman to woman. She leans on one of the high counter-stool chairs. "Look, this hiding goes way back, before you even were a married woman and my mother. You'll understand once I explain what happened with him. You'll see I'm not the little girl you used to con with trinkets like ballet lessons, and vacations on this very island." She glances away, focusing on the tiny bouquet of bright pink roses in the window, then climbs onto the stool.

"You're not making any sense!" Mother starts to fold the laundry.

Tania fishes for where to start. "Just listen a minute. You'll see."

"See what?"

"See that you picked a cold, dominating man like your father for your husband, just like I tend to do." She doesn't know why her mother refuses to see.

"Lower your voice, Tania"

"I'm angry," Tania retorts. Her eyes go to the floor. "You never gave me what I needed. All these years you put up with the way your men think. They could insult you and tell you with their actions that you were a nothing, and yet you *stayed*, and I was trapped with you. I'm sick of it. I never felt an emotionally 'present-in-the-flesh' mother who looked out for me. Even now you're standing here in front of me and I can't see a feeling in you."

Her mother shifts from foot to foot. She looks down at her wedding band, twists it around on her finger. Tania gazes at it too, wondering why this woman wears hers and "the king" doesn't wear his.

Mother also wonders, and thinks perhaps Tania is right, but . . . insolent. "You know," she says finally, you look very . . . I don't know, actually, you don't look so good, Tania."

"I just need to stop working all the time and feel the sun," Tania says. "My skin loves warmth." She stops. Her answer—as irrelevant as her mother's comment—comes automatically, and Tania kicks herself for going along. Her mother is as much of an avoider as her father, and she's letting her get away with it. Pam was right. It's not just him. She's got to grow up and face Mother, too. "But you know what?" she says, determined to force the issue. "You don't even like me . . . and I've been living in this delusion that you do."

Mother snaps. "Tania, stop!" Busy with the laundry, she slaps the folded sheets instead of her thigh as her temper rises, but her voice remains modulated.

"Really, Mother, do you think that talking to me as if I'm still to be controlled is helpful? All these years I wanted to believe the lie that we really were one big happy family. And we're not!" Suddenly she's shouting. She actually wants her father to overhear. She flings her arms wide, then brings her hands in towards her heart. "I'm a woman. I want real feelings from you. You two talk about stuff . . . cars, newspapers, beach dates. He doesn't even talk. I tried to have a real conversation with that dead person in the next room, and you know what, he can't call himself a father!"

"Stop it!" Mother says again and moves toward her, as if to hit her. "I thought I taught you how to control yourself." She turns away and takes a step toward the living room to call her husband to come and shut Tania up, maybe hit his uppity child with his belt the way he used to. When her daughters were still girls she used to tell on them to her husband, saying "Your daughter was terrible today and needs to be punished." But she thinks better of it, and turns back to her daughter, who is gripping the chair hard. "What *are* you talking about, Tania?"

"I'm talking about love, the way I'm loved by my friends," Tania replies.

"And you think I don't love you, is that it?"

"I think you think you do, but the truth is, it would take a heart for you to have a caring connection with me. Where was your heart when I was a girl and Daddy—" She stops, then begins again. "Do you remember those long walks we took in the park where you and Grandma used to walk?"

Her tone is challenging, not fondly reminiscent, but her mother chooses to ignore it, thinking she can calm her difficult child down. "Of course, darling," she says. "I remember we enjoyed nature so much, especially our walks around Sunken Pond. It was so big and deep it seemed like a lake. We liked fall best, don't you think? The red and yellow leaves and the evergreens."

"I remember you used to call the evergreens your 'delightful friends,' I guess 'cause they never changed. But mostly what I remember is you talking."

"Yes, we had lots of mother-daughter conversations in that park." Her mother's eyes mist over as she remembers those times when Tania would come back from wherever she'd wandered and they'd climb into her car, which she always drove when they were together even after Tania got her license and had her own keys. She'd park the car in the lot near the pond, and they'd stroll over to the place where, from the time she was a little Jewish girl, she'd felt a sense of community with nature, of some higher presence. She liked having Tania, with her short, neat afro, at her side because unlike her other daughters and, of course, her husband, she would listen without constantly interrupting. She wondered if Tania still liked Dentyne gum. She, herself, had lost her taste for it, but back then she always had some in her pocket and would offer Tania a piece.

"Mother, will you please stop thinking about our walks in the park? I need you to be *here* now."

"You're the one who brought it up, Tania. Besides, you loved nature too!"

"Okay, yeah, I did. And I knew it meant a lot to you and I wanted to see you happy. I liked seeing you do something besides sit on the edge of your seat at the dining room table listening while he talked endlessly about himself."

"I *was* happy." Mother fiddles with the bow on her butcher's apron, gazing out through the small kitchen window at the now cloudy sky.

"No. Don't. I know that's a lie. You're lying to yourself. For hours by that pond I listened while you complained. You were definitely not happy. We envied families where fathers came home and went to the park with their kids. We had a dad who was an emotional absentee! And sometimes, on the weekends, he was a real absentee. We kids wondered if he was too busy on the weekend to be with his family. Didn't you wonder where he was?"

"He was a wonderful provider. He paid all the bills along with me. Do you know how many Black men didn't or couldn't pay bills?"

"So he provided us with things! But that was *all* he provided. He wasn't a *real* provider, not of the important things like love and caring. He was an avoider! He made me believe men don't have emotions. I wanted to touch you and be tender and that's why I did. But it was wrong. You needed your *husband* to hold you. Instead I was smothered when you hugged me. I wanted to be my own person, but I couldn't stand to see you disappearing as he ignored you, year after year, so I went on those walks and listened while you talked. I didn't know how to ask you to get help . . . You could take a chance and do it even now. . ."

Her mother doesn't respond to this. The silence is deafening, as loud as the sirens back in New York City. Finally she turns on her heels and walks away from Tania into the dining room. She bends over and snatches at a plate on the dining room table, which is set for dinner with the good bone china, then loses her grip, setting it spinning like a wobbly top on the polished wood surface. Finally it falls to the floor with a crash and breaks into two jagged pieces. She stoops down to pick them up and carries them into the kitchen, pushing past Tania, who, instead of following behind her mother as she used to, has been standing still in the dining-room entrance watching her. Saying nothing, she lays the pieces of the plate on the counter, then takes the dustpan and brush, sweeps up the tiny shards and the dust, and returns to the kitchen.

The front screen door creaks. Both know Father has left the house. "I'm not going to stay here and be attacked, Tania," Mother says finally, looking sadly at the broken plate, which had belonged to her mother. Though it did not shatter, the break isn't clean, and there are too many bits for it to be mended.

Suddenly there are tears in Tania's eyes. She doesn't want to let her mother get away, doesn't want to give Mommy another chance to reject her. All the rejections from her childhood and her teen years stack up on top of each other, like the pile of bright yellow, everyday plates in the kitchen cabinet. All the times her mother let the family shut her down and stay stifled. All the times her sisters ganged up on her and Mother would say only "you girls work it out." The time Older Sister said she must have been adopted, and Mother didn't deny it, saying merely "stop fighting, girls, or you'll disturb your father." Still, she thinks, if they can just talk honestly, surely her mother will come through. But her wary inner voice, fearful of another rejection, keeps her from saying what she really wants to say: "Mommy, please don't leave. Mommy, please love me." And then her fantasy that, despite everything, her mother does love her brown-skinned daughter, that she even knows *how* to love her, breaks as surely as the bone china plate.

"It's time you realized that your father and I did the best we could," Mother says. "It's time we had an adult relationship. So calm down and tell me about one of the projects you're doing."

Tania stares in disbelief, seeing clearly for the very first time this woman with a white body and freckles, brown-gray hair, the never-going-to-be-Irish nose and green eyes. She doesn't have to leave the room to reject her daughter, to get herself off the hook. She merely changes the subject to something she finds intellectually satisfying.

"I don't *have* any projects!" Tania throws up her hands. "I'm a human *being*, not a human *doer*, damn it. I'm a bus driver, and I don't care if you think that's a low-class job. I'm one of the workers you claim to support, not somebody doing projects designed to enhance my status or yours, not somebody who's absolutely tense all the time trying to keep up with the Joneses. It's not that I don't appreciate the ideas about world peace and workers and bosses I absorbed growing up, it's just that I've learned that in this household they didn't amount to much more than intellectual posturing, cover for the conservative structure of our family's life, where the Man could do no wrong. You say it's time we had an adult relationship, but the fact is, you're incapable of having one on an emotional level. Not until you learn to face the truth . . ."

"And just what truth is that?"

"You *knew*, didn't you? About Daddy. Why didn't you protect me?"

"Protect you from what?"

"From him. I am *not* loved by you. I see that clearly now. Earlier today I asked Daddy for some answers, damn it, and I didn't hear the truth. And you must have heard something. But you knew all along, didn't you?"

"That's nonsense." Again the sound of her mother's hand hitting her thigh reveals the anger that the pitch of her voice does not.

Now Tania knows for sure that her mother and her father are on the same side! She takes several rapid breaths.

Mother stands there, raging. Her lips twitch. Then she shifts her feet. "Well . . ." she says. "Well . . ." She heads for the sink, where the day's dishes are piled up. "I like to keep busy," she says, reaching for the soap. "I better get these done and start getting ready for dinner."

Tears are streaming down Tania's cheeks. "Will you stop that and listen ?"

"Yes?" Her mother faces her again.

"Mom, I only wanted a life. I wanted people to talk with and be honest with about what's really going on inside me, inside us."

Mother says nothing. She wipes the sweat from her upper lip with her apron.

"He didn't admit to anything just now, you know. He never told me why he came upstairs when I was in bed. Why did he, Mother? Why did he? *Please*, can't we just sit down and talk about it?"

"Tania, you have said enough! What makes you think your behavior is likely to make me listen?" She turns her back on her daughter to face the sink as if only dirty dishes call out to be cleaned and not the whole stinking past.

"I know this washing procedure," Tania says hopelessly, still crying, her nose running. "You're as much of an avoider as he is. You knew I was forced . . . to be in pain. You knew that man did some things and won't admit it. And you still protect that lie. This whole damn family is hostile and keeps things so wrapped up." She is referring now to things she didn't even realize she knew. "So you can stop with the dishes. I'm not staying for dinner. I will not stay in this house with you and that monster man you tip toe around as if he matters more than love and truth." She snatches up her bag, which she had left by the kitchen door when she came in, and opens the screen door. "Do you hear me, Mother? I'm *going* to receive love in this lifetime and I'm going back to where I have a chance. I *do* have it, actually, though not from any of the men you thought I should marry who turned out to be just as distant and dominating as Daddy. I have love with people I never dreamed I would ever meet, real people, not phonies like you."

This daughter changes history as she moves toward the door. "I'm not going to die with you, Mother. You made your choice. I'm leaving right this second."

She hesitates, looks back at her mother, hoping against hope for a sign, but her mother is bent over the sink. "Goodbye, Rebi," she whispers, saying her mother's name softly, using the tone her grandma used to use.

Fleeing toward her car, she talks to her grandma in the wind that stirs the leaves of the trees. "I am not coming back," she says, wondering if her mother heard her goodbye. Yanking the car door open she jumps in and starts the engine before closing it again. Jamming the gears into reverse, she backs down the driveway, nearly hitting one of the trees. She wants her mother to run out and call after her, "Wait, come back!" But of course she doesn't. In the rear-view mirror, she notices her father returning. He makes no gesture, says nothing, as she backs out of the driveway, out of her family, and out of their class.

* * *

After Tania leaves, the eerie stillness of the fortress, which she had so hated as a girl, envelopes her father's stiff-backed chair, to which he has returned, and her mother, Rebi, standing at the kitchen sink watching her daughter's car exit the driveway. As the car disappears down the road, she happened, she reaches for the teapot and a cup and puts the kettle on to boil. Despite the summer's heat, she, like Sadstone, favors hot, brewed tea—peppermint for calm. In a ritual that goes back many years, she pours the hot water over the tea leaves and inhales the aroma as she puts the tea cosy over the pot and sets it, along with the cup and saucer on a tray. This she carries to the bedroom, to the table by the window, next to the picture of her mama, with her green eyes and a smile just forming and her hair in a bun of braids piled on top of her head, old-country style; she's wearing a blue dress and no jewelry. Settling into her chair, she gazes past the portrait at the sky, azure like her mother's dress, like her own dress, which she had planned to wear for dinner that evening, draped over the back of the other chair, Her mind drifts to the distant past and the day when, home on leave, she told her mother she was planning to marry a man who not only wasn't Jewish, but was a Negro to boot, and tried to explain why, tried to tell her about Sadstone, how kind he was and how handsome in his army uniform, when he walked into the Red Cross canteen where she worked. He was in a segregated unit, but the canteen in Hawaii, where he was stationed, was open to everybody. He knew all about the Trotskyites her brother admired so much, and even talked about running for public office to stand up against racism and anti-Semitism when he got back to the states. She would wonder later if her mother, slumped in the kitchen chair exhausted after a long day on her feet at her husband's restaurant-deli, had heard any of what she said beyond the statement of her intentions. If she did, she didn't let on. Instead, when she had recovered enough from the shock to talk, she said in a voice worn out from screaming all day about pickles and gefilte fish: "Have you forgotten we're Jewish? Why would you want to marry a goy, a Negro soldier at that? Is this what I worked my fingers to the bone for? Is this why I sent you to a nice college when I never finished school?" Her knuckles, gnarled and red, pounded the table.

Rebi had plowed ahead. "I'm marrying him because I love him, Ma. I want a man who feels like me or at least smiles with some kind of feeling. And he's interested in my passion for justice and enjoys hearing about my radio drama performances." She paused for a moment, then added, "Besides, I told you a long time ago I was planning to marry a man outside our culture. I was a Jewish girl only for you. I saw myself as an international person and I was going to marry for love. You didn't listen because I didn't have any male authority and you let my father rule you. You just said, 'We're Jewish and can't have a Christian for a son-in-law.' But Mama, even if the Jewish guys I dated were smart, they only talked at me. They never listened. They were just like Dad, Jewish and cold. Their brains impressed me, but they didn't make me feel loved the way I feel now."

They had both heard it then, the sound of her "son-of-a-rabbi" father at the door. Rebi felt a shiver in her spine. Her mother said, "I can't listen to any more of this," and threw up her hands to cover her ears, just as her own mother back in Poland had done when informed that her daughter was marrying a Russian boy.

They had never discussed the subject again until she told her mother about Sadstone, and her mother kept the information from her father, hoping her wayward daughter would change her mind. Not one word did she hear from her mother, much less her father, until she got pregnant. Her parents had refused to come to the wedding, even to the second ceremony she and Sadstone had had after they'd finished serving the military and the Red Cross and had returned stateside. They could have seen her marry him then without having to fly in a plane, but they had not. Sometimes she thought it was because they really didn't like Negroes, even though they'd always talked liberal and raised her and her brother that way.

Her thoughts turn to her brother, with whom she had been so close growing up. But when she and Sadstone got married, he was dating a girl whose parents were conservative and he, too, had refused to attend her wedding. Then, when their father died, he had taken the entire inheritance for himself, never splitting it with her the way he was supposed to. After that, the two families barely saw each other. Her brother's sons had even refused to invite her daughters to their bar mitzvah parties.

She pours another cup of tea and sits cradling the warm cup in her hands. She hadn't cared then that the whole society would be against them. They were in love, and their love would shield them and enable them to face down the taunts and the prejudice. But things hadn't turned out the way she thought they would. He was a Negro, and although she wasn't, their love wasn't enough to free them from all their bosses who looked mortified when they revealed their relationship, the white realtors she had to approach alone so the house or apartment would be shown, the white bank clerk who denied them the right to even apply for a loan the one time they had come in together to see the loan officer. She learned to keep going when, though he graduated from law school with honors, when Sadstone took the bar exam, three times he failed. The system didn't have to reveal the reason, but they knew: He was Black and that's why they failed him. Oh, she knew as well as he did!

Years later she had come to realize how little they had received from the structures that embodied American middle-class life, plucking and dodging for every crumb, almost like poor Blacks, despite the privilege that came with her white skin and their educations. Nothing had turned out as she expected, not her kids, not her marriage, not herself. Her mama's eyes come through her, as she lies down on her bed. She feels them following her.

As she dozes off, she is soothed by the room's colors, all special shades of light cream and coffee. She had shopped for the paint herself, guided by a kind, uniformed helper who knew a lot about tints. That's what I'll do, she thinks. In a little while I'll make myself a cup or two of café au lait, a delightful cup or two of dark coffee with cream and sugar. It will be cube sugar, like Mama used to use, and I will drink it calmly in the kitchen.

This is another of her rituals. It doesn't matter that she will have trouble sleeping afterwards. She knows what she must do to survive the empty evening that looms ahead of her, with her husband alone in the living room of a house still filled with her daughter's presence.

Later she shuts out any possibility of tomorrow's sunlight by drawing her kitchen's brown curtains, then sits down to drink her coffee, two full-bodied cups of Maxwell House as she had planned. As planned, a caffeine high eventually cuts through the depression, and she laughs uncontrollably, bitterly, as she goes to the phone and dials her daughter's number. She knows that Tania could not possibly have made it home, but she has no intention of letting herself talk with her directly. Instead, she will leave her a message, something that will keep her daughter from ever again hurting her the way she did today. She listens to the answering machine, mentally picking apart the incorrect grammar of Tania's Black-identifying message: "This be Tania's house, let me know who you are, and what you wanna say." Then she clears her throat and begins: "This is your *mother*. I have a message for you . . ."

That night, alone in the bedroom, she downs a Valium and stands for a moment in front of the full-length mirror. She looks like the frumpy old lady in the Charlie Chaplin movies she watched when she was a girl, the ones where the tramp will revive her if he can. But Charlie Chaplin is nowhere around. In the dark, the clock ticks so loud she wants to unplug it. "I hate my life," she mumbles, her words slurred. Her husband snores by himself in his own single bed. They had stopped sleeping together when she couldn't take his noise and fumbling anymore, once she had removed the blinder of her fantasies.

8 MOURNING BREAKS SILENCE

The leaves seem especially green as Tania drives her rental car past the trees. Under her breath she mutters, "O tree spirits, I've lost them. I gotta do this living on my own. Agua knows . . . she understands. And Pam. Thank god for them, or I'd be alone." The compact is zigzagging all over the road, almost crossing the white line. Her hand holds the steering wheel so tight, she feels a pain in the pads under all five knuckles. She tells herself she'd better watch out, her mother could be calling the police at this very moment, and they'd be pulling her over for reckless driving. She eases the car onto the shoulder and stops, then slumps against the door, laying her head on the head-rest. Pounding the steering wheel twice, she calls out, "Pam, Pam," Then opens the driver's side window to let air rush in to cool her brain, which is pounding too. She hears strong father wind whirring in her ears and soul. After wiping her cheeks with an open hand, she heads back down the road, driving fast, but careful not to cross the center line. She thinks about what she'll tell Pam. She'll shout it out: "I did it. I told those two I'm finished. I'm free. But Pam, why did they do it? Why don't they care? I gotta tell *myself* I'm good enough, 'cause they won't."

She presses her hand on her Adam's apple to suppress a cough, then sets the car veering again as she searches deep in her denim shoulder bag for tissues. Blowing, crying and spitting up phlegm, wiping her nose and crying some more, she realizes she'd better stop again and pulls off the road and lays her head back. The trees overhead wave gently, soothing her. "Thank you, Universe," she whispers. "You know, dear Universe, I needed to leave them, I just didn't realize it." She pops a cassette tape into her walkman. "O-o-o Baby, Baby. . ." The crooning of Smokey and the Miracles blooms into her spirit. "Stop caring about why they are the way they are," she whispers. She quiets herself as the singers' voices swell, carrying their tune and her to the airport and home to her city.

The ruby light on her answering machine is blinking when she enters her apartment. Pressing playback, she hears a soft voice: "I have a message for you.

This is your Mother. After the way you behaved today I never want to see you again. You can go kill yourself for all I care!"

"Oh my god." In shock, Tania just collapses the way Buttercup used to do, her legs sprawled open on the hardwood floor. Gotta tell somebody. Phone Pam even though it's late.

Tania's voice, unsteady: "Pam they hate me. I told them I'm done and I ain't . . . well, I mean I said goodbye."

Pam listens, waits.

Tania is crying. Finally, sniffing, she goes on.

". . . She left a message for me tonight. I heard it just now when I got back."

"Your mother?"

"Yeah. You know what she said?"

"What did she say?"

"My mother said, 'You can go kill yourself for all I care.'" Tania stops for a moment, then adds, "My mother, she ain't a mother. I don't have a mother."

"No, Tania, you have yourself. And that is the reality you face."

"Pam, I love you. Thank you for helping me." Tears flow. "I *am* facing this."

"Yes, you are . . . the loss of her as well as him."

Tania wipes the tears as best she can with her finger. She doesn't want to put the phone down to hunt up a tissue.

Pam says, "Thank you Tania, for letting me get to see someone who is no longer frail, but instead bright and grown up. You have passed through this now and there is no turning back. You know who you are. You're forging your Self. Write it, Tania. You are a writer and you can do it."

"I'm so tired, Pam."

"Just take care of yourself, and when you're ready make a start at setting down the emotions for the sisters in your writing group." The way Pam's tender voice conveys awe at a client's accomplishments and inspires confidence in future possibilities is part of what makes her special.

"I will, I will. I left those two, 'cause they were too cold."

"Yes, but you certainly have demystified a whole lot more. The crap they brought you up with. They didn't understand that, as Malcolm X said, it wasn't the American dream, it was the American nightmare they'd slept through."

"Yeah, they held on to their false beliefs and illusions." She sighs. "Thanks, Pam. Good night."

"Good night, Tania. Just remember, you did it! You went up there to take care of your inner child, little Buttercup, to face your fear of standing up to them, to tell them your true feelings. And you did it!"

Tania looks through her front window, with its wood shutters, into the night's black wholeness.

"I've got your back, Tania," Pam says. "You call me again if you need to. We can make an appointment if you still want one . . . or . . ."

Suddenly, despite Pam's encouraging words, Tania is filled with doubts. "Pam," she says. "I didn't. . ."

"Didn't what, Tania?"

"Pam, can I come tomorrow morning?"

"Hold on, let me check." Tania waits while Pam locates her appointment calendar. "I can squeeze you in for a half-hour first thing if you like," Pam says.

"Oh yes. Thanks so much, and thank you s-o-o much for picking up tonight."

"Okay, get some rest now."

"Okay, good night." As she hangs up, Tania, safe in Brooklyn, feels the warm breeze coming through the cracked-open window as a caress.

She walks to the bathroom to pee, then settles down on the cool, hard bathroom floor in the cross-legged easy pose of yoga to pet Power. "I can move past this," she says to her. The cat purrs.

"I didn't really believe they'd try to work it out with me. I didn't dare ask him again about the lust. I hate that I couldn't do it. And mother never honestly confessed. Yes, Mommy listened in on us but all she wanted was for me to stop criticizing her stupid, vicious husband." Power turns on her back and lets her legs splay out, inviting Tania to rub her belly. "It's been an okay life without them for this long while and now it'll be okay forever without their carcasses. Me and Agua and Pam and the writing group and maybe, one day, a new man . . ."

She yawns, stretches over and does the ujai yoga breath "ahhh," letting her mouth open and hearing the exhale like an ocean roar, then breathing through her nose, taking in more oxygen, and exhaling again. She sees Agua in her mind's eye, with her curly hair now cut very short, the brown-framed glasses that she puts on the side of the bed when she goes to sleep. She sees her bright gaze, those laughing, bubbly eyes over high cheekbones. Scrambling up, she walks back to the living-room window to stare out again into the beautiful black night. On the street she notices a lone woman, short like Agua, passing by at a New Yorker's rushed pace, probably heading home. Thankfully she and Agua don't often have to brave the streets so late at night, since they can stay over at each other's place when it's too late to subway it home. Having Agua in her life is a true blessing. She wishes she were with her now, wishes she could at least talk with her, but it's too late to call her.

Her body and mind beg for sleep. Black Power has already settled in for the night. "Come rest, in your real home, with a good skylight and spider plants," the cat purrs. "You can take a bath tomorrow morning." She crawls in and covers herself with one of the sheets. "Love yourself Tania," she whispers to herself.

After removing the red clips from her fluffy hair, she rests her head on the special neck pillow and starts finally to drift off.

"I know that my dreams will help me on the long path to recuperation," she mutters. She lightly strokes both eyelids, the way they do in yoga class, and whispers, "I love you, Tania."

During this sacred sleep, she dreams, but an intense urge to pee wakes her up. Her eyes stay shut as she falls out of bed, tiptoes to the bathroom, still smelling of Nam Champa incense, not sweet or pungent. Though there was a lot of rushing about and bleeding in her dream, she hopes nonetheless to resume it, so doesn't turn on the light, but feels her way. She is asleep again as soon as her head settles back on the pillow.

She dreams of a sweat lodge with some Native spirits. She sweats in all her blessed nakedness. "Make it right for us at work," she prays for people in the world, for two- leggeds, for winged ones, for this mama earth. The smells of cedar and sage waft over her head as the Medicine Man tosses herbs on hot rocks that steam up and hiss. She inhales and lowers her head to cool on this wet mother earth's mud. When she comes out of the sweat lodge, she cries '*I don't have a mother*!' The Native American women and men guide with firm voices. "Why don't you let the earth be your mother!" She wakes up stretching completely, so peaceful, instead of her usual jump up in a panic, brain on fire. Her eyes brighten as she remembers what they said.

Morning brings the need to tell another being about the dream, and she can't wait for Agua to check in, as she does every morning, and glances at the clock. It's after six and okay to call her.

"Hola," Agua answers. "Que pasa, amiga? What happened yesterday?"

Tania, sitting on a throw rug on the floor, says, "Agua, I'm glad I went, but before I tell you about that, let me tell you this dream I had last night, okay?"

"Sure." Agua agrees, but as Tania tries to recall the humble sweat lodge from her dream, she draws a blank. "I mean my dream was so damn *vivid*," she says.

"It'll all come back later today, probably." Agua reassures her, knowing the disjointed way the unconscious works. "What did you say to your mom and dad?"

"Sitting in his chair up at that vacation house, my father was nothing." As usual, Tania doesn't answer directly, but says a good deal. She massages a rage bump, a pounding feeling on top of her head. "He just sat there and I stood up to him and his walled-in deadness. But mother musta been listening in through the screen door or something. Here I was hoping she was gonna say to me, 'I'm so-o glad you've decided to have your own separate adult relationship with your father.' Instead, she said, 'Lower your voice.'"

There was so much to tell, too much for a phone call. Besides, Tania feels the need to hang with her friend, and in a few minutes she has to leave for Pam's.

Thankfully, Agua doesn't have to go to work for a few hours, so Tania decides to make a run to her place in the Bronx after seeing Pam.

"Good, I'll be here when you get here," Agua says. "See you later."

Pam is ready for her, with a welcoming pot of Tania's favorite tea on the coffee table, but Tania ignores the drink and launches right in.

"Mom didn't really understand me. I thought I was close to her, you know, Pam. But now I see she didn't care. I mean even when I was still with that idiot, Buster, and told her that I was being hit, being slapped, yes, slapped by Buster, she told me 'go into the kitchen and *cook*.' That's not enough."

"And instead you left him, your daddy representative." Pam, recognizing Tania's avoidance, encourages her by validating the courage she showed by leaving Buster, in preparation for drawing out of her that she did also leave her parents' house, and that this was a greater victory.

"But that's what my mother should've been saying to me . . . not just 'go into the kitchen.' She told me that when my father got excited and mad, she would simply go into the kitchen and cook." Tania looks down, realizing she has to move forward. "But Pam, despite what you said last night about how strong I was, the fact is I could only whisper goodbye to her—and he wasn't even there."

Pam inhales and blows smoke from her cigarette toward the open window. "What was the failure of nerve that caused you not to ask your mother straight out if she heard you say goodbye when you were leaving?"

Looking out the window, Tania tilts her head. "I guess I wonder if mother knows something, and I don't want to know."

"Your mother still stands between you and yourself." Pam implies Tania carries a fear of letting go completely and becoming aware of even deeper hurts.

Tania rushes on, to avoid letting what Pam has just said really sink in. "And I'll tell you something about my mother's response to my father and me that I figured out when I connected Buster and my father."

"Go ahead."

"When we were little and my father beat me, my mother didn't stop him. She hit us too, but not so hard. I remember one time, though, she slapped me really hard across the face." Tania's face becomes rigid and cold. Her memory takes over. Her mind drifts to when she was a teenager, back in Queens.

"Can you tell me about it?" Pam realizes Tania may be getting ready to make a connection.

As Tania answers, her body stiffens. It's as if she is her sixteen-year-old self again. "I was going out with this boy who was sixteen too. He'd kept me out late, and it was past my old midnight curfew when I came walking in. Mom was waiting up. I told her, 'You promised that I could stop having a curfew, once I kept my word and came home at the exact right time for a year. I did, so I don't have to keep a curfew anymore.'" Reliving her fury, she has begun to shout. "And then Mom came towards me, right in front of Walker, my guy, and backhanded me . . . humiliated me. I wanted to . . . run out of the house. Walker caught my arm." Burying her forehead on her knee, Tania beats the couch.

"She must have been beside herself by then," Pam says. She suspects that the mother's anger was fueled by a frantic fear of what Tania's teenage sexuality might mean, not only in her relationships with the males of her own generation she was now attracting, but in her relationship with her father, who she knew, though she couldn't admit, was molesting Tania. The fear of most mothers of teenage daughters that they would get pregnant was compounded for her by an inadmissible terror: that Tania might get pregnant by her own dad.

Gripping the soft fabric of the couch so hard her knuckles hurt, Tania spews out more, seeming to change the subject, but in reality making connections. "Pam, I remember the day my father smashed a huge dining room chair. My mother just stood there watching him beat the chair into the floor, shouting over and over, 'These damn racist bosses, these damn racist bosses . . .'"

Although Pam sometimes finds it difficult to know just when to drive a little harder, she risks it now. "Look Tania, if I'm reflecting you right, your mother accepting the rages of your father, telling you to go fix food instead of refusing to take abuse from a boyfriend, forces you to take a clearer look at this woman, who you thought would be on your side. Yes, racism is oppressive, but we have to fight the racists, not take it out on the family. Your parents hid their real terrors and, instead of getting help, punished their kids, especially you, because they felt helpless against the oppressors. Even if the kinds of help available now barely existed in those days for anyone but the rich, there were other options. Political options. What if they'd pursued their youthful socialist ideals instead of the false, unobtainable middle-class dream? Maybe then they could have escaped the isolation of the 'Father knows Best' nuke=liar family."

Having said this, however, Pam regards Tania, who is now curled up on the couch, and decides not to push her any further. Maybe it's too precarious a time for her to truly see and accept that both her mother and her dad had betrayed her more deeply. The half-hour is up, but she waits until Tania is ready to leave.

At Agua's place, the two sisters continue the healing. Tania has a real family in this friendship. Agua could have let her down and vice versa many times, but they have danced into a bond that overpowers the pain that Younger Sister and Older Sister seared into Tania when she was a kid.

Hugging Tania into her home, Agua comforts her. "Let it out. Hit this if you have to." She hands her a pillow from the couch.

"Guess I could beat it if I want to." Tania readies herself, dropping her pocketbook and kneeling on the living room floor.

"So tell me what the idiot said." Agua moves as if to put her finger down her throat to make herself throw up. They giggle. "And be sure you 'lower your voice,' like your parents say." They laugh again. Agua adds, "It's hilarious. The look of things is always more important than reality in your old family."

Their laughter makes Tania slap another pillow, one from a nearby chair, harder and harder.

Agua stops laughing as Tania interrupts. "I've been slapping this cushion the way my mother slaps her thigh when she's angry, instead of yelling. She did it more than once when I was there, breaking open the silence about the lack of love in the family."

"Yeah?"

"Yeah. And when I told my mother straight out I wasn't loved by them, she said I was talking nonsense."

"Damn," Agua murmurs.

Holding her chest, pressing on it with her hand as if she hopes it won't break inside like a levee broken by a hurricane, Tania looks at a photo of Agua's mother on a table by the television, her hair pulled tightly back so the African strands can't stick out to show the kinks. Agua, looking at it, too, remembers her own not-so-different confrontations with her working class moms.

"I wanna cry, Agua," Tania says. "But if I start, I'm scared I'll never stop."

"Go ahead, let it out. You're not alone," Agua says. She moves over to sit closer to her friend.

The sobs come in twos. Tania's voice interrupts her hiccoughs. "You know how when you feel like stifling something, but it burps up anyway?" She begins hitting the pillow again, beating it into the floor. After a while Agua stops her by taking her hand, but lets her cry. Raising her head a little, Tania murmurs, "Thank God I dreamed of Native American Spirit guides. I'm so happy I remember my dreams, Agua."

Agua lets the pause happen . . . It is filled with something almost tangible, something new coming . . . A new life?

Tania's eyes flutter as she recalls her dream. Out of tears and fears has come this gift. But remnants of her illusions clog her throat . . . She can't speak.

Again Agua breaks open her silence. "Was it a message dream, Tania?"

"Uh huh. There was a spirit, a Native American . . . it just felt like that. I even heard the big drums, a mother playing the huge drum over and over, like a heartbeat to calm the baby. I don't know . . ." For a few moments there is quiet. Then Tania remembers. "Yeah. The spirits said, 'why don't you let the earth be your mother?'"

Clasping her friend's other hand, so Tania can keep going, Agua adjusts her legs to sit comfortably, wondering at her friend's deepening understanding of Indigenous ways.

After another few moments of silence, Tania recounts another part of the dream, "A bird, a male bird, was in a nest and a baby bird was next to him He started to nibble at the chick. It was like he was going to eat her alive. I'm thinking that the father bird will eat his child alive because that's his nature. The father bird even had a sneer on his face. Then the father bird turned into a man, and I thought: This man is capable of real violence."

Pleased she can recall that much detail, she looks directly into Agua's eyes, behind her glasses, and adds, "Oh. Then after that came the part about the Native Americans! I remember more clearly now."

Massaging her friend's hands, maintaining a beautiful, soothing rhythm, Agua says, "There you go. You know now. You know who your mother and father truly are. You can't stay in denial anymore. That dying not to know was killing you . . . making you pick boyfriends who didn't really treat you good, 'cause that's what you thought you deserved . . . someone just like your parents, not available and able to suck your energy dry." Agua stops massaging. "That bird was your father, don't you think?"

"Oh?" Denial is still so seductive for Tania. Her lips quiver.

"Are you feeling like crying again?" Agua asks.

Tight lines form on Tania's brow. There are tears inside, but at this special moment she will not let them come out. She stretches her jaw and crunches up her face to release the tension and swallow them. She finds a resting spot for her eyes on another photo, this one hanging by the window, with the morning light filtering through the gray window gates. It's a photo of Tania and Agua performing their poems together.

A small smile begins to grow. Stretching herself out, Tania says, "Pam said I could write this . . . but, ahh . . ."

Immediately, exuberantly, Agua yells, "Yay! What a good idea! Do it Tania. Get all this stuff out. You can. Do it." Joyful, delighted almost as a child is delighted, by the thought that Tania can put the tragedy into herstory, she pulls back when she sees how nervous Tania seems. "Will you?"

Tania's throat holds Agua's question. She does not answer. But back home, the first thing she sees is Agua's scroll. Drawing close to it, she focuses on the last line of the poem, "We fight back." And suddenly, mysteriously, the scroll gives blessings, and a title for the play she now knows she will write: "She Fought Back."

Though it is only mid afternoon, she tumbles into bed and sleeps soundly. When she wakes up, it is early in the morning, barely light outside. Wiping both eyes with a long rub, she stretches. Power, purring beside her, lays a gentle paw on her cheek. She smiles at her kitty. "'She Fought Back," she says. "That's the name of my play. I could do a one woman show, talk and dance and have my characters all standing up with alter egos and everyone will fight back against those betrayers, mom and dad."

Crawling out of bed, one sock dangling from her foot, the other lost under the beaded bedspread, she makes her way to her computer. Her fingers on the letter keys, she reads the last lines she had written:

It was torture to be lusted after, but torture also was having the silence all those years of no one to witness my pain.

Then, repeatedly pressing the arrow key down, she rapidly types four words:

Title:
She
Fought
Back

9 NO DIXIE POMADE HERE

After this promising start, Tania writes nothing more for a week, and she spends her next Tuesday and Wednesday off work running every errand she can think of, making excuses to Power, to her computer: "It's too hot to write. I've got too many other things to do. I'm too tired." But then, as if on cue, Smoke, one of her women's writing-group friends, happens by, yelling from the front stoop while Tania's giving her plants their last watering before going to bed. Rather than throw her house keys out the window as she usually does, she races down the stairs. Smoke, with her broad hips, hates to climb steps, and will be waiting for her below. They hug.

"I was on my way home from a reading at a café here in Brooklyn, and took a chance you'd be in. Gotta talk fast, though. The trains run slow after hours."

Tania gives her another hug.

"I heard you walked out on them," Smoke says. "So, are you writing it?"

"I'm too tired," Tania moans.

"Just put down the bare outline so you don't forget. You can fill it in later." Smoke has left her mama, too, and knows the pain behind Tania's weariness.

"But where do I begin?"

"Anywhere!" exclaims Smoke, tossing her scarf over her shoulder and waving her hand goodbye in one smooth motion.

Inspired, Tania runs back up the steps and turns to a blank page in her notebook. She'll start with stream of consciousness, warm up for dialogue and scenes on the computer later. When, however, she goes to the wall mirror by her window to read the monologue she's created out loud, glancing up into her own wide-set eyes now and then, it seems nonsensical.

I'm so lost now. I ain't getting them back . . . but I never had them. They glossed over our lives with "I'll be there for you, Tania." He hurt me so bad.

In the margin she writes a note to herself in big black capital letters, going over and over them: **I NEED A COVER UP SCENE, SHOWING MY PARENTS HYPOCRISY**

Holding the notebook steady in her hand, she turns, walks to the bathroom, pees, leans on the sink, and again watching herself in the mirror, reads aloud some of her earlier notes.

Poems just come out and up, almost like stream of consciousness, but now she finds herself wanting to write dramatic monologues, which can be more complex. Can she do it? Can she take this wound and open it up and cleanse it with the herbs of writing? Maybe. Though she has to report to work almost every day/night, at least she has no child depending on her except her inner little girl. Suddenly, she feels certain.

She is sure she can use a writer's surgical knife, like the women who'd won the freedom to be doctors in the male medical industry. Other women of color were forced to take part in the workplace just to feed themselves and their kids. She has the freedom to create, and like a surgeon, cut and heal while she creates—not just a monologue, but dramatic dialogue, a play. A play the writing group will want to perform.

The group had started as a talk group for womanist consciousness-raising, with the sisters focusing on their journals and other stream-of-consciousness out-pourings, like spontaneous poems. Now it's evolved so there's an unwritten agreement among them that they'll use their true creativity—the discipline required to shape their artistic urges—to unburden themselves of their issues.

The next day she puts in for an AVA (Advance Vacation Allowance) day on a Saturday in December. She will present her play to the writing group and, for the first time since she started driving a bus, stay to the end.

Having made this commitment to her friends and to herself, every morning Tania shakes her head to wake up early, determined to write until she has to leave for work. Today is Labor Day, but her schedule has her working on holidays as well as weekends. At least on this holiday her work day is shorter. She'll be driving an older series Manhattan bus until exactly 9:03 pm instead of midnight. Lucky her. Finishing early means she'll have time to hang out at a barbecue she's been invited to by her friend Lisa, whom she met at a Non-Traditional Employment for Women forum, where the harassed women were being encouraged to keep standing up against the machismo at work. For once she'll arrive at a party before all the workers who have jobs in the morning have to leave to prepare for their next day of work, and the loneliness forced on her by late-night shift work will be relieved, at least for a few hours.

But as her Labor Day tour of duty drags on, the lingering stress from the visit to the vacation house catches up with her, and she can barely manage a smile in response to the friendly "Enjoy your swing" of her dinner-time relief driver, who is a good-looking man with a short afro and beautiful eyes. She does manage a wave from the street before he closes the door, then hurries off. Her break allows her only thirty-six minutes to swallow her dinner.

Barely moving her arms, she carries her tired body up the avenue to find that nice take-out place serving soups. "I'm gonna have cold soup," she thinks, but then suddenly realizes she feels nauseous, and places one hand on her forehead to see if she has a temperature. "I couldn't be pregnant, and I've eaten very little today, so what's up?" she mutters to herself. She can't afford to feel sick. She has to drive the bus, full of people talking over each other, shouting to be heard. Though there is no rush hour, holiday schedules, with fewer buses, are killers. She decides she'd better use the dirty restroom in the swing shack, where drivers sit and wait to take over their bus from the previous operator.

Entering the shack, she smells the odor of bodies that don't have enough space to breathe. A few chairs and a rickety table, big and wooden, occupy the center space. The toilet in the back runs non-stop, because transit never fixes it. On the way, she stops to make job talk with a guy called "Locks," who has a beard and a mustache, brown skin, brown eyes, and African locks pulled back in a rubber band. Like her, he's on dinner break, and is wolfing down take-out. Not long ago, he'd been one of her relief drivers, and after they've exchanged greetings, she listens while he gives voice to the disgust most of the drivers feel about the way transit authority management demeans its workers by insisting on a strict adherence to schedules and rules that take no account of their humanity. The dispatchers often don't think of themselves as union workers, and drivers see them management's enforcers. "There's no dispatcher willing to give a short sign, and that's a fact. You just have to keep on driving when you're late, no matter what the damn reason, whether you miss your break or not."

"Yeah, you got that right," Tania agrees. "At least today, I didn't have to ask for a pay ticket from the dispatcher, like I would've if I'd missed most of my break. Isn't that the worst, when you gotta cut short your break for a few bucks?"

Locks nods. "I'm willing to get to the garage late for my bus relief and get to take a full break, 'cause transit has already put a new bus out with a new guy, but sometimes they don't and you hardly get to eat. Damn this transit, they make the shortest breaks go with the longest shifts! Ten hours in the seat with a thirty-four-minute rest. Who thinks up these schedules? We drivers would do a lot better job of it if we had the chance!"

Just then a rat runs from the bathroom and into a hole in the wall.

"That's it!" Tania decides against using the bathroom or even staying a moment more. She'll just have to hold it. She walks quickly to the front door and pushes into the hot outside, then takes a quick look at her watch, which keeps her safe in her cage at transit so she doesn't get a violation for being late. She realizes that, given how crowded the take-out place always is, she won't have time for the soup, and retraces her steps towards the shift stop. There's a bench in the median strip of the avenue, where the powers that be had planted some flowers and a bush, as if a little greenery could erase the filth in the streets caused by the lack of garbage collection in this poor part of one of the richest cities in the world. She says to the seat: "Wow! A bench that has a back!" As her own strong back leans against the wooden one, her eyes scan the buildings on both sides of the street, hoping for a glimpse of sky. There is none, unless she puts her head all the way back.

Her palms seem like they're sweating, but this is a "come from the inside of the heart type sweat," not real sweat caused by the day's blazing heat. Her neck, when she touches it also feels too warm, but it's not sweating either. In a way she's glad for the fever. Her hands won't feel all wet and messy. She doesn't have tissues. Still, she'll have to cancel going to the party, and she'll have to do it fast or be late for her shift. Spotting a pay phone on the corner, she shoves her backpack aside and fishes for change in the little change pocket of her uniform pants. "Good," she thinks. "There's enough change. Now if the phone isn't busted . . ." The phone company hardly ever services the phones in this down-pressed neighborhood. She gets to her feet and trudges toward it, picks up the receiver.

It has a dial tone!

Her head feels as if a large truck is blowing its horn in there. She wishes she could just pull off this shift, and not have to go relieve the next driver pulling in for his break. But that would be an automatic violation from the cutthroat location chiefs. Tania has enough of those.

Noting an ominous crack in the phone, she says a silent prayer that it won't eat her change, then puts in her dime and dials Lisa's number. It's a long time before somebody answers and calls Lisa to the phone. She hears loud salsa and R&B music. Folks are dancing and obviously it took a while for somebody to hear the ringing. As she puts the receiver back on the hook, she stares into a tiny reflection of her own unhappy eyes in the chrome of the phone.

Taking another quick look at her watch, she sees she has a few minutes left to her break and decides to spend the time on that sturdy green bench. She has to be on time to the exact minute, and doesn't want to chance even walking into one of the crowded bodegas with all sorts of people talking at the same time and buying holiday cold beers and spicy snacks. Instead of eating, she'll just drink water slowly. On her way back to the median strip, she pulls the bottle of water she always carries and wets her hot, dry lips with a quick tongue bath.

Settled on the bench, she takes out the little cherry red notepad she carries with her everywhere. Shakily she writes: *I lost my family, but I am all right.* A couple of tears well up in the corners of her eyes. She knows her body feels sick because her heart is sick, and tells herself to keep on writing. *That was heavy to hear my mean father just snoring in the front room, while I was arguing with my mother in the kitchen about how she still trusts him and all those men who betray us.* Her right leg is crossed over her left, making a little "writing table" of her lap.

She feels uncomfortable in her body. Now chills climb up under her jaw and all over her skin. She takes her deep blue buttoned jacket out of her backpack and, and after patting out the wrinkles, puts it on. She spots the bus whose driver she's scheduled to relieve way down the avenue and stands up, stretching and hanging her torso over her feet in a yoga hang-down position." "I *will* do this," she thinks, then gulps a long swig from her water bottle. Her mind steadier, she walks determinedly, pressing a little harder into the cement pavement with each step. "I *can* finish this shift," she mutters to herself. It *is* less than four hours, after all. She will concentrate on the nice Epsom salts bath she'll run when she gets home. Craning her neck, she realizes the driver has "made the light" and will be in the bus stop earlier than she thought. She has to step it up.

Slightly out of breath as she slips into the hard plastic bus driver's seat, she quietly thanks her spirit guides: "At least I didn't get that bad-ass whiff from the bus seat after the other driver got out." Too often the previous driver's sweat has funked up the space.

"Bye," her tall, chocolate-skinned coworker says, then turns back on the lowest step of the bus and asks, "Want me to fix your route number for you?"

"Hey, all right, Smitty." She smiles in appreciation.

From behind her she hears passengers shifting and sighing, anxious to move. Sticking her hand out the window, then up inside the bus, she adjusts first the left mirror, then the right. Sitting still, ready to release the air break, she asks her spirit guides, as she always does, to make sure she doesn't have an accident.

On her days off she's writing non-stop, attempting to mold the material into clear written characters, dialogues of rage, and at least one climax. Often when she closes her journal, pressing it on her soft bosom, she wonders whether she can succeed. Until now, writing has been a kind of prayer, notebook after notebook filled with fragments of dialog and background notes and, in the margins, large, inked-in capital letters and doodles of plants with immense leaves long stems. Can she create a play from these ramblings? A real play, not just a series of choreopoems/monologues? Sometimes she wonders how it is she hasn't gone mad. "Musta believed in the right spirits," she thinks. "Spirits who cared and had eventually brought me friends to take the place of family." But how had that happened? That's what she's got to get down.

Finally, one day, she removes the pen from the spiral rings of the latest notebook and, breathing a long sigh, glances over towards the computer and the stack of notebooks beside it. "Tomorrow I'll switch to the computer, 'cause this thing's just growing like a weed," she mumbles to Power. The computer, she hopes, will help her shape what she's written. She feels lucky it was invented. The machine has become another friend. The workers who created it were good.

With the light of morning, she opens her computer, and starts with: *Please don't make me leave you.* It fits for a confrontation between mother and daughter. The computer's cooling fan hums, making sure the motor, running hot to keep up with her fingers on the keys, doesn't explode.

> *People listen when I try to ask them to hear this. Problems overcome people who act like they are listening. Mental worries: Who will be at the next rally,who will inspire them to rise up and shout "no!" To resist their bosses at their workplaces?*
>
> *We all need to shout we're not gonna go like sheep into the dustbins when our bodies can't survive after 30 years of being good, and coming on time and leaving late, receiving no overtime or being forced to work overtime.*
>
> *People listen sometimes with a kind willingness, when I try to find words and share why I hate compulsive types like my father, who seemed to just show up at the worst times of my life, like when I was trying to have a sexy teenage moment and he would barge into the party with a flashlight looking for me—HIS daughter.*
>
> *Words . . . good as water . . . People can read words when they're ready for the new clothes drawn on the page. They can be comfortable, even courageous, at their own pace. When they have to listen to someone read aloud they may not be ready to hear the message and tune out. On the other hand, when they have to listen to someone read aloud or perform, they may really hear and be shocked into consciousness in a way that reading doesn't usually do.*

Her cat places delicate paws on Tania's toes and listens as she reads aloud. "Power," she murmurs, "maybe a friend will say, 'I heard what you wrote, Tania, and it made me think about my life.'"

Buttercup always danced, and her grown-up self, Tania, rolls her hips. Then her arms swing. She scans through the last scene of the seed of her play.

> *Mother: "Use your palate, darling. Listen, I go into the kitchen and start whipping up some meal I like whenever your father gets on my nerves.*
> *Daughter: "How is that a good idea when a man is about to slap my face? I need something more!"*

At the end, she has written a prayer to her Muse: *Oh Dear Spirit of Writing, help me create and develop something good for me and for the People. And thank you for this computer, so I don't have to worry about forgetting where I put the latest typed pages any more.*

She sighs and releases her neck by making yoga circles, dropping her head forward first. Then, trying to keep her eyes open, she shuts down the computer and covers it. "I've put something sacred into this machine," she mutters to Power. The encouragement from Agua, Pam and Smoke has been a charm against the trauma that could have left her undisciplined and scattered.

Except for the daily phone call to or from Agua, Power is about the only company she's had for many weeks, since the confrontation with her parents. In fact, since Labor Day she's been sick on and off, with the flu or a drippy nose. It's as if, after facing her fears of her family and releasing her tears with Agua, she felt drained. Her body could only work, driving or writing. No parties with friends. No dates. Though she and Agua talk on the phone every day, they haven't seen each other for ages. But today is her Advance Vacation Day and the writers' group women have agreed to perform part of her play. As she looks at what she's written and adds a few more words, she isn't thinking about her throat being sore, because she is filled with anticipation, at once excited and scared. How she loves the writers' group, where the sisters will hear her ideas, ideas brought up from her belly. They will perform her play! What will their feedback be? She saves the manuscript to a floppy disk and heads for the copy shop to have it printed.

Back home, she dresses with care, putting on a jacket made by a member of the writers' group nicknamed Curly. Now that it's time to go, her heart feels like a lump in her chest. Her neck aches to be massaged. She wants to be loved and cradled, but her family can't or won't do that. They have lost her. "I'm good," she insists to herself. "I'm loving and sweet and kind with my friends, 'cause most of the time they want to know the real me." She picks up her journal and lets her feelings roll out: *Oh God*, she writes. *Oh God, old family, please don't make me leave you. But I've already left . . .*

She tears the page from her notebook and puts it in her bag, along with the four copies of the manuscript she'd had printed, and heads out the door.

The air outside feels fresh, like Freddie Hubbard improvising on how to step to the iron horse, as she hurries to the subway that will take her to the place where the group is set to meet.

As the hostess for today's meeting, a brown-skinned woman with well-groomed braids all over her head, opens the door to her tiny apartment, with its luscious green walls and silver ceiling, Tania hears a woman's husky voice in the background. "Hey, the liberation theologians died confronting the rich folk's lies that 'poor folks are stupid.' They were gunned down while they were giving mass to those who question endless poverty." From the doorway, Tania sees the speaker is Smoke. She looks beautiful today, her sepia-toned skin clear.

"Hi,Tania." Smoke shifts her behind, which seems to have spread since Tania last saw her. Maybe she's been over-eating out of worry over the difficulties she's had trying to self-publish her first chap book of poems. Trying to distribute it on her own takes so much money from her small credit union account that these days she fears looking at the balance. If she'd charge a fee for her open poetry readings, she'd have some money to buy ads for the book in the *Amsterdam News*, but that feels uncomfortable, so she doesn't.

The conversation turns into a loud, spirited discussion of Ronald Reagan's trickle-down-from-the-rich-to-everyone-else crap, aka supply side economics.

Curly, a slender Jewish woman with a well-endowed bosom and frizzy hair, who has spent fair amount of time in Latin America, says, "Yeah and in the same breath so-called President RayGUN is telling lies about the Sandinistas, who are *really* Latin American resisters to oppression. Resisters who actually beat the US-owned dictator of Nicaragua."

Agua agrees. "You're right. He just says the Sandinistas are a totalitarian regime to justify paying the Contras to bring back Somoza's people."

Looking in the mirror, unbuttoning her jacket, Tania says, "It's all part of the same US fascist conspiracy. Keeping poor folks down and backing the Contras in Nicaragua and the military in El Salvador that murders Archbishop Romero during mass, I mean." She turns back to the hostess, whose nickname is Conductor, and who, like many of the others, wears African locks without any Dixie Pomade. She takes Tania's jacket and hangs it in the closet.

As Tania glances from face to face, she focuses on remembering the nicknames she and Agua have given each of the group's members so that what they say at meetings remains anonymous. Almost all the women, who attend these meetings regularly, are stretched out in various relaxed positions. However, one, called Newbie, who has come back to the group after some time through a reconnection with Smoke, a friend of a friend in her writing class, is sitting with her legs crossed at the ankles, and her back stiff. Not nearly as radical as the others, she has an almost pained expression on her face.

"Wow!" says Tania to all of them. "On the way over here I was just thinking about Archbishop Romero and other priests who minister for peace, and here you all were talking about the same thing."

"Yeah, we're becoming pretty international," Conductor replies. She motions towards a hassock that is set slightly apart. "The seat of honor," she says. "Can you take off your shoes?"

Tania throws off her sneakers and sits down. "So where are the folks here in Brooklyn who'll finally dare to realize they can stop accepting generations of the same ole some ole as their horrible 'birthright' and rise up like those peasants? Nowhere, that's where. Mostly they just like to watch Americaca TV, and do nothing about stuff. And that's the way this country likes it."

Conductor nods in agreement, then, shifting gears, asks, "You want me to stand in for you as director, Tania, and read the stage directions and the back-story so you don't have to?"

"Sure." Tania appreciates her idea. She wants to observe this sitting back. "It's a first for me to step away and hear my own work! And I guess the audience does need to hear the back-story, don't they? I haven't written it, but there probably does need to be a director on stage, at least for now."

Conductor nods and begins flipping through her copy of the script, scribbling in the "role."

Agua's butt, cute but sometimes smelly, lets out a "ppah." If she does this at home, her son shouts at her to stop and runs away holding his nose. But she knows he's just teasing. Her little farts don't normally stink and she's an upfront talker, so she merely says, "Excuse me," and, smiling, announces that she'll play the part of the daughter. As she moves toward the area under the sleeping loft, which has been cleared to make a small stage, Curly gets up to join her, saying, "I'll read Ma, the daughter's white mother, okay?"

Conductor laughs. "You're the only white person here today."

Tania nods.

Scooting over next to Agua, Curly scans the script, picking out the mother's lines. As a young girl, she had spoken out about the mistreatment of patients of color, mostly Black people, in the hospital her father owned, and her mother, who had come from Germany, had allowed him to lock his defiant daughter up at age eight for "psychiatric treatment." So she has long recognized something of her mother in Tania's, as Tania sees something of her own Jewish mother in Curly's. All the women in the group know each other's problems. One of the group's principles is complete honesty with one another. And each of them has first presented her work—in Curly's case, her fight-the-patriarchy poetry—in the safe place the group provides.

Now, with dramatic flair, Conductor sets the scene, reading from the script:

"The mother and the daughter are at the beach talking without really communicating. The daughter, who is in her mid-twenties, is dressed in regular street clothes. The mother, who's wearing huge sunglasses, is sunbathing. She ignores her daughter, who attempts to bridge the gap by reaching down and almost touching the mother's face."

To demonstrate the emotional need, Agua, tenderly playing the role of the daughter, attempts to touch Curly's slender arm. Having heard the mother/daughter disconnect that is coming during past, private read-throughs over the phone with Tania, she's already fallen deeply into her character.

Conductor continues reading:

"But the mother ignores her daughter, partly pretending, and partly never actually feeling the possibility of their connecting. Finally the daughter gives up trying to ask the mother to love her and moves a few feet away on the sand, to the squawking of seagulls. The mother sits straight up.

"Mother and daughter freeze as other performers representing these two generations of women come onstage to perform a dance of intense anguish.

"Dancers exit. Mother takes off her sunglasses, revealing her eyes, which are blank."

Curly actually looks older for a moment as she identifies with the character she's playing, listening to but not hearing her child.

Daughter [Agua]*: "You sat there for years and closed your eyes, not in meditation, but in blindness that you did to yourself, while my father ignored all of us girls. 'Chicks,' that's all we were, just unimportant girls, not males, not essential. He even ignored you and you let him."*

Mother [Curly]*: "My dear darling, I'm going to walk away if you attack me."*

Daughter: "I'm not attacking you. I m telling you why I can't effing trust anybody now. 'Cause I couldn't trust you. I wanted you to help me. You let him touch me. That hurt more than his beatings with the belt."

Mother: "You need to set some goals for yourself . . ."

Daughter (shouting): "WHAT GOALS?"

Mother: "Like I say to my friends in counseling . . ."

Daughter: "Women, I bet all of them . . . no men at this time gots the guts to go for emotional help like counseling."

Mother (her voice rising in pitch, becoming almost shrill): "Like . . . I want to finish! . . . Please don't interrupt. The counseling isn't going to help if these women keep recapitulating the past. . ."

Daughter (not backing down): "I WANT YOU TO HEAR ME . . . Please. Please . . . I have a boyfriend, let's say, and I can never really trust him. I check on him, I spy on him, look through his pants pockets for women's numbers. I won't believe in him. Then I'll get involved with another one and every Black man that I've chosen so far is the same."

Mother: "Maybe try a non-Black man?"

Daughter: "You didn't try one! NO! IT'S NOT whether his background is Jamaican or southern Black or whatever. It's that I am repeating my stuff with my father . . . and NOW I SEE WITH YOU! You didn't help me. My father wanted sons, not daughters."

Mother: "He taught you to travel to the Long Island Institute of American Dance by bus . . . don't you remember?"

Daughter: You're not listening . . . it's like your ears are closed! I want to have a safe friend in you but you are dangerous. I can't believe any female friend, except maybe my best friend, isn't gonna betray me and think some man is more important than our time when we plan to be together as friends. I distrust
females . . . don't believe they can feel my sadness. I'm so damn broken by having had you as a mom . . .

Director [Conductor]: *"The mother sends frozen glare toward daughter. The daughter continues speaking."*

Daughter (tearily): "What kind of an educated mom can't think? No, it's that you refuse to FEEL. It's like, in your opinion, it wasn't INTELLECTUAL *to express emotions. Your heart is in words and eyes that are cold, like the ones telling me I'm in trouble for asking you this now. I gotta get outta here."*

Director: "The daughter gets to her feet."

Mother (slowly, revealing her depression): "Where are you going?"

Daughter: "I m going home . . ."

Director: "The daughter, almost shouting and just about ready to run, looks her mother in the eye."

Daughter (firmly, with determination): "I 'm going home!"

Director: "The daughter doesn't mean going home to her house. She means she's going to a place inside herself where she no longer needs this mother of hers to validate her as worthwhile."

Agua, playing the daughter, turns her back and sits very still. None of the women can see her face, but the shaking of her body lets everyone know she's crying. To wipe her tears, she wraps her Palestinian scarf, representing years of women revolting, around her head.

> *Daughter (jumping up and screaming): "Ma, I'm taking care of me. I'm taking care of me. Don't need your approval. I got my own."*

> *Director: "The daughter moves away. Mother and daughter part without a hug or even a quick kiss on the cheek. As the daughter leaves her, the mother sits very still, almost in a stupor not only from the sun's rays but from refusing to take her daughter's rage seriously. The scene ends with the daughter facing the audience, crying tears of joy and release, and also moaning for what she had wanted but hadn't gotten—approval from her mother for being eccentric and her own person."*

Conductor yells with a big voice, "End," then turns to catch Tania's eyes.

Tania's eyebrows rise, surprised, as the spell is broken. She has been focused on the end of the read-through. Agua and Curly, and Conductor, too, had invested her lines with so much emotion that it was as if they had rehearsed their performance. She smiles and thinks, "These women may understand my story."

Now, however, Conductor says, "Why do you go on and on about this mother, Tania?"

"Huh?"

"I mean, that mother worked hard. It's not easy to raise children." She throws her hands up and looks for a joint. Finding one on a table, she lights up and puffs. She's the only one smoking, but no one wants to share the reefer anyway.

It's not hard to understand why, in some ways, Conductor identifies with the mother. She doesn't want to face her own feelings about why she chose to let her ex raise their kids. True, he owned the house and they were in a good school, and she is a costume designer who felt she had no space of her own. But since she moved to New York City to focus on advancing in the industry that pulls at her, she rarely sees them. Their baby pictures, in a photo array on the bookshelf, seem to stare at her accusingly.

Curly, who is in a relationship with a white Jewish man for the first time, and who wants to face the alcoholism in her family and her own tendency to slip sometimes and use marijuana, now confronts Conductor: "I wish you'd stop smoking in front of me."

"This is my goddamn joint and don't you tell me what to do."

The other sisters shift uncomfortably, but then Agua leads in cries of affirmation for the piece. All of them except Conductor hug Tania. Then they form a circle around her, patting her back and throwing their fists in the air, shouting "WHOOO!"

While she had joined the others in the hug, Newbie hangs back from this circle. Many of the long-standing members of the group have been talking, performing poems, and reading short stories about the disconnect in the mother/child relationship since the group began, and Tania expects that's why they seem to like her piece But it's shaken Newbie for sure, and she now sits leaning stiffly against the back of her chair, both feet gripping the floor.

Conductor's attitude and Newbie's withdrawal still intrude, but Agua wants to keep the flow moving. Though everyone usually talks in a jumble when they give their feedback after the presentation of a piece, she senses this time is different, and asks Conductor to facilitate the discussion: "Hey, will you ask us to go 'round and share our suggestions and anything that just doesn't work for us?"

"Is that cool with everyone?" Conductor asks. Still smoking, she touches the cap she'd put on to play the director. Everyone nods yes. She puts out the joint.

Having organized this, Agua slides away from the area designated the "stage." Conductor assigns her to go first, and Agua's smile is broad, the white pearls of her teeth sliding over her red tongue, as she pronounces each word separately, then runs them all together once she has proclaimed her hatred of this USA system. "I'm so glad you decided, yeah I am so-o effing happy, Tania, that you chose, even in this early draft, to let us see the truth. You're removing the veil and breaking out, girl, from the damn so-called 'halo' around mothers, especially mothers of color, for some Black and Brown nationalists." For a moment she pauses, overcome by bottled up sadness, having lived lots of years on welfare both with her moms and with her son. "I mean," she says, "this capitalist system is disgusting and hates poor women, keeps us down and denies our families jobs, training and reparations. It hates all us workers, but how does the meanness travel into our very hearts, so that we actually believe we don't deserve nothing? I'll tell you how. It's through the conditioning and heartlessness of those close to us, through our own mother's denial of self and of us every damn day and through our father's lifelong disconnection." Finally, she explodes, breathing so deep her breasts heave: "And it's all got to be faced, in the Latina family too, I can tell you that. *Thank you*, Tania!" She laughs and hugs her best buddy.

Jewish soul sister that she is, Curly, her hair now almost a bush, since she's been running her fingers nervously through it, picks up the theme. "Yes, thank you, Tania. Thank you for showing the whole damn family system is messed up! My almost-rich white family put me into an insane asylum when I was a kid for talking about my father screwing around. Finally one of us has found the guts to talk about how families imitate this corrupt imperialist economic and social system that doesn't care about humans, and doesn't want to deal with it all together." Her eyes well up with tears of relief.

"Why did you write that piece, Tania?" Newbie whispers. She's now seated near Curly, fidgeting. Her tight manner is a huge contrast to Agua's waving arms and raucous laugh. Tania still calls her Newbie, though she's no longer new, because of how uptight she acts. Her hair is straightened and long. When you look at her nose it seems like it was sliced off a Greek statue. She was married it seems, but she never talks about her husband anymore.

Looking at Newbie's sharp features, Tania replies gently, so as not to put her off. "I want others to talk about their family aches too, so I am exposing this one family as having lots of contradictions and trauma. That way, maybe other people will talk about their troubles too. I mean, neglect may seem less important than the abuse by parents who don't face their own criminal acts towards their children, but emotional abandonment has to um . . . I wanted to expose neglect." She focuses on Newbie's bangs, lying against her ginger complexion, then looks deeply into her scared eyes. This thin woman with the harshly angled face had said when she first came to the group that standing up for herself with her parents was still pretty difficult for her, even though she was in her thirties. Though they were usually not home or not willing to go see her in dance concerts or anything she did at school, because they never hit her she confused their absence with just being too tired.

"You go, Tania!" Agua pipes in again, delighted that someone in the group has challenged this fixation that people of color sometimes have about protecting the secrets in the family because they're not "supposed to air dirty laundry." "Tu familia tambien," Agua would say at the end of one of her and Tania's readings.

Tania thinks carefully before responding further to Newbie's question, but then risks saying more, shaking her head as she talks. "It was pretty scary when everyone in our so called nationalist/progressive community was revering the Black family as only a place that stood up against the lynch mobs and the white racists' name calling. It's true, yes, the family can be a sanctuary and the family has also sometimes taken on the damn power 'over you' dynamic, you know?" Her heart beats faster. The group has never really had an in-depth discussion of their individual feelings about family/society's put down of the female, and how this does exist inside communities of color. But knowing that most of these sisters are 99.5 FM WBAI peace and justice radio listeners who reject the status quo, Tania believes they'll understand her view. After all, hadn't Samori Marksman, the general manager, just came on air announcing changes at the station so as to include more women's programming?

Almost all sisters nod, giving Tania courage. She clears her throat and swallows. Her throat's still sore.

"I don't know how you all think, but I believe this is fundamental. The family was and is a refuge. But it also gave in and became like massa."

She glances at Agua, silently asking her to help out.

Agua waits a moment, but the other folks stay quiet, so she plows ahead. "Yeah and sometimes when there's no man right there in her house, a woman, like my moms, will go and get a boyfriend to come over and treat her and the kids like shit, just so she can say 'I got a man.' I mean, my stepfather didn't even help with the bills, but he looked so good. To other Latinas she'd show off her *hombre*, even though he didn't give up no money and was really taking more than a little cash from her!"

Now Smoke, gesturing with her "pointer," finger, the only one whose nail is colored, by red polish, and tossing her head so that her grand, coffee colored, African wood earrings, which match her skin, dance wildly, asserts in a loud, baritone, smoker's voice, "This is a counterpoint to the vague generalization about the family being okay without thinking about what the internal mechanisms of the family are. Our parents imitated the plantation overseers by cussing us out, or whippin' us, or just ignoring us—their own kids! If I hadn't gone through my own changes, where I rejected not just my family, but all the 'big daddy' shit, I might fuss and fight when hearing this. Tania, you know"—she strongly emphasizes the word *you*—"even the concept of the nuclear family is shaky. I just gave up the illusion that family, with just two parents or even just one, trying to do it all, can succeed in this rich white folk's system without the system taking its toll."

Tania, relieved, jumps back in. "Yeah, I guess I just gave up on the idea that two people can raise a child too. With all the contradictions of the parents' past, and all the horrors of crapitalism's insecurity, we need to conjure up something else to try to build a healthy foundation." Stunned, the sisters take in how the word Tania's used sums up the system that's stunted their lives. Even though they have running water and flushing toilets, it keeps them down.

They smile and slap five in agreement about the failings of nuclear families. They each have a single friend, or even a couple, whose child they watch or keep on weekends when the mother is too 'out of it,' or just needs a break. Conductor speaks for them all when she says, "Yeah, we know we gotta help out and we do!"

Picking lint off her pants, Agua jumps into the convo. "Tania, I thank you, and all of you, who have helped me so much with my son Heru, taking him to and from school when I couldn't, and coming through for me when my old family turned their back on me for not wanting to go along with 'you have to kiss some man's ass to be a good little wifey.' Really, not a damn thing is sure in this imperialist messed up place, is it? Women, and men, too, for that matter, can't ever be sure we have the right to a job, or even a shithole place to live. These bosses try to make us hate men, and if the men do have a job, the bosses pay them more than us, but we NEED a cooperative way. New ways . . . are just needed. That's why I am a socialist." She grins.

Newbie glares at her. It's terrifying for her to hear a woman of color talk so clearly and use the "S" word with pride. "Wait a minute, does that mean that we're going to give up on Black folks and just let white radicals lead us?" she asks.

"No of course not," Conductor says. Look at Cuba. Yes, folks there are still just coming out of the colonized mind, but Black Cubans are taking more and more leadership roles. And there are anti-racism groups of folks of color and white allies exposing that superiority shit right here, like the People's Institute for Undoing Racism that just started a little while ago in New Orleans, I think."

"Damn it, how'd we get off on this subject?" Smoke growls. "We gotta get back to the mom and dad thing." She coughs, using her fingers to cover her mouth. The others wait until she can speak again. "Besides," she goes on, "how will the family actually look under socialism, anyway? Have you ever wondered about that, wimmins? Don't you remember we started this group in the first place 'cause most men on the left can't deal with women in leadership roles or step back to support writers who are female? Things haven't changed much since Shirley Chisolm published *Unbought and Unbossed.* Her life story still ruffles some feathers, believe me." She shifts in her chair. With her wide hips, Smoke is more comfortable resting in furniture, unlike Tania and Agua, who feel safe when they can stretch out and slide around on the rug or the floor.

"But I still want to have a boyfriend," insists Newbie, stroking her ponytail.

Most of the women smile in agreement.

"Well, I do, too," says Tania. "Just because we don't want a patriarchy where daddy is always right doesn't mean we can't choose to have sex. But let's choose caring men!" She tosses a pink throw pillow in the air, just an inch or two, then clutches it between her knees when it comes down.

"Yeah." Agua chimes in. "And besides having the boyfriend, if we change this shit, at least like in Cuba, we would have the right to a job, free healthcare and a place to live, not like here where we have the right to be homeless, and the bosses are throwing masses of us out of work like in the 1930's."

My husband had sex . . . I mean I chose not to have sex . . ." Newbie's voice trails off. She doesn't know why she even brought him up.

"Why did you stop having sex?" Agua sits up and leans forward.

"Well, let me tell you a quick story. My husband and I were together for months and I found out after bumping into him on the street with his 'girlfriend' that he had a different view of marriage. When I finished crying and asked him what was going on, he looked me dead in the eye and explained that just because he was married didn't mean he had to stop dating. I couldn't believe he was that crazy. It's one thing to be secretive 'cause you know people are not into that . . ."

"You mean he thought it was an open marriage?" Agua asks, knowing this was the "in" thing with some white folks she was acquainted with.

"What's that?" Newbie looks like she's about to cry.

"Never mind, it's just something where married people agree it's okay to sleep with other folks. I guess for people who have a lot to share moneywise it doesn't feel sad to share your partner too."

"Hell!" Newbie raises her voice for the first time. "If he thought I agreed to anything like that when we got married he had another think coming!"

Tania beams. People seem to be finding their true voices after having heard her piece about her mother and her. "Damn," she thinks. "That makes it better. Lost Mama, who covered everything up and was complicit with Daddy, but it looks like my story can really make a difference for some other folks."

She checks out her loving supporters as they chat, eat and laugh, then studies the vibe and the angry face of Newbie, who's just asked why she even wrote it. Obviously not everyone gets it. Newbie's like Mommy, an avoider who's like all the countries that don't deal with the US blockade against Cuba or don't want to associate with this new case about the Black journalist Mumia Abu Jamal. Ignoring her question, Tania turns away from her closed-up self and glances up at Chairman Mao Tse-Tung's extremely small book, perched above their heads in a niche in the green wall she'd helped Conductor splash paint on. Like Tania's piece, Conductor's oasis has the feeling of a work in progress. She redecorates with a wall hanging from East Africa or a curtain of cowrie shells, or some other global treasure, every season. It was Conductor who initiated the idea of sharing the black and white Palestinian scarf with the sisters, informing them that the urban refugees in the Palestinian homeland had begun to wear it in the cities as a salute to their sisters and brothers in the rural areas who usually carried it.

Tania bows her head and murmurs, "I'll sing a praise song to Mao instead of getting into it with Newbie." No one hears her. As she hums softly, the ideas about how to transform the institution of the family seem to flow around the candles, bending the flames. Conductor has set on either side of the Little Red Book, turning the niche into a kind of altar. She notices that the book looks a little dusty, not having been read in at least a month.

As the formal discussion of the play ends, the women stand up, stretch, hit the bathroom, pour each other tall glasses of Dominican tamarind juice, gather in groups of two or three. Agua, for whom the play brought up a lot, and who often wants to break out of isolation as a single mom but finds revealing her views in a group, even of these women, a little challenging, moves over to sit beside Smoke and picks up on what she said about the conditioning the family as an institution beats into people. "But Smoke, we parents gots to take responsibility for making our mistakes. We're only human, not perfect! Still, I don't say only parents can take care of and do all the loving of a child. We do need help from the society." Smoke nods, reaching for another cigarette, and asks if Agua can envision what a new type of family homestead would look like in real life, describing the collectives she's seen in Cuba, where she's been several times over the past few years as a volunteer breaking the US blockade. While she talks, Agua imagines going to her well-kept apartment alone, without her sidekick, Tania, so she could learn more. When Tania's around, she and Smoke sometimes talk so deep, Agua's mind can only focus on Smoke's African earrings or pointing finger.

But now, as Smoke talks, Agua can just imagine it. A group of non-blood-related women and men could take over a "squat" in a New-York-City-owned vacant building. They'd fix it up and all have separate, cozy studio apartments with clean bathrooms where the plumbing worked. They'd share a first floor kitchen and living room, and Heru could have more people to tell his stories to or hang up his drawings with, not just her.

"Squatters," Smoke says, "should consider themselves a new style of Chosen Family, like those in Brazil's Landless Peasant Movement."

"Chosen family." Agua likes the sound of that. She scans the faces of the others, remembering with clarity how some sisters have expressed to her in private their sadness about the way the system kills in them any desire to mother a baby. They have noticed how single parenting has woven wrinkles on Agua's forehead. Thanks, Smoke," she says, and sits back up, noticing some of the sisters are putting on hats, preparing to leave. She feels the afternoon has been liberating, that each moment has drawn her nearer to clear thinking. In her heart, she holds Tania close.

A precious, excited buzz fills the tiny studio as the women giggle, working words into hugs and smiles goodbye as the evening light shifts to the sacred call of night's darkness. Curly is upset when the velvet black is destroyed by the streetlights' glare, which wastes electricity and says to no one in particular, "Why can't we get more people into environmental activism?" Listening to her comments about paying for water being more crapitalism, and about one day having to pay for air, Agua's enthusiasm for the idea of communal living fades as she worries it's impossible, and she becomes depressed. She slumps back on the couch and holds a pillow on top of her belly, patting it like a drum.

The women all turn to look as Smoke, pulling on her coat, pronounces a benediction on the day. "So," she says firmly, "do we recognize that women, supporting other sisters by listening and discussing, show politics in action?" Heads nod. It's a relief for these women to realize they can free themselves from feeling guilty that they aren't "doing enough for the community" because they're writing too much or exposing personal contradictions.

Newbie, however, is not enthusiastic. Suddenly she realizes she doesn't want to deal with these man-hating women anymore. "Huh!" she snorts. "I don't know if *I* agree with most of what you're saying, and I don't know if I'll ever be back." She heads for the door.

Conductor says calmly, "You know socialism just means not as much competing and going at each other's throats as America pushes." She smiles goodbye.

Newbie refuses to smile back and pulls the door shut behind her.

As Tania and Agua prepare to run to catch a dirty subway, they share big bear grabs with the others. "No more illusions!" shouts Agua, her short arms just about reaching around each sister's waist, feeling how the group gives each birthing artist support, sisterhood and strength. Together the women build a new intimacy, a community of whole people. But at the train station Tania wonders to Agua, "What will other folks of color, especially people still wanting to idealize their family, really think, if this performance piece ever gets produced?"

"Who cares? You go for it, girl, and get past your effing fear!" Agua exclaims.

One evening shortly after the writers' group meeting Tania encounters an old neighbor from Queens, whose light brown face framed by rigidly straightened hair she instantly recognizes, stepping onto her Third Avenue bus.

Since Manhattan's busy streets and crowds look very different from their old neighborhood, the woman at first doesn't recognize Tania. She screws up her face when she sees it's a gal operating the big bus and whines, "Can you lower the steps?" As Tania turns slightly towards her to oblige, she looks directly into Tania's face. "Oh, my god, is that you?" she exclaims, recognizing her former neighbor, and attempts to strike up a conversation, mentioning that she'd heard that Tania's older sister had made a career for herself and going on to sing her praises for the way she cared enough about people even as a girl to run for office in the student government in high school.

God! Tania feels her stomach tighten. She has avoided thinking about Older Sister since she'd phoned Tania after her visit to the summer house and told her she that she had no right to talk to their parents like that, and that if she didn't apologize to them at once, she'd never speak to her again. At the time she hadn't mentioned the phone call to Pam, but the encounter with her former neighbor makes her so anxious that she can barely force herself to go to work, in case she should encounter her again, and she asks the counselor if she can see her. As usual, Pam finds time for her.

"So what exactly did this passenger who used to be a neighbor trigger?" Pam asks after pouring the tea.

Tania's voice is strained. "Older Sister has disconnected from me, Pam . . . My own sister wants nothing to do with me. She told me I can't tell my own parents how I feel. When we were kids she used to slam the door in my face when . . ."

Pam nods. "Whenever what?"

Sighing, Tania, as usual, doesn't answer directly. "Well, I mean, I realize Older Sister was only a part of the problem. Younger Sister also just stood by, saying nothing in my defense as a kid. And they both protected my parents in one way or the other from having to see how they hurt all their children. They all avoided talking about anything."

"And you?"

"I learned to shut down my feelings too in that sick nukeliar family system. I don't even know exactly what they went through, but now I do know that any time a family won't talk about feelings the whole damn group is nauseating. I may have stuffed things down too when we were girls, but I wanted to face it in the present, and Older Sister just cut me off when I had the guts to mention our father was running around with other women. She always backs them up."

Tania looks off into the distance, through the bay windows. She remembers how the other two ganged up on her, twirling the braids on each side of her head.

"You're at a precipice, Tania. "Let it go."

"I used to pull my own hair as a little girl, Pam. I used to scream and run away from my stuck up sisters." Suddenly feeling uncomfortable in her clothes, Tania adjusts the collar of her cotton turtleneck.

Pam sits very still, erect in her chair, glasses perched on her nose, waiting as her client makes the connections.

Tania's mind drifts. She looks out the window, and replays that last phone call from her sister. "At the end of the day, my sisters have always been closer to each other, though I'm . . . the middle child."

Pam nods encouraging her to go on.

"And they were closer to my mother. The three of them used to act together, like they were all in on something. They shut me out."

"So you connect your Older Sister's betrayal with your mother's?" The inflection in Pam's voice creates the question.

"What?" Tania closes her lids to think, then raises her head and nods grimly. "You know what? Yes. My Older Sister didn't have a boyfriend like Buster, and she didn't want to listen when I tried to tell her about the way he hit me in my face. Just like Mom did."

"That neighbor gave you a gift," Pam says.

"Really?"

Pam leans forward. "Yes. Because you met her you're going to take some action—now you realize your whole family, not just your parents, never accepted the truth-bearer you really were and the artist you are."

At home, Tania sits on the floor a long time, re-reading the draft of her play. Then she starts to write. The words of the poem pour out.

To Older Sister/Younger Sister

A resister to the bang up gang up
You did on the life of me—your middle sister.
A resister to the bang up gang up
'Cause I wanted to be loved and liked and
Didn't know how to tell you all "I'm very angry."
Tired of being shut out of your exclusive club
Called "we are liked by all the adults in this here fami - Lie"
And You Buttercup/Tania are the crazy kid, you said.
The one who sits in a room and thinks,
instead of coming out to be a part of the party with cocktail napkins.
You sisters said, "Only those poor-ass neighbor kids from down the blistering block play with you, Tania.'
You made fun of me, a girl, going every Saturday to play ball with thos boys,
Who made stupid home runs with only invisible men on base, you said.
Different kids, different kinds
Different kids, different class minds.
The sisters were smarter and prettier than me
more popular with the good kids at school, the ones who mattered & married.
Got to be on the honor roll while Tania was on the dumb roll
got to get more and more into those people who didn't want to go on vacations
Or if they did, they couldn't,
'cause they didn't have no prestigious corporate jobs,
Or even "Pretend to help the people" jobs
What You The Sisters Think: You, Tania, are a goner
And we are happy you left.
Now we get to be on the rollercoaster ride toward a fame, a get-knownness, and a bliss of not having to face what the almost rich almost always miss.
What I Think is this:
Bloody sisters, the tripping out on illusions
Will come back to haunt House niggas, you will never be really accepted
and the rich white anglo saxon protestant will keep you smiling and doing
Ruining any of your connection with working folks lives
Til you've worked all your ties to lovingness right away from under your eyes.

Having written it, she reads it through, then crosses it all out with strong, mad pen strokes, the rows of XX's X-ing her blood sisters out the same way they shut her down, and for the rest of the month she stays furious, and calls her soul sisters in the writing group one after the other for support. They agree with Pam that it's time to do something. They say, you can't keep ducking them, Tania. You got to confront them the way you did your parents. Go face Older Sister at her office, they say. They urge her to take the poem with her if she needs to.

PART TWO

10 TEDDY

Tania arranges with Older Sister to meet, so she can "give her something." It is early when she reaches the office building her sister commutes to, and she stands for a while across the street, gazing up at the Art Deco façade. She takes her carry-out-of-the-house notebook from her bag, removes the computer-perfected copy of the poem she's tucked inside it, and reads it through. The honking of car horns disturbs her. As she reads, on the sidewalk around her people's feet rush by, the women's high heels clacking, taxpayers and workers always in a hurry.

When it is time, with the poem in her hand, she walks as if through molasses into the imposing lobby of the building. "Don't come up," Older Sister had said. "I'll come downstairs when the security guard calls up and meet you outside." So, after speaking with security, Tania waits outside, glancing down alternately at the poem in her hand and her sneakers. She mutters, "Older Sister doesn't deserve this poem I created. I'm keeping it." And tucking the paper back inside the notebook, she returns it to her bag. She thinks, "I'm glad I didn't have to go up to her snooty floor where secretaries would have held me at the front desk with phony, official smiles." Aloud she mumbles, "Uh-oh there she is . . ." as she spies her sister in a silk business suit striding with powerful, hungry steps toward her.

The drone of traffic on the avenue almost drowns out what Older Sister says. She doesn't start with a hello to Tania, but launches right in. "I want to talk about you and me."

Although Tania shivers with fear, she tries to remember what Pam said about taking action now with Older Sister. "So do I. But how can we? You haven't called me back in months and you don't visit where I am, but always want me to come to your turf, like today." After a tense pause, with Older Sister holding back, she attempts to soften her tone. "I'm trying to find someone to feel with me. You just sat there when I was a child, while Daddy raged at me, destroying my sense of me, making me feel like I didn't even belong in that family."

"Tania—" Older Sister interrupts, waving her hand, but Tania plows ahead. "You just took the honors and kept quiet, never sticking up for me or saying that them always making me the scapegoat was wrong."

"What are you talking about? That I was smart and studied? That I had time for books and wasn't always in the street? Studying all the time was lonesome. It meant giving up certain things. I was different from you because I had different interests, and so, of course, they favored me." Older Sister tosses her head.

"Yes," Tania says, "We were different, our family was different, but not only because we are Jewish and Black." The two sisters are talking past each other, and Tania tries to get back in sync. "But, hey, at least we learned to deal with those stares from others and stuck together sorta, remember? Can me and you do that now?" She thinks about the poem in her bag and wonders whether she should give it to Older Sister after all.

Older Sister glances at her watch, which is a Rolex, gold with a black face. "What I remember is staying home and studying instead of going to parties," she snaps. "I had friends, but I had to wait 'til college to have a boyfriend. I only got to be in the band, and I didn't go to the prom because I didn't have an escort. Nobody asked me. And I remember, Tania, that you were always playing." Again she checks her watch.

"Playing? Just playing?" Tania's voice rises now as she walks toward the side of the building, as if she wants to avoid being seen by anyone entering the place. "I was getting to know the working class kids in the neighborhood. You stayed stuck up and stuck in the house, never really wanting to know the people across the street, who you thought were beneath your brilliance."

"Oh you are so stuck on working class this and working class that." Older Sister adjusts her stockings under her skirt, then twists the gold ring she always wears around her finger.

"No, I'm stuck on believing in people who care about feelings. Do you have any feelings? Or is staying in the spotlight the way you run from your feelings? Don't you remember you had migraine headaches all the time?"

"So what! When I get a migraine now I take medication, which I wish they had had back then, so I could have avoided all that suffering." She looks up the block, wondering if she should run to the store on the corner to pick up some aspirin and make Tania walk with her, while they finish this talk.

"Well, you could try that low-salt Gerson diet." Tania stretches out her hand.

"No! That's your crazy way, with all those things some of us can't stand like yoga, and whatever."

"Well, but there was so much tension in that house. Don't you want to talk about why? Maybe that's part of the reason you got those fierce headaches. You rolled around on the couch crying. I think the neighbors knew things were going on, but just like now, no one wanted to talk about Daddy's other women and . . ." Tania eyes a cloud in the sky over her sister's shoulder.

Older Sister wags her finger accusingly. "Tania, don't go there," and Tania acquiesces, returning to the external political. "About the class thing . . . it's true members of any class can betray you. But especially members of our almost rich class, no matter how much they talk about workers' rights, who want to be gatekeepers for the rich, betray the working poor." She nods toward a custodian in a brown uniform sweeping up infinitesimal bits of litter. "People like him! And me, now that I'm a bus driver. You, as a member of that almost rich class, have certainly betrayed me . . ."

"How? How, Butter, has anyone in our family betrayed you? You just weren't up to the standards of the rest of us." Older Sister looks once more at her watch.

"Don't call me by that old nickname. I am Tania. . . But okay, I'll tell you how. By not feeling anything and staying aloof and shut down, that's how our family betrays reality. By not speaking up when someone else is unfairly treated. By letting me be your scapegoat when you were really angry at Daddy for being away so much. I was not responsible!"

"I did *not* blame you. You're insane."

"And besides, when he wasn't busy chasing women, the little bit of attention he did give us you hogged." Tania wishes Pam were here, so she could help them hear each other. "Why don't you want to work this out?" she asks.

Older Sister moves her hand up like a stop sign, as if she could stop Tania physically from talking, but says nothing.

Tania takes a long breath and tries again. "I believed in you all those years. You could analyze things. You even introduced the word socialism to me. But you don't treat people well."

"What are you talking about? You just can't bear the fact that I got to be the star and you're out of the picture."

"Isn't that how you always wanted it?" Tania blinks back tears.

Older Sister ignores this. "You talk about treating people well, Tania. But the fact is, you've been out of the picture ever since you carried on with Mommy and Daddy the way you did. That's really why I agreed to meet you today."

Tania stands very still, her legs glued at the thighs, frightened by the rage in her sister's voice.

"Tania, I'm warning you. Don't you dare go again to my—I mean our—house on the island, and mess it up with your crudeness."

Tania cuts in. "Why bring that up? Don't desert this conversation. We were talking about us. I . . ."

But Older Sister's harsh voice overrides her. "I'm telling you, don't bother those two old people again." She stops abruptly as a truck accelerates at the light, its engine roaring. When it passes, she dismisses Tania with two more words: "We're through!" Before Tania can say anything else, she turns her back, strides to the building's door, pushes it open and disappears.

Bus drivers bring radios to work that crackle because of weak antennas, and are told there is no money for new ones while the mayor of New York bends the ear of one on-air host after the other about how the city has closed the peep shows on 42nd Street. "But," the mayor adds in response to a question, "we still got to stop the hoodlums writing graffiti on the busses and trains."

Evenings lately, in the break room on the way to use the bathroom, Tania has been walking past a new man, Teddy, or sometimes just Turner, who's one of the regulars shooting pool. She's become fixated on him, admiring his bald head, his mahogany skin, so like her father's, and his sturdy build as he leans over the table to make a shot. Most of all she likes his infectious chuckling. He looks to be thirty something years old, not yet forty anyway.

This evening, in front of some fifteen guys, he wolf whistles at her. She wants his attention, but feels on the spot when they all look at her, and says, "Nah, nah. Don't do that, Turner!" Immediately he stops, and though he says nothing, his clear brown eyes, connecting to hers without glasses to hide them, let her know his soul feels sorry. Just the fact that he hadn't immediately come back at her with a crack like "Shut up, you whore," the way the others in a group would've done, tells her he's special. He looks upset, as if Tania has caught him doing something the "guys" have put him up to. For that split second his gaze seems to hold Tania's for a lifetime. He's shot through her defenses with an uncanny ability to pierce her isolation. His lonely eyes meet her lonesomeness in the cramped, no-window, swing room of the North Manhattan bus depot, and they walk deeply into history as if they had known each other before. No one else in the room notices. The spiritual awareness of the other bus operators hasn't developed to that level of awareness where you can just sense the birth of something new. They have no idea that the sound of the 5 and 6 balls and sometimes even the 8 ball knocking against one another is calling out into the stale bus-depot air Tania's and Teddy's connection.

She turns away now, but she will latch onto his soulful eyes later, many, many times. Teddy . . . Teddy, with a fine bald head and mustache. She can see that his arms are the kind that pull open stuck windows and lift heavy chairs. In that soul moment, she and Teddy Turner become lovers.

As a matter of fact, however, that evening she takes a few more steps and quickly enters the bathroom. Leaning over the stained porcelain sink, she peers into the dusty mirror and wipes her eyes. "I don't care that I made Teddy look small in front of other men," she mumbles to herself. "He attacked my right to be . . . just be . . . just come and go like all the fellas." She wishes the other bus-woman who works out of this depot was here to talk to, but she works mornings.

She winces as she hears a guy yell at her though the bathroom door, "I hope the heels fall offa your shoes!"

"Who you talkin' to?" Another male voice says, laughing, "The bitch?" The noise of the balls smacking each other and men joking keeps Teddy, who's concentrating on his shots, from hearing these comments.

Inside, it doesn't matter that, with the plasterboard door behind her, she is physically safe. The sounds of male roughness come through.

Within a few feet of her, but with that bathroom door between them, Teddy continues shooting pool. She can hear him calling his shots and then shouting ever more loudly in delight as each and every pocket he "calls" receives the ball in its velvet-lined hole. A good player, yes. But Tania knows intuitively he has the potential to be so much more, a leader like the Nat Turner who led the slave rebellion in the 1800s. She believes his chuckling shouts of pleasure as he plays—so different from the roars of fury or triumph shouts of the others— will "gentlify" the ugly male-ruled atmosphere of the depot.

Tania renames him in her mind, and later will tell him directly: "Teddy, your name for me is gonna be Teddy *Nat* Turner, 'cause like that Nat from the centuries past, you seem willing to stand up for something , unlike all the other men in this bus garage who don't think they have to be supportive towards a woman like me who has the guts to take this job and walk around this place without another female to see, much less talk to. Teddy Turner, you at least know you don't have the right to talk down to me like I'm a piece of junk!"

A hot day! Brooklyn's less congested streets stretch the heat wide and wider still, beating on the two lanes of traffic. Cars easily pass one another without stopping, since rush hour has yet to come. Tania remembers her past choices and tries to remove some negativity. But her life seems to go by as slowly as a flu sick day in January, with sneezes and sniffles. She still struggles to wipe away the misery left from her long-term rageaholic partner Buster and the others after him who were similarly—unavailable. But as she dreams of Teddy, she tosses their remnants away, sticking in the garbage tissues and the store tag of a silky red dress she'd bought to show off in front of the worst of them, a completely unavailable married guy she'd tried to begin a fresh sensual life with. He called himself Deacon, but she called him other names.

Once during her time with Deacon, she'd gone to therapy, and, unlike Agua with her married guy, had told Pam what she was doing. Out of that usually calm therapist's mouth had come some profane, no-nonsense advice: "Stop being a weak pussy and picking all these replaceable dicks!"

Tania had told Pam Deacon had had a difficult relationship with his dad, who was a functioning alcoholic who had worked in a factory during the war and got fired when it was over and the white guys came back. He'd gone along with the oppressor and like most such fathers with their sons had come out of the side of his neck on Deacon when he got home from the lousy job he was forced to take. She'd noted in her journal Pam's suggestion that she tell him to his face that the problem with his father was that, like most Negro men, he'd been unwilling to stand up to stand up to the messed up the system.

Sitting in the open window reading these instructions, which she'd never carried out, she recalls Deacon's short, compact frame and the great massages he gave her. But in truth Pam had only confirmed what she already knew: Deacon's dad hadn't been able to confront the System, and neither could Deacon. He didn't even have the courage to face up to his wife's demands for the things the System said should be hers, so he had no energy to put into a real relationship.

Looking out at the cars going by, she mumbles to herself, "They were hard . . . those truth-hearing sessions with Pam." She rereads more of her journal: *After I saw thru the wall of silence that he used (like his daddy did and my father did too), I stopped seeing him. The wall kept a part of me from ever feeling close to him. I hope I don't have walls.*

She mutters to the cat, "I'm glad I realized I was betraying women. I sure wish Agua would see what she's doing by being with a married guy," then turns the journal page to a blank white space and writes: *I see a man who's married and "safely" unavailable keeps Agua and me from ever facing our fears of getting truly close to a man. I for one won't do it again.* Smelling the air outdoors, she closes the journal's thin covers and lets the weightlessness of the summer day surround her and lighten her spirit.

She has to pick up her paycheck. Slinging her bag on her shoulder and dropping in her keys, she walks outside into the sweet 85-degree-not-burn-sneakers-through-the-pavement type of weather and looks up at the blue sky overhead, so vast in low-building Brooklyn compared to Manhattan's, with its skyscrapers blocking the sun.

She is waiting for the light to change at the corner of Dekalb Avenue when a car pulls up in front of her, blocking the crosswalk, and the young man driving leans out the passenger-side window. "Is that you, Butter—I mean Tania?" He shouts over the blaring radio, and she recognizes her very own first cousin, Gerald, her father's sister's son.

Tania nods, speechless with surprise. She hasn't seen her Aunt Tantie or Gerald since she left home when she was a girl. He hasn't changed much, though. He has the same dark cinnamon skin and still wears wire-rim glasses—they'd both looked older than their years as teenagers. His hair is still cropped short so the kinkiness doesn't show. He waves her closer. "It's good to see you," he says, smiling, and she smiles back, realizing he's still the gentle, appealing person he was as a boy, more like his father than his mother, who was an overbearing mama. He's wearing a button-down blue shirt and smells of Brute cologne.

"Where are you going?" he asks, opening the car door. "Can I drop you?"

"You can give me a lift to the subway," she says. "It's almost fourteen blocks from here." She seats herself in his hatchback.

But instead of dropping her at the subway station, when he learns she's heading to the bus depot in northern Manhattan, just a half-hour by car from Brooklyn on a day like today when the traffic is light, he offers to drive her there. "It'll give us time to catch up," he says. He seems completely accepting of the fact that she works as a bus driver, and she smiles to herself, realizing how different his attitude is from what she's sure her Aunt Tantie's must be.

When she was a girl, Tania had somehow found out that her Aunt Tantie had used the evil eye to try and hurt her niece, holding spirit meetings to make her be a "good quiet girl." She had never understood why, only that, whenever her family visited their Jamaican relatives, there was a tension between her father and his sister that underlay the family gatherings. "How *is* Aunt Tantie?" she asks.

The question seems to open the floodgates. "She's okay," Gerald says, "except she doesn't like my wife, who she tells to her face is a lousy cook and doesn't keep the house clean the way she should. To me she says, 'How could you marry a lazy woman who doesn't do her job?' Even worse, she thinks she's a bad influence on me, 'cause we let our son cry when he's hurt or sad and won't give him war toys to play with. She says he won't grow up to be a man. What am I supposed to do? If he was a girl it would be okay."

"Good for you, standing up to her. Are you teaching him how to cook too?"

Gerald laughs. "Sure. And run the vacuum. I wish you could meet my wife. You'd like her."

"Me, too. I wish we had more time to talk, but here we are, and I gotta go."

Gerald refuses Tania's offer of a few singles for the gas. "Nah," he says, laughing. "That's okay." The two cousins promise to keep in touch as she gets out of the car. As he drives off, she thinks how amazing the encounter was. She and her Brooklyn relatives—and especially her aunt Tantie—had never seen eye to ear about anything much, but Gerald was one of them she actually liked! It is only when his car disappears around the corner that she realizes she doesn't have his phone number or know where he and his family live.

But already her thoughts are elsewhere as she strides toward the bus depot to pick up her check . . . and, she hopes against hope, to meet up with Teddy again, especially since she's not wearing the bus-drivers' uniform, which is all he's ever seen her in. Instead, she's got on shorts, with brown sandals that show off her long legs and great olive-colored skin—not really olive, that's how white folks describe Italians, but light brown, like *café au lait*—which is complemented by her green cotton top. Her hair, brown and curly, is piled to the side and looks sexy. Since becoming a bus driver she has never worn much jewelry, and today she has one silver ring on her unpolished forefinger; unlike some other women who do "men's work," she's never sought the "protection" of a fake wedding band.

She feels at once joyous and a little nervous as she remembers how Teddy had whistled at her when he was playing pool. She also thinks how great it would be to have his hands gently touch her back. "Yeah, I need a steady man. Me and Teddy. It's gonna be us," she murmurs, heading into the depot.

She glances around to see if Teddy is hanging out among the other guys, in and out of uniform, leaning on walls, joking and trading pay-day stories. When she doesn't see him, she prepares to truck to the third floor to pick up her paycheck. After she's got it she'll just go to see whatever's playing at the upper Broadway alternative cinema that she's heard is showing a post-'59 Cuban series and return to the depot around eleven, when she thinks Teddy will be pulling his bus in for the night.

Then her heart jumps. "Oh spirits of the tarot!" she mutters to herself as she spots him in the crowd near the domino players. He's wearing street clothes, which means he is off. Like her, he must be there just to pick up his check.

Seeing video tapes in his hand, she rushes over to him and asks, "What have you rented?"

"I'm returning them." He grins flirtatiously and keeps his eyes locked on hers, seeming to see right into her.

Suddenly, as if some irresistible force has seized hold of her, she boldly reaches out and grabs the tapes, then darts away toward the stairway that leads to the payroll office.

"Hey, give me back my videos!" He lunges for her, then, laughing, races after her as she flies up the steps.

When both arrive at the top, she asks him breathlessly, "Do you want to go with me after we pick up our checks?"

"Where are you going?" He's smart enough to ask.

"To the movies." Her voice is smooth.

"Okay."

He tells her he'll get his car and meet her on the side street by the depot.

She pockets her check and follows him downstairs to wait. He's stopped in front of her before she realizes his "car" is a station wagon, a family man's vehicle. What is his status, she wonders? She doesn't dare ask until she's made sure he might like her. At the movie theater, she hangs her leg over his, but he stays still. She doesn't know quite what to think. On the one hand, he's definitely been flirting with her. On the other, he now seems reluctant to respond entirely as she expects, though he's also definitely not putting her off.

What she doesn't realize is that Teddy, too, is uncertain. He knows her rep at the depot is that she has never had sex with any of the bosses. After watching the movie she's chosen, a Cuban docudrama about women's issues, he also knows she thinks differently from the other women he's known. While he's responded to her invitations, as she's responded to his, he senses that she's not a one-night-stand kind of woman, or one for whom sex is the be-all and end-all of a relationship. He even wonders if she might prefer to talk tonight—to listen to what's really been bothering him for a long time.

His question is answered when she sits apart from him in the car, and as it pulls away from the curb, she asks, "So, are you attached?" in a tone that tells him she's finally voicing the worry that's been nagging at her. Instead of answering directly, he sighs. "I'd really like to tell you something. Can I?" He smiles. She nods. She finds his smile endearing, crooked teeth and all, though she wonders why he didn't get them fixed, since Transit provides dental coverage. Probably scared of dentists, she thinks. Like Buster, who'd been traumatized by being used as a guinea pig at a poorly run dental school. In silence they drive a few blocks west to a place where they can park, listen to the ball game on the radio, and watch the river.

"The truth is, I'm facing a bad situation," he says finally. "For the past year I've been living with the mother of my two-year-old daughter, just sharing bills. She hasn't been speaking to me since I insisted she marry me. She refuses to divorce the 'Rican she married back in P.R. 'cause he owns a house. The only person who talks to me when I'm there is my daughter. Even her other kids, the Puerto Rican ones, won't talk to me. She's trained 'em to hate me. She hates me." Far from his usual joking self, he's looking down at the steering wheel, and again, for a few minutes, there is silence except for the unceasing blah blah blah of the ballgame announcer.

Hearing what he's just said with her eyes and her heart as well as her ears, Tania recognizes that this man has some integrity and she respects that. The fact that he's opened himself up to her, made himself vulnerable, instead of shutting down or distancing himself, brings her closer to him as a human being. For a moment she even thinks she should give him Pam's number. But what he's said has also put an end to her dreams. As he drives her to the subway, she feels her stomach sinking even as her heart still races with desire. By his own forthright admission, he is unavailable to the Tania, who has vowed never again to be with a man involved with someone else. Aloud she says, “Well, we can still be friends,” as much to herself as to him.

On the train, she opens her journal to read her latest affirmation: *I am glad to be a woman in the slums, reading Marxist books. Just now, Eisenstein’s Capitalist Patriarchy and the Case for Socialist Feminism.*

But just now the book doesn’t seem very affirming. While it may have given her some perspective, and the theories in it explain a lot, she needs concrete emotional sustenance. She chews her pen. Why, damn it, hadn’t she thought to find out if he was available before she got so enchanted? The truth was she expected that men who looked at her “in that way” would be single. In her thirties, she still really had no idea about healthy dating or the importance of finding out what was what at the outset. Her mother hadn’t “schooled” her to ask the important questions. Daddy hadn’t been any help either. He’d never once sat down and said, “Let me tell you how the males who go along with the system and see women as meat, Blacks as dirt and workers as nothing will treat you.” Not that her father would ever have broached the subject. Or Older Sister, either. The whole business was taboo in that family, though she had yearned for education of the dating kind. Even today she longs for a book to read with tips about how to build long-term relationships.

So until tonight she hadn’t dared to risk her self-esteem by asking questions. Still, she thinks, this is progress. Before she would have found out a guy was married or partnered up only after she’d already involved herself with him. But it had been progress at a price. She literally aches for Teddy, aches for him all the more because, unlike almost all the men she’s known, he hadn’t lied, hadn’t tried to take advantage. She aches for him, and she can’t have him. “We can still be friends,” she says again, to console herself. But her heart is still breaking.

And the two of them do become friends. Many days he’s there on the corner when she’s waiting to make her relief, and she lets him stand closer to her than any of her other co-workers, who basically shun or taunt her. Their routine is, he says, “I found you!” and she smiles. She complains about having to make a relief on one of the miles-long Avenue lines, which means she has to take over from the previous driver at the uptown end of a line that’s packed with passengers most of the time. “I hate this heavy shit,” she moans. “You can’t get a bathroom break downtown ’cause they only give you three minutes, you know?”

It’s not really a question, but Teddy comments, “Well it’s a job.”

“I know. But we get so stressed we could kill somebody out there and management don’t give a damn. We have to drive any day in any kind of weather, and when it rains it's slick and the public doesn't know the bastards give us bald-ass tires and bad brakes. And you get no help when you're told by the dispatcher to dump your uptown passengers and go back to white downtown to supposedly keep the schedule. The uptown folks are stranded 'cause the uptown so-called schedule has the longest waits between buses.

"Yeah, you can see that from the time points we have to make."

Another day he starts. "The public asks so many questions," Teddy says.

"Well, they do. But you don't seem to mind that much. And you're really caring with old people. When I relieved you last week, you gave that old man your arm as he and you got off the bus. But me, I get tired of white folks asking the same old question, especially those folks downtown." She mimics their phony politeness: "When will we make it through this traffic, sir, er, ma'am?"

"You're right. "It's like once you drive into their neighborhood below Ninety-Sixth Street, they have to ask, 'Can you tell that guy to pick up his packages and give me a seat?' 'Can't you hurry up?' It's like downtown folks don't even try to figure stuff out for themselves. And they're always asking you stuff while you're looking in the left mirror or changing lanes, and it's snowing outside." Teddy leans an elbow on her shoulder.

"Yeah, or when you have ten cabs all around trying to jut in front of you and a baby screaming in the seat right behind you, while the rain pours down and the bus management's put you in has windshield wipers that smear in the middle of the glass just where your eyes need to focus."

"Let's talk "bout something else, you're about to drive. I'll holler at you later on the phone."

"Okay."

It's not what Tania's used to. Sitting and adjusting her mirrors to begin her second half of the shift she feels horny and fantasizes about him leaving his baby's mom when, like he says, he can find a place in this tight city housing market. But no sex now for sure!

* * *

Tania isn't the only one fantasizing. Whenever Teddy thinks of her long shapely back he feels a tumbling in his belly. Whoops, it turns over. By summer's end, he has moved into the downstairs apartment of the building where his mother has lived with his aunt ever since she left his dad after he tried to throw her down the steps and threatened to shoot her with the BB gun he kept around for the rats.

Since he moved he and Tania have been tongue-kissing in the car. Now he plans to find Tania's bus on her route and follow her to the end. There's a smell of after-shave in his bathroom, 'cause he forgot to put its top back on, and he peers in the mirror at his overnight stubble. "Maybe I'll just do a quick shave so she can see my skin." He talks to himself the way Tania talks to her cat. "After a shave, it'll feel smooth to her fingertips, like Barry White's bass voice."

With a quick pull, he opens his medicine chest, takes out a disposable razor. Check. Yeah, he hears how her fingers could gently stroke his neck. He lifts and shakes the red and white can of shaving cream. Foam shoots onto his salivating skin. "Careful, bud. Careful, man," he says. "She's delicate, even though she drives those buggies, whipping through crazy four-lane traffic." Drawing more shaving cream off as he strokes down, the razor makes a soft sound, like wind. Carefully he trims his moustache, clearing a short path on the ends above his lip. Lips are made for talking, which Teddy doesn't do too much, except like now, to himself. A dash of musk oil placed behind his ears marks him as Tania's listener tonight. He finishes up, checks his hair, and heads out the door. Her shift ends soon, and he doesn't want to be late. He laughs out loud as he feels something like pin pricks on his chest. He sings, making a silly rhyme to calm his jitters. "With surprise she'll grin, when you find her driving, and you'll win!"

His plan is to offer Tania a lift. She'll be his Brooklyn-bound passenger and he'll drive her home.

* * *

Tania does a double take when she sees Teddy's car in the rear view mirror of her bus as she's completing her shift. She strains to make sure it's him, and when he pulls over beside her bus, smiling, she thinks, we finally gonna let it happen. For days she's been looking at her mountain of fear about what he will think of her when he sees her, not as a co-worker, one of the guys, but in her everyday clothes. She has tried getting past it by shedding her bus uniform and changing into overalls on weekends. And evenings, when she finishes work and climbs upstairs into "never-never land," also known as her apartment, she disrobes, looks at herself in the mirror and wonders how he will react to her panties, which are cotton and cute, not thongs, clear evidence of her disinterest in showing off the crack of her butt.

Now, on this night, after she's turned her bus in at the depot, Teddy gives her a ride home, parks and they walk to her place, their shoulders touching as he puts his arm around her.

"Hey, want to get some stout? It has Vitamin B," Tania says, smiling up into his eyes.

"Sure, I could get us some."

"Oh no, that's all right, "she says, having proved to herself that he's not cheap. "I've got some at home."

Almost every tree on the long Brooklyn block smiles at their shoulders and shoes. Harmonizing his step with hers, Teddy quickens his pace. The heavy

wooden door shuts behind them as they go up the stairs to her second-floor apartment. Tania wanted a Guinness to loosen up. Later she can do the kissing thing, even the tongue kissing. Tonight, she feels like taking it all off and letting it all in. But the beer will soothe and smooth the entrance, not a physical but spiritual one. His eyes feel this as she says,
"the beer's in the fridge. Feel free to get one and would ya get one for me?"

He wonders how he can tell her with his touch that she means too much for him to forget her quickly or ever. Maybe, he shouldn't even try to touch her? But damn, they have so many calm conversations—not at like it was with his daughter's mother, who fought first and then sometimes wanted sex. With Tania, his mind jumps into air balloons like a baby elephant riding for months inside his mama's belly, first developing the trunk so he can breathe. Later, after he's born, it acts like a snorkel to keep him afloat when he swims.

Once Tania told Teddy that Heru cracked a joke when he saw his photo. He said that Teddy looked like a tomato with legs. But the way she said it, with a soft smile, not holding back but biting her tongue before anything real cruel came up, was completely different from his baby's mom, too.

"Hey Tania , you want some of mine?" Teddy shouts from the kitchen where he has started to crack open the beer.

"Yeah, I'll have a sip of yours." Her shouted reply makes it into a song in her head, and an old "tape" going: "Yeah, yeah, I'll just take some for a little buzz, and then he can get close to me. It's not like I have to have the alcohol." Aloud she says, "It's nice to have a little beer to relax."

Smiles, hiccups, giggles blend together in a blanket that warms their hearts. Bonding had begun in their rough, dirty workplace, not in a designer stage-set like on TV.

Tonight their lives become their artist's studio. He convinces her to let his brush paint on her skin and inside her thighs. She convinces him that her canvas will take red and green and lots of his brown stokes. She can't let him fall down as he penetrates. Instead her hips hold him up high, and he feels he has become a plane and flies into air, far from where all the bosses, busses, bravado men, passengers keep crowding him . . . far from his baby's mother. Even his drinking dad, still driving his Buick after slugging ten beers, can't get near Teddy now, and as he flies inside and alongside Tania, he forces back into hiding his mama's shrill whistle of a voice, demanding that he be a good son and ride her to church.

Snuggling afterwards under the covers, naked bodies with his heavy leg stretched over her thigh, she murmurs, "I found someone to care, I found someone to care about me. Teddy . . . you scare me 'cause you care."

But then she starts to itch on her breast and in the hair above her vagina. She rolls away from him to scratch.

He notices and mumbles, “Maybe you’re allergic to me?”
Laughing, she rises and walks to the bathroom door. “I’ll be right back, let me check in the mirror and the light.”
He rolls the sheet over for her to climb in next to him again, then waits for her to return from the windowless bathroom, where she’s flicked on the light.
“No no, it’s something else,” she shouts back. His comment has burned a whole lot of fear in her. She doesn’t want to lose him. But as she stares in the simple mirror at the hives on her bosom, her eyes widen. “Oh no,” she whispers. She watches the red circles grow.

11 WORK BRINGS UP OLD ISSUES

One day on her way to work Tania unfolds and reads again a month-old clipping from the Island newspaper someone sent her. It is an article about Older Sister’s wedding, which she had not known about and to which she hadn’t been invited. Holding the thin paper now, she remembers how she and Younger Sister, when they were girls, would talk and joke about who they were all going to marry, especially Older Sister. There was no feminist/womanist moment when they discussed single motherhood or singledom or just living with a guy. Tania was sure Older Sister would hook up with some man with glasses ’cause she dressed in such a bookish way, and she and Younger Sister would roar with laughter, since the only guys who wore glasses were nerds.
As an elementary school kid, Tania loved her bike more than reading. Its indigo color reminded her of bluebirds, and on it she would speed away from that bookish tattler, Older Sister. “I saw you smoking and I’m gonna tell,” Older Sister would say. But when she did tell, Tania would be ready. “Why does she have to tattle?” She would complain, knowing Mother would avoid getting involved. “Work it out yourselves, girls,” Mother would say. For all of them it was most important that Father not find out. Older Sister would never tattle to Father. If Mother didn’t want to be bothered, Father was a remote and angry person, a bear everyone avoided making mad. Everyone also avoided talking about anything that was real, like why Tania was smoking.
Who in that closed-mouth society, it occurred to her now, would have listened if Tania had told the truth about her father. Or her mother’s complicity.
Now riding along with the other commuters on the subway, Tania lingers in her memories, staring out the window at the graffiti on the tunnel walls.
Older Sister had paid no attention to Tania as a baby. She’d been queen, and now this peasant baby had come to share the limelight that her parents had shined only on her. Still, it was lucky for her that Tania was a girl. If the new

arrival had had a penis, nothing she did could have kept the spotlight from shining on him. But Tania had only a vagina, so Older Sister was able to make sure that the light still shone mostly on her once baby sister was out of diapers, and that, if Tania was caught in it at all it was for "bad behavior."

The pattern hasn't changed. Leaving the subway, Tania reflects on what passed between them the last time they met—Older Sister's complete refusal to see her point of view, her failure to mention anything about her wedding plans—and mutters to herself, "So Older Sister got her wedding thirty years later and I got to work. I wasn't even invited." Outside, she leans against the railing of the subway station. . "We're not sisters," she thinks. "We're not even friends." Their class differences show in the way they speak, who they befriend, what they believe in, who they share power with, and not least in the way they dress. "Maybe they thought I'd wear my bus-driver's uniform to the reception and spoil the effect of all the clever Hawaiian decorations described in the article."

Later, well into her eleven-hour shift, while sitting at a red light, she takes out and then pockets the newspaper announcement. Her eyes drift to her next stop, just down the street. Boy, she thinks, these Midtown passengers are rude. She watches them shove each other, jockeying to be positioned near where they expect the door to open. The bus engine idles loudly.

Since no one has rung the bell to get off at 32nd Street, and there is no-one waiting at the stop—the crowd from Macy's jammed onto the bus at 34th—she decides to pull into the left lane to get passed a double-parked van and to make up some time. Her forehead wrinkled with concentration, she glances into the left mirror, then slowly, but with assurance once she spies an opening, inches into the rush-hour traffic. She's definitely moving now, no longer creeping along. Suddenly a woman passenger announces she "wants off" at 32nd street. The bus, still in the left lane, is approaching the stop. Passengers are piled up in the front of the bus, well ahead of the white line that means, "Standing behind this line is safe; cross it and you're on your own in case of a sudden stop." Letting the woman off will mean just such a short stop. She keeps the bus moving.

Suddenly she feels the woman's hot hand on her shoulder. Damn! The woman touched her! Immediately Tania brakes. In her mind, she screams, "I gotta stop this bus. I don't know what's coming next." She focuses on the street, keeping an eye on the cabs, as the bus swerves between lanes and roars to a short stop. People lurch forward. Those in front almost hit the windshield. Oblivious, the woman shouts! "Hey, I wanted to get off back there at 32nd Street!"

Tania turns to look at her, sighs, and calms herself enough to spit out, "Well you missed your stop. You'll have a chance to get out at the next one."

But the woman, who is fashionably dressed and white, points to the door and demands that Tania open it now. When Tania refuses and sets the bus in motion again, the woman shouts,"What's your badge number? I'm going to report you!"

A younger woman with red hair who is standing next to the irate passenger, and who has a working class feel to her, overhears. Tania recognizes her as a regular passenger, who rides Monday through Friday on her way home from work. Her presence is reassuring.

"Will anyone give me their name and number as witnesses to her grabbing my right shoulder?" Tania addresses the whole busload of passengers, especially the standees who've been thrown forward by the sudden stop. "You can give it to me when you get off."

"With pleasure!" the redhead hollers. She whips open her pocketbook, pulls out a small secretary's dictation pad, and tears out a page. On it she writes her name, address, and phone number.

People murmur, "She had some nerve, touching the driver! She must be 'off.'" "I mean, what is she thinking?"

"She isn't thinking," says a man, staring straight at the woman.

At the next stop, all watch as the woman steps off the bus and breathe a collective sigh relief. "Hopefully we'll make it to the end of the line without some other quote-un-quote incident," the redhead says. Tania smiles gratefully.

Every weekday, tempers flare on this rush hour line. The run starts at Manhattan's uptown garage at 4p.m. heading downtown, which means first trips feel like hell as the bus fights the tumultuous midtown traffic. But today had been the worst. Usually all the folks crammed into the bus just wanted to get to where they're going safely. They know touching the driver isn't a good idea.

After leaving her bus at the depot that night about 1:00 a.m, Tania trudges toward the subway. "Thank God, on my way to Brooksland at last," she mutters. Prepping herself to take the long ride home, she thinks again about Older Sister, a member of the same class as that woman, so individualistic, in such a hurry they trample on others.

She stops at the corner phone and calls Teddy. "You know, Teddy, I just learned that Older Sister got married a few weeks ago, in a fancy ceremony."

"Let's talk later, baby," he groans. "I gotta wake up in a couple of hours."

"Oh wow. I really need to talk, so when can it be?"

"I don't want to plan anything now."

"Do you even care?"

"Of course I do. I just can't make plans when I'm half asleep. I'll call you."

"Okay, I guess." She hangs up the phone. As she heads down the subway steps, she stares at the ties of her shoes, which end with ragged thin threads because the plastic fell off the tips. "Older sister loves showy shoes," she thinks.

"Bet she wore white heels or maybe silver with elegant buckles for her big day." Tania imagines the shoes, which were not described in the article.

Older Sister, through her marriage, has now tied their almost rich family to some other privileged family. Daddy has to be impressed. Mommy doesn't count as much. Tania imagines the cousins and Younger Sister laughing about the one who wasn't invited, the one they knew would never be back "in place" as a good girl in the eyes of the parents. In the past, Tania would have suffered mental weariness playing one-up-man-ship games, trying to outwit the next cousin, the next sister. "Ah, I'm relieved now of *that* pain, anyway," she mutters.

But how contradictory they were, her parents and Older Sister. Slumping on the train's bench, she remembers the political discussions they used to have, sitting around the long dining-room table. It was those discussions that had helped her think that workers could strike or go out and help make changes, instead of waiting for some politician to "Do something to help the people." When Older Sister used to speak about these things, even her parents nodded, admiring her logic, perhaps recognizing ideas they themselves once believed in passionately. But did they *feel*? Did ever it cross Older Sister's heart or Daddy's gut, for that matter, that the "looking downness" they inflicted on the brown-skinned child, Tania, was the same as the way they truly regarded poor Blacks?

Tania looks up and watches a homeless man walk from a two-seater at one end of the car to the two-seater at the other. His toes are showing where his shoes have split. He isn't wearing socks. "What this capitalist society does to people!" She takes out her dog-eared journal and writes, though the swaying of the train makes the letters curl erratically.

> *This wedding of my sister's prompts a lot of reflection on how angry I still am. This system robbed my mother, my father and my sisters of the ability to be caring. Every day going to these insane workplaces, where we aren't the people we really are, then coming home trying to be kind, feels impossible if we don't ever talk about how work robs us of our dignity, our ability to be gentle! I hate the bus sometimes. It even makes me uncaring at times, closing the door when I see someone's running for the bus 'cause I know the effing location chief will blame me if I'm late. It's crazy making. But I gotta continue this job for now. I gotta pay the bills. But I don't know how long I can do it, and this system don't guarantee a thing if something goes wrong like the Cubans do. I just hope they can hold on. I've got to talk to Teddy and Agua about this.*

She glances up as the train exits the tunnel and starts to rattle over the Manhattan Bridge to Brooklyn. Her handwriting gets worse. She herself can't even read it, but she goes on writing.

Los Cubanos fought those bastards and Domino Sugar ain't taking the lives of industrial workers over there at the same rate as they are here, 'cause they kicked those thieving corporations out.

I want socialism with free healthcare and free housing like they got there (once you've lived in a building more than a few years). I mean, landlords truly rake in money here in this amerrycaca. And these rich bastards stole money from the enslaved Africans who built their mansions and factories.

Yeah, the old family went along with this system, thinking "Oh, well, can we really change it?" But the big contradiction is Daddy didn't talk aloud about his own frustrations! I even tried to ask. He definitely wanted to cover up what he did because of his frustration.

No, Older Sister, Mommy and Daddy didn't "feel." Once I became a bus driver, my rating in my family went way down, despite the money I was making. Lower than when I was working as a "theater person" for free—though then they said "What kind of living can you make at that?" If they spoke to me at all. Still, I hoped for paid theater work until I realized getting it depended on operating according to the jungle mentality of having to sleep with agents, or "smooze"" with producers.. That made it repulsive to me, and I left "the professional world" then, though continuing with womanist art.

But like Pam says, making that choice put me on the road to stop being a victim, and I've just got to stop pretending I'll ever have a family supportive of my independent choices. Instead I've got friends. It's hard, though. Bus drivers with my "low seniority" have to drive the partygoers on Independence Day-July 4th, Labor Day, Thanksgiving, whatever, to their places of "fun" and don't get to walk off the bus at the "Great Sailing Ships" display on the Hudson River, or at 145th Street to go to the New Year's Eve party with the dancers. Which means I've got to fight to create friendship time some damn way when off from work, and it's draining and damn lonely to still be doing this after so many years—catching a little time with other shift worker friends after 9:00 p.m. on a Monday, just before my regular midweek regular day off, or spending a few hours with Agua when she's off on a Monday because it's a holiday, which is like three or four times a year. At least I'm not discussing shift work around some living room coffee table, with a pile of cheese and crackers in my lap on a napkin. I am in another class now. But time after time I still have to face my class background, as my identification transforms. Hard!

Over the barely functioning loudspeaker, the train conductor announces the next stop, her stop. She stuffs the pen in her pocket. "Watch the closing doors," he says as she steps off the train. Upstairs, the streets are almost deserted. It's 2 a.m. Only two cars pass as she hikes the long blocks, stomping in the heavy brogans that are unofficially as much a part of the bus driver's uniform as the pants. The shoes make her think again of the wedding. Older Sister got married and let the newspapers know, but left her out. Older Sister's class identification is with the rich, Tania's with the drivers. She remembers a quote from a fellow poet: "a sister not defined by her presence or absence but her actions instead hurts sometimes."

Suddenly, her eyes blurring, she remembers something else, something she hasn't thought of for a long time. When she was a little girl, she had loved Older Sister, who used to make bagels for her and Younger Sister in the morning while their mother got ready for work and they were still asleep. Then she'd wake them up to have breakfast before going to school. But those innocent days are gone! The gulf is a class gulf, and the tears of Tania the workingwoman dry up as she remembers the beginning of Older Sister's "career" as an assistant to some judge. Way back then, she'd complained to Tania that it was "too much" to have poor people coming before her every day, up on petty charges of stealing bread. She was "tired of it." Tania hadn't said anything but had wondered what it must be like to live a life like that, without enough cash to buy bread.

She tries to pinpoint when Older Sister became a phantom of caring. Maybe in her junior high days, before she started running for school office, she had still been a "caring" sister. Maybe before her escape into "being known" in order to escape her own pain at living in a family where emotions were shameful things kept hidden inside, she had wanted to like Tania. Maybe a part of her did have feelings. But sometime during their teen or early adult years her passage into the system—"you are making it as a lawyer"—disconnected the tie between them. So why does not being invited to the wedding hurt so much?

She unlocks the two locks on her apartment door, unties and kicks off the rugged shoes, and heads for the kitchen to brew some chamomile tea. Her mind is too revved up for sleep. She remembers watching Older Sister on the black telephone in the foyer, rubbing the first finger of her left hand against her thumb as if her nerves were on fire. What could've worried her so much? Could it have been the racism of the country under John F. Kennedy? Could it have been the Barbie doll sexism and limits on women's lives that Jackie Kennedy showed us? Could it have been father's fury at his life being stolen from him as he struggled to shift into a salesman's job, selling junk for the liars after being a union representative and being able to sort of stand up once in awhile, before the racist big-union heads got rid of Black left representatives? Could it even have been his self-hating touch? Had he done it to Older Sister first?

She sits with her mug of tea in the window seat, waiting now for Teddy to call when he gets up at 4:30 a.m. for his 6 to 2 shift. The apartment is a mess. She likes it that way, especially when Teddy is coming over and they meet in the soft dark space of her bedroom. Love starts in the front room with the beers they still usually drink, since transit would fire them if they were caught with reefer in their system. Maybe they can really hang together this week. She needs to be with him, after everything that's happened with her old family. But they'll have to plan for it. Because of the mismatch in their schedules, the time they spend with each other in his apartment or hers is rare and special. More often, they snatch a precious hour or so together whenever one or the other or both of them have driven to work. They meet in the garage on the top floor of the depot where the workers park their cars, in the interval between when he gets off his early shift at 2 and she starts her late one at 4.

It's 4 am and her mind is still racing, but now, thinking of how her and Teddy's schedules build tension between them, it's the depot that occupies her thoughts. That it's known as a "good location/easy runs" depot is a clue to the condition of the others, because it's a waking nightmare. Huge vehicles go out from it into Harlem, carrying live freight. No one seems to know the many names of the stuff used to clean these vehicles. They're certainly not posted for passengers or drivers. There's no sign saying: "Danger!" with a skull and crossed bones like there ought to be. Nothing that says, "Hey suckers, whether you know it or not, you're all being poisoned." They leach into the skin, passing easily through the blue polyester jackets and matching pants. Bus drivers breathe their last breath without knowing what smell murdered them. Once, Tania went to a naturopath holistic doctor. That integrative medical healer gave her acupuncture treatments and told her to leave her job. "You're too sensitive. You maybe pick up not only chemicals but also every damn vibration from the four hundred men you work with, the thousand passengers you see during the course of a shift and of course dirt, soot and smog."

Smog lies over New York City, a sweet candy smell. It becomes part of you as a New Yorker. Only when city folks flee to the countryside or to Cuba, far from greed's shores, do they realize the air is different in other places.

She's still sitting by the window as the pre-dawn traffic starts to pick up on the street below. Teddy does not call. She isn't surprised. Many times Teddy uses the phone to avoid. She'll be expecting him to call, waiting by the phone, grabbing for it before the third ring. "Hey, Teddy," she'll say into her screening machine. "Hold on, let me turn off the machine." But instead of responding, he'll start right in with "I'm calling you because I . . ." His deep voice climbs into her heart. And when she disconnects the machine, moving as fast as she can to press the stop button, he's gone. Whatever he intended to say, he had hoped he would miss her and could just leave a message, though they sometimes do talk more intimately over the phone than when they are together. But either way, he often can't seem to get the words out. Pam has explained that even caring men have trouble sharing their deepest feelings and thoughts. Women share these things with their friends because they're socialized to. Men are socialized to stuff it and be a man, to fix things, not to just listen. But however logical the explanation is, Tania feels Teddy's reticence as a rejection of her.

What she doesn't realize is that, much as he loves her, he is put off by her demand for a closeness that is, he senses, false. She doesn't really let him into her heart. When he calls her number, often his heart sinks when she answers, because he had hoped he would miss her and had wanted just to leave a message, to apologize for a recent quarrel, to suggest that they go to a ball game. He wishes he could relax and be with her, too, but it seems that he can't. There are ways of relaxing. With women it seems relaxing is all about talking, and sometimes they let you touch their softness. With men, well, the game on TV and the relaxation are free and easy. Those players just run around and make those fantastic shots. Yeah, men can be graceful. And then the other thing is the men on the basketball courts or the ball fields don't talk back, at least not to him. They strut in their uniforms and maybe beat up on the other player or mouth off at the ref or umpire, which is just what he wishes he could do after a long work day, spewing forth the cuss words that he would have liked to say to the irritable passengers and the white-shirt-white-car Transit spy/boss guy.

As he talks with Tania, leaning over the phone machine near the 50/50 canteen shack stuffed in the corner of the depot's first floor, adjusting the tight elastic of his blue running pants, he tries to explain to her why he doesn't always want to come over to her place on his days off. She accuses him of just wanting to watch TV. "Yeah, I do," he says. "And – and – and . . ." He stutters. Finally he gets it out. "And you don't have a TV so I can watch the Yankees."

"Who wants to watch a bunch of guys in silly uniforms running around after a ball?" she says.

"I do," he replies and hangs up. Blue is not just a static color. Inside it creeps a little green and lots of yellow. This is how it shares itself in a world of gray, the way men are forced to see it. Sometimes he sketches that world on the back of transfer books. Gorgeous grapes are green and sometimes purple. Those are Teddy's favorite fruit. In his teen years on his way to any basketball court, but especially that one over by Amsterdam Avenue, he'd grab a handful of grapes from his mom's fridge, pop them one by one into his mouth after tossing each separate grape into Harlem's air. Here was safety for him, walking and tossing up his imaginary pet and then catching it without any misstep or trip. He'd like to tip Tania off to the fact that if they could just watch the games together on TV, he could enjoy any afternoon with her. He'd lower the volume of the sports announcer's droning and play some sweet John Coltrane. He actually likes Tania, even the big other L word. But damn-it-to-hell, she excels at talking. Can't she be like his inner beating heart thumping with each moment, and yet hear him too in his silence? She hasn't found out that the schoolteachers in that almost integrated school he went to beat the words into hard wooden desks. His early times with Mrs. Burns keep coming up every time he sits down to write a card to Tania. "You kids will never rise anywhere. You talk and play and yell too much. You're beasts!" she'd scream at the top of her white lungs. Home was little better, what with his moms and dad always sniping at each other and telling him to stop whining when he was scared by the rats and roaches that lurked under the kitchen table. That's why Teddy became quieter.

Tania's blue fruit salads appeal to him. He also loves when she braids up her hair, sticking a blue, almost purple clip in back to hold each strand that wants to stray away. She likes to stray in her mind, but is stable in her heart, which is a relief to him. He's had too many girls—"women," Tania would say—who strayed into other men's beds hoping sex would help them escape from their fears of being independent able to trust themselves to lead their lives.

Though he's been with Tania so long, he's still thinking it's lonely to be a guy. He keeps hoping the words will come to him to help her see, but it hasn't happened yet. And since he continues to stay shut down, it's Tania who decides for them what they're going to do. He resents it but can't articulate what's troubling him, so they argue.

Some days later a brief make up conversation begins the road back together. Teddy looks for Tania when her shift starts to make sure she sees him waiting near the swing room and knows he's sorry. As he sips his drink from a take-out cup, she watches his lips. He invites her over to his apartment. She asks if he has to switch his idiot box on, and if he does, can the sound be turned off when the ads start? She reminds him that the programming isn't like European state-run television, and that here we have commercials everywhere trying to rip you off.

"Yeah, I know, it's buy, buy all the time. Okay Tania, sure." Teddy whispers his agreement. Their relationship in front of the fellas at the job needs to seem casual and friendly, not intimate.

"Okay, talk to ya later, she says."

With the argument smoothed over, she goes to his place when her shift ends, and the two lovers spend the night before his day off together, sleeping late and taking it easy until she has to leave for work. They lie on Teddy's firm, king-sized mattress, entwined in his favorite sheets, decorated with green and yellow leaves. They're her favorites, too. He and Tania have their love of nature in common. They keep their voices low. His apartment sits right below the one into which his mother moved when she left his violent, falling-down drunk dad. Tania hears her slippers padding back and forth on the floor overhead.

"Your mother has a way of being right over us when we're here, honey," she says. The false sweetness of her tone doesn't succeed in masking her irritation. "Is her kitchen right over this part of your apartment?

“Oh God, Tania, don’t start.”

“But Teddy, seriously, ever since that time she started bangin’ on your door and you came outta me when we was having sex, I never felt safe”

“All right, Tania, I get your point.” Teddy moves away and takes his arm from around her to put on the radio. Nina Simone singing “Mississippi Goddamn” fills the room. Thank god for alternative radio mixes.

“Tania,” he says tentatively, “I know this is the worst time to ask, but can I use your car to take her shoppin’ tomorrow?”

“I thought we were gonna do somethin’ together.”

“We still can. There’ll be time before your shift starts. Just let me borrow it first thing. She wants to load up on groceries at the discount warehouse.”

Tania blurs into an inner world, dropping out of the conversation to mull over his relationship with his family, as a radio version of “Someday I’m Coming Back” plays. The fact was, Teddy had never really gotten to know his parents. His momma worked twelve-hour days as a seamstress in the grubby garment industry, and was almost always too tired to attend much to her children. His dad slept for a good part of the day, and the rest of the time was a street watcher, studying the ‘morning’ folks rushing off to work while he waited for 5 p.m.—at which point, . just as Teddy was getting home from school, he would join the other Security Guards of Harlem who descended from six-story walk-ups to ride the A train downtown, where they’d watch over some rich guys’ building for twelve hours and come home with only the minimum wage and bulky beer bellies as compensation for the work’s loneliness. Instead of breaking out of this death-walkers’ routine, they remained stuck in their isolation. Instead of organizing, they dumped and beat up on their kids on their kids the way the master dumped and beat up on them.

As the song ends, she realizes suddenly that Teddy’s mother had latched on to Teddy as a boy to make up for the absence of emotional connection between her husband and herself. And now Teddy can’t or won’t let go of his momma, who simply wants him to drive her around shopping—in her car, since his is in the shop, which it often is. Between them they have just about one usable car, ’cause when his is working, hers isn’t.

Without answering him, she puts her hand on his shoulder, thinking about the vacation trip they’d taken to New Mexico that had brought them so close. They’d taken a long, slow route through Virginia and almost the entire states of Tennessee, Arkansas and Oklahoma, even detouring to his grandmother’s house in Virginia, where they slept together in her upstairs room. Teddy was clearly proud of her, and relished sharing with Tania the feast she served them—southern style fried chicken and collard greens she’d grown in her garden.

Except for the visit to his grandmother, driving through southern states had been hard for him, though Tania hadn't really understood all about why at the time. There had been one early clue, even before they got to his grandmother's house. At one of the diners where they stopped, in a small town, she had overheard Teddy ask the white waitress if she had a problem serving them. She said no, and Tania had thought nothing more of it until later, when he told her how, when he was a child and his father was driving him and his sister down south to visit family, they couldn't stop at most restaurants, even to go to the bathroom. They had to use the dirt behind the car, when his dad would pull off some back road. The south was also full of other reminders of his family's history, a history that Tania, with her Jamaican and Jewish ancestry, didn't share or even know much about, given the failure of the public schools to teach anything like the truth about what the South was like for black folks before the Civil Rights Movement began to force things to change a bit in the 1960s. As a child on those family trips to visit relatives in Virginia, he had seen chain gangs working on the roads. His own grandfather, his beloved granny's husband, had once worked on a chain gang, and *his* father had been lynched.

But when they arrived in New Mexico, Tania knew why he'd fallen in love with it all those years ago, when he passed through there on the way to Vietnam after being drafted. The weather had seemed perfect to them, with the days hot but with a dry heat completely different from the mugginess of New York in summertime, and the nights crisp and cool. And the air was so clear, with blue, blue skies—an ocean wave from above. The people were different, too. For one thing, most of them were native, white or Chicano. And yet they were not so different as to seem off-putting. After all, there were lots of pool halls and in the evenings, men could be spotted playing dominos and enjoying a beer.

When Teddy opens his sexy mouth to ask again about borrowing the car, she places a kiss on his mouth. "Do you remember how beautiful our vacation in New Mexico was?"

"Mmm." Teddy nods.

"Someday, we're going to move there, right?"

"Mmm."

"Remember the sunshine, the look of the moon over the Sandia Mountains? We made good love, remember? Inside the red clay canyon?" A sweet, delirious smile lifts her cheeks up.

Teddy gets up. "I'll be right back, hon,"

She smiles in anticipation and watches him as he goes out the door into the cold hall to use the toilet.

Tania leans over the bed fiddling with her slipper, when accidentally it flies under the bed. She takes her naked self off the bed, crouches down and reaches for her shoe. She can't get it. It's too far under the mattress. The flashback is upon her before she even knows it. Rising up she pounds her brown fists into the top of the bed. Spent, she flops onto her stomach, head to the side, and cries. It's the same hall bathroom that Teddy's mother tried to come into when she was peeing one day. Her mind races and other bathrooms reappear in her memory. The pink-tiled one with the towels embroidered with her old family's initials hanging in the towel rack beside the sink. Her mother Rebi entering while Tania, age twelve, was trying to insert a tampon, saying "I'll help you, honey."

Tania had *not* wanted to get help from her mother, but what could she do? She was still tight and her fingers didn't really know where to put the thing.

Next her memory flashes on her father in the shower . . . no, outside after he showers. He is naked. His thing is hanging down. Why did that seem strange to Tania? How old was she when she stopped finally watching him dry off after bathing? Why was she even asked to be in there with him?

Asked. The word sticks on Tania's tongue, lying there like thick glue. The tears roll out of her. Sobs and sobs heave down her skinny back. Teddy, back from the bathroom, draws a love touch on her shoulder. "Tania, Tan ... Tan ...? His deep bass voice wants to know, soothes her insides.

"Teddddddyyy, I had a flash back memory." Tania reaches her hand up for his. He holds it. He strokes her behind lovingly. He wraps the sheet over her and tucks himself ion holding her.

In the morning, Teddy whispers in Tania's ear, "I had a dream, Ton."

Tania moves her small ass, tucking it closer to his groin. She reminds herself to be cautious. Maybe it will be a dream like the one she'd shared with him about the hospital or was it the sleeping bag? "Is it okay that I'm close?" She asks softly. Teddy answers by pulls her closer, squeezing her with his powerful arms.

"Tell me your dream, Teddy," she whispers.

"Uhmmm. I dreamed that there was a scorpion in a glass in the refrigerator, coming for me. It had a face on it." He speaks slowly, enunciating every word.

"What did it look like?"

"It was brown."

"Was it a male or female face?"

"Female."

"Who did it represent, hon?" She's channeling Pam.

As always, he avoids going deeper. "Tania, I can't start into that now, I gotta get up and take my mother shoppin'." He pulls away from her and gets up.

She's disappointed, but not surprised. Teddy avoids getting into things. She keeps encouraging him to come with her to meet Pam, who has a lot of young working class men as clients, but so far he's resisted.

"Okay, I'll go with you," she says, appreciating his muscular arms as he pulls on his pants. She wants to witness him using the shopping to distract himself from his dream, and promises herself she'll zip her lip on the subject of his mother or anything else he classifies as "deep"—a promise she'll keep for a week.

By the time she's up, he's dressed and heading out the door. As she usually does when he leaves her alone in the apartment, she takes a quick look around, checking the inner recesses of the closet, his drawers in the dresser (she keeps a few things in one of them), the medicine cabinet in the bathroom and peering into nooks and crannies generally. What she's looking for she's not sure. As long as they've been together, she doesn't feel she really knows him, doesn't feel confident in his love. But instead of confronting him with her fears, sharing them, she snoops, looking for evidence of . . . whatever.

The truth is, neither Teddy nor Tania knows how to negotiate past the drapes in her back room and through the shades in his kitchen to unravel the hurts from their pasts. Love shouldn't have to hurt, but it does, because he, as much as Tania, crowds their bond with childhood memories. He remembers how his moms and dad, following the strict ways of their southern, rural roots, made him turn the TV off and go to bed just when the Yankees were tied with a man on third. Maybe his father was even drunk. He remembers how, when he was older, they weren't interested in any of his basketball games in junior high or in the pick-up games on the courts in their Harlem neighborhood. When he stayed out late on hot Manhattan summer nights to shoot hoops until two in the morning, neither one came by to smile "Good shot," though they, too, would be outside. Without air conditioning, it was too hot in the apartment to sleep. As for school games, well, both his folks worked, and when they got home, his father almost always went out somewhere drinking, while his mother spent the evening hours on the phone complaining to her aunt about his drunken, womanizing ways.

The screech of a bus turning too sharply and the wail of several car alarms going off intrude on these thoughts He has a sore ass from sitting so long, first in his bus and then in his car waiting for her to show up, and he snaps at her as he climbs into her car, which she's pulled into a spot not too far from his instead of telling her he's hurting. She senses it, however, and doesn't say anything about his latest failure to call her back. Avoiding what's really on their minds, they complain about the horrors of the job. Despite her years driving, she is still unable to get herself assigned to a less punishing shift. But she can't quit, even though the sexism is killing her. She's built her life around the great pay. He suggests she transfer to another depot.

"What makes you think working out of another depot will make a difference, Teddy? They're all the same. They'd make great holding pens for protesters, better than the stadiums they used in Chile during the 1973 coup. People could maybe get out of stadiums. In the depots, Massa could lock protesters inside. They wouldn't even get to see the sky."

"Right. Just those greasy windows up there and the peeling paint."

"Maybe if the protesters were held in here they'd start protesting the conditions we live with day after day. Do you know Agua told me there's asbestos in the ceiling where she works?"

"Yeah?"

"Yeah."

They decide to move to his car, which is more comfortable. Tania opens her door, starts to get out, then stops. "What do you think that could be?" She points towards the floor of the garage.

"What?" He leans over her to look. There's a large stain by the car door.

"Do they expect me to walk through that to get out of my car?"

"Here baby, I'll go to my car and bring it over to your spot. You move yours and put it in my slot, then come back here, okay?"

Tania nods, but the maneuver will cut into their time together, and something seems to burst open inside her. "Teddy, I can't do this job anymore!"

"Yes you can."

"Teddy, I can't. We gotta have an intimate life. We gots to have a *life*. These bosses are murdering us here, it's so dangerous. Kinda like the coal mines 'cause you can't see the poison in the air." Another car alarm goes off. "I can't stand it. The noise that blasts through my eardrums. People screaming at each other. The sound of stiff silence when the rat-ass bosses dock your pay for nothing . . . for being late getting to the time point in the middle of midtown on a Friday at rush hour . . . this is harassment, especially since the guys aren't getting the same amount of pay docked."

Teddy holds Tania's shoulders and peers deep into her brown eyes, and she cries. He holds her shoulders and pats her back, which is curved, like one of the wood sculptures in the Studio Museum of Harlem, which he passes every afternoon on his way home from the garage.

"These elite location chiefs stay cool in the office taking our pay away by giving us more time in the street. Oh God, Teddy, it's so unfair. We work for mean liars who make a schedule that's physically impossible for bus drivers to keep, then dock us when we don't." She bends her head, sniffling.

Teddy realizes that the explosion is finished for now. "Ton, come on, your shift'll be starting before too long. Let's switch cars now so we'll have some time together before you got to go."

"Yeah, I know. I got an hour and thirty in the seat comin' up, with no break."

He clambers out of her car and goes to his. After they've exchanged parking places, she settles into the passenger seat of his. She gifts him with her brown leather gloves with the tan tassels, placing them on his lap. "Look, Teddy, I love that you listened," she purrs. She plays with the silver buttons on his uniform jacket, while he eyes her. Blue jackets, dark as an almost-night-but-still-evening sky, sitting next to each other as if they were back in New Mexico enjoying the sweet smelling night they'd fallen in love with. A yellow moon rises on his dashboard, where he keeps a box of his favorite brand of tissues. The golden circle on the box appears to them like the full moon that gave the cool desert night a glow that Teddy, remembering his visit to the state while he was in the service, had tried to describe to her but that she couldn't really imagine until she'd seen it for herself. Now the poor copy on the tissue box, keeping its smiley amber face turned toward them, evokes for both of them the real thing. They put their arms around each other. Grace. Grace just flows.

Tania starts her shift at 100th Street, then loads up at 96th with a whole bunch of people in addition to the Harlemites who had already almost filled the bus. In twenty minutes the transit liars expect her to make it to 42nd Street. No way! There are infants being juggled up the steps along with their fold-up strollers, and older people she has to lower the bus steps for. The third time this happens, the air pressure increases so slowly afterwards that the bus can't be raised back up, and she has to shut it off to let the pressure build again. Finally, after three lost minutes, the bus rises to its normal position. Now the follower bus is right behind her—but at every stop the passengers still crowd into hers, because it stops first. As a result, she reaches the time-check at 42nd Street even later.

That's one reason she truly appreciates Teddy Nat Turner. He helps! Occasionally, when he works overtime, they're on the same route and if his bus ends up being behind her and he sees she's full up, he pulls out in front of her to help pick up some of the load. No matter how much the bosses push them, drivers like Teddy, like she tries to be, manage to remember they're carrying live freight, not steel pipes, and take care to keep crowding to the minimum possible. They're also careful not to speed up then jam on the breaks and jolt these breathing beings. Yes, Teddy's known for being caring that way. It's one of the reasons she fell in love with him. But he's also known for other things, and it's the jokes and stories he tells in the swing room, not his careful driving, that make him popular. Tania tries not to be bothered by the way, on his bus, he notices women, like the fine chocolate skinned sister he bragged to the guys about flirting with the other day. "These beads on my forehead are all for you," she heard he'd said to the passenger as he wiped the sweat from his face. "The sister drops a token in the slot and heads to the back," he says, mimicking her grin and her strut down the aisle of the bus. The way he tells stories, acting them out, has the guys in stitches every time. Another day, he describes an older white woman who kept pressing her hand on her head to keep the purple-tinted wig she wore in place. "You mean this bus don't give change for a dollar?" she'd asked. His audience roars as Teddy grunts the reply they all give to such complaints, which needed to be made to the Transit Authority, not the drivers: "No."

"'Oh New York is so-o-o backward.'" Teddy mimics her voice, then walks backward imitating her retreat down the steps into the crowd of waiting passengers, whom he also mimics, standing with arms crossed, unsmiling.

What he does not tell the guys is that the purple-haired lady sets him wondering if the busses in New Mexico have fare boxes that make change. When he and Tania drove there, they hadn't learned much about the transit systems. Nor does he share with the guys the fact that he and Tania sometimes think of moving there, though whether he'd have a shot at driving a city bus he has no idea and what the pay would be like in a place without much in the way of unions gives him something to really think about.

After six months of "preliminary" negotiations for a new union contract, it's leaked out that the rich white bosses want the workers to "give back" lots of hard won things, like cost-of-living allowances The suit-and-tie pretenders, who keep double sets of books, even want to deny the drivers the measly five paid minutes of "wash-up time" after their shift they now have. Tania reads this in "Hell On Wheels," the newsletter of a dissident faction of the union, of which she is a member. The dissidents are sick of the bureaucrat union heads, who just seem to go along with management at contract time.

Before her shift on the days "Hell on Wheels" is published she makes the rounds of different garages and drops off newsletters in the swing rooms. She's in uniform, so no one notices what she leaves on the dominos tables. Sometimes workers ask her about it and she suggests they read about the dangers they face on the job, and they laugh. Shouting, "You don't have to tell us!"

Transit and the "regular union" are scared of the dissident group because the writers of "Hell on Wheels" support the right of all the workers to know what's going on in the negotiations. They want a team of reps who'll really represent the depots, because they're afraid they may lose what little health insurance they have with the bastards trying to increase co-payments too damn much and the union not fighting hard enough. They want a team who'll fight against a system that lets violations pile up on drivers and where workers get no relief because the union doesn't mobilize them to stand up together at local garages. They want a system where, when workers dispute violations and have to take days off for hearings, and actually get an arbitration ruling in their favor, they get back the pay they've been docked. Also, give-backs like the 5-cent washing up time should be off the table from the beginning!

The dissidents want to run their own slate for office and try to replace the management cronies that always seem to win chapter elections now. They declare the big union guys, all white males, should make no more than the top workers. Some of them even know that in Cuba things like health care are totally free because socialists believe humans have the right to be healthy and cared for.

As she closes the paper, Tania reminds herself to talk more when she visits other garages about the demand that they keep the five lousy 'minutos,' which may not seem like a lot, but a day of bus driving—driving millions of people every day year after year—
takes a great toll on the body and the spirit of workers. The five minutes is just a little paid time to calm down and wash the city's grime and the Transit's carbon monoxide poisoning out of their souls.

Have those bosses ever sat in the hot seats of the 5000 series buses? Have they ever dealt with Manhattan's population straight up in the face, body to body? On the bus, drivers have no office window from behind which to steer the public's animosity for the cutthroat city mayor and his representatives to a waiting-room seat out of shouting-bumping-cutting you up-with-knives range. Once, while closing the window of his bus, Teddy got sliced in the arm by some man in the street. She, herself, puts up with some kind of assault, verbal and occasionally physical, almost daily. One time a guy with a belligerent, head-cocked-to-the-side, finger in the air attitude threw an umbrella at her. The union is fighting for a law to make it a felony to hit a bus driver. A felony! But damn it, why didn't they fight the system to improve the service? Then maybe the passengers wouldn't get so mad all the time.

The dissident union group behind "Hell on Wheels" doesn't meet with universal approval among the workers, especially those with positions in the union. One day when she's distributing the paper at a depot uptown, a different one from hers, a regular union steward, eyebrows raised as he twirls his moustache, shouts to her, "Don't leave that mess at this garage."

Even though her heart beats fast, she still retorts, "I will!" Her thin frame is no match for his burliness, but another guy, a driver with his cap turned back to front, asks, "Why shouldn't she leave them?"

She seizes the opportunity and urges her defender to take one. "Hey, why don't you read it yourself and find out what he doesn't want you to know?"

The driver takes the paper and opens it to the inside piece. She whispers, "Can you come outside for a minute?" He follows her, and outside, off the premises, she stuffs the rest of the papers into his hand. "Here, you give them out, okay?"

He grins. “Sure. And thanks. I’m tired of the bosses ‘upstairs’ screwing us by writing us up on violations about nothing, like whether our shirt is well-ironed, and then taking part of our paycheck!”

As usual, on Thanksgiving eve, Tania is driving. She is already pulling out of a northbound Harlem bus stop when a male passenger starts shouting, “Back door, back door! Let me off!” She has to ignore him to concentrate on the traffic. Seeing a car coming on the left, she maneuvers the bus in ahead of it, before the lane is closed off.

“You or your boss gonna pay for me missing my stop,” the man screams. Actually, he’d missed it because he had his radio blaring and didn’t jump off before the door closed. But once she’s pulled away from the curb she isn’t about to open it again. Bus operators were responsible for keeping three feet around their bus clear at all times. Besides, she remembers all too vividly how she once saw a cab, passing a bus on the right side, knock a passenger who was let out after the bus had pulled away off his feet.

While she’s stopped at the next street light, she watches the passenger in the rear view mirror. He’s not a big guy, but something about him sets her inner alarm bells ringing and makes her head feel tight. He’s wearing a scruffy jacket that’s too big for him, sneakers, and a little visor cap with deep, grungy wrinkles. He makes no move to get off at the next stop. “You gonna pay,” he says again, and moves to a seat in the front of the bus. Evidently he intends to stay aboard just to keep taunting her. At the following stop, a woman wearing an African head wrap and heavy shoes and pants marches past him up the aisle to exit by the front door. “You be Harriet Tubman now and Happy Thanksgiving,” she says to Tania. Tania nods gratefully as she lowers the steps. The woman smiles her thanks and climbs painfully down to the curb. As she hikes up the block, she turns to wave at Tania. Tania waves back and moves on.

The guy with the radio stays aboard past a few more stops, until the end of the line, where Tania has to drive around the block so she can head back downtown. Everyone else has gotten off —a bus almost always empties out completely at the end of the line—and she and the guy with the radio are alone. The streets seem deserted, though who knows how many crack-heads are lurking in the shadows? The street lights barely penetrate the dark.

“Just me and you now, bus driver!” The man laughs menacingly. His radio is still blasting. Thinking how people without consciousness like this guy make it hard for activists like her, she flashes on the “Class Consciousness” poster in Pam’s office and decides she has to make a move. She peers into the darkness ahead, and sees her chance.

Right at the corner where she is supposed to turn, there is a different depot from hers, one that houses a bunch of other bus lines. Its garage door is wide open. Instead of taking the risk of going around the block in the dark with the asshole, who got to his feet when she slowed down for the turn, she figures she'll turn in there. The vacuum guy, who collects the fare money from the buses that end their runs at the depot, can be a witness to anything that happens, even if he doesn't help. Gripping her steering wheel hard, she turns the bus into the garage.

"Where you going?" the man screams, heading right for her. "Where you taking me?"

Tania brings the bus to a screeching halt, throwing him off balance, lifts the parking brake and pops out from under the bar next to her driver's seat. Although he tries to block her exit, she squeezes past him onto the depot floor. He follows. She does a quick u-turn, runs back into the bus and shuts the door. The butterflies in her stomach settle as she backs the bus up and escapes, leaving him standing with his mouth open in mid-scream, for a second dumbfounded. She can no longer hear him yelling, only see his mouth moving "bla, bla, bla." As she drives the bus back out of the garage, she sees the vacuum guy running towards her, and thinks how she'll have to file a report about why she pulled into the wrong garage, and how she's going to be late at the time check at the start of her downtown run. She'll get a violation for sure, despite the circumstances.

She thinks again about the guy in the bus, and about the poster in Pam's office. That guy certainly wasn't with her or with workers in general. In fact the poor sucker might just as well be in the pocket of the bosses, who harass women too. The poor slob makes your life miserable by threatening your body with his mouth and sexist Black male privilege; the rich white boss threatens your existence, your livelihood and your soul.

A week after the encounter with the guy with the radio, Shitzano, the Location Chief at her depot, takes her up on charges for her sins: "Being Late for the Time Point" and driving her bus into the wrong garage. The boss, who is seriously overweight, sits in a plush chair behind a big desk. She and the Shop Steward with her have to stand. They don't give chairs to the workers.

"What would you have done?" Tania asks when Shitzano tries to justify giving her a violation for being late at the time-check, on top of whatever would almost certainly be coming her way for driving her bus into the wrong garage, and regardless of the fact she'd probably saved Transit a lot of money by avoiding being assaulted.

He doesn't answer directly, but suggests she should have gotten off the bus at the corner and called control from a pay phone."

"Sure!" The Shop Steward cuts in sarcastically. "And got herself mugged. It's ridiculous you don't have phones that work on the busses!" He makes a fist and walks closer to the boss's desk, though he stops short of pounding on it.

"I can't take this shit," Tania mutters to herself, wiping her eyebrow. Shitzano must be crazy. If she'd gotten out of the bus on the street the guy could've followed her and knocked her out and who knew what else. And even if he didn't, the street was probably crawling with addicts desperate for a fix, who would have found her an easy mark. And it didn't make any difference that they were probably victims of some government decision to flood the streets of Harlem with crack cocaine to kill any chance that the Black activism of the Seventies would continue into the Eighties, as Smoke, who had read about the CIA's role in drug trafficking in Vietnam, claimed. She would more than likely have still wound up in the gutter, maybe dead. Besides, pulling into the garage had thrown the guy off-guard. He probably thought Transit had an armed guard in the depot—though if there was one he would be there to protect the money, not the workers! On the other hand, maybe Shitzano was crazy like a fox. If she was hurt in the street instead of on company property, the bosses wouldn't have to pay her doctor bills.

She waits for her glare to knock the Chief back into the industrial wall behind him and off mother earth, but he is unmoved. Her Shop Steward makes a plea: "Come on, man, these suckers are out here assaulting our drivers every day. This was a night run!"

"We care about the safety of both passengers and bus operators," Shitzano says. "But who's to say what would've happened if she just did her job the way she's supposed to and drove around that corner?"

Both Tania and the Shop Steward smirk and let out a groan.

Shitzano ignores them. He has on a blue tie with an amerikkkan flag tiepin fronting a supposedly clean shirt, but dirt from his cover up and his insistence on being blind to facts make Tania want to puke. She gazes out the grimy window.

The Shop Steward ploughs on, shouting now. "This is really beyond me! If she stayed on the bus she might be dead now. Here we have drivers coming to work, doing their runs, but the buses Transit gives us to drive have radios that don't work so we can't call for help when we need it. And you're gonna stick her with a *lateness* violation on top of whatever else they're gonna throw at her?

At least her Shop Steward doesn't side with management the way some union sellouts in some so-called "professional" unions do. But Tania doesn't have much hope this first-step hearing will accomplish anything. She's learned over the years how the bosses con the workers into thinking they give a damn. Fixing her eyes on Shitzano's silly tie, she reminds herself that if he decides to dock her, and she appeals, then she's got to take a whole morning to go wait in the Bronx for the next-step hearing, which is such a miserable experience and costs so much time that the bosses count on workers not appealing. And after that, if she loses again, she has the right to go to arbitration, but that's an even more time-consuming and miserable experience and so biased in the bosses' favor that almost no one ever pursues it. All of which means if there is any justice, where the hell is it? Which is why we need a revolution! Only the spirits hear her heart-felt speech, as the phone on Shitzano's desk rings.

"Yeah, okay." The punk hangs up and says, "I have my next hearing waiting outside, so your time's up. I'm ruling against you." Then, staring dead at Tania, he threatens her: "And you better watch your step, young lady, so you don't lose this job one day." His white hand taps the phone back into its black cradle He doesn't even look up. His signature, as scrawny and tiny as his heart, on the white penalty paper means that now Tania for sure loses her pay for a whole day just for being late at the check point, whatever else happens. Unlike in white-collar industries, where a minor violation like being a little late at a checkpoint gets you a write-up in your personnel file, but they don't touch your paycheck, the bosses at Transit can and do take away a whole day's pay and more for nothing!

She makes her way out of the room to go back to the heavy traffic line, stopping in the bathroom on the way for a few moments of privacy. Tears had begun to well up and she doesn't want to be seen wiping her eyes with her sleeve as she leaves massa's office. As usual there are no tissues in either pocket.

She'll drive and drive her route until finally she can rest her aching right leg at 12:52 am. Her eyes blur while she waits for the shifter to pull out a bus, hoping against hope it will be one with power steering. As she paces back and forth, she composes a tirade in her mind she'll never deliver about how people in her mother's and father's and this boss's stinking middle-management petit-bourgeois class just mess around with peoples' lives and health and even paychecks without a second thought. That stupid class of do-nothings sit in warm or cool offices the whole damn day, then go home in fancy cars that are never more than a year old and sip martinis. As their vacation plans unfold, neither workers nor members of the public are on their minds. They never think about the guys coming to work every damn day, lung cancer and all, to drive the busses pulling hundreds of folks packed in worse than sardines, hour after hour, 24/7. The bastards just push the drivers down and take their lives—you have to call it murder when it's so tense and uptight at a workplace where there's heavy equipment being used. If a machine won't function right, folks can die, but they don't care, so the busses aren't maintained. Every day the workers who don't just push pencils and paper around in some office feel fear. They're afraid because they know that if they make a move that doesn't work they can run somebody off the road or even run over one of those people who like to stand in the street right by the bus stop to wave down a cab or a person on a bike in the blind spot of a driver whose mirror isn't working. No, the managers never think about the dead bodies of the bike messengers hit by busses, lying covered by tarps in the streets of Manhattan, surrounded by police cars. They don't think about the drivers who hit them because they are forced to drive over the city speed limits to keep the schedule. Even on Sunday, especially on Sunday, when they have to speed because there are fewer buses to pick up the loads of church goers and people just out biking for pleasure can be hit. The city doesn't give a damn about any of them. She'd almost puked the day the cops waved her past a person lying in the street under the back wheel of a bus from another bus line and garage.

Those bike messengers, too, are under pressure from their bosses, so they slide under wheels on icy streets or when it rains. No boss says "Go slow–safety first" and means it. Getting charged with a violation for being late means all such talk is so much garbage.

As she stands just outside the swing room waiting for her bus to come, again the tears well up. "I'm gonna kill one someday, for sure," she thinks. "Or a pedestrian. Oh God." She envisions the body under the wheels of her bus. Again she uses her sleeve to wipe her eyes. There's no problem about being seen doing it out here, where the black grit in the air swirls around the waiting drivers.

A short Caribbean driver passes her. "Hey, good lookin'." He waves hi. She clenches her fists at the greeting. Why can't these guys use her name the way they do when they greet each other? She stuffs her fists in her pockets.

Oblivious to her reaction, he turns back and stops beside her, lighting a cigarette. "How you like the new White dispatcher on the downtown line?" he asks, giving her an opening to do some organizing.

"Well, the new Black location chief is a junky mf!" she says. Shitzano has transferred out and the new man, while Black, seems to feel he has to prove himself to the bosses by being just as much if not more of a bastard. She moves away from the smoke. "In this bus garage, so called massa, stands to command us from a quiet office, no traffic, no knives, no rats, no carbon monoxide fumes blasting him. He talks to me and you and all of us like we're dirt. He may be Black like some of us, but he's completely forgotten where he comes from."

"I hear you," the driver agrees. "We only come to this dungeon 'cause we get healthcare and can die from homelessness if we don't come to work!"

She stops her pacing. "Man, companies like Con Ed and Chase and CBS and Tiffany and Pfizer and Met Life have offices in midtown or on Wall Street, where the trains and buses get their workers to them, but they pay not one cent in transportation taxes." She's on a roll. The guy had given her something real to be concerned about instead of time points and how many cute women were on the bus. She goes on. "Yeah, those corporate heads make sure of that." He agrees. She continues. "But folks from uptown and the far ends of Brooklyn gotta pay a whole lotta pennies outta their paycheck, which is just as many pennies more than the big corporations ever pay. *And* they're forced to ride on an always-late, crammed, decrepit, noisy insult of a mass transit system that keeps getting worse despite the fare going up just about every year!"

He nods and peers down the road to see if his bus is coming. "Worse for them and for us. Man, we drivers *die*."

"Yeah. Drivers and conductors and station agents and train operators and track workers and cleaners all die. Our lungs die." Tania kicks the ground. "Subway conductors can get their head chopped off if they put them out the window at the wrong moment 'cause management doesn't fix the metal that juts out where trains go into the tunnels. We all gonna die on this job."

He laughs nervously, scared she may really mean this.

She whips the "Hell on Wheels" newsletter from her back pocket. "We need a stronger union. We at Hell on Wheels are gonna wake up other workers and show the friggin' union bosses and management that it's *us* who really run the city's transport system and we're gonna shut this shit down."

His bus arrives and he grabs the paper and stuffs it in his back pocket as he hops in the bus to relieve the driver, leaving her standing alone.

Will he be with them when the time comes? She doubts it, especially if he's got a family. Men with families are reluctant to take the risks involved in an "action" like the one Hell on Wheels sometimes talks about. She knows this applies to Teddy as well, however much he might sympathize with the goal. Suddenly all the organizing seems so fruitless. Why does she keep at it? She wipes away angry tears with her sleeve as her bus pulls up.

After many trips up and down Manhattan, later that night she waits in the line of buses behind the garage, every muscle in her body aching. She's standing, leaning on the fare-box, trying to get some relief after so long in the seat.

The bus in front of her moves at last, and she jumps back into her seat to finish for the night. She pulls into the garage and turns the bus over to one of the shifters, who will park it for her. "F*** it," she sighs as she hops off, ecstatic to be finished, but so tired she feels like a zombie.

She looks back, and the vacuum guy waves as he climbs aboard, giving her a quick toothy smile, careful not to let himself be distracted so he won't get his finger cut off by the vacuum as, with a deafening roar, it sucks all the poor folks' change out of the fare-box. Cracking like thunder, quarters and dimes, no pennies, roll into massa's massive machine. To herself Tania, who knows this vacuum guy is "regular" union, cries, "All of us in this garage are in the same boat, so when are we gonna be standing together tight to fight?" To the vacuum guy she calls out only, "Good night."

The next time they're together, another battle erupts between her and Teddy. They're at her place. She's sitting on the window ledge in the bedroom.

"Yes." Teddy replies in a cold, grinding tone when she asks if he's leaving. After he chooses to say nothing more, but merely gets up from the chair he's squeezed himself into, she adds, "Why?"

"Why? You know I been working overtime this week to save up for child support. I need sleep, and I just don't feel relaxed here. I gotta get home." He's tremendous at putting on his scowl. It puckers his left lip where he usually has a cigarette hanging out. Watching old Marlon Brando movies helped him develop the look.

"But you promised you were gonna spend the day with me. It's a very spiritual day according to the astrological calendar. Come on, Teddy, don't be like this." Tania pleads.

She's gorgeous when she's raging, he thinks. But she's so uptight when he goes to touch her or wants her to touch him, and he's had enough of it. He shoulders the black duffle bag he carries his stuff in when he stays over in her apartment and heads for the door. As he opens it and walks out, he calls back to her, "I shoulda worked some more overtime instead of comin' here."

Her feet carry her back into the bedroom and the window seat, which faces the street. Trying to check on him through the window, she pushes up the screen to lean out. It goes crashing to the ground, but she ignores it. Thrusting her torso through the opening, she yells, "Don't call me again!"

Teddy, walking away, says more with his silent back than he could with any words. She pulls herself back inside, muttering, "idiot" over and over as s she stomps downstairs to retrieve her screen. It's fallen into the on the greenish brown hedge that graces the building's stoop.

WBGO jazz radio was playing the long Coltrane piece "A Love Supreme" when she left the apartment, and it is still playing when she returns. She slams the door and leans against it, gently tracing the smudged marks her fingers have left by the doorknob. Another effing Monday off, with Teddy gone. Slow tears come, running down her cheeks into her mouth, down her neck. She mutters, "I'll never get pregnant or have a little one or be able to truly relax in Teddy's arms." She wipes her eyes with the back of her arm, not finding a tissue handy, as usual.

Suddenly she feels as if her gums are on fire and goes to floss her teeth. An image of her father standing in front of her makes her skin crawl. She sits down and starts to write with her non-dominant hand, writing automatically, without thinking. Her unconscious has taken over: *These gums remember the force he used to open my oral cavity to his "member."*

The next morning, reading what she has written without remembering that she wrote it, she calls Pam to make an appointment. As usual, Pam responds quickly to her call, leaving a message on her machine that is like a balm. "Hello, Tania," she says, her voice clear and caring. "It's Pam. Anytime this Saturday after 8 a.m. is fine. We'll squeeze it in before you start your shift. I'll keep my phone line free if you decide you don't want to come all the way up here to see me in person."

The next day, Teddy calls. "Hi." He slowly inhales his cigarette. "I'm calling to tell you I'm sorry."

"Thank you," she says. She hesitates for a moment, then adds, "Teddy, you know what? I'm sorry too, for snooping around your apartment when I'm there."

"Oh?" He hadn't known she was doing that. Should he tell her off? But what would be the point? She's apologized and so has he. Instead of losing it, he says simply, "There's not much to see."

The two of them seem to be able to pull it together enough to at least see each other's side of the mess. "You know, Pam says we act out our feelings, instead of talking them out. Instead of letting each other know what's really bothering us, we do or say things that hurt without really clearing the air. I mean, she says I gotta stop taking your sudden departures and short temper personally. They say more about what happened to you as a kid, than about anything relating to me. To us."

"Okay, Tan. But, well, you know I don't like to get too heavy."

It's what he always says when their talk strays too close to the real issues between them. Or the real issues period. Like last Monday. She wishes he had someone like Pam to help him see that if you don't talk about the heavy stuff it just lies there like sludge. Maybe Pam, the master strategist, with her exceptional political awareness, could help him see that so many of his problems have roots in a system that forces people like him to work at jobs that are regimented and tedious—the same avenues, the same cross-streets year after year—and with no input into management decisions and regular harassment by the bosses. Workers and especially men, Teddy included, cover up despair and anger by isolating themselves, by going home and watching TV instead of admitting to themselves, much less talking about, much less doing anything about what's really bothering them. Pam has helped Tania understand, helped her have the guts to join the rebel union group, for example. Teddy just takes it. She knows he's scared of losing the job, that he's got a daughter to support, but still. . . Oh, he listens sometimes and even commiserates when she talks about how she gets hassled all the time 'cause she's a woman. But most often, like last Monday, he'll say he doesn't like to "get too heavy." "Well, sexism *is* heavy," she'd retorted. Instead of responding, he'd just gotten up to leave, the way he always did.

She sighs. “Can I just tell you one more thing, though?”

“Okay, I guess.”

“My father was short tempered and walked out or hung up the phone on me more than once . . .”

“I thought you said he never hardly called you.” Teddy likes things simple, and now he’s confused.

“That’s just it. He hung up by never hardly calling!”

Laughing, Teddy replies, “I get it! You mean he just wasn’t even there to pick up the phone,”

“Much less to slam it down.”

They’re laughing together now, and this unites them, heals their hurt a little.

“I love you, Teddy. I love you . . . and I hope I don’t mess things up too much, when I just can’t stand the isolation anymore and . . .”

He cuts in. “What do you mean?”

“I’m talking about the disconnects that happen between us. I just wish I could really *know* you’d be calling in a week . . .”

He replies sharply: “I do call, though.”

“I know. Mostly you do. But I get so anxious waiting”

Teddy apologizes. “I don’t mean to make you anxious. I guess . . . I guess I don’t know what I’m feeling and I just get . . .”

“Shut down?”

“Yeah, baby, that’s it. I get shut down. And sometimes I do feel like acting out with my ex.”

“Oh.”

“But I’m *not* gonna act out with her.” He sighs. “Okay, I’m gonna go fix some food. I love you, too, baby.” She can see him in her mind’s eye, grinning as he looks toward the fridge.

Suddenly she asks, “Will you drive me to my appointment with Pam on Saturday, maybe come in?”

“Does she have pets?” he asks. Teddy loves animals, and has won over Power to the point that she prefers his lap to Tania’s.

“She has a cat. But stop joking around. Lots of guys see her.”

He sighs. “I’m not going to say much,”

Happy that he’s agreed, she throws him a long kiss over the phone.

He returns it and hangs up.

* * *

After heating up some greens and rice and putting a little chicken gravy with a few scraps of chicken still in it over the top, Teddy sits down at his kitchen table. Before eating, he turns off Anita Baker and Stacey Lattisaw. He tries Max Roach, but the cut reminds him of how fast a drummer's hands can move. He flips through TV channels the way he flips bacon, and sips a beer.

He's thinking about last Monday, and about his daughter and how she'll have to face sexism when she grows up. Why had he walked out when he did? He should be glad Tania keeps bringing it up, so maybe he can learn how to help his female child, as Tania and that woman Agua always say—if he ever gets to spend time with his kid again. His ex is trying to get back at him for moving out and taking his bus operator's high wages with him by not letting him see his baby. He might have to go to court. At least with court supervision, he could be sure that the child-support money he sent was spent on the child and not the shopping sprees his mother and his ex still go on all the time. And speaking of his mother, why couldn't she be a proper grandmother, picking up his daughter and bringing her over to her place to make sure he could see her now and then? Just thinking about his mother and his ex partner makes him miss Tania. God, he loves her so much, even when she's bugging him. He picks up a pen and writes on an unlined art pad he has lying on the table:

> Hi Tania,
> I do understand your fear from Sexism. Males can suffer from it too because we shut down feelings trying to "Be the Man." But when you look at me, do you really see a potential for assault? I would never assault you, only try and defend myself as best I can. I WILL support you, even though sometimes my support might seem lacking by your standards. When your women friends run scared, I'll be here for you. We do need to learn to stop pounding on each other, because we know each other so well. Basically, we are the same emotionally but we react to our emotions differently. I go inside and you want to talk. We must learn to accept that about each other and talk about it.
> In love and struggle, TNT (Teddy Nat Turner)

After work the next day, he leaves the letter on the driver's seat of her car.

During the ride in Teddy's car on Saturday, Tania and Teddy don't talk much, but their silence is companionable. It's as if the time alone together after last Monday's blow-up is too precious for words. Tania hopes Pam will help untangle what happened then, a rift his letter has only partly healed. She stares out the streaked window at the Bronx River and the suburban supermarkets as the car rolls towards Pam's house.

By the time they get there, Teddy has decided he won't go in after all. He'll wait for Tania in the car.

Tania can scarcely hide her disappointment, but when told of it, Pam takes Teddy's reluctance to commit to counseling in stride. No sooner has Tania told her than she's out the door, heading toward the car, which is parked in her driveway. As she approaches it, Teddy jumps out and takes off his baseball cap.

"Hi," he says. "Did Tania tell you I'm not coming in?"

Pam laughs. "It's okay. You got her here safe and sound."

He smiles, feeling the vibrant spirit that seems too big for this tiny woman. "It's good to meet you finally, anyway," he says. "You don't really have to wait," Pam says. "I can drive Tania to the subway. Would that be okay with you, Tania?"

Tania agrees. Since Teddy isn't coming in, the drive with him to the depot would be excruciating, full of empty talk. And besides, driving to the subway with Pam is always special, more intimate somehow than the formal counseling session. And once she's inside the counseling room, alone with Pam, she remembers the journal, which she's brought with her, along with the cassette recorder, as she always does. Her issues with Teddy suddenly seem like light stuff, like pebbles on a sandy beach strewn with boulders from her past.

On the sofa, sitting forward, hot in her polyester uniform, Tania is glad Teddy's met Pam, but also glad now that he didn't come in. How had Pam sensed that the issues with Teddy she'd intended to talk about would seem trivial to her now? She fingers her journal, lying next to her on the couch.

Looking directly at the journal and then up at her client, Pam says. So what do you want to talk about?"

Trying to plunge in, Tania gingerly picks up the journal and extends her hand, holding the notebook open to the latest entry. Then, instead of handing it to Pam, she places it on the coffee table.

Pam sips a little tea, then puts her cup on the table. She crafts her next question carefully. "Do you want me to pick your journal up to read it aloud?"

"Yes."

Pam moves over to sit beside Tania on the couch. Tania shifts to make room. She has written a dialogue with characters named "Me" for herself and "Gums" for her gums. Pam reads only the character "Me," skipping the "Gums" part, while Tania's gaze remains focused on her teacup.

"My gum bones are letting go of the plentiful anguish of having to hold a fascist pop's dick. My jaws remember the day he took me in that auto, pushed my head onto his stupid thing. I wanted to bite it off. The urge to find a gun to shoot him was real, <u>but he was dead already.</u>

"A white lady, calling herself 'Mother, my protector,' let it go on.

"Ahhh . I imagine she looked at me like a toy/a p-p-p-paper to crush. Trust in humans was smashed for me then. Instead, a soreness lingers, telling me . . . I only deserve to 'be there for others.' No one, especially my mother, wants me to open my girlhood wounds, wants to help me clean out the distrust. I gnaw on my left gum, the way I did when they called me Buttercup & I sucked my left thumb."

Noticing a folded corner at the top of the next page, Pam asks, with a gesture instead of words, if it's okay to unfold it. Tania nods, and Pam's voice, like the voice of a songbird, ends the reading with:

"These gums remember the force he used to open my oral cavity to his member. But now no one not even mom wants to remember. What will help is gentle self 'into me see'. . . stroking myself with intimacy."

"Wow, Tania," Pam says softly, almost whispering. "Now you really know that you can know yourself. You can trust yourself."

"What do you mean?" Tania also whispers.

"That you can trust yourself to know what your father did. And your mother." Pam says no more, allowing her client to experience in the stillness the tremendous feeling of liberation that comes with consciousness of the truth. She is, of course, aware that there is more work to be done. Though the journal entry is a real breakthrough, in fact Tania hasn't actually *voiced* what happened with her father—she wrote it, but it was Pam who read it aloud, not Tania. For the time being, however, she pushes no further. It is enough that today Tania has revealed what she wasn't able to tell her mother. That she revealed it to a Black woman, not the White mother who she perceives willfully denied the truth, is an issue for another day.

After a few minutes, a low "*ahh*" comes out of Tania, like the sound of song. She stops gripping her necklace chain. The uncontrollable shaking of her left leg stops. She accepts that when she was a kid she told herself that her mother was not complicit, but now Pam. in her delicate voice, like the sound of a flute playing, has helped give form to her own idea: she is conscious of what her father did and of her mom's betrayal.

The client who had been scheduled to follow Tania isn't due for a while, which leaves Pam time to help Tania gather her thoughts and her belongings before driving her to the subway. Because Tania sometimes leaves things behind—something Pam in the past has taken as a sign that she wants to come back—Pam makes a point of handing her client the cassette tape of their session in its plastic case. "This healing session and breakthrough" she calls it.

They walk outside, through the door with is coffee-colored frame, and down the steps from the porch with its trellis of blooming flowers. Pam's cat, waking from a nap in her bed in the corner, meows gently.

"You know, Pam, I'm going to make a point of telling Teddy all about your cat. I mentioned to him that you have one, but I don't think it sank in or he wouldn't have been so stand-offish today. He's crazy about animals."

Pam nods. "I bet he grew up with people who neither talked nor listened. Animals at least listen." A breeze sweeps over the property, through the branches of the trees, giants compared to the sycamores struggling not to be overshadowed by the bus depots in Manhattan. Here, along this street in Black suburbia, where the revolutionary Pam hardly fits, they grow tall, unstopped.

Many times Pam has backed her car, a gas-sipping compact, out of her driveway, as she does now, to take Tania and other clients to the northern tip of the Bronx, south of her home, where the #6 subway line begins. She will drop Tania off and pick up her next client, another refugee from the city. Most of her clients are mass transit users, even those like Tania who own cars, to save on gas.

As Tania steps into the car, Pam turns off the radio, which is set as always to WBAI 99.5 F.M., so Tania can talk further if she wishes to. She's such an effective listener she can let Tania really settle in after that big revelation, and still deal with the traffic. A "transport angel" must be sitting on her shoulder, though. A crazed driver, attempting to get ahead of them, turns in front of her and cuts her off. Pam brakes calmly and there is no accident, but Tania is shaken and curses loudly, "What an effing idiot!" then settles back into peace as she regards Pam concentrating on safety, her hands steady on the steering wheel.

Tania murmurs, "I hate that I have to go to work now."

Pam asks, "Are they still on you 'cause you told the boss you have to use a real restroom, instead of a corner behind the bus at the end of the line, and that takes more time?"

For the first time that day Tania breaks into laughter. "Yeah, they're still on me, but I do take my full three minutes and go across the street to use to the bathroom in the diner."

"Defying the boss!" exclaims Pam. "Do you realize what strides you've made?"

"I guess so. I remember a long time ago, soon after I started at Transit, you asked me if I believed my boss was always right when he criticized me for something or other And it's true, back then I did believe my boss was right, most of the time, anyway. It was same way when I was a kid. My mom thought she was always right and I guess I did too when I was little. What it really was, though, was that she had the need to control me. She was imitating her boss, who controlled her."

"Do either mothers or bosses have the right to control us? Do you think they are justified?"

"This effing society thinks so, but I don't, not anymore."

"Well, that's progress. You know, your mother imitated that boss, thinking she could hide the lying by leaving stuff out." She emphasizes the last phrase.

They stop for a red. Tania nods. "So they both lie, either by leaving stuff out like she did, or just directly like the jerks at Transit who say the busses don't have bald tires and the brakes are okay. And put spies on my bus and threaten to fire me for not pulling out right away."

"Why do you think they lie?" Pam probes deeper.

Glancing down at her shoes, flats with no heels, and deeply scuffed, Tania is quiet for a few seconds, then says, "To maintain control. That's it, isn't it?" After a few more seconds, she adds "You know what, Pam? From the beginning you've tried to help me realize that it takes two!. And now I do realize it. I *and* my mother took in the bullshit. And it's liberating to realize that I don't have to be controlled, at least not in any way that counts, by believing the hiders of truth anymore. I may have to go to work and mostly submit to the bosses at Transit to make a living, and I hate it. But I don't have to pretend everything's okay. I can do better than my mother. My mother thought her boss was a colleague."

"And your father?" Gently Pam brings the talk back to the subject Tania has been avoiding. But the question hangs in the air. They have reached the subway station. Pam pulls up near the long flight of stairs leading to the train, which is an elevated here. They are painted a sickly green and the paint is peeling. Graffiti decorate the risers.

As she reaches for the car door handle, Tania says, "Pam?"

"Yes?"

"Here's the money for today. "

"Thanks."

"'I sent you last month's money as soon as I could," Tania adds.

"I got the money, sweetheart. Call me when you need to set the time for your next session."

Tania climbs out of the car, At the foot of the stairs she turns back. "Pam?" she says again.

"Yes?"

"I'm so grateful I stuck with you. I'm gonna nickname you clarity and spirituality!" She heads up the stairs.

12 PRESSURES HAVE TO BE DEALT WITH

With the old union contract about to expire, the "preliminary" negotiations for the new one have ended and "serious" talks have begun. While issues like the five minutes of paid washroom time and other wage issues are still not resolved, the focus has shifted to matters that directly affect the health and safety of drivers and their ability to have some kind of family life—matters that affect the public safety as well, because drivers who are stressed out or ill are not safe drivers. And the workers have learned that, far from considering changes that will relieve stress on the drivers, management is maintaining its hostile indifference to these issues, and indeed has proposed changes that will make the life of the average driver worse. For example, to maximize "efficiency"—that is, maximize the amount of work they can get out of the drivers for the least possible pay—they are pushing for a switch from "regular" 8-hour runs to 12-hour "swing runs," where drivers have to report at the crack of dawn to do the early morning rush hour, then hang around for four hours at half-pay before driving the four hours of the evening rush. Having to leave home at 4:00 am in order to be on time, they wouldn't see their kids in the morning before school and by the time they'd arrive home at 7:00 pm they'd feel too beat to check homework or read bedtime stories or even have sex with their wives. While most of the drivers may not have signed up for the political agenda of Hell on Wheels, all of them are upset at this prospect. Already, drivers' schedules are too inflexible, with little, if any, regard for their needs as human beings. The 12-hour swing run is a step too far, disregarding their very dignity as people, not machines. So an action has been organized. It's timed for midday, so the early-shift drivers and those who start driving later in the day can all take part. At around 1:00 pm, when the word goes out, participating drivers who are at the wheel are going to pull off the road "sick," park their buses and march to the hotel near the UN where the negotiations are taking place, to be joined by those, like Tania, whose shifts haven't started yet. They are going to say in no uncertain terms that "enuf is effing enuf!" And because they have a union, the protest won't be that of a few standing alone against the boss. Though this may not be an "official," union action—work stoppages by Transit employees are illegal—the drivers have the union's covert support.

Tania doesn't know if Teddy will be at the rally downtown. They haven't had a chance to talk about it. Even when they're together, he's too exhausted from working overtime to talk about much of anything. Besides, while there have been rumors of an action for some time, the word about when and exactly what had only just come down, long after Teddy had left for work and become impossible to reach by phone. Would he choose to stand up?

When word comes that the action is to begin, she has to calm herself down consciously, tell herself to at least breathe: At last the workers are going to let loose a big outburst of justified rage at the go-along-with-corporate America industrial thieves at Transit! And, today at least, she is one of them, a union worker. Even though many of the men can't stand that she won't have sex with them, her friends tell her they feel proud she chooses to stick it out, when most women are home watching TV or with their boyfriends.

She pushes her dark blue cap firmly down on her head, takes off her badge and puts it in her jacket pocket in case any police attack them and there's an arrest. Despite her excitement, as she walks with the others into the garage to ask the dispatcher for a slip stating she's sick, she feels her throat tighten with fear. Will the dispatcher shout "You got a write up" instead of giving her the slip?

But today the dispatcher is one with the drivers and a few moments later, slips in hand, they all walk out and head for the subway station. When she looks back she sees busses lined up on Park Avenue for a long way. Their drivers had just pulled in early and left them in order to join the protest. Again she wonders, Is Teddy's among them? A few minutes later, she is riding the local train with a bunch of the fellas, heading for the rally.

She's standing next to a clean shaven man with brown eyes who's a little taller than she is, and who once brought his daughter to ride with him on his shift and introduced her to the "lady bus driver." She knows him fairly well, since they work the same shift and often wait and joke around together in the rat-infested swing room on Sundays. To him she confides that this is the first time she's ever actually participated in a work stoppage. And it's true: despite her radical politics, handing out copies of "Hell On Wheels" is as far as she's gone—and even that has put her in the crosshairs of management and the regular union.

"What do you mean?" His body sways with the movement of the subway car.

"It's my first time to pull off the road for workers." She laughs. "Did you see all those busses that folks just left on the road behind the depot?" Her voice is high and excited. She feels good. For all their palling around, the two of them haven't talked politics before.

"You know, I like that you take the time to think about things." He grins widely, revealing a gap where a back tooth is missing.

"Yeah, and I like that you always talk to me about meditation. The public thinks we're stupid and don't have any other life."

"Nah, they're just ignorant. I listen to WBAI 99.5 on the radio. That's where I find out about police killings of Black folks and 'Ricans and stuff."

"Did you ever hear them talk about socialism as a system different from the shit we got here?"

"No, I musta missed that one."

"Yeah, they say capitalism is what we got now and workers gotta step up and take action so we don't have this rich folks' system killing us with industrial accidents and stuff."

"Tania, now you're kinda going too far."

"Going too far? No I'm not! Even Hank, you know him, he drives the Third Avenue line?"

He nods.

"Hank says we're stuck fighting for healthcare in our BS contract talks 'cause we as a nation don't have socialized medicine. The constitution in Cuba says everybody has the right to healthcare, education all the way from pre-school through graduate school, and you have the right to a home. And something like, if you've lived in your apartment for a few years, you get to keep it." She stops, observes as his mouth drops open, even if it's only a little 'cause hey, he has to keep his New York cool.

“Yeah?” His eyes, incredulous, widen a lot, like frog eyes.

“Yeah, Yeah.” She flings her hand up to give a high five and he slaps it hard, laughing.

“Well maybe that social—what is it?—got something to it.”

“Socialism.”

“Yeah, well, maybe it’s got something to it,” he says.”

Outside the rumbling train now she spots Teddy’s friend Clyde on the platform. The three of them walk together.

“This feels so-o-o good,” Tania shouts to Clyde over the black kinky hair of the other guy, who’s walking between them. Once they’re out of the subway, he drifts away as she and Clyde talk . It is a gorgeous day, clear and not too hot,

“"Yeah, we finally gonna say NO to the shit management tries to hide.” Clyde’s blond hair blows against his broad forehead as he talks. “Remember Hal, who died last year after 25 years in the seat, cancer of the lung and he never smoked?” He asks.

“Oh thanks for reminding me. At the last meeting on the negotiations, they said the bosses were claiming t our high rate of carbon monoxide poisoning ain’t Transit’s fault. Can you believe it? Management says that the busses are environmentally safe!”

“Does anybody believe that shit?"

“Nobody *I* know,” the two men say simultaneously.” The three of them laugh and slap five as they walk with so many others fast to reach the demo. Towering New York City buildings with gray fronts and too many windows greet them.

So many workers. “Look,” Tania says excitedly. “There must gonna be thousands of them, white, Puerto Rican, Haitian, African American. Jewish workers, for Christ sake. And we all work for the Transit Authority authoritarians!” She giggles.

Most of them walk in their dark blue uniforms, though of course their badges are off. Some have curly hair and brown skin, others straight noses and white skin. There are just three women, Tania and two others, who are marching together at the back of the crowd. Otherwise, the marchers are all guys, standing together for this battle. Some have their caps swung around with the brims to the back. There are no protest signs because this is a “spontaneous” rally, though one organized by the shop stewards, undercover—a show of strength to let the bosses know the members want their union heads to “Go in fighting.”

Tania listens while two old-timers behind her wonder aloud whether they’ll have to go on strike. One of them, who is wearing a big wide belt and his union pin on his collar says, “I hope not. I remember the last one.

“There won’t be no strike,” says the other, who has a gray mustache. “This guy ain’t no real strong leftist union leader like Mike Quill was.”

"You got that right. I doubt if his ass'd be willing to go to jail for us like Mike did back in the day." They continue to cast aspersions on the lack of courage in the current union president, then turn their caps back straight as someone rises ready to speak to the crowd.

"Oh man . . . there's Teddy!" Clyde grabs Tania's attention away from the speaker and points, smiling widely. In Tania's mind she shouts, "The universe is with us," and she grins at how in this huge throng of people she and Teddy could still draw together and connect through vibes. She's just so-o-o damn proud! He *is* on the same side, even though he doesn't write poems or go to the bookstore at the Brecht Forum and read Marx!

Coming up to her, he pulls her collar and she hugs him, bulky uniform jacket and all. Without letting go, she says, "You and me, the f***ing working class," then chants: "We, the working class STAND STRONG to win BACK five lousy minutes of wash-up time."

He chimes in. "Time to stare into a mirror or piss in a dirty toilet with rats running around." Their hug feels honest. They are comrades in something much bigger than them.

Teddy goes on. "Just a lousy five minutes after we all give yet another whole damn day . . ."

Tania finishes the sentence ". . . of our bodies' lives to the killer transit bosses of this city that we all slave and—" Laughing, she adds, "and make love in." Still hugging each other tight, they rock together side to side. The rally breaks up with cheers and hope.

Back at the depot, the thunderstorm that had been holding off during the last part of the rally breaks at last and a heavy rain beats on their backs as they run to pick up Teddy's car, parked in back of the garage.

From the passenger seat she smiles at him as he snaps into his seat belt. "Teddy, I want to share my piece titled 'Bus Driver' with you. I wrote it earlier today while waiting for the demo to start."

Eyeing his woman in the most loving way he can, he smiles back and nods.

She begins, reciting it from memory, not even looking at the paper in her hand, as he drives, focused on the no-traffic road, one hand with strong fingers resting on the back of her seat with her, sharing her heart. Because of the rally and the "pulling-off-the-road" action, they actually have time off together at the same moment in the day! It's a miracle.

"BUS DRIVER: A Communicating and Committing Bus Driving Woman Speaks"

Teddy nods approvingly at the title. Tania is the readingest girlfriend he's ever had and the only one who ever wrote anything except shopping lists. Her poetry writing is one of the things he loves about her.

She goes on, almost whispering. The softness of her voice embodies the intimacy of the moment.

"Same time of dirt
work grime oozing into pants,
industrial filth lies on Tania's blue shirt,
no cotton to protect skin,
as a driving woman she meets a driving man,
helping her win . . .
Working working days of small holidays
(presidents' birthdays)
working big holidays—Christmas/Happy New Years
working until—all of life: WORK
No days off with other folks to see spoken-word on a saturday
no sunday to go with other folks to a dance party show
or even an afternoon kinda "orisha" party.
Only tuesdays when no one else stays home in the day,
(until you find other shift workers)
only wednesdays as a day off
Years—silence
some serious sadness.
Yeah meat-eating/driving man came
had a name helping her reclaim
like Aretha Franklin sings: The Spirit in the Dark
"Amazing Grace, how sweet it is . . ." [Tania sings this]
Amazing, a man of a different class and Tania a lass
from almost-rich sass,
could bust ass
And make it out of the city."

"Yeah, you sure tell about this work junk just the way it is." Teddy squeezes her shoulder gently. "I could just *feel* the pressure." He glances at her out of the corner of his eye, then looks quickly back at the road rolling in front of them.

The specialness of having him with her for a whole bunch of hours allows Tania to ask, "So will you come in with me to see Pam next time?"

Pam has come to the station to collect Tania and Teddy for their joint appointment. For some reason, perhaps because Teddy is with her, as they drive along, Tania notices the ridiculous billboards that line the road from the Bronx to the edge of the leafy suburb where Pam lives. In almost all of them a white woman with bright teeth and breasts hanging out gives the impression that she comes with the convenience of the new car, or whatever, sleek and shining. It's a message that has been drummed into both Teddy and Tania from the time they were little, through the boob tube or the Dick and Jane books they read in elementary school.

The legend on one of the signs in particular catches Tania's eye. "Wait a minute, did I read that right?" she exclaims. "Blonde is in, Black is out?"

Teddy turns his head. "What?" He looks out the back window "That's what it says, all right." He sounds disgusted.

Pam says over her shoulder, without losing sight of the traffic, "All kinds of conditioning come through the media and the nuclear family."

"All these americanos." Tania gestures at the other drivers and pedestrians as they get closer to Pam's house. "All these americanos just taking in these lies from the advertisers and the government, not to mention our bosses' crap. We gots to stop that."

Turning into the leafy sanctuary of her driveway, Pam validates her client. "Right you are, Tania," she says. And, smiling at Teddy, her new, male client, she encourages him: "And you're dropping that stuff, that type of thinking, aren't you? Yes you are!"

Sitting beside Teddy on the couch, Tania exclaims about Pam's plants, which seem to have grown a lot since the last time she was here. Teddy, however, is watching the cat, which is stalking butterflies outside in the garden.

Pam, preparing the tea, asks about the demo and the bosses' reaction. Tania chuckles. "They're mad, and surprised, according to what we hear. The regular TWU isn't what you'd call militant, so the fact that the union supported the action did make them sit up and take notice. We'll see if it actually makes a difference, though."

"At least there hasn't been any retaliation, not yet, anyway," Teddy says. "I guess too many took part for them to write everybody up without putting the Transit system out of business."

"Did you realize Teddy was there, Pam?"

Pam nods. "You told me, remember? When you set up this appointment." Having poured the tea, she sets the pot down and sits in her chair, facing them.

"It was one of the best times we've ever had together." Tania squeezes Teddy's hand. "For once the fact that we work different shifts and different routes and don't have the same days off didn't mess things up."

Abruptly, Teddy pulls a little away from her. He hasn't agreed to come all the way out here to see the famous "Pam" to talk about his and Tania's incompatible schedules. For once it is he who wants to go deeper. He realizes that his relationship with his family is "off" and feels he's ready to explore that . . . maybe, though he's kept this to himself. He also wants to ask the counselor whether he and Tania are really good for each other. While she obviously enjoys sex, her pleasure seems purely physical to him, like the pleasure you get from being tickled. Emotionally she just isn't there. He's guessed the trouble comes from memories of what her father did to her, whatever that was, but doesn't know what to do about it, and her distancing is driving him crazy.

Pam notices his withdrawal. That Tania sees the demo as one of the best times she and Teddy have had together, with no mention of more intimate moments, much less their sexual relationship, is a sign that all is far from well. Indeed, she has heard often enough from Tania that when they have sex they end up quarreling. She intuits that Teddy really cares for Tania, but can't get close to her, and that this distancing, if not overcome, will mean that Tania will lose him in the end, even as she is coming to believe that he is a loving man, a caring man, a man she could have a child with.

Considering how she can help them, these two clients in their thirties who are searching for a way forward, she decides to broach the subject of their sexual relationship directly, putting herself in the mindset of each of them so she can reflect both their perspectives. Tania makes it easy by complaining once again about the way they are always arguing about "stuff," like coming to see Pam today. She had been sure Teddy would back out at the last minute. Which leads him in turn to accuse her of not trusting him to keep his word.

After some more back-and-forth, during which it is established that the arguing takes place while they are touching and about to have sex, or when they are naked after having sex, finally, Teddy blurts out, "You seem so distant when we're in bed, Tania, like you're scared of something. But I always use a condom."

"That's very responsible of you, Teddy," Pam says.

"Well, I don't to get her pregnant if she's not ready." He throws his hands up. "It's like I don't *feel* you, Tania, not the real you. Sure, you're really excited, but it's more like you're just high on something, and it's not being with me. I don't—"

Pam cuts him off. "That could be a seduction high."

"What do you mean?"

"That Tania's excitement is a way of escaping from something."

"I do know something's up with her," he says. "Something about her father."

Tania is suddenly uncomfortable. It seems that Pam and Teddy are talking to each other as if she's not there. But while there are things she could say about intimacy, she doesn't say them. Instead, she thinks to herself what being here with Pam and this man who loves her has forced her to see: that she has no desire for real intimacy. "Dear Teddy," she says soundlessly, "I want nothing to do with the closeness you want. I want to keep my distance. I may look sexy in my dress, but that has no connection to my body underneath the skirt. And that's the problem. You're loving what's underneath my skirt and I'm hating that you connect with me there. I'm blaming myself for having that bad part of my body. If I didn't have it, I wouldn't have this ugly stinking feeling, because my parents wouldn't have bothered with that part of me."

"I know something's up with her," Teddy says again. He looks at their intertwined fingers, golden and brown. Tania focuses on his dark brown hand, like her father's.

"Can you tell Teddy about your father, Tania?" Pam asks gently. "You know you're keeping your father and your mother between you and him. You may have written it down, but don't you see that you have to share it if you don't want the past and its secrets to pull you and this man who has come here today because he loves you, apart?"

"I can't . . . I can't speak it." Though she realizes she has to speak, not just write, the truth, she is still unable to do so, still trapped by the past. She withdraws her hand from Teddy's and stays extremely still, her eyes riveted on the cuff of his blue pants. No one hears what she is saying to herself. "Yes! Pam is speaking the truth. But . . . I can't tell anyone the horror details. I cannot."

She arches her back and glances at Teddy, then turns again to Pam, begging her with her eyes, those brown entry points for her soul, to stop asking her to tell, to signal instead that it's okay not to.

Instead Pam, who knows folks stay as sick as their secrets, says, "You never *have* to talk about it, and you *could* choose to let Teddy and his love in."

Teddy reaches for her hand. "I . . . I'd really like that, Tania," he says softly. Silence falls. Then Teddy asks the question he has come to Pam to ask. "So, are we good for each other, Pam?" As he says this, Tania takes his outstretched hand, and they bond delicately, touching each other mostly at the fingertips.

Pam nods and bows her head, speaking slowly as if pulling the words from the plant deva guides, "Yes, you match well because one of you—Teddy—has been afraid of the truth, but has finally come here to seek it, and the other . . ." She turns to Tania, taking her in with a gentle gaze. ". . . and Tania is still afraid of love. So however hard it is, you can help each other. Tania, you can help with facing things honestly, help him to be more self-reflective and face reality. And Teddy, you can help her allow caring to be a part of her life." With these few words, she confirms their breakthrough.

As they're getting ready to leave, she says to Teddy, "How about you come see me yourself one day?" She surmises that he picked Tania because his own family was dysfunctional, had emotionally abandoned him. He's picked a distancing woman because a distancing woman is familiar—not comfortable, but familiar. He doesn't have to think about how to cope. At the same time he's tired of being hurt by it. And he senses that with Tania there's the possibility of something better.

When he doesn't respond at once, she asks again.

"Or call you?" He hesitates.

"Sure." Pam smiles.

"Oh, that's a good idea, Teddy." Tania encourages him, acknowledging how much courage it has taken him to open up with a stranger. Pam's skill at mirroring human beings has put him at ease.

* * *

He does call, and over the next few weeks, tells her all about his alcoholic father and how he still drinks. Pam shows both her tough and her gentle side as she helps this brother, like most of the others she sees, check out why he feels the way he does about women by delving with him into his mom's ways: How she was always too busy working to bother with her kids; how she demeaned his father; how she still keeps Teddy at her beck and call. She reminds him that, in his grandma, he had had at least one female in his life who he felt cared, in whose house he felt safe. "Yes, Grandma was the one who loved me," he says. Then he tells her about the sister who died. She had been a few years older than he, and just after he was drafted into the army, she had died. He had never learned exactly what happened and never had a chance to deal with it.

But while he begins to acknowledge his deep fear of his mama and his anger towards her, he has yet to reach in and discover her most serious betrayal, her sexualization of their relationship, something Pam can smell, having worked with many men his age. Pam wonders whether his sister suffered abuse from his father—it is not uncommon for the sexualization of children to be a family affair—and she hopes that he will finally, all these years after his childhood, dare to confront what his dad may have done, as well as face off against his momma.

The more she comes to know him, the more she comes to believe that these two, Teddy and Tania, are indeed good for each other. Teddy sticks with Tania because, though she keeps secrets herself, she listens to others, and knows how important it is to have someone who listens. And Tania, if only she can accept his love, may at last find in this man one who, unlike her father, is truly caring.

It's Monday night and the end of Tania's work week. She's dropped off a crowd of late-shift passengers, mostly office cleaners and security guards, while coming up the avenue, and is now at end of the line, waiting to pull into the garage. For some reason there were fewer passengers than usual on the last run, so she's arrived at the depot on time, according to the official schedule. She hopes to finish up and sign out at as scheduled at midnight, without being forced to take an overtime pay ticket for an hour's extra work, which is what almost always happens, because the schedule is unrealistic and she usually isn't done before 1:00 am or later. She prefers to rest instead of slaving too damn long doing management-forced overtime, despite the extra pay. She shifts her bloodshot eyes away from the rear view mirror and walks down the aisle of the bus. The emergency brake is pulled up. Its yellow top glares at her. "It's sleep I want, not money," she says to herself, aware that she can afford to say this, having no kids.

She reflects again on the pull-off and the rally. She's full of doubts, not trusting the union bigwigs not to give in on the matter of the split shift. In their minds, and perhaps the minds of many of the drivers, the four hours of half pay they'll get for hanging around between the 9:00 am to 12:00 pm shift and the four-hour evening rush will compensate for the lost family time, the lack of sleep. It's part and parcel of the scheduling that forces everyone to work overtime most days. It seems never to occur to any of the bosses that they should just pay the same wage for eight hours of work that the drivers would obtain with the extra four hours of half-time pay or that they get now from forced overtime. She worries that revolution is a lifelong process, that the forces of the liars and the corrupt bosses can't be defeated. Then, recalling how happy she felt when surrounded by the others at the demo, she pumps herself up: Oh yes, they and their system *can* be overcome if we stay united. She opens the front door of the bus for air and peers down the block-long pull-in line, leaning out the door to count the busses in front of hers. Her optimism fades. Given the length of time it takes to be released from the job once the shift ends, according to the paper schedule, she knows she won't make it out of the depot before ten past twelve. You'd think that Transit would have a bigger depot or more evenly spaced pull-in times. But no. it's a messed up bureaucracy. Every bus will have to have the money vacuumed out. The bosses don't care if you're over your finishing time, and they ain't gonna pay you for going ten minutes over. But by the end of the year those extra few minutes at the end of the trips you finish on time add up to hours that Transit steals from workers.

To keep from screaming with frustration, she grabs her pocket notebook and starts writing. Once she had left her journal on the bus. When she realized her secrets might have been exposed if anyone had noticed it before she retrieved it, she had stopped bringing it to work. But writing was the only thing that dept the boredom of waiting on line from killing her, and for a while she had torn off the backs of transfer books to write on. Eventually, she had started to carry a pocket-size notebook in her breast pocket—her mini-journals. Now she often uses what she writes in them as starting points for entries in her "proper" journal.

At last it's her turn and she drives in, steering with one hand since today she had lucked up and gotten a bus with power steering. She can hear the grinding of the faulty motor even in the noisy depot. Thank God it didn't break down. Thank God nobody's bus broke down on the line tonight. Whenever that happens, as it had once last week, the shift doesn't end until the bus blocking the way is moved—which can take an hour or two, depending on whether the mechanics can fix the problem or, if they can't, the availability of the tow truck.

She pulls up, brakes, and drags herself off the bus. Leaving the vehicle running for the shifters to park, she says "bye" to the guy coming to vacuum out the change and heads for the swing room. The smell of the place as she opens the door makes her want to puke.

"Hey, Tania." The window man behind the dispatcher's gate calls her name. "You got a personal phone call," he growls. "You got an emergency. Call your sister! Here's the number. You're finished for the night, right?"

At his words, Tania feels a crawling tightness in her shoulders. The number in the dispatcher's office is a private number, unknown to anyone except Transit workers. She hands him her unused transfer books. He takes them in one wrinkled hand and waves her with the other towards the room behind the dispatcher's cage, where bus drivers never go. "Oh, okay," she says as he gestures towards the office phone. He's followed her, as if he wants to see her call for real, before she clears out. Tania dials the number. While she doesn't exactly think it's is a "fake" emergency, she expects the caller will prove to be one of her girlfriends who needed to tell Tania something important and told the boss man she was Tania's sister. It can't be Older Sister, because they never talk and Younger Sister is in Africa. But after connecting to the number, it is the voice of Younger Sister she hears on the other end of the line! It really is her blood sister calling, the very sister who's been living for years in West Africa! She had gone years ago, after banging around, still living with her parents, but knowing she had to leave them. When the chance came to study in West Africa, she had jumped at it. When in God's name had she gotten back?—And how had she figured out how to reach Tania while she was at work? The number in the dispatcher's office is a private one, unknown to anyone but transit workers. She clutches the phone and turns her back on the dispatcher.

"Hi, Tania, it's good to hear your voice." Younger Sister doesn't sound distressed, like there really is an emergency. It sounds like she's making a social call, just to catch up.

Out of the corner of her eye Tania darts a look at the dispatcher in his clean white shirt, pressed dark blue pants, and regulation cap, which looks odd indoors. His badge gleams threateningly. This bastard could write her up if the phone call turns out not to be an emergency. Social calls are forbidden. As if the depot were a military outpost, no outgoing phone calls are allowed, and violations are handed out for receiving personal calls, even if you didn't give out the private number.

Tania whispers, "Look, I'll call you back as soon as I can," and hangs up.

Before the dispatcher can say anything, she is out of his office and heading up the stairs to the pay phone on the top floor of the depot, as far from the dispatcher as she can get.

"Hi. So what's up?" she says after Younger Sister's initial hello. She doesn't make small talk, even to ask when Younger Sister had gotten back to the States, and neither does Younger Sister. Instead, she plunges right in.

"Tania, Daddy has Alzheimer's and I wanna talk face to face. Please come meet me."

"Where?" Tania asks, suddenly shivering.

"At the apartment."

"Oh no, I never go there."

"Please, I need to see you Tania."

"Okay, I'll meet you downstairs."

On her way to change out of her uniform, she opens the door to the union office. There has been talk of building a female locker room now that two more women have become drivers at the depot, but she isn't holding her breath. She stands looking out the cruddy little window, unzipping her uniform and removing her arms from her stuck-to-the-body shirt, sure that no one will see her through the thick film on the glass. She had written to Younger Sister when she first went overseas, asking for a phone number where she could be reached, but Younger Sister had never responded to her request. Or called her, for that matter. Still, she thinks, "Younger Sister was the only one in the family who loved me. And I loved her."

A little more than a year apart in age, they had grown up almost like twins, especially when Older Sister wasn't around to encourage Younger Sister, who also had straight hair, to tease Tania about her darker skin and her curls. They had played bathtub games together, and romped together on their beds in the morning before Mother came to get them up. The two of them had scrambled under the covers to the foot of their beds, which to them were ships. They had opened the "hospital corners" and peered out at each other's smiling faces, laughing as they steered their ships over the high seas. But when Tania asked Younger Sister why she was going to West Africa and she simply said 'to dance,' Tania had begged her not to go. "I need you here," she'd told her. "We're a team. We need to stand together." Younger Sister had left anyway.

When they were older, they had spent a lot of time together while their mother occupied herself playing Chopin on the piano and, during the summer, when they were staying on the island, tennis, a love of hers that her husband detested. Most of her waking hours, she would leave the girls to their own devices as, racket in hand, she went to play on the courts at the club. Before she got married, she had played with the white soldiers stationed in Hawaii, imagining that her Negro boyfriend might join her on the courts one day, when the racial barriers fell. But that hadn't happened. Only on the island was he welcome at the club, and by the time they bought the house there, he was too old to learn to play the game he'd come to loathe as much as she loved it. But if her boyfriend couldn't join her on the courts, he had wrapped his arms around her waist over her bathing suit and then over her nakedness, when they risked skinny dipping in the dark of the evening at Honolulu's oceanfront. Or at least, that was what Tania and Younger Sister imagined and giggled about together as they grew older. Neither their mother nor their father had ever admitted to the girls that they had had sex before marriage, though the date of Older Sister's birth confirmed that they had. Tania avoided thinking about how her father must have inserted his member between the young moist lips of his soon to be bride; the girls didn't discuss details like this. But they agreed that the mother they knew hid her sexuality in sturdy teacher shoes and slacks hung loosely over her flat behind. Flat or not, it had attracted their dad, but to acknowledge this sexuality to the girls, or admit her daughters were themselves developing sexually—this she could never do. Instead she had stifled it, in herself, and to the extent she could, in them. "She's such a hypocrite," they would say.

Still later, after Tania had left home, Younger Sister had described their girlhood to Tania as boring.

Boring? Shit.

Tania steps out of her pants, then changes her mind. Just wanting to run out of the place, she stuffs her street clothes into her backpack, remembering more with each push as she buries them deeper in the bag. She remembers feeling so damn depressed, and calling Agua every time she got a letter from Younger Sister telling her all about the African drummers and her life as a dancer. Tania had once thought Younger Sister would join with her to battle for their parents' honesty. And once she knew that wasn't going to happen, she had hoped for some real exchanges in their letters. But Younger Sister had avoided her direct questions in letters that took weeks to cross the ocean between them. She just didn't respond when Tania wrote, "Do you remember anything that ever happened between you and dad at night?" Instead, her return letter was a field report on the foods she was eating and the traditions of the Rastafarians she had met who were visiting. In a way, Tania didn't blame her. The trouble with trying to express reality in letters is that you can't smell the breath of the soul through the eyes. Would things be different when they met face-to-face, as Younger Sister wanted? Would she be willing now to go beyond what she had said about their family life being boring, and admit that maybe there were big problems? She wondered whether everybody experienced this level of distrust of the people they loved when they grew up. And would Younger Sister ever grow up with her? Would she talk about what had happened? Tania doesn't know. She only knows that she had loved Little Sister and missed her after she left.

Tania ties her backpack strings tight and shrugs into it, then turns for a last look in the mirror, pressing her hand to her head as she recalls her frustration at Younger Sister's silence, her avoidance. But she turns the gesture into a patting of her hair, avoiding herself how painful the deep wound still feels. Steeling herself, she returns to the break room and heads out the door. She speaks to no one, and for once the men are silent too.

Outside, she realizes there's been a shower and she breathes in the fresh mother earth air it has left behind. Slinging her backpack over one shoulder, she walks toward the subway station, head down, focusing on the hard tips of her work shoes. She wishes Younger Sister had come home before this. She wishes she'd been there when she had told them she wasn't ever coming back. She had so wanted to know then that at least Younger Sister was with her. She hadn't wanted to lose her whole family. But Younger Sister had stayed away, aloof as always. Now she was here.

Down underground, once the screeching of the train entering the station subsides, Tania puts herself in a corner seat and rolls with the lullaby rock of the train. Maybe she and I can finally tell each other face-to-face what happened when we were girls, she thinks. Her eyes are shut. Like the eyes of most of the passengers on this night train, taking night workers home, commuters commuting long after rush hour has passed.

A week after the phone call to her job from Younger Sister, Tania makes her journey to the apartment. It's going on 10:00 pm when she rings the bell in the lobby, and it takes several tries before Younger Sister finally answers. Tania says she'll wait in front of the building for her. Younger Sister agrees to come down, adding that Tania should make herself comfortable in the lobby instead of hanging around outside. An hour passes. Then it is not Younger Sister but Older Sister who appears, carrying a piece of yellow, lined paper. Her diamond wedding band sparkles and she wears velvet corduroy slacks and a thin silk jacket. She is trailed by Daddy, who looks bewildered and seems to have followed her down. What was he doing here? Tania wonders. Without saying anything, Older Sister hands Tania the paper. Tania takes it and reads, "I am upstairs waiting. In case you need to be reminded, it's 6D." The note is signed "Mommy." She has written precisely on the lines. Like the appearance of her father, the note surprises the hell out of Tania. She had only expected to see, privately, her younger sister. Will she even have a chance to hug her?

Still without having spoken, Older Sister disappears, leading Daddy back into the elevator, which has shiny brass doors. Watching them, Tania can barely process this new version of her abuser. His eyes are unfocused, blank, and his bumbling walk makes her feel that maybe justice has been done. But now, she realizes that he will never account to her for what he did. Years ago, he had failed to tell her that he recalled what he did; now, almost certainly, he does not. Pacing back and forth in the lobby, she thinks, I don't even hate the idiot anymore. I see that he feels dead now . . . walking around but without a brain. She rereads the note written in her mother's spidery hand, then crumples it. She had thought the idea was for her to be with Younger Sister. Maybe they'd set Younger Sister up to call her, knowing she wouldn't respond to anyone else.

But how can she leave without even seeing the person she's come to see? Does she dare go up there and ask Younger Sister to come outside? She mutters to herself: "I'll just go up there, ring the bell and say 'come *on*,' like I used to, and she'll come 'cause she'll want to talk to me for real, not in front of all of them, those lousy hiders and deniers." Convinced she feels brave enough, she presses the silver-colored UP button.

But, rising in the tall tower elevator, Tania's heart drops, and by the time she knocks on the wide, steel apartment door it's like a stone in the pit of her stomach. When the door opens, it is her mother, not Younger Sister, who stands before her. She notices that her shoulders are slumped now. She had always been so proud of her posture.

"Come in, Tania."

"No. I didn't even know you'd be here. I just want to talk with . . ."

"Coming. I'm coming," Younger Sister's voice reaches Tania from deep inside the apartment.

"I'll wait for you out in the hall," Tania calls to her. She looks at her mother. "Goodbye," she says.

"Oh, Tania!" As Mother huffs back inside the apartment, Tania catches a glimpse of her father's disheveled hair rising above the back of an armchair he's sitting in down the hall.

She is about to leave when she hears behind her the soft voice of Younger Sister: "Hey, girl."

Almost crying, but stuffing it down, Tania spins back around to confront her sister. She's wearing a pretty yellow, loose fitting top and a matching skirt that flares to a white frill at the bottom. Her hair, once cut short with bangs is now much longer, befitting the mature woman she has become. But a lost look, her eyes vacant and evasive, mars her stunningly beautiful features. Although she looks at Tania, somehow she seems veiled.

"Please come out and talk with me downstairs," Tania begs.

But Younger Sister motions with her slender arm. "Come in," she says. Her request carries little energy, however. Her evident despair scares Tania. She sees in her sister the lifelessness that was hers when she was in denial, that will be hers again if she ever reenters that place. Her fear, as she stands there before the open door, makes Tania harsh.

"You called me at the job, on the dispatcher's line. I could lose a day's pay for getting personal calls there. I never gave you that number. Then I told you when I called you back I would come all the way here to meet you, since you've been gone so long you probably don't remember the subway lines and would no doubt get lost trying to find my place. When we talked, you left out the fact that all of them would be here, not just Older Sister, but Mommy and Daddy *and* Older Sister, who I thought would be out somewhere like she usually is. Why won't you simply shut the door and come to the elevator with me and ride me down?"

Younger Sister just looks. Her turned-down mouth is open, but no words come out. The reckless rage Tania feels is making her heart beat rapidly, urging her to slap this woman, force her to face all the ways their family has killed their spirit. But instead, without saying anything more, she walks off. Her feet carry her numbly to the elevator where she presses the button with the down arrow.

Younger Sister closes the door and leans her back and her troubles on its sturdiness.

Tania steps to the street. It's crowded with cars and headlights. Her big brogan bus driver shoes clop along the sidewalk as she heads for the nearest subway that will take her home to Brooklyn. The line she wants is blocks away.

As she hikes, she goes over and over in her mind what had happened. Why hadn't Younger Sister come down? She'd waited for ten then twenty then thirty minutes, then a whole damn hour and she hadn't come down. Older Sister and Daddy came down and Mommy sent a note, but I was waiting for Younger Sister's presence. As she steps off a curb, a long car, a sleek black caddy, swerves to make a sharp turn in front of her. "My god! He nearly hit me, the bastard!" she shouts as she crosses the street. Where the hell was the subway station? She knows this area of town, but right now nothing looks familiar.

When she finally locates the station, she wonders whether she'll be able to take out her badge and flash it for the token clerk. Her arms and hands feel numb. In the end, she does manage that, but can't manage a smile as the clerk buzzes her in.

She thinks, "Younger Sister, you are gone!!!" and "Strange how I got born into that group," mouthing the words over and over as she waits for the train in the dirty subway station. A rat scurries under the platform to the uptown side. The dingy lights blink and flicker as if they will soon go out. The minutes become a half hour very slowly! "Where the . . . ? O Hell this damn mass transit. I hate it!" Other words rub against one another in her brain, words that can't rub out the full and clear feeling that all the old family is gone now.

In Brooklyn, sitting in the window seat in her apartment, still in her jacket, she looks up at the black sky as if searching for the star people she believes— hopes— she may be descended from, thinking "These humans sure ain't worth the earth they were born into." She sighs, and heads for the answering machine with its blinking red light.

"Tania, hey baby it's me, Teddy. I just had another great session with Pam." The message is such a non sequitur to her thoughts that she can't help but break up into laughter, and she rings him back as soon as she's taken off her jacket. She had barely mentioned to him the visit to Younger Sister or even the phone call because she hadn't wanted to worry him. His daughter's mother had decided the child should get started right by going to catholic school, and as a result his money problems had become overwhelming. But he knows how much she loves her sister and that she was coming back to see her for the first time in many years. As his phone rings, she unpins her bell-shaped badge and puts it on the mantel, so she'll know where it is. The ringing stops as Teddy picks up.

"Hello?" He sounds sleepy.

"Teddy?"

"Yeah, baby."

"She never came out." Tears form in Tania's eyes.

"Who, baby?"

"Younger Sister. I waited and waited and then Older Sister came down and then I read a stupid note from my mother and . . ." She stops mid-sentence.

"Get it out, baby."

"Teddy, she isn't coming back to me. I made up all that shit in my head. What was I thinking?"

"You love her, that's what."

"Teddy, I'm . . . I'm . . ." The crying interrupts her words.

"I know."

"Teddy, thank you for picking up. I know you were asleep. Thank you for listening. I love you."

"I love you, too, Tania." In her mind's eye, she sees him turn over and cradle his pillow.

"Oh. Hon, I am so glad that I can be held by you. People like my former family deny their feelings and always want to control those of us who have any emotions. My class is dead."

"Tania . . ."

"Yeah?"

"I gotta report to the depot at 5:59 tomorrow morning."

"Oh okay . . . "I love you, my Teddy. We'll talk later . . ."

They throw kisses to each other through the phone, and in their separate apartments, each walks to the bathroom. Tania starts running the hot water with the cold to make a good soak.

She won't beg even one more time for Younger Sister to be real and face down their family's bribes of money, trips, apartments to avoid feeling and healing, the shame of their secret. Younger Sister is gone and there's no one to replace her, not even Teddy. But Teddy has given her what Younger Sister didn't. He has given her hope.

She strips out of the big old boots and the blue itchy pants. She lets her hair out of the clip and places both hands in her bathwater to test it, then sinks gently into it until her entire body is submerged. With her hands over her ears, she sinks further under the water, into the silence that allows her to go inside to wonder and to heal, as her yoga meditations do. Only her nose stays above the surface. "Today I was in front of the sicko," she thinks. "I saw an old man."

13 LETTING IN A NEW GEOGRAPHY

Their time together recently has given Tania a strong sense of her and Teddy's love, but now, whenever she approaches the bus depot, she has a sick feeling. There's gonna be something inside there, she just knows. She thinks maybe this is why she hasn't been sleeping well, she thinks, even though she unplugs her phone before she goes to bed to make sure there are no interruptions. She has to protect her rest because if she's not alert, she could kill someone with the bus.

She had thought the new, younger Location Chief, even though still a male, might be willing to let go of the need the old fart Location Chiefs who came before him seemed to have to boss her around, to pull her upstairs for hearings on the stupidest things. She's had so many of their phony papers she never feels cool at all at work. She's always uptight. Once they even put a spy on her bus and threatened to fire her for not pulling out of the depot right away, even though it looked like a pedestrian was about to step into her path. Every day she worries about what discipline or cut-your-pay paper they'll hand her at the window where she picks up her transfers. The low-level boss could tell her she has to go upstairs for a step one hearing before she even gets on her bus. They were all dirty male supremacists. They just couldn't stand to have a woman among hundreds of men who didn't have to give sex to them and yet could still receive a "big" paycheck—a woman who carried her bus loads and was never early to pull in, racing to go home and thereby supposedly "cheating the company." Actually it was the transit system that cheated. Everyone knew they kept double books, so they could steal from the workers, the riding public and the taxpayers.

Yup. Her hunch was right, her sick feeling justified. The new Location Chief is no better than the old ones. When she goes to pick up her transfers from the crew chief window, there is the note attached. The dispatcher looks like he exists only when he's at work in this cage. Not even a hint of a smile indicates he's alive as he hands her the transfers and note. "Go upstairs to see the boss on your swing or before your shift starts," it reads.

She wants to get it over with, and the union guy has free time, so the two of them head for the gloomy top floor. The lights never seem to work in this stinking hellhole, or else Transit deliberately doesn't replace the bulbs when they burn out. Even though sun was peeking out from behind the clouds as she walked from the subway to the garage, there is no evidence of it in the depot, whose windows haven't been washed in living memory. The lack of light on the top floor makes her belly clench as she comes out of the long, even darker, stairwell. We're treated like rats in here, she thinks. As she reaches up to rub her aching left shoulder with her good right hand, her badge slides down on her right side. She turns it back over so they don't accuse her of hiding her number.

There is no greeting as she and the Shop Steward walk into the boss space. The first words out of his mouth are "You didn't have your right-turn indicator on yesterday when you changed lanes. That's the write up."

"It wasn't working," she explains.

"Are you kidding?" The Shop Steward protests. "They wouldn't let her take the bus out of service for such a small thing. Left-turn maybe. But right? No way."

"Well . . ." The Location Chief clears his throat. He sounds like her father. Even looks a little like him, with his hard eyes "You can't justify not having a working turn signal. You should have reported it."

The union guy shouts, "She did. You have the paper right there in your hand that states that the "operator" called it in to control. She did just what she was supposed to do. So let up already."

But Tania knows in her bones that this new to wanna-be-high-status boss, in his navy blue suit and glasses, has the same thoughts lurking in his brain as the old ones did. He was asking himself, "How can I tweak this woman, make her the way I want her to be, the way any woman ought to be? She's got no right to walk in here, proud, her head up. I want her to at least look like she's wrong, or scared or gonna be a follow-the-orders good girl. She's too damn arrogant, with her eyes looking straight into mine. It's the look of someone who knows that in fact I don't know what to do with only so many busses and too many passengers and almost every bus needing repairs."

"How does your husband deal with you?" He asks finally.

Tania rolls her eyes at him and the union guy, waiting. She expects the Shop Steward to mouth off and insist that questions like this are illegal. It's her personal business period. It ain't none of his. If he'd asked a guy a personal question like that, somebody would have gotten punched, But the union guy says nothing, and she decides that it's not a worker-boss thing, but a male thing, and that's why this union MAN ain't saying nothing. None of them want her to believe in herself.

But she holds her rage in her throat and says nothing. She's not about to go off on this sucker or the union man. Why fall into hot water? But if looks could kill, there'd be two dead guys in the boss's office.

The boss isn't oblivious to her silent defiance. He looks her up and down. His eyes focus on her shoes. They are slightly scuffed. Satisfied that he's got her, he says, "I'm going to write you up again today for shoes being out of code."

"What?" Her shoes are regulation black. What's he talking about?

"What's the beef?" The union guy has regained his ability to speak.

"They're dirty and not shined." The boss smiles an "I'm smart and pretending I care about how things should be presented nicely,"smile. Her mother used to smile that way. Who sees the dirty lies behind the phony smile in any of these exploitative situations? All these bosses count is the outer appearance, like a smooth shine on a plastic dental ad smile that hopes to seduce you into paying for whiter teeth.

The next operator with a write-up is outside the office, hunched over. As she turns to exit, the boss barks at her, "I'll keep looking into your file. One day . . . one day . . ." He doesn't incriminate himself, but she knows he means they think that one day they'll have worn her into a meatball and laid her down. But for today the attack on her is done—though she has another two write-ups on her record. She wants to believe both will be dismissed at the next level, and they probably will be. But they are never erased, and she's so tired of going to all these hearings. Every shitty day, she wants to be able to concentrate on the road, to enjoy the satisfaction of doing an important job well, to have time to be gracious when lost passengers ask for help. But mostly she's sitting behind that wheel stiff with fear, anticipating the next attack. They'd been trying to find some petty excuse to get her fired since she was hired; only the existence of the union, weak as it was, had kept her on the job. People in a non-union shop or even salaried workers in corporate Amerrycaca would probably have lost their gig right away. So, she thanks the Spirits for the union, and remembers to say bye to the union rep as she heads for the stairs.

She knows the attacks are aimed at wearing her down, but the truth was they are succeeding. "It's gotta be better than this in life," she thinks. She *has* to vision another society, one where there are other activists and people who are healing. She taps her heart, remembering the talks she's been to where young people from the Venceremos Brigade who'd been to Cuba and come back to explain how all the people there shared the frigging money that the workers made by producing *everything*, more or less the way Smoke used to toss over her shoulder at the poetry readings, sort of quoting Marx, "From each according to her abilities, to each according to her needs. How in that socialist country, people actually cared for their work and it was possible to have a life of integrity. But not here, not now. The impossibility of such a life, a life without harassment for doing a so-called "man's job," was the main reason she and Teddy had to leave this town. Suddenly she is clear. The sucker, and the others who would come after him, knew her history and would never stop digging, never stop trying to get her gone. "Before he can do it, I'm leaving," she says aloud. No one hears her, but she commits. She will quit right after her up-coming full-year anniversary and move with Teddy to New Mexico. The decision made, she walks outside to pick up her bus from the driver who had taken over her run for the first hour. After nine hours in the seat instead of the usual ten, her work day ends and she trudges out of the depot, looks back at the red-brick walls as the steel door slams behind her, wondering how she'll make it through the weeks until her anniversary without being fired. She wants to give her notice before the anniversary, so as not to be started on another year through inertia, but not too long before, because then they might come down on her and try to force her out before she reaches the date she's chosen and thereby screw her out of a couple weeks pay. "It's a hell of a life" she murmurs to herself as she tries to calculate the best time to make her move. Her left shoulder feels as if a truck wrenched it out of its socket. Or is the chiropractor's trigger point therapy working too slowly?

A few days later, having taken simultaneous Advanced Vacation Days off, Teddy and Tania have jazz from Les McCann and Syreeta playing while, as usual, their pillow talk is taken up by the way driving busses in Manhattan is killing them. "We see too much pain," Tania says, speaking over Syreeta's calming voice. "Poor folks' pain and even almost-rich folks' pain as they climb up and down those bus stairs on their aching feet day after night. I can't take it anymore," she adds. "I can't take their pain and I can't take my own, not anymore."

She has already told him about her latest run-in with the Location Chief and her conviction that they're just harassing her, looking for an excuse to get rid of her. He doesn't disagree. He has come to see the sexism on the job, among the bosses and most of the rank and file, through her eyes. Because he loves her, her pain and anger have become his. "Is it bad enough you think you oughta quit before they fire you?"

She hesitates only a moment.

"I can't take it, yes. I'm gonna quit," she says. There. She's stated aloud the decision she'd made after she left boss's office.

"Just like that?" Teddy props his head up on one arm and looks down at her. "What'll you do?"

"We've talked and talked about New Mexico," she says. "We can go there . . ."

". . . And find a new life," He finishes the sentence, slowly articulating each word as if he is finding them new one by one, though both have said them before, to each other and when talking with Pam. "Pam is supportive of us doing that, right? I do trust her."

"Yeah," Tania agrees. "If we move outta state we can start fresh, without our families of origin." She pauses, then goes on, stroking his shoulder. "Do you think we could become our own family?" She watches to see his reaction to this question. In the last year, it has become increasingly evident that the city has stolen his child. Time and again, even though he voluntarily pays child support, his ex just laughs when he calls to say he wants to pick up his daughter. And when he arrives at her place, she lets the child, all ginger colored, with big brown eyes, come to the door to say hi, and then slams it shut when his daughter says, "No, I don't want to see you."

"You know what," he says now. "My daughter, who's old enough to know she's Black like me, didn't want the Black doll-baby I got her. She's taking her mother's side."

"For right now, Teddy, that's true." Tania holds him tight, with a strong arm of caring. After five minutes of music, she reaches up and rubs his forehead gently with a massaging motion he usually enjoys. They look into each other's half open eyes.

"Our dream is coming." Teddy smiles at her, ready at this moment to leave the city, even the child who no longer calls him "daddy." Ready, except . . . it's so hard to let it all go, he thinks.

The music plays on as they fall silent, acting out the fear that forces them to lose the connection they might have through some deeper talking. They don't say aloud, "I feel scared, honey," so the terror of true intimacy remains. They don't go deeply into their differences. If they could only say to each other, that doesn't work for me, or we don't see things the same way. He prefers sex to talking about his sadness; she prefers sex to revealing what's still too painful to say. Instead of talking, together they choose sex to bond them.

One more visit, at least, to Pam's, before Tania begins the process that will allow her to fly the hell out of Transit. As always, Pam is pouring the tea that has comforted her client through so many sessions.

"Pam," Tania says when they've settled, Tania on the couch, Pam in her chair. "Pam. I'm gonna do it. I'm gonna get started on the paperwork."

A sparkle of light from Pam's bangle touches Tania's teacup.

"I just can't stand it anymore, the way the boss looks at me, big black dick with nowhere to go. He makes me think of my father and why I used to pick men like Buster and never see that I was *allowing* what they did. I'd say, 'I'm a feminist,' but I still depended on them to make me feel I was lovable, like I wanted to be loved by daddy."

This is ground Tania has covered before. As usual, having begun to push forward, she has pulled back into familiar territory.

"You know, yesterday he actually said to Teddy, 'I hear you wanna fuck one of our operators.'"

"O dear." Pam's words set both women to laughing.

"And Teddy . . ." Tania interrupts her own laugh. ". . . Teddy said to him, 'I might wanna fuck you!'"

Tears squeezed out of her by laughter roll down Tania's face.

"Go Teddy! WOOO!" Pam exclaims, making the OK sign.

They fall silent. While appreciating Teddy's quick wit and his nerve, both realize he could maybe get away with such talk because he, like the boss, is a man, and among men locker-room talk is expected. Still, what he did took nerve, for despite their shared male culture, Teddy is still a worker and the boss a boss.

Tania gets up and goes to the window. The cat is chasing leaves in the back yard. Pam watches her, contemplating how to redirect her back to her decision to quit her job and leave behind her friends and the life she has made for herself and strike out with just Teddy for a place she knows no more about than what she learned during the week she and Teddy had spent there. She senses that she needs intellectual buttressing to face and move past the terror she must feel, and suddenly realizes that the talk of Teddy has opened a way through.

"Tania," she says. "Are you aware that Teddy has given you a great gift? He knows in his working class bones that the boss man is supposed to try to keep you down and keep the rich white male in place. How many times have I said to you all, 'Analyze the ruling class. It's your idealistic ass if you don't'?"

Tania has resumed her seat. "You mean I still think that a boss is supposed to be okay, when in reality, under this shit capitalist system, he's *supposed* to jerk us around? And Teddy has known it all along?"

Pam nods. "Sweetheart, unlike you, he's *from* the working class, like some of your sisters in the Working Woman group and Agua.

"But are they always identified with their roots?"

"No, certainly not. Not consciously. But they know what you don't, at least not instinctively, which is that at all times the worker has to be ready for a boss to try and mess him up. In your case, the Transit bosses have a whole means of production—the transportation of millions of workers—that they worry about. And their bosses are the corporate bosses in every borough who need workers to be transported to jobs or they won't see any work done or be able to steal any more super profits. The workers are just pawns. It's the same everywhere except places like Cuba where people fought for their needs to be valued over profits."

"Yeah, they have free pre-k to grad school . . . I remember." Tania leans forward. "I'm gonna move the tape recorder so I'll be sure to pick up everything you're saying, Pam."

Pam smiles. "Well, shall I sum it up then? From us workers' point of view, the boss's power over us has both a subjective and an objective side. Inside we are filled with self-hate . . . and objectively, they really can fire us. They have power over us on both counts."

"And we in the United States of Americaca don't yet know our power, if we'd just join together to stand up, right?"

"Right. And Tania, you have to see, you really have to smell this. The boss tries to dominate you—the worker—and you *give* him the power over you. Instead of standing up workers go home and take it out on their kids, who grow up and do the same—submit or dominate."

"Umm, it's true. I look at that idiot boss on the job and think I'm pre-school age . . . and that he can totally isolate and destroy me." And so I go along to get along. Instead of standing up, I don't say anything." Except in the Hell on Wheels campaign, when maybe I said too much instead of biding my time, which put me in the union bosses' crosshairs."

"So you do know, Tania. You know how you give them the power over you. In every instance it's different, but really it's always the same and will always be the same given the system, and now you, like Teddy, know it in your gut. And while the union offers you some protection, even though they are damn sure bureaucratic and at times don't defend you too well, you have to see that that, too is a kind of trap, especially for people like Teddy with families to support. To even think of leaving a quote-unquote'good union job' takes courage, Tania, courage to face your fears, courage to venture into the unknown, maybe even the courage to confront and work to undermine the system."

Tania picks up and examines the framed photo of fighting Vietnamese on Pam's end table. "You mean like the Vietnamese revolutionaries who worked underground?"

"That's right . . . in those underground tunnels . . . Though there's a whole lot of consciousness-building to be done here before you start digging tunnels."

"But I can do that, Pam. I'm a writer, so, yeah, I can do that." Tania sounds excited. "You know what, Pam?" she says.

"What?"

Tania hesitates. Her eyebrows wrinkle and her eyes darken.

Pam says for her what she's left unsaid. "This is the last remnant of daddy. He's going."

"You mean my fear of big dick daddy is going?"

"Yes, because now you know he was really scared and needing legitimate power as a worker."

"But he showed his power over me rather than stand up to the thieving done by his bosses at his insurance gig and all those other messed up places where they called him 'dirty nigga' and hated his black guts."

"Black *and* a worker, that's what he was."

"But he thought that because he ate petit fours and used a credit card to pay for dinner at some sicko joint with us kids, looking down the cleavage of waitresses, he was a rich man. In fact he just had those stupid ideas of rich folks. He thought he owned us and controlled us, when in fact . . ."

Pam nods, urging Tania on.

"In fact . . ." Tania says again, "In fact, I did the emotional work in that family!" Tania is stunned by her own recognition of this type of labor. She leans back into her counselor's couch. It holds her with its springs and comforting fabric. It soothes her. It's as if she is with the workers on the line as they put the couch together, as if she is rolling along in the trucker's rig that carried it from the factory somewhere in the US of A , to the department store, where Pam and her husband picked it out. Suddenly she is crying. "But I loved him, Pam, in spite of everything. You know he's got Alzheimer's. The last time I saw him he was just a sick old man, nothing to be afraid of. But as much as I hate them, my old family, the love is still there along with the hate and the fear. Why? They're all cowards. My dad especially was a coward . . . that's what these men are, Black, white, damn it, any color, who don't want to jump up off their ass and do some changing of this oppressive, kick you-to-the-curb system. They, like the bosses, don't want to face their own inner self-hate and self-contempt while we—workers, wives, mothers, kids—who are their enablers don't dare reveal our real selves and stand up, but instead focus on their issues. We're always worried we won't have a home or a job that pays decent, 'cause there ain't no full employment law on the books, ain't no health care coverage like in every other country worth its salt . . ."And that's what these fathers don't want to face,"

Tania stops to catch her breath. The tape recorder has reached the end of the tape, but she hasn't noticed. Later, when she realizes it, she also realizes it doesn't matter. There's no way she'll forget what's been said today.

"You're right, Tania," Pam says. "We women have to stand up to them, and these men have the historical responsibility to stand up to the rich with us." She pauses, looking up at the wood-framed photo of Fidel in his Cuban armed forces fatigues, staring down at them from his place of honor on the wall. "And transform the world," she adds.

Tania almost whispers, "So quitting Transit and relocating is the first step to changing the world, is that what you're saying?"

Pam nods. "And you can do it. I think it might be helpful if you read some Womanist theorists."

"Like who? What can they tell me? I have a mortgage to pay!"

"After reading Marx I chose to study economics to learn how to maneuver in this shit. I suggest you figure out how to do a joint refinancing with Agua."

Tania looks up. "What would that mean?"

"It would be a way to support a working class sister by arranging for her to have the apartment without having to go on her own to a bank and apply for a loan, which she wouldn't get. You'd have to wait for her to pay you the down payment over time, but you'd be out of it, and I expect both of you would appreciate not having to pay closing fees to the bank. And Agua would have her own place. For it to work, though, you'd have to trust each other."

Tania mulls over this suggestion, not yet fully understanding it, but appreciating it as a possible way forward. "I love you, Pam. I love the way you give me practical ideas. I love your clarity . . . your dignity, your integrity." She stops, then begins again. "I think sooo much that if folks only had support from themselves and people who can think, and if they watch and choose the ripe time for change . . . the folks will do it. Rise up, build collectives, worker's co-ops and stuff like that I mean. Even a General Strike." She closes her eyes for a moment.

"I hope so Tania. I hope leaving Transit lets you keep your eyes open to the whole working world and explore outside of New York City and maybe even the US. Go see and hear for yourself. Start with New Mexico. The Spanish you picked from Agua will help you. "

"I will Pam, I will." Tania sighs. This has been a deep session. Then, suddenly hearing her inner goofy self, she says, "Pam, just today, I want to be silly."

"Well, it's your day off, so do something fun. We revolutionaries have to rest, too. It restores us."

"Okay, what should I do?"

"It'll come to you."

"Dance. I'll take all my clothes off and put on James Brown and dance around my apartment!"

"There you go." Pam's voice is sweet. Her neck is slender and heroic, like the neck of Nefertiti in the famous bust.

"Pam, let's not make another appointment," Tania says.

"No, you're ready to take wing. People move best when they're in pain, not too much, but some. Besides, as you know, I'm not some bourgie therapist who keeps people on a string every week just so he can pay his bills. And remember, sweetheart, you can call whenever you need to, from wherever you are."

"How do you manage?" Suddenly Tania is thinking about the practicalities involved in being on her own, without the high-paying job.

Pam gets to her feet, matter of fact. "Well, I've studied this man's banking system, and know that I can't go into dumb debt like so many people. Then, my husband carries the mortgage, so we survive, just like many conscious people. "You'll figure it out. Call me any time." She smiles.

Tania, too, stands up. It's time to go. "Thank you so much, Pam. I'll always remember my contract with you, to pass on what I've learned, to share it. Sharing is what socialism is."

The two women, client and counselor, friends, stand side by side for a while looking out Pam's big back window. It's late evening, and their gaze traces the long shadow of a tree toward the promise of sunlight behind it, in the distance.

Back home it's still Tania's day off, and of course she wants to do something with her man, not to mention share with him the excitement she feels after her session with Pam. But Teddy hasn't called—there's no message on her machine. And when she calls him, his machine answers.

"I'm sick of this," she says icily after the beep. "Why don't you call me when you know it's my day off? I hope you're not playing pool at the depot. I've got lots to tell you." She slams the phone down.

Later that night, around midnight, when she feels it's long past time he should have called her back, she calls again.

He answers groggy and sleepy. "Yeah?"

"Teddy? Teddy Nat . . ."

"Why you calling so late, Tan?"

His answering her with a question makes her angrier. Gone are the warm feelings, the understanding she'd had when she left Pam's. "Shit, Teddy, why didn't you just call me back? Maybe we should break up. Tomorrow's Wednesday, you know I'll be off again, but you didn't call me today to see if we could set something up after you get off work. I'm beginning to think you don't want to see me. You're just a big dodo who wants to stay away from me and be all up under your mama. You don't really want to think about leaving New York."

"That's not true. I'm just not focused on the same things at the same time as you are."

"Well, you better damn well get focused if we're gonna to go to New Mexico. When are we going to talk about it? If not now, when?"

"How about next weekend?"

"With you it's all the time 'next weekend.' I'm so frustrated I could scream." She wipes the backs of her hands on her head as she switches the phone from one hand to the other.

"Well, what's stopping you?"

"Don't give me that! Trying to push me into acting crazed."

"Why would I do that?"

"I don't know. We need to help each other, not be at each other's throats. Pam said so many important things today. . ."

"Tania, I am sleepy. I can't even think about all this now."

"So when will you think about it? Are you gonna back out?"

His body insisting that it be cared about, Teddy pulls the sheet up, just under his neck. "No, I'm not. But I gotta get some sleep. I report at 6 am."

"So when do we talk?"

"We'll talk tomorrow." He rolls over and hangs up.

She calls back. "You know what?" she says, cold as ice. I'm finished. Don't call me tomorrow. How dare you just hang up on me without giving me a chance to say okay, or 'let's plan for a time' or anything." She searches her ceiling for a soothing place to rest her eyes.

"Tania, what do you want from me? I'll call you tomorrow as soon as I get off. Right now I'm hanging up and turning off the ringer."

"Okay, Teddy, if that's the way you want it. Good stinking bye!" Crying with great, gasping sobs, she slams down the phone and beats her pillows.

After hanging up, Teddy lies staring at the ceiling, then lights a cigarette. He puts it out after two puffs and rolls over In a minute, he is sound asleep.

Still sobbing, she heads toward the bathroom. Back in her bedroom, she rips off her clothes and throws them on the floor, then curls up in a ball on the bed. She sleeps lightly, restlessly. Waking at 4:30 a.m. when Teddy wakes up on the other side of the city to get ready for work, she checks her clock, thinking one day Teddy could squeeze in another joint appointment with Pam and her to work stuff out. Would he do it though? She takes an herbal passionflower tablet to put herself back to sleep. Her eyes stay puffy.

Teddy wakes up, drags himself to his bathroom, throws water on his face, dresses and hurries to his car. He's late. Opening the car door, he sees that Tania left one of her scarves on the front seat. He holds it against his cheek as he waits for a green light. He is focused on the traffic, but he can smell the scent of her on the scarf and inside he feels her body, her softness. The cross streets, shops and traffic lights occur one after the other, and the routine calms him.

Days of this break up pass. They don't even like themselves, much less each other. During his swing at work, he parks himself at a table with five other guys right by where she has to walk when she reports to pick up her transfers. He ignores her, slapping white dominoes down, playing the men's game, talking rough the way they do. Tania ignores him right back. Her expression is glum, her mouth set in a stony fake smile that only halfway convinces her real self that she might make an okay day of it instead of a disaster. Then, eleven hours later, when she clears for the night and brings the unused transfers back to the dispatcher's open window, she glances at the empty table, remembering him sitting with his back to her.

The next day he sees her waiting outside to make her bus relief. She stands by a 5000 series bus that got pulled off the road for repairs, but the shifter hasn't had time to take it in to the back of the depot for fixing. She looks like a little kid compared to that forty-foot vehicle with its ten-foot high front end as she watches for her bus to come up the road. He knows she can't see him and he wants to go over and say hi. Instead, he stuffs his hands in his pocket and whispers to himself. "I love Tania. I love that woman. But she drives me crazy."

He looks up when a bald man who has just come out of the garage says to him, in a continuation of a discussion they'd been having on and off in the shift room about everybody owing something to the common good, "You'll never be a success 'cause, as you say, you don't do jury duty. That shit you be talkin', 'bout winnin' at pool upstairs, ain't nothin' but hot air. You gotta at least participate in the world away from transit. This ain't everything." He strokes his scalp and pulls on his chin, as if a wise-man's beard or at least a goatee would appear. Though Teddy usually appreciates the fatherly advice the older man gives him—so different from anything his own father ever said to him—today he just laughs and heads inside, away from the sage and Tania, slamming the door behind him.

A week goes by like this. On her day off, he calls. She picks up the phone and answers with a casual "Hello."

"It's me."

"I'm glad you called." She is crying but he can't hear her.

"I called to see how you are."

"Teddy I can't talk about it anymore like this. I'm not good at figuring stuff out sometimes. But I know that I love you, Teddy."

"I love you too."

"I know you do. But we've got to talk about the move. My next one-year anniversary is around the corner and if I'm going to quit, now is the time. When I talked with Pam she made me feel so sure I could do it—we could do it—but . . ."

"I'm tired of transit, yes. But Tania, I wanna make my ten years so I can take more of my pension contribution with me. You're so impatient."

"But that means we'll never be in sync about leaving, Teddy. You're the one originally wanted to go to New Mexico, remember?"

"Yes, and I do want a fresh start, but it's not so easy for me to just pick up and go. Bear with me, okay?"

"Okay, Teddy Nat Turner, okay."

"I gotta go now, baby." Teddy smiles a closed-mouth smile, relieved. He feels confident they will work it out eventually, and continues to smile even though she can't see it.

"Bye, hon." She slowly puts her phone in its cradle, looks for his photo tucked into the frame of her mirror. They are both smiling in that photo and she picks it up, stares a while, replaces it. They still have not had a real talk about the move. She had so wanted to share with him all that Pam said, maybe even the tape, and make plans for what they would do together. But there has been no chance, and before the end of the month she will have to go to the office to get the papers if she's going to quit on her anniversary.

One evening, on a drive out of the city, Teddy tells her he will not be moving to New Mexico when she does.

She cries out, "Why? You saw men out there you could relate to, like the guys playing dominos. You'll have friends."

"It won't be the same. I've known the guys at work for ten years. Like you and Agua and them. I don't see how you can just up and leave them."

"She'll visit. My friends will stay in touch. But Transit is killing my soul as well as my body. With you it's obviously different."

"Well, I'll leave once you set things up. I gotta make peace with this about the guys. They mean a lot to me. It'll only be a few more months."

They feel connected here in the car, far from the city's crowds and traffic bumper to bumper. Mother Earth helps them, along with Father Sky. After a few moments of silence, Teddy goes on: "You know, my family sent my aunt up north and she did day work and got settled and then sent for the rest of the family."

"Yeah, Pam told me a lot of Black families did that during migration to the north or outta Jamaica."

Tania agrees this is so. But the fact that his Black forebears and hers did it this way doesn't make up for her disappointment. She will be starting out alone on what she had believed would be their great adventure as a family.

After Teddy drops her off in Brooklyn her bedroom roots her, and she crafts a poem for other sisters, to express her feelings of panic.

An International Love Poem for Women, by Tania

NYC Strong Working women sewing love into every garment, we Filipina women push thru the sewing machine.
Turning and believing in the goodness in folks, in every London corner we drive the bus around.
Stamping an indelible print of nurturing in lumps of Kentucky coal we draw from the mine's walls . . .
OUR INTERNATIONAL BROTHERS and LOVERS, WE WANT SOME RELIEF, some stroking of our cunts, as you and we hunt for the inner peace.
We just want a 7-hour love
to make up for the 8 day shove, drawing us closer to our grave . . .
PLEASE BROTHERS, come toward our sensual hips/casual lips with an outstretched hand that's strong,
creasing the grayness outta our hair,
weaving, believing and screaming our freedom song!
It's long, it's long, not just your dick, but our struggle!
It's faith in our chance to change the small and Big fears we have
that keeps me and my sisters willing to juggle
some love time, some slave time, with some struggle time . . .
to make one endless moment of COURAGE!

Opening her Motherpeace Tarot deck of cards, she shuffles and, praying to the spirits for guidance, spreads them out beside her on her futon. Each card she chooses brings more clarity. One tells her she has to quit *now*. Another, which shows the Empress Major Arcana III, tells her she has to go without Teddy at first 'cause she can't trust the Transit bosses won't set her up so they can fire her for some infraction. Counseled by Pam's wisdom, she feels encouraged to trust in Teddy's process. After all, New Mexico had been his dream before it was hers. Now, reading the promise in the cards, she is sure it will be theirs together.

14 QUIT AND RUN

"You gotta notarize this form. You just can't come in here saying you're leaving this job," the Location Chief's male secretary barks at Tania. A Black man whose hair forms a perfect circle around the bald spot on top of his head, he withholds any sort of smile as he puts the white paper on the top of the ledge of the window between him and her. The window is open, but the air outside is so still that the paper doesn't stir. The man's aftershave smells too strong and Tania is repelled by his stubby fingers.

"You mean I have to do something else before I can leave this dump?" Her tone is scornful, not questioning.

"Hey, watch your language. You don't want the boss to hear you."

"Yes I damn sure do. I've had it with this hellhole, where the cockroaches and rats have a ball and we ain't got clean tables to eat on during our swings." She grabs the paper off the ledge. "Where the hell do I find a notary?"

"Try the bank down the block!" The secretary slides the window shut with a bang and retreats, turning his back and pulling open a file drawer as if to file something so she can't ask anything else.

An hour later that afternoon, after finishing with the bureaucrats and their shenanigans, she walks through the garage, waving a copy of the now notarized form as if to shake off the depot's dust, which clings to the sheet of paper. As she heads toward the huge doors at the back where the busses come in, the first person she passes is a man whose heavy frame seems to sit on his bones without much support. His beautiful brown eyes and well-shaped face have given him a lot of good luck with ladies, though he's gotten nowhere with Tania. Immediately he and several other guys who soon gather around realize that she's actually quit. They never believed she'd go through with it, and now they joke among themselves as she walks straight past them.

Finally it's the bus cleaner who shouts, over the noise of the vacuum swallowing the tokens and change from the bus that's just pulled in. "Hey, Tania. Did you really do it?"

"'Yes!" she shouts back. "I just QUIT!" Suddenly jumping and skipping, she waves the paper back and forth over her head like a flag.

"No you didn't."

"YES I DID!" As she throws her head back with a laugh, he reaches out and hugs her for the first time in all the years she's been there. "Yup, I finally did it!" she says again, and suddenly they're cracking up, laughing like a pair of maniacs.

Home at last, she settles into the chair by the window in her bedroom and kicks up her feet to rest as she has done so many times before. But the familiar apartment suddenly feels very different, not like home at all. And in fact, it is no longer hers. During the weeks it took Transit to process her papers, she has all but sold the co-op to Agua.

She and Agua had often talked about how Agua might purchase a co-op, since she had no ties to anyone who could lend her big bucks and, though she made good money at her unionized maintenance job, saving enough for a down payment on an apartment was almost impossible. She would get a few dollars in the bank and wham, there would be an emergency of some kind, like Heru's asthma attacks. Her mother Enid had a steady office job, but she too had trouble saving, and in any case, for a number of years she and Agua had not had any real communication. So during the months Teddy had been making up his mind that he was going to lie back and wait for Tania to leave first, Tania and Agua had talked about how Tania, who had quite a bit of money saved up, could finance Agua's purchase of her apartment. The idea was that Agua would become co-owner initially, with her name as well as Tania's on the papers, including the mortgage, which Tania would refinance at the new, low interest rates, so that Agua could afford the payments. Agua had learned from a friend who did paralegal work that the two women could pay a lawyer to draw up an agreement stating that Tania would relinquish her rights to the apartment even though her name would still be on it and Agua would pay her in installments over five years the amount of the down payment Tania had made when she bought the place. Also Agua would be completely responsible for the monthly payments on the bank loan as well as the monthly "maintenance" payments to the owners' corporation. The arrangement meant that Tania could "sell" the apartment while avoiding the bother and expense of advertising the place on the open market. And she could help her friend out, too.

So the two women have been doing business big time, and now that Tania has walked out of the depot for good, the deal can be finalized. All that remains to be done is to sign the papers that have been drawn up, Now that Tania walked out of the depot for good, the deal can be finalized. Tania picks up the phone, settles on the floor in the living room by the kitchen, and dials Agua's number.

"Hey Agua, it's me Tania."

"Hey Tania." Agua knows why she's called. "You've done it, haven't you? We can go ahead now. Just let me find my notepad." When doing business, it was important to keep careful records.

"I can hardly keep my mind on this business. I'm so damn glad to be finished with transit. I haven't even told Teddy yet."

"Yeah, I know, Tan. But I got to leave for work soon, so let's focus on the way the rent and other finances will go for right now, okay?" Agua is mindful of the way Tania can find talking about Teddy so much more interesting than talking about money stuff.

Suddenly finding her seat on the floor uncomfortable, Tania climbs to her feet and, trailing the long cord on the phone, walks over to the bed, where she leans on a soft pillow, the cat, Power, curled up beside her.

"Agua, you said I can stay in the co-op after the refinancing deal is signed, even until next year, December, if I have to, right?"

"Yes, Tania, and pay me rent, month to month, equal to the monthly payment on the loan and the maintenance. And I don't have to start paying you for the down-payment until you move out, right?"

"Yes, Agua, that's what we agreed. I'm glad I'm out of this shit. But if I'm paying you instead of you paying me, I gotta tell Teddy to be ready to go soon or

I'll go through what I've saved up for my new start in New Mexico before I get there. I can wait awhile, maybe pick up a part time delivery job while he decides what to do, but not forever."

"Tania, I can't go over your thing with Teddy right now. When we do the refinancing at the bank, I'll bring the agreement the lawyer drew up. We'll sign it together, all right?"

"All right. And thanks, Agua, for not being in a rush."

Agua chews the last piece of the cucumber she has been munching and wipes her lips. "That's okay. The delay gives me time here in the Bronx to save up a little, while you pay rent to stay there. Once the co-op, mortgage and all, belongs to me I know I'm gonna feel the financial pressure." I hope Heru gets a real job after he graduates high school, so he can help out more."

"It's okay for you, but I feel like I'm really effing losing money every minute I hang around here instead of living cheaper in the Southwest *and* collecting what you agreed to pay to me monthly to me for the down-payment. If only Teddy . . ."

Her worries furrow her brow and she shoves Power off her lap and gets up.

"I gotta go, Tania," says Agua. "When should we meet at the bank?"

After some back and forth, the two women settle on a date the next week.

As arguments erupt continually now between Tania and Teddy, she sometimes counts them in her imagination. Fight number five thousand and five . . . six . . . seven . . . she mutters as she sells her old furniture. Finally, after number five thousand and fifteen, with the apartment virtually empty, except for liquor-store boxes destined to be filled with the few essentials, like kitchen equipment and books and music tapes, she's taking with her, a couple of suitcases and the roll-a-way cot she's borrowed from Smoke, they reach out for help, agreeing to go for one last joint counseling session with Pam.

At the outset of the session, Pam's two clients settle into opposite ends of the couch, sitting by themselves rather than side by side. Their expressions are grim, though Teddy smiles as the cat passes on its way to the kitchen.

After pouring the tea and seating herself in her straight-backed chair facing them, Pam addresses Teddy. Her softly spoken words almost seem to be "channeled," a sharing with him of wisdom from another dimension.

"Until now you've been involved with very insecure women, Teddy, your daughter's mother and your own. I think you've already discovered that Tania isn't quite that way, at least not any more You believe the city has deprived you of your daughter, and that's so, but your ex keeps driving you away because that's her perverse way of keeping you on a string. Then there's your mama . . ."

"I think Tania thinks it's easy for me to move stuff—just pack up and go. She thinks they won't know I'm going," Teddy says sourly.

Tania jumps in. “Sure they’ll know, ’cause you won’t dare not tell ’em. Pam, he depends on his mama like he was still a child, and one minute she treats him like one and the next like some kind of servant at her beck and call. His mother will ask ‘how are you?’ and he’ll say, ‘I have a headache.’ And she’ll say ‘take two Tylenols.’ And he’ll say, ‘Yes, Mama.’ Then two or three hours later she’ll call him up and say ‘How’s your head?’ He’ll say ‘I took two Tylenols, but . . .’ She doesn’t let him finish. ‘Well,’ she’ll say, ‘your aunt is up here sick. I may need some help with her, so don't go out unless you call me and let me know.’ Can you imagine? Last night he dreamed he couldn't open his eyes. He pulled his sweater over his head and he tried to open them but he couldn't do it.” She sits back, having used her sharpest tone to fill Pam in, then turns to Teddy. “So I’m sure you’re gonna tell ’em. What I’m afraid of is that when your mother finds out you’re really moving, she’s gonna say she’s sick to keep you in New York.”

Now Pam comes in, speaking softly. “Tania’s right, Teddy. Your mama, when she finds out for sure you’re going move, first she’s gonna come out the side of her neck, and then she’s going play sick. The family you grew up in and the little family you created, they’re all going to say terrible things to you if you tell them.”

“I still don’t think I’d feel good if I just don’t tell them.” Teddy is sitting hunched over, looking miserable. He uses his forefinger to smooth down his purple jogging suit.

“Maybe so,” Pam says. “And I’m trying to be where you are. So’s Tania, even if you don’t always see it. But the truth is, even though you will have been respectful and told your mama you’re taking care of your own life and going to New Mexico once Tania’s settled in no matter what, she’ll still move on you . . .”

“I still don’t see why she should.”

“Because she doesn’t think you have the guts to go. And you do see that, really. You just can’t bear to be fully conscious of it. Remember what we said last time you were here and we talked about the dreams you’ve been having: the paralyzing scorpions and the cranes, which are scavengers even if they are beautiful. If you’re going to make a new life, a new family, with the woman you love, you’re going to have to free yourself from the clutches of the old one . . .”

Teddy cuts in. “But Pam, I mean, I don’t have to get all loud like Tania and just say to my mother, ‘Listen, I’m outta here!’”

“No, that wouldn’t be you, with that southern training. See, what you’re doing now is examining your relationship with your family, facing it, just the way Tania had to do with hers. But she’s scared you won’t go through with it and so becomes judgmental. She took ten years with her mother, and she’s afraid it’s going to take you that long, too. Does that help you to understand where she’s coming from?”

Teddy nods.

"And whenever you feel you want to, you just pick up the phone and say, 'Pam, this is Teddy, I gotta come in. I got something to talk about.' Okay?"

Again Teddy nods, and Pam turns to Tania, who has been uncharacteristically quiet, letting Pam speak for her. "As for you, Tania, you've got to leave this to him to follow his own path. You're scared because you know there's no way he won't let them know and you're afraid that if he does he won't ever make the move, and the new family you're counting on creating with him won't happen after all. So you delay your departure and camp out in your apartment, putting your life and Agua's on hold. You have to find the courage to go and trust that Teddy, who loves you so much, will follow. And if he doesn't . . ." She pauses for a moment, then goes on. "If he lets you down, remember, you can always call me from New Mexico . . ." She does not say that she knows that if this happens, Tania will be devastated not only because of the betrayal of her dreams but because she will think that once again, like her mother, she's chosen a man who cannot be the man she thought he was.

While Pam has been talking, Teddy has moved closer to Tania, and now he puts his arm around her and takes her hand. "Don't worry, Tania," he says. "I won't let you down."

Tania moves into his embrace, and after a moment, Pam stands up. The session is over. They leave the warmth of Pam's sanctuary hand in hand.

Moving day is here, and the inside of the co-op looks more and more empty. Filled boxes are stacked at the front door. Inside one that Agua struggles to close there are books: *Capitalist Patriarchy and the Case for Socialist Feminism*, by Zillah Eisenstein; *The Moon Calendar* and the *Moosewood Cookbook* as well as too many music cassettes—— jazz, James Brown, reggae—— for the size of the box. "What do I do with all these tapes?" Agua asks. "They don't fit."

"Oh here, would you like the ones by Judy Mowatt and Rita Marley?" Agua is a great admirer of Bob Marley's sister.

"Yes!" Both women smile as Agua receives the gift, then presses her hands down on the flaps, trying to get the four of them to intersect and close the box. In doing so, she stubs and cuts her finger, looks up and catches the eye of her friend, who is walking back and forth sweeping and finishing up. Teddy appears and hauls a few of the boxes that are already stacked by the door downstairs to the first floor and the waiting U-Haul trailer, which they'd managed to find a place to park only two doors from Tania's building. He continues going back and forth as the two women huddle together, out of his sight, in the bedroom.

"I'm gonna miss the hell outta being here with you, Tania," Agua says. Tania is searching in the box marked "Bathroom-Toiletries" for a band-aid to cover the cut on Agua's finger.

"Teddy can work by himself for a minute." Tania replies with a *non seqitur*. "Let's do a quick ritual to share our good-bye so we'll remember it with a smile."

Having found the band-aid, she sits in a yoga hero pose on the bare floor. Agua sits cross-legged across from her. They take two deep breaths. Agua extends her hand. Tania presses the band-aid onto Agua's finger. "With this tape may Agua be wrapped in love and support," she says.

"Yes!" Agua stands up, crying as she speaks. "And as Tania drives no more big busses, may her car and U-Haul help her steer her life to calmer streets far from an old family that wanted her dead."

Tania, looking up at her friend, seeing her tears, responds with encouragement. "Wow! We trust each other, don't we? I'm damn clear that, for both of us, leaving our old families helped us realize we need to be Family to each other. And like Pam said, financially independent of men, unlike our mothers." She scrambles to her feet and reaches out for a hug. "I feel so good that you understand me, Agua. I'll call you as soon as we arrive, in a few days, okay?"

Agua nods, but her tears continue to fall. The hollowness of the apartment resonates in her heart, but Tania, feeling the pressure of leaving and beginning the fast four-day drive, walks away from her toward the kitchen, where she checks that the AAA trip-tik is safely stowed in her shoulder bag, which lies on the floor. Back upstairs now, Teddy calls, "Hey, where's the car keys? The trailer's almost full and it's time to bring the car around to load the rest. I'll just double park it in front to load it."

"I have the key here in my bag, Hon," she calls to him, looking back at the empty doorway of the bedroom; she imagines Agua wiping her glasses, which will have steamed up from her tears.

Teddy, completely focused on the physical work, takes the keys from Tania, then hops downstairs, anxious to start driving. Tania has already given Agua the mailbox key; now she takes the last remaining key, the one to the deadbolt and puts it in her pants pocket. She pushes the few remaining boxes, small ones from the wine store, filled with odds and ends, the broom and dust pan, to the door, then returns to the bedroom.

"Here's the key Agua." She speaks softly.

"What?"

"Come on, woman, we'll see each other again before too long. You know we be best buddies."

Agua's sneakers carry her swiftly across the floor. She reaches out her arm and Tania slaps five with the key ending up in Agua's palm.

"Okay, Tan, I'll lock the door when you all leave and ride up to the Bronx to rest before I start to finish packing to move in here."

"I'm so glad you chose to wait a week before you moved in so you could take it easy." Tania tries to put some cash in Agua's pocket to thank her for helping her pack.

"No." Agua pushes away her friend's hand.

"But you'll need help with the bills at first, right? This mortgage is more than you've ever paid."

"No, Tania. You're my family now. You know I left Enid and them just like you had to let go of your deniers."

They walk to the door. Agua picks up the last box, while Tania, ignoring Power's protests, grabs the cat carrier, and together they head downstairs.

Teddy is a good packer, and has left space for the cat carrier on the back seat along with Agua's box, which will keep it from falling. The friends hug once more and Tania gets into the passenger seat. The car is her good-on-gas hatchback, but with the trailer attached, Teddy will drive them out of the city.

Leaving Agua on the sidewalk, they lurch away from the curb as Teddy struggles to get the small car moving, adjusting the gears to the weight of the trailer. In moments they are on their way.

He plays cassette after cassette and she glares silently out the window as they speed through New Jersey onto I-78 and head west, across Pennsylvania. This trip there will be no meanderings through Virginia and Tennessee, no lingering in bed together at various Kamper Kabins as they had done on their vacation trip. The drive will be a straight run to St. Louis, then Arkansas, Oklahoma and a sliver of Texas to Albuquerque, and from the beginning it seems like the whole time they're either rushing about or arguing. At their first motel, they push themselves out of bed at 6 a.m. to have as many daylight hours as possible to drive. "Hurry up Tania," Teddy calls as he leaves her in the bathroom, shutting the shower water off. "I've got the bag, and I left your clothes on the chair." He pounds quickly down the motel stairs to the car in its parking space and pulls it around to the lobby carport so Tania can hop in as soon as she's settled the tab and put Power in her carrier.

They're not long on the road the next morning when Tania asks him what he's feeling about going back to New York without her, and he doesn't like it. He's okay with Pam talking to him this way, not Tania, not before breakfast, anyway, and not when he's feeling the pressure of having put his job at risk by taking a four-day "emergency" leave to care for his supposedly ailing grandmother He puts headphones on.

The second night, however, he warms up as they snuggle in the motel's double bed. "Tania, I'm kinda worried about what's gonna happen when I have to face the guys back at the garage, especially when they ask me about my sick grandma. I don't know what to say." He pulls the sheet up over her to make sure she'll stay comfy if the night turns cooler.

"Tell them nothing. Cough and say it's too painful, you don't want to talk about it." She smiles.

He hugs her with one arm, but they're too tired from driving fourteen hours to make any real love. So they just spoon a little, and soon Teddy is snoring, and Tania, exhausted, also falls right to sleep despite his wheezing.

By the time they arrive in Arkansas, it's a fast in and out. They take turns driving until they reach Oklahoma, though he does most of it. He drives straight through the state, stopping only once, except for gas, at a convenience store off the highway exit, until they pull off for the night. On their previous trip, they'd noticed how Oklahoma's Native American roots stand out in the flat, high-cheek-boned faces of many of its people. This time Tania picks up a free Native Drum newspaper that lies next to the motel brochures in the lobby of the place they stay in, but Teddy doesn't really pay attention as she reads aloud from it.

At the Texas border, they switch seats and Tania drives while he stares out the window, studying the thin, dry looking sage brush. Despite the lack of magnolias and the poplar trees just right for lynching, he loses himself in memories of his boyhood self piled with his sister and the excess luggage in the back seat of his pop's car for those long drives through Virginia to his granny's house. He can just taste the fried chicken and greens, so unlike the tacos and tamales he's likely to have for supper today. Going west as well as south may still mean warmth in the afternoon sun during any winter month, but it utterly lacks the slow, dragged out sweet talking ways of southern Virginia, and all of a sudden he wonders whether he'll ever really belong out here.

Tania interrupts his reverie to ask him to change the station on the radio, tired of all the Christian radio announcers hollering "Praise Jesus" when introducing almost every number. He and Tania laugh about how Teddy's mom will feel right at home if she ever takes the bus to visit them once he moves out of the city and joins Tania in New Mexico.

"She'll have a church to pray in at every rest stop, I'll bet." Teddy says, glancing at Tania, who smiles lovingly. He squeezes her shoulder, glad that he chose a non-Christian, free spirited woman this time, unlike his mom and his daughter's mom, who'd claimed her Catholic upbringing kept her from having an abortion when she deliberately stopped using the pill and got pregnant.

She steers through Texas, heading toward the Sandia Mountains of New Mexico, now appearing in the distance. Glancing over at him, she smiles. "Thanks for making up that thing about your grandma and asking for the time off so we could start this new life on the physical plane."

He reaches out again to massage her shoulder. "I'll drive now, the last stretch." They've reached the New Mexico border. After they arrive in Albuquerque, they'll have only a few hours together before his plane leaves.

They pull off on the shoulder and switch seats. She picks up where she left off. "I wish you didn't have to go finish up those loose ends with your family before coming back to be with me."

"Well, I'm glad I helped you escape the hell hole of your life. You put up with transit long enough. You're better than those bosses ever tried to treat you."

Their excitement mounts as they look at the dabs of houses scattered along the mountainside as they race down the last stretch of I-40, then abruptly pull off at the Albuquerque Pet Food shop they've spotted, in a mall next to the freeway to pick up a bag of cat-food for Power. At the end of a huge aisle, with more space in it than there is in an entire bodega back east, they meet the clerk, who readily gives Tania a lead to an apartment.

Within hours, after meeting the New Mexican landlady, and having paid the rent, Teddy finds the tip of his woman's keys touching sharp metal edges of the lock to her apartment. He has gotten her here safe, and now he shoulders her boxes and carries them inside, making sure to see her all moved in before he has to fly home, wondering suddenly if it is back home . . . or just back east.

Tossing pillows on the floor of her new home, Tania flops down on the wall-to-wall carpeting and, breathing out a huge sigh, exclaims, "Wow, rent a place and move into an apartment within eight hours of arriving. No housing scarcity in the southwest, as long as you got that east coast cash!"

But the rest is a short one. Within moments they have to jump back in the car to take Teddy to the airport. Tania is driving, and Teddy shouts for her to speed up. "I gotta make it on the plane in time and get back to work," he says. At the airport, they barely have time for a single kiss, before he rushes to the gate and is gone.

Every day after Teddy leaves, Tania, alone in New Mexico, looks at the skies. Blue, only clear blue everywhere, ocean blue overhead, just the way she remembered it from when she and Teddy were together at the beach. She knows not a soul. Slowly it sinks in that she's left the city of her old family behind, that she's never ever going to bump into those people again, since Older Sister, Younger Sister and the parents don't have any idea she has left. "Let them drown in their denial alone," she mumbles to herself, lying down on her bed and looking out her window at the sky, deep as the sea.

***

Most weeks since he got back to New York, Teddy works seven days, even overtime on some of them. He'd started to make up for the time he'd missed, but it had become a regular thing, so he could avoid seeing his momma at his apartment door, all the time wanting him to get her something she needed or just scratch some itch she had. Several times, however, when something has happened that he needs to talk about but can't discuss with Tania in some long-distance phone call, he takes a break from work to drive up to Pam's home. At one session he tells her his father has died.

Pam sighs. "Another victim of alcoholism," she says, and he nods. "Do you feel relieved or . . .?"

"Yeah, I guess so. Now I can leave New York without worrying that Momma will go back to him. But . . ." He hesitates.

"But what?"

"But now I worry what's going to happen to her, now the house is lost." He had never explained to Pam how, when he was in high school, his parents had scraped together the money to buy a little house. But the move from Harlem had not worked out. His father had begun drinking more and more, and, especially after the death of his daughter, he had begun beating up on Teddy's mother, not now and then when he got mad, but whenever he laid eyes on her.

It is an old story to Pam. The isolation of living so far from where they worked and from the old, familiar neighborhood had finally broken Teddy's family. Also familiar is what Teddy tells her next. When he and his mother went to claim the property, they discovered that it had been lost because his father hadn't paid the taxes on it. "Just too drunk to remember, I guess," Teddy says. "And Momma not there to remind him,"

At another session, he asks her more about his mother. "Do you think Tania's right about my mother, Pam? Completely right?"

Without directly answering, Pam reminds him that they'd talked about how, just before he was really going to move across country to be with Tania, his momma would fall out sick or something.

He shifts uneasily as she speaks, and crosses one leg over his thigh.

Pam lays it out: "Your mother doesn't take your dreams seriously, Teddy. She still wants you to save her life and be her surrogate husband. And what you're doing now by working all the time is simply avoiding the issue. You're avoiding dealing with her and avoiding making the move." Pam wonders if he can make the connection, finally realize how his mother had sexualized their relationship—Do you recognize that her excessive possessiveness could have other implications—you know, as if you were her man?"

"Oh." Teddy gulps, then presses his belt buckle down hard on his blue uniform shirt. The pressure frightens his belly, and it turns over. His broad brown nose opens wider so he can breathe deeper. Her man? Glancing at the watch on his left wrist, he murmurs, "Ah, Pam I have to get back to work . . ."

Tuned in to his vibration, realizing he isn't ready to face these deeper issues, she asks, "Do you really not have any more time or will you be late for driving those passive passengers?"

Teddy laughs. He had told Pam about a guy yelling at him one day about a transfer and really mouthing off on him. "Mm, I better start, to—" He cuts himself off as he shifts towards the table and stands up.

"Call me when you need to, whenever you're discouraged. I'm sure you're going to get there." Pam reassures him as he heads for his car.

Sure enough, not longer after this session, his momma calls him on the first afternoon he's taken off in a while and tells him to come up to her kitchen. "I fell down the stairs today," she whines when he arrives in the small but tidy room, where everything is just so. There is no smile in greeting. Smiles don't come often to this Black woman's face, with eyebrows knitted in a permanent frown. He can see she isn't hurt, and suspects she's lying about the fall. Surprising himself, he says, "Well then, you'll have to go to the hospital. "Her small eyes dart across her son's shoulders as if to see if any more words are coming from him.

"I ain't being pulled into her trap," he thinks. He stays completely quiet, unwilling to come to the rescue the way her husband never did, remembering what Pam had said, suddenly understanding what she was getting at. Abruptly, he turns on his heels and walks out.

Back in his apartment, he stretches out on the bed and stares a while at the ceiling, then picks up the phone. Sometimes when he feels scared he forgets phone numbers, especially when they're new, but tonight he dials correctly his woman's Albuquerque number.

Tania picks up. "Yay! Honey, so good to hear your voice," she cries. She, too, is stretched out on her bed, staring up at the New Mexico sky.

Lying with his phone propped on his pillow, Teddy tells her about his mother saying she fell down the stairs and expecting him to do something. "I refused," he says. "I mean, I could see she wasn't hurt. She was just kinda manipulating me into having to take care of her again, the way I did that time when my father tried to push her down the stairs." He shifts the phone to the opposite ear. "Well, I did take care of her back then. But it took weeks to make her leave the house that he'd just let go to the dogs." He sighs. "Then when he died, I told her, 'Moms, don't tell me anything more about that man. You left him. And he didn't help us. But she told me she was going to his funeral, and acted all beside herself there." You know, Tania, my mother gets all religious on big occasions, but mostly it's just talk about going to church."

Listening to this stuff from his past, Tania rubs her neck, nodding her head as if he can see her, then brings him back to tonight. "Teddy, you ain't gonna let her come between us no more, are you?"

"No, I ain't." Suddenly he's resolved. "I'm gonna tell her I'm movin' for sure."

"Oh, Hon. I thought you were forgetting about me and you. But you really are coming soon, aren't you? I'd almost given up. You keep postponing and postponing, and now, finally . . . Your torture is over and mine is finished too." She rests her eyes, lightly closing them.

"Sure, Tania . . . I'll be seeing you soon! Real soon!" Teddy throws a kiss across the miles through his phone. Cradling it, he listens for what she'll say.

Tania holds her breath for so long she starts coughing.

"Breathe, baby." Teddy smiles into the phone. "Remember how you told me last time we talked I'd have a dream about sex one night and be coming right away 'cause that's what I missed . . ."

Despite herself, she chuckles.

". . . but I didn't, Tan. And I'm still coming, 'cause I miss you."

"It's okay, Teddy, I'm just so-o-o happy you're finally coming. You know, I never thought we were gonna make it." She grips the receiver and looks up at the ceiling of the little house with wood-paneled walls she's settled into.

They say goodnight and hang up, and she thinks, "I believe him. Finally, this time, I do . . . believe Teddy's uprooting himself and coming to build our dream."

***

On yet another smiling day, out in her back yard, which she calls her garden, Tania, as she often does, whispers to herself: "So many miles between me and Teddy." Despite his promises, he still isn't on his way. They talk often on the phone, and he keeps promising, but there's always some excuse. They avoid the real issues and often blow up at each other.

Today is her neighborhood's weekly garbage pick-up day, and she grabs the bin and rolls it through the gate, along the path beside the house to the street. She has to put it out in time or wait until next week. While she's about it, she will check her mailbox, which is just like the ones in the Dick and Jane books she read as a girl. You put the red flag up if you want Albuquerque's postal carrier to know there's an envelope inside waiting to be rushed across town, or across the country. This city is small-town, country style for sure, she thinks, looking down the block. Not one raggedy, homeless, or wealthy person even, anywhere in sight. Hardly anyone at all, for that matter is outside on this glorious day, except her tall Chicano neighbor, who is heading for his front door as she rolls the huge garbage bin out to the curb. He calls out a quick "Hi." She waves. The houses are spaced too far apart for them to be close enough to each other to start a conversation. They have seldom spoken to each other. But they know each other's business the way neighbors in small towns know each other's business—not by prying, exactly, but by close observation of comings and goings. It's foreign territory for Tania, who has lived her whole life in the big city, where even next-door neighbors are often oblivious to each other, and it is impolite to intrude.The high desert winds lift her hair.

She peers into the mailbox. She's got a letter. She knows it will be from Agua, sent with her monthly payment on the loan. So far, Agua is keeping her word. It's a good thing, too. Tania has not yet been able to find work, and so has been living on Agua's payments and her savings since she arrived. She is beginning to feel anxious about getting a job that will cover her living expenses. Pam had told her to hold on to her savings until she was an old lady, because she left transit before she got her pension, but despite the fact that the rents here are so much lower than in New York, she feels money is melting away.

She retraces her steps through the yard, past cactuses and cottonwoods, going back inside to read the letter.

> Tania hi!
> Those idiots at the bank hassle and hassle me so much over stupid things, like insurance and when did I make my bank mortgage "refinance" payment. But thanks to Yemeya, an African goddess I learned about from a Santeria priestess Pam put me onto, these corrupt lenders don't know anything about our smart women's side agreement! Yay! Thanks also to the working-person's lawyer who drew up our paper. And most of all, thanks to Pam, who taught us what any good Marxist knows, that it takes two, the victimizer and the victim, for things to fall apart. When the banks attack, if we the people don't have our shit together, we fall. We have to stand on a good base, and you and I have formed one, your new start there and my very own co-op here.
> Here's a huge laugh and a hug, Agua

Tania hears a pattering of rain outside and on her front door pane. A desert shower. When it stops, she walks outside again and picks one of the tomatoes that hang in long rows off the hard vine by the back fence. The vines had been there when she moved in, thanks to her landlord's mother-in-law, who had lived in the house until she had become too ill to be on her own. Tania thinks of this woman she never met as she brings the ripe fruit to her nose to savor the smell before dropping it into a straw basket. Dogs bark next door. The naturalness of the straw makes her feel safe and so does the wide open blue sky, so different from New York's. Now that the shower has passed, no clouds mar her view of father ancestor of the world of heaven. She can see this spiritual sky whenever she looks up, here in this pueblo, south of New York and west of the East River.

She sniffs the thin air, crisp and clean after the shower, without the soggy heaviness that follows a rain back east. Suddenly she hears the phone ringing, and rushes toward the kitchen like an Olympic runner, counting the rings. There have been just six when she snatches up the phone. Her fingers leave prints in the dust, which covers everything here thanks to the constant wind off the desert.

"Hello?" Tania gasps, out of breath.

"Hey, Tania, I'm here. It's Agua."

Tania dusts off her hands on her pants, but says nothing.

Agua, wondering if Tania has forgotten they'd planned this call, reminds her: "Remember, Tan? We said we'd call this afternoon when I got off work."

"Oh God, I forgot, but I'm glad you're so disciplined." Tania imagines Agua holding the phone, her nails shooting off red fire.

When Tania first arrived in New Mexico, she and Agua had talked at least once a week, the way they used to do. But after a couple of months, they'd looked at the phone bills and the long distance charges were seemed to be, as much as what Tania was paying to rent her house. That was just too damn much, and their calls became rare, and carefully planned.

"Did you get my check?

"Yeah, it arrived today. I'm so-o-o-o glad we did that. We learned a lot, huh?" Already Tania is adding "huh?" with a questioning lilt after her sentences, the way a lot of New Mexicans do. But despite her words, Tania realizes with a pang that her heart isn't in this conversation, a version of which it seems she and Agua have every time they talk. And as Agua rattles on about the wonderful deal they made and the woman power it took to make it, Tania regrets the money they're wasting on this long-distance call in which they just don't seem to connect the way they used to when their differences could be bridged with a hug.

Not long after this conversation, Tania finds this message on her answering machine: "Tania, I gots to write more, 'cause the long-distance bills and the monthly payments to you and the refinancing payments to the bank are kicking my ass." Maybe Agua had found their recent conversation as empty as Tania had. In any case, over the next weeks, there are several phone messages like this one, with Agua calling when she knows Tania won't be home, and eventually they stop talking pretty much altogether. And despite what she'd said about writing, Agua's letters never arrive—only cryptic notes with her checks. Tania starts to wonder about their friendship, but is afraid to mention her anxiety to Agua.

Conversations with Teddy are similarly unsatisfactory.

"Do you like the weather as much as we thought?" he asks.

"Yes, I love the dry heat and the rainbows that come when it rains sometimes. But I hate that your plans have changed again. How long are you going to make me wait? It's been months."

"Listen, Tan, I have to feel better about the money. I want to save more."

"But you promised you were coming when the stuff with your daughter. . . "

"You mean my child support was arranged?"

"Yes. When are we finally going to have what we planned together?"

"Please, baby . . . Give me some more time."

"You know what? Don't call me the next time you want to change your plans. Call Pam. I'm sick of it. If you'd been saving the way you say, you should have a small fortune socked away by now."

"Oh, Tan."

"Are you using the credit union, at least, instead of letting the banksters take shit out of your savings with all their fees?"

He doesn't answer this, saying only, "I'm coming, honey, believe me."

"Be the man, Teddy!" she shouts, and then adds softly, "I want you to see my garden. Bye."

Having finally landed a job, Tania watches as her new friends Becca and Becca's boyfriend, Joel, get ready to leave at the end of their shifts at the New Mexico Food Co-op, where they have both worked almost since the co-op was founded. Joel is responsible for deliveries, while Becca manages the cheese section. Tania who has just started, and is on probation, is bagging groceries. They stop when they see her watching them and Becca chats for a while about flowers that work with herbs, something about companion planting.

Becca is a tall, thin white woman with brown hair in a long single braid down her back. She has a lazy eye that causes people to look at her closely, as if searching for which eye it would be best to focus on to tap into the kind, eloquent soul within. Tania senses that she and Becca will become close. Already she has discovered that they have a number of political views in common and Becca, having learned that Tania is a writer, has invited her to contribute to the Co-op newsletter. She has also asked her to come with her to meet her friends, who gather at a little alternative healing and crystal book shop on Route 66 near Old Town. Tania is grateful, not least for Becca's readiness to accept her strong voice and ex-bus-driver arms that punch the air when she talks.

Joel, who has a Sephardic Jewish nose and a lot of hair that he pulls back into a tie, announces he has some planning to do for his latest woodworking project—if he could make a living at it, he would be a cabinet maker—and they need to be on their way.

Becca nods, smiles warmly, and says, "Joel's right, Tania, we've got to be on our way. I promised him we'd spend time together tonight doing home things."

Suddenly Tania is conscious of being lonely, of how much she misses Teddy, and she chokes up, though she does manage to say "Bye, you two. See you tomorrow," as they head for the door. Then she makes her way to the back to the store to schedule her probationary review with George, the big boss, who is standing by the window hole through which he watches the workers. He has short black hair, glasses and wears a white shirt, as he does most days. He tells her to see him with her immediate supervisor next week. She's sure the review will turn out well. After all, she's only bagging groceries.

Becca is true to her word, and the following weekend invites Tania to join her at a Shaman and meditation evening at the book store. Tania is eager to go, to get to know some people she can relax with, people who belong to a world far from the subways, the Bronx or Brooklyn. She is not disappointed. While most of the people there today are white, Rogelio, a Native American from the nearby Pueblo, who leads the evening's Shamanic drumming with his wife, Maria, also of Pueblo ancestry, seems pleased that she has come, a woman of color like them. He has brown eyes and Maria's are so dark they seem black. Their heights being almost the same makes Tania think at first they are sister and brother, or maybe it's the way they both tilt their head to the side when they look at her. His hair falls down his back in a braid and she has two braids, tied in the back with a beaded clip. Her long turquoise necklace falls just above her proud breasts. They invite her to come to their sweat lodge, which Rogelio and some of the men in the tradition had built with the help of the sisters out behind his home in the South Valley of Albuquerque. When she hesitates, Becca offers to go with her the first time, and suddenly she is sure, eager to be part of whatever spiritual tradition this wise man represents. She thanks him, adding, "I hope when my man moves here he can come too."

Within a few weeks, she has become part of a circle of seekers, centered around the book store, exploring the grounding world of Native Americans, whose traditions are still very much alive in the four southwestern states—Texas, New Mexico, Arizona and California— formed out of the territory stolen from Mexico by the Anglos in the nineteenth century. Here ceremonies still celebrate the old ways—so unlike in New York, where the rich white folks, descendants of the original settler-thieves, had had almost 300 years to kill the indigenous people off and steal their land, and where virtually all trace of them is gone now, paved over and buried in litter.

She devours books on the subject, and on mindfulness meditation, recommended by Becca and others in the group, and begins to understand how the ceremonies, like the sweats at Rogelio's lodge, are an indigenous form of introspection. She attends several ceremonies at the lodge, at first with Becca and then on her own. But attending a ceremony at one of the Pueblo communities near Albuquerque, which she yearns to do, is more complicated. Becca, whose many years of living in New Mexico have taught to respect the ways of the Pueblos, often goes to Native American ceremonies like the Corn Dances. But the Pueblos tend to be wary of outsiders. Many of the ceremonies are not open to them at all, and those that are open are often on the weekend, when Tania is working. Even those communities that welcome newcomers and tourists, limit their numbers, fearing that anglos may only attend to see a spectacle, not to appreciate a sacred ritual.

During another visit to the book shop, Becca introduces her to a neighbor of hers, a Black woman, who belongs to a group of artists—writers, painters, and theater folk—called Us N R Art that sometimes meets at the shop. Becca explains that Tania writes poetry, and on the spot, she is invited to read and to write something for the upcoming Juneteenth celebration." Tania is delighted. Though New Mexico, unlike the state next door, Arizona, does celebrate Martin Luther King's birthday, until now she has met so few Black people in Albuquerque that she is surprised there will be a Juneteenth celebration. She confides that back in New York she had been working on a play, and is also asked to join the group's informal theater workshop.

As she becomes more a part of this new world, New York recedes in Tania's consciousness—though not Teddy, with whom she still hopes to share her future, despite the fact that his coming is repeatedly delayed.

And Agua, too, is still part of her life. Though they are rarely in contact, except through the payments Agua sends every month, Tania thinks of her often, and imagines sharing with her the details of her new life, which now inform the poems she has begun writing again. Their relationship suddenly becomes complicated, however, after one of her payments to Tania is late. It is accompanied by a note explaining that she had been a little late in making her payment to the bank, and they had charged her a fee. She never explains how it feels to be a worker in New York who didn't grow up dealing with money and property. No one from her working class had explained that property comes with late fees to the banks that really own it. What a mistake it was to think you own something before you'd paid the banks off. With a sinking feeling Tania realizes that just growing up almost rich carries with it the class privilege she had wanted to leave behind her—had given her more instinctive knowledge about dealing with these things than Agua was likely ever to have.

Tania decides to write.

Dear Agua,

You and I are both dealing with all the issues that working folks go through when we meet the rules of the propertied class.

Pen in the air, she thinks a while, then resumes writing.

Did you realize you got to pay back that bank on time, or else there are always late fees, unlike in your old rental situation, when you could talk to the landlord sometimes, or they just didn't come after you for a lousy fifteen dollars, as long as they eventually got their overpriced rents for those roach infested places. But here there's no laws about tenants' rights like in New York, where folks organized to pass them. I'm struggling with the reality out here that in New Mexico the landlords can lock you out at a moment's notice if you don't pay on time, like they did my neighbor. This low wage state has no unions to speak of including at the food co-op, which pays barely minimum wage. It's okay. I'm glad you got my old apartment so I could get away from Transit and my messed up parents. And the cost of living is a lot less. But it ain't no gravy train. —T

Having folded the brown paper into thirds, her brown fingers stuff it into the brown envelope. She'd bought the tobacco writing paper at Joel's suggestion, "to be ecological." She hopes Agua gets the letter before the next payment to the bank is due. It had never occurred to her, nor does it occur to her now, at least consciously, that their different class backgrounds may affect what trust means for each of them, and how difficult it may be to make their arrangement, which is based on trust, work over the long term.

December starts out dismal. Tania looks at her calendar, with its photos of cacti, and wonders if she made the best choice when she left New York. She's been in the southwest for a almost a year! Who'd have thought she'd miss the change in the seasons, the onset of a real winter? She did *not* miss the Christmas glitz, however. She much prefers the *luminarias*, little candles stuck in sand in brown paper bags in front many houses. She wonders if Teddy will find these Latino symbols of hope as warming to the heart as she does, if he ever comes.

Then one day Becca approaches her at her new work station in the Bakery/Coffee section, where she's cutting brownies from a worker co-op, the Alvarado Bakery, for a customer. As usual, Becca's braided hair looks neat and her fingers are clean after cutting and wrapping all that European hard cheese. Her shoes are scuffed up sneakers, though.

The store seems very slow, no one shopping, really, except the customer who has just left Tania's counter, and no one has bought any cheese for a while. The hands on the huge clock on the wall seem not to move, until, as Tania now knows from experience, all of a sudden they will indicate it's quitting time and she and Becca will be able to leave.

Keeping an eye on the cheese counter just in case a customer shows up, Becca says, "Tania, if you want, we can go together to the Shalako ceremony at the Zuni Pueblo this weekend. I have a friend from the Pueblo who lives in Gallup, and she'll let us stay overnight the night before, if we go. We'll need the sleep. It's an all-night affair, and everyone who attends has to do as the Zuni do out of respect.

Tania is grateful that Becca trusts her enough to ask her. While this is one of those ceremonies where the Zuni do share their "ways" with outsiders, it is not open to all comers, and Becca, who has attended the ceremony several times, has had to get permission to bring her friend.

Becca turns to check the cheese counter again, but seeing that no one needs help, she goes on to tell Tania about her own experience of the Shalako ceremony and the feelings it has inspired in her, "It's that the night is precious *all through that night*," she explains. "Through the ceremony, the Zuni are revering the reality that the spiritual guides are preserving, which is the story of what has been since the first beginning, and I think the spirits actually take human form."

Tania's eyes widen. "Wow! I wish you could see the way your face is lighting up, I mean, I see this really moves you. You seem to be so much a part of it all for . . ." She hesitates, then decides to finish the thought. ". . . For an Anglo . . ."

"Yes, for an Anglo." Becca laughs with some silliness because she didn't grow up using that word to refer to herself. "So, will you come?"

"Oh, Becca, thank you so much. You know, until I came out here, and met you and Rogelio, I never knew there were still native peoples actually doing things in this country instead of being in museums, where the Europeans display their murdered remains. My friend Smoke used to talk about the way the Hopi had a prophecy and how they were 'relocated,' but that's about it."

Wanting to go, yet with her heart racing with anxiety about possibly putting a foot wrong and falling asleep, Tania hesitates. Finally, she agrees, speaking softly. "Okay, I'll give it a try."

"Good. It'll help you with your own rebirth and everything you already told me about you and your guy. He's still coming, right?"

"Tania ignores the question. "Oh? How will it help with that?"

"Because the men who dance in the ceremony have to lead inspirational lives. They do prayers and learn all kinds of things for twelve months before the winter ceremony. It will be good to be around that kind of male vibration."

"I hope Teddy's ready for that. I sure would like him to be." Tania picks up the bakery cleaning cloth and she starts rubbing the counter top.

"Um hum. Well, you'll see." Walking back to the cheese counter, Becca whistles the tune "The Earth Is Our Mother, We Must Take Care of Her."

In the afternoon the day before the ceremony, the two friends travel west of Albuquerque. The setting sun sets the massive red rock slabs along the road ablaze, and Becca, who has seen them many times before, but never in this light, exclaims "Look! Look!" at every turn while Tania sits in silent wonder. They sleep well in sleeping bags provided by Becca's friends on the floor of the living room in their small house. After the long drive, they don't wake until late, and the day is a lazy one as they prepare for the sleepless night to come.

Then the sacred night arrives and Tania sits waiting for the arrival of the Shalako—intermediaries between spirit and humans. She wonders again if Teddy would take inspiration from the men dancing. The night's cold doesn't penetrate. She wears her warm down coat, and mittens she'd bought in the small crafts department at the food store. In her heart, the strange cries and painted bodies of the dancers in the ceremony connect with her inner self in a way that makes her feel she belongs among these people. Her eyes are wide open, although she wants to rest the lids. It's so very late, so very dark.

Now, nudging her arm gently, Becca smiles and says, "Look, the Mud People," and Tania, not really understanding, but willing to observe closely, to learn, sees what look like huge beings covered all over with mud, except for openings in the faces to allow them to see. The dancing and the rattles and the general feeling of the people from the Pueblo, adults and children from babies to teens, group of adults and children from babies to teens, many wrapped in traditional blankets or wearing jackets made with the colors of the Zuni on them, seem enveloped in the ritual. Their eyes focus on the dancers and their bodies sway slightly to the rhythm of the rattles. Tania struggles to keep awake, her lids constantly falling, hoping her prayers go with everyone else's into the new year.

Then it's over. No Shalako has tapped her head with a rattle, so maybe she has stayed awake. The next thing she remembers, she has a pillow under her head and is dreaming of flowing water and the sounds of the chants. Becca rests near her. As she drifts back to sleep, she wonders whether she and Teddy will someday sit together on the mesa, held safe by the pounding of the drums, like a mother's heartbeat.

* * *

Weeks later, Teddy sets out by bus from New York. After he phones her with his schedule, Tania marks the special week preceding his arrival date on her cactus calendar, and in the evening, when she's alone in her house, her anticipation, combined with the smooth dust and pollution-filled air, which makes each sunset a riot of yellow-orange streaks, force her to work a little to breathe. She consciously pushes her lungs to expand as she gazes through her window at the mountains brushing the sky with their breasts. It still feels new to her, living so high above sea level. She wonders if Teddy will be able to adjust, or if the high altitude headaches she used to have will bother him, too.

* * *

Sitting uncomfortably in his seat, Teddy, eyes closed, listens to the engine as the bus rolls through Jersey to Philadelphia, then west through Pennsylvania as night falls. Whenever the bus stops, he jumps off to make sure his belongings, stowed in the luggage compartment underneath the bus, don't get stolen. That his things seem more likely than not to be swiped at every stop unless he is vigilant makes him too nervous to do more than doze even when the bus is rolling down the highway and the other passengers are snoring away. His hyper vigilance stems from his childhood, when he saw the thieving ways the high-rent-charging slumlords dealt with his parents. He remembers his father telling him to sneak new chairs into the apartment without letting the landlord's stool-pigeon super see him, because if the landlord knew about the new chairs he would think his dad had been given a raise and would raise the rent accordingly, and there would be no way to stop him, since the state's rent-control and rent-stabilization programs for the almost rich didn't apply to the crumby building they lived in. So when he travels, at each stop, whatever the hour, he rises to "stretch his legs," and watches to make sure that if the bus driver removes his luggage to get at something stowed in the back of the compartment, he puts it back in again. Reflexively he also checks to make sure his money belt is still secure. It contains the check from the Transit Authority for the funds vested in his pension, which he has already signed over to Tania, and the money he got when he sold his car. It was hard to sell it for so much less than it was worth, but at least the sign he'd put up at the depot at the last minute before he quit had attracted one of the new drivers, who'd wanted some half-assed wheels and could pay cash.

Long before the bus crosses the Mississippi, Teddy is numbed by the tedium of hours in the cramped seat, so much less generous, he realizes, than the bus driver's seat he's used to. He hasn't really faced the fact that he has quit, that he has left the only part of the world he ever lived in. Still, as the bus passes through the Texas Panhandle he smiles as he rests his head on the back of the seat to look out the window, watching a bird high in the sky that is following the route of the bus, heading west. The southwest will bring me luck, he thinks. He doesn't foresee that, for him, this low-wage place will be a beautiful hell.

A couple of hours later, the bus crosses into New Mexico, and his good feelings are abruptly dispelled as a man reeking of alcohol wobbles on and wavers to the seat in front of him. The guy's black hair rises above the gray cloth of the seatback. He falls asleep instantly; his snores sound like a foghorn.

After trying to shut his eyes and go to sleep himself to block out the drunk, he gives up and shifts his aching back and thinks about Tania instead. Lowering his head to look at his body, he pictures her small body lying on top of his large one, her small breasts and cute ass, her beautiful smile as she looks up at him. He grins when she gives a great, loud laugh at something he's said. He remembers the way she builds him up when he tells her about dealing with his daughter's mom, and how good that makes him feel. He wishes his daughter was coming with him, but he worries it's got to be years before that's ever going to work out. When, all teared up, he'd told her he was moving to New Mexico to be with Tania, she'd wailed, "Oh, Daddy, now I won't see you anymore. I have to live with mommy and mommy gets really mad about your girlfriend. I don't want to make mommy mad." He'd told her about the mountains and how she can ride her bike outside without having to take it down to the street on a smelly elevator. He'd explained her mother would have to let her come visit him because of the visitation rights. But he doesn't think he convinced her, and he sure hadn't convinced himself. When they'd said goodbye, she'd been hugging the Black doll he saved for her after her mother told her not to take it. How long would it be, after he was gone, before her mother tossed it out?

He pushes these unhappy thoughts away and remembers Pam had told him to wait to talk to Tania about his daughter until he got to New Mexico. Pam was right. Once he gets there he'll be able to hold Tania and explain that he used to fall for his daughter's mother's seduction, but doesn't any more. Now he's really, truly all hers. He glances out the window at a passing 14-wheeler. Tania, he'll think about Tania, about what it will be like to be with her again after so long. Yeah, I'll hold her and undress her and then ask her if she wants a massage. I'll tell her how much I missed her. He grins as he imagines the scene. But he can't stop worrying. I don't know, he thinks. I hope it's gonna be okay that I came so much later than she wanted. Then, determined, he tells himself, "We'll do this." How can they not? He's left behind the crowds, the transit liar bosses, the dark streets where he had to watch his back so nobody robbed him. He's left behind the fear that made him change out of his uniform before heading home, 'cause he didn't want people on the street to know he made good money.

Hearing a little kid across the aisle call out "Momma," he turns his mind to his mother, but he shuts the thought down, and drifts off to sleep. He doesn't hear the bus driver announce "Albuquerque next stop," but a jolt when the bus swerves wakes him, and looking out the window, he recognizes the mountain range. There are very few cars on the road. The sun streams in strong. They pass a road-work crew, Latino, light brown, and though the men are not chained together, somehow this reminds him of the chain gangs he saw in Virginia when he was a child. There must have been such work crews in the southwest all along the route he and Tania had driven, but he can't remember having noticed one before. The sight unsettles him, and his worries about fitting in out here return. He lays his head to the side. A tear runs down his face. He has made it out of the garbage and tension of the city. He stares out the window and watches appreciatively as the driver slowly edges them to the town he entered more than a year ago, with his woman.

When he arrives, Tania is still at work. He waits in the bus station, nibbling on a taco until he knows she'll be on her way home, then calls from a pay phone in the depot and leaves a message, saying he'll jump in a cab and be there in a few minutes. Now that the moment is almost here, he hopes to make love right away. He's missed her so much, her softness and her realness, even though the truth is hard t take sometimes.

Tania opens the front door. He enters. As she takes in his long leather coat, his leather cap and the few bags he carries, she reaches inside for the connection between them. Where is it? Teddy stands before her, but their love knot? Where has that link disappeared to? Untied, broken, buried under months of "seeing" him only by phone, without being able to smell onions, or musk oil, or even his cigarettes? How many times had she hung up wondering if he meant it when he said, "I'm coming. Please be patient!"

She can't move. Her brain lights match after match. What will happen now? Does he expect me to take care of him in this little place? I have two bedrooms that put together aren't as big as the living room I had back in Brooklyn. Will he want to come to yoga with me or go hiking? Can we talk? Looking down instead of touching his chest, she tells herself to open her heart to this man whom she's loved for so long, whom she's been praying would come for so many months. But she feels clumsy and not in her own body. Instead the anticipation she's used to, she can't stop the foreplay matches being struck in her head from feeling un-sexual, can't help wondering, Is Teddy really my man? She wants to cry, but she's been frozen solid by his procrastination, his eternal "I'll quit the bus job and come next month for sure, Tania." It's as if all their time together has been washed away. The wounds of her past, which she had fought so hard to stitch up, are open again, destroying warmth, leaving her as distant and isolated as ever when someone—even Teddy—comes too close.

Confronted by her silence, tears come to Teddy's eyes. Then he drops his bags and hugs the hell out of her. "God," he sighs.

She lets him stand there with his arms around her. Her heart beats fast, but memories of the angles of cars jutting out into the wrong parking space and sweet pancakes, like only Teddy Turner knows how to fix them, get mixed up and she begins to cough and spits into a wrinkled tissue she pulls from her pocket while he holds her.

Finally he takes his fingers from around her waist, and Tania mumbles, "I expected . . . I thought you weren't gonna come." She remembers how a few days before, when he had phoned her to say he had his ticket, she had imagined how their first night together would be, on her futon, cuddling. Instead, now, today, she shows him past her bookshelf, down the narrow hall that takes two steps to pass through to the "extra bed" in the second bedroom. "I got to get up early," she says. "You know how you snore."

He doesn't argue, just lays down his bags and squeezes her in another hug. "I missed you, Tania," he sighs, then begins to massage her shoulders. It's awkward facing her, though, and he drops the hug and tries to turn her around so he can smooth out the tension. But she resists, stays facing him, observing him, wondering whether, without the sounds of her old city, the sirens, and street conversations that never let up, the crowds of folks all the time to distract her—whether, without them, she's seeing Teddy for real now, her perception of him unclouded by expectations and illusions. Instead of receiving the massage, she says, "Let me show you the bathroom."

He can hear her radio playing in the next room, "KUNM, in Albuquerque, New Mexico, the best university radio station," the announcer says. Running water drowns out the sound as he takes a shower.

Tania doesn't go in and peek the way she used to, or lather him down on his back. They do hug for a long time when he comes out of the bathroom, however, and body to body, she realizes her freeze is thawing.

"A-a-a-ah." He smiles.

She waits for him to reveal more, thinking, He really did come, after all that delay. He'd prevented her from pinning him down to the point where she'd given up, and now, shockingly, he was here.

"You want to be with me . . . hmm." She responds to him, kind of smiling, too. He sits on the futon-sofa, and she kneels beside him for a moment.

But he can't open up for her either. Of course, he knows she likes to rush immediately to the root of a matter. But traveling a couple thousand miles in the back of that bus, the last bit behind a drunk, had exhausted him and he doesn't respond. Instead, moving his wide open hand with its strong fingers up her spine, he massages her neck. He wants to say, "I love you so much. Tania. I love you 'cause you've always had an aliveness in your soul that not many people keep burning." But he thinks, this isn't the time to tell her, not yet.

His eyes search his mind backwards through the rolodex of their intense touch-life together—her thighs, her waist, her lips. He longs to touch her in all those places, but he's nervous about what she'll do, what will happen. Finally he gives her a peck and they have one deep tongue to tongue kiss.

Then he says, "I have something for you," and rummages in his money belt for the check, which he hands to her. "I meant to come when I withdrew the pension money," he adds, "but . . ."

". . . But you didn't, did you? Your mother saying you ain't a good man 'cause you've failed her as a son must've still dominated you!" She is repeating something Pam had said once. Still, despite her disparaging words, she can't let go of his body and leans back to look into his face.

Teddy remembers his mother yelling to him from the top of the stairs about her so-called fall, and agrees with his lover-woman. "I guess you're right. Pam warned me Momma'd do something to try and stop me leaving."

"Yeah, Pam knew your momma, would play sick," Tania says. She frees herself from his hug and heads for the kitchen to get some water.

Teddy, watching the back of her head as she disappears through the doorway, heaves his aching body to his feet. He thinks, but doesn't say, "I still bought my ticket and packed, though," as he heads towards the back bedroom. His eyes cast down, he forces his thick body to ignore his fragile heart and move his suitcase into a corner in the darkening room to unpack. Tania has shocked him by telling him he will have to sleep alone in this tiny room because he snores. He tries to settle in. First out of the suitcase is his Jockey underwear, then a solid yellow sweat shirt and purple running pants and a peach shorts set—the bright colors he favors, so different from the dull blue most men prefer.

As he finds an empty drawer to put things in, he calls to her, "Tania, I did take the bus to meet you, baby." His voice cracks, but no one will ever see a tear.

"But it's been months and months since I left New York, Teddy," she responds from the hallway, wanting to go into his room, but staying out of it.

And so, here in their new homeland, each lies down alone, Tania by herself on the futon, where earlier they had sat together for a little while, he in the other bedroom. The lingering smell of his aftershave reminds her of her father and her teenage self and the sleeping bag on the living room carpet. The clock ticks loudly, and she sits up to set it for work next morning. She doesn't feel at all like touching, much less sexual touching. She thinks, Maybe on the weekend, when I'm not so tired . . . She tells herself that the reason they're sleeping apart really is his snoring. It used to keep her awake sometimes even in New York, but here in New Mexico, where the nights are still except for the occasional howling of a coyote, she's sure the sound will be deafening.

Coming into her room to say goodnight, he cries invisible tears in the darkness as he reaches down to her. She is still sitting with the clock in her hand. "I hope you had an okay trip here," she murmurs. She puts down the clock and reaches up so they can hug goodnight. "It was okay," he says as he closes the door to her room behind him.

PART THREE

15 PARTY DIVIDES

A roadrunner crosses in front of Tania as she makes her way to the backyard of her house. She is expecting him to arrive soon to set up a coyote stick fence, then help her prepare the soil for her garden. Thanks largely to Becca, who is as knowledgeable about southwestern gardening as she is about indigenous ceremonies, it is a real garden now, planted not only with tomatoes but with lettuce and other green things. She reflects sadly that it is still her garden and her house, just as it was when Teddy arrived in New Mexico, just as it had been in New York. After one night in her spare room, he had packed up and moved out, and it was twenty-four hours before he let her know where he was. When his anger subsided, as it always did, he had come back and, remembering how Pam had encouraged talking, they had discussed how disappointed she was that he had taken so long to come and how unhappy he was that she hadn't been more welcoming. Without Pam's direct input, however, they were unable to fully articulate the abandonment each felt, and though they both wanted to speak with her, they agreed that a long distance call to her so soon after Teddy's arrival would cost too much to consider. So while they made up, neither the breach between them nor the inner hurt each felt was really healed. She couldn't face the fact that he had loved her enough to actually come, expecting to share her life, expecting that she would share his. The truth was, she wanted love, but wasn't ready to let it in. He couldn't face the fact that his not coming within three months of her departure, as he promised, had left Tania terrified that he wasn't going to come at all, nor did he have the words to explain to himself or Tania why he hadn't come: that he had continued to hope that his mother and through her, his daughter, would get involved in his new life, and that this hope had finally exploded when his mother pretended to fall down the stairs to maintain what he realized at last, with Pam's help, was her uncaring control over him. But now that he's here in Albuquerque, he resents that they're not living with each other and thinks they ought to be. His mother and father, for all the misery of their life together, had stuck it out until he was grown up.

He had rented an apartment on the first floor of a run-down complex on the other side of town, spending down his savings on rent and other necessities until he landed the first of what would be a series of short-term laborer's jobs, as a roofer's assistant. The pay was low, not even up to the Federal minimum wage, because the outfits willing to hire him were so small and fly-by-night. For the first time in his adult life, what he earned barely covered his daily expenses, despite the fact that things cost so much less than in New York. Still, once he had work, they had begun to visit one another as they had in New York, though without the shared experience of their job at Transit—as much as Transit had torn them apart, it had also brought them together—they just don't feel the same closeness they had known in New York.

Now she hears his bike bell sounding and runs through the alley to the front of the house.

"Hi, hon," she calls out.

He smiles, staying quiet. Taking himself off the bike, he leans the sturdy black fender and thick tires against the side of the little bungalow. Automatically, he checks for punctures, ready with the tire sealant if any goat-head thorns have managed to penetrate the Mr. Tuffy tire liners he'd soon learned were a bike-rider's necessity out here.

She waits while he completes this ritual, then reaches out to him, smiling welcome.

They're doing better these days. Although the money is terrible, after being stiffed once, he has learned who the reliable contractors are and has been getting paid for his construction gigs. And if he has not quite embraced her tribe of artists, walkers, gardeners and bike riders, he has sometimes joined her in the activities she has come to love, like today, when he's come to help her with her garden. And whenever they can, they go bike-riding together, finding their way to Rio Grande, a winding old road, with lush trees overhead, nourished by the river. The trees are a green miracle in the midst of the predominant browns and reds of the surrounding high desert. Riding beneath them, peddling sort of slow, Tania and Teddy feel nourished, too.

But the dance and yoga classes she attends regularly, which always leave her feeling relaxed, are not for him. On a couple of occasions she'd invited him to the book shop to meet some of her friends. He'd gone and had had a good enough time but as far as he could tell, except for her co-worker Becca, that day they were mostly Native Americans, queer folks, and women of color. He'd liked them okay, and had enjoyed talking about biking with one "sister," Tam, a lesbian who'd joked that the town's name might as well be "Albuqueerque." But they just weren't interested in the same things he was interested in.

At one of these gatherings, Tania had made a point of introducing him to Rogelio, saying, "This is my teacher. He's a Native American elder and a spiritual healer." He had liked the smell of sage incense that clung to the loose-fitting cotton pants and woven vest he wore, but had declined his invitation to come with Tania to his sweat lodge, though he did take Rogelio up on going with Tania to a drumming out on the mesa with a group of women and men from one of the Pueblos who lived in Albuquerque. The drumbeat had soothed him, and he had closed his eyes, letting his ancestors' spirits rest. But he hadn't gone again. Truth be told, he missed the camaraderie of his buddies in New York, the men he worked with and played pool with. Here the men he worked with were almost all Latino, and while he got along well enough with them on the job, during breaks and at the end of the day they went their separate ways; that they spoke Spanish among themselves effectively shut him out.

"Want something to drink?" Tania asks, motioning to the house with her head cocked to the side.

"No, just bring it out to me. I want to finish before it's too hot."

They both know how the sun of New Mexico can beat down on you in the afternoon since they are 5,000 feet above New York's sea level. But they are good at rising early sometimes, like this morning.

She looks at the thick sticks for the coyote fence he's come to build lying on the ground, their brushed bark deep brown. The dirt holds them. He takes his saw from his back-pack and asks her to bring the high-power extension cord he'd told her to borrow from her neighbor or the store where she works.

While Tania runs in to prepare a cold juice and find the cord, Teddy picks up the sticks and lays them carefully against the house, figuring out the number he needs to enclose the little garden area and keep out any stray animals that might fancy some leaves to eat, once Tania's garden starts growing.

She returns with a mug of cold apple juice and the orange extension cord.

Once he begins she doesn't bother him. Instead, she places a few small plastic pots of already-started zucchini that she'd received at work on the ground ready to plant when he's done. She wants her garden to expand beyond "just tomatoes." Jokingly he sprinkles a little dirt on her feet, saying, "Tan, you think those sandals could use some leather oil?" She laughs and goes to the wall between her neighbor and her, where she digs in the dirt, making a gully so that when she waters the morning glories the water won't just drain off and the roots will get a good soaking. It's a trick she's learned from her Becca, who's an experienced gardener.

Teddy's sneakers, no longer white when he left New York, are now covered with good clean New Mexican dirt. After sawing the sticks to even them out, he places them one by one, in the hole he has dug for it, then uses wire to connect them. His strong back heaves as he swings the pick to start each hole, then shovels around it to make it big enough to hold the stake. He shovels the earth back into the hole around each one, pats it down to pack it, then with his feet stamps the top down hard.

Later, in the afternoon, when the fence is finished, they lie on the futon, cuddling and talking with Power, who is always glad to see him, no matter what's going on with Tania at the moment. Eventually, Tania gets up to prepare food. She returns and hands him what looks to him like a kind of hot cheese sandwich, but not what he's used to.

"What's this?"

"They call it a *quesadilla*." Tania grins, proud of her Spanish words.

After eating, they drive in her car to the Southwest Plants store, where they browse the rows and rows of desert flowers and easy-to-grow veggies. Herb names intrigue Tania: *Manzanilla*, Echinacea. They come to the tree section, and Tania exclaims, "Let's plant a tree in the yard. It's okay. I already checked."

"What price?" Teddy reminds her of the reduced state of his cash supply.

"No, I got it. You help me dig the hole and plant it, okay?"

"Sure, baby."

Within the hour they have returned and picked out the spot for their green-thumb project. He presses the shovel into the dirt, Tania creates a prayer for new beginnings and they make love that night enjoying laughing about their hard work together in this country style way. . .

"No more city slickers." He grins. "Yeah. We got creative, you and me honey." She kisses his bald head and they begin with oral sex. How do you want me to touch you? His eyes ask, deep and silent but talking through the quiet. She stretches her thighs up to his mouth and he gently motions to her with his right hand, indicating that she can relax. He knows what to do. His lips nibble on her hairs and then his tongue inserts itself in the very top of her woman's door. She moans, "Oh Teddy."

"Yeah baby."

"Oh . . ." her arms talk to his shoulders and he keeps at it until she screams, "Teddy-y-y-y!"

Then he wants to come inside her and she lets him in. Her wide open eyes show how much she wants him. She holds his butt to her with her ankles, her legs wrapped tightly around him. At the high point of his orgasm he raises the roof with a loud groan and they laugh. She doesn't cry out, but rests in his strong, muscular arms. They sleep completely naked.

It is not their last good time together, but it is the best. In the months that follow, the rain that sometimes builds in the usually dry clouds of New Mexico seems to fall into their lives, drowning them. Many sunny-on-the-outside, gloomy-on-the-inside, days pass. Teddy and Tania break up and re-patch. “Tania and Teddy.” It had sounded so new and fresh when, just before Tania left New York, she’d overheard Agua say to Heru, “Don’t be sad. Before too long, we’ll go out to visit Tania and Teddy in New Mexico.” But the steady march of their days: his menial work when he can get it, about which he has nothing to say to her; her work in the store, her circle of friends and their activities, in which he cannot or does not choose to participate, maintain a silence between them.

One day, desperately reaching out, they have a therapy session with Pam—a three-way call over the phone, with both of them sitting in Tania’s home.

“He just wants me for my body,” Tania says not long after Pam greets them.

Teddy doesn’t bother to respond to this. He complains, “Pam, you see Tania don’t care about me, the world issues are always more important to her.”

Neither is speaking more than superficially about what is troubling them. In fact, Teddy is distraught because his mother has not called him once since he’s been in New Mexico, nor responded to any of his many messages. But instead of going there, he deflects his feelings of abandonment onto Tania. She, still scared that the incest has made her unworthy of being loved by any man, is sure that Teddy cannot possibly really care about her. Neither is able to go deeper in the presence of the other. And in any case there is no time; because of the cost of long-distance the call must be cut short. All Pam can do is encourage them to keep talking to each other, to try to feel each other’s hurt as well as their own. She had offered the three-way because she hoped it would show them how they both need an individual session, and before they hang up, she suggests this to them. But though she expects that Tania will call her, she has little hope that Teddy will. She and he had had too little time together before he left for him to truly face the fact that his mother is incapable of adult love for her son and can only be dependent on him; that once he has left New York and is no longer taking care of her, she will in all likelihood no longer care for him. If Pam could talk with him one-on-one, perhaps she could help him see that his unhappiness has more to do with his mother’s rejection of him than with his issues with Tania. As for Tania, she would eventually come to understand that the incest had not made her unworthy of love, that Teddy does love her, that he is not her father. But Pam fears that by the time she does it will be too late for them both. And Teddy . . . Teddy might have moved across the continent from New York, but he holds in his belly his old disconnected nuclear family, entangled like shells, crabs and sand in a fisherman’s net. He cannot cut those strings! His mother does not call. He hears nothing of his daughter. Day after day he stuffs his regret deep back inside himself, smoking more than he used to, holding cigarette after cigarette in his full African lips, behind which he keeps his hurt inside.

One afternoon Tania calls and invites him to a performance. "Teddy, can you come please? You still don't really know most of the people who helped me while I was waiting for you to come. I'd like to introduce you to the others in the show."

"Are these the people we met before or some other people?" he asks.

"Well, some of the people you met are in this group that wants me to read. It's called 'Us N Our Art.' Remember, you met some of them at the book shop."

"Ah, I'm not sure. But do you want me to give you a massage to at least help you face the crowd beforehand?"

"Yes! Thanks so much, hon."

"Can you come by my place today?"

"Today isn't the performance."

"I know, but you'll be preparing." He chuckles and so does she. He wants to be the important one for her.

"Thanks baby. My poem is about my daddy and me. I want to be supported in revealing the incest publicly, and you are helping." Their conversation has to be short. He has to do laundry and clean his apartment, which is well-ordered, like his place in New York.

Early the evening of the Us 'N R Art show, as she strides into the room where she and others have rehearsed, Tania notices the arrangement of chairs for the spectators, with many seats scattered in the back for late-comers, or those who might have to leave early, and then ten rows with an aisle in between towards the front. There are bales of hay in front of the chairs for the kids, who don't need support for their backs. Whoever had set up the chairs had opened wide the windows on both sides of the room, letting in the dry yucca- and cactus-flavored breeze. Five-thousand feet above sea level, the strong, long-lasting twilight will still be gazing in when the performance begins at 7:00 pm.

From her place behind the gentle sliver of a curtain that serves to separate the audience and performers. As people enter and take their seats, Tania overhears various lighthearted male and female New Mexican voices exchanging greetings: "Hello." "*Hija.*" "*Hijo.*" They murmur in low, but excited tones, waiting for the show to begin. She hears children laughing, and for a moment, she wishes they were hers. Then, suddenly, a baby wails, and she remembers that infants take a lot of work.

All at once there is a hush as a brownie-toned woman wearing African culottes and her hair in Rastafarian locks steps in front of the audience to introduce the show. Tania, who is first up, steps from behind the curtain and onto the makeshift straw-bale stage, preparing herself to do the Yoga Sun Salutation to accompany her recitation of the poem she created to go with that movement. It is an old poem, from a play she had written long ago in the Voices of the Working Women Writer's group in Brooklyn. As she begins to speak, she slowly stretches her arms up, as if reaching for the sky. At first, reciting the title of the piece, her tone is low, so the audience is drawn in. Then, as the title blends into the verse, her voice is infused with passion and her whole body stretches upward, yearning for the life-giving sun.

"In Search Of Freedom from Pain. . .
She did the mother peace tarot, yoga asanas, and rested from toil
a boil had burst once more
in her heart was this sore
Mama had even gotten into seductress competition, over her position,
(right to lie prone, in front of daddy's-papi's throne). . ."

As she nears the end of her poem Tania looks up into the eyes of the crowd, women, men, white westerners and Iowans, shiny black southeastern faces, and a few Indigenous Pueblo friends. And way in the back she sees her man, whom she loves for his steadfastness. His loyal gaze causes her to burst into a wail as she cries out her last lines:

". . . again
& i ask you
what would you do
if you knew that papi had molested you too?"

As the applause of the audience thunders into the air, she sighs with relief. "Thank God," she thinks. "Thank God Teddy came and saw how good it went." She lifts her right foot and then her left, and step by step gathers herself to leave the makeshift stage. Once she's back on the floor, there are so many people crowding around that she can no longer see Teddy, but she heads confidently toward the back of the room, already feeling his strong arms around her, hugging her, so proud.

But after she has made her way to the rear where the drawings and found art of the show are sequestered in a small room off the big auditorium, she still can't find him. He has left. He came and went, peddling on his bike. She cannot even feel him. Only Goddess, bathed in the darkening alpine twilight and the red glow over the Sandia Mountains, witnesses his ride. He rides away from her.

* * *

Teddy had come to the performance to hug her with his presence while his physical body could. But he cannot stay. As she finishes her dramatization, the bags full of emotions—"Momma *is* here, inside Tania, I cannot trust even this female"—flood his heart. The thought that Tania is only interested in performing and giving to the public, not in her private life with him, arrives in his fearful brain. "She's selfish, like every other woman in my life," he thinks. But later, after the long bike ride, after he reaches his empty, lonely apartment, he realizes he can be with her. He wants to be with her. He calls, and says he's sorry he didn't stay, but he figured she'd be busy with her friends. And she says, "You're the one I want, hon. Please come over."

They hug as soon as he opens the door and never stop hugging as they lie down under the skylight in the living room on the futon on the white tiled platform he had built. She likes his big arms wrapped all around her waist. She likes him moving her hips with his ten fingers. It says into come towards me. But this time, as it has before, the trigger of his body touching her pussy reminds her of the sexual violence in her past and she asks him to stop. They know this pattern. It happens whenever her old memories of dad/mom invade. She moans, "Teddy I can't." And Teddy groans, but without protesting, he stops and holds her gently, as he has done whenever this happens. Not once has he complained. His desire to care rises above the ache of stifled sexual desire. He *feels* Tania.

On this occasion, however, for the first time ever, she cries out: "Teddy, why did my parents do this to me? Whyyyy?"

Teddy's heart wrenches open, and he speaks a truth that he had never realized before, not in all the times this had happened during their years together. Nor had it ever come to Tania that he would shout out what flew from his spirit that night.

"Because they were criminals, that's why," he shouts, making clear he's standing with her, facing the incest wound.

But he cannot stay. He sits up slowly, carefully, on the puffy cream-colored futon and puts on his socks and sneakers. He wants a cigarette. He wants a woman to hold and to hold him. He loves Tania. It hurts to walk away to find some space. But if he stays in that room he will start screaming and never stop. He will take all of his 5 feet 10 inches of Black power and started smashing things. What else do you do with that level of rage roaring through your veins?

Tania watches his slow walk to the door. She doesn't call him back.

On his way out, he thinks, I love Tania so much. If it wasn't for her monster father filling her head, we'd be fine. He twists the doorknob fiercely, and then he is outdoors, breathing in all the air he can. As he shuts the door behind him, he shouts to the wind, "I can't get in. I can't touch her." A block of ice as big as Antarctica stops him.

He picks up the heavy axe propped against the wall on the stoop, brown dirt on its blade. Thud, bang, down, down he starts splitting one of the logs in the yard, knocking out a stake to pound into her father's heart, then another and another. And into the hearts of her mother and her sisters, who hadn't done anything about it and just let it all be stuffed down inside. What was going on there? Was everybody just blind? He fears he'll actually break the axe handle with his force. With each blow, he thinks, That bastard broke us apart. *Broke us apart*. To his mind come lyrics from Teddy Pendegrass. And from another favorite singer man, the guy with the big bass boom . . . Barry White. Then one from Bill Withers. These black men love black women. He whistles, a great urge in his soul pushing the notes out, the familiar words in his mind a comfort: "Grandma's hands used to doo doo doo . . . on Sundays."

He cannot go back inside, but Teddy hugs Tania with his whistling through the glass windows in the clear New Mexico light. Give this beautiful bird of a woman I love some light, he prays. Give her a chance in life for hugging and good touching. I can't stand the shit she's been through. I know it's not her fault. I just have to pole vault over this right now. I can't act out. I'm her only family, so I can't find another woman to have sex with. I gotta stay here by my woman.

Indoors, Tania, lying on the futon, silently crying, hears the blows of the axe as Teddy splits the wood outside. That one, she thinks, is for my bastard of a dad. To Power, who has jumped onto the futon, she whispers, "And that one is for my unwilling-to-protect-me mom.

She cradles Power, who is purring, and thinks of all the times she and Teddy have made love since they've been together—on her futons, in the back of a truck, on blankets outdoors and on motel mattresses when they traveled together, in his apartment, with his mother and his aunt sleeping upstairs, in the upstairs room at his southern gramma's house. Most times the trigger hasn't spoiled things between them, but too often it has. Now she says aloud to Power what she didn't say—can't say—to Teddy. "Oh, Power, it was sooo brave of him to tell me what I didn't want to know. . . My parents were criminals. What my dad did is a crime and my mom was his accomplice. But the worst crime is that between them they destroyed my little-girl innocence." She blows her nose, and adds through her tears, "They took up all my space with their violence."

Power's purring stops. In the silence Tania sees her father in her mind, sees how his bigness could be confused with Teddy's.

"But Teddy loves the real me and I love the real Teddy," she whispers to Power and the purple Wandering Jew plant hanging by the window. The cat's yellow eyes stare into her own. She feels tiny curled up on the futon, like a child, and yet grown-up in her mind. "He came through!" she says with awe. He had summoned the courage to stand up, even though he, himself, was dealing with hurt, with shitty jobs and not getting any respect and not hearing a word from his mother or his daughter since he left New York. Pam would say he was facing what men everywhere in this shit-faced system have to face, that the system is filled with criminals, workers like her dad who go home and mess up their kids the way they've been messed over by their bosses.

Power hisses. Turning on her side, Tania strokes her arched back. Yes, tonight Teddy had made her feel witnessed. For the first time, she truly believes that he is the feeling male that her dad never was. But she does not go to him to tell him this, or how grateful she is that he takes out his frustration and anger chopping wood instead of hitting on her the way Buster did. Instead, she lies still, her eyes filled with joy enclosed by sad light. And in the following weeks, life returns to "normal." The moment, with its epiphanies and all its potential, is lost. Neither says to the other what they had understood about each other that night. If they had been able to talk with Pam, perhaps she could have helped them. But besides being expensive, the few three-way phone conversations they'd had with her since Teddy had arrived had been unsatisfying. Somehow they seem to need her presence. So things go on pretty much as before. Teddy finds enough minimum wage construction gigs to keep the wolf from the door, but just barely. By the time he knocks off work, he is too exhausted to do much but eat and hit the sack. Tania resumes working in the store and spends too many evenings with her friends, or so Teddy thinks. As the days go by, those emotional stinking thinking bags packed in his childhood and stowed forever in his body—his mother's seductive and manipulating ways, his father's rejection, making the booze more important than Teddy— become rounder and rounder. He puts chicken, steaks, biscuits, rice, corn bread and of course his famous Sunday morning pancakes into his gut. His bloated beer-and-food belly becomes harder and harder for Tania to rest on during the few nights they spend together.

The morning after one of those nights, Tania sees a slithering lizard on her porch, then notices two more on the side of the house. They have cracks in their backs and heads with too many moving parts. "I'm living in Lizard-town," she mutters to herself. Another lizard, to avoid the sun, has crawled under the belly of Teddy's beat-up car, which is pulled in behind her slightly less decrepit one in the alleyway beside her house. It is so hot it even smells hot.

She doesn't know that a few days before, a red-faced guy with black, pulled back "Ritchie Valens" hair, a trucker, has offered to break into the local trucking industry with Teddy if Teddy will hand over several thousand dollars. Teddy doesn't know the guy well, but his pitch is persuasive to a man fed up with the series of low-paying jobs he's been working at that barely pay the rent, much less the electric bill during these scorching summer days when New Mexicans have to keep the swamp cooler running when they can. The money is needed to make sure they can get the "right equipment." The deal has to be closed immediately or they'll lose the opportunity, but the demand for immediate funds has caught

Teddy short. He doesn't know how to tell Tania about the new venture.

Everything is so complicated with her. She lives in the spiritual world of the land here in the southwest. Just smelling the mountain air daily makes her aware of timelessness. And he does share her feelings when, only occasionally now, they go on a bike-ride together along the river, or sit side-by-side on some stones contemplating with awe the desert stars, sparkling white lights against the black, sacred sky that are invisible against the glow of the brash, blasting lights of New York City. But contemplating the stars with her is not enough, because, like many men, but especially a Black man in a state that has two percent Black folks and white men are always hired first, no matter their qualifications, he mostly feels desperate. Always running to catch up, he now plans to "make" the cash he needs for the trucking venture at the pool hall, which means getting more of his money from Tania, who he still wants to hold it. He figures he'll need another several hundred dollars from her to have enough to get started. He still hasn't found the right moment to ask her for it, though, and he has to leave soon.

Tania has come inside and, saying nothing to Teddy, has gone into the back room, where she now sits stroking Power and listening to him moving about, preparing for the game. His favorite stick and his gloves were already packed when he arrived at her place. Now he puts on his Yankees cap and pulls the brim down. He checks his watch. He wants to be sure to give himself plenty of time. But as he stuffs his cigarette lighter and a pack of smokes into his pocket, he forces out several of his lucky nickels, which drop to the floor. She hears them "ping" "pong" down and scatter. "What *is* that, Teddy?" She shouts.

"Oh, it's okay, just dropped some change." Teddy cuts her interrogation off before she can properly begin. He reaches down to the floor to retrieve the coins, making sure to get them all.

But instead of reassuring her, his offhand reply destroys her calm. Looking up at the ceiling, she rolls her eyes. "Where are you going?" she shouts.

"I don't have to tell you every place I am going," he shouts back.

"Well, I know you're going to play pool, 'cause you have your cue."

"You know everything, don't you?"

"No. I don't know what the . . . What's happening to me and you?"

He wants to stop this argument from escalating, so he makes no reply to this, but pats his bag and peers approvingly into its interior, looking for his car keys. No desert dust there. It's clean and orderly, the way he likes things. Glancing through Tania's thin curtains, which keep the dry smell of heat from entering through her window, he nonetheless can smell the dirt and tiredness that envelops his stick shift Toyota, parked just beyond it. He doesn't really want to go from Tania's cool spot indoors and walk the few steps under the burning sun to the car. But he opens the door. The sky's blueness jabs enough breeze into his armpits. Standing there, he figures he can just make it into the car without burning up. He closes the door again. He has to ask her for the money.

Power jumps off Tania's lap and wanders into the front room toward him. Her owner follows. "Your car's gonna feel like a furnace!"

"I know. That's why I'm glad I bought those seat covers." His tone defends the expense. The covers drape like cool iced drinks over the hard plastic seats to keep his bottom from feeling like it's on fire whenever he gets in the car after it's been parked in Tania's un-shaded dirt entryway.

Bending down, he strokes Power's back. The cat nuzzles into the love-taps of his gentle fingers. "By the way, Tania, I gotta ask you somethin' about my car."

"What does your car have to do with me?" Tania asks.

The crumpled bills in his pocket amount to just enough money to pay for the tune up his new white friend says he can get at a bargain rate from some guy he knows. But not today. He needs the car today, and wants to make sure it won't jam him up. Finally he gets it out: Today he's going to place a bet of a thousand dollars on the game. "Baby, can I borrow your triple A card and get another five hundred dollars?"

"What? You just got almost that much last week?"

"Because I really can't afford to waste time being broke down today. And it's my money you're holding."

"Oh God," she moans. This is the fourth time in as many weeks he has asked her for money from the kitty, though never this much before. She can't refuse him, though. It is his money, after all. "Okay.," she says. "But I need the card back before eight tonight."

"Why?"

"Because I want to go out tonight, and besides, we can talk then." Bending down, she picks up Power, then gently pushes the cat's soft, cuddly body into Teddy's chest. He takes her and drapes her over his sturdy shoulder.

"Oh, no, Tania, I don't want to fall into anything today. We're talking nice now. Just let me hold the card. I'll bring it back tomorrow."

She is too angry to argue. "Okay," she says again. "Tomorrow we'll talk." She returns to the back room to find her checkbook and the card. He waits for her, fingering open the zipper section of his bag to make sure he has the phone number of his pal Benny, the white guy who handles the betting at the pool hall. Again, some of the lucky nickels slip out of his pocket and roll across the floor, making a loud pop when they careen into the metal base of the standing lamp. Power jumps off his shoulder after them. Again, he bends down to retrieve them.

"No, Teddy." Tania screams suddenly from the back room "Teddy NAT TURNER where are you? What's happened to you?" She's angry at herself as well as him because she agreed to wait until tomorrow to talk. She's been wanting for weeks to thank him for the clarity he showed when he named her parents criminals. Now it seems to her that the Teddy from that night is slipping away. While he had come to New Mexico to be with her, he can't seem to stand up without the money he thinks he can win playing pool.

"What do you mean?" he shouts back, but the words are hardly out of his mouth when she returns to the front room, the check and the AAA card in her hand. "What in hell is the reason you keep dropping change?" She glares at him while he looks away. "I ain't gonna call you that blessed Nat Turner nickname no more. You sure don't act like you did when we were back in New York City, getting ready to start our great new life out here in this desert town! " What's happened to our dream? We were gonna use the money to burn down those plantation myths that said a woman should only be with a man 'cause she doesn't want to be alone. My mother stuck with my silent-as-a-rock father out of fear of loneliness and had a long life of nothing but that, and that's why I'm talking to you this way. We gotta talk now. It won't wait till tomorrow. I gotta know if we're still gonna buy that house together one day."

Teddy gives her a confused look.

"Hon," Tania goes on, pleading now. "I thought you believed a man could have feelings and share them with his woman."

He looks away.

"I thought you was gonna tell me when you're upset or scared. Don't you trust I'll listen?"

"No."

"Okay, okay. Or at least that I want to see you can be a person on your own?"

"I think you just want a back-up, maybe." Finally, with many more words than usual he releases his pent-up hurt: "You act like I'm not trying out here in this hot-assed town. Do you know how many lousy jobs I've had since I got here? Mostly standing Monday, Tuesday, Wednesday, Thursday, Friday for hours under this killer sun, with just my Yankees cap to keep me from drowning in heat and my ankles swelling up. And not one of them paying enough to cover my rent, much less to keep a house going."." He swats a fly away from his face.

"I don't wanna hear any more about your lousy jobs," Tania says. "I know they're lousy. I know it's been hard. But we had a back-up plan for that, didn't we? Isn't that why you took so long to come, so we would have more savings? Please . . . Can't we just . . .?" She stops herself, then says "Please, Teddy, just don't keep spending our, I mean, your money." She adds, "Please don't go," but so softly that his reply to what she has said covers the sound of her voice.

"I'm *not* spending it, baby, I'm making it. I'm making money so we *can* get the house we talked about with lots of dogs and your cat will have a place to fool around in outside . . . 'cause I'll make beautiful adobe walls high, high so she can't run away."He reaches for the check and the AAA card, and wordlessly Tania hands them over. He puts them in his chest pocket, right on top of his heart space, then turns away and opens the screen door, covering his nose as he does. He sneezes. He doesn't mention the trucking deal,

"Bless you," she says. Hot air smothers her cool blessing as he shuts the door behind him. He doesn't realize that Power has trapped one of his lucky coins under her paw.

* * *

The deal with his pal with the Ritchie Valens haircut doesn't pan out, but as the summer stretches out into the time of cicadas, the time when you can walk to and from anyone's house without the gushing New Mexico winds knocking at your head and almost tearing you down, Teddy is once again hopeful, because he's got a new job. And for the first time since he arrived in Albuquerque, it's not a dirty, dangerous short-term construction gig, but a job that could last a while. He's driving a van for one of the downtown hotels, picking up gourmet foods and other supplies and delivering them to the kitchen. Tania is less enthusiastic. She doesn't like it that most of his new co-workers are white and idealize the military, unlike the mostly Latino crews working construction. And the women working at the hotel are white, too. It's very unlike the bus depot in New York, where there were lots of Black and Puerto Rican and Haitian, and Jamaican men, as well as white ones. And of the very few women who decorated those gray peeling-paint walls, virtually all, like Tania, were Black. White women worked in hospitals and in stores and sold tickets at the movie theaters downtown. They didn't need to put up with having to eat lunch while a big gray rat smacked its teeth at their feet.

From the outset, Tania knew that Teddy was generally more comfortable with white folks than she was. After all, his buddies at Transit had included white men—there were several among the regulars at the pool table in the depot. Nor has he ever been drawn so deeply into the Black activism and Afro-centric culture that have engaged her since her days at the University of the Streets. Despite anything she might have said during their arguments, she wants to believe—still *does* believe—that he is her man, her proud Black man, her Teddy Nat Turner.

But now when Teddy and his co-workers at the hotel finally finish work, he and Tania are in totally different spaces. Before, sweating through those short-term construction gigs, he had never socialized with the men he worked with. They were never together long enough to get to know one another. Now, he has time to hang out with his co-workers, the way he used to do in New York—drinking, eating, playing pool, avoiding talking about his childhood hurt with Tania. So even though he and Tania have sort of made up since their last fight, their lives have become increasingly separate, and even the little time they spend together is filled with tension without Pam to help bridge the communications gap between them.

On top of this, there is an assistant cook at the hotel, a white woman named Dolly, who eyes him daily as he carries the supplies into the kitchen. He and she flirt at work the way a Black man and white woman can, in an unknowing/knowing kind of way. He enjoys her easy laugh and the flirty way she waves at him. He finds himself chatting too much, because she is white and "stacked" and he knows the other guys see her as a trophy.

Of course his daughter's mom has light skin and swears she's white even though she's Puerto Rican, but Dolly is different, a bona fide white woman who laughs when she sees him stride into "her" kitchen and greets him with a big smile, saying, "Hey big guy!"

Still, Tania is his woman, and when a party for people from the job is planned, he calls her.

"So when is it?" Tania asks. "Not tonight, I hope. This is Friday night and you know I'm tired from working all week."

"No . . . Tomorrow."

"Oh well, okay then. So are we going together?" She's worried his car has broken down again and he just needs a ride, and doesn't really want to see her. She looks for his answer the way she looks for roaches in her kitchen.

"Yes," he replies. It's the first chance he's had to introduce her to the folks at his job, and he hopes it'll work out. Will they like her and will they be able to talk with one another? He hopes she'll blend, even though most of his co-workers had supported the Gulf War and some still wear those yellow so-called "patriotic" ribbons, and have them stuck on their cars even though the war is over. There's one on the truck he drives. Mostly they've stopped shouting "you're un-American" at anyone not wearing them, but no one says anything against the military or war.

"Well, Tania, will you pick me up?"

"Yeah," she replies, with very little mint and no sugar in her tone, as if she'd just bit into a real sour lemon.

"Then let's go," he says.

After setting the plan for her to pick him up at seven o'clock the next day, they hang up.

Tania is filled with foreboding. She longs to talk about her fears with a girlfriend, but is afraid even Becca will not understand, not the way Agua would. For one thing, though Becca has a working-class background, she and Tania's other friends in Albuquerque, are a hodgepodge of values, beliefs and class identification—mostly leftist and artistic, perhaps, but not working poor like Agua, And Agua, of course, is far away and mostly out of touch.

Saturday evening she waits in her car for Teddy to come out of his apartment, listening to an oldies tape on her Walkman. Aretha Franklin takes her back to a time when she was a girl and her father and mother were in the dining room after lunch. A few days before, she had overheard her mom say on the phone to one of her friends, "I needed a man who could stop thinking of me as 'a little doll.' That's how the white guys in the Red Cross canteen referred to me. Your dad seemed different," But on the day Tania is remembering, her mother stands stiffly next to the table. Her father has raised one of the heavy wooden chairs over his head. Tania feels about 10 years old. Her breasts have not come yet. She is watching from the doorway of the dining room. Dad is yelling, but she doesn't remember what. The yelling frightens her. What will he do next? The chair is rising higher. Her mother is just standing there. The chair is coming down . . . crashing down . . . smashing in front of her. It's threatening every fiber in Butter's short body.

She snaps back to the present when she hears Teddy say, "Tania, open the Goddamn door. It's hot out here."

She unlocks the passenger side and he pushes his big body into the tiny hatchback car. She reminds herself to "stay present," as Pam says she should, so puts away the Walkman's ear-buds. His sneakers and sports socks look good on his powerful legs. He wears shorts and a fancy turquoise State Fair of N.M. sports shirt. She glances at her unpainted nails, clean and clear. "Look, Teddy, I trimmed my nails so I could do a massage on your feet later tonight, maybe. What do you think?" She smiles. "You know, I've been wanting to say thank you for understanding about my parents' criminality and saying it aloud that night, you remember . . .?"

Teddy nods and gives a slight smile and reaches for her shoulder to give her a love tap, then looks out the window while Tania drives and wishes there were a radio so he could listen to something, or better, they could listen together, the way they used to when driving together in New York. He yearns to shove a cigarette into his mouth. He fingers the Kools in his pocket, making sure he has matches. He knows Tania won't.

"Teddy, can we leave around midnight?" She asks.

"I don't know," he says flatly.

"Well, you let me know and I'll try to let *you* know when *I'm* ready."

Their dialogue is short, just informational, the way it usually is now with these two, who do not touch. When they lived back East and even here, they used to help each other through stress by stopping to connect, with their hands on each other's thigh. She misses that so much. She reminds herself of Teddy's coffee-brown eyes, which match his deep brown skin. They shine in a soft, subtle way, so he doesn't come across as the kind who doesn't listen. He does listen, and take in women's stories, including Tania's, with his kindness. But not now.

Glancing sideways at her, he thinks about how she's driving in an absentminded, erratic way but he doesn't try to interfere. His mind shifts gears as Tania goes into high to power onto the freeways, first I-40 and then, at the Big Intersection, making the switch to I-25. Here her professional concentration and skills as a driver kick in and he can relax. Dolly will be at the party. He likes to joke around with her at the job, 'cause she isn't so serious, the way Tania always is. She reminds him a little of a German girl named Ana he dated when he was in the army stationed in Germany. He's never mentioned her to Tania, the fun they had together. But Ana didn't drink, and Dolly does, and when she does she looks sloshy and acts silly. He's even caught her taking nips at the job. But he figures he can handle it. Besides, Tania, who loves Blackness, is still his woman, even though she's high strung and he's nervous around her because she pushes him.

He shifts his weight in the too-small seat and reaches over to gently touch her shoulder, but she shoots an irritated look at him, her glare pressing his hand back to his lap. He raises it again to wipe his brow, then with sweat sticking to his fingers reaches over to turn on the radio. He'd like to listen to some Les McCann or Nina. But his hand remembers in mid-air that there is no radio. Silently he curses himself for not having the money to keep his own, bigger car running. It's an old wreck, but it does have a radio. And he hates having to have Tania drive him places. Fidgeting in his too-tight seat belt, he wonders why he keeps spending money. It's as if his fingers are slippery and the dollars just slide off.

Tania's leg, long with a graceful curving calf, presses down hard on the gas pedal. As she steers, focusing on the light traffic, she thinks about all those New York City streets that she and Teddy Nat Turner used to drive buses on. She wants to say to him, "Remember how we used to have so much fun, had such a 'hum' when you met me after work at the depot?" But she says nothing, and he responds with silence.

Silences between them used to be their special language, their unspoken love messages, but not this evening. She thinks, now I'm driving him 'cause he probably hasn't got enough money to gas up his car. She knows he's still playing pool and losing, that his shot ain't like it was when he was that big city bus depot pool shark. For a long time she's wanted to thank him for understanding about her father but damn it, there's never been a chance, and now he was just sitting over there so silent and shut down. She hates these disconnects. She knows he needs to talk too about how low he feels. He must have realized by now that his momma isn't ever going to be interested in him or her or their move. The two of them are out here together, away from her and his memories of his pops. Teddy's pops! At least Teddy had moved his Momma out when his father threatened to kill her with the BB gun. Thank God! But now Teddy is gambling the way his father drank. And he never talks with her about any of it. His insight into her father's behavior—calling him a criminal, which he was, but which she had never acknowledged until that night—had clarified so much for her, had been a breakthrough as profound as any she had had with Pam. But his withdrawal from her since then, his neediness, his frequent requests for "his" money from the savings account, had made it seem as if it had never really happened. It seemed like she and Teddy had become as far apart from each other as his mother and father, and her parents, too, had been. Still, she can't accept that this could be true. "Teddy?" She speaks with hesitation. "Thanks for letting out your rage at my shutdownness by cracking that wood last time."

"Yeah. Okay."

Yes, she thinks. He is still with me. But neither of them says anything else.

The silence is finally broken when Teddy says, "Tania, the exit is coming up. We're almost there."

She looks up and sees in the distance the majestic Sandia Mountains, holding the promise of the Native American ways. Recently she has been taking workshops and studying Reiki healing and pressure point therapy with a woman named Milagros, a *Mezcla* Latina with a strong indigenous spirit she had met at Us 'n' R Art. The energy work is all connected.

She says, "Teddy, I think we're connected spiritually in ways we never knew. You showed it to me when you said my parents were criminals and cracked open that wood. You really clarified something for me when you used that word."

What she says touches something in him and he shoots her a loving look, gazing at her turquoise earrings, thinking about a dream he had once about Native American men, who wore thick turquoise stone bracelets. He recalls the ceremony circle he joined at the drumming he went to, and wonders why he hasn't given those Native American ways more of a chance. But the thought is fleeting as the approach to the exit takes them away from the view of the mountains, and he is distracted by the cars speeding by, regular American ones like they drive out here, except for a hippie looking van with a multi colored paint job and a line of motorcyclists that jump in front of Tania's car as she slows down for the exit. No "low riders" in spruced up old cars with shiny golden chrome exteriors are out today.

Following his terse directions, she pulls off the highway and after a couple of turns, pulls into the parking lot of a modern apartment complex in the northwest part of town. She notices at once that few of the people walking about are Chicanos and there are definitely no Blacks, as there are in the "Sticks community" over by the airport. They get out of the car. Teddy walks slightly in front of Tania, heading towards a wide, low building without steps

"Where are we going?"

"To the rec room."

"Oh, the tenants can use it for special occasions?"

"Yeah."

At the door, Teddy walks in first and holds it for Tania, who comes in behind him. The first thing she notices, besides the whiteness of everyone's skin except hers and Teddy's, is the music. No African or Native American drums play the way they do at the gatherings Tania usually invites Teddy to. The second thing is that most of the women wear jeans and sandals, though not Birkenstocks like Tania's, and she feels overdressed in her strappy summer sundress. She wishes she'd asked Teddy what kind of dress these people might be into. A man playing CDs puts on "I Would Never Let You Go."

Once in the room, Teddy sees Dolly right off. She's one of the few women wearing a skirt, and it's short, above her knees. She's standing at the bar, where most of the men are also clustered, within easy reach of the Johnny Walker Red and Bacardi . There is wine, too, low-key, but not Manischewitz, and salsa and corn chips in a big plastic bowl. Even as he takes Tania's hand and pulls her towards the crowd, calling out a broad "hello" to everyone, his mind is on Dolly. He eyes her breasts, which stretch the fitted top she wears. Tania has lips and eyes and hips, a nice Black ass, he thinks. But she ain't got no tits. Tania has legs and can move, but she don't have Dolly's dimensions!

He introduces Tania by saying, "This is Tania. She's a New Yorker like me." He allows his accent to be strong, right out of Harlem. After folks nod he adds, "And she brought her tarot cards!"

At this they all smile white-folk smiles, and Tania returns their smiles half-heartedly. Frankie Beverly and Mays sing out, "I would never never let you go . . ." The guitar plays, conga drums keep the beat, supporting the male singers, with a few snapping tambourines delivering a gospel feel to what is still a pop Rhythm and Blues song, a straight up Black urban sound. "I can't understand it where did we go wrong? / I won't be happy, girl / I gotta make sure I'm right before I let go."

Now the chorus: "Baa bam bap." "Oh baby," the backup singers croon. Tania's heart stays caught in the fabric of the music. She moves towards some children, who are playing with pretzels on the other side of the room. They are taking one pretzel and then another out of the bag, shrieking with laughter.

After a while she starts to feel a little sick. She wonders when Teddy is coming over to be with her. She shoves a pretzel into her mouth, deciding to wait for him, instead of going back to the bar. Feeling the music, she wants him to ask her to dance, but worries that he'll act all macho and touch her breasts while they move, the way he did once at a party they went to in the Bronx. But would that be worse than being ignored? She continues to wait, watching as he pours himself another drink and banters with the guys. She wonders what would happen if she mentioned that she listens regularly to Amy Goodman on K.U.N.M. She wonders which of the people here owns the car in the parking lot with the bumper sticker that says "If you don't like America then leave." These folks believe America is always right when it invades brown people's countries, are still stuck on doing whatever is good for low gas prices. They're not likely to trust some Black New York woman trying to open their eyes to the sins of Americaca due to the education system hiding the truth that our country was founded on invasion, genocide and slavery.

She overhears a woman saying, "My husband just got another yellow ribbon for the truck," and wishes she could find a more politically conscious working class to talk to. She wishes Agua were here. Since she didn't work with these white people wearing jeans, who all knew each other from the job, she had nothing to say to them, nor they to her. It wasn't like at the bus depot, where working-class political consciousness might not have been profound, even among union leaders, but where she could have friends because at least they could at least all talk "bus talk." Or like the Natural Foods store, where everyone cared about the environment and she and Becca could talk about Pueblo ceremonies.

She notices some women and kids wearing bathing suits who have appeared in the room from a hallway, and decides to head for the place they have come from, another space . . . . She leaves the party without telling Teddy, who is still over at the bar, joking with the guys, his white teeth shining in his brown-skinned face. She walks into the passageway and heads toward that other space, where, from the chlorine smell, there must be a swimming pool.

On the wallpaper in the hall there's a drawing of a huge mountain. She mumbles to herself, "Will my fear be lifted in this place where the kids are? What am I afraid of anyway? Maybe I know there's no room for an independent, politically aware woman in this crowd. These working class people have a good time partying!

At the entrance to the room where the pool is, she hesitates, shifting uncomfortably and swaying back and forth. A big broad-leafed plant striving to grow greets her. Some of the women have let their kids, who are too young to go in the water in the absence of a kiddy pool, take their shoes and socks off and dangle their feet in the warm water. They sit really close so they can snatch the children if it seems they're likely to fall in.

She smiles at the mothers, wondering if Teddy will come and look for her. She had wanted to be Teddy's daughter's step mom, but that won't happen, it seems. She chats with the women about the plant. No one seems to know what kind of plant it is.

A blonde woman warns her son to watch his sister.

Sunday—tomorrow—brings yoga class. Tania thinks how restful it will feel to connect deeply with such positive energy. Her anticipation brings her chin to her lightly closed fist. But, she thinks, there is no point in mentioning yoga, or the Reiki healing training she is about to start, to these people.

Unable to bear her feeling of isolation anymore she leaves, carefully avoiding a little girl who is chasing a boy around the pool. As slowly as she can, she walks back toward the party room, thinking, "Damn, where the hell isTeddy? Why didn't he come after me? He must have seen me leave the room."

Approaching the other end of the hall she can see what is happening. She sees Teddy with his arms at his sides. Dolly is pulling at them, trying to position his hands on her waist. He and Dolly look into each other's eyes. Her big breasts are pressing against his chest. Tania thinks: "They are acting like lovers." Her mind races. What should she do? Should she just walk out, go down the path to the parking lot and vent her wrath on the Toyota? Drive as fast as she can to wherever she can?

No, No, No. She would go tell Teddy she wanted to leave.

"Outstanding" is playing. "Girl, you knock me out / Excited (I'm so excited, baby) / It makes me want to shout (Baby) / Gee, I feel so lucky, girl . . . / You blow my mind, baby / I'm so alive with you, baby . . ."

This music lights Tania's anger. Singers of Blackness crooning to this messed up turn of a party night. Finally, standing beside her man, she says icily, "I'm ready to leave this party, Teddy." Her eyes try to engage his. She is working hard to keep herself from shouting.

"Okay, Tan." Teddy lets go of Dolly. He makes no eye contact with Tania.

"I'm going to the car."

"Okay."

She turns and heads toward the bright red E X I T sign, politely saying goodbye to a white guy who just happens to be coming into the room as she leaves.. The wailing chorus of "Outstanding" follows her out. She hates the song, though before tonight she and Teddy had enjoyed it together.

She slides into the driver's seat of her little car, wipes her eyes, then checks them in the rear view mirror to make sure there's no sign of tears. She wonders, Is he coming 'cause he's thinking 'Okay, gotta go, 'cause this damn town don't have no bus service up here at night'? Or is he coming 'cause he knows we have to work this out? His appearance with Dolly traipsing along behind him answers her question to her bitter satisfaction.

She unlocks the passenger door. The heat in her car matches the heat inside her. Teddy packs himself into the front passenger seat. She doesn't open her window, though Dolly, who is clearly wasted, tries to get her attention. "I'm sorry . . ." she says through the closed window, the words tumbling together so what she says sounds like Immmaaaasor . . . ee."

Tania starts the car, but Dolly lingers, so she gives in and rolls down the window. "I'm sorry," Dolly says again, carefully.

Teddy leans over towards the open window, crowding Tania. "Bye, Dolly," he says. "We're leaving. You better get away from the car."

Tania backs her car out the parking spot as fast as she can and heads down the street, driving with a vengeance. "I'm not saying not a f***ing word," she mutters. The sounds of the gears shifting make her words inaudible. At the first red light the car lurches to a stop as her mind rolls over and over the sight of Teddy's arms around Dolly.

"Whoa, whoa baby!" he blurts out.

"Don't call me baby! You got your baby. I am *Tania*!" For further emphasis she spells it out: "T-A-N-I-A!" Loud and clear. "And from today on, I'm gonna remember that you . . ." She stops herself from saying anything more, anything that might reveal her contempt and put him down. Instead she jeers with one word: "Shit!"

Teddy stares out through his open window at the fast moving cars on Albuquerque's freeway, which runs alongside the road they're on. The hot desert air does little to clear his head. He wishes he had a car that wasn't always broken down. He wishes memories of holding Tania didn't bring up what he never wants to look at. He wishes he had money so he could buy her some gas, since despite her evident hurt and fury, she is driving him home. He closes his eyes and concentrates on keeping his lips frozen, so he won't yell at her and threaten her the way his father used to do to his moms. She's driving like a madwoman, car swerving, but he just hangs on, sensing no room for talk that will make any sense.

Tania waits for him to say something, anything, but he remains silent, chewing the last bit of sugar out of his piece of mint gum. "Why don't you apologize?" she says finally as they arrive at his apartment building, unable to hold herself quiet any longer.

He doesn't reply, but unfolds his big body and climbs out of the car. The door shuts behind him and he reaches for his cigarettes. He's been itching to light up since they left the party, but knew better than to ask while they were in the car.

"I'm sorry," he says, bending down to talk through the car window.

"For what?" Tania hisses, trying to hold back tears.

"Let's not talk now . . . Later, okay? You know how we can get."

“You call me!” She barely waits for him to step back before flooring the gas pedal. The wheels screech as the car pulls out into the street. As before, she drives without slowing down until red lights catch her off guard and she has to stop short. It’s a good thing the small town cops, busy with nothing to do, keep away from her route that night. Arriving at her house, she parks the car and sits a while before going inside. As the silver rays of the desert moon shine down on her, she screams silently, “Ahhh,” and then, “No more!”

Finally she stirs. She fishes for the house key on the floor by the driver’s seat, then climbs out of the car, moving in what feels like slow motion. She plugs the key in the door, turns it, and stomps into the house. The scent of a cedar branch, cut earlier in the day from the tree in her backyard, fills the room. “Oh I forgot to take off my shoes,” She checks herself.

Mother moon keeps her gaze on Tania through the glass rectangle in the top of her door as she sits on a rug woven with Zuni symbols, holding herself. *Prisoners of Childhood* by Alice Miller and another book, *About Men*, stare at her from her bookshelf, which Teddy had painted purple for her. “I *can write*,” she says to herself. The journal calls to her. But she stalls. Better to take a bath and dream. Her dream-self will validate what happened. But it is her daddy, who betrayed her, who comes in her dream. She grinds her teeth, and works into so much pain she won’t feel good in her jaw at work tomorrow.

16 REVELATION, HONOR N. Y. C.

Teddy hears the screech of the tires as Tania pulls away from the curb in front of his apartment building and reaches for a cigarette from the pack of Kools stuffed in his pants pocket. “God! What made me do that?” He draws the smoke deeper than he usually does into his lungs. A least he didn’t shout and threaten her when she hauled him away from his friends the way his father used to do his moms. Not that he and Tania don’t know how to tear into each other; they just don’t do it in front of other folks. But maybe her icy silence is worse. He closes his eyes and takes another puff, scanning the clear black sky for the moon.

He wonders what Pam would say. She’d told him he had to think things through for himself and not depend on Tania to make him face reality, figure out what’s really bugging him, the reasons for his actions. Thinking about Dolly, it occurs to him that he likes the way she calls him “big guy,” instead of making him feel like he’s good for nothing, a piece of shit. His mind turns to New York and earning good money driving a bus and being his mother’s big guy, taking her around, shopping and all.

Still emotionally off balance, he fights inside for language. In New York he wasn't exactly Tania's big guy, but he was her Teddy Nat Turner and her equal. Here in New Mexico, he can't help but feel that Tania is much more successful than he is. She has a better car, and has to drive him places when his breaks down, which is all the time. Sure, she lives in a rental, not a co-op like the place she owned in New York, but it's a house with a garden, not a dump like his place. In New York, they spent as much time in his apartment as in hers; here she rarely comes to his place and never sleeps there. Despite all his efforts, the cockroaches won't be defeated. So out here he's not anybody's Big Guy, not really. Out here, as far as he's concerned, he's a failure.

Fingering his keys, Yankees cap in his left hand, he lowers himself to sit on the steps. That Dolly is white isn't the most important thing, though it was nice seeing those white guys' faces when Dolly flirted with him. But damn, when Tania came back in from wherever she went and saw him and Dolly together, he felt like shit. He knew at the time that she hadn't read the scene right. She thought he only let Dolly hug on him 'cause she was white. He wanted to tell her that it wasn't because Dolly was white, but because she says "hey, big guy" when she sees him and he feels good 'cause everything out here is such a mess for him otherwise and he doesn't ever hear from his momma. He wanted to tell her in the car. But she drove like a mad woman, swerving back and forth, and he couldn't do anything but hang on. Probably he wouldn't have found the words anyway.

He stubs out the cigarette and returns to his inner sanctuary, shutting both eyes, while the almost noiseless night secures him. New York sirens no longer make his heart race, but this shit does. He hears an alley cat shriek, and lays one hand against the back of his head, propping himself on his elbow, looking at the night sky. Filled with stars and the silvery light of the desert moon, it was one thing that was better out here than in New York. He sees a falling star, bright even in the moonlight, but it doesn't lift his mood as it usually does. The truth is, he thinks, he needs support too, and he feels he's not getting it from Tania. Dolly means nothing to him, but just by flirting with him she builds him up. And if she has issues, he doesn't know about them, thank god. He hates himself for thinking this way, but it's so goddamn hard dealing with what Tania's been through. She doesn't really trust him . . . can't help mixing him up with that criminal father of hers who hurt her so bad. He doesn't know how much more of it he can take. He says to himself that he should call Pam, but he can't do it now because it's two o'clock in the morning back east. And besides, talking with her on the phone doesn't really work. The time it takes to get deep into things, the way they did when he was in New York, would cost a fortune. And it's hard to go deep on the phone in any case. Besides, Pam would ask him to start thinking about what his mother didn't give him, and he can't bear to think about that, about the fact he hasn't heard from her once since he left, or his daughter either.

The pressure of living now on much less money than he made bus driving is killing him. Also paying rent to some unforgiving stranger of a landlord compared to how it was in New York when he rented from his aunt. He had left a secure job before he retired, so could take only the money he had put into his pension fund, in order to come and live with, and he thought, love Tania. But it hasn't worked out. Tania weighs on his brain. Why couldn't she trust him? He had trusted her and moved his entire life out here to this desert town. He forgets that Pam had told him to move only if he wanted to do it for himself. He focuses his resentment on Tania, not on his family for not even calling and finding out what he's doing now that they can't depend on him.

He sighs, itching to light up another cigarette, but having to pee, gets to his feet and unlocks the door, hoping the fridge will have a last beer in it. He knows there's no food. The sounds of insects crackle in the night.

* * *

It's a couple of weeks since the party. Teddy had left a very short message—"I'm sorry"—the day after, but didn't say anything else. Tania wants to talk in person and left him that message. Now, finally, he calls and she answers. He can imagine her resting on her futon with her legs in the air, leaning them against the wall to bring the blood down from her calves. Although she knows he probably still just wants to talk on the phone, she says, "Teddy, please come over, I need to find out what's going on here." She sighs as the silence between them lengthens.

"Well, I really didn't call for that," he says eventually. He wishes he could move the conversation around to his need, but cannot. He strokes his head with one hand, looks down at his sneakers with their white shoelaces. The black jeans he wears fit him, but his belly has started to really hang over. He wears his red tee shirt outside his pants to cover it up.

"Come on, Teddy, we need to face whatever it is, in front of each other."

"Okay, I'll come tomorrow." He thinks it's best to wait. He needs her to give him some more of his savings.

He drives over the following afternoon, after work.

Walking up the path he smells trouble in the air, hot, dry and no clouds. She must have heard his car pull up, 'cause she looks out the window, then goes right to the door and lets him in.

They look at each other. He sits on the one chair she has in the kitchen. He watches as she washes dishes.

"So, Teddy, you know we never finished that . . . you know, what went on between us . . . you know, about the party. . .

"Tania, I told you I was sorry. Anyway, I told that woman I don't want to have anything to do with her."

"I know, but why, why did you fall into that fix?" Tania can't let it go. She wants him to stand and put his arms around her from the back, like old times.

Teddy stays seated, looking first at his sneakers, then staring out her kitchen window at the cedar tree. He thinks, this woman isn't going to be willing to talk about money. I better not ask her.

"Teddy what's up?"

"I need your help."

"What?

"I thought you were working. Your dumb-ass bosses didn't say anything about you and that woman, did they? I know they deny they compete with Black men and might have harassed you. Did they?"

"Tania, it's just. . ."

She cuts in: "I haven't really heard from you since the party. Oh yeah, thanks again for the apology. Can we talk about us now?"

They talk over each other, can't hear each other.

"It's just my paycheck is nowhere near the money we made in New York. You know I can hardly buy groceries."

"So come with me to the food co-op, you could be a member and you'd have a discount," she pleads.

"No baby. I'm not into that, and you know it. Besides, their prices are too high even with the discount. I support your ideas and stuff, but right now I just need some cash. I have a big game tonight and I need to put some real money on it, so I can win big. You know I'm a good player. Okay?"

"No." She glares at him. "No money for games."

"Are you worried, I won't repay you? I promise I'll pay it back after I win."

"That's so unrealistic. We've been here before." Her voice rises and she slams the sponge into the sink.

The neighbor's kids, who are playing outside, are laughing deliriously, and the sound tears at Tania. She pounds him: "Are you willing to take this relationship as seriously as you do money?" She shoots him with her eyes.

"I didn't come here to argue." He tries to keep his voice low.

"Then what the hell did you come for? You wouldn't apologize to me in person. You wouldn't stop holding that woman as soon as you saw me. You even got yourself into that mess. Just 'cause she was sloppy drunk, do you expect me to believe it was all her fault?" Tania thrusts her face towards him, holding herself back by gripping the sink behind her..

Teddy moves away.

"Now you're going to run." She tries to cut him off at the door.

"Tania, excuse me. Excuse me." Teddy doesn't back down, yet wants to keep it cool, so they don't physically hurt each other.

"No. You stay here and work this out with me."

"No. I can't pay my bills. You say I can't live with you. I had to put my last big money on gas for the car to drive here. I have to pay the stupid phone company or they will shut off my service. I'm so behind, I have to make this extra money." Finally, Teddy asserts himself, though suddenly he realizes that he played too much last month and did lose a little cash. He's sure he'll make it up easy, though, if he can just get into the game tonight.

"I won't front you the money, if that's the only reason you came over here."

"Okay."

"Okay what?" She steps back, hoping he will admit he misses her.

"Okay. I'm leaving." Passing her, he walks toward the door.

"And don't come back. Don't you come back." Her hair feels like it stands on the end of her neck ready to dig into her skin. The heat bursts into her temples.

He turns back towards her. "Tania, it's my money and I want it."

"No. Damn it, you're breaking it all up. I don't want to give you the savings. Teddy . . ." She reaches towards his back, arm raised as if to hit him, as she cries.

"Don't even try that shit, Tania!" His voice pushes her hand down. She knows his fury could erupt into violence. She'd better stop.

Teddy walks fast, out the door, glad they avoided hitting each other, his anger and his sadness held in by his tightly closed lips. He can't run but he can't slow down. Damn it, how can I talk with her so she understands? He wonders. Defeated, he strides towards his broken down car without looking back. He revs the engine and his fury forces the car to move.

She drops into the kitchen chair. A half hour passes as she sits and wonders what to do. Finally, moving slowly as the day's heat burns into her home, she rises, finds her beat-up checkbook, cries and writes out a check for his part of their savings—the money he had brought with him from New York, less what she had already given him. Numb, she takes an envelope from the box on the shelf by the table where she does her writing, puts the check into it, seals it and stamps it, after addressing it to Teddy. Then she throws it on the floor and dials Pam. "He's crushing our dream," she says, sobbing.

"Listen, Tania." Pam cuts to the chase. "Have you ever talked with any of your woman friends—Agua?—about how so many of you women who've been abused as children stay with men who you think need fixing 'cause you couldn't fix the adult who abused you?"

Tania drops her head and stops crying. Could this be possible?

Pam, hearing the quiet, tells her to send him the money. "It's his money," she says. "He has to be his own person and face his own demons. You can't save him. You've got to let go."

A month later, Tania's body stays still as her eyes drift into deep REM dreaming. Her most recent poem "#1005—You Are Finished," hangs over a copy of the radical Jewish women's magazine *Lilith*, which a customer from the Nahalat Shalom congregation had given her at work. Books line up next to it, near the futon she rests on. Many a night of heavy sleeping has eased some deep creases into the cushiony "bed," so much more comfortable than a traditional mattress. Tania needs to fluff it up or turn it over, but her torment over Teddy has kept her riveted to her writing, to the neglect of housekeeping chores. She had written Poem 1005 in bright red ink, with exclamations at every line's ending, after Teddy had had nothing to say when she told him, "Don't come back." After she sent him the money, which she knew he had received only because the check had cleared. She has made herself strong enough not to pursue him since then, and actually sleeps well at night the way she sleeps now, having given herself some of that healing Reiki energy before going to bed, as she had learned to do recently.

The loud ringing of her phone jolts her awake. Though they haven't spoken since their break-up, she knows it has to be Teddy, calling in the cool dryness of the dawn. She had thought it was their last ending, imagining that Dolly had taken over where Tania had been. But he's the onlyonewho would call so early.

"Did you get my message?" He hurries right into conversation as soon as she picks up, not waiting for her slow, sleepy hello.

"No." Tania Shocked at the tone of his voice, she's suddenly wide awake. It's lower than usual, maybe because it's so early, or maybe because he's been drinking.

"I left you a message . . ." Teddy's tone implores Tania to have a heart, let him know he is important to her.

"When?"

"Didn't you listen to your machine last night?" She imagines his eyes darting back and forth, imagines him wiping the sweat from his forehead with the back of his hand.

"Teddy, please tell me what you said. Tell me now. I'm on the phone with you right now." She begins to taste ugliness in her mouth.

He slams the phone down.

Tania quickly rises and presses the playback button on her answering machine. "I can't take it anymore." Teddy's voice on the machine pauses and the silence fills her head. Then she hears, "I'm gonna take myself out." Again silence. Then the machine announces the time he called: "12:01 a.m."

"Last night he left *this*?!" She says aloud, then begins to laugh uncontrollably, doubling over. She can't stop laughing, as she grabs a pair of orange drawstring pants, which she pulls on over her pajama bottoms, and the first top that comes to hand. She puts on her sneakers.

Her laughter changes now, her short puffy screams filling the little bungalow, threatening to burst outside to awaken the still-quiet town and scatter the wild creatures who live on the slopes of the mountains to the east. She scrambles for her pocketbook, searches frantically for the key ring with the yellow Zuni flag that holds her car keys. She finds it on top of a pile of books in the hallway.

Running to the car, she stumbles and drops the key ring in the sandy dirt, stops to pick it up with her left hand. Her right clutches her bag. Now, she walks, looks down at the ground, concentrating to make sure she doesn't stumble again. Her next door neighbor's rooster crows. It's 7 a.m. on a solid Sunday in this churchgoing town, and there's no one else in the street when she gets into the car, with her pajama bottoms under her orange drawstring pants, hair wild, pulled up in a rubber band . . . Her heart screams.

Driving, she remembers all the times she dropped her keys back in New York City. She used to go to Teddy's house at 1 a.m. after driving that big, overwhelming bus on the 4 to midnight shift. He would be too tired and uptight to be with her then, and, leaving almost as soon as she arrived, she would drop her keys in the snow, or on the ground, as windy weather beat her face. Or, scrambling into her old used car, she would drop them by the driver's seat, and have to feel around for them in the dark, so she could go home. Every time she was "off," crazy with need for Teddy to fill her, she would call him, even though he had said "Don't call me until tomorrow." In that darkness when she would enter her own apartment back in Brooklyn, she would still pick up the black phone and dial his number . . . And Teddy would answer.

He would always answer. And now here, she not only didn't answer, 'cause they had broken up, she didn't even listen to what he said into the answering machine, 'cause she had gotten in so late and was tired and went to bed. Besides, as a rule she only listens to messages when she feels ready . . . and now, she realizes, "Oh man . . . Teddy . . . Teddy is ready to take himself out . . ."

"Teddy, wait, Teddy wait," she cries silently as a red light stops her.

When she reaches his apartment, she knocks so hard the wood frame shakes. As she pounds on the door, he opens it. He wears dark colors, all maroon and burgundy, not the bright ones she's used to, They suit his somber, anguished expression. It shows, she realizes suddenly, that her Teddy, whom she had seen as strong and resilient, who had always answered the phone when she called, had been smothered—smothered by life. His family had beaten up on him as much as hers had on her. The only difference was, his was working class, hers almost rich.

But both killer tribes had been out to make the 'American Nightmare' work, just like Pam said. She doesn't remember Pam also warned her he had to save himself.

"Teddy . . ." Her cry is a drawn out wail. She holds out her right hand to touch him. But where? They're not lovers anymore, so where does she dare to touch him?

"Tania . . ."

With her there, he notices the bills piled up on the table near the door, the two from the landlord on top. He can't pay, and with his rent two months overdue he could just be locked out and lose everything. In New Mexico there are even fewer tenant protections than in New York. Or job protections. He's about to lose his, will lose it if he misses one more day. Out here there's no union help for workers in trouble.

He begs the wall for support. He places his back, the broad shoulders that she loves, on a spot on his wall, then rolls his head too, so it touches the dirty cream-colored space. He sighs . . .

"I lost the money," he says,

"All of it?"

Tania touches the wall with her hand, near his shoulder.

"The money . . . It's all gone. I kept on playing, made bets . . ." He is crying.

"Don't hate yourself," she whispers. I love you, Teddy," Tania leans on the other wall, facing him, just giving him her eyes and her heart and listening to him let it all come up, without her body in the way of his release. She knows he has to let go of all this. "We gotta value ourselves and our work, baby," she says, 'cause this system sure don't."

"I don't know what to do . . . I called you Tania . . ."

"I know Teddy. I know . . ."

He hangs his head so she sees his bald spot on the top.

She moves close to him and with her fingers gently rubs the top of his head. He reaches up and she hugs him as hard as she can. "Teddy I love you. We can make this work. We need to find a way to help you. Find some help."

She glimpses new-day sun streaming in through his kitchen window—intense, as only the light the southwest sun, 5000 above the polluted mists of the valleys can be. She wants to move with him to sit in that light at the kitchen table, to calm him. But she senses that the gloom of the hall suits his grim mood and doesn't want to suggest it.

They step back from the oneness of their hug. Tania slowly strokes his face with her left hand and then her right one. It's been days since he shaved, and the soft stubble caresses her fingers. He turns away, leaning his side against the wall this time, his back to her. Something has changed, and she takes his hand. They walk together down the hallway toward the simple chairs and Formica table.

She sits in the chair facing the window and the brilliant sun. He opens the Fridge, which the resident roaches haven't figured out how to get into, and pulls out cornflakes, then milk. He takes the last clean bowl from the counter beside the sink, which overflows with dirty dishes.

"Are you hungry?" he asks. Tania sees this invitation as a good sign, that he can think of eating, and eating with her. She has to go work today, and now she feels she can. He will be okay if he gets some help.

"Call Pam . . . will you? She sighs. Promise me you'll get help. You scared the shit out of me. Get some help. As long as you do, I'll stand by you."

Teddy starts again with Pam when she fits him in for a phone consult after he's off work the very next day. At the close of the session, Pam tells Teddy, "Besides everything we talked about the family, why don't you check out the 12 step programs like Gamblers Anonymous. Call Tania and tell her you want to hear some of what she's written about capitalism and the family. She needs feedback and it will help you too."

"How?"

"It'll help you see the domination and submission that went on in your family, too, so you were left feeling like a nothing, which gets triggered when you don't feel useful at a job."

"Yeah, I feel like I'm not doing something important like I did in New York, taking care of people's lives."

"Yes, that's it. Men connect their importance with their jobs and the way they're treated at work. The way Tania's father did."

"Huh? But I'm not anything like him."

"Not in the way you react. You beat up on yourself. He violated his daughter. He needed to dominate her because his job made him feel small, forced him to submit to racist and capitalist rules that stole his humanity. Your dad beat you up for the same reason. The system perpetuates the violence and we end up hating ourselves.

Teddy whispers, "I never knew that it is all connected."

"Yes. So read that piece she wrote. It'll help you find a new perspective, so you know you're not alone." Pam is trying to give him something tangible to hold onto. But she knows Tania's paper and their phone conversation can only bring him so far. He has to be ready to come out of his bottom, to do the work of healing himself.

He hangs up, and calls Tania, though he knows she's at work, and leaves a message. "Pam says I should read some of your writings about capitalism and the family. Just wanted you to know." She calls him when she knows he's at work and says she'll leave a letter in his mail box. He gets it and reads:

Dear Teddy,

My thoughts on *Capitalism's "Don't Feel, Don't Share, Don't Tell Policy"*:

The system has infected me and you. We did not yet get the courage, and have not had the model to sit and face each other with truths. Capitalism's denial strategy came through our parents' eyes...eyes filled with rage about their work days and how the society looks at them as low class and low-life. And the bosses get over 'cause we as workers, you and I and all of us don't realize we make the whole society run. And we don't fight for wages, housing, pensions, everything! And damnit we are to be valued. Teddy, your mom was a seamstress in the Garment District for years, your dad watched over other people's wealth as a security guard. But in a society that measures your value only by the money you make, their low wages couldn't help but make them feel low. And they took that out on you and on themselves, instead of opening up about their pain. Instead of maybe organizing other tenants and workers, they just sat and watched t.v.

I wonder if, as a teen, you felt the neglect in the eerie quiet, as they silently endured? Teddy, the policy of the rich and owning class came through every time you sat down to a shut-down meal—brownies, fried chicken and grits but no talk. The repression of our real selves came from the workplace and edged up right next to our parents' hearts, yours and mine, so they violated our need for warmth and communication.

Teddy, I want to be there for you emotionally, the way you've been there for me around what my parents did to me. Will you let me?

And racism from the 1500's stayed all up in them and hurt my family. How did it hurt yours?

Love and struggle for justice,
Tania

PS- Teddy, we have had breakthroughs and loved being and talking in a new way . . . Don't let it die . . . Your parents and mine did not love us the way we needed to be loved . . .

PPS- Maybe if you continue to get help over the next year or two, we can make a real partnership and even talk about living together. Maybe if you stop gambling and come to meditation in the sweat lodge with me, it would help us.

Crumpling up the letter and leaning into his easy chair, Teddy takes a drink from a Johnnie Walker Red bottle. Within an hour he finishes the whole thing, crying and drinking, drops of liquor spilling on her words.

He does not call Pam again. When he picks up the phone to dial her number, the phone feels like a stone, so heavy that he has to replace the handle in its cradle. He does not call Tania either.

* * *

After she doesn't hear from him for several weeks, Tania snaps. Gone is the beginning of hope. On the weekend, she replays an old Teddy Pendergrass tape, one she had made in New York of her favorite radio DJ. Musical words fill her. The guitar expresses her mood even more. Pendergrass screams.

Cuing up the next set, the DJ says, "And for the men . . . I Don't Love You Anymore." Pendergrass blazes: "We can't work it out / No not this time . . ."

And then the next song helps her seethe problem is bigger than just her and Teddy. She lies down and listens on her futon. With guitars and violins backing him up, the singer croons "Wake Up Everybody."

> ". . . Wake up all the doctors, make the ol' people well / . . . Wake up all the builders time to build a new land / I know we can do it if we all lend a hand . . . / The world won't get no better if we just let it be / The world won't get no better we gotta change it yeah, just you and me . . ."

Over and over she plays the same tape, thinking about the singer's silky voice and good looking brown-skinned maleness, releasing tears and screams, but always stopping herself from picking up the phone to get back into trying to rescue her Teddy.

A few days later she calls Rogelio. "Does Teddy want to grow? Does he want me?" she asks.

After thinking a while—in her mind's eye, she can see him stroking his chin as he talks—he says, "Teddy wants what you represent, but he is too scared."

"What do you mean . . .?" Tania leans in, as if Rogelio could see the urgency in her body through the phone wire.

Rogelio responds, "Umm . . . "In the past he made the decision to struggle with what you represent. Not you the person, but the future, the capacity to have courage. I think he still wishes to struggle for that capacity."

Shifting her seat on the hard floor, where she has chosen to sit for a contact she expects to be brief, Tania realizes how badly she wishes Rogelio will say she hasn't lost him, and asks again, "What do you mean by 'what I represent'?"

Rogelio elaborates, as always, gently: "You know, your spirituality, your forthrightness, your ability to keep yourself together . . . He wants that."

Tania explodes, jumping up, but keeps her voice low and intense. "But not with me, Rogelio. He doesn't want to struggle anymore . . . not with me!"

Rogelio simply waits.

"I can't let him go, Rogelio!" She begins to cry.

"Come for a sweat," he says. "You need to cleanse."

The next weekend, as she has many times before, she drives down to the Valley. This time she passes by the Eugene Fields Elementary School, where she had volunteered to listen to the kids read during the last school year. She'd learned about the program from one of her friends in Us 'N 'R Arts, whose daughter went there, and had signed up because there were a lot of Black kids in that area and the school, and she had increasingly found herself missing her people, with whom Teddy was now an unreliable connection.

She exits on the one-way heading for the Rio Grande River, then turns left after passing the water, where she and Teddy used to ride their bikes when he first arrived, and pulls into Rogelio's driveway. She's wearing the light cotton sun dress that she will wear inside this sweat.

Other people sit around in the back of the house. Some are Native, or Latino and some are white. None of them are people she knows, although she recognizes some of them from previous sweats. Listening to their talk, she hears snatches that stick with her. Sacred words are sacred actions. She allows her mind to retain only those parts of what people say that signify good praying. Rogelio, wearing, as he almost always does, a long shirt from his tradition and brown straight pants, and a bead necklace, is standing in a relaxed way, leaning with most of his weight on one leg.

Some of the people there have attended ceremony and prepare to leave as others make ready to enter. They stand around near the fire pit, drinking *atole,* a corn drink, from earthenware cups, breathing in the scent, at once heavy and light, of the copal burned earlier. As the sacred grandmother and grandfather rocks heat up in the fire, Tania waits with the others, eyes downcast, listening to the slight crackle of the fire and the murmuring voice of the fire-keeper discussing with Rogelio how much longer it will be before the rocks are hot enough for the ceremony to begin. The man, who wears shorts and a white tee shirt, with a bandana tied around his head, has short black hair, and appears to be Native, although so much mixing has gone on in the southwest that he could have Latino roots as well.

When the rocks are hot enough, Rogelio crawls through entryway into the lodge and gestures to the group of eight or nine men and women who are waiting to come in and sit in a circle around the pit. Trailing the others, Tania is moving slowly towards the entrance when she sees Becca running to join the group. She waves, beckoning eagerly to her, grateful that this sister, whom she doesn't see as often as she used to—they now work different shifts—can sit next to her.

"It's been much too long," Becca whispers. She hands Tania a small stone. "For you to hold, if you feel like it. Or you could lay it down next to you. I got it while camping at Jemez Springs." Tania attempts a smile. The stone is flat and smooth, and fits in the palm of her hand. She places it beside her.

Rogelio casts ladles of water from a bucket next to him over the hot stones and the steam rises. By the end of the first round, sweat pours over Tania's neck and thighs. It is a cleansing sweat, nothing like the sticky, grimy wetness she endured driving her bus on hot summer days, and she feels the tension in her body melt away. She touches the stone next to her to stay grounded. The fire-keeper asks permission to open the flap over the door and brings another bucket of clean water to Rogelio, who offers ladles-full to the people. Each one drinks some, and several use the ladle to pour a little over their head to cool themselves. As they pass the ladle, Rogelio starts a chant.

By the third round of the sweat Tania has begun to cry. A rebirth of the desire to go on rises as it ends and the singing in the lodge reaches a crescendo that rocks her. Now she too sings: "The earth is our mother, we must take care of her. The earth is our mother we must take care of her."

The rhythmic repetition of the voices of the people holds her and she lays her head on the cooler earth. In the dark, no one, not even Becca, can see her tears. The ancient grandmother and grandfather rocks have given her new life.

Again Rogelio casts water on the rocks, and steam hisses up into the desert air. Hotter, hotter. The air swells. Tania prays into her pain and out of it as the heat pushes her sadness to the top of her throat. After a while, she begins to feel a slight headache coming on. Rogelio always says participants can leave at any time, but as she wonders whether she should go, the last round ends. Holding the stone in her left hand, she crawls behind Becca into the cooler air outside the lodge, where she stands and turns to face the mountain range.

She feels open in her heart as she watches the deep blue and lighter blue of night falling. The color stretches across the wideness overhead, more all-embracing in this part of town, which has fewer buildings than where Tania lives, closer to the center. Here the plains are dotted with homes and flat roofs. The salmon-colored paint on most of them looks like it needs a new coat. But the owners have clothes for the kids or gas to buy and of course electric bills to pay to the greedy, lying, never-fix-it-when-they-say-they-will Power New Mexico.

Closing her eyes, she exhales fully. Opening them and looking up, breathing in, she feels her whole body fill with the pleasure of her pores opening to the dry heat and her mind opening to the possibility of something different. She looks at Becca, whose face tilts to the side with a shy smile and openness to listening. Tania appreciates Becca's readiness to accept the way she punches the air with her strong ex-bus-driver arms when she talks.

"Becca, you were so right to give me the stone. It helped me. I feel much lighter, really better."

"Yeah," Becca says. "I had a feeling I needed to be here. I had a dream you were dealing with something and would come today." She doesn't mention Teddy, who was also in the dream. She thinks of the anxiety around her man Tania has spoken about ever since they first became friends, while she was waiting for him to come. She hopes her friend has delivered all that to the steaming water of the lodge.

"I've missed hanging out with you at the job," Tania says. "So much of what has been good in my life here started with you—the pueblo, Rogelio, my garden, which you helped me have faith would grow."

"Tania, you know a garden is like a reflection of your heart. When you open up to life it grows. The vines climb high, though, and even entangle your favorite plants, when you feel anxious."

Tania laughs bitterly. "I guess it's got my number, then. The other day I had to cut back a vicious tangle of vines."

"I figured." Becca pauses, and when Tania says nothing, goes on. "You told me something about Teddy the last time we talked, Tania . . ."

"Yes, I told you Teddy was gone from my life. But the truth is, he's not truly gone, 'cause I can't leave him in my heart. I'm afraid . . ."

"I know, Tania. I could hear that *susto* in your voice. I hope you threw it to the rocks in your prayers today."

"*Susto*?"

"Yeah, fear." Becca wants to be gentle but it seems as if a spirit, one of her strong Polish guides, is talking through her now. "He's a parasite Tania." She jerks her head, half regretting her bluntness, yet feeling that the time for evading the truth is past.

Tania, however, doesn't flinch. Instead she takes Becca's hands in her own and makes them into the traditional Namaste yoga pose, palm to palm.

Becca bows, then adds, "And you were a great host."

Thinking about what Becca said on the drive home, Tania realizes that her friend and Pam are coming from the same place. She wishes she could talk with Pam, but Pam has moved out of New York, and their phone conversations have lost the grounding they used to have when Tania could imagine her mentor sitting in her chair, in the place where they used to meet, the tea pot on the table nearby and the cat curled up on the window-seat.

The sweat has given her new resolve, however, and as she pulls into her parking place, for the first time in a while she thinks about Agua. They haven't spoken for a long time, but somehow she knows that her old friend is the person she should call. And indeed, when she does phone, Agua answers as if they had never been out of touch.

They waste no time on pleasantries. It's as if Agua senses the urgency in Tania's voice before the words of her usual greeting, "Hey, woman," have even reached her. "What's the matter?" she asks.

Tania, mindful as always of the cost of long distance, wastes no time telling her friend that Teddy no longer hangs out with her, that their lives have become more and more separate. "The lovingness is there . . ."she says finally, "but . . ."

"But . . . ?

"But the commitment to spend energy and. . ."

"Yeah . . .?"

"Well, to work at communicating and accepting each other's ways is blocked."

Before Agua can respond to this, Tania blurts out, "I don't know what to do, Agua. Talking to Pam still helps but not as deeply as before, when I could see her face to face."

"I don't see Pam either, since she moved away from the City, and like you I need to talk with someone whose eyes I can see. I said this to her the last time we did talk, and she told me about a woman she called Madrina who could help me explore my African and Caribbean spiritual roots. I've been seeing her for some time, ever since Pam told me about her.

"Can you tell me more about her, what's she called, Madrina?" Tania asks.

Agua smiles. "Oh, are you interested in seeing her? She works out of a store she runs with her husband in the Bronx, a real old-fashioned botanica, with all kinds of herbs and soaps for spiritual baths for sale." Agua speaks fast, at once conscious of the time and eager to give Tania as much information as she can. "She's a spiritual warrior, a Latina with African roots, a Santeria Guide who is a practicing descendant of the Yoruba people. Before Pam moved, she was exploring her own African roots with her guidance. Madrina means *godmother*, and that's what she is to us Pan-African socialists. That's what I call myself now." Agua chuckles. "You'll have to come back to New York, though. She doesn't give spiritual advice over the phone, at least not until she's met you and read for you."

"What?"

"You know, interpreted your life with the tarot cards. Why don't you come home to New York for a while? You can stay here with me. Heru has moved in with his girlfriend, so we'll have the place to ourselves."

In no time the plans are made. Tania will take a vacation from work—she has the time coming—and spend it in the city she fled. She decides she will not call Teddy to tell him she's going.

New Mexico's landscape seems so big, Tania thinks, looking down at mountain tops from her seat as her plane lifts off from the Albuquerque airport. There are only a couple of million people in the whole state, and its vistas, like its Red Rocks, make the life of humanity seem ancient here. When she lands in New York, she is filled with trepidation. In this city, she remembers, the buildings cramped together side by side block everyone's heart every day. How can people ever connect to their inner spirit and feel nature here?

Surprising herself, however, despite the big-city sirens, she sleeps well on a pull-out sofa in her old apartment, which Agua has made her own, and wakes early. Agua states she needs more sleep time, and Tania slips outside for a walk. In her southwestern homeland, she loves to walk through the sagebrush, and among fragrant trees like cedar and pine. Even the spiny yucca contributes to the feeling of timeless quietness that wraps around her there, despite the grief she feels about Teddy, whom she hasn't seen or heard from since the day of the sweat ceremony. She has learned to commune with the Great Spirit of the Native peoples, whose ancestors' bones nourish the soil even as they still walk on the Sacred Mother. Now, mourning inside, the muggy summer heat crawls on her neck and she wipes the sweat trickling into her eyes from under her hair as she navigates back to the apartment. She feels more of a stranger in Nueva York than she had expected. She yearns for the quiet streets of Albuquerque, the gardens filled with tomatoes and chilies, the ever present smell of sage, even the lizards, which, despite their secretive ways, are at home in the sun, unlike New York's rats, which scurry for cover as the sun rises.

Back inside, she grins as she hears Agua shout, "Damn, it was so late last night when you arrived we couldn't really talk." She is making her bed.

Tania takes a quick tour of the apartment, marveling at the work Agua has done on the place, including building a loft for Heru that looks like the work of a professional carpenter. She stops by a table where she picks up a a photo of Agua and Heru at his graduation. "Agua," she exclaims, "you've done such a lot of work on this place. And look at this photo. Heru's much taller than you now. He's a young *man*. You did a lot to keep him clear about this lying system."

"*Gracias*, girl. I miss him sometimes, though, now he's living with his girlfriend. You know, after you left, I had support raising him from that Non-Traditional Working Women's Group you were in. Remember when I did that performance of your poem for you? I joined it just after you left. You encouraged me. We all missed you, though. I'm really glad you're here."

In the kitchen, the two women nourish their bond through deep talk.

"Hey, woman," Agua says, "I bet you didn't really realize the true purpose of your trip was to learn how spiritual teachings and practices from Africa as seen through the Santeria tradition relate to socialism." She laughs.

Tania laughs, too. "You mean I didn't come back for the Statue of Liberty vacation tour?"

"Yeah," Agua says. "You gotta come back to New York every now and then to be with Black and Caribbean folks."

"Yeah. Teddy was my Black connection and it's hard now in New Mexico. I don't see Black people every day."

Agua gives Tania a reassuring hug and hands her the number and address for Madrina's shop in the Bronx, where she does readings.

That same day, Tania calls the number and is lucky enough to get an appointment before she has to take the plane back to New Mexico. Meanwhile, while Agua is at work, she reconnects with old friends. At the WOW Café, she has tea with Smoke, who catches her up on what's been happening in the writer's group and among political activists. Thoughtful soul that she's always been, she reassures Tania that the experiments in African socialism that had so excited them had not been totally destroyed by American intervention, the way those in South America had been. They agree that socialism and African spirituality can blend; Smoke is sure Tania will find a way to become whole. One day, she stops by the Harlem Rec Center, where she used to go, and discovers there is a new yoga teacher, Maisha, whose name means "life" in Swahili. From the moment they meet, Tania feels that this mature, bold African-American woman, who has a to-the-scalp-cropped afro and always wears African-style clothes, will play an important role in making Smoke's prediction come true. The spiritually intense chanting yoga she teaches draws Tania back to the center twice more before her meeting with Madrina.

At the same time, however, walking the city's streets, riding the subways and buses, she notices the absence of faces revealing openly indigenous roots, and remembers New Mexico, where she has developed such a strong belief in Native American blessings like the sweat lodge and drumming to find her "Power Animal." How, she wonders, will the African-centered spirituality she now seeks here, so far from her drum circles, connect with what has engaged her in New Mexico. Often she finds herself humming to center herself as the noises of Manhattan, Brooklyn and the Bronx mix around her. She used to hum when she was going to see Pam years ago. It had been a way to white out the roar of the city, something she had felt no need for in the silent spaces of the West.

On the day of her appointment with Madrina, Tania follows Agua's directions to the Botanica. During the long subway ride from Brooklyn to the Bronx, she takes the photo of Teddy she has carried for years out of her wallet and murmurs, "I loved that me and you left this big-ass apple." Then, as she kisses the photo, a tear comes to her eye. She pulls out her pocket journal, and finds her muse in reflecting again on her longest relationship. He was her New York and New Mexico family. Teddy knew all these different addresses that she had. He knew her strong kick ass, bus self. He knew her light work in-the-garden, pull up roots self. He knew her "let's hop in her car and pick out a Vitex tree" self. They chose to plant their life in the earth. They knew not to become pregnant with a baby. She looks at her belly. They became pregnant with re-rooting in a new, expansive, full clear sky together. She still cannot accept the fact that, as an incest survivor, she was conditioned to yearn for love instead of being with someone who could be emotionally present for her in everyday life.

In the Bronx, as she heads for the stairs from the elevated train platform to the street, she finds herself following a gorgeous, dark Latina woman in stiletto heels. Each clack of the shoes shakes her up. Maybe if she had worn sexy high heels like that, Teddy would still be in her life.

She has almost reached the store that is Madrina's Botanica, and stops a moment to adjust her clothes to look somewhat presentable and uses an Afro pick to fix her hair, using a car window as a mirror. The sound of drumming coming through the open door of the storefront erases the street noise. A spiritual singer with a lovely male voice sings laments alongside the bap op, bop bap drumming, which sounds like the clickety clap of a trotting horse.

She steps into a long, narrow shop, where, along with herbs and healing soaps, a row of statues of different *santos*—Osun, Yemeya and Shango—are on sale. Next to them the carved face of a strong Indian with a beautiful feathered head covering calls to her. The *santos*, yellow, blue and white and red, seem to hear Tania and send her a vibe: she has to share deeply with Madrina. She fingers the silver necklace with a heart that Teddy had given her long ago, thinking, I don't want to leave Teddy.

She marvels at a box of *cigaros* in a red and brown box stowed under the see-through counter, surrounded by candles and small bracelets and amulets. The cigars are probably for ceremonial use, like the smoke used by the indigenous folks back in Albuquerque. Madrina's husband, who is Puerto Rican like her, stands behind it minding the store and the saints. At the back there is a partial wall that separates the tarot reading area with its small waiting room from the rest of the Botanica.

As she sits in Madrina's waiting area, she can still hear the beating of the drums, although the sound is much softer, since the speakers are in front of the store. Through the beaded curtain between the waiting room and the table, she can see Madrina's tarot cards—as far as she can tell, a regular deck, not like the round cards of Motherpeace and other feminist decks she has seen in the book shop in New Mexico.

Finally Madrina beckons her. Tania walks in and sits down at the table. Madrina sits opposite her and quietly takes in the vibration of the younger woman. She dresses in regular street clothes when not leading a traditional Santeria ceremony. Then she'd be all in white with even her head covered with a white *panuelo*. She has five strings of beads draping down over her breasts.

Tania can't help staring at the woman, who has great curves, very shapely for a woman her age, and wears her white hair in a short boy-cut. She wears white bracelets that stand out against her dark brown skin. She waves her hands rapidly, the way some people from Puerto Rico do, as she greets Tania, exuding such love that Tania is immediately at ease, and breaks the silence by asking, "What can I do about these sad feelings that keep drowning me?"

Madrina takes the abruptness of the question in stride, and pulls the cards out of the deck. Having done this for years, she's drawn to which ones to pick. After laying them out face-up, she stares with equal attention at both the face cards and the plain numbered ones, clearly engaging both her physical and spiritual self to read them.

"I especially want to see if there is any answer to how to be . . . how to relate to the best man so far in my life," Tania asks in a soft, scared voice.

A deep, husky voice, speaking English laced with a Spanish accent, comes from Madrina. "You need to be committed inside to putting your spiritual self together. Come back to the city and work on that. You will attend ceremonies and be involved with Santeria. You need to work with your *muertos*."

"*Muertos*?" Tania leans forward.

"Your ancestors who want to help clean you, the dead ones whose good spirits will keep watch. The spirits of the dead are always present, and they are honored as long as they are good spirits. Santeria is the practice of seeking their guidance and protection." Madrina's rough hands shuffle the deck again. An ease pervades the room. Madrina's fingers have relieved many people of the burdensome spirits in their auras. Her gift has prevented those unseen negative forces from spoiling hundreds of lives. She sits a moment more and realizes the negative spirit of a man, recently gone over, lurks in Tania's aura, and wonders how much to say. "Tania, I will work with you on cleansing you of the effects of a recently deceased *muerto*."

"But isn't there anything you can tell me about me and my guy?" Tania implores her. Under the table, her legs cross.

Madrina chooses to follow where Tania goes. "Your guy is on another path now, and you are on a spiritual one. He is here in this card." Madrina's right hand points to a male picture card.

"Oh, god, does that mean we have no hope?" Tania peers at the cards, which are, after all, just plain old playing cards, and badly wants not to believe anything this woman has said.

"The hope is in the spiritual path. Come back home."

Tapping her foot, Tania thinks, "Oh man, why did I come for this damn reading?" She needs New Mexico and its peace. She won't ever be at home back here in the city, where there's so much noise. She wants to be able to fix things with Teddy. She wishes she could talk with Pam, but realizes that even if she could talk with her the way she used to, Pam wouldn't have anything to say except what she's said so many times before, that Tania is a willing host, allowing herself be a victim.

"Well, I guess I . . ." Tania begins, hoping the woman will interrupt her. "It's nice to be back in the city for a while, but I can't *live* here anymore. I can't move around or even breathe in this closely packed umm, madness."

Madrina nods a yes, but then says, "Oh, yes, one more thing. Do it soon."

Tania, a calf whose gentle eyes search for a mama, returns Madrina's soft gaze. "The move you mean?"

"Yes, as soon as possible. By the way, you have always had an Indian spirit that walks with you. And the *muertos*. They say you have to act." Madrina smiles and begins collecting the cards, signaling the end of the reading. "You may call me if you wish," she adds surprisingly, and hands Tania a business card.

Tania moves away from the table, her shoulders drooping, her head full of unanswered questions, and returns to the store to pay Madrina's husband for the reading. She is again conscious of the drums beating, especially the rapid hits of the conga players, and the sound brings back to her what Madrina had said about the spirits of the dead. Suddenly she wants to know more, not about her future with Teddy, but about the African mysteries that Madrina has hinted at and that have been denied to her. She asks Madrina's husband for advice, and after he points to a few things, she collects several books on the religious traditions of West Africa, and cassettes and CD's of an Afro-Cuban singer named Lázaro Ros, who sings the sacred songs. As she waits for her receipt, she notices a small row of different colored candles in boxes to match—light yellow, pink, green, blue. The boxes are all lined up, in order. She wishes her life would be half as orderly as those colored boxes. A bright purple one seems to reach out to her, and she picks it up and holds the sacred candle to her heart.

"I will light this candle when I see my home in Albuquerque," she murmurs to herself. "It will tell me if I really have to leave." She purchases her omen guide, turns toward the door, and the concrete form with cowrie shell eyes that stands in a pot beside it. Although she does not know it yet, this deity is Elegba, guardian of path-ways. Unaware that he is guiding her thoughts, she realizes that her journey is over and she has to fly back to face reality in New Mexico.

On the flight home, she begins reading the books she had bought, and through them exploring the new spiritual world—strange yet familiar, as if she had always known of it in her bones— that Madrina and the botanica represent. She reads in particular of the Mountain God Obatala, who helps people make wise decisions, and of the *orishas*, spiritual beings who represent mountains, rivers, seas and other natural forces for the Yoruba people of West Africa, and who bless and watch over the people—her people, she thinks. She yearns to know more, more than books and tapes can tell her. She thinks she will have to do what Madrina says, and return to New York, but when she deplanes in Albuquerque, the smell of piñon fills the air, overpowering even the stench of jet fuel. How can she even think about leaving? And not only, or even primarily, Teddy, though finding out about their future together had seemed so important during the reading. How can she ever say goodbye to this southwest, to the enchantments of the pueblos and the ceremonies at Rogelio's sweat lodge?

In the next couple of weeks, she calls Madrina several times. These spiritual conversations always end the same way, with Madrina saying, "You got to come back and deal with your ancestors." And when she hangs up, Tania wants to pack up her computer, her red robe and her still-paid-up New York City bus driver's license that had cost so damn much, and be on her way. Daily, in the sun-scorched afternoons after work, as she sweeps the dusty front yard, she yells into the hot dry air at the barking dogs. Then she leans on her tall broom and eyes Father Sky overhead, so blue in the dry air. How can she trade that sky for one that is occasionally blue, but more often gray from the fumes of a million cars and trucks jockeying for space on a couple of tiny, overcrowded islands? She thinks, "Maybe I will only relocate to the Big Mango for a few months."

During this time Teddy only calls once and leaves a message. He probably needed money. That's why he always calls when he expects her to be at work. She wants to see him in person. Let him call again.

Then one day, he does. She's been sweeping the pebbles in the garden, the sun almost burning her bare shoulder, and has just gone indoors to pour a glass of juice when she hears the phone. She picks up the demanding thing on the 3rd ring and is surprised to find Teddy on the other end.

Her suddenly over-excited energy erupts and her face flushes as she holds the phone cradled against her ear. The hoop earrings she wears, crafted from Native beads, knock against it. What has made him call after all this time? She's been waiting for so long to talk with him, though not admitting it to herself. Maybe he will ask her to go out to take a long stroll and hold hands while he apologizes. She wants to see him so badly. Her fantasy builds as her eyes focus on the way a tiny breeze outside lightly lifts the branch of the vitex tree.

On the other end of the line Teddy sits in the dark, then stands feeling his empty pocket. The cheap fabric makes him sigh. He knows he can't ask Tania for money, but he has no one else. He has already borrowed from everyone at the job and no one believes he will pay them back. He had found it hard to pick up the phone. He expects she won't be home, as usual, and he can just leave a message.

"Hello," she says brightly

Teddy murmurs, "Hi." Shocked that he's actually talking to her, not her message machine, he blurts out, "Tania, can you lay some cash on me?"

"What?"

"I can't ride my bike to the bus stop and take the bus to work 'cause at night I get off so late there's no buses and I can't ask you to pick me up. So I gotta pay to fix my car."

Her eyes widen and she shouts, "Teddy!"

He can't stop himself. "You can pass by the job at the end of my shift and leave the money. You don't have to see me if you just don't want to. I'd like to be with you a little, but the landlady said I had to pay or move, so I got to go straight to her office after work to pay the rent.

Tania doesn't respond, so he adds "It's just a loan, I mean."

"Oh," she bursts out. "At least you aren't making believe you even really want to see me. It's always been about the money, huh?" Her free hand pounds the air.

"Look, I'm working in the tourist industry. It's a big improvement on the construction gigs 'cause it's regular, but the pay is lousy."

"Yeah I know, but . . ." She knows she needs to get off the phone, but she doesn't. Instead she extends the cord to the maximum to go into the kitchen and get the juice container out of the fridge. Trying to juggle phone, glass and juice carton, and figure out what to say next, she stands helpless as her hand slips while she's pouring and the carton falls. Yellow pineapple juice "not from concentrate" splashes onto the floor.

"Oh no-o-o . . ." She steps over the juice. "Teddy, I can NOT do it. I cannot f***ing do it. You and I are completely over . . ." Her voice rises very high and shrill. The vitex tree's thin leaves watch her through the window.

"Tania, I don't know why you wanna say that now." Teddy hangs his head fingering his bald spot.

"I'm saying it so I can effing believe it. I can't stand the way we've become. From now on, keep yourself to yourself and don't pick up your goddamn phone ever again to say you're stopping over 'cause I'm probably moving."

"What? When?"

"I don't know, but I won't tell *you*." She lowers her head and musters up her voice, which has just left her. "Good bye." She slams the phone down and heads outside, banging the screen door behind her, seeking the calm to be found in the space in the front of the house, her own little swept-earth place with paved path to the street and the new red *chile ristra* Becca had given her as a welcome-home present hanging on the gate.

But the vibrant red of the chile pods and the bright sun don't suit her mood and she goes around back, where the sun can't reach her. The petals of the morning glory flowers have folded in the heat. She sits down on the bench crafted from a cottonwood trunk that Teddy had made for her, back when he was helping her with her garden.

Stroking her braids, she murmurs to herself. "Where the hell is my man? Fact is, I'm my own old man. I'm alone." She stares at the rocks in the dirt, aimlessly pushes a couple of them with a stick. Tears fall. "But I love him," she insists. "He don't love me, but I love him, and that makes me a sucker for his call-Tania-up-and-drop-by-her-place-to pick-up-stuff routine. It's like I'm an addict." She hauls herself to her feet and trudges around front to check the mailbox. There is a letter from Pam. Excited, she tears it open. The note inside, which is folded over an obituary notice for her father, says simply, "You're free."

Without realizing it, she had been holding her breath. Now she blows the air out in a great sigh of relief, expelling the past, letting it go. But while the relief is real, the memories cannot be erased. The conflict within is suddenly unbearable, and to the good spirits of her ancestors, she cries out, "I can't deal with this," and rushes back into the house to find the purple candle she'd bought at Madrina's Botanica. She takes it from her jewelry box, where she'd stowed it when she got back from New York, and puts it in a small jar. This she sets carefully, reverently, on the velvet cloth that covers the little table by the door. She lights the candle with a long-stick match, like the tapers used in churches. The glow from the flame is very steady and strong, and as she watches it, she takes the certainty of that flame as a sign. She remembers that Madrina had said there was a man, recently dead, who she'd need to cleanse from. Was this the end or the beginning of that cleansing? Seeking to use journaling the way Pam taught her, as a technique to break out of the isolation of thinking she suffers alone by communicating with the friend she has in herself, she picks up the pen with the feather on its end and lies down on the coiled rug that looks like a snake to write. But the words won't come. She realizes the journal isn't enough, she needs a real hug. She calls Becca.

After the usual hellos, she gets right to the point: "I need to work something out, Becca. Can I come by, or is your honey at home?"

"What's up? No, he's not. Come on over. Or do you want to do it on the phone?" Becca knows Tania and her patterns of fear, knows she likes to keep a certain distance.

"No, Becca. I need a real live sister-friend."

"See you in a bit, then."

At Tania's knock, Becca opens her door, which is decorated with a long red chile ristra. The two women hug.

Becca has clearly been cleaning up for Tania, whose house is always neat, and welcomes her with broom in hand, "Just talk, don't help," she says.

Tania perches on one of Becca's wicker chairs and proceeds to do just that. "Becca," she says, "I'm thinking of moving back to New York." She does not mention her father's death. Only the spirits know how liberating it will be to never have to face him again.

"Damn. I thought you got that out of your system on your quote unquote vacation."

Instead of responding directly, Tania sighs. "It's broke up, Becca. Teddy and I aren't going to make it. I failed and he did too, damn it. I wanted so-o-o bad for us to be able to make it as a new family; you know the new kind of feeling man and the new independent woman. But money comes between us. Sports on TV come between us. My effing issues . . ."

"I hear you." Becca's steady tone grounds Tania.

"Oh, man, Becca . . . You know, I realize something. Teddy has smoked cigarettes during our whole relationship. I watched him blow smoke up around his head and I thought he was cool. I think this means I really don't want to be present for him any more than he is really present for me. I like looking at him behind a smokescreen, 'cause then I don't have to tell him I'm scared to death he's a gambler. I can just be angry at him. I want him to apologize for being sooo unwilling to talk. But the fact is, I'm not really *hearing him*, either."

"Wow, Tania, New York helped you to do some thinking!" Becca heads for her kitchen and the stack of dirty dishes by the sink.

Tania follows, settles on the stool, and picks up where she left off.

"I mean, my father damaged my inner self, so I really can't be with anyone, not really, 'Cause I can't really love myself. But with Teddy, who really does understand what happened to me—he called my parents the criminals they were—I could pretend we had a real relationship. But if I go over and say, 'Teddy I want you to stop smoking and I want to stop being behind the smoke, I'm letting go and I choose to be alone,' because I'm brave and not because I can't stand watching him self-destruct with gambling, smoking and maybe on the way to being an alcoholic—if I'm going to do that, then I have to love me."

"You can, Tania."

"I hope I can, Becca. But however much I talk about being alone and brave, the truth is I want a man in my life, but . . . What's wrong with me? Did I *choose* this life of having relationships only with men who are afraid? I wish . . ."

Turning the hot water on and starting on her pots, Becca cuts in, "Are you afraid of taking a healthy risk and finding someone else, including yourself?"

"Yeah, I guess I am. I'm so-o-o lonely."

"But you've told me that you're lonely with him in your life, too."

Tania can't bear to hear this. She wishes Becca would be less clear. She looks at her friend's pale face framed by thin rope earrings and a bead necklace the same color as her blue eyes, and sighs. She looks so gently alluring.

"Aren't I attractive and . . . can't he see how I care?"

"It has so little to do with us and who we are. You know these men have been brutalized as kids by this macho system. It hurts men and women, all of us, Black and white! Men weren't taught that they have the right to any boyhood feelings except anger. Even today, admitting sadness or fear is out, especially once boys become men. It's still hard for Joel and he's white so he doesn't have Teddy's other pressures." She gestures towards his smiling face in a photo on her fridge.

"And they shut down, like my father," Tania blurts out.

"Yup." Taking a dishwashing break while the burned pot soaks, Becca, after offering and Tania waving "No thanks," chews some lettuce and soy cheese, dipping it in a sauce that's always on her counter. She smiles encouragingly, "You letting the fantasy go girl."

"But Becca, I want to be loved."

"We all do. But I've learned I've got to be prepared to let go. If the connection between Ron and me is meant to be, then he'll pick up his courage and find me again to talk it out."

"But I *banked* on this one. Teddy was the man I put all my heart and soul into. I remember when we left Brooklyn and my friend, Agua, cried, I felt sad to leave but had such a good feeling in . . . in my center . . . about creating a nest away from New York and both our past families,"

"Yeah, but that's just the problem," Becca says. "We can't do that, girl." The fact is that if the man, Teddy in this case, is too wrapped in terror . . ." Becca stops, understanding this is hard for her friend to hear, realizing she already knows the conclusion.

Tania does know it. but she waits for Becca to say it: "Then we take ourselves in hand and remember there is a world out there, and a system to dismantle. We involve ourselves in making change for a sharing world. In New Mexico and I guess New York. Even though for right now, our heart is breaking and we are . . ."

". . . shaking." Tania finishes the sentence.

At the door, Becca hugs Tania bye, and says, "Maybe you really do have to go back to New York. Maybe you're ready to complete this with Teddy. . ."

"Thanks, girl," Tania says.

Back in her own yard, Tania sits quietly for a while on the bench Teddy made, having cried long enough. Not for the first time since she and Becca met and became friends, she feels amazed at the way the spirits had brought her together with this woman who had come to New Mexico from the east coast several years before Tania and who was politically aware, *conscious* even—not like Pam, of course, but enough to be a kindred spirit. Finally she gets to her feet and picks up her key ring. She needs to face the man who has given her the one thing she couldn't give herself, both sensual openness and a mirror in which she saw the shut-down dad she at once honored and despised.

She drives slowly. The heat of the desert claws at her heart. It but it is heat without moisture, so sweat never comes and her brain beats on her stomach.

Arriving in front of the cheap apartment complex she has rarely visited, she notices for the first time that nothing about the place gives a sense of the southwest. No adobe, no smiling-sun sculpture. Only the sound of gravel under her feet reminds her that landscapers here try to avoid the expense of watering by simply dumping a layer of these pebbles that roll under foot when she walks along. She finds the sound annoying.

Teddy opens his door to the cool indoors and she stares at him. His big gut sticks out, although he has it covered with an extra large t-shirt, the color all white, like the guys he's been hanging around with for weeks who don't seem to want to do much work at the job. He turns away from her, wordless, and she follows him inside. Neither greets the other.

"I am so so . . . so . . ." Her voice trails off. She doesn't know how to start.

He turns away from her and sits down in front of the TV, which dominates the wall space on one side of his living room, and has sports on all the time.

"Can we at least shut the idiot box off? Please, Teddy."

He nods and reaches for the remote. His chair squeals under his weight.

"Thanks, now I can hear myself think." She pauses, realizing she doesn't know how to say it.

He looks up, expressionless, staring at her. Only his eyes are alive.

She stares back. "I loved you like a family. I am . . ." Her voice cracks. She pauses, pushes ahead. "When I first left the parents who hated me, I wanted you to come and be with me in this non-New York place, our new home-land. And you did, But by then, it felt so late for me. I mean, by then, we couldn't find the way to be deeply part of each other's lives. I . . ."

Teddy is not up for this. He crosses his white sneakers and looks up at the ceiling, thinking about his unpaid rent, which, as usual, is long overdue.

Ignoring his indifference, Tania moves towards him, and goes on. "It was like my mother, you not coming to help me. I waited for her to help me year after year, night after night. That feeling that I associate with her I put on you, Hon." The familiar endearment falls naturally from her tight mouth as she tries to take responsibility for her part in their break-up. "Teddy, I wasn't able to let you in."

He looks over at her again, and she realizes she has to tell him. "I'm going back to New York," she says. "I gotta grow by myself without these cactuses, and pine trees and dry fucking sagebrush and everyone saying 'You betcha.' I'm making myself return to the crowds, the millions of people, the excitement that maybe could make me able to live without you." She stops expectantly, waiting for him to say, don't go.

But he stays motionless. The silence explodes like distant gunfire, pop . . . pop. Finally he lets out a deep sigh that turns into a groan of loneliness.

"Teddy? . . ." She steps a little closer. Her voice wavers. "My friend . . . You meant the world to me when we first planned this. You have the fingers that unlocked my tired secret with your sex and your care. But now I don't dare . . ."

He only looks at her, his expression somber, deadened. Now his eyes are blank, turned inward. It's as if he has no capacity to move his lips.

She raises her hand to touch his cheek, but lets it fall. She exhales. "I'm gone," she says, realizing the basic goodness of his character cannot stop her from going, or help him wake up.

On the way out, she stumbles on a beer can. Trembling, she works the knob to open the door, which sticks because the builder didn't put it in right.

17 ALREADY LEFT

A subtle wind grows down from Teddy's neighborhood until it pushes back and forth across Albuquerque's boulder yards and yucca gardens. He opens a letter from Tania.

> *Dear Teddy,*
> *I'm going back to New York .I can't stand watching you die, which you are doing day by day the way you are acting. I still believe you can do it on your own, though, and I hope you'll reach out for some help. But now I have to take care of me.*
> *Tania*

One day, while watching him smoke and hoping he'd quit, she'd sent him the Reiki healing energy she'd been learning, but it hadn't worked—nothing she tried had. Her letter misses its mark just as surely. He rips it up and lights a cigarette, one already smoked nearly to the butt. Not satisfied, he abandons all thought of the cost involved and, with a slow, methodical movement pops a whole, new Kool stick out of the pack. He twirls it carefully between his left thumb and forefinger, as his eyes, like those of a turtle, peer around for his new lighter, silver gray with the latest child's stop top. His inner voice talks to him. She won't ever see this lighter or ever again come by his place, smiling as he opens his door. They moved here to be together. Now she's gone.

Kicking off his Adidas, he settles onto the couch, remembering how, the few times he'd invited her to his place, she would plop down cross-legged on the carpet next to it. He could never manage to do that. His knees are too stiff. Sometimes they'd have quick sex, just for the fun of it. Other times, he'd be real and they'd make slow, passionate love on this smooth, thick carpet with a blanket underneath them. But he never could get down on the floor, so he would sit sprawled on it, and let her lean against his leg for support. His mind argues with itself about their life together. She had just used him to get away from that bus job. Nah, she had really wanted a new start out here with him. He studies the thin white paper of the cigarette, with the pale blue letters K- O- O- L placed just so. He knew Tania hated his smoking because she loved him—but she just wouldn't be quiet. She would go on and on about it or whatever else she didn't like It was as if she lived in another time, wasn't there with him at all.

Itches come to play with him. An eye twitches. He swipes his hand across his sweaty forehead, then uses his forefinger to massage his left arm. His belly heaves as he breathes. Maybe she'll call instead of writing again. He glances over at the pieces of her letter, just so much litter on the floor, and stumbles to his bedroom. His steps are slow, heavy, but when he stops by the bed, he feels the soft carpet through his socks and the sensation calms him. He catches his breath, then kneels down and finds the green and black shoebox under the bed, pulls it out and dumps it. Everything is there, Tania's letters and the other writings she had shared with him, some with faded ink. "Tania . . ." In his mind he says to her what he never could say in person. "We just couldn't live together and get close, you and I. You needed distance because of what your dad did and your family ignored. So you wrote. But I needed to be *with* you." Still, caressing a few of the notes connects him to her again, and then his heart seems to burst in his chest. The pain becomes more than he can bear. He reaches for the phone to call 911 but it's too late. "Tania," he gasps.

* * *

A poem she wrote when she first came to the southwest is Tania's talisman, waving at her from where she had taped it on the door to the glove compartment, as she drives along the Rio Grande, past patches of yucca, and plants with lilac leaves and others with twinkling red-light colored berries. Smiling, they say goodbye to her as she steers her car past them. She catches glimpses of the river, which had kept Teddy from feeling landlocked. Soon she will be near the sea again—the sea she and Teddy had loved, though they had only gone to Orchard Beach a few times. When they did go, Teddy didn't go in the water above his knees, but after she had had a swim, they used to sit together in silence, just listening to the waves.

Once she had decided to heed the urgings of Madrina and move back to New York, plans had been made and goodbyes said quickly, except for Teddy. Perhaps surprisingly, finding a place to live in the city had proved more complicated than she had first thought. After a phone conversation or two, it was clear that she could not stay with Agua, not for any length of time. She and Agua had always lived very different lives—and Agua, who was again seeing a married man, liked her privacy, as did Tania. In the end, it had been Agua who had come up with the solution. Tania could rent a room from Agua's friend Lis, whom Tania had gotten to know at meetings of the United Tradeswomen. Since Lis also remembered Tania, the two women readily made an agreement over the phone. Soon after, Tania sent Lis a deposit and Lis sent her the key.

Letting go of Albuquerque had been easier. Becca agreed to take Power, who was too old for another cross-country move, and she and Rogelio's partner, Maria, and sisters from Us N R Art arranged a give-away of clothes and furniture.

Now, leaving Old Town, headed for the freeway, she passes through other neighborhoods where, nowadays, it seems that eyes of New Yorkers and Californians peer out of every other house and car. More and more of these people have been buying up property cheaper than can be had on the east or west coasts, splitting open this southwestern town, as they don't even try to fit in. Some of them come to escape from east-or-west-coast city bosses beating them up with their demands for overtime. Some stretch in their limos, just greedy for land, smelling cash. Soon they'll sell it at twice what they stole it for, after laying up adobe walls, skylights, and stunning vistas in a realtor's brochure.

Tania had thrived during the years she spent in the small city,, still a mostly easy-going place, compared to where she is heading. It had brought to her the clarity of meditation and the powerful spirit of the Indigenous Sweat Lodge. She won't forget. Nor will she forget the way some of the smaller-town folk had accepted her, apparently reasoning that, since she hadn't grown up here, they couldn't expect her to take things slower and calmer, the way they did.

"Hug me please, Teddy, hug me please." As she drives onto I-40 she talks to the air, talks to him the way she hasn't done for ages. "I loved you, Teddy. Together we planned to make a new home for *ourselves*. But it didn't happen. You were desperate for your mom's support for our common law marriage and it never came, while I . . ."

After a time, she pulls off to the side of the road and sips tea from a small thermos, inhaling the aroma. She reaches for her cassette recorder, which is sitting on the passenger seat, and turns it on to record. "When I first met your moms, I liked her, but then she revealed her dog claws and bark. She never even called you to ask about our life in New Mexico. You had to phone her." Tania's hand strokes her lids softly, massaging them.

She is leaving the man who opened her up, the man to whom she told the secret about her father's violation of her, the man who named what her parents did a crime. Even though he will not be with her in New York, she carries back to the Atlantic coast the beautiful anchor Teddy was before it all went to pieces—Teddy, who had helped her in her struggle against the macho ways of the bus depot guys. The struggle had strengthened her as she came out of her twenties and moved into serious adulthood, so that she now knows that no bullying males can stop her from working a job not many other women have, with a paycheck many other women wished they did have.

Heading into Oklahoma, she passes the big white Christian cross on the side of the road on the Texas side of the border, and wonders how Jesus would feel here. It's one bit of landscape that's hard to miss, in contrast to the vast sameness of most of it. She struggles to keep awake. Finally the signs announcing where the freeway heading directly to New York splits off from the I-40 come into view. From the outset she had been clear she didn't want to retrace the route she and Teddy had taken when he drove west with her and left her on her own while he returned to New York. Instead her plan is to take the I-40 all the way east to North Carolina, then turn north, and she slows down to make sure she gets it right, forcing herself to ignore the wind-rush from passing tractor trailers.

At the next filling station, half hoping to attract a man to distract her with a flirtation, she pulls up to the pumps behind a white guy topping up his tank. He smiles, stares. She smiles back. He starts to walk toward her. A woman returning from the convenience store jumps in the front seat of his car. Reality hits, and she Tania enters the store and asks the clerk for the restroom key. The bathroom is dirty and stinks, but at least there is toilet paper.

In the evening, when it's cooler, she pulls into a rest stop and dares to depart from the grey plastic interior of the car to stretch her legs. When she spots a lonely pay phone with a sign over the booth saying in huge letters "$1.00 call anywhere in the US," she thinks of calling Teddy. She starts to walk over to the phone, and the apple she was biting suddenly drops out of her hand. Could that be a sign telling her "No"? Back in the car, she realizes she has to find a motel soon. Her eyes drift to closing as she drives, then jerks herself awake. The sunset in the rear view mirror looks like the end of a show on stage, life's curtain going down for the night on Tania howling over her loss and failure.

Finally, at a motel near the Arkansas border, she curls up in the big double bed and sobs: "I needed Teddy so bad. I needed him to be my family. But now I gots to need myself." Remembering how Pam had told her to use whatever she could to get through the night, she spots her copy of the latest issue of the New Mexico Food Co-op Newsletter in her bag. It contains an article she wrote about water rights and corporations threatening to limit healthy food choices. Reading it, she's glad that, while in New Mexico, she had remained part of the Movement through her writing.

Laying down the paper, she rolls over onto her back, stares at the ugly gray curtains with big yellow-flowered borders. She drifts into dreams of Teddy. But he walks away. She starts to run after him, when a voice asks, "Hey"? She turns to look and sees a man from the Zuni pueblo. She cries out to him. "Oh!" At the sound, Teddy turns to hug her. "Goodbye," he says, as the Zuni wraps him in a sacred blanket with stripes and fringes. Then both are gone.

Morning comes, bringing strong sunlight in through the crack between the two curtains. She wonders what the dream means. In daylight the yellow flowers brighten. Tania slowly eases up on her elbows and then steps over to the window. She peeks behind the curtain where the sunshine blesses her face and sparkles on the motel pool, in which she can't resist taking a swim before checking out.

She doesn't stop often. When she can't stand the country music on the radio, she plays the tapes of reggae music she'd recorded back in Albuquerque from the University of New Mexico's radio station, KUNM. Boredom finally releases somewhere in Tennessee, She pulls off the highway where there are a few bushes to hide a quick pee. After doing some yoga stretches, she hops back into the car, and has started on her way when the urge to touch herself comes. A light stroke of her fingers down her left non-driving leg tantalizes her mind. Ooo. She allows her finger to fondle her pussy through the shorts she threw on in the morning.

By North Carolina her back actually feels stronger, though her shoulders burn. She knows it will take a lot more hours to bring her to her hometown, but being in North Carolina is a kind of balm in itself, and she exits the highway for a few miles to revel in the presence of large numbers of Black folk in the small towns and the parking lots of shopping malls. In Albuquerque, the only time there were so many people of African ancestry in one place was at the annual Juneteenth celebration.

Back on the highway, she tops a hill and stops the car for a few minutes to survey the long stretches of tobacco fields, thinking of how the harvest, which takes place during late July or early August, the hottest time of the year, and is now accomplished with the assistance of machines, used to be done by hand, with long lines of Black folk using sickles. Suddenly she recalls Purple. She hasn't thought of him in years. She remembers North Carolina was his birthplace and his descriptions of the summers he spent with his grandma in Gullah-Geechee country. She also remembers how supportive he had been of her writing. Familiar with African American writing, he could critique her work in a way that Teddy, no matter how much he loved what she wrote, could not. For the first time in a long time she also thinks about "She Fought Back," the play she had first written with the women in New York supporting her. She had worked on it with the Us N

R Art sisters before Teddy's arrival had complicated things. Now, she thinks, when she's settled in New York again, maybe she'll get back to it.

For a while, she considers detouring to the section of the North Carolina coast Purple came from, but when the choice must be made, she heads north, aiming straight for New York on Route 95, focusing on her driving in the heavy traffic. It's after dark when, suddenly, she finds herself approaching the Lincoln Tunnel, with the lit-up towers of the World Trade Center dominating the horizon to her right. She has missed the exits that would have taken her more directly to Brooklyn, and now will be delayed by the traffic in Manhattan.

The slow passage through the brightly lit tunnel lets her stop concentrating on the mechanics of driving and sets her wondering what will show up for her in New York City this time. During one of her phone calls, Madrina had said, "It's time to make a spiritual discovery as to who has your head." "Who *are* her eguns, her ancestors?" she wonders.

It is nearly midnight when she reaches her new place in Brooklyn, but no matter. Neighbors in the big city won't mind a woman unpacking her car and stashing her boxes in the common basement of Lis's building. Thanks to the New Mexico swapping, there isn't much, which is a good thing, since there isn't a bunch of men available to help out. Lis lives in a neighborhood where single women have their own apartments and cook for their guys much less than in the southwest. Many times they tell their men, "Get take out, I'm too damn tired," or "You do the cooking," and sometimes the men do. Other times, they move out, so there are fewer of them around.

One good thing about the neighborhood, though, and about New York in general: She will no longer be living near people who watch a person's every move. No one will pay any attention to whoever might be moving into the tiny room where now she can rest.

Back in New York City, Tania finds the noise pollution overwhelms, but here she is near the Atlantic Ocean, where so many of her African ancestors lie buried. Here she feels close to them, feels that now they can claim her and she them. Now she can think about finding out "who has her head," as Madrina put it, about getting into spiritual work with the Orishas who watch over her. But she wonders whether that protective blessing has really been hers since her born-time. If the Orishas have been keeping watch, how could they have let all the shit happen? What is the lesson? And what do they have to do with aiding her in finally, truly digging up the torture and tell others about it, so she and they can make it past the pain that cripples them?

At first, as she struggles with these questions, she finds the phrase "My God"—no, now "My GodDESS"—comes to mind more readily than the name of any African deity. The women in those southwestern "circles," whom she had learned to love, had taught her to attach a feminine face to the creator. And Pam, too, comes to mind, with her uncommon common sense about it all.

Then, one night not long after her return to the city, a dream message comes: She's with Madrina, who looks a bit older; she fears Madrina will die soon, and wants to share her deepest feelings with her before that happens. She tells Madrina she loves her. Madrina is arguing with her husband, a padrino (spiritual godfather), whose relationship with Madrina is less-than-functional. He is worried because he wants to use the same space at the same time that Madrina and Tania have an appointment to use it for a ceremony. He needs to be out of there. Madrina fusses. Then Tania hugs her to ease her nerves and descends to the foundation floor of their home, into a room filled with books and a beautiful sculpture of brown wood. Content, she gazes into the area where brown and black images representing her spirit guides are sitting on a corner table. The peace of the lit candles makes her want to live in this tradition of the people in New York City who are descendants of those who used it to resist their enslavement when they were dragged from Africa. It now draws her in, even deeper than the spiritual traditions of New Mexico.

Days later Tania goes to the Bronx botanica for a ceremony. She carries a hold-all containing a white blouse and skirt, which she has been instructed to bring. As before, the botanica is filled to overflowing with statues and candles and gourds. As before, by the door to the noisy outside, a tall purple vase filled with water holds a bunch of the wide, flat, bright green leaves on strong, brown stems known as "lucky leaves." Her fingers want to touch the offerings of copper pennies to Elegba, which surround the pottery dish containing his image. She remembers him as the deity representing the crossroads where people can choose to begin again. He is the opener or closer of pathways. The pot emits the scent of cigars, whose smoke of which practitioners blow over him as they pray to be shown the right path. Tania likes the way this clay bowl feels. But her eyes are drawn away from it to a conch shell that sits nearby. It's as if together they shout, "Feel the spirits of Madrina, who speaks this different language."

Madrina has Elegba music playing. The plaintive voice of Lázaro Ros, the Afro-Cuban singer of sacred African music, fills Tania. The spirits draw her into the back room, where she had her reading, and then towards another more private room with a door. Madrina stands beside it, motioning for her to enter. It has been prepared for the ritual. In the center is a chair, on which Tania sits after she has changed into the white clothes she has brought. On a table near the chair is another vase full of Lucky Leaves, a white plate, and a small bottle whose label proclaims it *botella de agua*—Florida water from Cuba. Once Tania is seated: bare feet firmly together and planted on the floor, her back straight, Madrina "draws" a square on the floor around the chair, then sets a candle on each of the four corners and lights them. She then picks up the white plate and circles the chair, holding it over each candle in turn, so that the smoke from the four of them together makes a unique black image on the white surface. Still holding the plate, she hands Tania the small bottle of Florida water. For the first time, she speaks: "See the design on this plate?" She wastes no time with extra words. "It's the man's dirty penis!" She is very clear. "It's deadly."

Tania's amazement shows in her eyes. She has never told Madrina about her father raping her. But the protective spirits know. They have revealed it to Madrina in this ceremony. Tania stays very still. She wants to be blessed. Her white shirt and white skirt are gathered around her like a flower, enfolding her, caressing her skin and her gunned-down heart. Maybe this unsmiling woman's powerful energy really can help cleanse her, so that she can let trust in.

"Your father hurt you!" Madrina announces. Her Latina accent, her almost-closed teeth, make the "Y" in "your" sound like a "J." "Jour father did bad things." Taking the lucky leaves, she brushes the air around Tania and motions her to stand, while the ugly vibes lift and tears release Tania from her bondage. Again, Madrina, still unsmiling, commands her: "Okay, now cleanse your body with the water." Her crackly voice is nevertheless as smooth as the Caribbean sea that wades through her tones. Tania pours Florida water into her hands, breathing in its uplifting scent. Annointing both her palms and the backs of her hands, she lets this fragrance, like a breeze, a *brisa* from the Spanish Islands, waft over her aura. She holds her palms first to her face to bring the smell close, then moves them down her front as if bathing the air in front of her, to wash the bad vibrations away. Soft and safe like the gentle Caribbean wind, her hands carries the *brisa* over her back, her legs, again in front of her sweet breasts, and into her special place between her legs. Thighs vibrate, as with the freshness of a bubble bath. Her yearning whips through her mind. She is brushing the junk of daddy away, she thinks, moving away from his wanna-be-ness of the elite class. Her soul rises. As she raises her two hands, almost as if possessed, she cries inside "wash and wash and finish with Daddy the Dominator." Now, she scoops up handfuls of the clear, scented water and tosses it over her body, throwing it hard, then almost beating herself as she claps, claps, slaps the white garments, now heavy with water, clinging t her skin. Then, spent, she moves her hands slowly over and over her thighs, and the sounds of her hands as she rubs them on the cloth pass like the sounds of sacred night. There is a soft, rustling as she rids herself of the hard violence of his presence.

Finally, Tania is once more aware of the godmother, with her short curly white hair and spry brown eyes behind her glasses. Stunning! From the corner altar, her African images, black cotton faces with great eyes, look lovingly at

Madrina's new godchild. The peace of this sacred room surrounds her. Yes, these guides are good.

It's been weeks since the ceremony with the signs on the plate, and Tania has now attended many others, where celebrants dance with repetitive movements to the drumming of the men. She particularly likes the sound of the three drums that the men play for the Bembe ceremony, where the orishas are praised.

Every morning, to drown out the hum of the street traffic below, punctuated by insistent horns and sirens, that creeps into her room, she puts on a Santa Barbara Africana cassette, her favorite of those that are played at the ceremonies. The tape features Lázaro Ros, and she allows the Yoruba chants he sings, and the rhythmic drums punctuated by the ringing of iron cowbells, bop ba baa, to waft over her body. Immersed in these sacred African sounds, she processes the immense revelation the spirits have shared with her through Madrina. Thanks to them, she senses that she is cleansed, that the beast of her past is washed away. Feeling light, unburdened, she sighs in relief. Lázaro sings "Elegba, Elegbaaa," And Tania knows this is the time of the opening. Elegba, the god of gateways, is opening the way to some new part of life. When the singer hits the highest notes her heart wants to cry. Cry for days . . . This singer, these chants, are the sounds of soulful freedom, sounds that aren't anything like the harsh, metallic sounds of cars, computers, or dishwashers. These are root sounds, from the earth.

Every morning she lies on the bed and plays the sacred tape over and over until an hour passes, a whole hour before she does anything else, and even then, as she dresses and dusts and cleans, the music fills her soul.. It brings to her what she loves, and, lying in bed, she moves with the sound, turning on her belly, on her side, again on her back, gazing at the patterns embossed on the tin ceiling of her room, still the silver color it was when it was installed at the turn of the century, listening intently to the repetitions that are not mere repetitions, for with each chorus the intensity increases. Today she notices the part of the music that brings in "Ochosi," the deity of hunting, She remembers him being mentioned at a ceremony for a woman from Brazil, who, after the ceremony was over, continued wearing her all-white clothes, including her hat; someone said she did that come summer or winter. She walks, they said, in a special time of these practices, because she never wears any colors. Her blouse, pants, even shoes are always white. At one point in the music, Lázaro says something that sounds like "okay okay," but these are Yoruba sounds, not English noise. Then a chorus of child-like voices repeats "ooookay." Tania also cries out, "ooo." The drums never let up. Tania thinks, "O my god, I love Babalu Aye, Spirit of the Earth, and Shango, Divinity of Thunder and Lightning." A husky-voiced woman sings "Baaba luu oo aye" and then pauses, silent against the steady, unhurried drumming, the slow click clack of sticks, the slap slap of the shekere gourd, covered with a net woven with wooden beads and cowrie shells. The drum sounds harsher than the other drums, like there is metal in it. Tania remembers that someone told her Babalu Aye can bring epidemics as well as cures.

As the music plays, sometimes she gets up and reaches for the broom to begin sweeping. Other times she jumps off the bed and sways to the music, remembering the dances she's seen others do. But whatever she does in response, the music moves her heart to feel that it's good to be back in the city she once ran from. She recalls how she and Teddy couldn't stand the crowds, the noise, the lack of peace back then. But somehow this music, with what she once would have thought of as too many screams and too much rapid drumming and too many sounds all mixed together, harmonizes—and puts her spirit in harmony with her inner essence.

The wondrous story of the deity Ogun, who worked in the forest, enchants her. She knows from her reading that when you are looking for a job, you pray to Ogun. Putting her room in order, thinking of Ogun—she knows this is preparation to receive a vision of the new, more fulfilling work she will find, and soon does find, a position as an administrative assistant in a community Art Center in a section of Broolyn not well-served by the New York subways, so she has to drive to work, the way she did in New Mexico. The job pays little, but is far more rewarding than clerking in a food store. The work itself is not so different from what Agua had done at the University of the Streets all those years ago.

She likes driving to work because it gives her time to think in a way the noisy, crowded subways cannot, and possible because of the nature of her job, her thoughts often turn to Agua. She becomes aware of how, during these past several weeks, while she's been going to ceremonies, looking for work, and reading voraciously about African-Caribbean traditions, she hasn't much noticed other things, in particular the absence of Agua. Agua didn't call her to ask if she could help her move in and get re-oriented in the city, which has changed a lot since she's been away. When Tania visited New York and stayed with her, it was as if they'd never been apart, but now the intimacy they had shared is gone. Partly, she realizes, the problem is Agua's job. High-paying though her shift work is, the hours are horrendous and irregular, not in sync with any kind of normal human life-rhythm. Working for Transit, Tania had experienced the dehumanization and isolation of this kind of work first hand, so on one level, she understands what has happened between them—that Agua cannot plan her life with other people because she is off on different days each week and people with "regular" jobs cannot be that flexible. Still, there must be more to it than this, More than once she resolves to reach out, but does not, as she works to recover from her hurts by looking internally.

Then, one night, she has a dream in which that swelling Spirit voice that she and Agua used to hear together speaks to her again as the rooms they met in and the faces of women from their former writing group pass before her eyes. The Spirit voice speaks to them both:

"Tania/Agua, you once had nights of sleeping over in each other's Bronx and Brooklyn apartments. You made the business deal, with Tania refinancing to get Agua's name on the deed. And then Tania moved out as planned and the apartment became Agua's. You avoided the taxes due on closings. Good for you."

When she wakes up, she writes down what the Spirit's has said, feeling this is a message dream to guide her forward to a change in her relationship with Agua now, Without having to worry about business at all, like Agua's checks being late, maybe they could reacquaint themselves with their deeper emotional bond.

Sure enough, her trust in the universe is not misplaced, and the dream is a predictor. One day she receives a phone message from Agua. She has found a buyer for the apartment. The amount will more than cover the mortgage and yield a nice profit. Can Tania call her back as soon as possible?

They finally get to talk. Agua, ecstatic, explains how she will now be finished with paying off the loan to the bank, and will be able to pay what she still owes to Tania plus some extra. And she will be able to afford to buy a less expensive place of her very own. Though Tania will have to take un-paid time off from work to come to the bank to sign the papers, the deal marks the two women's ultimate victory over the f ***ing rich banks and their rules of private property—a small one, perhaps, but a victory none-the-less, not only over those multi-millionaire bankers but over the whole real estate industry that robs poor folk and then wonder how come so-called "minority development" efforts fail. "One day," Tania says, her emphasis on every word showing her rage, "one day under socialism, everyone will have the *right* to housing, and workers won't have to scrape together down payments and mortgages and those red-lining banks won't get to foreclose on people's homes."

"That was a good speech, Tania," 'Aqua says, and they laugh together like old times. But the moment is brief. "The closing will be the afternoon of the fifteenth of next month at the bank's offices downtown. Don't forget to write it down." Agua knows Tania sometimes loses herself in ideas and forgets practical information like the dates and times of appointments if she doesn't write them down. "I'll call back with the exact time later. I gotta run now, or I'll be late for work. If anything changes I'll phone you, Bye." She hangs up.

As she scribbles the information on the pad she keeps by the phone, Tania realizes she didn't even get a chance to congratulate her friend on finding a buyer. She also realizes that she'll have to take time off from work to attend the meeting, and that this will mean losing pay, because she is on probation at the Art Center and, unlike Agua, with her union job, is not entitled to paid time off.

Delighted though she is, as she keeps telling herself in the weeks before the closing, Tania can't help also feeling a deep sense of loss. Her conversation with Agua, the first long one since she had returned to New York, had been about business. And when Agua called back with the time of the appointment, she left a message, the way Teddy used to do when he didn't want to talk. The dream had been a predictor, perhaps, but not of a renewal of intimacy between them. Part of the problem is that they're living such different lives now, with Agua working irregular shifts for good pay but with almost no control over her schedule. When Tania got her spirit-destroying shift-work job at Transit, Agua's low-paying jobs had given her the flexibility to adapt, to make their friendship work, to continue sharing Tania's passions for poetry and politics, and being a sounding board for her writing. But that had changed, Tania thought, when she moved to New Mexico, and despite the fact that it had been Agua who introduced her to Madrina and to her African-Caribbean spiritual roots, when she moved back to New York to explore these roots, Agua had not been part of her journey. She was, Tania feared, now trapped in the kind of job and the kind of life that Tania had escaped—the kind that paid well, but didn't give her time to attend Madrina's ceremonies, or listen to poetry, or maintain meaningful, intimate relationships.

Tania checks her watch as she drives away from the Art Center. The closing is scheduled for 3:00 p.m., and the Art Center has only given her a half-day off. She had thought there would be enough time to drive, instead of taking the subway, but the traffic, even this far out, is heavier than she had expected. Thankfully, she had had the forethought to grab a grilled cheese sandwich, which she nibbles on whenever a light turns red.

By the time she reaches downtown, she is increasingly worried. The traffic here is fierce, and as the hour of the meeting comes close, she finds herself driving around looking for a place to park the car without feeding a parking meter or paying the high fee at some garage. Finally, after circling for what seems like forever, she leaves the car at a sidewalk spot with no meter but some distance from the bank where she needs to be in a few minutes. Out of breath and racing toward the office, she mutters over and over to herself, "This effing, thieving bank," but then, in the elevator she takes a deep breath to calm herself. "Oh God, my reputation is on the line," she thinks as she is led to the conference room, steeling herself to apologize for being late.

While Tania has been looking for parking, Agua has arrived at the bank well ahead of time and been ushered to a seat at a large glass table in an upstairs conference room, where before long she is facing a trio of white male suits, who offer pleasantries in cold voices, and a woman, also in a suit, whom she recognizes as the real estate agent. For a moment, she regrets her decision. Through these indifferent intermediaries, she is selling the investment she and her friend Tania had made to some stranger, whom she has never met and who isn't in the room. But as she waits, and as it looks increasingly like Tania will be late, her mood changes, and she wonders whether she really wants to get back being close friends with Tania. They are living such different lives. When Tania visited New York and stayed with her and first met Madrina, it had seemed like old times. But looking back, she realizes how lucky she had been to get a weekend off, and in fact, for most of the time Tania was there, they had hardly seen each other. And now—her job pays well and is allowing her to get her very own place with her very own mortgage. But the schedule is crazy-making, and has caused her to lose touch with a lot of people, especially women like Tania who want to be connected as friends and share their lives and go to political rallies and art shows and poetry readings. Since her mother died, when Tania was in New Mexico, she hasn't really felt the need for a friend whose shoulder she could cry on about her mom, and besides, she has been dating another married man and doesn't want to talk about it with Tania, and face a conversation about her "flings," which, she tells herself, is all she has time for.

"Is your co-signer arriving soon?" The question comes with a false smile from one of the officials from the bank, or perhaps he is a lawyer. She can't tell. "If she doesn't appear in ten minutes we're going to have to call off this meeting and maybe the buyer will back out of the deal."

"Yes." The realtor chimes in. "I have to show another apartment in an hour." She taps her notebook with a ballpoint pen.

"She'll be here," Agua says, but mentally she is tearing her hair. Where the fuck was Tania? The suits are right. If the bastards call off the closing, the deal will probably fall through. To buy time, she stands and excuses herself.

As she searches for the light switch in the women's room, she starts the mental tape running. Why didn't Tania take the whole day off so she could beat the traffic and get here early? I know how she is. She probably just squeezed out of her job at the lunch hour thinking she could make it here in thirty minutes

Exiting the bathroom stall, she feels around for the light rose lipstick and essential musk oil in the bottom of her black bag, then heads for the sink to wash her hands, which she wipes over and over on the two or three paper towels she's pulled from the dispenser. Peering into the mirror, she decides against refreshing her lips, but dots some of the oil on her wrists. Finally she straightens, inhales with a deep Yoga breath, saying a short African blessing in her head as she opens the door and, her eyes on the heavy carpet, returns to the conference room. When she enters, all the white males look at their $5000 Rolex watches and shift in their chairs, then straighten their blue silk ties. One asks again whether "the co-signer" is on her way. Agua thinks, "If Tania doesn't get here, I'll be stuck paying this mortgage for the rest of my life. Maybe I can't trust Tania right now."

Then, suddenly, Tania appears in the office vestibule. Agua spots her through the glass doors and motions to her to come into the conference room. And there, seated at that big, ugly glass table, the two single women activists sign where they are told to sign on the five sets of papers passed around. Her eyes focused with determination, Agua says not a word..Tania, too, says nothing, except to ask the suit who hands her the papers to hand her another pen when the one she has been given unexpectedly stops working. When the transaction is completed, the two of them stand and, after perfunctory goodbyes, leave the room and stride towards the elevators, their walk the subtle, winning strut of those who have won a victory. In her hard-working Latina hands, Agua holds the sheaf of white paper and the certified check from the bank that say the sale is d-o-n-e. They smile because they know they did it! They smile because Agua had found a buyer who offered a price that will allow her to move into a more affordable place. They smile because no man was involved. When the 'down' elevator arrives empty they jump into it like kids and, with a yell they double over laughing.

Agua shouts, "We two single cullid gals bought and sold property in the same century when those white boys used to be able to keep us from even voting."

"Yeah, we figured out a way to do it!" Tania agrees, smiling at her friend. Outdoors, they feel the cool breeze.

Then the mood shifts. "Tania, what happened?" Agua can't let Tania's lateness just slide. "You were late, Tania," she says. "I was scared you wouldn't make it in time."

Tania doesn't say anything, hesitating to come clean about parking in a space where she wouldn't have to pay even though it was so far from the bank that she had to run all those blocks to avoid being even later than she was.

"You know," Agua goes on, "part of the reason I haven't called you for very much socializing since you got back is because, frankly, in the past, I was too scared to tell you when I was upset. Half the time when I tried, I felt you weren't listening. You would change the subject or go off on something else, or just shut down. But now I've got a job that pays really well and will soon own my very own place, not one I sort of inherited from you, so I feel different. Not that I'm not grateful for the way things worked out, but maybe that's the problem. I feel I got to be grateful. My class of folks never had property. My mother was on welfare my whole childhood, just like almost my entire neighborhood. I'm the first person to work outside the house almost all my life. But welfare is work too, believe me. You gotta sell your time waiting on those long-ass lines with your kids crying for some chicken shit money that barely covers rent, and for f . . .

king food stamps, and health coverage. Forget about transportation. You remember how I had to walk everywhere. We single moms create the next generation of workers for that rich class of owners, so the warmongers can send them to their death for rubber or oil or whatever."

Tania says nothing, wishing they could talk about all this class stuff deeply one day, when they're not coping with just having come out of a closing at a bank. She looks down, preparing to cop to her mess about being late.

But Agua is not prepared to listen anyway. "You know what," she shouts, with one eyebrow rising as she pushes her simple, round eye-glasses back up on her nose. "You know what? I'm finished. I'm not going to pull some damn understanding out of you. Take your intellectual rationalizing self outta my life." She turns on her heel, sizzling again the way she was when she was in the bank waiting for Tania to show.

Finally, Tania finds her voice. "Wait, Agua, I did want you to be out of that pressure. I just wasn't being in your shoes. . ." She grabs at Agua's elbow.

Agua shakes her off, but stops and turns back. "When you make a mistake, Tania, admit it right away. You gotta get real some day."

"I am so sorry. I feel bad and sad. My heart hurts. At least it's out." But Agua has turned away again. Tania, following her down the street, again reaches for her hand. Again waving her off, Agua throws back Tania's apology: "I'm not sure I can continue this with you. I have to think about all of it and we'll see. I'll send you the check by registered mail."

In Tania's dream that night, Agua sends a message, saying, "Yeah, I remember when I was late sending the payments to you, , Tania, you didn't charge a late fee, like the bank did, like anybody else from your almost-rich class would do. So I trusted you and we found financial wisdom under this crapitalist shit together. But your former class loomed too large in my poor childhood on welfare, for me to forget it, or for me to be sure it was really your *former* class." She is laughing at every fourth word, but what she's saying isn't funny. "And now I see, Tania, your class issues will always be coming up, not all the time, but every now and then for sure, and when they do, *I have to confront you on them.*"

Tania says, "Thank you, Agua. I love you, my friend. You are the friend who taught me how to feel! I remember you asked me years ago, 'What are you feeling, Tania?' and I was stunned. My almost rich class only talks about 'I was thinking,' or 'I'm hoping,' but 'I feel sad, or afraid . . .' never." She takes a deep, long, solid breath.

Then the scene in the dream changes, and Tania is resting her back against a tree with long branches. "Agua, bless our lives. I was too concerned with me, and I am so-o-o grateful that the spirits got me to the closing in time to sign."

"Yes, Tania, I am so-o-o glad, too." A glimmer of a smile appears on both their faces. Agua goes on: "It used to be hard for me to tell you I was angry. But I've learned it's my ass if I don't stand up to your class." The two women grin at the joke, then stand facing each other, each looking at her own reflection in the eye of the other.

Tania looks away first. "Agua, I never expected to be so deeply touched by someone's upsetness."

"No, I never expected to tell you. I guess in some way, deep inside, I do trust you." replies Agua.

In the dream, they begin to fly, and their blouses become like wings. The dream dissolves, and Tania reaches back to waking life.

Tania cries and screams and kisses the letter from the sisters at Women's One World, which informs her that her script *She Fought Back* has been approved for the fall line-up at the W.O.W Café theatre where she had performed poems with Agua some twenty years before. Then the presentation had been one among many by the WOW sisters, who ran the space. Now her play would be the entire bill for a three-performance run—in just a few weeks! As a returning WOW member, at Smoke's suggestion, she'd applied to have her play performed, and luckily she'd done it before Agua called about the sale of the apartment. Now she can concentrate on the production without any distractions. For a moment she's sorry Agua won't be part of it, but then she realizes she wouldn't have had time for it anyway.

After an initial moment of panic as she absorbs the news, especially the pressure of having only few weeks until the performance, she is energized in a way she hasn't been since—she can't remember when. The WOW sisters leave the production up to the playwright. She'll have to find a director, and a cast that understands political "socialism- type" thinking, as well as how to really let feelings live. The man in the piece, who is seventy years old, has to be of African ancestry. Who is going to come and audition for a freebee? Who will help this dream live so many years after Smoke first suggested she write her story down?

In New York, unlike in New Mexico, she benefits from others having unionized. While the staff at the Art Center isn't organized, and she can't take an afternoon off whenever it pleases her, she can count on being able to leave work promptly at five o'clock to focus on the true vision of producing her "baby"

:putting together the cast; designing the publicity; locating tech people and a stage manager, all of whom must be volunteers. The task of stage manager, which turns into a combo position that involves assisting with the lights as well, is taken on by her friend Maisha, her yoga instructor from the Harlem Rec Center, who has become a confidant, a true sister. Not only is the yoga she teaches spiritually powerful, Tania has discovered that Maisha is also a Reiki practitioner who teaches Reiki healing. It is Maisha who draws the dynamic green and white sketch that will become the vehicle for the show, appearing on posters and programs. A video guy named Rolando Perez signs on to tape the show and the audience dialogue afterwards. A Latino activist with socialist leanings who is among several gay men who work regularly with WOW, he had read Tania's play and asked to help early on because it spoke to him as a gay man who had suffered the same kind of denial and rejection from his family as Tania's heroine.

In the end, she decides to direct the play herself, because no one else truly understands how racism is affecting the white mother-Black daughter relationship. "Oh spirits, help me get this done," she prays every morning when she wakes up to another day of coping with the routine at the Art Center, followed by the long drive to Manhattan, a hectic, late night working on the play, then the drive home to her apartment in Brooklyn, where she falls into bed well after midnight.

Before going to sleep, she cries with exhaustion and worry, conscious as she hadn't been before of how cramped her apartment is, with its loft bed and a table that doubles as a desk, now piled high with papers. At least the skylight in the bathroom lets in some light from the ancestors, to whom she continues praying, but whose presence she rarely seems to feel, except when she's attending to her physical self, sitting on the white porcelain and plastic toilet bathed in their spiritual glow, Otherwise, while she practices "receiving their message" as before, some days she shows a damn rude side, brushing them off, along with any of her acquaintances not connected with the play. It is Milagros, the Afro-Dominican actor and dancer playing the main character's alter ego, who finally confronts her about her one-track mind. Tania listens, because the dancer, who has the same name as her Reiki teacher in New Mexico, embodies the same quality of intense caring, and so is someone Tania respects spiritually.

She still feels overwhelmed, however. There are so many details for one person to remember, and as rehearsals proceed, it seems at times that the white actresses don't understand the role of racism in the USA, don't always see why, for example, the white mother in the script has to be directed to act out covering up repressed fury every time she enters the stage. "Look, the mom denies her own feelings, and represses so much pain," she explains. "To silence the daughter, she forces the child to fear anger and submit. There's no love around."

On the other hand, the two men of color who play the father and his alter ego do understand, and it gives them the capacity to enrich their acting by taking risks in rehearsals. They know about Black daddies letting down their children. Their attitudes and performances actually cause Tania's thinking to shift. Instead of holding to her previous narrow view, which perceived all men of color, except

Teddy, as being like her dad, she sees that other Black men besides Teddy—and, she suddenly realizes, Purple— —are *conscious*. She shows her gratitude to them by making a special thank-you card for opening night.

As rehearsals progress, Tania thinks more deeply about the forceful sister who plays the lead female. She watches the actress enter the stage, her afro shining, how she brings out the pain of a young 29-year-old woman, the character she's playing, who is scared yet willing to face her fears as she struggles to recover from the racist materialist system's attacks on her self-image and its limits on her life choices. She brings her own insight to the role as she, tries desperately to connect onstage to her Jewish mom. What a tender moment it is in one rehearsal, when the actress's tan hand goes up to touch the white face of her stage mom, and the mom's eyes stay closed, her heart evidently forever closed off from her Black/Jewish daughter,

Another rehearsal has Tania actually shouting "Yay" to the cast at the end, clapping with approval. She nods to the lead actress. "I am so-o-o pleased with the dance you all helped to choreograph." Turning to Maisha, she smiles. "We *all* be doing it—bringing this production together!" She gives a high-five to her friend. Smiles all around! Even the white actresses, who had initially had trouble understanding their roles, now seem able to transcend their white privilege, showing a willingness to be led into the reality of a mostly Black cast, a Black writer-director. They show up on time, committed. She decides and announces that she will share with the whole cast the part of the take from the ticket sales that doesn't go to WOW.

Central to it all is Maisha, who creates a story every day just through her outfits. On her feet are usually sturdy shoes, then pants with African patterns of great baobab trees and matching fitted tops of every color. Today/tonight it's vivid aqua, yesterday the bright red of flame trees. Tomorrow . . . tomorrow, who knows? Her face has a trace of a giggle always waiting to burst through her thick, luscious, curvy lips, which at times she paints with lipstick. Her Native American beaded earrings, made with cowrie shells, flow well with her eccentric personality. After hearing Tania's cheer, she gives her a hug, then fills her curvy body with laughter, so that Tania, too, cannot help but laugh.

Then, the very next day the actress playing the white mother's alter ego resisting change, phones. "Do I have to take the subway all the way to that rec center in Harlem for the individual rehearsal?"

"It's just five stops from West 72nd street!" Tania's eyebrows rise. I'll see you there," is all she says before hanging up, but she is shocked. This actress, who she believed had truly gotten into her role, apparently didn't want to come up to a Black neighborhood for a private rehearsal. She sighs. "It still can all work out," she whispers to her angel guides, and once more sinks into despair. Maisha, seeing the change from the day before, insists that after the next rehearsal, the last before opening night, Tania find the time to come to the circle of Reiki energy-work practitioners that meets regularly in Maisha's home and that she had participated in until the play became all-consuming. Immediately after returning to New York, Tania had been taken up with exploring and enriching her African spirituality through Madrina. But thanks to Maisha, she has also found strength again in the spiritual healing of Reiki. Now, as the pressure on her ramps up, she is doubly grateful for its healing energy, and she kneels, praying, 'Thank you, African deities, for the timing, for sending Milagro, who taught me in New Mexico and Milagro whose dancing embodies her spirit, and Maisha, my true Reiki sister. Thank you for Reiki's power to transcend time and soothe old wounds." She realizes that part of the tension she has been feeling is bound up in disappointment: Agua, from whose poem she had taken the title of her play, will not be there to see it performed. She had told Tania it was because she had to work that weekend, but Tania wonders whether Agua has forgiven her for her being late to the closing, and worries that maybe the breach in their friendship will not be healed.

After the circle, she returns to her apartment to change clothes, for the opening night of her play. Leaning on her white stove in the cramped space she fills it with singing from a tape while brewing some African Roibos tea for the trip in the wet weather. Fortified with the tea, she steps out into the drizzling rain. She notices an older Black couple in front of her, holding hands. They help each other down the steps to the subway station, then ride in the same car and get off at the same Lower- East-Side stop as she does. As they walk off into the rain, they are still holding hands, even though their hair has grayed. He carries their umbrella, keeping her head dry even as rain drips from it onto his old-school afro, the droplets making his hair sparkle in the street lights.

She wonders at this Black couple showing their love for each other in this hippy-dippy part of town, surrounded by mostly white folks as well as back in Brooklyn, where there are more Black people and it's okay for them to touch. She wonders where they're going. Maybe shopping at one of the local thrift stores.

Suddenly she thinks of Teddy and how they went shopping for plants for her garden after he came to Albuquerque. They didn't shop together for clothes. He wanted her to dress what he called "regular" and casual, with matching shorts and tops in solid colors. "That's not me," she'd say. "I'm a mismatch-and-layer-it-up woman." Sighing, she presses her lips together, watching the couple stepping carefully between parked cars to cross the narrow street. "He probably still kisses her with his tongue," she thinks, "not like Teddy at the end, giving me those pecks and then nothing, and when we had sex no kisses at all, and I begged him to say some words, anything, and he told me, 'The sky is blue." Once she had thought to grow old with Teddy, like this couple.

She stops at the edge of the curb, almost about to step off. Wrestling with her compulsion to retreat, longing, into the past, she fiddles around by walking back and leaning against the DOWNTOWN subway sign, wiping her eyes with an almost clean tissue. "I'm going to the WOW Theater. I'm doing my show. The actors are good. My directing is fine." She jumps in the air lightly the way the lead actress does in the opening dance of *She Fought Back*, breathes in deep, then races with long steps, towards her show's opening.

Upstairs! She allows herself to tell no one, except Maisha, who is at the front of the theater stacking the programs, how heavy her heart is: The opening of the show is the beginning of the end. Will anybody even come? And sister-woman Maisha shows care through her attentive listening, not interrupting, letting Tania dig it all out.

Finally, taking a deep breath, Tania pushes the "play" button on the tape recorder, and the pre-set music, which she has taped off the "New York Sunday Morning Classics" program on WBLS radio, begins playing "Color Him Father." She has chosen it for its contrast to the story of a father's betrayal and a daughter's liberation in the play, so that as a multi-racial audience enters and finds unreserved seats, they hear a Black male singer's deep, solid voice singing, ". . . think I'll color this man father / I think I'll color him love . . ."

It's dark on the stage as the house manager, a thin young woman of color, with her baby strapped on her back, stands in a spotlight, inviting folks to make a contribution after the show to support women-produced theater. Then the play begins with Milagro doing brilliant, interpretive movements in a modern dance.

Closing night arrives before Tania knows it.

After the opening dance, the thick front door opens to the hallway one more time and the audience filters in Just before the lights go down, two women of color enter wearing interesting clothes. One of them catches Tania's eye. Her African style headdress is multi-hued. Tania, standing in the lighting booth with Maisha, makes a mental note, then refocuses on the board, so she isn't distracted by the latecomers. The show has fabulous energy, as all actors stay completely on point tonight. The rhythm flows. All the actors help build the tension. The audience cries as mom and daughter cannot connect and father denies lusting after his daughters.

All afternoon, Tania has basked in the afterglow of another Reiki circle with Maisha that ended just before she ran downtown to help with the lighting board, which had given them trouble during the previous performance. The healing energy of the Reiki continues to help her center. As Maisha knew it would, Reiki has turned out to be the perfect way to prepare for the close of this theater experience, and for the close of her more-than-a-decade-long relationship with Teddy. "Reiki works to heal the emotional, physical and spiritual Self," Maisha said, and it was true.

Hearing the closing lines of the play, Tania brings her attention back to the theater, as the audience applauds and the lights come back up. She treads lightly down the few steps from the lighting booth to sit with the cast and hear feedback from the audience, since this is a "work in progress," as all Tania's work is.

Before taking questions, she thanks the beautiful cast. After all the difficulties, it turned out that every one of them, Black and white, had given so much to the show. Confronting things in their own past, they seem to have been transformed, so that all of them can stop being controlled by "wanna be" parents, in effect stand in front of their mamas and their papas and say "I move to live life forward." . And they have shared the message with the audience, as the look of reflection on everyone's face and the silence before the burst of applause prove. She takes the notebook out from under her arm to jot down comments from the audience and the cast, as she has done every night after the performance.

A white woman from the audience, seated on the left, looks upset. Her mouth is pursed. "Why was the mother soooo angry?" she asks.

Another white woman on the other side of the audience says with a tight voice, "Yes, I mean, I didn't understand what made her like that all the time."

Tania hears them, and writes.

A Black woman seated in the center, who, Tania knows, is involved in an interracial partnership with the white man sitting next to her like the mother and father in the script, says "I'm so glad you had the courage to create this and ask us to think about it."

One of the Black women who arrived late has had her hand up. A medium-built, cashew-colored woman with a flair of a hat, she is restless, squirming in her seat, but Tania still has not noticed her. As a latecomer, she has sat near the back by the recording equipment, and now the video man Rolando tries subtly to attract Tania's attention to her with a tilt of his head, as if to say, "You forgot about this Black woman, who has had her hand up, while you have been giving the white folks the floor.

Tania turns to this woman and apologizes, "I'm sorry if you're angry. I was distracted by the folks over there."

"No, that's not why I'm angry," the woman in the hat fires back.

Tania's ears perk up. She thinks, "This woman's voice is my voice. It has the same quality and rhythm. I hear the tone and it's my own. It seems like the spirits of my Jamaican aunt are all around her."

She stands up and, walking to the front of the stage, squinting to see the woman more clearly, finally recognizes Younger Sister.

She cries out, "Oh my God, you had the courage to come." She lets tears flow in front of everyone and reaches out as if to embrace Younger Sister, who has stood up. She wears her bright African-designed clothes well.

The crowd lets out a general "ohh." They don't know what they are witnessing, but a feeling in the air grabs them. Tania's brain turns inside, words come out loud: "I am awestruck by life." Younger Sister puts her hand to her chest and slips back into her seat. Tania returns to hers. As if in a trance, she reaches for the arm rest, and sits. She looks down at the stage floor, takes a breath, looks up into the lights and only then feels able to go on.

One by one, the actors leave the set and mingle with the remaining audience. Younger Sister and her friend stand up, but make no move to leave. Tania, pulling on her sweater, realizes her heart is pumping wildly. Will Younger Sister want to talk with her now? She flashes back to the time when she was still a bus driver and had gone to see her sister. She had not wanted to talk then. Does she want to talk now? Younger Sister is chatting with some of the cast. She calls out, "Buttercup." It's been years since Tania heard that name. Inside she cries and can't look directly at her sister. Unsurprisingly, Younger Sister looks older. Is she finally mature? Her hands look the same as they did when they were teens, though—small with short fingers. But there are many rings on those fingers now.

"Buttercup, hi." Younger Sister repeats the childhood name.

She motions to the hallway, where people are preparing to leave, chatting about what train to take. Despite their presence, it feels more private than the theater. There are candles, so the vibe evokes peace. They stand, for the first time in many years, together.

Younger Sister's hands go to her face. "Buttercup, did Daddy rape you?" She asks abruptly. Tania's revelatory play lies across their reunion like a blanket of snow, leaving space for nothing else. "I mean . . . in the script . . . our family."

"Yes, Gerri, you made the connection." Tania confirms this horrible fact for her sister. "Gerri . . . Gerri . . . Gerri." It's strange for Tania to hear herself say her sister's name.

"Oh my God." Younger Sister's mouth hangs open like a gas pipe.

"Yes, Gerri." Tania says again, seeing her sister's eyes now fill with tears.

"Did he rape me too?"

"You'll have to find out for yourself, Gerri." Tania replies.

The tears and more tears declare a path down Younger Sister's soft cheeks, a path only lightly marked because she is wearing no make-up.

They hold hands. Tania's long arms, unable to take this pain away, nevertheless wrap around Younger Sister's fragile, boney arms offering comfort, with the hug they couldn't share before.

Why had her younger sister come tonight?

"Hey, Tania." Gerri, fearing to go deeper, interrupts Tania's thinking, "Hey, one thing you need to know. I have a son. His name is Quilombo."

"Really Gerri?" Her sister Gerri, who has a son with an African name, stands here, by her side, after all this time, after all those sun-filled years in New Mexico. The universe has broken her apart from Teddy, who had been in her thoughts every day. But look who has come back into her life!

Before they part, Gerri invites Tania to come over to her place the next week and Tania agrees to come, though she senses that Gerri is eager to find out more about what happened during their childhood, while Tania wants to focus on building their sisterhood as adults.

She is not really surprised to learn that Gerri is living in the co-op apartment her parents had had in the city and that their mother still owns. She had probably turned it over to her when she returned from Africa with her son in tow at the time of their father's funeral and had the money to live in the city (though not, Tania learns later, to pay rent, which their mother doesn't require her to do). It's a nice apartment, with two bedrooms and an eat-in kitchen. Gerri is lucky to have such a place to raise her son. Tania had thought about the place more than once when she was considering moving back to the city after her father's death, how nice it would be to live there. But even as she considered it, she knew it would never be passed along to her. After all, she thinks now, "I knew those parents would never give me this apartment." They had rejected her and she had finally learned to accept this, which was good. Pam would say that when you don't need them anymore, you can accept that the passage is complete.

As she enters the lobby of the building, she remembers the last time she had been there, after Younger Sister had called her at work and begged her to come. The name on the bell has not been changed. Younger Sister buzzes her in.

That time the steel door to the apartment had been shut like the door to a prison, and when it opened, she had stood in the doorway, looking down the short hallway, and asked Younger Sister to come out and talk. Today the steel door is ajar, and as she knocks and pushes it open, Gerri calls out, "Come in, is that you?" and she walks through the door into that the small hallway. It is decorated now with brightly colored African beaded necklaces.

She marvels all over again at the woman who comes to greet her, so unlike the Younger Sister who had always before been unwilling to talk about their past all those years ago.

"Oh, you fixed the place up so different from when Older Sister used to stay here," Tania says "It looks African in this hall, and alive."

"It sure is messier, anyway" Gerri says. "But let's talk about other things before my son comes back up."

"Where is he?" asks Tania, her head turning toward the door.

"Doing the laundry downstairs. It's a lot to wash, so he'll be gone a while."

Gerri sits comfortably in her home. Her very posture, feet up and one hand draped over the cushy back of her sofa, shows she feels she owns it. But before she says anything, suddenly she rises and offers to show Tania the rest of the place. She leads the way to her bedroom, navigating among stacks of papers and a rack of shoes, overflow from the closet. The bedroom is big enough to hold the entire shack of a southern sharecropper, and every available surface, it seems, is covered with clothes of all kinds: fancy slacks, beautiful jackets for day and night. Even Gerri's bed has a big pile of clothing on it: cute short-sleeved cotton shirts designed to go under the vests worn under the jackets, most of which have shoulder puffs. There is only one empty space, on the right side of the bed, where Gerri must sleep.

Gerri waves her in and Tania follows, walking the narrow path into the room, from the door to the bed. She points to a photo in an ornate silver frame on a table by the mirror. It's an old and totally grey-haired version of their father. "That's the photo that was in the newspaper when he died," she says. "I missed you at the funeral. I'm so sorry you weren't around to be there."

"I'm not." Tania stands proud. "Besides, they never invited me."

"We didn't know where you were," Gerri says.

"You could have found out easily enough," Tania retorts. She changes the subject. "So, how's your relationship with mother?"

"Um, well since we're getting right into things . . ." Gerri pauses and then, stroking one of her jackets, she says, "It's okay, I guess."

After another silence, Tania, her mouth with the corners down, says aloud something she's now realizing she always knew. "Listen, Gerri, I just didn't feel *heard* by our mother. Her whiteness got in the way. She was so unwilling to face the racist reality of the shit society she became part of when she came back from Hawaii—the society that put a white woman who married a Black man down. From growing up in a white neighborhood with good, well-funded schools, she was now forced to live in a beaten down one with lousy schools if she was gonna live with her Black husband and Black kids. White neighbors even moved out when she and Daddy moved in. And by the time we were coming up, well, I mean, in the schools in our neighborhood, you remember as well as I do, you could do a good project or your teacher might think you were inventive or curious, but it didn't matter. There wasn't any serious college prep. So Mom worked like hell to get Older Sister into that junior high school where mostly white kids went. I didn't get to go, though, and neither did you. She never explained why, so I figured she had just been going for white, which I would never be, not like Older Sister, with her light skin and good hair." As if exhausted by this long speech, Tania sits down on the floor facing the bed.

Gerri, willing to get more intimate, flops down on her bed. "Maybe she was just worn down by the time we came along," she says. "After all, my hair isn't at all nappy even if my skin is permanently tanned." As soon as she says this, she wishes she could take it back, but Tania seems not to have heard. To compensate, Gerri adds, "I always felt she was a bit racist, you know. I never said anything, but I think that may be why I went to Africa."

"Okay, Gerri, yeah . . . But there was no getting around the fact that I *was* Black, and she would just ignore my needs. I mean, like when she told me *NEVER* to listen to that *vulgar*—that's the word she used—Black music playing on WWRL She and Dad only wanted to listen to the news or some damn classical music station." Tania flies her hands up in the air.

"She told you that?"

"Yeah. I'd cut my eyes at her but it made no difference. I could have maybe understood if she'd said she didn't like it, but I could listen to it when she wasn't around. But no. That music was never to be heard coming from our radio. I had to listen to it with kids in the neighborhood . . ."

Gerri, who has been absent-mindedly folding the shirts lying on the bed, drops one on the floor, but Tania doesn't notice, she's so busy finally getting this out. "And damn it I don't want to say this, Gerri, but . . ."

"Go ahead. I'm so glad we're talking." Gerri pushes her hair back under the African *gele* she's wearing, which is red and white with yellow swirls.

"She *hated* my blackness. I just smelled it. She wanted me to be proud of Harriet Tubman but she didn't want me to *become* Harriet Tubman and lead her anywhere. She wanted me to be shut down about sexism, too. I was not to mention things she could—no, *would*—not deal with."

Gerri smiles and nods, and Tania takes this as an invitation to jump into even deeper conversation, and does so at once, afraid Gerri will pull back if given the chance and try to distract them both by talking about just anything instead of real feelings. "Gerri," she says, "I want to tell you what happened in the past that caused me to distrust *you*."

"Okay," Gerri says uncertainly. "I guess." Her voice is too bright, but Tania plows ahead.

"I never felt part of that family, the way you seemed to do. All those historic places we went to and museums we visited, all that normal family life, was just a façade as far as I was concerned. But you seemed to be okay with it, like Older

Sister, or at least feel perfectly comfortable. Didn't you feel the lack of love? Daddy may have sold life insurance, but love insurance is something no company can guarantee."

"I went to Africa," Gerri says defensively. "But you speak about them like they have no connection with you. They were our *parents*."

"Well, they *are* disconnected. More than disconnected. Don't you *understand*? You saw the play. I was *raped* by them and then had to live behind the façade they maintained so the image of the happy family could continue to be presented to the world."

"We didn't know," Gerri says. "Why do you say you were 'raped by *them*'?"

"*You* didn't know, Gerri, but *she* did. *They* covered it up. *They pretended* to know nothing. That's what made me so-o-o crazed inside. I knew they knew. I knew because he was the damn perpetrator. *He* did the touching and the violence to my soul and she closed her eyes and didn't even try to protect me. And when I was older and confronted him, he denied it. And so did she. She kept the fantasy going, pretending he never hurt me or brutalized my sense of self, refusing to acknowledge the effects of that silence even after I was long out of the house and on my own. That he denied it wasn't all that surprising. That she wouldn't admit it even then was beyond belief." Tania finds herself almost screaming, and crying so hard she has to run to the bathroom for some tissues.

When she comes back into the bedroom, Gerri cocks her head to the side. "I do hear you, Tania. I did see the play. But whatever happened, Daddy is dead now. And Mother and Evangeline, Older Sister, as you call her, are our family."

"No, Gerri, they're *your* family." Gerri still doesn't fully comprehend, though she herself has implied it, that their mother had treated them differently because Gerri, though her skin was brown, had straight white-people's hair. Even as she has begun the process of trying to get to know the truth of her childhood through finally hearing Tania out, she still wants to hold on to the myth that everything was okay.

"But you are in the family, too." Gerri speaks softly. She wants to warm Tania and nourish her. She wishes Tania had had the same gifts she'd had from their parents—or thinks she had. She tries again. "You know, Tania, Evangeline took it upon herself to take care of everything when Daddy got sick."

Suddenly, her tone changes, as she goes on to explain that Older Sister had obtained power of attorney and had made herself sole executor of their father's will. She still controls all the family's finances.

"She *says* it's so Mommy and I don't have to worry, but . . ." Gerri shakes her head. "Mommy and I try to fight her, but we just don't have the strength."

Tania throws up her hands. "And this is the family you want me to be part of, Gerri? A family is a group of caring people, not just people who happen to be born into the same group of bodies." But Gerri doesn't hear her. Suddenly she has stood up and is headed for the kitchen. "I gotta do the dishes," she shouts over her shoulder.

Tania follows her. Gerri puts her hands into soapy water, where the dishes have been soaking. The sound of rinse water splashing over the plates fills the air.

Gerri mumbles, "Sorry, I hope you don't mind, I gotta wash these dishes before I leave. I'm taking the boys—my son and a friend of his—to the movies. She pauses. "Do you remember this china? Mommy gave it to me when I moved in here."

Tania shrugs. "You see, that's just it, Gerri. How can I trust you will see and feel what I'm talking about when I don't want what you want."

"What do you mean?"

"I mean I don't want a connection to so-called family members who stay silent about horror."

"'Stay silent'?" Gerri washes another plate.

"You remember I said I confronted them? It was right after I started bus-driving. I visited them on the island. You were out of the country,"

"Yeah. I must have been out of the country."

"And later, when you came back to the US for a visit, do you remember you wanted me to come up into this apartment with all of them? You didn't tell me they would all be here."

"I guess," Gerri says. "I didn't understand what was going on, about you and Daddy, I mean."

Tania's eyes widen. "Could it be you didn't *want* to understand?"

An awkward silence falls. Gerri puts down her dishrag. Tossing the words over her shoulder, she says, "Oh Tania, how do I know? We were kids. But it must be hard not to have any connection to family, I mean . . ."

Tania's stomach has a butterfly feeling. Not the butterfly feeling you get before you're about to go onstage to perform, but the feeling you get when your soul is on edge. She wants Gerri to like her, hopes Gerri will want to come over to her and hold her. She wants Gerri to go back into the past and heal the hurt by saying she would have been there for Tania if she'd known.

Tania keeps thinking, but why didn't I *tell* her? Why didn't I trust her back then, when she reached out by calling me at work? Is it because she used to wipe my kisses off her cheeks when she was four years old? Is it because they babied her and gave her special attention and left me waiting in the dressing room while they shopped? Because it was always Gerri and Mom and Older Sister, with Tania left out? No, she had never felt wanted, even by Gerri. But she hadn't voiced any of this when she was young. In her family's culture they didn't talk about feelings.

And she's not going ask Gerri about it today either, when they're just getting to know each other again . . .

But then Gerri asks her own question. "Tania, did Daddy rape me too? I'm ready to know."

"Gerri, you asked me that at the theater, and like I said then, I can't figure it out for you. Incest is a violent crime. It's about having power over others, 'cause the perpetrators are weak and self-destructive, but they try to take others down with them. Victims of such crimes often repress the memory of them. But whether you were a victim like I was, you're going to have to figure out for yourself the way I did, by going for help." Tania twists the ends of her hair. "For a long time I had only clues about what happened to me. I have even fewer about what things were like for you."

After another silence Gerri says, almost whispering, "Tania . . . I do want to talk about this . . . but there's something else I want to tell you now, before Quilombo comes back upstairs. I never married his father."

"Oh?"

"He was a married man." Leaning back against the counter, she adds, "My son has problems because of that secret."

"Who knows?" "Mom knows. Daddy knew, too."

"Older Sister?" asks Tania.

"Yes. No one else, though. The thing is, they were all upset that I never married. And money has always been a problem."

"Yes, I hear you, they're bourgie, and if I'd still been connected, they sure wouldn't have liked it that I had boyfriends and didn't pay the state to issue official agreements legitimizing my relationships or break-ups!"

Abruptly Gerri starts rummaging for rubber gloves, preparing to scrub a burned-black pot that has been soaking. Clearly what Tania has just said does not sit well with her, and the air turns tense.

Tania shouts, "Damn it Gerri, isn't finishing this conversation important to you?" Then she stops, shuddering. What they've been saying has been cutting too close, and Gerri won't face it, not now, anyway.

Gerri confirms her sister's thinking by avoiding the issue, saying defensively, rushing the words, "Yes I do. But you don't understand. I have a kid and it's the weekend and I have some things to do, otherwise the whole week is crazy."

"Okay, Gerri. But take care. I don't want to believe you're going to be just like Older Sister." Tania moves toward the living room.

"Wait a minute," Gerri says. "What do you mean?"

"Well, years ago, when I tried to tell *her* about all this she just said she felt our childhood was a happy and interesting experience."

"O my God!" Gerri almost drops the pot.

"Yes, Gerri, O my God." Tania resumes her place, leaning against the wall. She senses Gerri has suddenly become *aware* of the past in a way she hasn't been, and that they have to take this more deeply now, whether Gerri's kid walks in or not. Still, she is floored by what Gerri says next.

"No, wait a sec, Tania. I want to show your script to Evangeline . . ."

"What?" Tania straightens up in disbelief.

"I want to show the script to Evangeline. She'll show it to Mom."

Gerri admits that after seeing the play, she had told them what was in it. Tania raises an eyebrow. "You did?"

"Yes, I did. I guess I should have mentioned it before, 'cause now I don't have time to hear your thoughts about it. My son is due back from the laundry any minute, and we both have to change clothes before going out." As if on cue, her hair under her *gele* starts to drop as the scarf comes untied, and she heads towards the bedroom to search for another one. Tania, speechless, follows.

As they pass the front door, it slowly opens and Quilombo enters with the laundry. He's a beautiful brown boy, tall for his age, but still slightly chubby. His height makes him tower over the sisters.

Gerri smiles. "Quilombo, this is my sister, Tania, your aunt."

"Hi." A shy smile forms on his face.

Tania, who had felt she would meet him today, extends her hand, then opens her arms. He responds, and they hug.

"What should I call you?" Quilombo asks.

Tania grins. "How about Tantie Tania?"

"Tantie?"

Tania laughs. "It means 'Auntie.' Didn't your mom ever tell you, when we were kids growing up we called your great aunt Tantie 'Tantie Tantie'? Not when the grown-ups were around, of course. But we thought it was hilarious that our aunt's given name actually *meant* 'Auntie.'"

But Gerri is not laughing, and there is an awkward silence. Clearly she has not shared this tidbit with her son. Finally, Quilombo says, "Well, I gotta put this laundry away and hang some of it." He walks slowly down the hall to the back, past his mom's many pairs of shoes.

The next time she sees her, Gerri gives the script of Tania's play to Older Sister, who, she is sure, has given it to their mother. She has no idea—the same way Tania, years before, had had little awareness of the reality—that neither woman will like it that she has reached out to Tania or that Tania has responded. They do not want Gerri and her son to continue the relationship. And after they have read the play, the full reaction comes.

Gerri is home waiting for Quilombo when the phone rings.

"Hi," she coos.

An accusatory question, in Older Sister's voice, shatters her mood.

"Why didn't Tania mention any of this before? We were so close," Older Sister exclaims. "If it was true, why didn't she tell Mother? I don't believe a word of it. Mother was in tears after she read it. She said it was too painful to be true."

Before Gerri can manage more than a "But . . ." Older Sister says, "I'm hanging up. Goodbye."

Gerri then calls to tell Tania what Older Sister said.

Tania can barely let Gerri finish before responding in anguish. "Close?" are you kidding? In all the years after I left home and was living in the city and you were in Africa, did she even once try to connect? One time I went to see her at work and she wouldn't even let me into her office."

Gerri rolls her head to release the tension building in her neck. Confronted with this reality, she tries to deny it. "Well, Tania," she said, even if that's so, it doesn't make what she said about Mother's reaction to your play *untrue*. She *cried*, Tania. She said it was too painful to be true."

"Oh God!" Tania says. Just as she thought, they were still dying not to know.

They hang up. This short, intense conversation flips Gerri's stomach over. She doesn't really know why. Some unformed memory? What she does know is that she doesn't dare call Mother now to find out whether Older Sister is telling the truth. And she can't believe that her mother—*their* mother—could really have gone through the play page by page and still deny that any of it was true.

PART FOUR

18A HEALING, ORGANIZING, RECONNECTING

Not long after the play closes, the job at the Art Center ends and something else besides the family becomes a battle for Tania: finding a new one. She keeps sending out emails and puts her resume into several online job banks. Her rejections come in the desolating silence of no bosses writing back. Then, just as WOW's acceptance of her application had come out of the blue, so an email from the play's videographer, Rolando Perez, about an opportunity to train as a union organizer appears in her inbox. Within a few weeks she has sublet her apartment in the city and taken up residence in eastern Pennsylvania, where she is a paid organizer-trainee.

The setting for the series of workshops is a room which includes a photo exhibit as a backdrop: Mother Jones, A. Philip Randolph and Cesar Chavez posters lean against the backs of chairs set along one wall. Tania is especially taken with the portrait of Mother Jones, the only woman in the group—her fiery eyes and rumpled hat that kicks to the side, then tilts up. "Pray for the dead and fight like hell for the living" is the caption at the bottom of the poster.

Nearby, on the wall, photos of strikers from the 1930s holding picket signs, with some guys standing off to the side drinking from cups or bottles, catch Tania's eyes. The strikers had closed down the auto industry in a bitter fight for better wages, but Tania is struck by the evidence of drinking even on the picket line. It occurs to her that the more truly conscious organizers of today might start support groups to help folks deal with alcoholism and family dysfunction, in addition to agitating for better wages and working conditions.

From the first session, Tania is a leader among the trainees. She is not a complete novice, after all: Basically, she has been doing consciousness-raising, organizing work from the day she started writing. Her long-ago poetry performances with Agua had helped to rouse the down-pressed. The two of them had loved the mysterious power of performances, of poetry to inspire to action. When working folks heard the truth in their poems, they sat afterwards and talked with them, often revealing their own family systems of exploitation and abuse. They would talk about their mind-numbing jobs and irregular, unforgiving schedules that made no allowance for life beyond work and how they became conscious of having to set things clear in their minds when they came home from work. Their kids were not to blame for the shit they were enduring, even in so-called "professional" jobs.

As she talks with other trainees about the way many workers use alcohol to numb the feelings of isolation that are the inevitable consequence of jobs that don't let them have a voice, she begins to think about making the organization of such groups the focus of her union work. They would have to meet in union spaces, because no one really wants to tell people in so-called Human Resources Departments that they have a serious family problem. Who can trust that this confidential information isn't going to find its way into the files of the very supervisors who pressure the workers all day and then warn them about taking time off and drinking too much. Who wouldn't be driven to drink by seeing industrial accidents or being told to overlook "white collar" corruption?

Then, after a workshop about Third World workers at "runaway factories" needing to be supported by the unions of the industrialized nations, Tania's thoughts turn to unions as part of a movement, as they had been when her father was a union leader, before they were transformed into organizations that looked out for their mostly white members and avoided political controversy as America embarked on its great anti-communist crusade—organizations that had driven her father out. Excited, she says to the woman sitting next to her wearing the *Si Se Puede* tee-shirt, "You know what? This workshop reawakened something in me. I think it's realizing the importance of encouraging masses of people all over the world to organize themselves again into unions to fight these violent bosses."

The Latina woman encourages her with a smile. Tania adds, "Back in the movement in the seventies I used to write poems and perform them at rallies." The two women laugh.

The class makes Tania recall her parents' talk about rallying the workers to fight the bosses before her father had been fired from the union and forced to take up selling life insurance. She had been too small then to understand much, but she clearly remembers him telling her, during one of the many talks about true American history he'd had with her when she was older, how a strike was a great tool for changing bosses' minds, and how a general strike as a part of a movement could change countries.

After the session, she shares something of these thoughts with her workshop leader. The training was good, she told him, and she appreciated the vital importance of combating the decline in unionism by organizing department store workers. But had he ever thought about the connections between labor and people outside the labor force, outside the country even? She knew all too well what had happened to U.S. participation in the international labor movement her father had been part of after the Cold War set in, but what about now? Why couldn't the labor movement be a connector for people again?

A month after the last workshop, an organizing gig at a department store chain comes along. Tania, who is assigned to work mostly with women workers, is stationed at one of the chain's stores in the same small city she trained in with a white man who had been in the same program. They meet with workers in a nearby McDonald's to find out what folks consider their issues. In this part of Pennsylvania, most are white women with blonde hair and green eyes, but they are working class and they want a union. They say they are among the few people in the store who are "safe," and don't ever rat to the boss. They're interested in having regular shifts instead of horrible hours that bosses can and do change at any time, even when they themselves are about to leave promptly at 5 pm and pick up their kids at the babysitters. These women, familiar with union power, leave excited about the possibility of gaining respect through joining their own.

Before she has been at it very long, Tania realizes that this union work has lit her fire more brightly than almost anything she's ever done. She approaches each day with a purpose she hasn't had since . . . perhaps has never had, even when she and Agua were performing together. Certainly, never before has her work been so in sync with what she considers important. Even her writing cannot compare. She now sees that as an avocation, something to serve her true calling. Happier than she has ever been, she approaches each day with gusto.

Tania's phone rings. She picks it up. It's the bass voice of Rolando Perez, calling to remind her about the Northeast Black Radical Congress rally coming up in a few weeks, and enlisting her help in lining up speakers and performers for the event. After they have made some initial plans and arranged to be in touch again the following weekend, he says, "By the way, have you decided what you're going to do this weekend for Juneteenth? Are you going to the Middle Passage Tribute at Coney Island?"

Suddenly, Tania realizes she's been putting so much energy into her union organizing in white-bread eastern Pennsylvania that Juneteenth has crept up on her. Now is her chance to put that aside and reconnect with her African roots.

She laughs. "Thanks for reminding me, Bro. I've been so tied up here I actually forgot Juneteenth was coming up. You're a messenger from Spirit telling me to stop for one day trying to figure out who's a Number One worker and who's a Number Four."

"What the hell are you talking about?"

"Number one workers are all-in for organizing and number fours are scared and totally unsafe 'cause they resist the very idea of collective job actions."

"I'll take your word for it. So will you be there?"

"Yeah, I'll be there. Maybe we'll meet up."

"Maybe. But trying to find a person in those crowds is almost impossible. Let's leave it to fate, okay?"

The morning of the celebration is sunny and warm. She can hear birds through the open window of the furnished apartment the union has rented for its reps. She rubs her eyes awake, eager to go to the ceremony on the beach, to feel through the sand the vibrations of the Africans who have gone before, and look out over the waters of the Atlantic, where so many of them were lost. As she fiddles with the dial on her radio and adjusts the antenna to tune in to 99.5 FM WBAI, she appreciates the fact that, while she is now living in a place where nature is part of daily life, the way it was in Albuquerque, she is also close enough to New York City to be able to tune in to *Democracy Now*'s progressive alternative to the corporate news and other radical, international radio programs whenever she chooses.

She jiggles the antenna one more time, then bends down and puts her ear next to the speaker. Yay! A cart about the Juneteenth event in Brooklyn is playing with Rita Marley's reggae voice in the background. She is singing about

Juneteenth, about how it commemorates the announcement in Texas, on June 19, 1865, of the abolition of slavery in the United States. The Emancipation Proclamation may have been issued in 1863, but it didn't take full effect until after the war ended more than two years later. But news of Lee's surrender in April, 1865, in Virginia, conveyed mostly by stagecoach, along with Union troops to enforce the Proclamation, took weeks to reach Texas, the most remote of the slave states. Only after that happened could the formerly enslaved Africans truly celebrate their freedom.

The reggae music ends.

She smiles and looks out at the green of the trees, breathes in the fresh scent of them. It's because the "movement brother" reminded her that she will go to the celebration today despite the long drive. She will choose to let life happen. "Thank you universe," she says aloud and, tuning out the radio cart, she finds herself mulling over her relationship with Teddy.

She remembers how it had been through the years: Teddy holding her, even moving cross-country to live near her, the tears in his eyes when he would see her after one of their many breakups—everything that kept her going back to him time after time. Now that she has started a new life, a career helping workers, women and men, organize to fight back, she grieves the breaking of that tremendous tie. Teddy had been a worker, but he had mostly chosen only to work, not to be a worker who would fight for his own best interests.

Still, she doesn't have the heart to realize fully how to face life without him. She has mourned him, done Reiki healing energy, and written passage after passage in her journal but none of it has helped. The black and white marble notebook that is the latest volume is on the floor. Shifting her position, she reaches for it. Nah. Leave it there. She gets up and stretches her body into a big yoga half-moon pose, with arms overhead and then flopping down, before washing and getting dressed. She chooses her clothes for the day carefully: bright yellow shorts, and an African style top given to her by Milagros, her Reiki sister. With its fitted bodice and ruffle waist, it suits her figure and goes well with her hair, which she picks, creating a bush of wiry curls.

Taking one last look in the mirror, she grabs her bag and carefully folds into it the Juneteenth poem she had written in New Mexico, which she has chosen to bring. Slinging the bag over her shoulder, she picks up the bouquet of flowers she plans to place in the Atlantic as an offering to honor the courage of those ancestors who chose to defy destiny and engage death rather than be used by the plantation owners in Jamaica or North America. At the door, she pauses and takes a regretful last look back at the journal, still lying on the floor. When she reaches for the house keys pain shoots up her right arm. Is the pain telling her to stop? Should she go back and write something, or reread what she once wrote?

Nah, she decides, it's time to move out. She'll leave the remembering to another time. She steps through the door, locking it behind her.

Her steady horse, which some folks call a car, waits outside for her. She unfolds the quick scribble of directions she had written down while the WBAI radio announcement played and lays the paper on the seat beside her, next to the flowers and her copy of Ralph Ellison's book about Juneteenth, which has finally been published these many years after he wrote it. She has brought it with her as a talisman to dip into if she gets the chance.

Considering its age and the miles it's traveled, the car starts readily and runs smoothly. Through the open window, the wind feels gentle, as men can be. Reflecting on enjoying the beach, relaxing, she chants softly, "Om Shanti . . . Om Shanti . . . Om Shanti . . . Ommm," trying to rekindle that peaceful, sacred feeling that fills her being when she's taking a Hatha Yoga or Astanga or even Kundalini class. The Om brings to mind the image of the small group led by a teacher of the Kripalu method that Tania attends now, where participants listen to the sacred poems of Rumi while resting in Yoga Nidra, that deep Yoga rest. The sessions are satisfying, and no one snores, but she can't help missing Maisha, who is her true teacher. She will have to drive into the city for a session with her when she has a chance. She wonders whether Maisha will be at Juneteenth.

She waits in Brooklyn for yet another street light to turn green. She is almost there. The traffic near Coney Island doesn't disturb her approach to the beach.

Drums play on the boardwalk, loud and strong, and walking toward the crowd she hears the 6/6 beat, and is aware of it connecting her to something she had missed in New Mexico: that "Black thing" on a mass scale. Most people in the crowd are African Americans, and on this day many, both men and women, show off the flowing clothes made of the bright African cloth they love. *Geles* cover the women's African-style locks, framing and complementing their brown, vanilla, or deep rust-colored faces. Men in Kufi caps, or with Rastafarian locks under huge straw hats with visors, stroll by. Tania walks well with the crowd.

"Hey, Buttercup?" She hears her old nickname, coming from a man standing in front of her who is wearing a straw cap with the Jamaican flag printed on it and a Bob Marley tee shirt, along with clip-on sunglasses and sandals. Sandals! Not many men of color wear sandals. Most stick to sneakers, even at the beach on a hot June day. She stops and looks into his face, which is brown, with smooth skin and a beard. He seems familiar, but it is the tone of his voice, soft and gentle, that brings him fully back to her. She hadn't recognized him because of the beard and because he has slimmed down. He doesn't seem fat to her any more.

"My name is Tania now," she says. "Just Tania. Hi, Purple." She smiles.

"*Tania*," he says. "HELLO!" They hug. "How you doing? Where you been all these years?"

She giggles. "Well, for several years I drove a bus, and after I quit that I moved to New Mexico."

He smiles again. "Oh, yeah, I remember now. You became one of the few woman bus drivers in the MTA. And a union activist. We heard about you . . ." His voice trails off, and for a moment there is an awkward silence. Then he says, "Remember when we were in my room with Malcolm X hanging on the wall?"

"I remember, but I was only interested in bad boys with leather jackets then," she says. "And once I started driving . . ."

"Well, how are you in relation to the brothers these days?"

Oh, man, she thinks, at once scared and excited. He's bringing their conversation into the present, so they are not only reminiscing. There may be some new dynamic unfolding. "I'm trying to be open," she says.

"Well, call me sometime." He hands her a purple business card.

"Oh you're still with that community activist group!" she exclaims, glancing at the card.

"Yeah, I'm still pushing the envelope against capitalism. Still organizing tenants, pretty much full time now." She remembers the rallies from twenty years ago and how he had helped move her early poetry out to the public.

"Can I see your eyes without the shades?" she asks.

He flips up the dark glasses and spirits connect.

The wind blows as seagulls wheel around overhead, diving down occasionally to snatch a scrap of the garbage that litters the beach. Looking toward the ocean where ancestors are buried, she watches Purple out of the corner of her eye. She wants to reveal something but her throat feels dry as if it can't say it.

What she actually says is, "Purple, I wanna let you know something."

"Yes?" He seems eager to listen, as open as he had been all those years ago, but just then a Latino couple with their child in a stroller comes by and stops to greet him. They are tenants he has helped stay in their apartment, and are soon engaged in conversation with him.

Tania thinks, "Oh well, a missed opportunity . . ." and turns to walk away, saying with a wave, "it was nice to see you again, Purple, take care."

Purple turns back towards Tania, reaches out for her shoulder. She feels the tenderness in his touch. "Wait a minute," he says. "Let me introduce you."

After the greetings, the woman asks Tania what is going on, pointing to the crowd of African descendants who are gathered at the water's edge listening to the drums and speeches. Many, like Tania, are holding bouquets of flowers.

"It's part of Juneteenth," Tania says.

"Juneteenth?" the woman asks.

Purple explains that the day is mostly a celebration of the end of slavery. Gesturing toward the food stands and the drummers, he says, "Every Saturday at Coney Island is like a carnival. This one is just special."

The woman nods, but points again to the group standing at the water's edge. "That doesn't seem like a carnival to me," she says.

"You're right." Tania speaks up. "It's a ceremony honoring the long road back to our spiritual and ancestral homeland by thinking of the Africans who jumped overboard rather than be enslaved. The flowers are for them."

"That explains it, then. People's bones are in that sea, real deep . . . "

"Yes," Tania says.

"I'll let you go, then." She turns to say goodbye to Purple, but Tania has started rooting in her bag.

"What are you looking for, Tania?" Purple asks.

"It's a Juneteenth poem I brought with me. It explains . . ."

He nods, and says to the Latina woman, "I think my friend wants to read something to you. Right, Tania?"

Tania likes that he intuits, and nods yes.

But the woman is distracted as her son begins pulling on her hand. "I'm hungry, *mami*," he complains. Roti smells draw him and his father further down the beach. "I wish I could stay and hear it, but I better go," she says.

"Take these flowers then and put them in the sea for me," Tania says.

"I will," she says. "And thank you. You make me feel connected." She waves goodbye.

Tania, noticing Purple's hand is back on her shoulder, trusts his gentle touch. She takes the Juneteenth poem from her bag. "Here I found it," she says. "Do you really want to hear it?"

"Yeah, I do. But why don't I treat us to some roti from that food stand over there, and we can sit and eat and really talk, and you can read me the poem?"

Tania throws her head back to laugh. "Oh, it does smell delicious. You mean share a meal?"

He nods and smiles and she tucks the poem back in her bag, as they walk side by side to the roti stand, comfortable together. Then, plates of roti and bottles of traditional Jamaican ginger beer in hand, they sit down at one of the wobbly tables and tuck in.

They eat in companionable silence, like a couple that has been together for a long time, taking in the end of the water-side ceremony and the continuing celebration. Finally Tania, drinking the last of her ginger beer, sighs contentedly and says, "Thanks for this treat, Purple," then reaches into her bag again for the poem. "Shall I read now?"

"Yes," he says simply, and she begins. Her long voice, the one she uses to bring an audience in to claim its intimate space, opens up and she almost sings.

"Afree ka / Africa aka . . .
Dedicated to those who celebrate Black folks leading a world to face truth!

Juneteenth Compañeros . . .Yemeya's Deep Sea
Chaka Zulu, like my old love
Ted Nat Turner
fighting back liars
of family of origin
Chaka Zulu and Hannibal of the long march in our Motherland
A free ka—

A movement catches her eye, and Tania pauses and looks up. A small crowd has gathered to listen, and a woman standing beside a little girl says, "Would you tell my daughter who Chaka Zulu is?"

"Chaka Zulu was an African leader who stood up against the Europeans when they came to enslave his people. The rest of the poem tells the rest of the story. Shall I go on?"

The little girl nods her head, and Tania starts reading again.

"Then these of Euro
Euro money
Euro pean & Euro peon
Taking/shaking/raping/& working my great granny's Granny and my nana's nana . . .
Mi abuelo & granpappy's great uncle
Damn it to hell
This country does well . . .
at hiding.
Nanny from Jamaica, Denmark Vesey, Harriet Tubman, So journey woman Truth . . .
Freedom fighters all.
The 1st person murdered under British killers in 1700's North America/usa's so called Revolutionary war: Crispus Attucks, be an African in amerrycaca.
Come on! Bust this open!
For those of still unsure of Amurderousica (America)
Both up and down, Brazil to Brooklyn
Had mucho money made off our backs,
While they be sitting, Worked us—watching rich whites' kids.
Spaniards, Dutch, Brits and Germans, all these Euro peons
Enslaved other humans.

Damn it to hell
This country does well...
At hiding.
But in slave-ship basements,
We See, with the clarity of our deep private Inner eyes, chained
We Smell our fellow tied sisters, cousins, brothers, nephews, nieces ***Blood***
We Fought back, by throwing ourselves into Yemeya's sea deep.
Yet millions of Norte americanos who never heard of 19 June 1865,
Never gonna keep our youth alive
If we all stay without consciousness.
if we all do not celebrate those of our people who
Jumped into sharks' bellies, instead of being hung in lynchers' trees.
See See do you, do you?
Damn it to hell
This country does well...
At hiding
&
when we from Texas, still living with the lies of the Texas senate, who knew . . .
when we, now but a small part of the Holocaust of African enslavement, found
out in June 18hundred65, that rich killers robbers rapists named
Jefferson, Washington, Robert E Lee,
Were no longer able to legally sell us . . .
We cried on 19 June.
We danced, Drummed delicious Bata, conga, shekere
Even though stagecoaches did not bring the news fast (at all),it
Made our music come up outta Hiding.
And now hundreds of lives later, our Ears Hear
in Mama Ocean's waves: "Come my chileren, honor the bones of all ancestors,
antepasados, *from the maroons of Jamaica,* hermanas desde *Cuba and Puerto*
Rico, shaking our Brazilian prophets, honor them for
Refusing to be used for Pro fit, Pro killing, Pro drilling, Pro cotton stealing!"
Damn it to hell
This country does well
At hiding.
We be Protect full of our spirit . . .
Dying to become unchained to Massa Imperialism's military games.
We Shout up to Father Sky
Human needs Matter . . . matter . . . matter . . .
Juneteenth compañeros:
Celebrate Black folks leading a world to take and face TRUTH."

Purple claps and slaps five with Tania's left hand. "Love those last lines," he says. "And the chorus: 'Damn it to hell / This country does well / At hiding.' I hope folks remember that." The people listening nod their heads vigorously and slap five with one another. "We will," they say.

Tania's eyes glow as she takes in their appreciation. Suddenly as exhausted as she is elated, she sits down again.

"Do you want some ice cream? Purple asks. "They have mango."

"No. Just another ginger beer, please. I'm thirsty."

He grins. "I bet you are. That was a great performance."

A few minutes later, as they savor the taste of-the ginger beer, Purple says, "So what did you want to tell me before we got interrupted?"

Surprised he remembers this, she shifts on her chair. "Should I tell you now?"

"If you still want to . . ." He keeps his eyes on Tania's.

Taking a deep breath, Tania puts her napkin down. "Am I trusting this man with too much?" she wonders, even as she says, "I mean, I know we just bumped into each other after a long time . . ."

"I've never forgotten," he says. "But only tell me if you want to." His words encourage her.

"Yes, I do. I really want to. But I'm so-o-o scared, Purple."

"Yes, I get scared too."

"Oh, God, thank you for admitting that." She honors his emotional bravery, so rare among men.

"Tania, we all have our spaces inside that are stuck." His face softens. He leans in, wanting to listen deeply to what troubles her.

"I wanted to say sorry for the way I treated you," she says. To explain."

"There's no need," he says.

But she goes on. "You see, my mother and my father did not have a happy relationship. When we were talking with that couple, I kept thinking, 'that woman could have been me if I didn't have so much distrust for Black men.'"

She tells herself to look up at the man who took the time to read her poems decades ago, who didn't think her strange for wanting to kick her shoes off and run barefoot in that Brooklyn park they'd gone to so often. She doesn't know what else to say. She believes her spirit guides are watching over her. Somehow he knows, and she knows he knows, the *essence o*f her story. He knows her fear of men taking advantage even though he hasn't heard her say those words.

Looking directly at her, he pulls out a cigarette, but seeing her pull away before he lights up, decides against it. He places his hand on the table palm up, inviting her to place hers in it. Slowly she does so, and they sit together feeling the rhythm of the Rasta drums, the drums of Nyabingi time. Watching him now, a gentle guy swaying to the Caribbean music, her half-Jamaican self feels that Jah, the great spirit of the Rastas, is bringing them together.

"I'm so glad I came to Juneteenth," she says.

He nods. "I am, too. But I've got to think about heading out."

"Me, too, before the traffic gets too bad."

Still holding hands, they walk together down the boardwalk, oblivious to the crowd dispersing, even to the setting sun watching over their stroll.

Their talk is the talk of good friends, and the subjects are various—not intimate, but the kinds of things people who share values and concerns talk about. The litter left behind by the crowds draws their attention, especially all the plastic that the receding tides will soon take out to pollute the sea. The pollution of the sea leads them to discuss the pollution of the air, the haze they can see over the city even on such a day as this, and the threatened destruction of the ozone layer and the treaty nations have signed to try and heal the hole that has formed in it by gradually halting production of the pollutants that created it. It is a minor miracle, that treaty, but it amounts to not very much in the face of the catastrophic destruction the Amerikan system, spread world-wide, has unleashed on the natural world. She tells him some of what she learned from the indigenous people in New Mexico about taking care of Mother Earth.

After a while the talk turns to racial politics. "Do you remember the Central Park Five?" he asks. "I hear they might be getting a new trial or that the whole thing with DNA now could help overturn their conviction. . ."

He notices her blank look. "Oh that's right, you were out of state when it happened, I guess it wasn't news in New Mexico when the white Mayor of New York called the rape of a white woman supposedly by a group of Black and Latino teenagers the 'crime of the century.' That sucker convicted those brothers long before there could be a trial . . ."

She nods. "And white folks pretend they ain't racists! It's the same in the southwest. The governors and lawmakers there are racists too, only it's more about Latinos and the indigenous people."

He presses her hand, appreciating her consciousness.

They arrive at the exit from the boardwalk, and the concrete ramp that leads to the parking lot. It's an unforgiving surface, contrasting harshly with the soft sand of the beach and the wooden slats of the boardwalk, and as one they hesitate before stepping onto it.

"So Tania," he says. "It would be a shame to lose touch again, don't you think? Can I have your number?"

She replies "yes," but then, still cautious, wanting to check him out away from the magic of this day, she adds that she will email it to him. "I have your card here in my pocket." She waves 'bye and heads down the steps without looking back.

On the drive back to Pennsylvania, Tania's mind is full of thoughts of Purple, of how he has changed physically since she knew him before, but how he is essentially the same gentle, caring man he was when, in the park, she confided to him that as a child she had been called Buttercup. When they parted she had hesitated to give him her number. By the time she gets home she has no doubts, and emails him at once. It is the first in a long series of exchanges during the following weeks, by email and by phone, and through an instant messaging service, a form of communication that they discover lets them share thoughts in the moment, almost as if they are having a conversation. Both discover there is an unexpected intimacy in this long-distance relationship, and they tell each other things that, in person, they probably would not have revealed.

They talk about their work. She especially likes that, even as he has become ever more prominent in organizations campaigning for social justice and still keeps his hand in as an occasional photojournalist for radical publications, he now works full time at the grass-roots level, as a tenant organizer focused on helping individual families deal with their landlords. Unlike so many men (especially men, it seems to her), he has remained true to his principles on the most fundamental level and now lives in a tiny studio apartment carved out of a Brooklyn brownstone, the latest in a series of downsizings since, as he had predicted, urban renewal, really urban removal, made the rent on the one-bedroom where she had first visited him too high. They speak about Cuba, which he has visited, and where he saw with his own eyes that people actually *own* a home after they have lived in it a certain number of years, and that no one goes hungry or without basic medical care. Both of them appreciate how the Cubans continue to stick to their principles despite the overwhelming hardships that followed the West's destruction of the Soviet Union. She talks about how her father had been a union organizer right World War II, so in becoming one herself she has found her dream job and when she is promoted to project organizer after the women at the department store chain vote to form a local, his reply is an all-caps YOU GO GIRL!

She tells him how her father was driven from his position at the union because, they said, he was a communist, but really because he was Black, and how she had come to understand the roots of this betrayal in the racist capitalist system thanks to the insights of her radical therapist. He knows immediately who she is talking about. Though he has never met Pam, he has learned much from her through her publications. He has read *Lessons from the Damned.*

She tells him about her spiritual journeys, how she has been enlightened by the insights of Native Americans in New Mexico, and then those of her West African ancestors through Madrina in New York, and the Reiki practice that has come to mean so much to her. In this connection she mentions Maisha, and is delighted to learn that Purple knows her well, as a fellow activist. "Amazing woman," he writes. "Always wears African-style clothes, which evoke the spiritual energy of our people."

He tells her about his own spiritual journey towards Africa and revolutionary, independence-minded thinking inspired by the Rastafarians. While his Geechee roots had always provided a connection to African culture, Rasta teachings and the music of Bob Marley had made him feel part of a movement to change the way Black folk think about themselves, though he could never join outright because of the Rastas' views on women. Mostly, though, for Tania, their communications recall the conversations they had had in the park all those years ago, with Tania trusting him to *hear* her even when he disagrees or thinks she is going too far. She tells him how the child's pet name Buttercup had become, as she grew up, the humiliating "Butter," until she became strong enough to insist on "Tania." She tells him about the pain of never truly feeling she belonged in her family, and how she became bitterly estranged from them. He tells her how sorry he is about this, because his own experience growing up with roots in an extended African American family in the south was so different. While there were serious issues—among other things, his pops had regularly stepped out on his moms—feeling he didn't belong wasn't one of them. His parents had returned to the south—gone home—after his pops retired, and were buried there.

He confides that his moms, unable to have more children and neglected by her husband, had focused on her "little man," and how he ate and ate to make her happy. After her death, he had come to understand this, and was able to break free, thanks to the insightful advice Oprah Winfrey offered to Black men and everybody else on her show. Free therapy on TV! But maybe because of it, and despite Oprah's insights, he has always been wary of forming lasting attachments. "I don't do relationships," he says.

Tania is touched by his willingness to share his feelings with her, to risk being truly open, to make himself vulnerable. He has moved past the conditioning of most men. She responds by sending him a copy of her play and explains how she and her younger sister, Gerri, had found each other again because of it, but her older sister and her mother had denied it, and her. After reading it, he understands, more than Tania realizes, and hopes she will someday be able to come to terms with what he sees as a tragedy for all concerned.

He says nothing along these lines at the time, but in the Fall, on a day when a blustery wind whips New York's streets, rustling the leaves of the trees outside his apartment, Purple engages in another instant message exchange with Tania.

"Hey, Tania, what are you doing next Tuesday? I want to surprise you with something." He clicks *send*.

"Oh? What's up?" *Send*.

"I have something special I plan to go to and hope you'll join me." *Send*.

"What? Where?" *Send*.

"It involves Older Sister." He inserts a smiley face and writes, "See, I'm gonna call her by the name you use." *Send*.

"What about her?" *Send*.

"She's giving a presentation in connection with the publication of her book. Folks in the community are talking about it and I want to hear what she's got to say and get some pictures for an article. You haven't seen her in so long. Maybe she's changed. People do, you know. And she *is* your sister. " *Send*.

When Tania doesn't respond, he writes, "Well?" and clicks *send* again.

This time she replies: "WHY NOW AFTER ALL THESE YEARS?"

"To see her eyeball to eyeball and 'get into it' if you need to, but at least see her. She's your family, your blood." *Send*.

"Maybe you're right. I don't think so, but I'll go with you 'cause I want to be with you. It's been a long time since me and you have seen each other." *Send*.

Purple inserts a smiley face and a heart and clicks *send*.

As she and Purple approach the venue for Older Sister's talk, Tania wonders whether the place will be a bookstore or a battleground. Certainly it is no small, feminist shop. The first floor is taken up by piles of best sellers and cash registers, ringing up sales for the corporate owners of the chain. Upstairs in the harsh gleam of the fluorescents, the "area for book talks" feels like a clearing in a forest of bookshelves, each one hiding a canon aimed at her. There are about thirty people present, both Black and white. Tania and Purple take seats in the last row of seats near the aisle, so that he will be able to get up and take pictures.

Tania wishes she could escape to the children's section, where there are lots of colorful books with teddy bears strewn about for hugging. Why does being an adult mean one must become used to dull brass and green-hued carpets strewn with images of dead fish on which chairs, arrayed in regimented rows, face a massive table that stands between the author and the readers?

Older Sister arrives about ten minutes before the presentation is to begin. She is wearing a wool suit and high heels, which contrast jarringly with the radical symbolism of her black beret. On her way to the table, piled high with copies of her book, she glances at Tania, but says nothing to her. Instead she turns away and speaks briefly with a few other members of the audience before making her way up front.

Purple, shocked, squints to make sure this is in fact Older Sister, whose face is depicted on posters all around the store. Surely she recognized Tania, who looks almost exactly the same as she had years before. His shock turns to sadness for Tania's sake when, from behind the table, Older Sister looks right at him and Tania, then deliberately looks away to arrange the pages of her presentation.

When Older Sister begins speaking, Tania hears a woman who has a commanding voice and enunciates carefully, explaining how Black folks can get ahead. "I want to be crystal clear . . ." she says, her index finger puncturing the air. As she talks, Tania realizes this is not the woman/girl she grew up with, but instead a public figure. She feels like a doofus for going along with Purple's insistence that she try to reconnect with this woman. The fact that they are "family," as Purple says, doesn't make it so.

What happened to her? The woman standing behind the table doesn't mention the socialism Tania remembers Older Sister had explained to her when they were girls. Tania had fallen in love with socialist thinking then and still believes passionately in the "we" politics it embodies at its best, not the individualistic shit that is the so-called American Dream. "The right to have our individuality and sing our individual songs in harmony with a society that shares. That's the kind of socialist identity I want," she murmurs inside as Older Sister talks. Their personal lives have been politically changed by emotional distance.

The presentation draws to a close and Older Sister invites questions from the audience. The long sitting has made Tania's old bus-driver's backache return. Gotta get up and stretch, she thinks. No one will notice. But she remains seated as audience and author engage one another on the details of how to reform capitalism, to make it more "fair." No one suggests what Tania mutters to Purple under her breath: that the system is rotten and cannot be reformed, only destroyed, that it depends on the exploitation of people, especially Black and brown people, for its very existence.

"Not to mention that the US is a militaristic empire set on destroying the planet," Purple whispers in response.

When a man sitting up front asks, "What do you mean the U.S. isn't fair?" Tania has had enough and heads for the restroom. When she returns, the crowd is lining up to purchase one of the signed copies of the book on the table, or get the author to sign copies they have already bought. Seeing them, white and Black, standing in this orderly line, Tania is suddenly aware of how middle class they are. Their hands are smooth, with no rough nails, and their smiles are restrained, not broad and unself-conscious. Definitely not working class. Maybe some of them are wannabes with working-class roots, like her father was. She wants to tell them that they will never truly belong, will never have real power, that Older Sister's pitch is a lie. But she says nothing as she sits down again.

As if reading her mind, Purple asks, "What's your feeling about these sellouts, Tania?"

"Well, they're folks who think going over to massa's side by forgetting that workers make this stuff, even the very chairs they're sitting on, is gonna help them rise."

Purple agrees, but adds, "Outside of here, many folks have to work overtime, or two jobs, to make ends meet. In either case, they wouldn't have time to come here either to support the book's argument or to object to it. That's not going over to the other side."

"Yeah, that's true," she agrees "But, Purple, those guys, and definitely these folks here, not to mention union workers who aren't active organizers, don't realize we can BRING THIS WHOLE UNJUST SYSTEM DOWN WITH A GENERAL STRIKE, THE WAY CUBA DID IN 1959." She says this so fiercely that several folks in line turn to stare, and she lowers her voice. "We're so stuck on little, everyday concerns, Purple."

"You're right, Tania, we don't make the connections to bigger strategies. To revolution." His theories and hers come together.

But Purple is still thinking about Tania and Older Sister. Tilting his head to the side, he says, "Hey, wanna get on line, too, ask her to sign a book? Surprise her? I'll take a picture of the two of you together."

Tania looks over at his charming face. His eyes smile but his forehead is wrinkled with worry. She wonders at his concern for her, and, instead of simply saying no, she responds to it by trying to explain. "My dearest Purple, I'm not unhappy you suggested I come and find out for myself who my blood is. But you see how she pretends I'm not here. Me being seen as *Tania* is still impossible for my family, even Gerri, who comes closest."

Still, she gets to her feet with him as the end of the line passes them. They squeeze each other's hands as it moves forward, until, suddenly, they are at the table, and Older Sister is greeting them as she has greeted all the others: "Oh, hello, how nice of you to come," she says. "I hope you enjoyed my talk." She rushes the words together, red lipstick smiling, and extends her hand to Tania. A formal greeting for a stranger. The right hand of this former leftist thinker extended ratchet-like, to attach itself to the book-buyer in front of her. Then her body stiffens as she recognizes her sister. "Hello, Tania," she says. When Tania stands silent, Purple steps into the breach, introducing himself as a friend of Tania's who has come not only to hear the talk but to take photos for a piece on the ideas in the book. He hands her his card, and then, holding up his camera, he asks her and Tania to get closer to each other. Neither sister moves. He snaps the photo anyway, then urges them to pose for another, "Could you stand here . . .? Could you stand next to her?"

Tania thinks wonderingly, Maybe it is possible Older Sister will look into my eyes as he asks, and see herself, a person from the same culture . . . family. She moves an inch closer to Older Sister, who once made bagels for her in the morning, who, when they were children acted like the responsible one. They stand rigidly side by side. Purple snaps the photo.

Older Sister blinks and turns away to shake the hand of another book buyer. Tania also turns away and Purple accompanies her back to their seats. Gently he taps her shoulder to show her the photos in the camera.

"No, I don't want to see them," Tania says. Then, feeling she has to explain, she adds, "New Mexico warmed me, Purple."

"I bet!" Purple laughs.

"In New Mexico I learned I deserve to be around warm and loving people. But Older Sister is frozen into this severely dressed, hair down and done person you see up there greeting her public. I'm not her sister. I'm simply one of the . . ." She searches for the word Older Sister might use ". . . you know, the lowly masses. She doesn't have a heart." Still, she waits. sitting as before, beside Purple, in the last row of seats near the aisle, while Older Sister lingers in chit-chat by the table. Tania's palms grip each other, and then, to calm her nerves, she strokes them with her fingers. "I learned this in New Mexico in a workshop on self-massage," she says. Purple nods. He is looking through Older Sister's book.

Tania tries to talk lovingly to herself, promising herself that she will take a good lo-o-o-ng bath with lavender oil when she gets home. "Purple?" she says. "You remember I told you about how, after Younger Sister came to my play. . ."

"Gerri? I remember."

"Yes. After all the years that had passed there were warm looks and tender tentative touches, like we could maybe bridge the lost time. As you can see, that's not so with this stranger wearing stockings and heels and an expensive suit with a black beret . . ."

"Maybe you haven't really given her a chance," Purple says. "Let's wait 'til everybody else has left. Maybe she'll come over here then."

"I bet she won't. The whole damn charade of our lives has always been about keeping silent. She's not about to start communicating now."

"Yeah I hear you. But did you ever think maybe she's scared?

"Older Sister scared?"

"Tania . . . Can you let yourself feel what she might be feeling? You say it's always been about silence. Is it possible she's afraid being close to you might expose things she needs to keep buried? But I guess you're right. I guess she ain't coming over to see us. The bookstore people are the only ones left up there." He reaches over and hugs Tania.

She wants to cry, but holds it in and sets her mouth, resolving now to stay. The simple black Timex on her wrist ticks loudly. A young man asks her the time, then leaves. "Purple, I'm not leaving until she comes over here. If we leave now I'll never know for sure that she wants nothing to do with me." I mean, we're here to see her, and not just at the end of some line. I've been away for years, but I'm still on the planet and she"s gonna have to deal with me. I'll wait even if she stays over there chatting 'til this place closes at midnight"

She shoots another look in Older Sister's direction. Now the space between the table and where she and Purple are sitting is completely empty, so Older Sister can't pretend they are just part of the crowd anymore.

And perhaps surprisingly, she does not. Instead, she waves good night to the last bookstore representative, pulls on her elegant wool jacket, picks up her bag and gloves and briefcase and comes over to stand in front of them, the priest before the congregation.

"Hello," she says to Purple, smiling at him as she had before.

He rises and extends his hand, and he and Older Sister chat about the event. Tania, still seated, doesn't hear what they're saying.

Finally, Older Sister gives Purple her business card, then, as an apparent afterthought, turns to Tania. In the silence between them, Purple excuses himself and heads for the men's room.

Looking Tania up and down, Older Sister says, "Is that all you wore?"

"No. I have a coat." Tania wears a lovely red corduroy Chinese jacket that graces her slender frame, but she can tell by the way Older Sister's lips twitch like their mother's did when Tania came to visit, that she thinks it's too bright. She refuses to defend herself, to answer back the way she would have when she was younger. She no longer feels like Older Sister's Little Kid. Instead she waits, still hopeful that something healing will come of this. Surprisingly, Billy Holiday's song "Strange Fruit" is playing on the music system, and Tania identifies with the song's desperate lyrics, belie her hope. Her heart beats fast.

Finally, as Older Sister makes a move to step away from her, Tania forces out words, "You can look at me like that, all you want, but I am not going back to being your baby sister."

“"No one's asking you to, but for God's sake, can't you dress like a sensible adult instead of some aging hippie?"

"How come my clothes are always more important than my feelings?" Tania stands in Older Sister's face now, "My feelings have been shut off by you for years, and I don't know why I thought tonight would make any difference. Purple thought it might, that I should give it a try. But now I finally realize you're only interested in me behaving, never in me opening my true self to you."

"Look, what I'm interested in is not being embarrassed by you and your loudness, your brash way of dressing and your downright crude manners. I've got a reputation to maintain."

"But I loved you. I loved you and Younger Sister and Mommy and Daddy. I believed you all cared about me. I trusted *you.* But what I've come to learn is what an emotionally dead place I survived in."

Older Sister begins to button her jacket, pausing deliberately at each velvet-covered button.

Suddenly, Tania doesn't want her to go. She wants to try once more to pry open the box of memory that Older Sister has nailed shut. Failing that, she wants to be the one to turn her back. "Wait," she says. "I want to tell you something."

"No, I don't have time."

“”"I want to tell you what happened."

"No! No, don't tell me. You've kept it to yourself all these years. Besides, it's all lies anyway if it's anything like what you wrote in that awful play."

"No, I want you to listen to me."

Older Sister now has her jacket buttoned. She throws her gloves into her bag without stopping to close the latch properly, so they stick out, and grabs her briefcase.

"Goodbye." She stumbles as she strides away.

Tania realizes that this is truly the end of any fantasy she might have had about making the new start with Older Sister Purple has tried to encourage. She studies her as she walks away briskly, her shoulders hunched. Suddenly she straightens, tosses them back, as if tossing Tania out with the movement.

"Don't go," Tania wants to call after her. "I can't wait for Purple," she thinks and runs after her. The store's escalators are all headed down now, and Tania jumps on one of them, not the one that is carrying Older Sister away, but another one. She sees Older sister opposite her and tries to catch her eye, then again on the mezzanine landing. Older Sister is staring straight ahead, clearly pushing down her feelings, keeping her face emotionless, the way members of the class of the almost rich do. She heads on down, and is already stepping briskly off the escalator onto the carpeted ground floor before Tania starts after her, springing down the escalator, trying to spot the security guard who, she knows, will be standing by the exit. But she is too late. When, breathless, she reaches the exit, Older Sister is already disappearing into the cold New York night.

"I'll call Purple later," Tania says to herself, embarrassed by the old desperation that has made her chase after Older Sister like the little girl she once was. What must Purple think? She had told him she wasn't sure how she would react to Older Sister after years of not seeing her, but still . . .

A gust of wind blows her back into the building's lobby. Suddenly she can't leave without him. She stands by the bookstore exit waiting. Tears want to come out of her very skin. Please let him use this exit, she prays.

She imagines his reaction as he doesn't find her when he walks back to the chairs they had sat in. Doesn't find Older Sister either. Probably he thinks they've left together. Maybe they needed to talk. Thinking they're together, he takes his time heading towards the exit, the ground floor. He stops to take photos of the covers of books by brown and Black people, even riffles through one or two of them. But, she imagines, something calls him to the farthest exit. And there, just outside it, he sees Tania.

And he is real, standing there in front of her in his black and brown cloth jacket,. She waves and smiles. She breathes. Her heart jumps. His smile back comforts her. He is Purple, and now she knows she can count on him. She buries her head in his chest.

"She's gone, Purple," Tania says. "She just left. Purple, hold me tight."

He folds his arms around her. "I understand now," he says. "I understand the ice that almost killed you."

She pulls back a little to look up at him and touches his fuzzy beard. "Purple, remember when we first knew each other . . .?"

"Yeah?"

I didn't understand then that people are a lot more than the way they look.I wanna ask, will you forgive me?"

He strokes her hand. "Tania, the person who needs to forgive you is yourself."

Her heart hears him. A tear and then another roll down her cheeks. "Purple, thank you so-o-o much. I wanna tell you more. Is it okay?"

"If you want to. But let's go outside. I know it's cold, but I feel sort of exposed standing at the entrance to the bookstore. We'll find a place out of the wind."

Hand in hand they walk through the doors of the building into the night, and around the corner they do find a sheltered place.

"Well, Tania says, "just let me say for right now that my distrust of men like you, who are Black and also thinkers comes from my fear you will use your tremendous smarts and your mind to, you know, to con me and . . . "

"To use you?"

"Yes, Purple," she murmurs and then, for the first time with Purple, speaks directly about her dad. "I want so-o-o much to trust, but when I look at Black men, I think of my father. He hurt me so much, Purple. He had a lot to say about Malcolm X and Paul Robeson, but . . ." She pauses, then goes on, her eyebrows raised in surprise at the understanding that has just come to her. ". . . You know,

I'm just realizing this now, he didn't use words to express his rage at the viciousness of the racism he faced all the time. His anger didn't turn into emotional courage. Instead he brought it home and took it out on us, on me."

"I hear you," he whispers, gathering her in. They stand together holding each other's hearts closer.

A few weeks later, Tania leans against the wall in the kitchenette in Purple's cozy apartment reading aloud from the book *Breaking Bread* by Cornel West and bell hooks, while Purple cooks. "Listen to what they be saying *here*," she says whenever his attention seems to stray. They have both read the book before, but never together until now.

Since the evening at the bookstore, when Purple had brought her home and sat with her and held her until daybreak, his apartment has come to welcome Tania easily. The thought of driving back to Pennsylvania after that event had terrified her, and going home with Purple, instead of calling Maisha, had felt right. Unlike when she visited his apartment all those years ago, now she feels safe with him. She feels she can trust him.

Tonight, after they have eaten, they sit together on his sofa as they had that night and as they have come to do whenever they are at his place. He has his legs stretched out, displaying his socks. He likes to take his shoes off at his front door, just like Tania. The sofa, which is upholstered in soft shades of brown and purple, is also his bed, but they have never opened it, at least not yet. They are learning how to be close to each other without sex, to build the kind of trust in each other that knows no fear of betrayal. As they often do, they are contemplating his precious Malcolm X collage. It takes up most of the opposite wall and is one of the few things he still has from the apartment he'd lived in twenty years before. When she had first seen it back then, hanging in his bedroom, she had been too distracted, too disappointed at the discovery that Purple, too, wanted her for sex, to take it in. Now, every time she sees it she finds something new in its portrayal of this real history-loving Black-consciousness raising leader of the masses. Woven into his hat, the black old-ways style hat, are various images: Malcolm in jail, in Africa praying. In the bottom right-hand corner there is a huge yellow sunburst. Its rays spark out in bold, electric type phrases from his speeches: "Ballot or the Bullet!"; "Message to the Grassroots!"

Under the collage are chrome racks and shelves that hold all the tapes Purple has ever worked on, including the back-ups he made for Tania when she traveled about performing her poems with Agua, along with a collection of vinyl records and a few CDs. There, as well, are books on tenant organizing—how to get groups of folks in a building to stand brave together to face a ruthless, thieving landlord in housing court and win. His audio equipment, along with his computer and several cameras, occupies the alcove where there would normally be a bed. A mix-tape of Bob Marley and Miriam Makeba is playing.

She is teasing him about how much time it had taken him to call her after the bookstore night, and how, when he finally did, it had been to ask her for a suggestion about his health, since, in one of her emails, she'd mentioned the healing cleanses she'd learned from *curanderas* in the southwest. Since he had trouble walking, she had brought the potions to his place.

He grins. "Yeah, I remember. When I pinched my nerve,"

He rubs his back, where it once ached.

"Okay, Purple, I see what you were getting at now." She returns to the conversation they were having at dinner.

"It's global Tania . . . invasions of Panama, Grenada, Nicaragua. Haiti. Somalia. A drug factory in Sudan, for god's sake. Damn, we gotta be political."

She nods emphatically, adding, "And they do it without our, the people's, permission. This government just steals our money and puts it in the U.S. military. And for us, you and me, to be learning how to love is political, like Audre Lorde says."

"That seems like a jump. What do you mean?"

"Because we are supporting ourselves. As Mao said, 'preserve oneself, defeat the enemy.'"

Purple's thigh rests beside hers, and she reaches out to stroke it. "Hey, my friend," She smiles, and withdraws her hand, providing for his heart to rest. "We've been woken up by there being no feel-good jobs, no health coverage here in the u.s.a. We've been woken up by how you and I had families we loved who did no political resistance and let this amerrycaca madness continue."

He laughs. "I do like that term," he says. "It fits the bill. But I still gotta wonder, Tania. As a socialist labor activist, how do you deal with being born and raised middle class?"

Tania laughs, too, "Well, it ain't been easy. Step by step, I learned how to disconnect not only from my family, but also from that whole crap idea that it's necessary for one's well-being to be seen at the best restaurants."

"Yeah?"

"Yeah. I mean, even now there are temptations. Gerri tried to seduce me back in by saying I could stay in a vacation time-share she and Older Sister inherited from my father. I said no, but I confess that for a second I was tempted, before I realized how disgusting the whole idea was."

"Disgusting?"

"Yeah, I feel disgusted now by the bourgie energy that drives the exploitation of people and the planet in the name of success and progress. The fact is, I learned to see the world as it really is, that it's working people who actually make and produce or drive or serve everything I interact with, even my clothes. My supposedly leftist family talked about it, but didn't mean it."

"Tania, I'm glad you and I can talk like this."

"Me too, Purple. Me, too. I'm also glad you can cook."

He grins and goes on, "You know, Tania, my working class family had bourgie ways, too. My pops was always working, not to mention running around, and my moms thought she had to stay with him for my sake."

"I don't buy that explanation," she argues. "These moms seem to always say it's for the kids when they're just too scared to be on their own,"

"Yeah, maybe you're right. Moms worked as a singer and sometimes a beautician, so I guess she could have left him, since she had her own money and, well, like she left the first guy, 'cause he was hitting her. But what she could earn on her own ain't big money when you got kids." He laughs bitterly. "How's that for bourgie thinking?"

"That worry, that parental agony about work and everything else, took up all the oxygen in my house and in yours. Emotional justice? Hah! They dressed you to be only mama's, to never let no other woman receive your truth and kindness."

Deep inside he feels a flower growing, as he strokes her knee.

". . . They dressed me in 'Don't let a man place himself inside, 'cause he'll be gone, after he done shook up your world.'"

"No more." Purple moves to get up off the sofa, but Tania pushes him back down and jumps up herself. She loves dancing to the drum beat of Marley's music, and now struts her stuff as he sings "Get Up Stand Up." "We can change, yes we can, yes we can," she chants. Purple grins, appreciating her, and when the song ends, grabs her hips and they fall back into the couch, lie still . . . just enjoying quiet for a few minutes. Breathing together. His belly raises her back. A half hour of holding each other's bodies and resting passes. The late afternoon sun lets its eyes close. Tania strokes him on his shoulder and chest, as Purple, now asleep, breathes long and complete at last.

Laying her head on the back of the sofa, she gazes up at the cream-colored ceiling, listening to the sweet sound of Makeba singing "Malaika." It's funny, she thinks, how much men will pay for audio equipment, though she appreciates the way the full stereophonic sound of the music curls around her toes. She feels so safe here, protected by the heavy green curtains Purple has hung in the window that looks out on the landing at the base of the stairs leading up to street level, where the trash cans are stored between the sanitation department's scheduled pick-ups. Whenever Purple moves from one street-level or below-street-level apartment to another—apartments on higher floors usually cost more—he washes the two curtains and installs them in the window facing the street (there is never more than one) in the new space. They keep his "sweetness" safe, he told her, grinning broadly when she asked about them. They protect a man's bear cave from the fake gold-digging women their mamas warn them about. Unlike Tania, with whom he connects by phone before she steps into his brown-bear den, those tigresses, if they see a man inside, scratch on the funky old glass of the window with sharp nails until he lets them in.

The Makeba-Marley mix tape ends and in the silence that follows, Purple stirs. His full hand strokes Tania's leg. He likes the soft feel of the non-jeans—never jeans—she wears. In fact he has never felt this woman in dungarees. Fully awake now, he smiles with his nose buried in her shoulder, then gets up and, goes to the tape deck. After pushing "rewind," he moves toward the shelves of mix-tapes to choose another.

"Don't change it," Tania begs. "It's the one I'm feeling in my heart tonight."

Purple nods. "Me, too," he says, and turns back to the tape deck. He pushes "play." In a moment the rhythms of Makeba's irrestible "Pata Pata" fill the room, and once again Tania jumps up to dance. This time Purple joins her. When the song ends, as one they flop back down on the couch side by side, breathless together. Once they have caught their breath, he opens his arms on the sofa back, then cradles Tania in his left, and they pick up where they left off.

Tania, as usual, is the brave one and goes first. Realizing that the things he has just told her about his mother represent a breakthrough, that what he had admitted in their long getting-to-know-each-other-again email conversation over the summer was not so easily discussed in person, she broaches the subject carefully. "Baby, your moms was smart enough to leave her first husband, who beat her. I know that's why you like me, 'cause I stood up also. I told *my* pops he couldn't have me in his life no more, since he wouldn't admit what he'd done."

Purple, however, doesn't follow her. Instead he picks up on what she has just said about her father. "Not *wouldn't*, Tania. *'Couldn't.'* Your father couldn't admit what he did, even to himself, 'cause of what this shit system did to his brain." He avoids mentioning his mother again.

She nods. "Yeah, Purple, what it did to his soul! After the white unionists betrayed him, he bought into the middle-class climb-the-corporate ladder shit as the only way to make a life, selling life insurance for god's sake. And he was good at it, but being Black he never got rewarded the way he deserved, or promoted. It's like Malcolm said, north of the Mason-Dixon Line is just 'Upsouth.' So the only way he could be a man was by treating his wife and daughters like shit."

"Yeah, Tania, people think what happens in the outer world, outside the family, is just that, but it ain't so. And it ain't just the racist attitudes. When unions go along with the bosses' thinking, or with the government that's siding with big business, that's a real problem. If they've bought into this so-called okey-doke system, the working class my moms and pops brought me up in lives the same shit your middle-class folks did. They don't believe in themselves. The bourgie white folks make them hate each other for being poor." He falls silent. Mental images elaborate what he remembers.

He feels his father womanizing at the factory and Bertha, his moms, crying, while little Purple, her "little guy," can only watch. He leans forward and lets himself look deeply into the photo of his moms, framed in gold and hung over his TV. She is wearing the big white hat she wore to church on summer Sundays, and her vibration seems to linger now in his apartment, even though she never visited him here, and even though he is no longer the six-year-old boy she made into her "little man," her little husband she could control, but an independent adult, thanks to the passage of many years and Oprah Winfrey's wisdom.

He sighs, lays his head on the back of the couch again. He knows Tania wants him to talk about all this. He even thinks what he might say: "Moms allowed me to think I could make up for Pops not being home." But he says nothing. Instead, his hand gently touches and reassures her shoulder.

Realizing that, with this touch, he has said something important—"I'm here with you, but I just don't want to verbalize right now"—she slides her arm off his lap and places it behind his head and looks caringly at his tender brownness. "Let's step outta this Purple," she says.

"Step out? Sometimes you say things and I don't know what you mean."

She strokes his shoulder, touches his hand, keeps lovingly connected as she says, "You told me you don't "do" relationships. Yet we are doing one. You kept in touch after we ran into each other on Juneteenth, even though we hadn't seen each other for years. You mix music tapes you know I'll like, and we share them 'cause you like them too. You cook meals for me a lot better than I can." She gestures towards a book he has been reading about societies' hatred of women and how men can stop it, which sits where he has left it, next to his computer and his clean green ashtray. She appreciates that he doesn't smoke when he's with her, or even inside his apartment, so it stays fresh for her. "You read books about things you know are important to me," she says. "You've all but given up smoking. So now, if you ain't ready to talk with me about some things and resist getting counseling for your own self, like I've done, I still accept you. I know Black men don't always trust that even a Black radical therapist like Pam, who helped me face how my father and my whole family betrayed me . . ."

She stops. Before she can resume speaking, he says, "You may not want to hear this, Tania, but the fact is, before he died, I told my dad I loved him."

"Aw, my god, Purple, when?" Tania swells inside with tears. "Did your father truly *hear* you after all those years?"

"I don't really know. But I came to realize he worked all the time to give me books and things, not just food and an apartment in the Bronx. He didn't hug me or stay home or laugh with me. It was like he was addicted to work. But he worked so hard 'cause he'd truly bought into the bourgie idea that this was the way to make life better for his son, and when he was dying. . ." Purple stops, as if he sees something. "When he was dying I walked into that hospital room, Tan, and told him, 'I love you. And yes, he heard me." He lowers his eyes to avoid her grave face. Her eyes are closed.

Finally, she says, "Look at me, Purple. Please?" Gently he raises his lids.

"Purple, my situation was different. I had an ongoing betrayal. There was no deathbed scene. I wasn't even there. But long before he died he'd lost his mind to dementia. And afterwards . . . Even now, only Gerri, not my mother or Older Sister, acknowledges what happened. So I've fought through that pain mostly alone, with the support of therapy. That's why I'm motivated."

"To do what?" He closes his coffee eyes. The lids, looking like two miniature overturned saucers, face her.

"To open my eyes, hon. To see that our parents' betrayals are *theirs*. I don't . . . We don't have to keep their pattern going by refusing to admit what we've done . . . We're different." She strokes his lids with her little finger.

"When we first got close all those years ago I was in the middle of torture. You looked at me as a friend to talk with and listen to Malcolm X with."

Waiting for Purple to open his eyes, she touches his chest while kissing out her next words: "We've taken almost twenty years to bring ourselves to a place of almost having sex, and . . . "

Purple grins.

She goes on, "What I mean is, I figure we got to just wade through our differences. I'm many cultures. You're basically two, male and African-American southern, and have had to learn to believe in females, which I appreciate. But having gotten through that change, you wanna rest. I wanna control. You want me to accept you without asking any questions, I need you to tell me when you're scared, and when you don't tell me, *I* get scared, and then I push too hard . . ."

He groans. "Yeah, and then I gots to tell you to stop! Remember? So stop. Let's don't think about that now."

His arm curls protectively around her and they laugh together as Malcolm X smiles down on them from the collage. Bob Marley is singing "Redemption Song."

18B HEALING, ORGANIZING, RECONNECTING CONTINUED

Tania's friend Maisha emails her: "A new support group for survivors of childhood sexual abuse is meeting and has space for you." Maisha had bumped into Purple. "You know, when I saw your man, he told me about what happened with your sister at the bookstore, and I thought you deserve support if you want it, right now. How about letting this group be a part of your life? They have this grant to help women work through trauma."

The following week Tania goes to sign up at a wellness center located next to a Quaker meeting house. It consists of a meeting room with a couple of tables, several comfortable reupholstered armchairs and posters of Frida Kahlo self portraits and Georgia O'Keefe flowers on the walls. Books of poetry by African American women like Audre Lorde and texts such as *Courage to Heal* by Ellen Bass and Laura Davis, along with copies of *Mother Jones,* are displayed prominently on a stand in the middle of the room. Tania sits in one of two chairs in a corner and waits to meet the facilitator, who will interview her in order to "feel her story," as she had put it when Tania called.

Within a few minutes, the facilitator appears, a tall, kind-looking woman with striking ebony skin, who introduces herself as Grace. "We use first names here," she says, and goes on to explain: "I facilitate by gradually bringing out info on this issue of incest and the family and encouraging the sharing of your experience within the safety of a group, if you wish." She hands Tania a clipboard with a form several pages long to fill out.

Tania, who has stood to greet the woman, responds to this with a nod, then settles back into the chair with the clipboard in hand. At first the questions are routine, but towards the bottom of the first page, she tugs her cap brim down and wriggles her small nose as she ponders how to answer, "Was your family aware? Was the sexual abuse only with one person?" Her mind drifts. She thinks of her friend Rolando Perez, who, because, he said, he trusted her, once shared his family pain with her, describing the unity he felt in retreats for male survivors he attended. His openness is such a rare and precious quality, especially in a man.

At this point, however, Tania is not trusting enough to respond to these queries with anything other than "I don't know" and "we didn't talk about it," and is relieved when the questionnaire turns to more philosophical issues. Maisha had told her the facilitator had been a union organizer before taking up recovery counseling, and as a result, Tania feels the two of them must be on the same wavelength, so she can answer these questions in a deeper way. In response to one of the last, "Can you tell about how participating in this group relates to your thinking?" she writes: "I hate the corporate empire we live in. This system conditions parents to make their children their property! Kids are just another 'thing,' like parents as workers are 'things' for the boss to control and use! My incest was a part of that, and I can heal by being open. I am not the criminal. Parents who hurt us and this brutal system are criminal. I have learned, through my past work on this issue, that I'm guided by a deeper source than parents. I realize that although this work has brought a lot of growth, still capitalist social relations, like capitalist economic relations, will take lots of revolutionary transformation of both us and the world. Doing this personal work is as important for me as my commitment to struggling forward on the road to economic and spiritual change." Finally she signs the form on the line stating: "I will commit to doing the emotional work of this group for the complete time that it will meet. I will show up."

Soon after this, as a member of the group, Tania is driving to the city every Friday evening to participate in the sometimes hours-long sessions, which start at 7:00 when the women and Grace settle into the chairs, now arranged in an informal circle. Most of them have brought something to eat. Before they arrive, Grace has set out bottles of water and tissues, and sometimes handouts.

At first Tania is more reticent than some of the other participants. Despite what she had revealed in her play and in her other writings, she had never opened herself up directly in the way Grace and the group seem to expect, except in her sessions with Pam, when the two of them were alone, or alone with Teddy. And despite the literature on the bookstand she isn't sure Grace has the same understanding as Pam about the invidious role capitalist society plays in family relationships. Certainly she practices radical therapy in a much less formal way. But it is not long before she is responding to Grace's broad smile, which, along with her words, encourages the survivors to share. "Take a deep breath," she'll say. "You're being real and not stuck in your head, and are doing such great work." And listening to the others, hearing their stories, Tania soon begins to feel she belongs with them the way she never felt she belonged in her family.

And, she is now beginning to think, with Purple. One Friday, they arrange to meet up at the bus stop on the corner near the wellness center before she goes inside and he heads uptown to a tenants' association meeting. They have not been together since she joined the group, and she wants to tell him something. Despite their growing closeness, such brief hook-ups are often all they can manage. While her schedule as a union project organizer is flexible, his, as a tenant organizer and free-lance photographer is often irregular, even chaotic, dependant on the cruel whims of landlords and what is happening in the lives of the folks he tries to help.

"I'm so grateful you told Maisha about what happened at the bookstore," she tells him after a quick hug.

"How come?"

"Because without that I wouldn't have found this group, and when I'm in group I feel better about myself. I realize you are not in my life to heal me. I go to my support group for that . . . and . . ." She motions towards the building.

"And?"

She thinks: "In the group, the pent-up trauma of my childhood is beginning to release, allowing me—preparing me—to accept the joy of being in a loving relationship with an adult man who loves me, an adult woman. Meaning you, Purple." But aloud she says only, "And you play the music I like and kiss me gently and sometimes we even have so much fun being playful and I don't have to ask you to hear my tears anymore. I can cry them by myself now, with my group. With you, now I can. . ." She pauses, then says simply, "Now I feel maybe we can love each other, Purple."

He says nothing, taking this in, then bends his head down and kisses her. She lightly tongue kisses him back. The precious moment cannot last. Over her shoulder, down the block, he sees his bus, stopped at a red light. Quickly he takes a cassette he has made for her of Malcolm X's speeches out of his drab olive knapsack and hands it to her just as the bus pulls up. He hugs her tight and they smile bye-bye as he boards.

Inside the wellness center, the group settles into the chairs—each has her "own" now—and opens up the cartons of food she has brought. Then Grace says, "Take a deep breath, and share with us, if you like, how the trauma of your childhood has made you feel powerless at work, in relationships, in life." And Tania, for the first time, opens her heart up in front of Grace and the others. It all spills out, not in the disciplined format of a play or in a setting that immediately puts what she says in its social-political context, but in a complete release of feeling. She cries and cries . . . being heard. Her tears drop onto the carpet as she bends herself over her lap. She feels united with the other survivors. "Un-alone" is what they say to one another as they prepare to leave the comfort of each other's company. Grace summarizes: "Today we have begun the work of exposing the power of those who have long been seen as victims—the power to survive and resist, to stand up to the people with power over us!"

At the end of group, Grace customarily gives a hug to everyone and receives one in return from everyone—except Tania. Grace understands that this is not a rejection. She realizes that Tania does not yet feel secure, is not yet sure she can trust. Even today, after Tania, at last feeling safe enough, has released her pent-up feelings, as the others hug Grace and are hugged, Tania hangs back, still not sure about being touched by an adult with even a little authority. Recognizing this, Grace honors Tania's soul by letting her avoid the good-bye hug, saying simply, "Thank you, Tania, for your courage." There is no pressure.

One Sunday when they are both off from work, Purple and Tania are sitting side-by-side in his neighborhood Laundromat. It has become usual for them to do laundry together, especially since she began leaving a few things at his place. They don't talk about much beyond the logistics of washing and drying clothes, because, as has also become usual when they are at the Laundromat, each has a headphone plugged into one of his Walkman's two jacks, and they are listening to music together—today one of his mix tapes of samba, mambo and *plena*. They take turns disconnecting to do the chores associated with washing clothes until finally the dryer is done and Purple turns off the Walkman and puts it and the two sets of headphones away. They work together folding the linens, then she folds the clothes as he packs them into his shopping cart. Out of the corner of his eye, he watches as she moves gracefully to fold the few pieces that belong to her, then turns to the long-sleeved shirts he wears to protect himself as he walks around in the old New York City buildings where he does his tenant organizing.

"Be careful," he says. "Maybe asbestos got into the seams. It's in a lot of old buildings and the landlords don't do anything to fix it unless they're renovating in order to raise the rent in gentrifying neighborhoods." Sensing his worry, she stops folding and gives him a quick hug. "I know that," she says, "but I didn't realize it might cling to clothes even after they're washed."

"I bet you didn't," he says, laughing. "You ain't got the right background." He teases her.

"Well, you, yourself, learned it on the job," she retorts. "Your family may have been working class, but your pops had steady work in a factory. You didn't grow up in a tenement."

"Got it." Purple laughs and resumes carefully placing the folded laundry in the shopping cart.

Before they leave the Laundromat, Purple plugs the dual sets of headphones back into the Walkman, which he carries clipped to his belt, and the two of them move together in time to the music, almost dancing, down the street.

Back in his apartment, after they put the clean clothes away, Purple heads for the kitchenette. "Put some music on, will you? Sam Cook." Horns and drums. He loves the mix.

She does so, then snuggles her body into the cramped kitchenette.

"I wanna read something from my journal to you . . . okay?"

He fixes his eyes on the fridge, thinking about what to prepare. He usually likes to be quiet when he cooks, and would rather do this on the couch in the big room, but he lets it go. "Okay, yeah," he says, "while I fix us something."

She reads, "*I'm damn sure happy to be recovering Purple from the toxicity of this society, so filled with general lies . . . amerrycaca.*

"*Not to mention recovering my own self, having my shortcomings removed. I am reclaiming, I guess, the little one, you know, my sure, innocent inside self that I came onto planet earth with.*"

She then circles back to read a question that precedes these entries and is one of the many writing prompts in her journal: *"How have you been shown what actions to take as a shortcoming is removed?"*

Purple puts down his spoon and hugs her, but he is puzzled. "Hey, baby," he says. "What do you mean when you talk about 'recovering' me from this amerrycaca society? Can we ever recover the innocent self we were born with?"

When she doesn't respond, he plows on. "And about those shortcomings. What actions *do* you take as one of them is removed? What do you do when you make a mistake?"

"I pray by breathing in goddess! I know you call it Jah, so let's say I call in healing Rasta love." She nods toward the large, well-thumbed bible bound in brown leather on the table beside the couch—the "bedside table" when the sleep sofa is open. Purple calls it his Rastafarian bible, and it is often fleshed open, like a morning glory blossom at noon.

He chuckles and shakes his head, and though he sometimes prays to Jah about the bond between him and Tania, he says uncomprehendingly, "But what does that *mean*, Tania?"

His attention on the stove, where his veggies, rice and eggs, with a side of leftover home fries , need tending, he doesn't see her wide-set eyes narrow to slits. Although consciously she may realize he's not paying close attention simply because his focus is on his cooking, deep down it feels to her that he just doesn't take her emotional writing seriously.

During dinner, however, he returns to the subject of what she does when a shortcoming is removed, showing her he has heard more than she thought.

"I take actions like remembering Harriet Tubman, never stopping, mostly just lying down for a while when her 'sleep' would come over her from that gash on her head, you know, the one from the plantation sucker's abuse, and I rest in meditation to find the deepest answer in me to stay clear."

He smiles at her genuineness, which brings magic to him even as her answer still leaves him puzzled. He squeezes her hand, then returns to his food, as does she, both listening to the smooth horn riffs of John Coltrane and then the falling-water sounds of his wife Alice's harp, followed by several numbers from the Neville Brothers 1990 concert in New Orleans.

As ever, Tania gets off dancing to the cool jazz, the riffs of alto sax, the slow guitars with violins over-laced in the background, the sweet sounds of Aaron Neville singing "Arianna," and Charles Neville playing "Healing Chant," and after they eat, she appreciates sharing her sensuality, while he watches from the sofa.

"Damn this shit has to get better," she says when she sits down. "Your generation of men . . ." She gets up again and turns down the music so they can really hear each other. "I mean," she says, "your generation of men seems at least to know that if they're not just going with the mainstream, or are at least semi-conscious, they can't be hitting on our faces, and bodies no more."

"Where did that come from?" he asks. "You think I'm like my mom's first husband?" Scared Tania will lose the overall mood of their day off and get too intellectual, he motions for her to move nearer to him.

"You know I respect you, right, Tania?" He eases any underlying fear by looking at her from behind his horn rims.

"Yeah I do," she replies. "But I wanna ask something."

"Why do you do that, Tania? Why don't you just ask straight out?"

"Oh, when I was younger and going to Pam . . .

"You sound nostalgic," he says. He touches his ears, almost like he's cleaning them, preparing to hear something deep.

She nods. "I miss her so much. She was so much more than just a therapist, you know. She was the one who was really responsible for developing my working-class consciousness. She says it's up to us to face the acute contradictions and change this monstrosity."

"I know," he says. "I've read her writings, remember?" Purple's head tilts slightly, and they rest that conversation, his arm now giving her a light touch.

"Okay, back to what we were saying," Tania is encouraged by remembering. "I'm glad you're open to thinking about all this."

He glances over at *Facing Love Addiction*, a book she had brought him that he reads in every now and then, when he's at his computer waiting for downloads. It's open to the chapter on avoidance.

"Well maybe, I guess so . . ."

Tania lays her head on his shoulder. She realizes he needs to relax more before going deeper. "In my case," she says, "'cause my pattern from my father and him being unavailable emotionally and . . . and other things . . . well, my pattern is to know a man may have stuff to talk about and I either push to get it out of him, or I allow him to neglect our connection totally and become a busy-aholic where he just stays busy all the time."

"Wow, that's a term I never heard before."

Tania keeps going, "Well, I mean with all the stuff that's always going on in this system, we could stay fighting it all the time."

"Tania, I take breaks so we can just be together." He straightens his glasses.

"I know and I appreciate that so much."

"We can move people to organize and shake this thing up."

Tania nods. "And deep caring for each other while we do the outside stuff is shaking it up too,"

As if on cue, Isaac Hayes sings, "someday we're gonna change all this . . . some are looking for tricks . . ."

"Yeah." He squeezes her hand. They kiss, lips lightly touching.

"Yeah," she repeats, but again she circles back. Still, I get scared you'll leave when it gets tough. And sometimes I think you work to help others only and don't take care of you."

"Let me get what you mean. You're afraid I'll leave you? Have I shown you that?" His smile is lovely. Not a big grin that would set Tania off, but a gentle, genuine one.

"Not really. I mean, even after you get scared and don't call for a while, like a week or more." She stretches out the word *more* to show him how it affects her, this need of his for space.

"We've talked about this before. Remember, I gotta process how close we're getting," he explains. "It brings up a lot for me too."

It feels like an opening. "Purple, are you thinking about your mother?" she asks. Though in some part of her she knows the question will upset him, knows how scary it is for him to talk about these things, she can't resist probing. For the truth is, she *is* afraid. Afraid not only that he will leave her, but even more afraid that, if he won't share his feelings with her, she will have to leave him in the end, the way she had to leave Teddy emotionally long before they parted company. The only way she and Purple can move forward together is with mutual understanding. They cannot continue to speak different languages.

"I don't know, Tania. You're so . . ." His voice shows irritation.

She can't stop. "Did she shower you with food and keep your clothes really pressed, do your hair for you and ignore your dad whenever he found his way home? Did she stay so focused on your emotionally absent, but come-home-and-sleep-with-her dad that they both didn't give you true mother/fathering? Seems like you had to be momma's special 'little man,' cause her husband didn't wake up. And *he* put you in the middle, Purple, by neglecting her and you! And—"

Purple cuts in, putting a stop to her unwelcome analysis. "Maybe all that's so, Tania, but . . . How did you know? You know everything? You think you do anyhow." He shows sad eyes to her through his fingers, covering bitter shadows with two of them pressed hard on his lids.

She starts to say he'd told her, in their email exchange over the summer, but stops herself. He had not told her these details. She is sure, from all she has learned over the years and from her many convos with Pam about mothers and their sons and fathers not wanting to share power with mothers, that they come pretty close to the truth, but he is not ready, and she stops, then begins again. "And then, Purple, I come in, and you come into a relationship, and we try to love each other and your moms gets in our way, 'cause you're afraid . . ."

Purple starts to move away, then stops himself, accepts what she is saying. "Okay, so maybe she got too close. Maybe she let me think I could make up for

Pops not being there." His tone is reflective, wondering, the tone of someone who has recognized a truth. "And I am afraid, Tania. You say you're afraid I'll leave you. Well, I'm afraid *you're* gonna leave *me*," He says this softly, leaning on his elbow, on the arm rest, so she can see his eyes, then sinking back. He breathes deeply, trying to make the connection between Tania and the woman he had counted on when he was a boy, thinking *this* woman is different. When she doesn't respond, he presses on, saying something she might have said: "But I'm beginning to feel you won't, that maybe, like you said, we really can love each other, 'Cause we ain't betrayed each other."

She nods, recalling what she had said at the bus stop, and moves closer to him, curling up in his embrace.

For a few minutes there is silence. Then he says softly, "I got something I want to share with you, Tania. Something I think is really special." He reaches over, picks up a CD that is lying on the bedside table, half-hidden by his "Rastafarian" bible, and hands it to her.

She takes it wonderingly, surprised. Neither she nor Purple can afford to buy much in the way of commercial CD's (he still creates his mix tapes mostly by recording from the radio, refusing on principle to download freebies from the internet). She recognizes the artist, India Arie. The album is "Acoustic Soul."

"This just came out," he says. "It's her first album." He gets up and inserts the disc in the player, As he sits back down, India Arie's haunting voice holds them both in the sofa's soft folds.

Tania is enchanted. She has heard some of the songs before, on the radio, but never when she could give them her full attention. Every now and then a breath of coconut incense enters her nostrils. She inhales, exhales, blowing in his ear. When she kisses his scalp, she tastes Irie Rastafarian hair oil. His soft cotton shirt fabric stays loving. Many threads, many soft ties blend under her fingertips.

* * *

The next time the group meets Tania arrives a few minutes early so she and Grace can walk in together and she can express her own gratitude. As they take off their coats, she says, "Grace, I just wanted say I am so-o-o-o grateful to the people who write grants to get healing circles like this going, for those of us who need great relieving from the deceiving." She laughs at the rhyme.

Grace understands what Tania is now signaling, and once everyone else arrives and settles into their chairs, she expresses the theme of security really clearly. "When we are children, we put all our 'safety needs' into the hands of these huge people, these adults, who then betray us. And as we get older, we carry within us that little child who still needs to be parented. So we are re-parenting our inner kid."

"Can we be good inner parents and treat ourselves with compassion instead of putting ourselves down the way our real parents did?" The question comes from a Latina who always wears a flower print blouse. Tania has mentally nicknamed her "Flower."

"Yes, we can become good inner parents instead of the uncaring ones our blood parents were forced to become by this society, which made them powerless."

"You mean I can stop yelling at myself and give myself a pat on the back for what I'm doing good in this world? Even when I'm with the family?"

Grace nods, "Yes. Though it's not always easy to do."

The woman sits back in her chair and shakes her head. "But what if you can't even feel part of your family because they won't talk about what happened. I can't bear to show up at any family functions. I didn't even go to my youngest cousin's wedding as a bridesmaid because I couldn't bear to see all those liars. I couldn't hold on to my dignity because so many of them have never reached out to me since I left home, only my youngest cousin. Or if they did they wouldn't talk about the dirty secret."

Grace suggests that perhaps, "by showing up here with new people who share that experience, you'll become more brave and ready to face them. And, if you wish, to figure out if you have any other allies in your family besides your youngest cousin."

Tania feels that Grace is speaking directly to her, that the last barriers to complete trust are gone as the group shares some of the same fears she used to have, before she confronted her parents. She is sure now that she is not alone.

After the session is over, she stays behind to help Grace put the room in order. "Grace?" she says when they have finished and are putting on their coats. "Grace, do you feel I'll ever become strong enough to stand up to the deniers in my family in some group"

"Yes," Grace says confidently. "Yes, I do."

With a heartfelt smile, Tania hugs her tightly

The next week, the woman who wears flowery tops does not come to the group, although she is a committed member. Afterwards, Tania, who has again stayed after the session to help with the cleaning up, comments to Grace, "I feel so much grief. Like maybe I am going to lose a person who had shared her story and listened to mine." Grace nods. "I'm worried, too. But let's wait and see what happens next week." And the next week "Flower" comes back.

"I'd like to share this poem," she says as soon as all are seated. "I mostly feel too scared to let my real family know who I am. My birth family, I mean. I feel like you're my real family now."

The others encourage her: "Let's hear it."

Sitting forward in her chair, she begins haltingly. "The title is 'Descendant's Ladder Climb.'

"After Ashtanga Yoga class
"Hammered like dead bolt locks
"Onto 'wombmons' tops
"Rungs of a ladder:
"1st rung - deny sexuality
"2nd rung - once she accepts "A chest has grown a breast, cover the new blossoms"
"3rd rung - act like she's still treated the same, although what she thinks and knows is now less, much less important than how her bosom, ass, thighs, bless a man's gaze.
"4th rung - ladder ices over with a marriage promise as her 4-leaf clover
"5th rung - awaken through Yoga work. Teach bodies to stretch, sister healer of alternate nostril breath gives back the freedom, her girl-self feels.
"6th rung - female student becomes the adept
"7th rung - healing women give chakra crystal health, designing safe space where humans can care!

"The Ani DiFranco song about how to be in a female body played the whole time I was writing this poem, "Flower" adds. "I love that Annie sings about how I haven't felt at home with this body since I was a little girl."

Everybody's eyes glow. As a Black woman, Tania feels the poem, with its evocation of the powers of Yoga, has spoken to her in a special way. "Mm. Mm" she says emphatically. "Your real self is here. So glad you came back."

Grace adds, "So you see, the rapists don't always win! *We* win when we tell our story in the safety of the ears of good loving people, when we are ready!"

The group sits quiet. The soft-white light from the lamps envelopes their circle which is further enclosed by the drapes that shut out the lights and sounds of the street. Her head lowered, this brown Latina sister gazes at the red ruffles on the front of her flowered blouse, touching each trimming. Then, shyly, she looks up at the others, just taking in the energy of their response. "I'm glad I came back," she murmurs softly, and everyone hears.

The following week, Grace invites the group to recall their last session and to think about all they have learned during their time together. At the end, she reminds them of what she had said then: that victims of child abuse win when they can share their stories. In group, they have found the courage to do this with a small number of people like themselves, whom they had come to know and trust. Now, if they feel ready, they may be able to help others, by finding the courage to go public with their stories, to share them not only with each other and with family members who are willing to hear them, but with strangers. She goes on to explain that child sexual abuse occurs much more often than most people realize. It damages men as well as women, and their whole families over generations, as well as their communities, especially in societies where the System makes folks feel powerless and therefore worthless. But little can be done about it unless those who have been abused are willing to tell what happened to them and to seek justice.

Having said this, she scans the room and adds, "Let me tell you about an organization called Generation Five, which recognizes that at least five generations of an incest family, along with their communities, are harmed by child sexual abuse. That includes everyone from the parents of the perpetrator to the victim's siblings, children, and grandchildren. It aims to foster healing among all of them if they are alive and willing to engage, so that the violence of child sexual abuse doesn't lead to more violence when victims become perpetrators, which happens all too often. Remember, we know that most abusers have been abused themselves."

Seeing by the nods of agreement that the group is with her, Grace goes on to describe how Generation Five attempts to aid healing through the practice called Transformative Justice, in which victims, perpetrators and enablers of violence may be brought together to seek understanding and forgiveness. This requires awareness in place of the denial and silence that enables the horror of child sexual abuse to be perpetuated. So to make healing possible, Generation Five also works to expand awareness through the facilitation of retreats and other events and activities, some more public than others.

"For those of you who feel ready to take this next step and share your experiences more widely," she says finally, "there will be a Survivors' Retreat later this month. I, myself, will be among the facilitators. Before you sign up, however, I want you to know that some of the victims will be men. One in six men has been sexually abused as a child, and females as well as males are perpetrators."

* * *

The morning of the Survivors' retreat, Tania gathers with other survivors, Black and white, in the wellness room of the institution hosting the event. Some dress in artsy clothes, very colorful with dots and tie-dyes. Tania, herself, has on one of her bright African tops and her hair in braids, which she has pulled together into pigtails instead of letting them hang down. Others, especially the guys, wear jeans and sneakers and their hair straight, white folk style. Some look like the people you see on the bus and the subway after rush hour, or coming out of the gym in running shorts after having de-stressed from office jobs.

After introductions, the group breaks up into getting-to-know-one-another workshops named "Intimacy," "Relearning Healthy Touch," and "Letting Go of the Abusers and Our Patterns," with participants switching among them. Then, following lunch, they reunite in a circle of folding chairs for what Grace announces will be a healing exercise or game called "Shamebusters." Several of the participants, who have been to other retreats facilitated by Grace, seem raring to go, but Tania sits hunched over, thinking, "Wow what a title." She wants to leave, but she doesn't. She trusts Grace.

Once everyone is settled, Grace introduces the game, which involves folks moving from one chair to another when they hear something described that happened to them. To Tania it sounds like a version of the kids' game musical chairs, which she hadn't much liked even when she was little, but it seems that Grace has this misperception in mind when she explains that no one ever *has* to leave their chair, giving everyone the emotional space to decide for themselves how much to reveal, if anything. Finally, she invites all to play, adding that everything will become clear as they go along, and nods to a tall guy standing beside her to lead off.

The man, who is mostly bald, with a short gray ponytail at the back his neck, moves to the center of the circle. "Here's how it works," he says. "Whoever is in the center of the circle—for the moment, me—will make a statement. If that statement describes something that happened to you, if you can say, 'Yeah that's me, that happened to me also,' then you're asked to get up and run or walk real fast across the room and take an empty chair. The last person standing takes my place in the center of the circle." He shifts his weight, then adds, "Remember, no one ever *has* to stand up and move. You can always choose to remain seated, so everyone can always feel safe. And in case anyone feels anxious about something, Grace here is available for individual sessions all next week. After the game a closing ceremony helps bring everyone together. Okay?" Most people nod tentatively, and after a quick look around, connecting with each of them, he opens it up with, "If you were ever molested, change seats." Suddenly Tania's heart is beating like an African drum and she can barely breathe, much less move. Everyone else, it seems, has immediately jumped up to switch seats. Only she has stayed put. Many of those popping up and moving fast to empty chairs, missing out and heading for others, are laughing and giggling like the kids they once were. Finally, the one left standing, a woman of color like Tania, moves to the center and calls out, "Switch chairs . . . if you've been molested in a car."

Again, Tania can scarcely breathe. It's been years since she thought of her father in the car, but the memory now is so clear. Still she doesn't move, and she continues to remain seated as one after another, folks left standing move to the center and call out things she endured but has never before heard stated aloud.

Then, suddenly, she finds herself giggling as she watches a girl wiggle her behind into a seat just ahead of another woman, both of them laughing. The woman moves to the center and says, “If you were incested for years, change chairs.”

Still Tania doesn’t move, but she realizes that the beating of her heart has now changed. No longer does it pound with the fight-or-flight response to terror. Now it pulses with healthy excitement. She tilts her head back, watching as people race across the room. She thinks, “I’m identifying with others. We are not alone. I have found people who shout out loud what happened to them simply by being here and getting out of their seats and changing them, whether they end up standing in the middle or not. Suddenly, her feet want to move, and she stands up—and immediately sits back down again when she realizes she was so happy to feel connected that she hadn’t really been paying attention, because the command from the person in the center had been, “Switch chairs if you told a classmate what happened and they laughed.”

No, that had never happened to her. But now her blood is rushing and her feet are tapping as the energy shifts lighter and higher. She finally takes the risk on the next statement that fits: “Switch chairs if you have been incested as a teen as well as a child,” and rushing with all her athletic vitality, she bounds over to the other side of the room, slides her butt into a chair, and gleefully watches the much younger woman who had also been aiming for it stop in her tracks and look around. Seeing that there is no other free chair, the young woman makes a sweeping bow to Tania and, hand to her mouth as if to stifle her giggles, goes to stand in the middle of the circle.

The shame-busters game ends after about forty minutes, when Grace calls them all together for the closing ceremony. Candles have been lit and flowers set out. Tania bows her head with the others as they salute their ancestors in a universal prayer. She places her hands on her chest, one over the other, then opens them to send Reiki healing energy to all in the circle, while also setting an intention of peace for the other members of her regular group, who had evidently not felt ready to attend. Her eyes rest, her mind breathes, and suddenly, in this moment, she is clear. Safe from her old role as scapegoat in her blood family, she is ready to reach out to them, to try to break the chain of silence that has imprisoned them, to expand the links of awareness. She’ll start with Gerri, who had had the courage to come to her play, but not to face down the denials of Older Sister and their mother.

* * *

Tania’s body feels stretched out today. This morning, after Purple left, she has spent an hour engaged in deep, luscious breathing. Now she spends several more minutes looking at the collage of Malcolm X. Every time she sees it, she sees more in it. Maybe that's why she stays over at Purple's so much more often nowadays. She can lie on the couch or, as now, on pillows on the floor, taking in the greatness of that leader of the masses against colonized thinking. Last night, after they had kissed a while, she had felt like sleeping alone on the pillows instead of beside him on the couch. Purple didn't complain. He accepts her. They understand each other.

Although it's fairly late in the afternoon when Purple returns, having gotten off early from work, they decide to celebrate the extra time together with a subway ride to Coney Island, where they had found each other again. They will be there in time to watch the sunset.

At the beginning of the trip, she takes her journal out of her bag and tries to write, but the train's lurches and jerks make it almost impossible, and before long she gives up. After that, they remain peaceful, meditating together. He holds her right hand in his left palm. She loves his neat fingernails and the smoothness of his skin. There is no hair on the backs of his hands.

When the train comes out from underground, it suddenly stops. The voice on the loudspeaker announces they will be moving shortly and thanks them for their patience. For a moment Tania and Purple simply bask in the silence and the late afternoon light filtering through the train's dirty windows. Then Purple, taking advantage of the quiet, asks her to tell him about what she has been writing.

"A piece about the white, rich British and the over-privilege white folks get from dying not to know, in other words, denying they reap the benefits of a racist society. The history of centuries of labor stolen from Blacks. Family history."

She shares that she's been thinking about how her father's mama—"my nana"—was rejected by her white father's family when he died, how they threw her and her Black mother off the land! "You know, this was years after slavery officially ended. Jamaican post-slavery society so-called was filled with the same kind of trauma there had been when the slave-owners worked African folks till they died. So my nana, who was just nine years old, was forced to leave the only home she knew, and then a relative had to take care of her, 'cause her traumatized mother couldn't handle anything after having been raped repeatedly over the years."

"So what brought this on?"

"It's the direction the Group is going in, how sexual abuse and violence and trauma are passed down from generation to generation because the victims are forced to keep silent. My nana was never allowed to say that her mother had been a sex slave and that she herself had likely been "incested" by her own white daddy. You remember that retreat I went on?"

"Yes."

"That was the first step, ending the silence not just within the confines of the group but publicly. Everybody there had been incested and we all ended up admitting it, in public, as part of a kind of game like musical chairs. I know it sounds weird, but it was liberating, being able to shout out, loud and clear, what had happened to me. Not the details, exactly, but the essentials."

"Liberating? How do you mean?" Purple had felt a change in her mood since the retreat, but had put it down to the advent of spring.

"By letting me be open about *what* had happened to me, it left me free to try and understand *why* it happened. So I've been trying to recall what little I was told about slavery and its sexual domination in Jamaica, or gleaned by listening to what the grown-ups let slip when they didn't know I was around. And I've been looking into how my family history fits into history overall."

"Yeah, history in the Caribbean."

"What do you mean?"

"The biggest slave revolt in history was in Jamaica in 1831."

"Yeah, but I'm focused on my family."

"Well, were they involved in that Christmas rebellion?"

"I don't know. How many rebelled?

"Sixty thousand, out of a total of 300,000. It began on Christmas Day in 1831, and lasted eleven days. A couple of years later slavery was abolished in the British Empire."

Suddenly Tania is wondering why she doesn't know whether her family was among the 60,000 who rebelled or the 240,000 who didn't—and embarrassed that she doesn't.

Sensing her feelings, Purple strokes Tania's fingers and returns to the personal story she's already shared. "Do you think your nana took out her pain from colonialism's racism and degradation on . . .?" He pauses, then continues resolutely, ". . . on your father?"

". . . on my dad?" She looks at him wide-eyed, "You mean . . .? I don't know. When he was a little boy she left him behind in Jamaica with his older sister, my Aunt Tantie, or Tantie Tantie as my sisters and I used to call her behind her back when I was growing up. But it's definitely true that as a child he was the one product of her labor she had some little power over."

In her piece, Tania has written that the torrential rains on Jamaican fields could never wash away the stench of what owning people does to them and their children and their children's children. The trauma will last forever—unless and until the construct of ownership is broken, as happened in Cuba. But she has not related this insight explicitly to her father's behavior, and says no more about it now. Instead, after a silence, she reads Purple these lines from her piece, then adds, "We can do it, Purple. We can be the generation that changes things. You and me and the leftists all around, from Brazil to Uzbekistan to Vietnam."

"Why not?" Purple urges their conversation toward solutions. "How about we circle the world with our worker-led cooperatives, and our condemnation of Capitalism?"

Tania nods, but says no more. With the train moving again, talking is difficult and she takes her pocket radio and the dual set of ear-buds out of her bag and says, "There's an interview with Joy Leary on WBAI in a couple of minutes. Want to listen in?"

"Who?" he asks reflexively, then remembers. "Oh yeah, that sister who talks about the effects of slavery's trauma on young Black men today. I heard she was gonna be talking about her theories. I'll have to catch her another time, though." He hugs her and smiles. "I gotta catch a few z's. The never-ending 'no heat no hot water leaks in the roof rats under the bed' horror stories wear me out. Just give me a nudge when we get near our stop." While Tania plugs in her earbuds, he puts his elbows on his knees and his head in his hands, then relaxes, looking down at his feet, tuning out.

Tania hears Joy Leary's forceful voice. "Every psychiatrist, "she says, ". . . every one of them, knows that, other things being equal, Black children start off just fine." As she goes on to explain how her research shows that violence among modern Black youth is related to the violence of slavery, Tania has a sudden insight. The truth Leary speaks relates not only to the violence among modern Black youth, but to the violence of the whole culture, white as well as Black. She had read somewhere about how in colonial times the white Kentuckian and the white Virginian used to fight ferociously, gouging out eyes, tearing off ears, and breaking noses while crowds watched and applauded the bloody victor, carrying him in triumph on their shoulders. For the upper classes, dueling formalized the violence, but it was always there. The violence whites inflicted on their slaves was reflected in the violence they inflicted on each other. Suddenly it is so clear to Tania that the seductive, intimate violence that afflicts so many folks, and not just Black folks, but especially them, is related to all the violence, all the seductions/abductions and rapes of slavery. In a sense, slavery *made* incest. Even the white kids who get incested are from the same culture of violent domination and submission.

The interview with Joy Leary is over, and with the stop for Coney Island approaching, Tania turns off the radio and puts it away. Purple is still asleep; watching him, she is reminded of Teddy and how he, too, would sometimes feel the need to "catch a few z's" when she hoped to engage him in something that was on her mind. Was this how some Black men sometimes chose to deal with white society's constant onslaught on their humanity, not with violence, but by shutting it out for a bit, closing their eyes to go within?

Smiling, she reaches out to touch Purple's shoulder. A few minutes later, hand in hand, like teenagers, they leave the steel and plastic train with its hard seats and dirty windows and walk to the beach. A stiff breeze whips up whitecaps on the Atlantic Ocean, and as they settle on a bench, he puts his arm around her for warmth.

For a while they are quiet, absorbed in the inner quietness that comes with the rhythmic sounds of waves lapping on the almost deserted beach, the occasional cry of a gull. Then Tania's mind drifts into beginning another poem and she reaches for her journal. When the pages lift in the stiff breeze, Purple moves a little to shield her as she writes.

"Do you want to hear it?" she asks. "I've only got a couple of lines, but . . ."

"Sure," he says. "What's the title?"

"Um, 'Poem number . . .'? I don't know, let me share what I got. It's just a couple of lines," Tania replies.

"Sure," he says again. He has always appreciated her poetry, ever since he recorded her performances with Agua twenty years before.

After focusing, and pausing to clear her throat, she reads: "*Won't carry your shame / Won't be bringing your fear/ Daddymama drama / Daddymama trauma*"

She looks up. Purple is looking toward the west, and the setting sun. "Purple, will you please look at me?" she asks. Her voice is demanding.

Purple's voice caresses as he replies, "I will, if it's not a command." Once she would have heard only his words, not the loving tone in which they were said, and would have been irritated. But thanks to the Group she has come to feel—and he has come to understand—that he does good when he stands up to her fearful controlling tones. For Tania's very life force was controlled by that bastard, the abuser, and as a defense she took on his controlling behavior. Purple standing up to her is helping her stand up to her father.

Their bodies move closer, into their energetic bond. She feels his loving male friendness. She trusts his black cotton shirt and matching black pants and shoes with a sandal feel. He envelops her like a pleasant warm evening. "You know, Purple," Tania says, "in our beginning I had learned through my recovery and counseling to open up slow . . . no instant intimacy."

"I remember, and I'm not pushing you, am I?" He has removed his sandals and lets sand ooze through his naked toes.

Tania doesn't answer directly, but settles her body against the protective warmth of his. She catches herself doing shallow breathing, and, aware of how good she feels when she deepens her breath, she takes in a big gulp of delicious oxygen, then unravels more of her feelings.

"Purple, I won't lose. I won't stop trying."

"And succeeding," he whispers. His lips brush her neck.

"Yeah I won't stop loving 'cause of how childhood was." She smiles.

The setting sun casts long shadows on the beach, shadows of rocks and boulders and a few straggling beachcombers. One of them is whistling. Tania rests her shoulder on Purple's chest. She is crying. Gently he rocks her as she says, "Purple, my father used to whistle. Whistling was an expression of his aliveness. Other than that he was deadened."

Purple kisses her on top of her brown plaits, and they are quiet together, listening as mother/father ocean Yemeya, Olukun and even an energy of Obatala the mountain god waves at them both. Each spirit takes in the ocean's rolling.

* * *

Gerri looks through her overstuffed closet for just the right outfit to wear to see Tania perform. Figuring her look should be casual, she chooses an African top and jeans, then bumps her head as she tosses shoe boxes aside looking for a pair of low heels. "Ow!" The pain momentarily masks the anxiety she is feeling.

Tania has invited her to attend a "Generation Five Special Event" (according to the email announcement) in which survivors of childhood sexual abuse will make public, through performances before a general audience, what happened to them when they were young. After explaining Generation Five's mission to spread awareness of childhood sexual abuse, she announced that she herself would be performing something she has written for the occasion, and she very much wants her baby sister to be there for moral support. Unlike the play Tania presented at the WOW Café, which fictionalized what had happened to her, so people could dismiss it as a morbid fantasy, her presentation at this event will be more explicitly personal, and she wants to know her sister, who was there, will be listening. Gerri, who has found a kind of peace in the embrace of her sister after being estranged from her for so many years, could not say no. Besides, while she had avoided thinking about the past before seeing Tania's play, recently, despite her fears, she has found herself wanting to know more, to *understand.*

"I am Gerri," she thinks, "I have the same sad eyes as Buttercup. And anyway, no one in the audience will know Tania and I are related, or that I myself . . ." She cuts this thought short, and goes to the bathroom to scrounge a herbal headache remedy and comb her hair, then responds to the screaming tea kettle in her kitchen, deciding she has just enough time to drink a cup before heading to the jazz and poetry club where the event is to take place. After only a sip, however, she realizes she is running late and, grabbing her bag, dashes out the door and down to the parking garage, worrying about whether the car will start (it does) and whether she will find a parking space (she does).

"I didn't need to bring anyone with me," she thinks as she drives, "although I wish I had been brave enough to ask Quilombo to come. Tania wanted me to ask him, but I just couldn't. Besides . . ." she excuses herself, sighing, "my son comes nowhere with me these days. He's all grown up. But my sister Buttercup, my sister, my dear . . . dear sister, she will love me with her eyes from the stage. She asked me if it was okay to honor me by telling the audience I'm there to support her. I felt so touched that she asked me that I said it was okay, as long as she doesn't point me out. I'm glad to be there for her. We are the two sisters. She says she doesn't even have another sister."

Inside the café, the small stage opens in front of Gerri and the stage lights warm it. Looking for a table with an empty seat, she shifts uneasily, like a cat who, about to settle in its special nook, senses the worrisome energy of a dog close by, and has almost decided to walk out when she spots Tania busily searching for her presentation piece in her large knapsack. She looks gorgeous in a long, elegant Afro Am style dress Gerri had given her. The tan and cream color with brown trim suits Tania, Gerri thinks. She can wear subdued colors like that.

"Tania, where do you want me to sit?" she asks nervously.

Tania throws her answer over her shoulder with a quick smile. "Wherever you feel good and can see the stage, okay?"

Gerri picks a spot at a table near a wall, where no one will be sitting behind her to be bothered by the big puffy blue hat she's wearing. A woman seated in a rollator-walker is already there. She is chocolate skinned, with medium-length hair in African locks, wearing glasses and huge West African ebony earrings. The woman nods a silent greeting, but seems focused on the candle in the center of the table and the slow melody of John Coltrane's "A Love Supreme" coming from speakers overhead. Together they admire the mural behind the stage, a wall of lavender, blue, and grey with red accents on which faces of jazz greats line up one after another. The show will start soon.

"Thank God I didn't come late like I usually do," Gerri says, stroking the wood table top. I wouldn't have found a seat." The woman sitting beside her nods. "I don't know why I can't seem to get to places on time," Gerri goes on. "Time is my downfall."

"Mine, too." The woman gives her rollator a pat, and Gerri is immediately mortified. This woman has a good excuse for being late, whereas Gerri, it seems, always finds herself frantically inventing them.

Thankfully, her cell phone rings. The call is from Quilombo, but with the show about to start, there's no time to talk with him even if she were ready to, so she whispers, "I'll call you back later," and turns the phone off. She wishes Tania were not so preoccupied with welcoming other members of the audience, people who, like Gerri, have come to support the survivor-performers. There is one white woman in particular Gerri notices when Tania greets her. Not quite five feet tall, she has short, curly hair. Jewish hair, Gerri thinks, and is reminded of her mother, the Jewish woman from Poland and Russia by way of the Bronx who had dared to marry a Black man from Jamaica. Suddenly she feels the sting of tears in her eyes.

How different their lives might have been if only . . . Neither she nor Tania had found someone to marry. Older sister has a husband, but as far as Gerri can tell, they live separate lives. She remembers their mother complaining about Tania's boyfriends, the brute named Buster and the man she went to New Mexico with, who was "only a bus driver." Thankfully her mother hadn't known anything about her own inability to find a man whose life she could share, and by the time she showed up with Quilombo, Rebi was too preoccupied with her husband's declining health to bother much.

"Are you okay?" Suddenly Tania is beside her, handing her the bag she's carrying to watch for her as the lights dim.

Gerri nods. "Break a leg," she says, and watches with huge saucer eyes as her sister heads for the stage, full of purpose, watches until she disappears among the other survivor-performers. Then her gaze is drawn to the bag Tania has entrusted to her care, and she starts her inner tape again. "Buttercup, I mean Tania, I'm scared. I can watch this little bag your elegantly dressed-up self has left with me, but I'm not sure I can do what you want me to do, whatever that is. All I can do is help you look great by giving you scarves and silk jackets and long Afro Am dresses that I never should have bought anyway."

The audience's clapping for Tania, who has just stepped downstage, startles Gerri, and she eases back into her seat to get more comfortable. But her head starts to throb again. She hopes the remedy she took before she left home will hold off anything worse as Tania begins to speak.

She doesn't hear much of what Tania says. She doesn't have to. She is watching as Tania hikes her dress up to just above her ashy knees, revealing anklet socks and Mary Janes, the kind of socks and shoes they used to wear when they were children. The socks are mismatched. In her mind, she says, "Those are the anklet socks you wore, Tania. You're announcing to the world that your four-year-old self is still here. I get it. I know why the socks don't match!"

Rocking her body forward, leaning on the table, she shies away from this thought and takes her inner monologue in a different direction, reaching up to touch her hat, glad she was able to find a seat where she wouldn't have to take it off and let her long hair hang loose. When she's out of the house, she always wears her hair tucked inside a hat. "It's one of the reasons," she explains silently to Tania, "I'm scarcely able to do anything like work outside, so I have to put the food on my credit card and don't have money in the bank to get cash when I want to 'cause Geraldine doesn't give me enough. Tania, remember how Mommy liked to wear those stylish Linda Wood hats? Remember how she used to go shop at that boutique? I love shopping. Thrift stores are my best places to browse. I loosen up in there . . . lose myself in the taffeta, the silk, the suede. Touching those fabrics I forget. I forget the old touch that you told me about and I know was no good. Oh, Tania, help me if you can. I'm dying.

Suddenly Gerri realizes everyone is applauding, so she pats her two hands together and looks up. She realizes that Tania must have left the stage a while ago, because a video called "Healing Sex" is just winding up. She has missed it. She wishes she had watched it, instead of being distracted by her thoughts. Her sex life has been a mess from day one. She remembers her first sexual encounter, how drunk she was, how the man was rough and didn't care, how she freezes when she has sex. So, she wonders, is the first act of sexual abuse the "first time"? No, that can't be right. The "first time" is the first time you have sex as a consenting person. But had she ever really consented to sex, even when she wasn't drunk?"

Now, as the end of the program nears, a woman with a flute takes the stage, and the audience abruptly hushes as she begins playing the melody of a song by the musical group Sweet Honey in the Rock. Suddenly Gerri is half-remembering lines from a poem she read once. "Your children are not your children, they are the sons and daughters of . . ." Of what? She can't remember, but now, all at once, she can remember Tania's performance, the last part of it anyway, after Tania had becomes an adult again by letting down her long dress to hide her mismatched socks and Mary Janes. Usually so scatterbrained, she remembers clearly every word of the letter-poem Tania recited. She remembers that it was dedicated to a lesbian poet/incest survivor who had asked, in her one woman show "Lagrimas": "Is that really the first time?" "Dear Sistah," Tania had begun and Gerri thinks, "She was speaking to me."

"Dear Sistah,
Don't carry your shame,
Don't be bringin' your fear
Daddymama drama
Daddymama trauma"
Dear Sistah,
Child sex abuse is not sex. It is the very first torture
Using Sex as a weapon
Deployed against the Powerless
By those the System makes feel Powerless themselves.
Deployed across the Generations
(All five of them)
Bound one to another by hidden chains whose links are silence.
Damn it to hell. Hiding is what we do well.
To break free we gotta shout it out. TELL! TELL! TELL!"

"Tell Tell Tell." The words run through Gerri's rocking brain as the flutist's performance comes to an end and the audience stands to applaud. Gerri also stands and applauds, but her gaze is fixed not on the flutist or on the other performers, including Tania, who have come onto the stage to take final bows, but on one of the faces in the mural. He reminds her of Daddy, his gray Afro and something about his brows. Is she imagining it? Those heavy brows that mark Sadstone's daughters as his. And his grandchildren. Suddenly she is thinking of her precious Quilombo. Suddenly, she knows what Tania hopes she will do. What she is called to do. She needs to tell Quilombo.

* * *

One evening not long after the Generation Five event, Tania drives to Gerri's to choose once again what she likes from the new outfits her sister has bought but decided don't suit her after all. She hasn't seen her sister since the Gen5 event, though she senses it has had an impact. She, herself, has been inspired by the movement's emphasis on history, and by Purple's questions about her family's participation in the Jamaican slave rebellion of 1831, to do some research of her own, something she has time for since Purple has been away at a training.

"It's been two weeks," she had murmured to herself early that morning as she checked the calendar on her wall bulletin board. She had been listening, as she does most mornings, to WBAI's rebroadcast of the previous evening's peace and justice news. Today this had been followed by a show about rapes of women around the world, including the possibility that a leftist from the Sandinistas has been abusive in his personal life. "We need socialism, shit, but we also gots to effing deal with male supremacy," she had muttered to herself, and scrambled to find her new cordless phone, cursing, as she always did, the up-to-date gadget that never seemed to be where she was sure she had left it. She wanted to connect with Purple on this issue, if only briefly.

She now calls Purple regularly between their times together, leaving short messages on his answering machine about the next time she will visit, still honoring what they had agreed to—that she would always call before coming to his place—and sometimes just responding to the urge to share an idea that has come to her or something she has heard.

"Hi!" she would say. "Hi! Just wanted to say I heard something on the news today that let me realize how glad I am to be involved with you, a man who cares to be a world citizen and despises this so-called 'I'm an American' junk! Also, a man who doesn't act like he's God's gift to women, but supports them instead. I do appreciate your support." She'd had the phone in her hand, had already punched his speed-dial number, before she remembered he would not be there.

Still, as she put the phone in its cradle, she'd imagined what would have happened if he had been there. His answering machine lets him screen calls, and this morning, having walked out of the bathroom just as she was reaching the end of her message, he would have picked up the phone. "Tania, hey, baby," he would've said. "Hey, why don't you come by later? I'll pick you up and we can come back from the train together." She has stopped driving to the city when she is planning just to spend time with him because of the virtual impossibility of finding overnight parking in his neighborhood.

"Oh . . . You're still there. . ."

"Yeah! I just found out I only have to work this morning and then I'm off tomorrow! And you're between projects, so . . ." He likes hearing her voice, and wants to smell her close. And she feels the same about him. But today, of course, he was not there to pick up his phone, and now, after a day spent mostly catching up on paperwork and researching the colonial slave-history of Jamaica, she is on the way, not to his place but to Gerri's, frustrated that she can't share with him what she's learned and what she now suspects about her family's history.

"Look Purple, she would say to him when she had the chance. "I know now that the Great Slave Rebellion in Jamaica in 1831 is called the Baptist War 'cause it was led by a Baptist preacher. But my great grandfather was white, remember? He was the owner of the plantation where my great grandmother worked and where my nana, who was his daughter, was born and spent her childhood. So I think that under slavery my folks were house servants, not field workers, and more likely respectful Methodists. Not the sort to risk their lives rebelling."

"Why were Baptists more likely to rebel?" he would ask.

And she, marveling at how the friendship between them is deepening with historical communications, would say, "Maybe 'cause Baptist congregations chose their own local leaders. The point is, my nana might have had choices, but her mother and slavery's whole way of being made her so white-identified she puffed up her hair in a bouffant hairdo, wore chiffon dresses to the big church she went to in Brooklyn, and crossed her pocketbooks, while praying to nothin' even though she attended church. My father was only a boy when he came here. I think he stopped going to that respectable church and rebelled against his bourgie family when he discovered the labor movement in the 1930s. What he taught me about Black history was American history, not Jamaican history. He never went back to Jamaica. He took us to visit nana and the rest of his family in Brooklyn just because they were family."

In the back of Tania's mind, as she nears the apartment house where Gerri lives, where her parents had once lived, is the realization of how terrible it must have been for her father, given this history, to be forced back into a bourgie life—to be sold into bourgie slavery by his selling job. But she doesn't have time to dwell on this, and soon she is standing in Gerri's bedroom, a white linen jacket and a gorgeous brown taffeta dress for her to try on draped over her arm. Suddenly Gerri, who has been acting even more distracted than usual, says, "Aunt Tantie, you know, Daddy's sister, died over the weekend. Will you come to the funeral?"

At first Tania hesitates. For years she has had no real contact with her immediate family except for Gerri and Quilombo and the fiasco with Older Sister at the bookstore, much less her extended Jamaican family. Even growing up, when there were Jamaican Family Occasions in Brooklyn her father dragged them to, she had looked forward only to playing with her cousins, especially Aunt Tantie's son, Gerald, whenever they could escape from the adults, But participating in the group and becoming active in Generation Five have given her courage, and instead of avoiding the issue, as she has done for so long, she sees a possible opportunity and makes a new choice.

"Yes, I'll go," she says. "When is it? And where?"

Gerri moves toward her phone, an elegant ivory model on her bedside table. "Sometime this coming weekend," she says over her shoulder. "We don't know where yet. Excuse me, I have to call Mom and a few more people."

Tania clears away some of the clothes spread out on Gerri's bed and sits down, her new-found courage suddenly dissipating as she wonders how she can face the relatives.

"Do you have to phone right now?" she asks Gerri.

"Yes, if I don't do it right away I won't do it, and Mom might find out from someone else."

"I'll take these, then," Tania says. "Call me with the details."

By the time she has reached her place in Pennsylvania, it is late, and she is exhausted, but as soon as she has taken off her coat, she dials Maisha, whom she knows she can call any time. Despite her growing closeness to Purple, whenever she feels she is not strong enough for some task, she remembers the power of the symbols of Reiki and calls Maisha, who knows how to work those symbols for healing. She explains about the funeral and asks her Reiki sister if she will come and walk with her down what she knows will be a path full of pitfalls.

"Okay, I'll be glad to go. I don't have anything else on for this weekend, anything I can't get out of at any rate. I know what these folks can be like, my family being from Jamaica and all, and you'll need somebody to run interference. When exactly is it? And where?" Maisha had been asleep when Tania rang, but doesn't let on. Her body, even half asleep, easily holds her desire to support the woman who has become her Reiki healing sister, as she had become Tania's.

"Sometime this weekend. I don't know the details yet."

Suddenly Tania is weeping, deep scary wails revealing the anguish at the loss of her family she could not share with Gerri or even Grace and the group, or with Purple, at least not yet, but has no fear of sharing with Maisha. "You know," she sobs, "this will be my first family funeral since my grandmother died when I was a little girl. When my dad died, remember, I was still in New Mexico, and they were *all* toxic for me. And then Pam invited me to feel free, knowing that my abuser's carcass had risen off the planet. But of course, I wasn't free, not really. . ."

"Yes, I hear you, my sister." Maisha reassures Tania that she knows her family history. "Shall we send Reiki energy?" she asks.

Tania's sobs have begun to subside, and she nods yes, knowing that Maisha will sense her feelings. There is a silence. Then Maisha begins saying the Reiki symbols for distance aloud, while the spiritual energy heals them both. Then Tania says, "You know, everything, even death, seemed more natural in New Mexico, where I could live filled with the life of the mountains and the streams and there were no buildings blocking the blue sky."

Sighing, Maisha nods. "Yes. It's hard to get that feeling here, except through spiritual practices." Both women feel the Reiki energy confirming that it's good for them to be with each other.

Finally, Maisha says again, "Of course I'll meet you at the funeral. Just give me the exact time and the address."

"Okay, as soon as I know them."

Maisha blocks out the weekend in her date book, then says, "Bye now, my sister. Be well."

After she hangs up, Tania sits a while in the "easy pose." Her inner turmoil does not disappear, but she has a sense that there is a way forward, that all the spiritual roads she has explored are joining to become one road.

* * *

After Tania leaves, Gerri puts down the phone and begins washing dishes and sorting herbal teas as she resists making the call she's been assigned to make.

Finally, when she is sure her mother will be asleep, her dutiful self picks up the kitchen phone. She rubs her finger over some spots on the receiver, making a mental note—"need to clean this"—and dials. When the answering machine answers, she leaves the message she has been rehearsing since Tania left.

"Hello Mom, I'm calling to let you know that Aunt Tantie died over the weekend. We just found out. The memorial will be this weekend. I don't know the details yet, but . . ." Her voice trails off for a moment, then she resumes. "You can come down by train and stay at my place, so we can go to everything together, if you feel up to it."

As she hangs up, her thoughts turn to the bitterness between Tania and their mother, and she wonders what it will be like when the two meet at the funeral, assuming Rebi feels well enough to come. After she told Quilombo about Tania's performance at the Generation Five event and what it meant, she had thought about telling Rebi, too, but could not bring herself to do it. She remembers what happened when she gave her and Evangeline Tania's play to read, how she had said it was too painful to be true. Besides, telling Quilombo had been hard enough, though he had never known his grandfather except as an old man with dementia. She had seen the hurt in his eyes, the question she is grateful he did not ask: "What about you, Mama?" The truth is, she doesn't remember much about her childhood, only snatches of dreams. And she had left home and headed for Africa as soon after the family moved out of Queens as she could.

Suddenly she realizes she hasn't told Tania that Quilombo now knows the truth. She had intended to tell her when came over tonight, but then Aunt Tantie died and the funeral overwhelmed any other thoughts. With her head pounding, she heads for the kitchen to brew a pot of the herbal tea she knows will ease the pain and calm her enough to let her sleep, at least for a while. Just making the tea is soothing, and carrying the mug, she goes to the bedroom, where her bed is still piled with clothes for Tania to choose from. She pushes them aside and pulls others from her closet, clothes appropriate for a funeral. She likes to dress up and is already thinking about what accessories to wear with her black linen suit.

* * *

Rebi checks her phone messages as she always does after she has had her morning coffee at the table in the kitchen of the house where she has lived alone since her husband died. When she hears the message from her youngest daughter about her sister-in-law's death, she moves slowly to the soft sofa she had bought a few years ago and sits with her head bowed, her now aged, bony hands placed carefully in her lap. A tug of war goes on between her two palms announcing her worries. Will I go to the funeral and see Tania, if she comes? Will I not go, so I can avoid being reminded again of what she told me, of the accusations she made that weekend that wracked my brain for years until Sadstone's disease overcame any hope I had of trying to work something, anything out with my daughter . . .? That girl was like me, confronting me the way I confronted my mother. And like my mother with me, I didn't support her. But how could I support her? I merely insisted on marrying the man I loved, who was Black and from a different culture. Tania insisted that this man had . . . No! It can't be true.

Closing her eyes, Rebi turns inward even more, thinking of her mother and her mother's death. She thinks, "I have my mama's Polish Jewish eyes, green as a meadow of uncut, sweet-smelling grass. I loved her so much, but I couldn't stand the way she let me down when I married Sadstone." Her thoughts circle back. "And then I didn't stand with Tania. That's what she was saying in that play of hers, that I let her down. I understand that now. But how could I, when what she said . . .?" Her veined hands move from her lap to her face, and she speaks aloud into them, the words wrenched from her.

"Mama, couldn't you see I was scared? After Sadstone and I got back from Hawaii and I saw how things were going to be, I was petrified, Mama, and you didn't help me. Why didn't you help me? You could have, you know. Lived up to your own ideals, the ideals you taught me. With Tania and me, it was the same, but it was different, too. You had recognized Daddy's cold and controlling nature before your honeymoon was over. I loved Sadstone until he died. We had been through so much together. And I *couldn't* help Tania without turning on him and I could never do that. By the time she left home, she was a bundle of fire and rage and when she came to see us that last time and started crying, I just froze up. When people cry, I'm numb, the same way you were. I do the same numbness you did. We aren't so different, you and I. Do you know how much I miss you? I miss Tania, too. So much. I haven't seen her for years, because she wanted me to choose, and I couldn't do that, especially after Sadstone started to get sick.

"Even when she came to see us that last time, he wasn't right. Tania couldn't see it, but it was so. How could I leave him to die alone of dementia? She looks at the photo of him on the end table. He is standing on the beach in Hawaii, young, strong, half smiling, the corners of his mouth slightly turned up.

"In the year before he died he couldn't even remember my name." The words stumble out of her trembling lips. "Mama, why didn't you let me see that you were . . . trapped by marriage too? Maybe, then, I would have known how to make Tania understand."

She lays her head back on the couch pillow and sobs. Waves of sobbing wrack her body like some inner waterfall.

When finally she is calm, she gets painfully to her feet. After her husband's body finished with life, she had never walked fast again. Her legs ache, like her heart had ached during the decades of their marriage and the girls' growing up. Slowly she walks around the room, stopping beside each African sculpture, and the death masks on the walls. She has changed nothing significant since her husband's death, except for the new couch and laying down throw rugs to brighten the shadowy grays of the carpet and the shades of tan and cream on the walls, the carefully chosen color scheme that had once soothed her but that she now found depressing, Sometimes she selects an orange shag, other times a small mat of sisal that Gerri brought back from Ghana. One thing she and Sadstone had given all their girls, Tania included, was knowledge of their roots in the great kingdoms of West Africa, deeper and stronger than any connection with the humiliations of Jamaican plantation culture.

She has decided not to go to the funeral. She wants to see Tania, but is afraid her daughter will not be willing to speak with her.

* * *

The weekend comes fast. Maisha and Tania stand outside the big church with stained glass windows.

"Let's go in," Maisha says, and leads the way inside. She takes a seat in the back. Tania sits down beside her. She avoids any eye contact with members of the family who are still arriving and making their way to front of the church. Instead, gazing straight ahead at the stained glass window above the altar, she thinks of her dead aunt's son, Gerald, her favorite cousin, who should have been there but is not, because he had died years ago, before the age of forty, before his own son had finished high school. It had happened while she was in New Mexico, but she had only learned of it after she returned to New York and she and Gerri reconnected. How come Gerald hadn't outlived his mother? Tania remembers how kind he was the day they ran into each other on the street and he drove her to her old bus depot job, just as she was hooking up with Teddy. She remembers with horror his account of the way his mother humiliated his young wife. Had it all been too much for him? For a moment, the music coming from the front of the church distracts her, but her thoughts soon return to her cousin as she had seen him that day so long ago, his skin the color of butter. She hears his gravelly voice as he tells her about the way his mother treated his wife and how much she disapproved of the way they were raising their son.

The recollection makes the heat rise in Tania. Aunt Tantie was a b-i-t-c-h. She wants to say this aloud, but of course, does not. Her aunt is dead now. And besides, women don't need to label other women. Women should reflect on their own actions instead!

But right now Tania isn't in any mood for self-reflection. ~~Aunt Tantie had been no wellspring of hope.~~ How she had learned the way Aunt Tantie felt about her she does not remember, only that, instead of trying to find out why her brother's middle child acted "crazy," she had, Obeah like, used the blades of tiny symbolic knives to try and cut the life-force from an innocent girl's heart. True, she had had a hard life. She had done an adult's work in Jamaica's fields from the time she first leaned into a tall sunflower, at age ten. Tania's father had explained how, long after the official end of slavery, into modern times, white families on the island continued to own the plantations whose fields of sugarcane and, later, bananas were worked by Jamaicans of African descent. The whites covered up and lied and said Black Jamaicans were too stupid to own their own country free and clear. Most of it, anyway. Horsecrap attempts at land reform had put small holdings in the hands of some Jamaicans, including some members of Tania's family. While there wasn't enough land to farm profitably, they clung to it fiercely, even as they made lives for themselves in Kingston, even after many of them, like Tania's nana and step grand-dad, headed for the USA in the years before 1924, when the U.S. Congress had slammed the immigration doors shut on pretty much everyone except northern Europeans. The children were left behind, to wait in Jamaica while their parents made a way for them to follow. Aunt Tantie had packed up her little brother, Sadstone, and taken him with her to the family farm, where, day in and day out, they pricked every finger picking sorrel tea leaves, which Tantie traded for pennies in the market in Kingston.

The fact that her life had been hard didn't really explain why Aunt Tantie had been so mean, but Tania, now observing the members of her extended family, the light-skinned and the dark, suddenly has an idea. Aunt Tantie had known from a very young age what a dark-skinned girl like her would be made to suffer. And not only by Jamaican society in general. The tall, dark-skinned man who had been her and Sadstone's father had died young, and their mother, Tania's nana, had remarried a light-skinned guy. The extended family Nana and her husband joined in Brooklyn when they came to the US had been largely his blood relations. Had they been truly welcoming to Nana's dark-skinned children? And who knew what had happened to Tantie when she went alone as a girl to that marketplace in Kingston? For the first time in her life, Tania wonders whether her brother's light-skinned children had been a torment to their aunt, somehow symbols of all she had suffered, and though Tania was the darkest of the sisters, she had been, she realized, the least compliant. Though all three had giggled about "Tantie Tantie," it was Tania who had come up with the joke.

When the service ends, Tania leaves Maisha and finds a way upstairs to the balcony so she can observe the crowd of friends and relations, some of whom she remembers from childhood, along with many other people she doesn't recognize at all, mingling below. As she leans over the balcony rail, she spots Gerri, who is talking with a woman wearing a wide-brimmed black hat covered by green dots. Some impulse makes her sister look up and Tania waves. Gerri waves back, and the woman in the hat, seeing this, also looks up. Tania can imagine the exchange between them. The woman, one of many "aunties" Tania remembers from childhood but whose name she doesn't recall, asks who that is and Gerri explains it's her sister Tania. The auntie scowls and avoids Tania's gaze while nudging an older woman standing next to her, another auntie, who also looks up. Both women then make a show of looking away. Gerri, still looking up, mouths the words "I told him," pointing to Quilombo, who is standing nearby beside another young man Tania doesn't recognize.

Then Gerri is engulfed by mingling relatives, and Tania, who had felt in her heart that the Gen 5 event had had a powerful effect on her sister, but had not realized she had found the courage to tell her son, now turns her attention to him and to the young man with him. He is tall and skinny, like someone who will put on weight later, and she thinks he must be Older Sister's child. She has never met him, but she has heard about him. Certainly, he could have inherited his height from her. Older Sister had cried buckets when she grew to be six feet tall, and incessantly begged their mother to do something to stop her growing.

When she sees the two young men head for the back of the church, she runs down the stairs to intercept them, stopping first at the pew where she had been sitting to get Maisha and collect her things. Spotting her, Quilombo smiles broadly. He has bulked up since she last saw him, and as he introduces the young man with him, she notices his voice has deepened. "This is your *other* nephew," he says to Tania, gesturing towards the tall, thin young man . . ."and this . . ." he announces to his cousin proudly, nodding towards Tania, ". . . is Tantie Tania."

As the boy reaches out politely to shake her hand, she notices that he has not only Older Sister's height, but also the thick, sweeping eyebrows all three sisters had inherited from the molester, as if someone had sliced Sadstone's pain from his forehead and stamped it across their light cashew skins.

"It's nice to meet you," he says. "Quilombo has told me about you."

"Does your mother ever mention me?"

"No," he says. "I just know you left home a long time ago."

She expects Older Sister will be upon them in no time, and she may never have another chance to make sure he knows what has been hidden from him.

"Do you know anything about why I left home?" she asks.

"No, I just know you did." He stands still, but his eyes are wide open, curious.

"Oh, well . . . I wonder if I should tell you."

Quilombo says, "I know, so why shouldn't he?"

"You know because your mother had the courage to tell you. But this is different." For a moment she thinks, "Why not let Quilombo tell him?" but only for a moment. This is her responsibility, to prevent the silence from crippling another generation, as it had crippled his grandmother and his aunts and his mother. She looks gently up into his eyes, trying to make this moment live, knowing she may never see him again. "Your grandfather molested me," she says.

"Oh . . ." A long pause. His face remains expressionless, an indication to Tania that he has been well trained not to reveal his emotions. She expects he is worried that he will be in trouble for listening to his Aunt Tania. She keeps her hands at her side, but mentally raises them to massage his shoulders and be kind to him as he takes in this blast of truth that no one has prepared him for. Then she feels the menacing vibration of his mother behind her, and looks around to find Older Sister heading her way. Her rage is all too evident. Alarmed, Tania motions to Maisha, who, intuitive soul sister that she is, moves at once to intercept the approaching Fury—who, professional woman that *she* is, stops to say a formal hello and introduce herself.

Relieved, Tania turns back to her nephew while Older Sister is preoccupied with Maisha, and says, "I would rather you be spared from any clash between your mother and me. You can contact me any time through your cousin."

"Okay," he says, also relieved. Tania doubts he will ever call, but still, watching the back of his head as, accompanied by Quilombo, he moves through the crowd towards is mother, she hopes against hope she may hear from him.

She doesn't want to be watching when they meet, and, suddenly needing to pee, she maneuvers through the crowd of relatives and friends of her late aunt to make her way to the bathroom. None of them stops her or makes any attempt to speak with her, although in truth, it is unlikely any of them except the aunties who were with Gerri when she waved from the balcony would even recognize her. She looks for Gerri, to tell her what she's done and warn her Older Sister will be on the warpath, but doesn't see her.

From one of the stalls in the church's quaint "Ladies Room," with its white pedestal sinks, she hears the door open, and when she emerges, she is face to face with Older Sister. "There you are," Older Sister snarls after a moment of startled silence. Without missing a beat she comes to the point, although the language she uses continues to avoid. "How dare you tell my son you had issues?"

"Do you really want to know?"

"You have no right."

"I guess that means you don't want to know, not really, but since you asked, I'm going to tell you anyway," Tania says, refusing to let herself be silenced. "I work with a group called Generation Five."

"What does that have to do with anything?" Older Sister asks.

"If you just let me finish . . . Generation Five teaches that *all* the family of a survivor of childhood sexual abuse, including their siblings and their siblings' children, are damaged by the domination, control and submission that are essential parts of it even if they are not abused themselves. And the only way to even begin to heal is to break the chain of silence and denial and acknowledge the truth."

"What truth? You tell lies about Daddy just to cover up your own craziness. You've even got Gerri believing you. You may even believe yourself. But it's not true. You broke Daddy's heart and Mama's with your lies. Now you want to make my son ashamed of his Jamaican grandfather. I won't let you do it." She tries to push her way past Tania to a stall.

"Tania, you have to move. I have things to attend to."

"No I won't. You have become something, I don't know what. No longer a sister . . . you have no feelings."

Older Sister again tries to make a move, but Tania doesn't let her pass. "You're crazy, Tania, and everyone knows it."

"Who are you calling crazy?" Tania spits the words through her teeth, as Older Sister abruptly turns to leave the bathroom and finds herself face to face with Maisha. Immediately she pulls herself together, again the professional woman, encountering someone she has just met.

"Hello, Maisha," she says calmly. "Tania, I have to go."

"Yes, Evangeline," Maisha says, "that's a damn good idea." But Evangeline, Tania's former sister, is already gone.

Tania sits on a big floor pillow and remembers the soft constant lapping of waves on a beach. She draws her fingers through the pillow's tassels, sifting them like she used to sift the tassels of pondweed through her fingers when she was with her mother in the park, when she was a child. It is late in the day. She doesn't remember leaving the church or the drive home from the funeral. "Ocean Waves," an environmental music tape, is playing on her cassette player. Water has always welcomed her and comforted her: the pond in the park, the lake at summer camp, the ocean near the house on the island, before she left home. The river in Albuquerque, which Teddy had loved, too. Long, hot baths. Yes, those liquid places hold her body, soothe it like one of Madrina's rituals. But she feels un-held tonight. Tonight the pain is too great.

She reaches for the phone on the floor near the pillow. Her fingers automatically press the buttons for Maisha's number. Maisha, who senses it is Tania calling, does not have to say hello. She simply listens. Tania is crying. Without preamble, she says, "My mother ain't a mother. I don't have a mother."

"No, Tania, you have yourself. That's the reality you face."

Tania nods. "There's just the woman who gave me blood. She and my blood father never touched me lovingly at all. Never ever. No, they didn't. Never never never . . ." She repeats the word over and over, the pitch of her voice rising, until Maisha, understanding that the funeral has triggered the little girl within her friend, suggests gently, "If you can, Tania, tell me, how old you feel now?"

"Three." Tania is so shocked by her own response that the phone drops from her hand. She picks it back up. "Sorry." she says.

"No, that's okay." Maisha comforts her. "So, Tania, go ahead and cry . . . a three-year old would scream and yell and beat up her teddy bear. So go ahead and do that. Let your little girl tell you, the adult you, her *real* parent, her *real* mama, everything."

"I *can* face this," Tania sobs.

"Yes you can. You *are* facing it. The loss of her as well as him . . ."

"I love you, Maisha. Thank you for encouraging the release, just like Pam used to do."

"I love you, too, Tania."

Each retreats to her own mind as they hang up.

Tania gets up and walks over to her futon-bed and picks up the big double pillow, long and fluffy with curves on the cover's edges. She beats the pillow, then falls onto the bed and moans into it, her grown-up self using the pillow to stifle the sound so the people who live next door won't hear her, aware even in her anguish, that we do not have a society where we are allowed to scream in our homes to release our pain. Her strong adult hands grasp her elbows as she rocks. The elbows are little Buttercup's elbows. Her inner child, Buttercup, cries out. She tells her adult self, her real mama, everything: "I feel really scared, Mama. I'm wishing Mommy and Daddy would ho-o-old me, but they never do. I'm so angry. They say I'm a bad girl. Aunt Tantie says so, too. And they're right. I'm bad, Mama. I'm very bad. I can't get outta here. Help me, Mama, help me."

Great, heaving sobs wrack Tania's body even as the musical ocean within her never stops singing. When the tape ends, Tania reaches out and flips it over, no more conscious of doing so than the automatic record changer had been in the Victrola they'd had when she was a girl. The sea is Tania's friend, mother, lover, daddy. The mother sea within her cradles and rocks her, and Tania floats in the water-music as the sobs subside and she is still floating.

Finally she moves. For decades her energy had stayed connected only to the wounded programming her society, her schools, her family conditioned into her life. Now she thinks, "I have grown up. For every damn year from age one minute to age seventeen when I finally left their house I've eaten and run and walked and kept drinking healthy liquids, so I never disappeared or got suicidal and cut myself or went crazy like the aunties said I would. I got help from Pam and my writing, and, yes, from Teddy, who loved me but in the end couldn't face his own demons, much less mine."

Now, finally truth has come with Maisha's wondrous, wild question: How old do you feel now? Maisha, the wise seer who somehow knew from the beginning that one day Tania's loving inner adult would become the guide for her wounded small self. Her soul now knows that her nervous system no longer has to activate the little three-year-old Tania going on four, or the school girl or adolescent. The sea, the cradle of life, its very Soul, envelops all of Tania, speaks through Tania and to her. "You were never bad," she says. And again, "You never were bad and today you are whole and healed."

Fully conscious now, Tania rubs her whole body into the futon and rolls over, looking up at the darkness in her closed eyes, realizing, finally, that she is no longer alone, except in the way that every human being on this planet at times feels alone. Then, speaking to all those who feel the same loneliness she had felt during her entire childhood, she says, "Please know now that someone else knows and feels you in the vibrations of the universe. And someone else decided to stop keeping scared to tell everybody. Know that you can tell each person, tree, rock or ocean you want to tell. Know that. Tell and tell and tell. It keeps the years unravelling. It lets the wound get air and sunlight."

With the back of her hand she wipes her eyes, then goes on. ". . . When it scabs over it is safe. The wound has transformed into new TRUST for those who can believe you. Some won't. They have their own pain, and they are insane. So they will deny and lie. When they speak, these people who live only physically, but are emotionally dead, ignore them. Go hold your ocean, like I hold mine."

Now, with her head down, she moves across the apartment and opens her computer. While she still writes in her journal, from this moment she will no longer keep all these thoughts to herself. She is ready to share them with the world. As she types, watching them appear on the computer's screen, she cries, but gently now, listening to the wondrous sound of the seagulls in the background of Oceans Roar on the tape. Her mind rolls over. "I love life," she thinks. And then, "I love Purple." She opens her email and finds one from him, telling her he'll be home in a few days.

She leaves her computer and draws a hot bath. Sitting in the water, she does yoga postures: forward bend, head rolls, and the stretch up to the sky, holding her hands in a diamond position in the warm water. "Om Shanti, Om Shanti." Her chants rest in night air. She steps carefully from the tub, wraps herself in a towel. Sighing, she lights an incense stick of sandalwood to keep the air in the apartment cool. More will be revealed in this new beginning.

19 A PURPLE ROSE BLOOMS

When Purple returns home, Tania has the conversation in person she had imagined having with him on the way to Gerri's apartment, before she learned of Aunt Tantie's death—not an unusual conversation, but an ordinary one. After all that has happened, she draws comfort from the return to what has become a familiar routine, a customary intimacy. Though she knows he got back late the previous night, she calls early. His answering machine picks up, and then, hearing her voice as it is recorded, he lifts the receiver, stopping the machine. "Tania, hey, baby" he says.

"Hey," she replies. "You're awake. I've missed you so much."

"I've missed you, too. Why don't you come by later if you can? I'm off work all day tomorrow. I'll meet you at the train and we can walk home together. Maybe pick up some supplies. The cupboard's pretty bare."

"Okay. I'm off tomorrow, too."Again, Tania is comforted by the ordinariness of the exchange. It's almost as if all that happened while he was away—the Gen5 event, the funeral—has not happened, or, rather, that all of it will somehow flow into their life together. She asks, "Can you hear a piece I've been working on with your name?"

"Sure, whenever you want."

"When I see you," she says. "I have some things to do before I leave. We're getting ready for a new campaign."

"I hear you. I'll get in a couple hours more sleep and meet you on the usual platform at 4:00, assuming that works for you." He makes sure their life together respects her autonomy.

"I'll see you then." As she hangs up, suddenly, for the first time in months, she is thinking of Teddy, and of how different their fraught relationship was from the life she now shares with Purple.

The train is running a little late, as usual, but when she steps onto the platform, Purple is waiting, as she knew he would be. They hug, or try to. Purple laughs as her backpack frustrates them. "Give it to me, baby," he says, and slings it over his shoulder.

Smiling, she hands it to him, and together they climb the stairs into the sunlight of a perfect afternoon, the air clear after rain the night before. It is too beautiful not to savor before they get down to the business of grocery shopping and return to his_apartment. There is a small park near the subway station and they settle together on a bench. She rummages in the backpack for the poem she wants to share, but as often happens, cannot find what she is looking for, and in the end, she speaks from memory, her voice soft, like a cat purring.

"P U r-r P L E
P for you Purple and me and being true to telling smelling smiling.
U for YOU (poetically "u") under the reality of this eat-you-alive-want-to-keep-you-homeless system and you with me in the struggle to FREE MUMIA.
R for Real and funny and my honey and the Righteous anger we both feel
R also for Regard for my well-being that shows when you hesitate to make too many sexual moves before both of us are Ready (another R) to groove.
P again. Here goes this letter of Patiently listening with lovemanship and brothermanship that reveal to you that my Parents of blood would have put me in an institution instead of listening if I ever finished the sentence of what was really happening. Silence kept me alive 'til I turned twenty-five.

L for Like and for Listen. I Like to eat your Jollof rice and home-made ginger tea. Like to Listen to your unveiling of secrets, how your dad, the working-class man, was an emotional Runner who provided money like men of that time but left you in an emotional deadness, how your moms ate you alive emotionally, making her son responsible For Her Hurts With Him and all Men.
E for Each and Every time we get a communication, a touch of our eyes behind glasses so wise . . . Each and Every time we allow a bond of our ancestors, those of this land of the Turtle Island to mix sticks from West Africa's Yoruba people, Roots from Jews escaping the Russian pogroms, music and healing energy grow. Caribbean-sweet coconut blending in a flavor of relax it now. Escaping stones that sting and potholes that bring you down past revolution to suicide.
Hide no more. Hide kills. Hide won't uplift, like a sail going up in the wind. Hide stays in our Past.Today we join with millions in Venezuela and Trinidad, Canada and Cuba's land,who recover/who sponsor Ms.Truth."

Watching him as she speaks, Tania feels supported and held. He has on the Free Mumia tee shirt he got that day last December when they demonstrated for him down in Philadelphia where he had been sentenced to death for supposedly shooting a cop, but was really convicted for being a supporter of the Black Panthers and, as a journalist, sharing the truth about police brutality.

A couple of hours later, Purple is in his couch, 'cause when Purple gets "in for the night," his belly full of Geechee home cooking, he ain't leavin' his couch too much. Tania, beside him, relaxes her head on his shoulder. "Tell me about the funeral." His melodious voice unwinds his woman. It is a mark of his caring that he brings up the subject. He likes to remember people as they were when they were alive and doesn't like to attend burials.

"Can I lie down?" Tania asks. Without waiting for an answer, she settles with her head on his lap. "Okay?"

"Okay," he says, touching her cheek, then cradling her head in his hand while she talks. He listens by paying attention. She can get to the point, because he *gives* her his tender ears, not "lending" them the way most people do. There is no doubting, no questioning. He simply hangs in there, accepting, listening to what many find difficult to hear. She loves how he actually hears her heart.

"I've been reflecting on the funeral a lot," she says. She describes it to him, the big church, the bourgie "aunties," the light-skinned and the dark, and how she now thinks her Aunt Tantie suffered from hurts so deep, from being the dark-skinned child of a white man's rape, and probably a victim, too, that she couldn't help taking out her suppressed rage on her brother's uppity light-skinned children.

"Did you talk to anyone about your dad? Did you learn anything? I can assume but I don't want to. I'd rather let you tell me, if that's okay."

For a long moment, she doesn't breathe. "About my father. . ." She stutters to start. Then the words tumble out. "I told Older Sister's son he abused me. Gerri told Quilombo after the Gen5 event, and Quilombo introduced me to him and was going to tell him but I decided I had to do it. Older Sister was beside herself. She said I was trying to turn her son against his Jamaican ancestors. It's a good thing Maisha was there. In her presence, Older Sister couldn't help but play the successful professional woman, in command of her emotions.

Still telling, she sits up, leaving the protective circle of his arm. His eyes are caring behind the glasses he only takes off when he goes to sleep. They are also tired, and in the momentary silence he reaches up to rub them under the frames. When he speaks, it's kind of like the water pump in a fish pond gently giving air. "About your father," he persists. "Did you learn anything?"

"Like what?" She is bitter. "All the history of enslavement and rape and incest doesn't change what he did to me. He violated me, Purple. He took so-o-o much from me. He did unspeakable things and then denied it."

"But did you *learn* anything, Tania? "I can hear you if you don't have condemnation in your voice."

She pulls away from him. "Oh Purple, no," she thinks frantically. "Don't let me down. Don't make me be a good girl, make me be talking in a calm voice." She wants to scream, but instead, her hand rises to cover her mouth.

"I think my mother was incested, too," Purple says softly. His revelation eases Tania. It is not surprising, but that he has said it, has *told* it, lets her see that the rape and incest in her family history are also part of his and cements the bond between them. Looking into his eyes, she reaches up and grabs him and pulls him down to her and he holds her and holds her. It's the way Teddy Nat Turner used to hold her, but this new socialist man is not Teddy. He has the capacity to think real deep and she knows it. "But God damn," she says to herself, so quietly he doesn't hear the words, muffled as she nestles her head against his shoulder and chest, lips pressed into his tee shirt. "He's wrong to tell me not to know what my life knows, and to ask me not to condemn. How can I not?" The drool of the saliva at the corner of her mouth eases into his clothing, lightly. Gently, tenderly, they release each other's bodies.

Purple kisses her cheek lightly, then very lightly kisses her lips. He caresses her hair by stroking the ends of the braids, just like her grandma used to do. A siren wails outside.

"Oh, Purple, I miss my grandma, who really loved me," Tania says, making the connection Purple is unaware of—the connection between the two people in her life who loved her unconditionally. "Thank you for coming into this friendship and sticking around. I used to feel I wasn't worthy of long-term deep friendships. I used to think that one day I was gonna do something so terrible the friend would leave, and not come back to work it out."

Purple waits until he's sure she has expressed everything inside, then speaks just one short sentence. "Like your father and mother left, huh?"

She doesn't answer immediately, wondering at his insightfulness, which she would have expected from Pam or Grace and the group or, perhaps, Maisha. But, she realizes, now she can count on Purple, too. "Yes, you're right," she says finally. "The rapes were abandonments over and over. The group helped me see that. I thought they were only invasions. But either way, the "secret" hung like a cloud in the background, Even on my good days, I didn't really feel there was any sun . . ." Eyeing the sunburst on Purple's collage of Malcolm X, she adds, "I used to think friends who had neglecting parents had it really bad, 'cause they couldn't point to a specific rape and say that's what made them furious with their parents. But in fact, I had neglect too." She wants to keep making realizations, but at the same time, basking in Purple's caring, bit by bit she calms down until, for the moment, the wounds of the past no longer sting. His ability to listen and listen is a wide river washing over her.

"Tania, you are good enough." Purple still strokes her braids with his short brown fingers, the nails clipped and clean. He twists the ends of her hair around, very gently. She lets her yielding body be wrapped by his, for their mutual cocooning. Their eyes close, rest, as they retreat together into sleep.

A profound, clairvoyant dream comes to Tania. She and Purple stand side by side in North Carolina, on the coast where his Geechee ancestors were enslaved, where he spent summers with his grandma. She knows it's the south by the dense humidity in the air and the wide open sky above the small town, his hometown. Then the scene changes. Tania is walking in Harlem with Daddy, who is tall and still young. He, looks down at her and says, "My mother used to make me put my dick in a coke bottle. I think one time Tantie was watching, too."

Shocked, Tania says, "That's not right, Daddy. She was your mother!"

Daddy waves his hand in that Caribbean-male gesture of dismissal, and says, "She was only a woman."

"No," Tania says again. "That is not the way a mother needs to treat her son, Daddy." She keeps walking in Harlem. Both daughter and father know the weather would be warmer in New Mexico.

The *sueño* . . . the dream . . . ends.

Waking up, still nestled in Purple's arms, she gazes again at the sunburst in the Malcolm X collage. Whispering to her spirits she says, "My father has come from the dead to visit. He has told me a truth I should have sensed all along. He did to me what was done to him!"

Purple has asked that she let him know the truth of her girlhood without condemnation in her tone. Now the Spirits and ancestors have gifted her with this night experience that helps her understand.

Tania slides out of Purple's embrace. She feels the need for a shower—not her usual long, luxurious bath, her body safe under sweet-smelling bubbles, but a shower, with her whole body-self naked for an extended period of time. Just recently she's become totally okay with this. As the water washes over her, she prays for a spiritual color to tell her how to approach him, how to let him know she is ready. She sees Green. Goddess Green.

The sound of the shower running rouses Purple, and he slips into the bathroom to brush his teeth. He sees Tania's wet body through the thin clear shower curtain. Her back stirs him, but not wanting to disturb her, he leaves the room without saying anything. She hears the heavy bathroom door shut behind him, sliding solidly into the door frame in a way that speaks of the craftsmanship that went into the construction of these old New York houses. She feels a stirring in her pum pum, knowing he must have seen her nakedness before he left.

Purple is back on his couch as usual, his legs stretched out. He listens to the water running as Tania wets her hair under the tub's spout to rinse off some soap that hadn't come out under the shower. He loves Tania. He loves the smell of her in his tiny apartment. He loves her toes and her soft breasts he has held while he sleeps with her, without penetrating her, spooned up together like animals. Checking on his heart-self, he thinks, "I used to worry that she really loved me and that her love would be too much. But now I know I am really into her, too, and we can argue without drama and take space and come back and talk stuff out. I'm lucky, especially when I think of men I know who are with women who think they ain't got no problems.

When he hears her brushing her teeth, he gets up and opens the sleep sofa. He can still smell the lima beans from the soup he had made for supper. Then, she emerges from the bathroom, and her aura mixes into the limas' lightness and transforms it. She slips into the side of the bed he likes to find her on when he rolls over. His eyes catch hers, and she looks away.

"Purple, I love you," she says, and then, shyly, "and I want to be loved. I have told you about this before in a way, that what was most missing from my life was love. When I was young I had things, I had vacations. I know how the privilege of that shit sometimes seems to overshadow the unspeakable betrayal. But it does *not* overshadow it. Purple, I trusted. . . " She almost shrieks, but instead, as she breathes deep, sobs come out. He holds her hand so that her chest freely heaves and her other hand beats the soft sofa. "I trusted a man and a woman who claimed to be parents. Purple, I have so often been in friendships with people who don't want me to tell this. They run from the friendship when I ask them to hear me about this or other things. So I realize I picked people who are afraid of feelings, just like my parents. But now I realize I can't stay around unavailable people. It hurts me. I got to stop staying around so they don't get to pretend anymore.

"But with you, Purple, we are telling truth to each other, and I thank the universe for it. And here is another truth. My Jamaican granddad died when my dad was little and his mom's very wiring was like this: BEAT to a pulp the soul of the person who is in your power."

"Where is all this coming from?"

"I had a dream just now. In the dream my daddy told me that my nana violated him when he was a little boy by watching him in his very private moments. No one ever said so, but I just *know* my dad's mama was used as a little girl by that damn white father of hers, and now Daddy has told me how she passed the secret on: dominate your kid through secret sexual acts that build shame on him. And what I finally understand now is that he was compelled by his life to build shame on me."

"Oh man," Purple says.

"Purple, I keep remembering what you told me about how when your father was dying you told him you loved him. Not that you forgave him, but that you loved him. At the time I didn't understand. I thought . . ." She stops, then goes on, dragging her words from deep within herself. "And I know we're talking about me now, but your openness about that gives me the courage to trust you, my friend."

Her head just rests on his shoulder. He picks up her face gently and, looking into her eyes, he says, "Tania, I don't look at you as damaged because of the stuff your father, your family, did to you. I look at you as whole and softly forceful and wonderful and . . ." He takes her in his arms and holds her tight.

"Oh, Purple, I am so-o glad." She removes the robe she put on after her shower. He looks at her luscious breasts and she eyes his chest. Tania feels his love, doesn't have to beg for him to use words to show his feelings. She's had enough of fakey words of love. Instead, she simply lets his love come to her as he grabs her in a bear hug.

They kiss deeply. She takes a condom from the drawer in the table by the bed, unrolls it and lovingly eases it onto his hardness. "So hard," She smiles, touching the tip. And at last he serves her, and she receives all his stem with welcoming vaginal lips holding him, making him swell. After they climax they are both exhausted, so they stop and, as one, they look down at themselves and laugh. He grabs her head, kisses her nose, both eyelids wide apart, and then these lovers rest in a nest, tucked away like his soup, stored in his fridge in the pot he cooked it in. They both know there will be more spice to come.

"Solid, you feel solid," she murmurs.

"And you're soft. I need softness in my life." He snuggles her back.

Turning out Purple's lamps, they prepare once more for sleeping. And it is good, so good.

On the weekend, Tania is back in Purple's spiritually cleansed apartment. It is a hot day, and the room is very warm, but in solidarity with those who can't afford it, the air conditioner is off. When she arrived he was meditating with Nadi music, something they had started doing together after the day they went to Coney Island, when she had felt close to him in a way she hadn't before, though they hadn't had much time together before he had to go away. The meditation helps them both, and she loves that he does it on his own now.

Since they last were together, she has found herself thinking often about Teddy, choosing to write to clarify the difference between him and Purple. As if he is channeling these thoughts, Purple goes to the tape deck and puts on a new mix. The lead song is Marvin Gaye's "Purple Snowflakes." One of her jokes on the universe when she was with Teddy had been to listen to winter music in warm weather and hot summer-fun songs when January was killing New Yorkers with freezing winds. How Purple has intuited this she isn't sure—she herself had lost the memory when she was in New Mexico and the seasons didn't change the same way, and Teddy, himself, was lost to her. Now, hearing the familiar words—'Softly they fall, where do they go? Purple snowflakes . . .'—she laughs delightedly and dances into Purple's arms, then away, appreciating him.

When the song ends, she removes her earrings of hoops and cowrie shells and places them beside Purple's sea green ashtray, recalling how Teddy (Nat) Turner had a similar one. Teddy (Nat) Turner. He hadn't really liked that nickname, the Nat Turner part. She thinks now he just kind of went along with it, that night they gave each other gifts of their new names.

Suddenly she remembers the conversation about Teddy she had had with Rogelio before she went to New York and met Madrina and started on her way down new paths. Teddy, Rogelio said, wanted to struggle with what she represented, not as a person, but the future, the capacity to have courage. And she had replied, "Not with me. He doesn't want to struggle any more, not with me." But she sees now that she had been wrong. Teddy had wanted to go into the future with her. But he was so damaged by the racist system that threatened the very lives of Black men every day that, far from the structures in New York—the steady job, the union, the friendships—that offered some protection, and cruelly abandoned by the mother who had dominated his whole life, he had fallen apart. Neither his love for Tania nor hers for him was enough to make them whole. She had to move on. He was unable to. And now, in her mind, vivid as it had been all those years ago, is her last memory of Teddy: not the wreck she'd had to walk away from, but the man in the dream she'd had after leaving Albuquerque for New York, the man wrapped by the Zuni in a sacred blanket, saying goodbye. She understands now the dream meant that Teddy had died, but the realization doesn't affect her the way it would have done back then. No. In the dream Teddy was whole. And now, so is she. Not whole as a state of being, but of becoming.

Looking over at Purple, who is now in his usual position, his head resting on the back of his couch, she smiles and says, "You know, Purple, I'm glad you don't mix up the spelling of my name, like my ex did."

"Oh, yeah?"

She walks over to cuddle with him. "Yeah. He first saw my name at that bus depot on the list board, and he thought it said 'Tony.' I got him clear. I said, 'I spell it "T-A-N-I-A." ' Teddy just smiled back at Ms. Smarts-me. He didn't know Tania was Che Guevara's compañera."

"Why do you want to tell me about him?" Purple asks. Then, deciding he's secure enough in their relationship to be able to listen to her talk about her ex, he says, "But okay, go ahead."

Tania brightens, relieved. "I called him T.N.T., 'cause Teddy did stand up for me to our bastard boss, one of our many vicious location chiefs. And he was the first man whose sensual caring and listening showed he was willing to stand up to other men's idea that the man in the family is always right." Purple nods and squeezes her. "But he also . . ." She stops, then starts again. "I want to explain by reading the poem I'm writing . . . about staying with you, Purple, after years of remaining stuck with someone I loved and who loved me but who I saw as a non-political man."

It's a lot for him to digest, so Purple changes the mix-tape to one including Herbie Hancock's "Prince of Darkness" solo from "Sorcerer," followed by Artie Shaw, a slow number with the sax, then disappears into the kitchen to fix something to eat. ,

Getting her long body out of the couch, Tania locates her bag and pulls out her notebook, sets it down on the table beside his bible, then sways to the music while Purple finds some leftovers to work his grandma's magic on. As he lowers the flame on the root vegetables and greens he's heating up and returns to the couch, she stops moving to watch him, then sits down beside him and picks up her journal. "It ain't got a title yet," she says. "Or, actually, it's got three: "'*P O E M (untitled).*' Or '*We are opening up all our E y e s.*' Or '*Purple, I feel so happy we're together!*'"

When he makes no comment, she goes on:

"I loved a man who took a stand,
Held my hand

Against only my father (but that was also big!)
He worked with me,
We had bosses to see,
We fought them back off our sensuality.
Then it was many times
My lover's other political ideas and mine
Showed fear and difference
My lover could only watch balls,
(basket ones and foot ones)
Running bases,
doing chases.
He closed his thoughts when I talked of corporate
u.s.a brutality & poverty
Or standing for social change and demos
"Come to a meeting about nuke-liars from Los Alamos," I'd say.
My lover, back then, preferred State Fairs.
To be fair, he did care . . .
But damn it, he chose to do what most folks (U.S.ers) do
(African American or white, Latino or from Asia,
even newer immigrants, too!)
He chose to accept His Flushing Toilet, and His Hot Water
He forgot about standing up to Exxon and Shell beating/robbing the hell
outta poor folks in Nigeria, Congo & South Africa.
He didn't want to stand up to people exploiting others.
He chose to avoid Cuban Baseball
Fidel wasn't even in his mind
And Purple (new man), I tell you that's why I ran from my ex lover . . .
No longer was I willing to be giving my time
helping that man to face his own fami-lie meanness.
He truly understood family domination,
but with the social madness he refused to make the connection:
Our fami-liars, imitate boss liars / propping up government liars,
protecting rich liars!
Years later, Purple, here comes you,
My political lover—we're doing something new!
Our spirit connection forming the base of our political struggle . . .
of being able to just "know" that will help uproot this shit.
Hanging with you is revealing
as we take back our emotions from nuke family destroyers,
(busy dads, too absent or too criminal to love with care)

(moms too dependent, too wanting of the "good white picket fence" idea to protect their children when they are beat, ignored, raped)
As you and I cry,
we also think outside our personal world. You've helped me unfurl, a timely way of remembering.
Our ancestors jumped, fought, kicked, yelled, defeated master's ideas,
And We Can Too.
Thank you, Purple
(for your consciousness)
Sometimes in my life, I had to step away to reclaim love
a livingness with deeper waters,
clearer skies.
Thank you, soul/brother & lover.

"That's it," she says. For a long moment, she looks into his bright eyes, glistening behind his glasses. Then she lets the journal fall, and with both her hands massages his scalp.

"Wait a minute," he says, smiling. He picks up the precious notebook and places it carefully back on the table. "That's better," he whispers, and holds her, tying them together.

She and Purple have won. Together, ruggedly, they have uncovered the truth . . . Now both of them get to face it and transform.

THE END

REFERENCES AND RESOURCES

This list is not intended to be comprehensive. Rather, it is intended to lead the reader to additional sources, to open up other possibilities.
Nor is it confined to sources available to Tania. The novel ends at the beginning of the new millenium. The issues are still with us, and the work continues.

An invaluable resource is the Schomburg Center for Research in Black Culture in Harlem, one of the New York Public Library's research libraries. It is named for historian, writer, collector and activist Arturo Alfonzo Schomburg (1874–1938), a Puerto Rican of African and German descent who researched and raised awareness of the great contributions that Afro-Latin Americans and African Americans have made. His collection of literature, art, slave narratives and other materials of African history became the basis of the Schomburg Center, now a world-leading cultural institution devoted to the research, preservation, and exhibition of materials focused on African American, African Diaspora, and African experiences. http://www.nypl.org/locations/schomburg

HISTORY

Http://www.howardzinn.org
Website devoted to the life and works of historian Howard Zinn (1922–2010), author of *A People's History of the United States* (1979).

Lessons from the Damned: Class Struggle in the Black Community. By the Damned. Times Change Press, 1973, 1990. The book is unavailable, but the text may be downloaded at pmrbio.wordpress.com

The New York Times 1619 Project is an ongoing initiative that began with the August 18, 2019 issue of *The New York Times Magazine.* August 2019 marked the 400th anniversary of the beginning of American slavery. The project aims to reframe the history of the United States by placing the consequences of slavery and the contributions of Black Americans at the center of the national narrative. https://www.nytimes.com/interactive/2019/08/14/magazine/1619-america-slavery.html

Post Traumatic Slave Syndrome: America's Legacy of Enduring Injury and Healing. By Joy Degruy Leary. Revised Edition, 2017. Joy Degruy Publications, Inc. Paperback. (Originally published in 2005 by Uptone Press)

https://www.youtube.com/watch?v=lNAtEXavTF4 "Post Traumatic Slave Syndrome," Part 2. Joy Degruy Leary. The Black Bag Speakers Series. PSU. 2006 https://www.youtube.com/watch?v=wZ2mnoHINyE Joy Degruy. Post Traumatic Slave Syndrome p 1. July 18, 2020. Melanated Vibrations - YouTube channel

Sojourner Truth: Post Traumatic Slave Syndrome. New York-WBAI 99.5 FM New York City, Pacifica Radio. Wednesday, December 30, 2020. https://www.wbai.org/archive/program/episode/?id=18754 2003

Post Traumatic Slave Syndrome. National Public Radio, Hosted by Tavis Smiley, December 2002.
https://www.npr.org/templates/story/story.php?storyId=863362
http://www.npr.org/programs/tavis-smiley/2002/04/08/13052089/

Post Traumatic Slave Syndrome: The Play. Off Broadway, New York 2001. Read review: https://www.nytimes.com/2001/09/14/movies/theater-review-foraging-in-the-mind-where-slavery-s-scars-linger.html

LABOR / POLITICAL & SOCIAL ACTION / SOCIALISM

http://labornet.org/video.htm

labornotes.org

bringmumiahome.com

prolibertad.org

PEOPLE OF THE AFRICA DIASPORA/WOMEN/BLACK RADICAL FEMINISM

Words of Fire: An Anthology of African-American Feminist Thought. Edited by Beverly Guy-Sheftall. The New Press, 1995. Essay co-authored by Patricia Murphy Robinson titled "A Historical and Critical Essay for Black Women" in Chapter 3 ("Civil Rights and Racial Women's Liberation")

Black Women's Blueprint: Reclaiming Ourselves and Transforming Harm

https://www.blackwomensblueprint.org/

Fight Back! Feminist Resistance to Male Violence. Cleiss Press, 1981. http://www.cleispress.com Lupe Family contributed to Chapter 6 of this book under another name.

SEXUAL VIOLENCE (INCEST): CAUSES AND CONSEQUENCES

Generation Five. *Generationfive.org*
"Ending Child Sexual Abuse: A Transformational Justice Handbook" (Available as download at Generation Five website)

Survivors of Incest Anonymous. www.siawso.org

Sex and Love Addicts Anonymous. www.slaafws.org

Http://www.12stepsoberliving.com/recovery-info-line.html

Http://www.harrietfraad.com
Dr. Harriet Fraad: *On the Pursuit of Happines: A 12-Step Program and Platform*
"Capitalism Hits Home" by Fraad and another young woman on YouTube

RADICAL THERAPY

www/radicaltherapy.org

www.alice-miller.com

HONORING PATRICIA ROBINSON

www.blackwomenradicals.com/blog-feed/unearthing-the-life-and-leadership-of-black-radical-feminist-patricia-robinson

https://www.instagram.com/patarchives/?hl=sen

Made in the USA
Middletown, DE
30 November 2022

16479730R00232